DYING

TO BE

WIDOW

Other Books by Edward Allen Karr

SERIES: Risk and the Killers
(Adult Urban Fantasy)
Below the Bay – Book One
* * * * *

SERIES: Thrills N Kills in the Hills
(Racy, Comical Horror in Beverly Hills)
Dayzee Dazzle and the Kildare Killers – Book One
Dayzee Dazzle and her Manic Mansion – Book Two
Dayzee Dazzle and the On-Set Onslaught – Book Three
Dayzee Dazzle and the Cadaver Collectors – Book Four
* * * * *

SERIES: Socrates Lewis Stories
(Psychological/Religious Fiction)
Crosswinds – Book One
Crossovers – Book Two
* * * * *

SERIES: Fringes of Infinity
(Contemporary Fantasy Fiction)
Lin Finity and her Mayhem Rising – Book One
Lin Finity in Holding On – A Novella
Lin Finity and the Words Unspoken – Book Two
Lin Finity and the Islands of Time – Book Three
Lin Finity and the Flights to Forever – Book Four
Tayo Tersoo and the Hunter of Souls – Book Five
* * * * *

SERIES: A World So Close
(Middle-grade Fantasy Adventure & Coming of Age)
Jayden Blue and the Gift to Imagine – A Prequel
Jayden Blue and the Sword in his Shadow – Book One
Jayden Blue and the Call of the Wings – Book Two
Jayden Blue and the Lair of the Iron Lions – Book Three
Jayden Blue and the Journey to Val ka'Yoom – Book Four
Jayden Blue and the Forest of Night Fallen – Book Five
Jayden Blue and the Wait of the Sun – Book Six
* * * * *

DYING
TO BE
WIDOW

Risk and the Killers
Book Two

Edward Allen Karr

LAKESIDE
LETTERS, LLC

Lakeside Letters, LLC
30628 Detroit Road, #247
Westlake, OH 44145

Dying To Be Widow
Risk and the Killers Book Two
©2025 Edward Sechkar.   All rights reserved.

First Edition, 2025
www.LakesideLetters.com

Cover design by JD Smith Design

ISBN-13: 978-1-950886-69-2

"Isn't she adorable, slave?"

"Yes, Widow. Yes. But—"

She looked up at the mutant in the attic, keeping her chin snug between the crafter's breasts.

"There's only one way she could be perfect: if she were dressed like a little girl."

"A little girl, Widow?"

"Mm-hmm. Not by force. Oh, no. If she had dressed herself like a pretty little girl just for me. To offer herself to me. Mm, that would be perfect."

While Igor was speaking, she gave each of the crafter girl's nipples a kiss and a soft nibble.

"But Widow, probably no little girl could ever get here. Not with what it takes. You must know that—"

"Slave, I speak not about a true little girl. No. A grown woman who dresses in teasing little girl clothes. Mm, that's what I want."

From Chapter 60 – More Than Her Own Life

Table of Contents

Chapter 1 – It's All Consumption

"Mm, this is like some kind of meal served only in Heaven."

Daniel scoffed softly and said, "Scarlet, that means you'd have to be dead to enjoy it. We can't get deliveries there. And come on, you can't like this food that much."

"If it takes being dead, hmm, maybe it would be worth it."

She grinned and bit the other end off of a spring roll, then dipped it in the special house sauce, making it ready for the next attack.

"You and your appetites. You can't really think that—"

"Plural, Daniel? Uh, we're just talking about food, right?"

He laughed and said, "The lines between them aren't as crisp as we might think. Maybe food and—"

"Sex? You're comparing eating to sex now?"

"Yeah, food and sex—maybe they're all—"

"I already know what you're going to say: that it's all consumption."

Laughing, he said, "Huh? No, Scarlet, I was going to say it's all enjoyable. Consumption? That's your word."

With a grin, she said, "Well, consumption can be enjoyable."

He pointed at her and said, "Either, or both, with you."

"You're sweet."

"And I'm eating with you."

"Yes, you are. You and your theories," she said before taking another crunchy bite, then talking around it while also chomping. "It's just really good—that's all I'm saying."

Daniel paused his next bite to smile at her, then let his heavily loaded fork rest on his plate.

"No argument here. Can't beat a high-end Chinese feast, but you'd probably devour just about anything right now."

Scarlet hurried to swallow and answer her husband, but she'd rushed the bits down before they were ready and had to cough a few times. If her long and thick black hair hadn't been tied up in a controlled, elegant fashion, she would have bounced it all around and maybe dragged it across her plate.

Daniel laughed at her modest distress and said, "Hey, that's what you get for letting yourself get so hungry. Maybe we should put it all in a blender?"

She managed a muffled laugh, mixed in with more coughing and the beginning of her blue eyes watering, apparent even through the thick lenses of her eyeglasses. But she also held a hand up and shook her head.

"Oh, a blender, Daniel? Really?"

"Yeah. A liquid diet for you. You could just take your time and sip it all down, just a drop at a time."

"Take my time? How long would it take to finish a meal one drop at a time?"

"Okay, that's kind of an exaggeration. You could just slurp it all down real quick too."

She scoffed and said, "You're being silly. But you're right about being too hungry. Mm, I do want to keep stuffing this all down, just more carefully."

He grinned at her chopping off a bigger bite, one slathered with more colorful sauce. She only bobbed her eyebrows a few times, kept smiling, and chewed and savored every crunch.

"Happy anniversary, Baby," he said.

Quickly, she blinked softly as she paused her chewing, but her smile didn't retreat.

After another quick swallow, but one without any difficulties, she said, "Aw, thanks, Honey. Yes, the anniversary is a happy thing."

Daniel's smile faded, and he studied the tines of his fork probing around in a plate of sloppy noodles. He nodded before looking up at her again.

"I'm so sorry about . . . things. If there was any way I could change it, or anything I could have given to—"

"Honey, no," she said. "I didn't mean it that way. I promise, I'm not thinking about it—just how happy I am to be celebrating here with you."

His smile returned, and he said, "Uh, yeah. With me . . . and the food."

"Oh," she said with a grin, "you're worried that I'll get obese?"

He laughed at the ceiling, then said, "You? Not possible. You have a figure most women would kill for."

She tipped her head and waited.

"Alright. Most men too. I'm trying not to think about that."

"Well, I don't want them to think about it either."

"You dress so modestly that hardly anyone would ever notice. I'm lucky. I get to unwrap that package."

"Hmm. Only if you're good."

He'd been listening while finishing off his glass of rice wine, then he set it on the crisp white tablecloth.

"Check your mental notes and do a quick analysis. Like you're at work."

She paused her next bite into what was left of her spring roll.

"Analysis of what?"

"Of how good I've been."

He began to count off with one finger at a time.

"I got us the best room and a table at the best restaurant in Chinatown. I did not forget our anniversary. I've complimented you on how outrageously gorgeous your figure is and now, I'm telling you how absolutely captivating your smile is."

He waited with four fingers held up. She smiled and waited.

His thumb joined the fingers, and he said, "And I'm going to state for the record, right now, that your kisses are addictive, could get me to do anything, and should probably be outlawed because—"

"Stop!" she said, laughing as she looked around.

He stopped, smiled, and let his counting hand relax.

Scarlet tipped her head back enough to look toward the ceiling, and her eyes rhythmically moved from side to side several times.

Looking into his eyes again, she said, "Okay. I'm done."

He squinted a glance toward her plate, which hadn't gotten even close to being emptied.

"Uh, there's still—"

"No, silly. The analysis. Yes. You're being a perfect husband. Thank you."

"So, you agree that your kisses are—"

"Stop again. That's sweet, but you're exaggerating. And being so complimentary. My analysis tells me that you probably have some secret agenda with all that."

He rubbed his chin, nodding, and said, "Shrewd. Yeah, you sure can analyze the crap out of things. Yes, I do have a, um, suggestion."

"And what might that be?"

He looked down at her silverware, saw that she wasn't holding any of it, not even the knife, then sighed and looked back up at her.

"You love the stars probably more than anything. Well, except for me, of course."

"Of course," she said with a soft giggle.

"And the stars love you right back. They sent me a secret comm today, and they—"

"A secret comm?"

"Alright. Maybe it was just my imagination."

"And what did you imagine the stars telling you in this secret comm?"

He smiled at her smile, lingering on the sight of her lips, then looked through the lenses of her glasses at her soft blue eyes.

"They said that they want more than anything to—"

He jacked up his eyebrows and looked around them, saw that no one appeared to be listening, then focused on her eyes again.

"They want to watch us make love. Just for us and for them to witness. Scarlet, they want to watch."

"You're terrible. Stars don't want things like that."

"They don't? Have you polled them and analyzed the results? No, I doubt that you have. You can't prove my contention about them wrong."

"Well, no, I guess I can't. But Honey, our balcony has no privacy, and—"

"No. No, Scarlet. Me and you, out on the roof. Right after this meal."

"Oh, Daniel, no. I love you, you know I do, but that's not my style at all."

"Your style takes my breath away."

"Hmm. I've never seen you stop breathing. I'm not that stylish."

He laughed then said, "I exaggerate. But just because your work is so serious, with all that figuring and stuff, doesn't mean you can't cut loose sometimes too."

She scoffed, barely hiding her grin, keeping it at bay long enough to respond.

"You think I'm a prude."

"I didn't say that. It's just that—"

"It's just that I'm too much of a—"

"Prude. Yeah. Deadly gorgeous, though."

She looked down at her plate, smiling, and said, "Gorgeous is nice. Deadly, though?"

"Just a figure of speech. And maybe prude isn't the right word. You know what I mean. I just think you ought to try letting yourself go a little sometimes."

"Making love out there on the roof is a little? Oh, Daniel."

He nodded at his largely untouched meal, then looked back into her eyes.

"I know. But maybe we need to, I don't know, kind of get out of our lane. Something kind of crazy that's really not all that crazy."

She stared at him across the small table, slowly shaking her head and unable to completely hide her smile.

He gave her reluctant smile a quick look, then said, "It might, um, help us get past things. At least for a while. What do you say?"

"Daniel."

"You could kiss me and make me do probably anything."

"Daniel, no."

"You like having that kind of power over me. I know you do."

"Daniel, you're being—"

"It's not just about me. Scarlet, think of the stars."

"Oh, the stars. I do love the stars. But it's been cloudy all day, and they're all—"

She stopped at the sight of him pointing to the window next to their table. Just beyond the small patio, across the darkness of the deserted rooftop, a full and bright moon was peeking over a low parapet.

"Oh, um. Uh, the moon's out."

He nodded and said, "And it brought along a whole flock of—"

She giggled and said, "Stars don't gather together in flocks."

"They'll flock themselves up to watch you."

"Daniel."

"When I unwrap you, showing them just how gorgeous you are."

"Daniel, you really should—"

"And when your kisses, like the sweetest drug possible, get me to the point where—"

"Okay!"

She giggled and looked around them.

"Okay, Daniel. Um, but just a, uh, a—"

"A quickie?"

"Yes. That."

"Deal. The stars will just have to pay attention and not miss anything."

"You're terrible."

"Happy anniversary, Scarlet, my love."

"That's better than calling me a prude. I'm not, you know. Not really."

He grinned and said, "You won't be after the stars watch you being so bad."

* * *

Daniel held the top rail of the low chain-link fence bounding the patio. All of the wrought iron lampposts were off, and the tables and chairs were stacked and stored away, leaving a clear view of the other diners inside staying busy with their meals and oblivious to the couple sneaking away.

"We probably shouldn't even be out here, Daniel."

"I didn't see any signs. They're practically inviting people to come out here."

"People? You think there are more people out here?"

He laughed and said, "Would you like that? With what we're going to do?"

"No! I'm not like that. That's a very private thing, and I'm—"

"A very private and practical woman. I know. But drop-dead gorgeous too."

"I'm not sure I like being drop-dead anything. But thanks."

"Calls 'em as I sees 'em."

"Oh, boy. Funny."

"Just get a hold of that top pipe, then swing your leg over, and you—"

"Ooh, I don't even want to touch that. There could be bugs."

"There aren't any bugs. They don't just sit around this high up on a building. Oh, but maybe that dress is kind of long."

She punched him softly on his arm.

"You're always wanting me to shorten that, aren't you? This is quite a nice dress just the way it is."

"And you look fantastic in it. But your legs are even more fantastic. You'll just have to hike that up some to climb over. Better yet, let me help you."

She slapped at his hands and said, "I'll manage. It's really not much of a fence anyway."

"Sure. I'm going to watch, though. With the stars."

"You're terrible. Alright, I'm going over."

"Not down?"

She giggled and said, "You're impossible."

"How about hopeful?"

With a smile, barely discernible in the dark, she said, "Maybe if my analysis says you've earned that."

He pumped a fist and said, "Yes! I mean, yeah, I think I have."

"Terrible."

She pulled her dress up quickly, just enough to get one leg over the low fence, then quickly brought over the other and let the dress back down.

"It was too dark," he said, "and you were too quick."

"Did you see any bugs? Are there bugs about to get me?"

"There are no bugs, Scarlet. You're safe. But you're too quick. I didn't see anything."

"You did say that you wanted something quick."

"Funny. Not that."

"Anyway, you've seen it all before."

"Oh my God, yeah. Up close too. Like, so close that—"

"Will you just get over that fence already? Before I change my mind?"

"You can't," he said, and she saw that he was pointing straight up.

She sighed when looking up at the black dome above them, too high above San Francisco's lights to scare away even the faintest of stars. The sparkling dots all crowded together, dancing around to form constellations and clusters and seeming to blink softly to sneak their light down to the appreciative blue eyes trying to take all of them in with a single look.

"They won't let you, those stars. They just told me that you can't go back on our agreement."

"Ooh, just like an attorney. I didn't sign anything, did I?"

"Well, no, but I think it was a, um . . . you say it. What kind of agreement did you make?"

"You're so bad, Daniel. I'm not saying it."

He hurried over the railing, sat himself back against it, and pulled her in close. Together, they looked up at the bright pinholes in the tight black fabric above them.

"Say it, Scarlet. What kind of agreement?"

"No, I'm not saying it."

"It's just a word. You can probably tell that I'm already imagining that word coming from your lips."

She shifted her hips around, grinding into him, then giggled softly.

"Oh my, yes, I can tell. Even without me saying it."

"Still, say it. You might even like saying it."

He smiled at the sound of her letting out a deep breath before she said, "Oral. It was oral, an oral agreement, you bad man."

He laughed softly, then said, "The man in the moon really liked you saying that."

She squeezed his hand and looked across a rough gravel field still hidden in the parapet's shadow.

"He said he wants to hear more."

"Oh, you're impossible."

Looking down near them for a moment, she watched as the line between shadow and moonlit roof surface crept away from them, as if conniving to coax them toward the brightest light in the sky.

"Hmm," she said with a modest scoff. "What about the stars?"

"Oh, I'm afraid they expect much more than some dirty talk."

"I wasn't talking dirty."

"Not yet. That was part of the agreement too."

"It was not!"

"There's no arguing with stars, Scarlet. Like your kisses being somehow kind of toxic to me, they—"

"Toxic now?"

"Uh, you know what I mean. Tasty toxic is what I meant."

"I'm not sure that's too much better."

"Okay, but the point is, stars always get their way with you. You love them."

"Yes, I kind of do. And while they're getting their way with me, you'll be getting your way with me too?"

"A deal's a deal."

She turned to gaze at the moon, its lowest edge kissing the low brick wall. He inhaled and nuzzled around her neck

"Yeah. And it's working, Daniel. I am kind of forgetting. A little."

"That's the whole point."

"No, it's not," she said, laughing softly and still focused on the moon. "You want your way with me."

"On the roof."

"Yeah, on the roof."

"It's for the stars, Scarlet. Can't argue with stars."

"For the stars."

She sighed and started a slow walk toward the moon, his hand in hers, and her low heels were all that broke the silence on the lofty, moonlit and starlit roof in San Francisco.

* * *

Hand in hand, Scarlet and Daniel approached the waist-high brick wall capped with smooth, flat sandstone. With every step, the full moon rewarded them with more light and cast their shadows, which they'd never turned to see, farther behind them, almost far enough to reach the restaurant's patio.

10

He stopped her and turned her to face him.

"First," he said, then removed her glasses, using both hands. They were quickly folded and tucked into a pocket.

The moonlight seemed to approve and provided enough light for him to see her smile, which remained when she said, "And second?"

He reached around with both hands, and each found an ass cheek. Each got a gentle squeeze, then a few pats for one of them, before he started rubbing both.

"This. Oh, that feels so nice. You're really kind of spectacular."

"You kind of have to say that, you know."

"I do?"

"Yes. Or my toxic kisses will make you say whatever I want."

"Just the thought of those kisses could make me say whatever you want."

He leaned in, she tipped her head back enough for their lips to meet, and the moon, planted amongst the stars, watched quietly.

"Mm," he said, keeping their lips close. "I really liked hearing you say what kind of agreement you made for tonight."

She rolled her eyes just enough that he could notice, then said, "I might even say it again."

He waited, looking down at her lips, which were full and red and curled slightly into a smile.

Her lips formed the word, "Oral."

He gave her a quick kiss, then said, "What about it?"

"Hmm. You just want me to keep saying it."

"Uh, yeah. I sure do."

"Okay. I, um, like the word 'oral.'"

He laughed, gave her ass a tighter squeeze with each hand, and said, "Again. Leave out that bit about it being a word."

"You're terrible."

"Only because you kissed me. It's overpowering."

"Huh. Yeah, I can see that. Okay. Um, I like . . . oral."

Daniel groaned out a deep sigh but didn't let her go. But he did dare to go back for another dose of her hypnotic kisses. Before leaning away, he moved closer, enough to whisper in her ear.

"It's kind of a *giving* thing, you know. Maybe you should add that. You know, just to be precise."

In his ear, she whispered, "Oh, you are such a bad man."

"I can't help it. I kissed you. Try it again, and remember to show how generous you are."

She giggled softly, still close to his ear, then whispered, "I like . . . giving . . . oral."

He gave her ear a kiss and said, "Mm-hmm. Oh, yeah, and you like talking dirty too."

"Since when, Daniel? That doesn't count. That was just because you're pestering me. Maybe that moon is pestering me too."

"And the stars. Don't leave them out."

"Anything for the stars. Yeah."

"Oh, yeah. Now, you're talking."

"What?"

"You just entered into another oral agreement. You committed yourself to keeping the stars happy."

"I did not! So, just out of curiosity, what would it take to please them?"

"Remember that they just showed up minutes ago, just for you."

"Yeah, it was cloudy all day. Okay. Sure."

"So, you owe them."

"What, exactly?"

He leaned forward and whispered in her ear.

She leaned back and slapped both hands against his chest.

"Stars aren't perverted like that! They don't want that!"

"Uh, someone does. Alright, maybe not the stars."

"You, Daniel. You want that."

"I want what?" he said, grinning in the moonlight.

"You want me to say that too?"

He nodded and said, "Oh, yeah. Yeah. Say it."

While she was shaking her head, her eyes blue enough for the weak rooftop light, he reached up and found what she'd used to restrain her hair. The few pins and clips were quickly lost in the parapet's shadows, and Scarlet's very long, thick black hair cascaded down over her back.

"And I suppose that's necessary too?"

"Yep. You probably even feel more daring with all that hair down."

"Hmm."

"Go on. You should still say it. Tell me what I want and maybe the stars do too."

She put her arms up over his shoulders, gave him a quick kiss, then backed away just enough to smile, keeping her lips close.

"You want me to . . ."

"Go on. Keep going."

"You're horrible. Okay. You want me to . . . masturbate. For you to watch."

"Oh, God, I sure do."

Holding her waist, he turned her back toward the roof's edge and began nudging her backwards.

"Um, Daniel. What are you doing?"

"Nothing. Just kind of lean up against that wall with the moon behind you."

"How long have you had this all choreographed?"

"I worked out the last detail when I cracked open that last fortune cookie."

"Oh, I really believe that. It told you to arrange all of this?"

"Well, sort of. Not exactly. It was something about taking chances. Daring to hope for more than a mere human deserves."

They'd reached the wall, and she leaned back to sit herself into it. He let go of her waist to brush her mane back over her shoulders, then leaned down to kiss her.

"I'm the mere human," he said. "You? You're something else."

He took a few steps back, then stooped down, watching her silhouette. The light breezes toyed with wisps of her hair but kept them back and off of her face.

"I'm something not human, huh?"

"Um, just trying to say that you're so much more."

"Sweet talker."

"Yeah. That's part of it too."

"What is?"

"Talking. While you're, um, you know."

"You're too much sometimes. What exactly am I supposed to be saying?"

"Oh, I don't know. How about a play-by-play kind of thing? Oh, pretend I'm blind. Yeah, call it like that."

"What is going on with you?" she said with a soft laugh. "All of this from a fortune cookie?"

"Well, no. My imagination sometimes gets—"

Something metallic rattled in the dark distance, far away in the roof's remaining shadows.

"Daniel, what's that? Is someone else up here?"

"No, Scarlet. No way. Don't worry about that at all."

"You neither. I'll protect you."

Laughing, he said, "You? No, you're too sweet and innocent. I don't see you ever doing anything even close to violent."

She sighed and said, "I suppose that's true. You're sure there's no one else up here?"

"I'm sure."

She turned enough to look out from the roof, then gave a quick glance down.

"Hey," he said. "Careful, alright?"

"Me?" she said, laughing once. "This was your idea. You put me here."

She stood up and said, "Never mind. This is silly. We shouldn't even be out here."

He almost whined, saying, "We had a deal, Scarlet. You can't change your mind now."

"Oh. That agreement."

"Yeah, that. If you really change your mind, maybe I'll, I don't know, throw myself over the edge."

She laughed and said, "No, there's no way you'd ever do that. And besides, that would make me a widow. I don't want to be a widow, Daniel."

His grin was obvious in the moon's light, then it was like a celestial hand somewhere had snapped a silent switch, and the entire rooftop went dark. They both looked up.

"No moon and no stars," she said. "Only clouds again."

"It's a sign."

"A sign of what?"

He said, "They're all just giving you a bit more privacy. They'll see you. The moon and stars will see you just fine."

"You're impossible."

"And they'll hear you. God, that's so important too."

"You're a terrible man."

"Damn fortune cookie."

Chapter 2 – Mm, I Love to Rub It

"Sure," she said, "blame it on a cookie."

"Yeah, that's pretty lame. So, lights are out, and it's time to get back to it."

"Back to me, uh . . ."

"Say it. Go on."

After a half-hearted scoff, she said, "Back to me masturbating."

"And talking dirty."

"A play-by-play?"

"Yeah. I mean, yes, please. Hey, you'll have to lift that dress up to, uh, you know."

"Now, you can't say it? But you want me to?"

"I can say it. But this is your show, so you—"

"It's a show? Really, Daniel?"

He laughed once and said, "Well, yeah. For the moon and stars. Somewhere behind the clouds. Okay, it's a little for me too."

She scoffed and reached for the hem of her dress. She cleared her throat, then her voice took on a different tone—that of a narrator.

"I'm reaching for my dress."

He watched both of her hands holding the hem, then he said, "And do you feel your legs?"

She stopped and scoffed again.

"Uh, sort of."

"Talk about that too."

"But I'm barely even touching my—"

"So, make a better effort. For the moon."

After a deep sigh and a smile that he could just barely see, she began to slowly peel her dress up along her thighs. He leaned enough to get a better view of her fingertips gliding along her skin.

"This dress needs to be out of the way. And my thighs, which I'm touching, are so smooth."

He coughed softly and said, "And you like that, right? You like touching them."

She scoffed and said, "I'm touching my legs, and I like how smooth they are."

She pulled the dress up more, and Daniel only watched silently.

"They're so smooth and soft."

He still hadn't said anything.

"I touch them all the time."

With the moonlight hitting him head-on, she could plainly see that his eyes were locked onto her hands, and her dress, and her thighs.

"Every chance I get."

"Why wouldn't you? Even when I'm not around, right?"

She stopped her progress and tipped her head, waiting for his eyes to meet hers.

When they finally did, she said, "Daniel, this is silly. You really want me to—"

"Me and the moon and the stars. Yeah. All of us."

She laughed and said, "That's a lot."

"One more. The most important one."

"Oh, my," she said, looking around. "That noise a second ago. There had better not be—"

He laughed and said, "No, Scarlet. You. *You* really want to."

"I do?"

"Close your eyes for a second, and imagine a steamy orgasm waiting for you—just moments away."

She grinned but closed her eyes.

"Okay. Uh, yeah. Steamy, you said? That's always nice."

She kept her eyes closed, and he said, "You want to masturbate. You want that orgasm, don't you?"

Her grin faded, and she began folding her dress up along her thighs again. He stayed quiet, and Scarlet needed no more prompting.

Using her narrator voice again, she said, "I really do touch my thighs all the time."

She kept going with the dress, and Daniel smiled at the sight of her panties as she got the dress up around her waist, then tucked it around behind her.

"And there we go. That's out of the way."

"You even like undressing yourself, right?"

That got a grin and nod from her, and she said, "Oh, yeah. It's an excuse to touch my soft skin all over. Like I'm doing with my thighs. My smooth, soft thighs."

With eyes still closed, she rubbed her fingertips along the insides of her legs and said, "But touching my thighs is only a start. It's never enough."

She traced paths up to her belly, and rubbed around there for a few moments. Daniel, shaking slightly, dared to look up higher. He saw Scarlet's eyes closed still, but she also was teasing her tongue along her upper lip.

"Mm," she said, and he was quick in looking back down between her thighs.

With her palms against the bare skin above the delicate elastic band, Scarlet poked her fingers inside, then wiggled them enough to drive them in behind the silky fabric.

"Never enough," she said. "Oh, no. I always want to touch my . . ."

He held his breath, eyes locked on the fingers that were still motionless inside her panties.

". . . pussy."

Daniel was shaking his head, staring at his wife just beginning to masturbate for him on a deserted Chinatown roof.

And telling him all about it.

"Mm, it feels so good to touch my pussy. Mm, I love to rub it."

He swallowed hard.

"I know just what my pussy likes."

He watched the cloth moving in the moonlight as her fingers found just the right places.

"Oh, just like that," she said, and it was obvious that she'd gotten a finger or two inside.

Even as he watched her left arm making gentle, rhythmic motions, and knowing—imagining—what she was doing to herself, he didn't even realize that he was reaching for his zipper.

"In and out," she said, her eyes still closed and her motions steady and determined and appearing well-practiced. "So soft. Just the right amount."

He'd gotten his zipper down and was fumbling around inside.

"And I don't ever want to stop touching my pussy until I—"

Another loud creaky rattle coasted through the darkness from some area of the rooftop still buried in shadows.

"What was that?"

"Nothing, Scarlet. It's just an old building."

"Old buildings are creepy and scary. Is there someone else out here?"

"No. No way. But why don't you imagine that someone's watching from the shadows?"

"What? You can't be serious."

"What are they watching you do?"

She giggled and said, "Masturbating."

"More detail," he said, laughing softly.

"Touching my pussy?"

"Yes. Maybe someone's watching you touch your pussy. It's so soft, isn't it? And your fingers know just what it likes?"

"Hmm. Yeah. They sure do."

She closed her eyes, and he watched her arm begin its steady motions again. He'd fought with a large, stiff part of himself to get it out into the moonlight, and he stared at her hand as he gave himself modest strokes.

"Mm," she said, "my pussy is so wet."

"Show me."

"God, you're a terrible man."

With one hand, she made sure that her dress was up and out of the way. She slipped the other out from inside her panties, then slid her fingertips down, then up the inside of one thigh. Then, the other.

"God, even in the dark, I see it."

"Mm-hmm. Ooh, my pussy needs to get even wetter."

Still holding her dress, she wiggled her fingers back under the tight fabric, then went a little farther, bringing out a soft moan.

"Say you love it."

She smiled, never slowed, and said, "I love when it's all wet."

"Not just that."

She smiled, shook her head, kept her eyes closed, and didn't stop.

"You really are terrible."

He shrugged, but she didn't see it with her eyes closed.

"Damn, Daniel. The things I'll do for you."

"Especially when you're about to cum."

"Hmm . . ."

Her breaths were sometimes choppy and deep enough to extend her breasts out with each inhale.

"I, um, I love my pussy. I love my wet pussy."

"Oh, yeah. You sure do. It's all wet and juicy, isn't it?"

"Mm-hmm. It's so juicy."

"And you love that."

Her breaths got choppier, and her arm was moving more quickly, more forcefully, keeping wet fingers busy and getting her so close.

"Mm-hmm, I love my wet and juicy pussy."

"And just the juice?"

"Mm, I love my pussy juice."

"Oh, yeah. Too many words, though."

"Really, Daniel?" she said, pulling in a sharp breath.

"Yes, really. With what you're feeling, you have to play along."

She scoffed with a smile, then said, "Hmm. I love, um, pussy juice."

"Oh, yeah. And you love to make yourself cum?"

She panted a few times before answering.

"Mm-hmm. Oh my God, I am. I'm so close."

He kept stroking himself, watching fingers beneath the fine cloth of her panties rubbing more quickly. His glances away from her action were quick, but they were enough to see that with each breath, she was jutting out her breasts, straining them against the thin fabric of her dress.

"And you love to cum? Tell me you do even if you don't mean it."

"You're getting even sillier, Daniel. Mm, oh yeah. I sure do love to cum."

"You love making yourself cum?"

"Mm-hmm. Because I love my—"

"Too many words."

"Daniel!"

"My anniversary gift, Scarlet. Come on."

"Fine. Because I love pu—"

A loud thump, then a rusty squeal, rolled toward them from the darkness.

She didn't open her eyes, and neither of them stopped.

"It's nothing. Say it. It's part of the agreement."

"Because I love . . . pussy. I bet you like me saying that, huh?"

"Say it again. I mean, really say it."

She shook a couple of times before she spoke. And she didn't show the slightest smile.

"I absolutely love . . . pussy. More than—"

"Aw, you're just say—"

"Uh-uh. More than anything at all . . . mm, I love pussy. I really love pussy, Daniel."

"You do?"

"Mm-hmm," she said, more moan than anything else, shaking with every stroke of her hand. "Mm, so soft and all that . . . juice. You never . . . asked me. You don't . . . mind . . . do you?"

She tipped her head to hear his answer, but Daniel didn't say a word.

So, Scarlet delivered the final, expert touches to send herself into a spiraling climax, touching what she'd just told her husband she liked the best.

* * *

"Oh God," she said, listening but not hearing Daniel, who had gone completely silent.

"Mm . . ." she said, gasping softly as her fingertips skillfully touched in just the right ways. "I'm glad I told you."

Before opening her eyes but never slowing her fingers or weakening her still-growing orgasm, Scarlet said, between urgent breaths, "Oh, that feels so good. Oh! Oh, here it goes! Mm . . ."

She groaned out a deep breath, rubbed with more pressure, and said, "But you still have to fuck me. I love that too."

Grinning, she added, "I'm talking so dirty, and I want so bad to be fucked. Daniel? I said 'fucked.'"

Then, quaking from the ecstasy, she opened her eyes just enough to see her husband's reaction.

And though her hand locked itself in place, with two wet fingers deep inside her, her climax was just too strong to stop for anything.

Even the sight of a giant ragged hand couldn't halt it, a hand coarse and black and leathery, like a weathered black glove covering Daniel's mouth and so wide that it almost blocked his staring eyes.

Scarlet's orgasm wouldn't fade even when she saw a snarling, gargoyle-like head high above her husband's, and large, sinewy black wings extending out far to each side, pumping slowly and quietly.

Through the strong ripples and tingling, she found the will to scream.

"Daniel!"

He groaned and wrestled and got free from the hand just long enough to yell, "Scarlet! Run as fast as—"

The hand nearly crushed his face as it trapped the rest of his words inside, but Daniel kept fighting to break free of its grasp.

Scarlet, electricity still pulsing through her from her daring masturbation for her husband, did nothing but open her eyes wider. She had no time to speak or scream before Daniel was on her, his arms flailing out as he tried to grab her.

She saw that the beast behind him, so black everywhere that it could almost have been a sinewy slice of the night that had ripped itself free, was reaching for him with both of its hideous hands. Long claws on every one of its fingers, all as dark as the rest of the creature, were about to rip into him.

"Scarlet! You have to—"

One hand smothered him again and started to pull him backwards. Scarlet fought to not get dragged with him, but he'd gotten tight grips on the sleeves of her dress.

The nightmare bat thing easily lifted Daniel from the gravel, which then yanked Scarlet upright onto her heels, then higher. But her dress was still wrapped around her waist, showing simple, modest panties that were dark enough to conceal any wet spots. And her long black hair was a mop dangling down over the busy street far below.

Her legs hung limp as she watched the bat open its mouth to scream.

But all it did was laugh like something that knew very well its level of vileness and reveled in it.

Scarlet screamed, then screamed again when a second bat appeared from the darkness and grabbed at her husband too.

That one laughed as roughly as the first.

Daniel, his face gouged and ripped and bleeding, struggled and twisted around to get his mouth free and yelled, "Scarlet, not you too!"

"Daniel!"

"Run! When I let you go, run, goddammit!"

"No, Daniel! I'm not leaving you!"

As if it understood the words spoken by the anniversary couple who'd been enjoying a new experience to forget their past, the first bat flapped its wings just before Daniel was about to let go of Scarlet.

That single pump of its wings lifted them all up more, and it also moved husband and wife closer to the edge.

Too close.

Only Scarlet's ankles were touching the parapet's top sandstone layer when Daniel lost his grip on the flimsy fabric, and her eyes, blue even without the voyeuristic moon's light, stared into Daniel's.

She stared even as she fell, heels in place, tasteful dress still bunched up around her waist, and her wild black hair flapping madly and pointing up at Daniel.

A single scream, an odd mix from a woman knowing that she'd be dead soon but still twisted up from the rapture of an uncommonly robust orgasm, reached upward to her captured and brutalized husband.

The bat held Daniel there, clutching his neck and not letting him scream his final goodbye, as it and the other bat, and Daniel, all watched Scarlet and her dwindling scream falling toward the street many stories below them.

"Hate humans," it said, then it began a steady driving of its oily black wings, lifting itself and Daniel higher above the gravel.

"Eh," said the other, also winging enough to hover there. "They have some value."

"Some."
"Only some."

25

Chapter 3 – More Like Hell's Door

"You can't play for shit," said a thin, sloppy teenage boy, covered in grimy denim and pausing his nose picking long enough to sneer while offering his uninvited critique.

His friends, not as thin but almost as dirty as the streets, snickered and giggled. But the sparse crowd surrounding the homeless musician, who was sitting on the sidewalk with his back against the building's brick wall, mostly ignored the comment. Some shook their heads, and others scoffed and searched their pockets for more change for the donation bucket adorned with a crude sign reading "Blind. Help Feed Kat."

And one in the audience, a slightly older fellow obviously dedicated to serious gym time, dropped his backpack, pointed and the crass critic, and said, "Hey, leave him alone."

"Wade, not again," said a wispy blond woman holding his arm.

"Relax, Ginny," he said, never taking his eyes off of the wisecracking punk.

A punk who said, mostly for his friends, "Somebody's whipped."

His back got patted, and the youth to his left elbowed him and said, "That's telling him."

"Dammit, you—"

"Wade, no. Just let it go."

He frowned at the entire laughing group of them while saying, "Fine."

Tipping his head to his own strumming rhythm, which barely moved his bushy, matted mop of hair, the man seated on the grimy concrete grinned beneath dark glasses as his sudden musical outburst aborted the pending fight scene. Both the rude young man and the aggressive, slightly older man let their hostilities slip away, and each even managed a smile at the nighttime curbside concert.

The guitar man's cat, leashed and sitting regally on a small square of carpet near him, had been looking from face to face, then scooted himself back down into a scruffy bunch of fluff when the onlookers calmed and the music played.

But the cat was the first to look up, following two swiveling ears that had reacted first.

The cat was the first to hear a woman's screams as she rocketed toward them.

The blind musician looked up next, then the crowd, everyone craning their necks to watch a body somewhat clothed in a stylish dress, still wearing heels, and with a cloud of snapping black hair racing toward the canopy roof beside them.

All watched in silence as Scarlet's scream emptied her lungs, and she became as quiet as the onlookers. But her impact, ripping and shattering through the canvas and supporting structure, drowned out even the car engines.

Her fateful flight was fast but not fast enough to send her completely through. One of her ankles caught a loop of power cord as every part of her got sliced and gouged, and she jerked to an abrupt stop, hanging from that one snagged leg.

Only her hair, carrying bits of debris but otherwise looking quite photogenic, appropriate for an anniversary dinner out with her husband, touched the sidewalk.

And only the cat had eyes sharp enough to watch beads of blood tracing paths along strands of hair to begin forming a small, shiny pool.

Muted, the standing audience and the seated blind musician and his cat all watched as Scarlet's lifeless body spun slowly one way, then the other, then back again.

With each pass, her dead, blank eyes studied them before scanning either the street or the building wall. The wind from falling had failed to restore her dress to any level of dignity, and her free leg, unhindered by any of the canopy's construction, pointed nearly straight out to the side.

"Holy shit," said the guitar man, standing and watching Scarlet spin.

"Hey," said the punk. "Not so fucking blind anymore?"

He only waved to be left alone as he stared over his glasses at the spectacle.

"Wade, help her down!"

He laughed and said, "Uh, Ginny, it's kind of late to help her with anything."

"Well?" said the street punk. "Play some fucking music, at least!"

He got his guitar ready as he focused on the young man sneering at him and said, "Least I could do."

"Since you're not fucking blind anyway. Shit, we should all get refunds."

"You little fucker. Ever hear of performance art?"

"You're lame. Just a fucking phony."

He shrugged and said, "Well, fuck. It's a living. Sure, I'll play for you, you greasy little prick."

He looked around at his audience, most of whom were still staring in shock at dead Scarlet, and said, "For all of you," then began a very familiar tune about a bell dinging and donging and a witch being dead.

"Hey," said Wade, "maybe show some respect, huh?"

He smirked and said, "It'll cost you."

Ginny fished out a few bills, mumbled, "Bastard," and hurried to drop them into his bucket. When her hand was close enough, the cat hissed and swiped at it.

"Jesus. Nice cat."

"He can see that those are only singles," the man said with a grin.

"Yeah, so can you," said Wade. "What a fake fucker. Play, dammit."

"Sure. Why the fuck not?"

He grinned, still meeting as many eyes as he could, and strummed out a tune about someone knocking on Heaven's door.

"That's funny," said the punk. "You're a funny fucker."

He only grinned and boosted his strumming.

Wade snorted out a loud laugh, looking from the punk, to the guitar player, quickly at the cat, then lingering at the sight of Scarlet, hanging upside down and still spinning slowly.

"More like Hell's door," he said.

Ginny gave him a sharp elbow.

"No, really," he said. "She was headed straight for Hell. Like a goddamn bullet."

"Yeah," said the punk. "All she had to do was punch a hole in that fucking sidewalk. She gave it her best fucking shot."

Wade looked straight up, pointed, and said, "She tried. She picked the highest fucking—wait, did you see that?"

Most of them looked up, and the punk said, "Uh-oh. More falling corpses?"

He got elbowed, and his buddy said, "Dude, she wasn't a corpse till she hit."

"How do you know that?"

"Look at her. She was up there getting fucked, I'd bet."

"Yeah, looks like it. But plenty of people fuck dead bodies. It happens more often than—"

"She's still smiling. Sort of. Nympho dead bitch."

"No, things just look different when a bitch is hanging upside down."

"Oh, yeah. Probably. I mean, even both of her—"

"Shut up, you idiots!" said Wade. "There were some big fucking wings up there. You didn't see that?"

"Birds. Dude, birds are everywhere."

"It wasn't a goddamn bird. Too fucking big."

The punk smirked, then looked at the formerly blind musician until he looked up at him.

"Hey, blind man. Know any songs about giant birds fucking hot dead chicks on a Chinatown roof, then trying to shoot them straight to Hell?"

"Yeah, you little shit. I wrote a shitload of them last week about exactly that. How much time you got?"

* * *

"Only this one?"

"This time," said the first bat, and it worked its wings enough to draw itself and Daniel away from the roof's edge. "No dead ones."

"Can't work. Yeah."

Daniel, hanging with one unyielding hand around his neck, had kicked and swung his arms and watched Scarlet fall. The bat had allowed him to watch her strike near the street, almost disappearing without a sound so far below them. Then, it had jerked him back, pumped its wings, and lifted him higher.

His clean dress shoes sometimes scraped across the gravel but mostly, the bat kept him high enough to not make even that sound. His zipper was still down, but he was showing far less enthusiasm than when Scarlet was moaning and masturbating for him and telling him what she absolutely loved. Grasping with both hands at the much larger one around his neck left him no chance of hiding it away and zipping up.

Looking ahead, he saw moonlight glinting on the fractured metal housing of a ventilation duct cap. The large unit's sides were peeled back, torn and jagged, and the blackness inside was absolute.

"Hate this."

"Yeah. Tight."

The bat carrying Daniel tucked its wings and wiggled through the opening, then pulled its captive in too. Keeping its wings folded tight, it began scraping its way downward, claws scratching against the damaged steel sides of a square tube leading down from the roof.

The other bat followed, sometimes snorting and cussing.

"Tired of hiding."

"Yeah. Should just hunt."

"Not hide."

"Not."

Daniel led the way, with a grip on him loose enough that he could breathe and pray in a constant, desperate mumble. The shaft seemed to go on forever, and he could barely groan out a protest whenever he got banged against the sidewall, sometimes ripping clothes and skin if sharp edges were lined up just right.

They continued dropping, long bat claws fighting for traction, oily wings folded, scraping, and a human held tight. On and on, through total darkness. Daniel showed no signs of bravery, letting tears flow and fighting for every breath.

"Fuck," said the trailing bat. "Finally."

Straining against the leather glove almost choking the life out of him, Daniel tipped his head enough to see the faintest of orange glows. It was just a pinpoint, like a star in the sky but in the wrong direction. And the wrong color.

With a heavy thump, Daniel's bat landed and blasted an aggravated snort. He heard the thing spread its wings, but he was still dangling above emptiness with a dim orange glow some unknown distance farther down.

He heard the other bat land and groan as it spread its wings too.

"Fuck. Home."

"Yeah. Go."

The second bat became a tangled shadow with its wings compact at its sides. It sometimes hid the orange and sometimes circled around in it as its size decreased from its rapid descent.

"Hate this crack."

It waited, but Daniel couldn't answer.

"We go."

But Daniel could hold his breath, what little he had, as he and his bat began a freefall, their speed increasing rapidly as they pursued the other bat. As the orange glow grew, he could see that they were spiraling down through a rock passageway. Jagged walls were close front and back but to the sides, there was only darkness.

The first bat through the rocky passage begin whooshing its wings and seconds later, the rock walls flying past them ended. Daniel's bat laughed as they fell for a few seconds before it gave its wings a start.

The sudden slowing nearly removed Daniel's head, but the bat seemed to know how much a human could withstand without getting ruined during transport.

The scorched air billowed up in waves, wedging around Daniel's eyes, under the lids, and his tears dripped away toward fires far below them. Still, he tried to look in every direction as his heart gave a strong reminder that he was still alive.

A world shrouded in black sprawled out below them as the two bats hovered high up, close to the rock ceiling and its crack that led to a basement and an abandoned ventilation shaft in a tall Chinatown building.

Directly below them, too distant to see any real detail, a maze of haphazard streets divided old buildings into silent groupings, some with a few lights in windows and others with small fires burning on their roofs.

Straight ahead of them, the dark city met its end where a slick black plain flooded out farther. Far beyond that, a wide fire raged, and black dots circled all around it.

"Go," said the other bat.

"Yeah. Buckets."

"Two."

"Two."

Both bats maneuvered themselves to face all three of them the other way, and Daniel tipped up his head up enough to point his watering eyes that way.

Not far in the distance, the city with its buildings and fires abutted a shoreline. And beyond that, there was only fire.

A sea of fire, stretching as far as he could see.

And the bats were taking him there, flying below the jagged rock ceiling and high above a dark and desolate city.

Chapter 4 – Like a Delicacy, I'd Say

Without clumps of her thick black hair as a cushion, Scarlet would have felt the coarse stone floor of the alley against the delicate skin of her cheek. She lay facedown several paces from the street, wearing the same dress and same low heels, and her arms were straight along her sides.

She moved her fingers first, just those on her left hand, and touched a filmy warm liquid there. She let them rest then tried her right hand, and sliding the fingers from side to side moved them easily on the rough but lubricated surface.

With a modest groan, she reached around with both hands and found some of where she lay to be slick and other places dry. Her hair tickled her nose, and she snorted weakly, trying to move it aside, but that minimal action had no effect. It was trapped.

"Oh, God, where am I?"

Lifting her head, then opening her eyes, didn't help at all. All she saw was night as if her eyes were still shut tight.

And all she heard was a buzzing so low that it could have gone unnoticed.

There was nothing to see, but the sound of footsteps somewhere behind her got her lungs to lock up, and she lay still, listening.

The steps, some of them splashing and others only clopping, got louder then began to fade.

Groaning again, she fought herself up onto her feet and bumped into a brick wall, which she confirmed by patting it all around. Then, she put her back to it and looked first to her left, then to her right.

And she saw very dim light like through a doorway. She took a step toward it, then froze and pressed her back against the wall again.

Something large, easily twice her height and much longer, had begun lumbering from right to left, crossing that opening, a thing thick and smooth and snorting softly. In the faint light, it appeared black. Slick and black.

She caught her breath and stared as three more followed after it.

Their sharp footfalls on the brick pavement dwindled as the small pack meandered away, and Scarlet stayed frozen and fought to calm her breaths.

When that area with the only light that she could see had stayed quiet for a while, she ventured toward it again.

She reached out and felt the sharp edge of the brick wall and held it as she leaned out just enough to see what part of San Francisco was out there.

All she saw was a narrow, barely visible street lined with tall dark buildings. Looking up, she saw that only a few of the many windows housed some kind of light, as if it were so late at night that everyone was asleep.

"What zoo did those come from?" she mumbled to herself.

More footsteps were approaching. The sound of running. Desperate running, coming from the left.

Scarlet ducked back into the shadows and watched a shabby older man running past, sometimes looking behind him, and wheezing from the effort.

The sound of his steps hadn't diminished any before the beasts she'd seen before—big and oily black and snorting—charged after him.

"Oh, God, what is this?" she whispered.

She heard a scream and more frantic running mixed in with the sound of durable hooves striking the bricks.

Another scream. Louder.

And no more steps of any kind.

Just deep grunting and growling and fighting somewhere down the street.

"Don't look, Scarlet. Just don't."

She did look and saw the tail ends of two of the escaped beasts, both jostling for position, bumping into each other and snorting gleefully.

One reared and turned its head, and what could have been a human arm dangled from its jaws.

Scarlet retreated farther into the shadows, muttering quietly, "No, no, no! What the hell is this?"

Her chest rose and fell, and she found no way to stop it. Those breaths needed to rush in, then even more quickly back out.

The sound of a bone snapping—at least, it could have been that—came from the direction of the beasts and the fleeing man who hadn't fled quickly enough.

"This can't be happening. No, it just can't!"

Tears began to gather, hot and thick, and they broke free to fight a tight course down her cheeks.

She rubbed at them with both hands, then gasped.

"My glasses! Where are they?"

She patted around and found only a dress without pockets, and no handbag was there to search.

A scared laugh began then died, and she nodded quickly and tried to laugh again, on command, but the tears didn't give any ground.

"I didn't see that right," she said, still rubbing her eyes and shaking from a stifled sob. "That was something else. Not what I thought."

With her arms at her sides, she kept tight against the wall and gazed toward the street.

"It couldn't be what I thought. No, I didn't see that!"

She sucked in a sharp breath as quietly as she could when something big and dark even against the darkness out there fell from above in a jerky pattern. What looked like a head, a silhouette of one, bobbed one way, then the other.

It jerked from side to side, then held still and made no sound. Seconds passed, then it hurried low, then high, then froze and stayed quiet.

Mouthing the words, "No, no, no!" Scarlet forced her eyes closed and leaned forward, letting her black hair have a chance at hiding anything that apparition might see.

She heard it snorting softly and held aside just enough of her hair to look.

From the thing's sides, large parts of it were moving rhythmically up and down, even as the head continued to tip like a metronome. It drew in long breaths, then snorted them out quickly.

Hiding behind her thick hair again, she heard an angry, gravely voice say, "What? Something?"

The thing looking in relaxed, gave its dark appendages a decisive final flap, then grunted out, "Thought a human."

The other said, "Hate humans."

"Yeah. Eat, though."

A gravely laugh, then a rough voice saying, "Good to eat. Yeah."

Scarlet stayed hidden in the shadows and listened to what could only be massive wings being pounded against the stale, dark air. The sound of them leaving gave way to silence and faint buzzing only seconds later.

She looked up and confirmed that they—whatever they were— were gone.

The sobbing started before she could turn and press her face into the warm bricks and inhale their scent of oil.

And before she gave herself to a hearty cry, she hurried to fluff her hair up and around to hide her face as well as she could.

Then, she cried, with her palms flat against the wall. She cried a lot.

Quietly, though.

* * *

She'd been wiping across her cheek when she first heard the voices.

Somewhere out there, out on that street with its mysteries that she couldn't have seen clearly without enough light or her eyeglasses, humans were approaching. She heard their voices.

A man and a woman.

They were talking pleasantly and sometimes laughing.

Scarlet inhaled sharply, chasing away the last sob, then wiped at each eye one more time before turning and walking quietly toward the street.

Again, she held the wall's corner and looked left, then right, and she saw a couple approaching from the right.

Still mostly lost in the darkness but coming more into focus with every step, they walked easily, hand in hand.

"Hey!" she called out even before she'd stepped into the open. "Over here!"

"Oh, Isabella, look. A new arrival, I'd bet."

"Jonas, Honey, you think you're so fucking smart, but you don't know squat. Maybe she lives around here."

"Huh. Lives, you say? You know that can't possibly make a damn bit of sense."

Jonas waved as the couple drew near, then said, "Well, hello! What the hell brings you out along a dark street like this?"

"Hello. I, um, I think I'm kind of lost. What part of Chinatown is this?"

The couple looked at each other for a few seconds, then both smiled at Scarlet.

Isabella said, "Uh, maybe the lower end?"

Jonas blurted out a single loud laugh and said, "Good one, Honey. More like China Underground, though."

"Even fucking better."

She faced Scarlet and said, "I'm Isabella, and this son of a bitch is Jonas. What's your name?"

"I'm Scarlet. I don't know where I am. Can you give me some directions?"

Jonas cleared his throat, grinned, then said, "Take off your dress. How's that for some goddamn directions?"

He got a sharp elbow from Isabella, who said, "Honey, shame on you, you dirty fucker."

To Scarlet, she said, "At least he started that last word with a letter 'd.' Would have been more interesting without that first letter, though!"

"What?"

"Think about it!"

"Look," said Scarlet, "I just want to—"

"Oh, I know," Isabella said. "You don't know where in Hell you are."

"Uh, Chinatown, right? But what part of it?"

"Let's give him another chance. Jonas, Honey, try again."

Jonas nodded, maintained a silly grin, and said, "Up is way better than down."

"He's right," said Isabella. "But I think he's mostly thinking about 'going down.'"

She chopped him again with an elbow, and Scarlet noticed, even in the faint light, that the skin on her arm kind of sloshed around for a second, even though she didn't appear overweight.

"She's just looking for an excuse to talk about sexual types of things," said Jonas. "I love that about her."

"He loves a lot of things about me. Oh, the things I do for him."

"*To* me, you mean. You do all kinds of things *to* me. Some are fucking mean!"

Scarlet had been looking from one gaunt face to the other, listening to them chattering on, until they stopped and focused on her again.

"Oh, my dear," said Isabella, "you have a little bit of crude there on your pretty cheeks. Let me."

She took a step closer, and Scarlet let the woman reach out and lightly touch under her eyes, wiping both ways. Then, she wiped more. And yet more.

"Um, I think maybe that's good. Thanks," said Scarlet. "Um, I really could just use some directions, you know? I don't even see any street signs."

Jonas snickered and said, "Not much sign of life either, huh?"

"What?"

"Never mind him. He's a joker. Well, Scarlet, Sweety, you sure can't navigate by the stars."

Scarlet looked up and for the first time, she saw nothing but solid black. Not gray like cloud cover. Just black. And no stars.

"Dark clouds?" she said. "That's why?"

Isabella roared out a hearty laugh and said, "Yeah. You just go with that. For as long as you fucking can. It'll help keep that pretty head together."

"She does have a pretty head," said Jonas. "Pretty. Good head for head."

Isabella tipped her own head, studying Scarlet, and said, "Hmm. Maybe even prettier when not together."

"Mm-hmm," said Jonas. "Pretty head *not* together. We should find out."

Isabella grinned at Scarlet and said, "He's always planning ahead, this one."

"Ha! A head!"

"Um, look," said Scarlet. "I think I'm taking too much of your time. Can you just point toward Chinatown?"

Jonas chuckled and said, "My thing is already pointing that way. I can show you. God damn, I want to show you. Let me just—"

His reaching for his zipper got stopped by a grab of his arm by Isabella.

"He's joking, dear Scarlet."

"No, I'm not. I'm, uh . . . really pointing. Hardly pointing too. Oh, boy. Oh, yeah."

"We don't get too many fresh ones here," said Isabella. "You're new, right? Just arrived?"

"Is that like coming?"

She elbowed him again and kept grinning at Scarlet.

Scarlet said, "I think I might—"

"How was her skin, Isabella? Was it soft? It looks soft. I like soft. Even though I'm almost always so—"

A sharp elbow to his gut forced him to wheeze out, not leaving enough air to finish that thought.

"Yes, Jonas. She has very nice skin. It's really quite exquisite. Like a delicacy, I'd say."

"I'd say that too."

"Um, Chinatown? Please?"

"That's, um, going to be a bit of a problem because,"—she turned her eyes down to examine Scarlet's legs, not much of them visible beneath the hem of her modest dress—"ooh, looks like good muscle tone too."

"I like muscles. That's second best. Not my first choice. Guess my first choice, Isabella. Guess it!"

"You're being crazy, Jonas. I damn well know your first choice. Same as mine, right? You'd know if you had any brains at all to—"

"Ha!"

"Look, really!" said Scarlet. "If you don't know, you can just say so. It's fine. I'll—"

"You need Mortimer. He's kind of like our lead fucker around here. Maybe he can help."

Jonas snickered and said, "Help himself, more likely."

Isabella said, more quietly, "Horny old goat."

Scarlet coughed and said, "Where's this Mortimer at?"

Isabella grinned over at Jonas, who tried without success to stifle a deep laugh.

"She's just setting them up, isn't she?"

Jonas said, "Oh my, yes. Shall I?"

"I'd rather. Allow me."

Isabella reached out and caressed Scarlet's cheek, looked her in the eye, and said, "He's coming. He's almost always coming!"

And Isabella didn't laugh until Jonas laughed. They both laughed.

And Isabella kept helping herself to the soft skin until Scarlet took two quick steps back.

Chapter 5 – No Pay for Dead Flesh, Dammit

"Hey," said the bat without human cargo. "Don't kill."

"Want to."

"Yeah. Don't."

"Alright."

He switched his grip to hold Daniel under his arms, allowing him to cough and suck in as much of the hot air as he could.

"Maybe it talks."

"Too stupid."

"What the fuck are you? What the fuck is going on?"

"It talks."

"Hate humans."

"Where am I? Oh God, take me back! Please!"

The bat shook Daniel around, laughed about it, then said, "Could drop."

"Don't. Need for trade."

"No, don't drop me! Good God, what is this place?"

Several long moments passed with only the sound of heavy wings flapping against the still air.

"Don't know," said one.

"You know?" said the other while shaking Daniel around.

"No, I fucking don't! Am I dead? Is this Hell?"

Daniel looked up enough to see his bat turn its large, scaly head to look at its companion flying close by.

"Could be," it said.

"No," said the other. "Below, maybe."

"Yeah. More below."

"This is some kind of fucking nightmare. God, I have to wake up. Please, just let me—"

A loud boom cracked the darkness and echoed off of the ceiling and the ground, then raced past them and toward the endless burning sea.

"Hate that."

"Hate wind."

"Because fly."

"Hard to."

"Yeah. Hurry."

Daniel felt claws sinking through clothing and skin as the thing's powerful hands tightened their grip.

Then, both of the beasts beat their wings, picking up speed and hurtling them toward the fiery ocean.

"Almost."

"Hurry. Reactor safe."

Daniel sucked in a deep breath as they all began a sudden freefall, and he saw, near the fires, a cluster of dimly lit buildings with patchy pools of smooth black surrounding them.

They swooped so low over a chain link fence that he screamed and lifted his legs, narrowly escaping having them shredded from his body.

"Don't rip," said the companion bat.

"Won't. Much."

Daniel's carrier bat sailed low, dragging his feet across the gravel lot and tearing off one of his shoes.

"Could just eat."

"No. Trade."

"Fatter."

"Fatter. Buckets tastier."

The wind came up from behind them in a hot, violent squall just as Daniel was carried and sometimes dragged through a wide, low opening into a dark, empty building. He groaned when the claws released him, and he was already too low to the ground to fall.

But with each tumble, sharp little stones dug themselves in. And his final slide pushed a few in deeper.

He lay there bleeding, eyes welded shut, without even a sob to clutter up his shallow breathing.

Until two sets of claws pinched into his ribs and lifted him up.

* * *

Daniel's feet, one torn and missing a shoe, dragged along the cracked linoleum of a hallway in one of the reactor buildings. Even with their wings tucked back, the two bats walked one behind the other, and Daniel's legs were the farthest back.

"Alive?"

"Enough."

They rounded a corner, and Daniel didn't resist his battered legs banging when they bumped a wall as they made the turn. He got dragged a few more steps, then dropped facedown when the forks jabbing into his sides released him.

A low humming and comfortable, constant vibration of the floor gave him no reason to try moving. Even the smell of burning oil, like from hundreds of old lamps, seemed welcoming, but the unmistakable stench of rotting bodies mingled with the soot, choking him.

A disinterested human voice, raspy and scratchy, spoke nearby.

"Is he alive?"

A bat said, "Enough."

"Fucker. I'll be the judge of that."

A modest kick from a hard boot caught Daniel's already bleeding side.

"Hey. Dead or alive? I'm not paying these fuckers for dead flesh. No pay for dead flesh, dammit."

Daniel turned his head some, opened his eyes, and met the inquisitive stare of a tortured, oil-stained face.

His hard hat carried its own smears and streaks, and denim coveralls, that long ago could have been blue, bulged in odd places. His tired eyes stared down at Daniel as he smirked.

"Close enough," he said, then poked stained, mangled fingers around up under his helmet.

Daniel groaned and rested his head, then let his eyes snap shut as the odd crowd bantered around him.

"Try to keep them more alive, will you? You fuckers."

"Hate humans."

"Me too, now. Straight fucking humans, I mean—they think they're better than the rest of us. Still, we need to squeeze some useful work out of these fuckers before they expire."

"Funny. Expire."

"I'll give you one goddamn bucket, and you two fuckers can split it."

"Bucket each."

"He's almost dead, this goddamn straight fucking human."

"Hate humans."

"Yeah, I've heard that. Like a fucking million goddamn times, so save it, you fucker. One bucket."

"Large."

The workman nudged Daniel with his boot, trying to roll him over, but that wasn't enough. So, he kicked him, getting only a groan. He kept kicking until the bruised and bloody man rolled over onto his back.

"Uh, that's not exactly large," he said, pointing at Daniel's open fly and what he'd never even thought to hide back away. "Not now."

"Was."

"Was with human female."

"Yeah. She wanted fucking."

"Was bigger then."

"Was going to fuck her."

"You fuckers. So what? We're not running some kind of stud farm breeding operation here. Strong backs—that's what we want. He could have a monster cock and unless he can shovel dirt with it, it's useless to us. Got that? One fucking bucket."

"Two."

"One, dammit."

"Big."

"Big bucket."

"Oh, fine, you fucking goddamn bat freaks. Next time, try beating a little less fucking shit out of the guy, alright?"

"Hate humans."

Daniel heard "You guys" as the reactor worker turned and walked away.

A few seconds later, he heard him returning, and the bats laughed in a low, calmly aggressive way.

"Big? Not."

"Bigger. Or two."

"It's fucking big enough. You take just this one or you can just bring this beat up fucker outside and eat him instead."

"Entrails."

"Yeah, that's right. The entire bucket is entrails. You like that, don't you?"

"Good."

"Tasty."

"So, we have a deal? More entrails in that bucket than in this fucker?"

"Yeah."

"Yeah."

"Pick that fucker up first."

Daniel groaned as two sets of sharp nails poked him like a baked potato and stood him up. They held on long enough for him to prove that he wouldn't collapse, then they backed away.

He opened his eyes and gazed without comment at the man who had just traded a bucket of entrails for him.

Beyond the oily man, he saw two pairs of giant black wings, folded and tilting from side to side as the laughing bats hiked away and carried their bucket toward the outside.

"If you have a name," he said to Daniel, "just forget it. You're done with that bullshit."

Daniel looked down and saw that when the man had gone for the bucket of slop, he'd also brought back a shovel.

"But you will need this. Except for all the cuts and scrapes and bruising and broken bones and—oh, shit, what good are you? Can you still fucking work, or should we move this train wreck along and just incinerate you?"

"I can work. I . . . can work."

"You're just filling me up with confidence. Alright, fine. We'll give you a try. I, myself, think those fucking bats beat all the good work out of you. But fine, let's get you going."

"Where am I?"

"At the reactor. We're the sons of bitches that actually try to keep this giant evil machine running. It isn't easy, let me tell you."

"A reactor? Uh, but where? What happened to—I was in San Francisco, and—"

"Yeah, with some woman that wanted to get fucked, so I hear. Funny. Now, look at you. Beat to shit and about to shovel dirt over some goddamn evil radioactive crap."

Daniel only stared, shaking his head slowly.

"Yeah, you're right. That's not so fucking funny. But that's— shit, I almost said 'life.' Imagine that."

He turned and took a few steps, then stopped and faced Daniel again.

"Two things," he said, holding up one full finger and one missing most of it.

He saw Daniel glance quickly at his hand, so he lowered it.

"Forget the fingers. Really, two complete things. One: follow close and don't stray off whatever fucking path I walk. Got it?"

"Uh, yeah. Sure. But just where the hell is—"

"Two! For God's sake, pull up that fucking zipper unless you're planning on fucking someone or something."

The man laughed while Daniel looked down, then fought with his zipper. But he looked back up when the man continued.

"Or maybe you'll be looking for some head. Yeah, that might be it. You might get lucky and get head from two. Imagine that. And that would all be from just one mutated fucking thing where you're going."

Daniel's mouth quivered, but he didn't speak.

"No, don't even think about it. I know it sounds good. But anything with two heads, giving you head, or heads, is most likely just scheming to bite your fucking balls off."

He turned and walked away, whistling a happy tune.

Daniel swallowed hard, held the shovel in one hand and his crotch in the other, and hurried after a man who had a large lump moving around under the loose fabric of his oily denim work clothes.

*　*　*

The man leading the procession of two stopped abruptly, and his whistling stopped five seconds later. Then, he turned to look at Daniel.

"I'm Willie. My brain is fried."

Daniel tipped his head and stared without answering.

"Maybe like fried rice."

He grinned and pointed at Daniel and said, "But don't be getting the idea that you're going to crack open this melon and dip an oily spoon in there for some. Oh, no. They need me here. I have value."

He turned to resume the walk, then stopped again, causing Daniel to bump into the lump on his back.

"I have value not just as a tasty snack, I mean. My fried rice works just good enough to hand out shovels to new guys like you. Got your shovel?"

"Uh, yeah."

"Got your fucking shovel?" he yelled.

"Yeah. Yeah, I do."

Calmly, he said, "Let's march."

He led Daniel through a maze of hallways and down many flights of stairs, and the temperature climbed with every descent. Through open doorways, in unlit rooms and corridors, wailing and screams and hideous laughter competed with the grinding of gears and whining of powerful motors.

Before passing through what looked like a hatch on a submarine, Willie stopped him.

"It was the radiation that did it. It's got a funny fucking way of cooking things on the inside. Like my heaping serving of fried rice stored away up top. I swear on the God of bats that—hey, you suppose those bat friends of yours have a god?"

"My, my friends?"

"I'm just being stupid. They're probably not your absolute best friends. I mean, you only just met somewhere up there,"—he pointed up and bounced his eyebrows—"when you was about to fuck some living human woman. She was living, right?"

"Huh? Yeah, she was—"

"Not that there's anything wrong with fucking a dead one. Oh, no. You won't hear that from me. Even if she was dead, and even if she had noodles for brains, fried or not, and even if—wait, was it noodles or rice?"

Daniel shook with his sobbing, and his shovel clattered to the oily concrete floor.

"Rice," Daniel said.

"What?"

"Rice! Fried fucking rice!"

Willie blasted out a sharp laugh and said, "Anger isn't very becoming, you know. You got to learn to roll with the punches here because—wait, maybe it's burn with the radiation. Yeah, that's it.

Learn to burn with the waves. They come in fast, all hot and ornery."

Daniel rubbed his eyes with both hands and shook silently.

"Aw, there, there, young fellow. I was just being silly. It's kind of all I have left. Look, I was just kidding around. Oh, shit. I forgot all about the goddamn bats and if they have a goddamn god or not."

Daniel wiped at his eyes and got his sobbing under control.

"That was funny. A goddamn god. How could a god be a goddamn god? That's some serious self-loathing from a goddish goddamn god type of thing. See? Isn't that alone worth your scary, freaky ride here?"

"What? Huh?"

"It's all about the radiation, son. It cooks, it burns, it rattles things around. Mostly, though, it's got a fucked up imagination, and it sure does like to experiment with shit."

"It, it has imagination?"

"Nah, no way. Don't believe every fucked up thing some blasted fool tells you. Oh no, it's worse than that. It's random as fuck. It does things even a goddamn god would never think of. If the god had a brain. A fried one."

"What? What the hell are you—"

"Frying is easy. Growing fun shit is the real adventure. There's no telling what any one of us is about to grow next."

"Grow? Huh?"

"Yeah, young man! Like that floppy sausage you had hanging out just a second ago. Want another? Huh? Oh, hey, maybe it'll puff up like a bloated dirigible leading a goddamn parade! How about that, huh?"

"What are you talking about? What's wrong with you?"

"It isn't me, kid. Goddamn radiation. Do you feel it? You're already sponging it up. It's some goddamn awful evil stuff too. I seriously don't know what the fuck this place is. Do you?"

Willie stared and waited for an answer.

"Uh, I mean . . . what?"

"Never mind. No one knows. Can't be Hell, though. Even Hell has higher standards than to take in the kind of outrageous freaks packed into this hellhole. Not Hell—just a hellhole. Huh. That's kind of funny too. Imagine a goddamn god living in a hellhole that's not actually Hell. No, it's something fucking different. But hey, there's work to be done."

"What . . . why? Can't I just—"

"Can't you just go back to fucking the dead babe with roasted macaroni for brains? That it? No, young man, no! Let's get your ass to work!"

Sobbing again, Daniel picked up his shovel and followed after Willie.

Who had resumed whistling a very pleasant tune.

Chapter 6 – Orgasming Your Brains Out

"I, um, think my eyes are okay now. Thanks."

"Nonsense. Even in the dark, I can still see a few stubborn smudges. A little rubbing will do it."

"Always works on me," Jonas said with a satisfied groan.

"Never mind him."

Scarlet watched Isabella closely and saw that her eyes were roaming all over her face, then she reached out again, and Scarlet took another step back.

"No, really. Thanks. I, um, think I need to talk with Mortimer, then."

"He really is coming," said Jonas. "Like, way more often than you'd—"

"Shh!" said Isabella. "Hear that?"

In the still air, on the deserted street full of wrecked and abandoned buildings, the sounds of approaching tapping and scuffling and scraping carried over the incessant low buzzing. Isabella held a hand up as they all stayed still and listened.

"Boars," said Jonas in a weak whisper. "Maybe it's those goddamn—"

"No," said Isabella. "Those things have hooves. They clatter when they're hunting in the city."

"I saw them!" Scarlet said, straining out her whisper. "I thought I was imagining them. They're huge."

"Big heads," Jonas said while holding his belly with one hand. "And you know what that means."

"We've tried, Honey. Even when we swarm them, they're too strong and oily. We can never even get close to cracking open one of—"

"It sounds like people," said Scarlet. "Maybe it's Mortimer?"

"Oh, it sure could be Mortimer."

Jonas scoffed and said, "Not exactly people, though."

Scarlet stared at Isabella, who only nodded, then she squinted at Jonas, who shrugged.

The footfalls grew louder, and they watched a small band of jovial people appearing out of the darkness and coming their way. Leading them was a kindly looking older man in a long white shirt, not tucked in and hanging like a grease-stained lab coat. Atop his head was a teased-up mound of wavy hair, pointed in every direction as if he'd dragged his fingers through it constantly but not enough to remove globs of thickening crude.

When they'd gotten close enough, he stopped his small horde and stared at Scarlet and her companions through small round glasses that magnified the size of his eyes.

He gave his unruly hair another poke, then a scratch, then said, "Well, what do we have here?"

"She's new," said Isabella.

"Fresh," said Jonas. "Very fresh."

"New and fresh—just what we need here."

He tipped his head and focused on Scarlet.

"I'm Mortimer. Welcome to . . . uh, where we are. Right here. And you are?"

"I'm Scarlet. Like I was telling them, I'm just kind of lost. This is a part of Chinatown that I never—"

"Oh, dear me! No, fresh and new Scarlet. No, this isn't Chinatown."

While he was smoothing down his hair and adjusting his glasses on his nose, many pairs of eyes stared at Scarlet from each side of him, some leaning to look over his shoulders.

Grinning, Mortimer added, "Close, but no cigar, as they say."

"I never say that."

"Shh, Jonas," said Isabella. "Don't interrupt him."

Mortimer slid his backpack off of the shoulder where it was looped and set it next to his leg. Several in his group did the same with theirs.

"No. Not Chinatown. Never heard buzzing in Chinatown, did you?"

They all stayed quiet, watching Scarlet as she turned her head, listening to the soft buzzing that seemed to come from everywhere around her.

"What is that?" she said.

"Right now," said Mortimer, "that's something you probably need to keep hearing. Am I right?"

He turned each way, smiling at the others laughing and nodding.

He kicked at his backpack and said, "We're out setting these mobile units up, trying to hook them into the power grid."

"What? I don't know what any of you are talking about."

"All you need to know, fresh Scarlet, is that buzzing is good. You want that buzzing."

"I don't," said a woman off to one side. "I'm itching for some crazy."

The man next to her fluffed up her matted hair and said, "You're itching for way more than that."

"Please," said Mortimer, "you're getting my brain off its tracks."

"That's funny," said Isabella. "Your fucking brain."

Mortimer cleared his throat, then focused again on Scarlet.

"Scarlet, my dear," said Mortimer, "it's probably best if you forget all about that goddamn Chinatown. Whatever memories you have of that place are just—"

Scarlet groaned and leaned over, crossing her arms over her belly, shaking a couple of times then standing back up.

"Oh my God. I remember. I remember what happened. As soon as you said 'memories,' it came back."

Mortimer took a few steps closer to her, and his very interested troupe stumbled to form a half-circle around her.

"You made me remember. I don't know how. Oh, God, what is this?"

Mortimer looked down at Scarlet's hands still against her midsection, then back up at her eyes.

"Soft flesh, I'd wager."

"I'm not betting against that," someone behind him said.

"Soft and fleshy. Oh, very fleshy," said another, then Mortimer held a hand up, silencing them.

Scarlet snapped her hands down to her sides.

"What is it that you remember, dear Scarlet?"

"I fell. I fell off of a building!"

Mortimer smirked and said, "Come on, now. We all know it takes more than some simple kind of dying. No, Scarlet. We already know."

He looked to each side repeatedly, saying, "Don't we? Don't we all fucking know?"

"Fuck, yeah! We know!" said a woman to Mortimer's left.

A man to his right said, "Shit, yeah! We know it had something to do with your—"

Mortimer shot his hand up, got them quiet, then focused on Scarlet with a genial smile.

"Something to do with your . . . pussy."

"What?" she said. "What are you talking about? I was on the roof, and I . . ."

Scarlet paused, squinting at many of the eager faces around her.

"Mm-hmm. Go on," Isabella said as she moved to stand beside her.

She slipped an arm around her waist and said, "Tell us what you were doing on that roof."

"I, uh, it was our anniversary, and we—"

"We, who?" said someone farther back.

"Two of you? Three? Dammit, more than three?"

"It was a goddamn orgy!" a woman said as she held Mortimer's shoulders and grinned past him at Scarlet. "You had yourself a sexy, perverted fuck fest orgy on the roof!"

Scarlet pulled free of Isabella's arm and said, "No! Just my husband! He wanted to—"

"Fuck you," Mortimer said, nodding calmly. "Of course. Anyone would, with all that new, fresh flesh of yours."

"Won't be fresh forever," said a large character two rows back.

"He does have a good point," said a shorter man near him. "Clock's ticking."

"That's just stupid. There aren't any fucking—"

"Stop, stop, stop!" yelled Mortimer. "All of you! Where are your goddamn manners?"

A voice came from the back, saying, "We left them in Chinatown!"

"Ignore them," Mortimer said to Scarlet. "Now, tell us what you were doing. This husband of yours was fucking you, wasn't he?"

"No! Look, all of you, I just want to—"

"Yes, you want to keep fucking him. Any one of us would too. Well, you can't. That fucking is what got you here for us to—"

"No, I told you—he wasn't making love to me!"

No one spoke, and only a low, disapproving murmur came from many of them.

"That language," said Mortimer, shaking his head. "That'll never do. Use the word, 'fuck.' Go on. Say it right."

Scarlet looked around at all of the grim faces, then said, "He, um, he wasn't . . . fucking me."

Mortimer got a big smile and said, "There. We like that so much better. Always talk dirty, Scarlet. Always! Okay, so who *was* fucking you, then?"

"No one!"

"How many were fucking you? Huh? One after another after—"

Jonas snickered and yelled, "Someone was doing something!"

Isabella had closed the distance again quietly, and she got her arm back around Scarlet's waist.

"He is so right. Something fun was going on with your pussy. Who was having all that fun? With your pussy?"

Scarlet, near tears, turned to look at Isabella, who only bounced her eyebrows a few times.

"I," she said, "I, uh, I was."

"Oh, sweet!" yelled Mortimer. "Yes, that's nice. That's really nice. Say it. Say it for us."

"What?"

"Look," said Mortimer, "we know this is all kind of unsettling for you. It would be for any human."

Scarlet looked around at many nodding their heads.

"But we do so love to hear it. We want the words. Say it right, and we'll move on to whatever else you want to discuss."

"He means it," said a man in back.

"Okay. Fine. Um, I was, uh, masturbating because my husband—"

"That word lacks so many important details," said Mortimer. "It just glosses over all of the tastiest parts. Try again."

"He said 'tasty!'" yelled a man from the small crowd.

"I was, um, touching my—"

"Through your dress?"

"Well, no. I, uh, lifted it up."

"Show us."

"What? Why would I—"

"Oh, okay. Just tell us, then. Details, Scarlet!"

"Okay. I, uh, lifted up my dress, then I—"

"Did you go right for your pussy? Just like that?"

Mortimer turned to look behind him and said, "She's doing fine, Wesley. Let her talk."

Facing Scarlet again, he said, "Please. Continue. Oh, he does have a good point, though. Did you give yourself a little foreplay?"

Voices all around him hooted and hollered.

"What's wrong with all of you?"

Jonas shrugged and said, "We're horny as fuck."

Scarlet felt a tighter squeeze around her waist and turned to Isabella, who said, "Like you can't fucking believe."

She broke free of the embrace and took two steps away.

"Okay, fine. I, um, touched my thighs first. Then—"

"Then, your pussy?"

"Yes! Dammit, yes, I touched my pussy! It was just for my husband."

"Touched it a lot?"

Scarlet looked down and said, "Enough. Yeah."

"Then, you fell? While you were orgasming your brains out?"

"Yeah."

Someone said, "Her brain came out? That's all it takes?"

Mortimer said, "Hush. Figure of speech."

"I'm trying that next time," said someone else.

"Hey!" said Mortimer. "Now, Scarlet, you understand as much about this fucked up place as we do."

"Huh? What do I understand?"

"You died in an orgasm. That's the ticket here. Must have been one hell of an orgasm too."

"What? Why?"

"It lasted while you fell . . . how far?"

"Um, pretty far. Okay, yeah. It was a good one."

"Hey, how did you fall?"

"I, uh . . ."

She winced and held her belly again.

"Oh, God. I forgot about them. Those things."

She sucked in a quick breath and looked all around, then up.

"They're here too! God, those things are here too!"

"She means those greasy goddamn bats."

"I agree. That fucker Demetrius is right."

"Hush, everyone. Now, Scarlet, you're saying that bats threw you off of the roof while you were touching your pussy?"

"Uh, kind of. They grabbed Daniel, and he—"

"He wasn't fucking you, right?"

"Uh, no. He was watching, and they—"

"I'd watch that any day of the week."

"Any minute of the day!"

"Enough. All of you," said Mortimer. "Scarlet, this Daniel character, he wasn't orgasming his brains out, was he?"

"Again with the brains," said a young woman nearby. "Mortimer's making me crazy."

"And horny!" yelled someone farther back.

Mortimer kept a steady grin pointed at Scarlet and said to the group around him, "I do that on purpose, you know."

"What is with you all?"

"Like any of us could fucking explain it, Scarlet. Okay, look, the bats took your husband if they didn't kill him right there and eat him."

"What? They eat people?"

"Gosh, you say that like it's a bad thing."

They all got silent and stared at Scarlet, who stared back at them for a moment.

Mortimer continued.

"No, they brought him here. He's probably not dead yet. Soon, though. That reactor. Hoo, boy. There's some serious fucking frying that goes on there."

"What? Daniel's here? Where?"

"The reactor. It's an evil thing, but it keeps the goddamn lights on."

"Sometimes," said Jonas. "Until it doesn't."

"Right," said Mortimer. "And then, it switches off our fun little transmitters too. I need to find some other way than to tap into streetlights."

He looked at Scarlet and said, "If you hear that buzzing stop, you'd better just—"

"Run!" Isabella yelled in her ear. "Because we sure will. We're not as fast as we used to be, but we can still—"

The buzzing stopped.

Isabella bared her teeth.

Jonas snarled, Mortimer's jaws snapped, teeth clunking together, and all of them advanced on Scarlet, hands out and grabbing for her.

A low growling erupted and swept through all of them like a hungry spirit awakening.

Scarlet gasped and began backing away along a street lit only by a dim orange glow from the burning ocean beyond the reactor.

Then, she ran just as Isabella got a grip on her dress, ripping it as she fled with the stomping of her heels echoing off of the old buildings.

* * *

Panting and with tears streaking her cheeks, mixing with oily smears left by Isabella's eager touching, Scarlet scurried and sometimes scraped against the weathered bricks of the buildings on one side of the dark street. Each time she passed the absolute empty black of an alley entrance, she held her breath and coaxed her legs to deliver enough speed to get her past but never quickly enough to stop her wide-eyed stares into the dark.

Behind her, the sounds of mindless snarling and growling and pounding of worn shoes began to fade. And when it had grown quiet enough, she stopped to listen, straining to hear whatever buzzing had stopped and had driven Mortimer and the rest of them mad.

But there was no buzzing to challenge the silence of the dilapidated city. Scarlet paused, her back against the wall, and looked each way along the street. He chest heaved with breathing that she managed to keep silent, and nothing on that dark, deserted street conspired to create any sounds at all.

Until someone around a nearby corner screamed, "Help!"

Scarlet clenched shut her eyes and tried to submerge herself into the warm bricks at her back, shaking her head and mumbling, "No, no, no!"

She listened and heard again only silence.

Until someone, from the same direction, yelled again, "Please, help!"

Groaning softly, Scarlet unlocked herself from the bricks and took a few quiet steps toward the corner, but she stopped before reaching it and only listened.

She heard nothing, so she kept moving toward the corner with as little sound as possible. With one hand resting on the sharp, warm corner of the brick walls, she gave her agitated breathing a chance to settle.

But her lungs had no reason to relax, so she started to lean and peek around the corner. And she froze just before she could see.

"Oh, God, somebody help me!"

It was a weaker call for help, not even really a scream. An actual scream might have covered the sounds like soft, wet twigs being snapped.

And slow, easy whooshing.

And laughter. Soft, satisfied, and scornful laughter.

She leaned more, just enough to give one eye a view, and the pungent air that she'd been breathing in stayed inside.

In the gloomy darkness, two giant bat things were hunched on each side of a prone human man, a young one—barely an adult. Their wings were keeping a steady pace, whooshing on the up strokes, then shaking their way back down like falling leaves.

One of them was feasting on the man's thigh, leaving a puddle beneath it, along with a few chunks of flesh, as it snapped its jaws, grinding into bone as the leg twitched.

The other bat was devouring what it could of a shoulder, near the neck, while lifting the torso off of the ground. The man's head hung loosely, bobbing lazily from the feeding, and his mouth was moving slowly.

"Help. Somebody . . ."

The words were too faint to be more than whispers mixed with gurgles as blood got squeezed up and out of his mouth.

"Hate humans."

"Guts are good."

"Yeah. For dessert."

"No. Now," said the bat chomping on a leg as it raised its head, then jabbed its jaws into the man's belly, sloshing slop out to splatter on the street's bricks.

Scarlet's hand over her mouth smelled like oil but it helped contain her soft gasp. The man being eaten said no more, and his head got clunked repeatedly onto the warm pavement until the other bat, the one enjoying human shoulder, joined its companion.

Two large, leathery mouths were working at the man's middle, digging in, unraveling long innards, then ripping pieces loose. Both heads came up together, the ends of a long strand of gristle in each mouth, and they laughed while chewing their way toward the middle.

The one that mostly had its back turned toward Scarlet spun its head around to face her. Blood ran down from both corners of its mouth and dripped from the end of the short tubular segment of intestine before it got sucked in and swallowed.

"What?" said the one that was again poking around in the open body cavity.

"Heard. Breathing."

"Boar?"

"No."

"Dead?"

"No. Alive," it said, then rose up to its full height, facing Scarlet with its wings held high and still.

"You hunt. I eat."

The standing bat sniffed the air for several seconds, then twisted around and hunched low, letting its wings whoosh at a leisurely pace.

"I eat too."

"Still warm."

"Warm. Hate humans."

"Good to eat."

"Yeah."

Scarlet gasped into her crude-stained hand and retreated out of sight, then crept along the building's warm wall, letting her anniversary dress snag on every little burr and crack.

She'd just passed a building's entrance, a recessed pit of blackness that revealed nothing of itself, then reached the far corner after only a few more steps.

Waiting before looking, she pressed her back against the wall and listened to human voices approaching in the gloom. The voices carried through the night, but they were still too distant for their footsteps to be heard.

"I kind of hate the early shift," said one.

"You are a foolish brute," said another.

"No," said the first. "I'm a guard."

"You're not an amusing guard," said the second. "Besides, how would you define 'early' in a place such as this?"

"Stop," said a third voice. "Both of you have disappointing intellects. Your idle banter isn't helpful. Neither of you is even marginally useful as a guard."

The owner of the first voice laughed, then said, "Guard this."

Scarlet heard what sounded like an open faucet trickling water onto the pavement and dared to grasp the jagged corner and look around.

But only for a second, then she hid herself back behind the corner. Her chest, barely calmed from the slaughter and feeding of the bats, launched another round of rapid consumption of the oil-tinged air.

She'd seen three dogs pointed her way, and one of them, the last one that spoke, had lifted its leg and was urinating on a wall.

All three had human faces.

"No, no, no!" she groaned softly through the fingers of a hand clamped over her mouth.

"See?" said the third dog guard. "How is that helpful?"

The faucet got cranked down to a trickle, then it stopped.

"Helped me. Whether you two guard it or not."

"Okay," said the second. "That was kind of funny."

"I'll tell you what's not funny," said the peeing dog guard. "Archie."

The voices were again drawing near, but the pads on their paws kept them quiet as they trotted closer to Scarlet.

"Huh," said the second. "The boss. Yeah. Not funny."

The third said, "His job isn't to be funny. It's to keep the reactor working. Nothing more. Nothing less."

"Nothing more?" said the first. "I'd stop and piss again over that, but my reservoir just spilled it all. His job seems to always be more than just the reactor."

"Careful how you talk about the boss," said the second. "He has spies all over this place."

Scarlet fought to corral her ragged breaths as she ducked backwards into the dark cave of the building entrance. She kept going until she could feel sheets of glass behind her, smooth and warm, and she waited there as the guards turned the corner.

They got as far as her hideaway, then the second one stopped and said, "He can spy this."

In the dim light, Scarlet watched the dog with a face lift its leg and urinate in her direction.

"We're going to be late," said the third guard dog. "Pee on the clock."

The second dog gave it one final squirt, lowered its leg, then said, "You mean on company time. Not on the clock."

"You're a real hound for details, aren't you?" said the third.

"See? That's funny."

"Hound. I get it."

"Alright, you two. You both know there's no clock here. To the reactor. And no more badmouthing Archie."

"Why not?"

The third snickered and said, "Because it's just one more excuse for him to rape you."

"Not again. I don't like that too much."

"You'd hump his leg if he'd let you."

"Well, yeah. You would too."

"Guys! Get your hairless human faces pointed toward the reactor, and let's march!"

Hidden in the blackest of shade, Scarlet watched as the lead guard led two grumbling human-faced dogs out of sight. Seconds later, after hearing their voices trailing away in the night, she stepped close enough to lean and look around the corner. And she saw three tails swishing before the gloom swallowed them.

Above their heads, just a tight low region in the distance showed a faint orange glow.

"The reactor," she said to herself.

She let her breaths fight at their own pace and began walking after the dogs.

"Daniel . . ."

Chapter 7 – Yes, We're Mutants

Even after the trio of guards had turned a corner, Scarlet could hear their polite, good-natured conversations and teasing jokes like a homing signal to lead her on.

Staying far enough back and taking careful steps, she followed them through quiet, unlit streets. Several times, a soft buzzing had arisen all around her and each time, the dogs had commented favorably about it, welcoming the sound.

Far ahead but with their wagging tails still in sight, she watched them pass through a damaged gate in a chain link fence, then continue toward a cluster of low buildings that appeared wrecked and abandoned. But several windows glowed and hinted that there was some activity inside.

Scarlet hurried to get herself to the gate, then watched the dog trio trot across a wide expanse of gravel and toward a large open roll-up door. Beyond that, dim lights glowed and made clear that the building contained a cavernous area.

"Oh, God. Daniel's in there?"

Clutching the fence, her breathing again drumming up a quick rhythm, Scarlet looked toward the dogs, then back behind her, then each way. She snapped her head all around, then focused again on the buildings, the dogs, and the faint orange glow that reached up weakly from behind the structures before the absolute blackness of the sky choked it off.

"Wait!" she yelled, and the dog guards all spun around, pointing their human faces toward her.

"I heard that."

"Me too. Sounded human."

"You don't. Too hoarse."

"I'm not a horse."

"Shh. Maybe soon."

The second dog barked several times, then howled at the black sky, giving its co-workers reason to snicker and shake their heads before they, too, yipped and howled straight up.

After a single, shrill howl, the lead guard leveled its sights in Scarlet's direction, picked her out of the shadows near the fence, and set its tail into some frantic snapping left and right.

"Okay, lady. You got us waiting. What's on your mind?"

Scarlet stared and before she could answer, the first dog said, "Are you a villain? The kind we're tasked with guarding against?"

The second one said, "She doesn't look like a criminal that's determined to wreck the reactor."

"Guys, shh. You, by the fence. Ignore these dolts. Come closer if you wish to speak."

"She might be an outlaw."

"A thug. She looks like a thug."

"You two! She doesn't look like a thug or an outlaw. She looks quite pleasant."

"And she might have treats."

"I haven't had a decent treat since I grew this face."

"I'd be ashamed of that face if I were you."

"You're almost me. Look in a mirror if you—"

"Stop, you two!"

The leader advanced toward Scarlet, bounced up and down on its front paws a few times, then said, "Really, don't mind them. Come closer. It's fine."

Scarlet looked behind her, then to each side, then again at the three dogs. She began a steady walk toward them, and she didn't wait until she was right upon them to plead.

"Do you know Daniel? Is he here? Please, I need to find him!"

"Who's Daniel?"

"He's my husband. He, um, he didn't—"

"Didn't die during an orgasm? I bet that's what you're going to say, isn't it?"

"Uh, yeah. I guess that's how—hey, wait a minute. What exactly are you? Am I losing my mind?"

"First," said the dog group leader, "that's correct. That's how you got here. I'm surmising by your comments that this Daniel character just plain died and didn't get his rocks off at the same time."

"Uh, maybe he didn't die. I don't know. But I did."

"Hmm, tell us about it."

"No! Not again! What kind of insane place is this?"

The leader tipped its head, and the other two turned to look at each other before again focusing on Scarlet.

"It's, uh, the best and most insanest place ever. That's what!"

It led the chorus in howling up at the unbroken black above them.

"What are you? Oh, this can't be real. I hit my head, or I'm imagining things, or I died and went to Hell, or—"

"Well, see, that's just too many options. Stick with what I told you: it's the most insanest place ever."

"What the hell are you? Are you a dog?"

"Yes. Well, used to be."

"But you . . . you got some kind of—"

"Human face? Yes. Used to be that too."

Scarlet stooped down and covered her face with both hands. She shook softly with her sobbing.

"There, there. It's not so bad."

"Sure it is," said human-face dog number one.

The second one snickered and said, "Uh, no. It's worse."

A loud sob shook Scarlet enough that she fell back and sat on the gravel, and her hands never left her face. But she did stretch her legs out in front and leaned forward, still sobbing quietly.

"Don't mind them, lady. They—hey, what's your name?"

With her hands opened like two swinging doors, Scarlet said, "I'm Scarlet. My husband is Daniel. Is he here?"

"He might be. Sure. Maybe. Why don't you just have a nice little cry, just get it all out, then we'll help figure this all out for you."

She accepted its advice and sobbed into her hands. Half a minute later, she heard the leader and one of the others snickering and felt something disturbing. She looked.

One of the lesser guard dogs was happily humping her leg and grinning at her the entire time.

"Hey," it said, "never thought I'd have to resort to this kind of doggie style."

Even the leader laughed, saying, "That's a good one. That came from the human part of you."

Crying, Scarlet said, "Please make him stop!"

"Eh. He'll be done in a few seconds. What a lightweight."

She covered her face and shook from sobbing and humping where she sat on the gravel outside the array of reactor buildings.

And it was right. The eager humper finished its business, dragged itself around to clean up, barked once at the black above, then stepped back, wagging its tail calmly.

"It feels better. Maybe you do too?"

"What? Everyone here is crazy!"

"Oh, I see. Everyone except you. Sure. If that's true, it's only because you're so fresh and—"

"That's what they said! They said I was fresh!"

"Who? Oh, you must mean Mortimer and those mindless freaks that flock around him like he's some kind of god in this hell."

Scarlet looked down at her leg and had just enough light to see a few sloppy streaks and puddles of some kind of gelatin slop.

To herself, she mumbled, "I just want to go home. Please, can I just go home?"

"No!" barked the leader. "You have to find Daniel!"

She looked up and screamed for the first time at the sight of human face on a dog, bouncing its eyebrows and grinning.

The bouncing stopped, and it said, "That doesn't do much for my ego, you know. Screaming at the sight of me. You wouldn't like it."

She buried her face and sobbed more, then it added, "Alright. Now that you've been humped, we've all had a few laughs, and you let yourself cry out some of those tears, let's go see about your husband."

She looked up at it with tears trickling down both cheeks.

"Sound good? We'd better hurry, you know. Radiation spikes happen all the time and always bring a few surprises."

She only stared up at him.

"Okay, I'll say it. Like what happened to the three of us. I'll just tell you, Scarlet, since you might not be sure and you're just too polite to ask: yes, we're mutants."

It watched her steady flow of tears from wet, staring eyes.

"There. Now that everything is squared away, let's go. Come on. Get up and follow us."

The three of them turned and began a slow trot toward the wide door which opened to a giant, dim interior.

The leader stopped a second later and turned back toward Scarlet.

"Look, something else is just going to come along and hump some part of you. You might as well tag along."

It turned, continued its trot, and Scarlet jumped to her feet and followed. The dogs stopped at the doorway and waited for her to catch up with them.

"In there," said the leader. "Just wait there, and someone or something will be along to size you up."

"To do what?"

"Don't let them put you to work. Be ready to run. Seriously, just inquire about your husband, then run."

She wiped at a fresh tear and nodded.

"Okay. I'll run. But I want to find Daniel first. I was told he might be here."

"We really do wish you the best. But we have to run along and patrol the grounds. Good luck!"

Amid a chorus of happy barking and a few yips straight up, the group of wagging tails succumbed to the shadows along the building as they all left Scarlet standing just inside the wide doorway.

She looked around, saw some movement, and watched as a figure approached and didn't maintain a steady gait as it ambled toward her from the far end of the vast insides of the building.

* * *

Willie held up a hand, stopping Daniel behind him. He sniffed to the left, then to the right. Daniel saw an open submarine hatch door on each side of them and beyond those doorways, there was mostly just darkness.

And pathetic moaning.

And sometimes a shrill cackle.

"Take your pick."

"I, um, would rather—"

"Try to keep up, son. When I say something funny, you really ought to consider laughing. Even if just to humor the fried-up old coot named Willie that used to be, in some other life, not quite so fried-up."

Daniel stared.

"Okay. That Willie was already a little fried. He was into some weird shit. No, listen, young man . . . what I said was pretty goddamn funny."

"Huh? What the hell are you—"

"Try to recall. I told you to take your pick, remember?"

He waited, staring at Daniel with a crooked grin.

"I, uh, I don't—"

"Look in your hand, there, sonny boy. That isn't a pick. It's a goddamn shovel. Get it? Get it? I should have said . . . what?"

"Uh, take your shovel?"

"Well, young man, yeah, but you still have to take your pick."

He giggled, then held himself still with a silly grin. His eyes looked left, then right, then left again.

"What's the difference?"

"No difference at all. Nope. It's just the last reasonable choice you'll have in this hellhole that isn't Hell, presided over by a goddamn god. So, which one for you, young fella?"

Daniel wiped a tear, sighed, and pointed to the left.

"Oh, boy. Big trouble."

"What?"

"Just messing with you. No, the other one is big trouble too. Anyway, you're down to your last reasonable choice in . . . well, I'm not going through all that descriptive bullshit again. You got it down by now, I'd bet."

"What's my last reasonable choice? What are you talking about?"

"Why, checkout time, of course. Most blokes with oily shovels make that decision real damn quick. That's not to say it's easy, though. Oh no, that's some traumatic bullshit infecting your brain when you're considering that big checkout."

"Checkout?"

"Yeah, man with a shovel. Talking to an old fool with a skull full of soup. Or something. Checkout. Like, adios. Goodbye, cruel world. See you on the other side. Oh, wait. Unless this is the other side. Where you'd end up, then, I have no fucking clue."

"Maybe, um, I'd—"

"You're right. You're a goddamn genius! Yes, you'd find yourself down a few levels, where the temperature is higher, the radiation is sicker, and the shovels are so goddamn heavy you can barely hoist them up. Yeah. That's where you'd go."

Daniel's tears flowed and never slowed as he shook his head at Willie.

"Well, no sense getting all teary-eyed about it."

He pointed toward the selected hatchway.

"In you go. You took your pick. Now, take your shovel. I'll follow you. Go on."

Daniel faced the open doorway, then took a few steps through, where the increase in heat got him sweating profusely in seconds. He stopped, wiped across his forehead, then spun around at the sound of the hatch closing behind him. He watched as the wheel mounted near the middle of the door spun, then hit some kind of limit. A loud clunk followed.

"Willie?"

A voice from behind him said, "Willie isn't stupid. He won't come in here and find out what we think of him."

Daniel let out a choppy breath and turned to look into the shadows surrounding a shallow trench filled with glowing pieces of metal. Some were torn and curled sheets, others were cracked and worn machine parts, and many more evaded any easy identification. But all were steaming hot.

"Good. You gots yourself a shovel. Come on, then. Help us out."

Daniel got his feet moving and taking slow steps toward several men sweating near their hot work.

"Who are you? Start with that."

"I'm Daniel. What is this place?"

"End of the road, my friend."

Daniel leaned, wincing from the heat, and studied the man's face. Behind the overgrowth of whiskers, ash and oil clinging and clumped to it, and beads of oily sweat dripping everywhere, sad eyes peered at him, then one closed as something in the trench popped, sending a tiny boiling bit of garbage onto the man's cheek, where it sizzled and smoked.

"Hate when that happens."

"Happens all the time," said the man next to him, who looked about the same.

Another snap sent a burning metal bit up high enough to land on the first man's hat, where it began to smolder and smoke.

"Hate that too," he said with his eyes turned up.

He closed them when his co-worker slammed his shovel down on the other's head before the fire could take hold.

With closed eyes, but without a flaming hat, he said, "Hmm, hate that too."

"What is this place?" said Daniel. "I just want to get out of here."

"Oh, we don't blame you, newbie. Yeah, of course, you want out. You'd be crazy not to. Come on. I'll show you the way out."

"Do I need my shovel?"

"Nah. Just drop it."

Daniel dropped it.

"Alright, let's go. Don't fall into that goddamn trench unless you want to."

"It's, it's hot. All that stuff is—"

"Radio-fucking-active. Yeah, you got that right. At least the heat is some treacherous but natural kind of thing. Those rad waves, though? Hell, no one knows. Some twisted shit. Come on."

He turned to lead the way, exposing a large hump high on his back, off to one side and stretching his soiled and singed t-shirt. As the man stepped, it flopped from side to side.

The other man, walking beside Daniel, pointed and laughed.

"If you last long enough to want some head, Benny, there, has an extra one. Sick fucker."

"What? What are you talking about?"

"Radiation, my friend. Funny stuff. Willie didn't mention that?"

"Willie? Willie is—"

"Fucked up. Oh, yeah. But he's pretty good at laying down the facts. Like about the sick shit that goes on down here. He told you, right?"

"Uh, radiation? Yeah, he said that."

"Well, there you go," he said, pointing at the hump.

"Where do I go? What are you—"

"Benny. Hold up, will you?"

"No way, Jerome. We're almost there."

He kept shuffling through the ash and grit, sometimes kicking hot metal parts to the sides, and rounded a corner.

Daniel and Jerome joined him, and all three looked into a room where monstrous machinery was working like some diabolical engine. Giant wheels were spinning, pistons were sliding, hinged parts were flapping, and everything glowed like a strobe light, brightening and dimming all together.

At the base of the complex creation, large sprockets and gears were jerking around, their teeth meshing and sometimes grinding.

"What the hell is this? What is that thing?"

"Well, now, Daniel, it might be just what you want."

"Huh?"

Benny spun himself back around, showing that another speck of hot metal was burning a hole in the skin of his forehead. He grinned and pointed at it.

"Yeah, I feel it. I just don't care anymore."

"Benny," said Jerome, "we got him here. We did our part. I'm tempted to join him."

"I won't stop you, J-freak. We—"

"You know I don't like that name."

"No, don't suppose you would. But you are a freak, right?"

Jerome looked down and kicked at the cinders.

"Yeah," said Benny, scoffing. "Exactly. So, like I was saying, you can follow after him but first, he might like a little fun. Whatcha think?"

"Oh, yeah. He needs fun more than anyone I know."

"You don't know anybody."

He kicked the hot gravel again.

"Yeah. Exactly. Again. Let's give him some fun, then we can all jump the fuck out of here."

"Miranda?"

"Oh, yeah, Jerome. It's . . . showtime!"

Benny spun himself around and dropped to his knees, then sat back on his heels.

"This is fun," Jerome said, giggling. "Watch. Watch!"

Grunting with contortions and twisting himself around, Benny was dragging his filthy t-shirt up, up, and up over his hump.

To reveal another head growing right out of his back.

Calm blue eyes looked up at Daniel.

"He grew a . . . God, how did—"

"Damndest thing," said Jerome. "Damn radiation made him sprout a damn good-looking woman's head right there on his goddamn back."

Over his shoulder, Benny said, "She's beautiful, isn't she?"

"What? What is—"

Still talking over his shoulder, he said, "Look, Daniel. Forget where you are and how there's only one way out. Forget the goddamn radiation, the fried chicken Willie has in his skull, and the starving, savage bat freaks that brought your regretful ass here. Just forget all that shit. Just look at my girl, Miranda. And tell me: isn't she beautiful?"

Daniel winced and leaned to get a better look.

Miranda batted her eyes and puckered up to kiss him.

"Wait!" yelled Jerome. "Wait just a second!"

He bent over, dragged two fingers through the soot on the floor, and brought them up, all coated with a reddish ore dust. Gently, lovingly, he dragged it all across Miranda's lips, then pulled his hand back.

She puckered, rubbing her lips together, all while gazing up at Daniel.

"Lipstick. Well, sort of."

"Beautiful now?" Benny said over his shoulder.

"You guys are all—"

"Oh, come on. Live a little," said Jerome. "Like Benny said. Forget all the lame shit all around you and just look at the doll growing right there, the one looking right up at you. Isn't she hot?"

"I mean, this doesn't make any—"

"If you pried that head loose and put it on an actual woman's body, what then, huh? Pretty damn beautiful, right?"

Sobbing again, Daniel nodded and said, "Yeah. Yeah, she's beautiful."

"Tell her, then," Benny said, trying to look back toward Daniel. "Huh?"

"What woman doesn't want to hear that—"

"God, that's not a woman!"

"Uh, no. We kind of know that. Some of the time. She gives damn good head, though. Go on. Get your pecker out."

"What? Huh?"

"Get your pecker out," said Jerome, "and bring it up close. I mean, she can't actually come to you, right?"

"You want me to . . . what?"

Miranda started licking her lips, getting her tongue coated with bits of ore and metal shavings.

"Ew," said Jerome. "That's going to cut a little bit. Still, though. It's head."

"That's funny," Benny said. "Head giving head. Go on, Daniel. Get some head from the head."

"Do it," said Jerome, and Daniel felt the hot point of a shovel at the back of his neck. "She wants it. Girls need some fun too. Get it out."

"I, I can't. This is—"

Jerome pressed the sharp edge hard enough to start digging into Daniel's neck.

"Just get that pecker out, and give that pretty little thing what she wants. Do it!"

"No, I can't! This is all so—"

"Do it! Miranda wants to suck it! Give it to her!"

"I don't want head from a head! Please, I just—"

"I'll cut your fucking head off. Put the damn thing in her mouth! Now!"

Daniel tried to lean away from the hot, sharp shovel blade, looked down at a head that was licking its lips and batting its big blue eyes, and took quick glances at the grinding and clanking gear teeth at the bottom of the ghastly machinery.

"Let Miranda suck it. You know you want it. She sure wants it. That's one horny little momma, right there."

"No! No, no, no!"

"Let her—"

Jerome stopped to watch, and Benny spun around to watch, and Miranda had to look away as Daniel, flailing his arms, dove head first into the jerking, stuttering gears, which kept turning and meshing and pulled his twitching body in.

And jammed it up completely.

"Oh, fuck. Not again," said Benny.

"Yep. I think it was his hip bones that got all crunched up in there."

"No, Jerome. I think it was the skull."

"Oh, yeah, you're probably right."

"Damn skulls. Hey, Jerome, we done got little Miranda all worked up. Help her out, alright?"

Jerome whistled, then hooted and said, "I was going to anyway!"

Benny spun himself back around, Jerome stepped closer, and Miranda smiled and licked her ore-crusted lips as she watched scarred and burned hands pulling down a rusty zipper.

"I like that she can't talk too," said Jerome.

"Yep," said Benny. "Damn near perfect woman, that Miranda. Just wish I could figure out how to get some of her action. Maybe if I mutate more?"

Chapter 8 – No One Can Protect You

Across the well-lit hangar interior, the woman walked toward Scarlet, who waited near the wide roll-up doors. Behind her, windows near the floor and the glass portions of several doors flickered with an orange glow. But higher up, near the ceiling, windows were only black squares pasted in place.

Still many steps away, the woman called out, "Hello! I'm Betsy!"

Scarlet coughed in her hand, then said, "Um, hi. I'm—"

"Save your voice, Sugar. I'll be with you in just a second."

The nearly silent footfalls of the woman's ragged brown boots came into focus, as did her appearance. She was about Scarlet's height but with sloppily cropped shoulder-length black hair. Her clothes were torn and stained khaki trousers and a splotchy gray t-shirt that was shifted and twisted to one side.

Her smile appeared pleasant and cordial, but her eyes were borrowed from a caged animal, whose leg was in a trap, and they rarely focused on anything before scanning somewhere else.

And she wore many bandages: wrapped all around her left upper arm, completely covering her right thigh, a patch taped onto the sweaty skin above and between her breasts, and another hiding the entire right side of her face.

All of the dressings remained white only on select parts of their perimeters. But the middle areas of all of them were red, spongy wet, and oozy.

Despite all of that, her figure was flawless: strong, trim legs, a slender waist, and full breasts. She had the face of a model only slightly past her prime.

She came to a stop five paces from Scarlet and locked her hands on her hips.

"Okay. Whew, that's kind of a long walk. Name, please?"

"I'm Scarlet. What is this—"

"I take it you're new, huh? Just arrived?"

"Um, not too long ago. I heard that—"

"I hear voices sometimes, too, Sugar. And sometimes, I even listen. What do you think about that?"

"I, um, maybe I—"

"Right. Don't think about it. That's best. Now, let's see about getting you to work before things get too interesting for you."

"Uh, interesting?"

"Place is full of surprises, Sugar. Things change quickly. Even things you never thought could change so drastically."

"Huh?"

"Never mind that. I just like to talk."

She tapped her temple on the side that wasn't patched over and swampy.

"Heads are the first things to go. You'll see."

"Wait. I just came here to find—"

"Walk with me."

Betsy stepped closer and extended a wet hand toward Scarlet, who gave it a glance, then looked back into her eyes.

"Um, alright. I'll walk with you."

"Fine," she said, then wiped her hand on her pants. "Stay close. I'll protect you."

She turned and started walking, and Scarlet said, "What? Protect me from what?"

Calling back over her shoulder, Betsy said, "I was fooling with you. No one can protect you. Come on."

Scarlet looked all around at the shadows and dark corridors leading away, then hurried to walk alongside Betsy.

"I already know your story. Tell me anyway."

"You too? Why do I have to keep—"

"You've already told someone how you got your ass here? Who?"

"Um, some people on the street. It was Jonas and Isabella, at first. Then, someone named Mortimer came around with—"

Betsy laughed and said, "People? Oh, that's rich. Uh-huh, Sugar. Uh-huh. Look, forget them. They—"

She yipped, held her bandaged thigh, and stooped down.

"Are you alright?"

"Do I look alright, Sugar?"

"Well, it looks like you've had some kind of accident, but I don't mean to pry into—"

"Oh, it was no accident. Help me up, will you?"

She reached up a hand that was still slick and slimy.

"Uh, sure."

Scarlet took her hand and helped her get back up on her boots.

"Whew. Some movies just can't be over quick enough. Know what I mean?"

"What movie? Look, Betsy, I'm glad you're trying to help me, but this is just—"

"No one here is ever going to help you, Sugar. You best learn that lesson right from the get-go."

"But why? What is this—"

"Learn to help yourself. That's all. You take, Sugar. You take whatever you can before this freak show smears you down into a puddle of crude."

"Huh? I just want to find—"

"Keep walking. We have to get you some better clothes for work. That pretty little dress of yours isn't going to make it. So, I know you had a sex and death party somewhere up there,"—she poked an oddly crooked finger straight up—"but give me some details. Nothing like a book, though. Just a few of the fun points."

"If I do, then you'll help me? With why I came to this place?"

"Wait. You came to this nightmare reactor dump on purpose? Please, no one's that foolish. No matter how new they are."

"I came here looking for my husband. He might be here. I have to find—"

"Just keep walking, Sugar. Look. Tell me about you and your husband. Just get it out."

"Fine. We were on a high roof, and I was, um, . . ."

"Fucking him?"

"No, I was—"

"Giving him a blow job. Yeah, that would be nice on a—"

"What? No, I was, um, masturbating, and then some kind of bats—"

"Oh, I get it. You were creaming when you died, but the old man, he was just a stiff, horny guy, and those bat freaks took him."

"Yes! And he might be here. If I could—"

"He was watching you mess with yourself, is that it?"

"Yeah. It was our anniversary, and that's what he wanted."

"I'd call him a pervert but dang, I'd like to watch that too. But we don't have time."

"Why is everyone here so, uh, so—"

"Crazy? Look around, Sugar. It's kind of the only option. Now, since your husband was a normal alive type when he was brought here, they would have put him to the hardest, most god-awful work possible. No one lasts long at that. So, we need to get you—"

"Wait! He can't be dead! I have to find him!"

"Forget about him. He probably got himself ground and shredded into just a streak of messy crude like a second after he got to work. It'll be the same for you unless you have some kind of useful skills."

"No, I have to find him! Take me to—"

"Skills, Sugar. Keep that brain focused while you can. This place wreaks havoc with all the synapses and cells and other mush up there. Now, tell me you have some skills so I don't have to see you just get tossed into a furnace or something."

"Huh?"

"I'm joking. No, I'm really not. So, what can you do?"

"I'm, uh, I was an engineer. Mostly automation kinds of things, with motors and linkages and control systems. I could automate just about anything."

"That's good. This reactor needs all kind of technical stuff to keep it running. What else?"

"Uh, chemistry. I know all about chemicals, compounds, mixing things. And, uh, physics and math, programming—I can write code for just about anything, and I—oh, please, I don't want to get tossed into an oven!"

"You'd rather get stretched out on a hot radiator, make some quick Scarlet jerky?"

"What? No, I just—"

"Another joke. I really ought to stop that."

"Yes, I wish you would."

"Okay, Sugar. Sure. I can tell this is just a little bit stressful for you."

"Yeah. A little."

"Yeah. Okay, hold up."

She held a bandaged arm out in front of Scarlet, stopping her at a wall of dusty metal lockers. From inside one, she dragged out a balled-up mess of clothing and a pair of old work boots.

"Here. This is your new style. In this place, you'll never have anything nicer than this. Bet you liked dressing up all fancy when you were normal alive, didn't you?"

"Normal alive?"

"Yeah. Before you died and orgasmed your way here. You liked dressing sexy?"

"Uh, no. I've always been kind of modest."

"Well, Sugar, you got the body for some serious fashion statements. Too bad that's all in the past."

She pointed toward a cracked wooden door hanging from only one of its three hinges.

"In there. Say goodbye to that pretty dress and nice shoes and all of that. Get those work clothes on, and we'll see what's next."

"Then, you'll help me find Daniel?"

"Daniel, huh? Nice name. Look, we can ask around. First, though, get that body of yours out of those useless clothes and into something more practical."

"In there?"

"Sure. It's safe. Sort of."

Scarlet took the jumble of dusty clothes, wiped at a tear, and creaked the door open enough to pass through.

*　*　*

Leaving the door open and hanging crookedly behind her, Scarlet paused to look around the dim room, unlit except for a weak orange glow coming through two cracked windows.

To her right, a conference room table had become home for abandoned coffee mugs, papers, and oily machine parts. And from its grimy surface, two bloated rats lay on their sides and stared at her, sometimes sniffing the air and twitching around their whiskers.

On the left side of the room, two doors, employing all of their hinges, remained shut. One of them occasionally shook and rattled from something hitting it from the other side.

"Oh, God."

She walked over to the windows, still clutching her work clothes, and gazed out, holding her breath and shaking her head. Only a short distance away, across a swath of gravel and beyond a chain link fence full of holes and sagging sections, everything, all the way to the horizon, was on fire.

It was a sea of flames, all churning and convulsing and sending random bursts up to lick at whatever parts of the black sky they could kiss. She held her hand up, felt the warmth, then gingerly touched the glass.

But her instincts recoiled her finger before she could register the heat, and she backed away, toward the table.

Behind her, a tiny, squeaky voice whispered, "Run!"

She spun around and watched as the two curious rats used only their front legs to drag their bodies and back legs to the table's edge, where they promptly fell and broke open like sloshing balloons full of syrup.

"Oh my God."

Scarlet leaned enough to look at two overlapping puddles, each with a tail and a head. And each head had eyes focused on her.

"Did you—one of you—talk?"

The head on the left managed a pained grin, then its eyes rolled back, then closed.

The other rat in its own puddle only stared and when Scarlet waved her hand around, the eyes stayed frozen open.

"Oh my God. This just can't be."

The frozen eyes closed.

She sobbed once and dropped her clothes on the table, tipping one of the mugs and causing a slow spill of some gelatinous slime.

She pinched the soiled fabric of her new wardrobe, then let it go and looked down at what she was wearing. Her hands moved to her thighs, and she rubbed along the cleaner, finer material, pulling at it, tugging it up until she could grasp the hem.

Lifting that, she looked down at her lean, toned legs, the skin soft and smooth, then she let the hemline drop again.

"Oh, the things I was doing for him. The things I was saying."

She eased the dress over her shoulders on each side, then wiggled it down far enough to let it drop to the warm concrete floor. After stepping out of it, she held each calf up and to the back to remove her practical heels, then stooped low to retrieve the dress.

Dumping those items on the table upset another mug, and she hurried to set it upright, but she never allowed her eyes to look at the spilled slop or the rat puddles beside the table.

With the heat from the sea of fire trying to cook her nearly naked body through the windows, Scarlet straightened out her underwear, then got a hold of the work trousers, which she stepped into quickly. Passing on the boots, she next got her arms into the thick, faded flannel shirt and buttoned all the way up except for the very top one.

Only then did she force her bare feet into the rough work boots, which were two sizes too big, and tied them tightly.

Standing in the room heated by a burning landscape, she reached out to touch her dress, letting her fingertips trace soft circles around on it, then tip the hem up a few times.

She kept fondling the soft cloth and wiped at a tear with her other hand.

"I should never have been a prude with you. Oh God, why didn't I just dress sexy for you when I had the chance, Daniel?"

The tears flowed from both eyes, and her sobbing turned into crying as she pulled in a few choppy breaths.

But she suspended all of that at the loud rapping on the broken door.

"Hey! You want to cry? I'll send something in there that'll really make you cry!"

Scarlet winced, kept her breaths at a minimum, and pulled back her hand.

She whispered to herself, "Something? Oh, God."

"Hey!" Betsy yelled through the gaps around the wrecked door. "We don't have all day. Well, as if there really was something like day in this dump. Whatever. Get your fine ass moving!"

"Okay. I'm, um, almost ready."

"I'll give you just ten more seconds! Ten! Nine!"

Betsy's kick swung the door madly about on its only good hinge, and she stood there sneering in at Scarlet.

"I lied. Time to go."

Scarlet said, "Okay," and scooped up her old clothes.

But Betsy came directly at her, grabbed all of it, and threw it back down on the table. Scarlet watched as the dress hung over the side, and one of her shoes tumbled off of the edge and into the rat sludge puddle.

"I want to keep those. It's all I have left."

"Sugar, you won't be needing fine things like that anymore. Especially those shoes."

"What? I might—"

"Heels are stupid in a place like this. Steel toes is what you want, if you can find them. No, Sugar, those fine legs of yours will never again get all teasy in any kind of heels."

"But I—"

Betsy gave her a shove and said, "Let's get out of this hotbox. That damn ocean of flames is a bit much sometimes."

Scarlet stopped where she had a good view out through one of the windows.

"What the hell is that? Is this Hell?"

"Sugar, you really think there's any dry land in Hell? Come on. Don't be stupid."

"Well, what is this place, then?"

Betsy scratched at the outside of the soggy bandage hiding half of her face.

"Beats the hell out of me. No one knows, Sugar. But if you want to visit Hell, I can kick your ass in the right direction."

"What?"

Betsy pointed down, snickering.

"Down there. Oh, shit, there are levels and levels. Least, that's what I heard. You want to get your ass running down some hot stairs, see what you can find down there? Huh?"

"No. No, thanks. This place, this is—"

"Bad enough. Yeah. Alright, let's get moving."

She popped her eyebrows up, held them there, and pointed to the ruined door.

Scarlet sighed, gave her modest but expensive shoe, the one resting in a puddle of ruptured rats, one last look, then turned and walked toward the door with Betsy close behind.

"Wait. Stop."

Scarlet stopped.

"You should know, Sugar, that you look pretty damn fine even in those old work duds."

Scarlet shuddered once but didn't turn around.

"I . . . I do?"

"Well, mostly just your ass. Can't tell with the rest. That ass, though? Hmm."

Scarlet shuddered again and resumed her walk out of the hot room.

Chapter 9 – A Hypnotic Sexiness About You

"Hey," Betsy called from behind Scarlet, "don't get too far ahead. It's a scary place if you don't know your way around."

Scarlet stopped, then turned to face Betsy as she walked toward her from the overheated changing room.

"Shit, even if you do."

"Yeah, it really is," Scarlet said. "What is this place? Some kind of reactor?"

"Some kind. Yeah. We don't know what kind."

"I'm kind of familiar with the process at most reactors. This doesn't look like anything I've ever heard of. Shouldn't there be cooling towers or something?"

"Sugar, you're asking the wrong girl. I just work here. All I know is that this whole operation is one evil mess. Stay away from it if you can."

"Can I? Can I just—"

"No. You're not going anywhere. Especially not dressed all sloppy like that."

"Huh? But you said I couldn't—"

"Forget your old clothes. You'll never have fine things like that again. No, I'm talking about how you must have just thrown all of this stuff on. Here, let me help."

While Scarlet was saying, "Thanks, but I don't need—" Betsy had walked close enough to stand directly in front of her.

"Shh. Just stand still a sec."

She pinched Scarlet's shirt near each shoulder, then twisted it around, getting the line of buttons exactly midway between her breasts. Staring at those breasts, she grinned and shook the shirt, along with Scarlet's breasts, a few times.

Then, looking into Scarlet's eyes, she reached for the highest fastened button and popped it open. Then, the next one down.

"Wait. I don't think—"

"It's just on account of the heat, Sugar. Just trying to help."

She gave Scarlet's breasts another study, then tipped her eyes down and leaned to one side.

"Huh. Trousers too."

She grabbed at the waistband with both hands and tried to twist the pants around, with her eyes on the zipper the whole time.

"Better."

"It was already—"

"Hush, now."

She circled around behind Scarlet and got a fresh hold on the top band of her work pants and again shifted them around. She reached around, tightened the belt one more notch, then laughed and smacked Scarlet's ass.

"There. Much better."

Scarlet started to turn, but Betsy's hands on both shoulders stopped her.

"Wait, Sugar. Final check."

She guided Scarlet's arms straight out to her sides, then said, "Hold that for just a sec."

Scarlet complied, and Betsy reached around with both hands until she'd found the line of buttons, and she checked one down low, near her belly.

"It's fine. Really, it should—"

"Well, let's see. Straightening out those tight pants of yours might have messed up the shirt. It'll only take a sec."

Scarlet looked down at the scarred, gouged, and blood-streaked hands as they slowly crept upward, fingertips checking each button.

"It's good. Really. Everything is fine."

"Sugar, you don't know your way around, do you? Best be a little more cordial."

"But I—"

"Shh."

Scarlet watched as Betsy started checking the last buttoned button, one right between her breasts. Her fingers tugged at it, then pressed it down against her skin. Leaving her fingertips just lightly touching it, she pressed her palms slowly down on both of Scarlet's breasts.

"Hey, that really—"

"Shh, now. Have to be sure it's in the middle."

She began shifting her palms around, rubbing Scarlet's breasts through the soiled work shirt, then she ignored the button and cupped each of the breasts, squeezing them, lifting them, and caressing them with her fingertips.

"It's fine! Stop!"

Betsy gave them a long, gentle squeeze, then pulled one hand back around.

"Easy for you to say. Details matter, you know. Just a quick final check of your total work getup. Hey, just look up for a second."

Scarlet sobbed once, then squinted, holding in tears, as she tipped her head back and looked up at a tangled maze of burned out pendulum lights, rusty and collapsing catwalks, and ladders zigzagging up to closed hatches mounted in the roof.

"Let's just see here."

She kept squeezing a breast with one hand, and she used the other to rub and lift each of Scarlet's ass cheeks. She squeezed one side, then the other, patted her once, then reached around and stepped in closer.

"Hey, I just want—"

"Shh, Sugar. Just hush a sec."

She slipped her free hand around and stroked her fingertips up along the inside of Scarlet's thigh, then down, then up again gently, all while her other hand was squeezing and rubbing a breast.

"Yeah, almost there, Sugar. Just have to be sure."

Betsy let her hand travel all the way up Scarlet's thigh, then she wiggled her hand in, palm against her leg, and began a steady pressing upwards.

"That's it. Hmm, just imagine if you had some fine, sexy clothes on. Close your eyes and imagine the two of us in a swanky hotel room, just getting started with—"

Scarlet said, "Stop!" and took each of Betsy's hands and dragged them off of her body, then spun herself around.

She glared at Betsy with fresh tears on her cheeks.

"Had to be sure, Sugar."

"Sure of what? You're not checking my clothes!"

"No, probably not."

She stepped closer to Scarlet, grinned at her flinching, then reached up with both hands to fluff back her long black hair. Then, she flipped it around and played with it until it was all balanced and lying on her back.

Scarlet groaned and took a step back, freeing her hair from Betsy's hands.

"Hey, enough. What do you think you're doing?"

"Teaching you something, Sugar."

"Oh, yeah? What's that?"

"That you'd never make it in that brutal world outside of the reactor complex. You're just too weak and compliant. Anyone and anything will do whatever they want with you. Is that what you want?"

"No. And I'm not that weak like you say."

"Still, I just did some nice feeling up on you, didn't I?"

"I, um, you caught me by surprise. Oh, come on. This is so traumatic. I just want to find my husband, then—"

"Then, what? Go back to fucking on a roof somewhere?"

"We weren't making love. I already told you that—"

Betsy scoffed and said, "Even the way you talk. Sugar, you're just too fragile. Better toughen up if you want any chance in hell. That's almost literal, too, Sugar."

"I'm tough. And I'm smart."

"Yeah, no doubt. But even the way you just said that isn't very convincing. Put some force in that voice of yours. You have a nice voice. It's kind of sultry when you're not whining."

Scarlet looked down, pouting, and said, "I'm not whining. I just, um, this is all too much and besides, I'm married."

"Probably not anymore."

"What? How could you—"

"It's a brutal place is all. So, if you weren't married, you and I could maybe—"

"No. I'm not, uh, interested in—"

"Bloody, bandaged women? Is that it? Just say it."

"It's not that. And what happened to you anyway?"

Betsy scoffed and said, "You don't want to know. This place is a horror show. Come on. Let's get you a quick tour before you meet the boss."

"I don't want to meet anyone. I just want to—"

"If you don't get an interview with the boss and convince him that you have some value, you'll end up in the most ungodly hellhole this place has. So, you wanna change your mind about that?"

Scarlet wiped once under each eye, then frowned at Betsy.

"Sure. I'll see your boss."

"Good. After a tour of the fun stuff. Right that way."

She pointed toward a closed door that vibrated and sometimes shook. Scarlet brushed her hair back and turned to walk toward it.

And Betsy smacked her ass and said, "Thanks."

Scarlet stopped and turned just enough to say, "For what?"

"For the most normal sex I've had since I got here."

"Um, you . . . you're—"

"You're sexy, Sugar. You got this kind of a hypnotic sexiness about you."

Scarlet scoffed and said, "I'm just scared. That's all."

"Hmm. Fear is sexy sometimes. Remember that."

* * *

They hiked side by side along a wide corridor that sloped downward too steeply to be walked comfortably. Closed doors with padlocks were mixed in with boarded-over windows above crunchy piles of broken glass. An occasional dark hallway, with randomly blinking lights dim in the distance, led away to the left and right.

"See? You'd be in serious trouble, sweet Sugar, if you had some sexy heels to stomp around in."

Scarlet scoffed but didn't smile when she said, "Stomp? Oh, I don't think so."

"No, of course not. Lady like you probably has a sweet little strut. That's all in the past."

Scarlet stopped and leaned over with her arms crossed over her belly.

"Something I said?"

"This is just too much. If I could go back, see Daniel again . . ."

"You'd what?"

She held Betsy's gaze, whose eyes were darting quickly between both of her own.

"I'd, um, dress sexier. He deserves it. And I'd, um, I'd strut all goddamn day for him."

"Now, you're talking. That's a superpower, Sugar. Yeah. If you could go back. Come on."

She took Scarlet's arm and got her started, then quickly stopped her when they both heard a scream up ahead and saw flickering light from flames inside a room off to the right.

"No. No more. I don't want to see whatever is in there."

"Oh, it's alright. I just want you to meet someone."

"I don't want to meet anyone. I'm happy enough with—"

"With bloody Betsy feeling you up? Yeah, Sugar, I'm good with that too. But I still have to deliver you to the boss. Come on."

Betsy led the way, sometimes holding Scarlet's arm and dragging her along until they were near the doorway. Another two steps and they'd see whatever was screaming in there.

"No! Don't make me!"

"I have to, Sugar."

She turned to face Scarlet and stayed close.

"Best I can do is delay it for a few minutes."

"What? How?"

She slipped her hands around Scarlet's waist.

"Here's the best deal you're going to get. We'll stay right here and forget that room just so long as you're kissing me."

"What? You're crazy. I've never kissed a woman."

"Alright, let's see what's going on in—"

"Wait. Oh God, I'm scared. I'm so scared, Betsy."

"Mm. Yeah. Best time to kiss you."

"What? No."

"I'm not asking again."

Betsy leaned forward, turning the bandaged side of her face away, and stopped with their lips about to touch. She looked into Scarlet's eyes for a few seconds, then smiled, then pressed her lips into hers.

Scarlet groaned softly but didn't try to escape, even as Betsy wound her arms around her waist and pulled them together.

She kissed the new arrival for thirty seconds, then backed away just enough to say, "Damn. Something about your kisses, Sugar."

Scarlet sobbed and laughed and said, "That's what Daniel told me."

"Mm. So glad he saved some for me."

She resumed their kiss and reached down with both hands to hold Scarlet's ass cheeks, then broke the kiss only enough to whisper loudly enough to carry over all of the reactor noise.

"Mine too. Go on."

"What? No, I—"

Betsy stifled her with a wet kiss, and Scarlet groaned and reached down to hold Betsy's ass too.

After another thirty seconds of kissing and fondling, deep underground in a buried reactor in a burning city, Scarlet fought her way free and stepped back.

"No, I'm married, and I don't, uh, you know. Not me."

"Alright, Sugar. That was nice, but we do have a schedule to keep anyway. Come on."

Betsy stepped over enough to look inside the room, then Scarlet joined her. She winced from the heat billowing out, and the smell made her cough and gag.

Ten paces inside the room, a large metal box with an open door was filled with flames and unidentifiable lumps piled up and burning. Outside the burn box stood a young, brown-haired man wearing only tight khaki pants and heavy work boots.

His body rippled with muscles so thick that he likely couldn't touch his own head, and his elbows were locked far from his body. Legs like the building's concrete columns stretched the pants into a ripped and tattered coat of paint.

Sweat poured from his unmarred, perfect skin like he was playing in a sprinkler.

He turned and looked their way, showing the face of an overgrown child, a child whose eyes got big and whose mouth snapped into a gigantic smile.

"Mama!"

"Junior. You working hard?"

Scarlet shuffled over to stand behind Betsy and peeked over her shoulder.

"Always, Mama. I'm almost caught up. Got any more? Huh? Any more?"

Betsy held a finger up, prompting Junior to be patient while she turned her head to speak to Scarlet.

"My boy. He's kind of a big one, isn't he?"

"What? That's your son?"

"Mm-hmm. Quite a strapping boy, huh? He's the hardest working employee in this reactor."

"Mama, I'm hungry! Any more? Huh? Any more?"

Betsy held up her finger again.

"What's he doing? What is this?"

"Oh, Sugar, he's just burning body parts."

"They're making him—"

"Oh, no, he volunteered."

She turned back to Junior, and Scarlet hid herself further when Junior said, "Her? That one? Is she next?"

"Junior, no," said Betsy. "She's still alive, you silly boy."

"That's okay, Mama. That's okay! Is she next? Huh?"

"Junior, forget about Scarlet. I just wanted her to meet you. We're taking a tour."

"Okay, Mama. Okay. Then, you bring me more? Huh? More?"

"Sure, Junior. Just be patient. There's plenty to burn and . . . whatever."

"Okay. Okay, Mama."

Betsy turned her head enough to say, "See? Kissing me was a damn good deal, right? Instead of seeing that?"

At hearing no response, she turned farther and saw Scarlet staring at Junior, mouth and eyes open wide. So, she turned to look again herself.

Junior was standing and flexing his sweaty muscles and raising a detached arm up to his mouth. He offered a flash of red, gummed-up teeth with sharp points just before he bit loose a chunk.

With a full mouth and chewing, he said, "More, Mama. Okay? More, okay?"

"Soon, Junior. Soon!"

He grinned, took a bite, then laughed and stood near the oven and sweated with his cheeks packed.

"Come on."

She pulled Scarlet along behind her, away from Junior and his body oven.

"My God. That's really your son?"

"Well, more than he used to be. He was always into bodybuilding and stuff. Now, here, doing the work he's doing, and—"

"Eating people? He's eating people?"

"Uh, I don't think they're actually people when he's eating them. Just meat that got left behind."

"Okay. Sure. But how did he get so gigantic?"

"I can't explain it good for that scientific brain of yours but here, around the reactor and its awful radiation, things, uh, kind of happen to people."

"From the radiation, you mean? They . . . what? Mutate?"

"See? I knew you'd understand. Anyway, Junior gorges on all of that and, well, you see what that gets him. He's a genuine monster."

Scarlet, walking a step behind Betsy, said, "Oh, no, no, no," and stopped.

Betsy stopped, too, and turned to see her.

"What? Time to kiss again?"

"No! I don't kiss women."

"Could have fooled me. Seemed like a pretty natural thing for you once you got going."

"Hey, this isn't fair. I don't belong here. But I kind of know how I got here."

"Yeah. Go on."

"It was sex and . . ."

"Death. Yeah. That's the ticket."

Scarlet coughed and said, "So, you and your son are both here. So, does that mean . . ."

"Grand prize. You figured us out. Yeah, we were doing something nasty when the gas line to the trailer ruptured and kaboom!"

"You . . . and your son?"

"Hey, don't judge. He, uh, he—hey, you really want to hear this?"

Scarlet looked around and let out a panicked laugh.

"As much as I want to do anything here."

"Yeah, I get that. Alright."

They were standing near a wall, facing each other, many steps from Junior and his howling for more food.

"So, I just got back from work, and Junior was out under the tarp doing his usual weightlifting stuff. He heard my truck backfire when I shut it down, and he called me over. He was about to do some bench press lifting, and he wanted me to kind of guard him, or whatever they call that."

"Spotting, I think."

"Sure. Okay. So, I got in place, and I watched him lying there with pumped up muscles and just these skimpy little shorts. And I mean, just the shorts. Can you imagine that? Can you see it?"

"Yeah. Sure."

"He seemed way too excited just from lifting weights. Know what I mean?"

"Uh-huh. I think so."

"So, he did his lifting and didn't need any help. He plopped the bar down on the rack, then he just lay there. And it took me a second to realize he was looking up my skirt! That sweaty pervert!"

"He's still sweaty."

"Yeah. So, I was kind of high, and I thought I'd mess with him. I asked if he saw anything he liked. And I was about to laugh at my own joke, then he said he sure as hell did. Oh, I never should have done what I did."

"What? What did you do?"

"Damn, I just lifted my skirt and stepped forward, still thinking it was like some kind of weird joke that we'd laugh about later. But that boy grabbed me, and I sure couldn't get away."

"He was too strong?"

"Damn right, he was too strong, even before this place and the shit he's been eating. He had me by my ass and just pulled me down right onto his face. I fought but, uh, not for long. I kind of got lost in watching his chest and waistline muscles flexing and sweating and flexing and . . . well, you get the idea."

"Then, what? The explosion?"

"I'm not even done with that first psycho time with him! No, Sugar, he wanted more than that, that big healthy boy, and who could tell him no? So, I strutted around and straddled that boy on the bench, and it's a good thing I wasn't barefoot because—"

"Gym shoes?"

"Oh, hell no. I had these sweet, sexy little boots, kind of short, with really high, spiky heels. You should have seen them. They laced all the way up the front and were just the thing to drive all the hicks crazy where I worked. You can ask where, if you want."

"Okay. Where?"

"Strip club. Those seedy perverts sure loved those boots. So, I thought that boy was flexing those abs when I had his hungry face covered. Shit, you should have seen those tight muscles when I was—"

"Okay! I get it. So, you two were doing that, then that gas line—"

"Oh, hell no. That blast was about two years later. And let me tell you, that was a sweet couple of years. Just bad luck that the gas done blew up the place right when we were—"

"Doing the weight thing again?"

"Oh, Sugar, no. That was only that first time. We were in bed. Oh my God, I can honestly say that I barely even noticed the place blowing to smithereens—it kind of always felt like that."

"Uh . . ."

"Come on. One more stop."

She took Scarlet's hand and pulled her along the dim corridor.

* * *

Still holding Scarlet's hand, Betsy stooped down to lead her through a short, oblong doorway with a rusting hatch door detached and leaning against the wall nearby. She brushed aside a few cobwebs, then took a step inside.

"Watch your head."

"Good advice. It looks like no one ever comes in here. What are we doing here?"

"Oh, I just kind of wanted to see it. I haven't been in here in a while."

"Uh, okay."

The metal grating beneath their feet came to an end, and rough planks were positioned across the support beams, just wide enough for single file passage.

"Uh, I think I'll hang on here," Scarlet said and took her hand out of Betsy's.

She reached out to both sides and held the pipe railings at waist height, then stopped to look down.

"I don't want to be here. Can we just go back?"

"The walkway starts up again, Sugar. It just, uh, got blown up over here a while back."

"All the more reason."

"Aw, come on. It isn't so bad."

The planks ended where more metal grating continued, and Betsy waited for Scarlet to catch up and stand beside her.

"Look over the side. Not so scary, right?"

Scarlet saw beneath them a concrete floor, so close that she could have stepped down onto it. Stacks of cardboard boxes and wooden crates were piled haphazardly all around, almost all of them covered and connected by the remains of thick spiderwebs.

"No, but I still wouldn't want to go down there. I don't like bugs."

"Oh, bugs aren't so bad. Anyway, we're not going down there. I just want you to see an ugly part of the reactor that hardly anyone even knows about anymore. Come on. It's right up there."

"Betsy, this is too scary. Can we just go back?"

She stopped and turned to face Scarlet.

"Sure. We could."

"So, let's go, alright?"

"Nope. Same deal as before."

"What deal? What are you talking about?"

Betsy grinned in the dim, flickering light and said, "Bet you wish you didn't ever go look in on my boy, Junior. Right? Eating arms and shit?"

"I could have done without seeing that. Yeah."

"And all you had to do was keep . . . what?"

"No. I'm not going to kiss you again."

Betsy reached for her waist, and Scarlet backed herself into the railing.

"Alright. We can skip that and get to something better. That's what you want?"

"What? No! That's why you brought me here?"

"Well, Sugar, you're just so easy to scare and get all sexy. Can't pass that up."

"Well, you're going to have to. I'm going back."

Scarlet turned and took one step before Betsy reached around her waist with both hands and stopped her on the metal walkway behind the reactor.

She held her close and said, "Mm, even your hair smells good. Not all oily like everything else."

"Let me go! You're some kind of addict, aren't you?"

Scarlet struggled but only ended up turned around and facing Betsy and still in her arms.

"Yeah. Always have been. Junior knows better than anyone. Come on. Start with a kiss. I'm still one-hundred percent woman, just damaged. Nothing about my woman stuff got mutated. Yet."

"What? What can happen?"

"Nothing, Sugar. Forget I said that. Come on. Start with a kiss."

She leaned in quickly and planted her lips on Scarlet's, who tipped her head from side to side to evade her.

"Stop! You're all insane here!"

Betsy cackled and said, "No, Sugar, you're insane for not taking what you can while you still can. Treat me nice, and you and I can both go back and get Junior nice and busy and sweaty. He'd like that. He'd do us both and never get tired."

"Stop! Let me go!"

"He's a big, healthy boy. He could handle both of us. More than once each too."

"No, that's crazy!"

"Shh. Not so loud. You might wake something up down here."

"Huh?" Scarlet whispered. "Like what?"

"God only knows. Well, if God cared enough to look around down here. But he never would. Probably scared to. Look, really, you'd better stay nice and quiet for both of our sakes."

Scarlet trembled and looked at the deep shadows all around them, and she didn't notice that Betsy was leaning toward her again.

She groaned but didn't fight too loudly as Betsy forced a long kiss, with one arm around her waist and a hand holding her head in place. After a few seconds, her groaning stopped, then Betsy backed away but still held her close.

"There. That's better. Afraid and quiet and actually kissing me back that time. Mm, that's the way to serve it up."

"No," she whispered, "just let me—"

"Mm," Betsy could barely say with their lips again squeezed together.

She held Scarlet tight for a minute of kissing, then whispered in her ear.

"There's a scrap of cardboard right there. All you got to do, Sugar, is pull that over, then stay very quiet while you get on your knees."

"What? No! No, I'm not doing anything like that!"

"Think about where you're at, Sugar. Remember that you're never getting out. And you're probably not going to last. You do me, then I'll do you. Really, Sugar, what else do you have going on?"

"I don't care! I'm married, and I—"

A siren began blasting up ahead along the walkway, and screaming erupted from some of the shadows. Scarlet and Betsy watched as shapes like men wailed and hurried past them on the concrete floor below, crouching low and keeping their faces hidden.

"What's going on? What is this?"

"We should be running like them, but I just don't care anymore. I'm ready."

"What? No, I still have to find Daniel! What's going on?"

"Reactor's going to blow. It's my lucky fucking day!"

"No! We have to run! Let me—"

The shock wave from a mighty blast blew both of them off of the walkway and onto their backs on a sloppy grouping of cardboard boxes.

Scarlet screamed and wiped at dusty spider webs plastered all over her, thick like cheesecloth. She'd just cleared enough to open her eyes, and she saw a dangling spider, as big as her hand and wiggling all of its legs around as it lowered itself down.

Right onto her face.

"No, get off of me!"

With its long, hairy legs shifting around, tickling her face, she flailed around for something to hit it with, or brush it with, or just smash it, then . . .

. . . it hit.

A silent, hot wave swept through her, stirring around her insides, messing with things that shouldn't be messed with until it had passed.

Looking up again, cross-eyed to focus on the suddenly still spider, she watched as it staggered, one leg at a time, then curled itself down into a tangled, dehydrated mess before she gasped and pushed it off of her face.

Then, the sweating started.

Quicker breathing began on its own.

She stopped reaching for something to strike the now-dead insect.

"Scarlet!" Betsy called from nearby. "Oh, God, Scarlet, we have to get out of here!"

Scarlet sat up and plucked some of the webbing off of her arms and legs, then turned to see the anguished look Betsy was giving her from two boxes over.

"Something bad happened to me, Scarlet. We never should have come down here. I fell into some kind of . . . I don't know, nest or something. God, there were hundreds of them!"

"What just happened? What the hell was that?"

"Radiation. I'll explain, but we have to get our asses out of here before it hits us again. Get your ass up!"

Betsy clattered about clumsily until she was free of the boxes and climbed up onto the walkway. Scarlet stepped out of the mess and easily got herself up to join Betsy.

"Was it worth it?"

"Huh? What are you talking about, Scarlet?"

"To get me afraid even more. To try to make me, uh, you know."

Betsy managed a terrified smile, then said, "Yeah. Oh, hell yeah. But we really have to go!"

With a wet hand, she took Scarlet's, and they both ran back down the walkway, over the planks, then sprinted until they were clear of the danger zone

"Okay," Betsy said while wheezing and bending over, "we're far enough out of there."

"Uh, are you alright? You got a little—"

Betsy snapped a hand over her neck, on the side that wasn't bandaged, and said, "Oh, Scarlet, something bad is going on. I can feel it. Do you feel alright?"

Scarlet kicked out each leg, then stretched her arms out to her sides.

"Yeah. I'm fine. I think that running did me some good. My legs feel good."

"Oh, shit, I don't feel so good. God, I fell right into them!"

"Into what?"

"I don't know. Centipedes? Millipedes? I don't know how many goddamn pedes were there, but it was a shitload of them!"

"Well, you're fine now. Grossed out, sure, but they can't hurt you."

She stayed low and held her face in her hands.

"Oh, Scarlet, you don't understand. Just be glad you didn't land in that nest with me."

"Yeah, I'm glad about that. But I did get a—"

"Oh, shit, we have to go. The boss is going to be pissed if we don't get there quick. Come on!"

She grabbed Scarlet's hand and raced with her up stairways, through dark rooms, and along dim corridors with flashing lights.

They finally stopped at a door with a sign that said there was a boss behind it.

Chapter 10 – He Can Sniff Out Females

"Oh, hold up, Scarlet. I can't keep up with—"

Betsy groaned and doubled herself over, her head almost against her knees.

"Are you alright?"

"No, not even close. Oh, Scarlet, I think I'm in big trouble."

She straightened up, then stretched back to look at the ceiling. Before she could cover her neck with a hand, some thin, worm-like growths began popping out in close lines, up and down each side.

"Betsy, what's wrong? What's going on?"

"Radiation, Scarlet. Damn, we never should have gone down there. It's your fault. Your fault!"

"My fault? It was your idea!"

"Your fault that you're so goddamn irresistible. Even in those damn work clothes. Oh, I—"

She turned away quickly and slapped her other hand against her forehead, but the same thin, wormy things wiggled up from behind her fingers and waved to Scarlet, some of them snaking through Betsy's hair first.

"Oh my God, Betsy! What's going on? Can I help?"

She scoffed while rounding up the wagging worms and pinned them all under her palm before turning around.

She cackled and said, "Yeah. Call the exterminator."

"What? What do you—"

"You sure you feel alright, Scarlet? Anything feel different?"

"I, um . . ."

She ran her hands down both thighs, then slowly back up. She reached around back, squeezed her own ass cheeks several times, then ran her hands up her sides till they were under her breasts.

But she snapped her hands down to her sides and said, "Uh, no. Not really. I, um, just feel kind of good."

With one hand on her neck and the other trapping things against her forehead, Betsy squinted and said, "You're taller than you were."

She looked down, then back up.

"Huh. You didn't sneak those heels back on, though."

"What are you talking about?"

"Nothing. Never mind. We don't have time anyway. Time to see the boss."

"What's he like?"

"Hell if I know. I've never met him. Sure heard stories, though."

"Oh. Like what?"

Still holding back squirmy things, and sometimes letting Scarlet see a waving tip before she could corral it with the rest, Betsy looked both ways along the dark hallway, then again at Scarlet.

"Some folks call him a madman. Which doesn't say much in a fucked up world like this. Unless he's really, *really* a madman. That could be."

"I, uh, maybe I should just go get to work or look for Daniel. Let's get out of here."

"No, it's too late. He knows we're here."

"How?"

"Like a dog on a hunt. I heard he can sniff out females, just pick out each one of them. Males, too, though. He doesn't care, I heard."

"Really, Betsy, let's just run anyway!"

"I'd try to cut a deal with you, make you do some seriously sweet things for me, but that train has sailed. I'm not just bloody Betsy anymore. Oh, no, I got some weird—"

A long, delicate, finger-thick stick jutted out from between the fingers of the hand trying to contain the rest up against her forehead.

"Oh, God."

It grew as Scarlet took a step back, and it poked around in different directions until it finally pointed at Scarlet's head, then it started to stretch toward her.

"Betsy! What's going on with you?"

"Radiation. Oh, God, I'm done for."

She used the hand from her neck to grab it, exposing feathery lines of the same leg-like growths, all wiggling and waving around. All down the front of her shirt, nearly down to her waist, the cloth was twitching and bouncing.

"Can I help? There must be something we can do!"

She cackled, wrestled with her new body parts, then glared at Scarlet.

"Shit, no. I'm done. Can't say that it's been a pleasant time here."

"There must be some—"

"Promise me, dear Scarlet, that you won't feed me to Junior when I'm done."

"What? Why would I? That's so—"

"Not even before I'm done. I can't be doing that anymore."

"What? What does that mean?"

"Oh, hell. Might as well tell you since my throat's going to be packed with these things soon."

"No, no, no! You can—"

"Listen! It's like my final confession, dammit. Me and Junior, we had some wild times, then our sorry asses ended up here. He got into that biting and eating people and all that shit, but he still wanted his Mama because there's just no one like his Mama, right? So, we gave it a go here, and that pile of sweaty muscles took a nibble out of me. Just a nibble, but it hurt, Scarlet! Like a sex-crazed fool, I went back for more, and that freak took another bite."

"Your bandages? That's all where—"

"Shit, yeah. Chunks are missing. That muscle freak digested them all, and he wants more. But don't let him, Scarlet, not now! Not after that radiation got me!"

"Okay, I promise. Oh, I can't believe I'm saying this. Okay, Betsy, I won't let your son eat you while he . . ."

"Say it. Say it!"

"Uh, while he . . . fucks you."

"There. My heart is at peace. I'm ready to go, or become something else, or whatever. Why the hell should I even care?"

She let a squirming patch of legs on her forehead breathe some fresh air and held her fist near the boss's door.

"There might still be hope, Betsy. We could—"

"Last chance, Scarlet."

"Huh?"

"You want to kiss bloody buggy Betsy some more or see that madman boss?"

"I, uh . . ."

A wormy, fleshy stick fought its way out of Betsy's mouth until she sucked it back in like a strand of escaping spaghetti.

"Um . . ."

"Mm-hmm," she said while holding her lips tight together. "Mm-hmm."

She knocked.

*   *   *

"This better be something I care about!" the boss yelled through the closed door.

"No turning back now," Betsy said, then sucked in a wiggling noodle. "Same with me. No going back."

Scarlet sobbed, looking into eyes that Betsy allowed to peek between fingers and twisting, tiny little new limbs.

"God, I just want to go home. Find Daniel and—"

Betsy cackled weakly and said, "You're fucked, Scarlet. Can't go home and scared to see the boss. Maybe you should be more scared of the freak nightmare I'm becoming. What are you going to do?"

"I, uh, think . . ."

"Yeah, that's the spirit. Let's go."

She pushed the door in, and a squirmy little twig whipped against the worn wood surface, leaving a sticky track.

They stood side by side, against each other until Scarlet felt a few tickles on her arm, didn't look, but took a step away from Betsy.

At the far side of the cluttered room sat a bulky plain metal desk, its top surface littered with papers, file folders, oily machine parts, and knives. Seated there was a man with a short gray beard and intense black eyes who watched them closely. A gray ponytail dropped down to one side and lay on his chest.

He glared at them from below the brim of a plain and faded black fedora, one lacking a decorative feather or any other kind of embellishment.

Despite his obvious age, the short sleeves of his black polo shirt were straining around thick biceps, and his broad chest kept the fabric tight all the way around.

In one hand, he held a long, clean sword by its handle, and he was scraping it methodically over a whetstone in his other hand. He paused to look over his new guests.

"Well, get your asses in here. This better be important."

Scarlet and Betsy gave each other a quick glance, then stepped into the room.

"Well?"

"New arrival," said Betsy. "She—"

"Slave labor. Good. Why the hell you bothering me about it?"

"Uh, yeah, she could do some labor. But she has skills that—"

Three snake-like growths sprouted out of Betsy's mouth, gagging her until she could groan and suck them all back in.

"You're disgusting," he said to her. "Radiation?"

"Yeah," said Betsy. "We just got a big blast. We don't know if it was a bad kind or—"

The boss laughed and said, "There any other kind? Don't fucking kid yourself. You're well on your way to being a god-awful freak. Good for you."

He laid down the sword and whetstone and turned his eyes to Scarlet.

"Not you, though? You some kind of goddamn miracle that's immune to that shit?"

"I, uh, I don't—"

"What's your name?"

"I'm—"

"Never mind. No one cares."

Betsy was leaning forward, holding her neck and her belly, when she laughed once, hysterically, and said, "I call her Sugar! I . . . I—"

She got choked and had to suck in more legs.

"Disgusting. Back up."

Betsy, still slurping, took a step back.

"No, come on. You're a disgusting fucking mess and getting worse by the second. Back yourself all the fucking way over by the door."

She'd managed to get her lips closed, held it all in, and shuffled back toward the open door.

The boss turned his eyes back to Scarlet.

"I'm Archie. I run this place. I own it. Why are you—"

He shifted his eyes to look past Scarlet, and she turned to see too.

Betsy had given up trying to hide the slender, wiggly things growing out of her. The ones from her neck had gotten long enough to feel around and tap on the door against which she was leaning. The two crowded lines of them twitching around under her shirt had grown down far enough to bounce around the pants over her thighs. And she'd begun to use both hands to force her jaw to stay closed, trapping inside however many were trying to get out into the air.

"Holy shit. That's new."

"Oh my God. Betsy!"

"Hey."

Scarlet turned back toward Archie, who was again looking up at her from his desk.

"What about you? You about to grow some scary shit too?"

"I, uh, what? You think I will?"

"Nope. Would have by now. You say you got hit with whatever the fuck got her?"

He picked up his sword and pointed it at Betsy. Scarlet didn't turn around, even at the sound of her gagging and dozens of tapping rhythms against the door.

"Yes. But, I, um . . ."

She took a deep breath and rubbed her hands down her thighs, then back up, then started feeling around behind her before she jerked her arms straight down at her sides.

"Uh, maybe it missed?"

"Yeah. Maybe. Either fucking way, you still look pretty damn good."

He looked higher to study her hair, then down to her breasts for a few seconds, then down as far as he could see of her as she stood near his desk.

"Damn good."

His eyes focused unwaveringly at a precise region between Scarlet's thighs, high up, even though the baggy khaki work pants weren't providing any special kind of view.

He snapped his eyes up to gaze into hers.

"Oh, yeah. Damn good. A sexy new treat."

* * *

"What did you say that thing's name was?" he said with a tip of his head.

Scarlet froze and wouldn't turn her head at the gurgling from Betsy's throat and the drumming and swishing from the legs already out and the many others that had just begun sprouting.

"She's Betsy. Is there anything we can do?"

He laughed and said, "What? She's not mutating fast enough for you?"

"Huh?"

"Look, forget about that. It's over for that thing. You, though, might be of some use. Before she became . . . what was her name again? Bugsy?"

"No! Her name is—"

"Oh, I know. I just don't care. We'll deal with her in a second. You. You have any skills that I can use around here, or should we just bury you with some glowing fuel rods or something?"

"What? Why would you—"

With his eyes back on Scarlet's crotch, he rubbed at his chin and said, "Hmm, just kidding about that."

He looked back up into her eyes and said, "Really, what can you do, fresh arrival, in our fucking wonderland?"

"I, um, I'm an engineer, and I—"

"Were. You were an engineer. Then, you . . . what?"

She looked down and said, "God, it's all of you. Everyone wants to hear it."

"Forget that. Whatever I imagine is way better than whatever lame sex you were having that got your pretty ass here."

Betsy snorted out a laugh that ended in more gurgling, then slipped her back down along the door until she and her eager insect parts were seated.

"Alright, so you did some engineering. That's good. What else?"

"Um, automation."

Scarlet shifted her eyes to the side at the sound of Betsy, behind her, moaning and gurgling, then she cast her eyes toward the floor in front of her.

In an exhausted monotone, she said, "I could use almost anything to automate almost anything. Programming. I did a lot of that. All the major languages. I could also—oh, please, can I just find Daniel and go home?"

She stared at Archie, trembling, as Betsy twitched against the door and groaned.

"Who the hell is Daniel?"

"My husband."

Archie opened his mouth to speak but stopped and tipped his head to watch as Scarlet unfolded her arms straight out from her, then rotated them several times lazily. She curled them back in close, then slid her palms down her sides, past her waistline, and down as far as she could reach along her thighs.

She left them there, drawing Archie's careful scrutiny, then he looked back up at her eyes.

"What the hell is going on with you?"

"I, um, nothing. I hope. My husband? Is he here?"

"God knows, pretty treat, and he isn't talking. Not to me. You just forget trying to find anyone."

He pointed past her, and Scarlet didn't turn at the sound of gagging and wheezing and chittering of countless little legs against the wood of the door and floor.

"He's like Bugsy, there, or worse. Now, get back to your damn resume."

"Okay. I, um, know a lot about mathematics, and chemistry, and physics, and industrial processes. I've never worked at a reactor, but I've studied them and can probably—please, I just want to go home!"

"Get it through that gorgeous head of yours, you whiny little baby. You died there."

She stared at him, and one tear escaped to weave a path down her cheek.

"And you fucking enjoyed it. That's what got your sexy ass here."

"But if I could just find Daniel and—"

Behind her, Betsy was giving up quick, short groans as she staggered her way back up onto her feet, dragging her back and excited new appendages along the door.

"You really got to see that," Archie said, laughing and pointing. "Fuck."

"I don't want to see what—"

"Look at her!" he yelled. "Look at Bugsy!"

Scarlet turned to look and gasped, but she turned back to Archie when he said, "I'm a patient man, sort of, but this is just too much."

He stood and picked up his sword, then walked around the desk to stand beside Scarlet.

"I mean, really, how much absolute fuckery am I supposed to put up with?"

"What are you going to do?"

"I never really know. It's always a goddamn surprise to me too."

He reached around her waist with his free arm and pulled her in close.

"See? Didn't know I was going to do that!"

He walked toward the standing and gurgling and snarling mutant known as Betsy or Bugsy and took Scarlet with him. She fought to get free but couldn't get away from his arm, which had locked solid like a big metal hook.

"Let me go! Stop it!"

Betsy wailed, sending the tendrils from her mouth into an undulating frenzy, and left a wet mess on the doorknob as she pulled in the door.

"Oh, something's about to stop. Help me, sweet little girl!"

His hook of an arm unhooked enough to grab Scarlet's closest wrist, and he forced her hand to join his other one on the sword's handle.

"Yeah! Fucking teamwork!"

He raised the sword up high, and Scarlet appeared to be helping him.

"Just like this!"

Together, they swung down the sharp blade and caught Betsy's head, near the top but on the side with the bloody bandage oozing out tiny, curious fingers.

"Ha!"

They pulled the sword out of the deep cleft which had opened to let out more of the squirmy little things growing out of her everywhere. Many had poked through her clothing in packed, parallel lines. They wiggled and waved and sometimes snapped around enough to send a few drops of blood out like from a damaged sprinkler.

Betsy's eyes rolled back, and she fell out of the room, toppling rigidly onto her back with no bending at the waist. Almost instantly, all of her new limbs found the floor and after some gentle tapping and exploring, they worked together to mostly lift her body up off of the tile.

"Well, son of a bitch. Just when I thought I'd fucking seen it all."

Archie kept his arm around Scarlet's waist, and she made no effort to get away from him. They both stared through the doorway and watched what was left of Betsy and what it was doing.

Only her boots and hair were still touching the floor, and all of the legs were almost getting coordinated with each other. Her body spun a little bit one way, then the other.

All while she stared up at the ceiling, grinning and with a bouquet of tendrils wagging up and out of her mouth.

"That shit has to get out of here. Dragging down my reputation."

He walked toward the spectacle and took Scarlet with him. They stood over Betsy, both gazing down at her.

Scarlet sobbed silently.

Archie chuckled and reached for her with his free hand, but he paused before grabbing any part of the no-longer-human commotion on the floor.

Looking back up at Scarlet, he winked and said, "I'm really not a nice, uh, man."

He focused again on Betsy, grabbed her work shirt where it was buttoned up between her breasts, and ripped it upward. He quickly flapped it open, exposing two very well-shaped breasts.

With slithery vines slipping around and across them.

He stood back up, held Scarlet close, and said, "Huh. Thought I would have enjoyed that more than I did. That's just too fucking weird."

"God. You're just leaving her there?"

He snickered and walked backwards with her, back into the office, and left the door open.

"Isn't much of a 'her' anymore, precious thing. Nope. Just a bug. A bug with some luscious breasts. If you could stomach all that bug stuff growing out of them."

Still watching, and still sobbing, Scarlet said, as the body almost danced in circles, up on all of its tendrils, "So, you're just leaving her there?"

"We have workers that'll clean that up. God, I sure as fuck hope we do."

Scarlet swooned with a loud groan and would have fallen to the floor, but Archie's hook arm had her locked up against him.

"Hey. You feel kind of nice. Even better than you look."

Chapter 11 – Never a Dull Goddamn Moment

Archie spun himself around, still holding Scarlet, and easily lifted her till her boots didn't touch the floor, then carried her back to his desk. He swept her around and sat her on the edge, then held her in place with a hand on each shoulder.

"Hey. Don't zone out on me."

He let her go long enough to lightly slap her cheek a few times, then used a hand under her chin to hold her slumping head upright.

"Course, I could just slap you more. That's kind of—"

He snapped his head around at the sound of Betsy's garbled wailing.

Her hundreds of new legs were still undecided about which way to spin her, but they kept trying. And she'd tipped her head to one side to try screaming past the lush growth blooming out of her mouth.

"God, that's ugly."

He let Scarlet's head hang, then laid her down onto her back on his desk.

"Stay."

He strode to the doorway and looked where Betsy's eyes were looking. Two men with shovels were approaching, laughing like loons as they materialized out of the hallway's shadows.

"This should be good."

Walking back toward Scarlet, he said, "Let's just hold up on the key part of this interview. We'll get to it. Oh, we'll surely get to it."

He sat beside her, rubbing and squeezing her thigh, and grinned and watched the doorway as the sounds of footsteps and voices got louder.

"What the fuck is that?" said one, still out of sight through the doorway.

"Well, shit, Mikey. Look at them tits. That's your next wife."

"Yeah, yeah, those are some fine tits. What's all that other shit, though?"

"Oh, nothing. She's just part bug."

"What kind, Dax? What kind of bug?"

"Like it fucking matters. Just a bug. A centipede, maybe?"

"Yeah, yeah. Uh-huh. That's a lot of fucking legs."

"She's dancing for you."

"Hey, maybe she was a dancer before she got here?"

"Yeah, probably. Maybe you should fuck her, see if you want to marry her."

"Oh, no, Dax. I ain't getting married again. You go ahead and fuck her."

"Mikey, you're a kook. You know better than that. I wouldn't fuck that thing with either one of your dicks."

"Huh. Yeah, but . . ."

"You're thinking about fucking that, aren't you?"

"Well, maybe with my second dick. I don't care what that thing does. Help me hold her still."

"It ain't really a 'her.' It's a goddamn insect."

"Uh, kind of. Mostly. Yeah, yeah. Grab her ankles."

"You're stupid as fuck. I ain't touching that shit."

Betsy kept spinning one way, up on hundreds of legs, then the other way. Dax stuck the point of his shovel between her knees, causing the spin cycle to shorten up, then he looked into Archie's office.

"Oh, uh, sorry, Boss. We were just, I mean, Mikey and I were—"

"Hey," said Archie, "don't sweat it. Just pretend I'm not even here."

He flicked his hand toward him and added, "Carry on, you and Mikey. Just, whatever you do, make sure that shit gets the hell—"

Betsy's many extra legs had grown and learned to coordinate their efforts. They ran her free of Dax's shovel first, then, with her wailing through the waving stalks planted in her mouth, they swept from her head to her feet, wave after wave, and started carrying her down the hallway.

"Gotta go, Boss!"

"Yeah, like he said. Yeah!"

Archie saluted as the two workmen chased after a runaway insect woman scrambling toward the left.

"Shit," he said to Scarlet, who had picked up her head and watched the entire exchange, "never a dull goddamn moment. Don't go away."

She sobbed quietly, her eyes wet and staring up at him.

"Hey, that's kind of cute. Keep that up. I'll be right back."

He got up and watched two men stabbing their shovels, trying to snag the giant slithering insect as it scurried along quickly. But they kept missing as it twitched up against one wall, then the other, leading them away from Archie's office.

The next shovel strike elicited a muffled screech as it squished into a human leg and held it in place.

"This should be fun," Archie said, then turned, grinning, to look back at Scarlet.

She still reclined on the desk where he'd left her, but she was up on her elbows, slowly kicking out one leg then the other, and staring into his eyes.

"Huh. Awake. I guess that's good too. Just a second, new girl. Things are heating up out there."

*   *   *

Archie watched the hallway drama again and saw one of the workers—it was too dim to know which one—stabbing down repeatedly, sending loud squeals and cries along the hallway.

"She'll never marry you now, you dumbass!"

"I might still fuck her, though. But not with my real dick. Not with that one!"

"Go ahead, then. Give me your shovel. I'll try to pin down both of those legs."

"Shit, those other ones are still growing. They're almost as big! I'm not fucking that with any dick I have now or might still grow."

"That's funny, Mikey. But a lie. You'd fuck anything with any dick."

"Hey, you let her go!"

The centipede with a human head and bared breasts was scurrying back toward Archie's office, and two laughing men with shovels were chasing it.

"The things that happen around here . . ."

"Stab her, Mikey! Don't take that shit from your new bride!"

"I'm not marrying her! Probably!"

Archie looked back at Scarlet, who was still kicking lazily and still staring at him. But she'd also tipped her head to one side.

"Radiation," he said to her, tapping his temple. "Not good for the brain."

Scarlet tipped her head the other way and kept staring.

"Huh," he said. "Alright, then."

He looked back out into the hallway just in time to see the menagerie of insect and shovels and maniacal workmen almost at his door.

"Shit!"

He closed the door and left it open just enough to watch the sport.

"Stab it, Dax! Stab that bitch!"

He did, and the Betsy thing shrieked.

"Again!"

The shovel met the floor, and several of the new bug legs were free to roam about on their own.

"Oh, shit! Dammit, Dax, you chopped off her legs!"

"Mikey, those were something else's legs. Hey, that gives me an idea, though."

He started stabbing with his shovel all around Betsy, lopping off legs left and right, all of which wiggled around on their own like blind snakes.

"Let's trim her back down to human woman size for you, Mikey. She'll be a blushing bride for you in no time."

"I'm not marrying her! I already told you that I only want to—"

"Ah!"

Dozens of the loose legs had scurried over and climbed right up on Mikey and were writhing and wrestling around, completely covering his face. He opened his mouth to scream, and the nearest ones slithered right in.

"Mikey! Quit fucking around!"

He only gurgled and spasmed and clawed at his face as he leaned against the wall.

"Shit, we got to get out of here!"

He stabbed at Betsy's torso, yelling, "Goddamn bug!"

What was left of Betsy shrieked and scurried away on a feathery set of twitching bug legs.

Dax dropped his shovel, grabbed Mikey's arm, then ran with him in the same direction as Betsy. The rest of the severed, wiggling legs started crawling toward Archie's door.

"Oh, fuck no!"

Archie slammed the door and locked it, then leaned his back into it.

"Alright, pretty baby. I got something for you before anything truly spectacular like that happens to you and your sweet body."

Chapter 12 – That Fucking Mouth of Yours

Archie stood near his office door, smirking at the scratching and thumping from something trying to get inside. A cluster of smaller taps and scrapes came from just one top corner, then a lower corner, then from everywhere on the door.

"Crazy," he said, then he tipped his head to match Scarlet's.

Her unblinking eyes stared back, so he gazed at them for a second, snapped his fingers in their line of sight, then scoffed at getting no reaction.

"Huh. Something's getting started in there. Better get the fuck going on this."

He got himself close to her still slowly kicking legs, watched them for a few seconds, then grabbed at one. She pulled it back and kicked him in his gut.

"Damn. Wanna make it fun, huh? Fucking fine by me."

He gave the constant scratching at the door a quick turn and a short look, then focused again on Scarlet.

She still hadn't blinked, even from kicking him, and she still stared in the same direction. He scoffed at her, then got solid grips on her ankles and smirked at her offering no resistance.

He started lifting both of her legs and said, "Yeah. Nice and easy. You just lie back and—"

"Stop."

He stopped, cocked his head, and stared at the woman who had just spoken slowly and calmly after having kicked him.

She didn't meet his gaze, and he stayed where he was but leaned slightly to try to see her eyes.

"Hey. Don't fucking tell me what to do. No one's ever going to listen to—"

"Stop. Archie."

He held his breath, gazing at Scarlet as her legs remained relaxed in his hands. A few seconds of silence passed, except for the bug legs trying to tunnel into the room.

"Shut up," he said. "Don't talk anymore."

She winced, kept her eyes closed tightly, and whispered, "I don't know why I said that!"

Then, she relaxed and resumed her stare in the same direction, and he squinted while watching, waiting for her to blink. But she didn't. Long seconds crawled past.

He lowered one of her legs, watching her closely, then he let the other down, too, but he didn't let them go.

Scarlet kept staring.

"Shit," he whispered to himself, and got no reaction from her.

He let go of her legs, and they bent at the knee and hung down toward the floor.

Then, they started their lazy kicking again.

"What the hell? You must know I'm about to fuck you, right?"

She gave no reaction.

"Good. Glad you got that. Now, let's just—"

"Don't."

He sucked in a quick breath and held it. Seconds later, he let it out and spoke.

"Goddamn it, you're really pissing me off."

He checked her eyes, then her chest, and didn't notice any blinking or breathing. As her legs continued their easy, rhythmic kicks, he watched her closely and leaned forward.

With a hand on each shoulder, he gently sat her up, and that got her legs to stay down. But she still hadn't blinked.

"Bet you got some sweet tits in there," he said, reaching for the buttons of her dirty flannel shirt. "I insist. Let's get those out where—"

"No," she said, her voice calm.

His fingertips froze where they held the cloth and the top button. His breath oozed back out of him slowly as he watched her face.

He shook his head, laughed, and said, "Oh, right. I get it. Hypnotist. That's on your goddamn resume too. Well, that shit doesn't work on—"

"Go away."

"Goddammit. You listen here, bitch. You keep that goddamn mouth shut or—"

"No," she said, then frowned and locked her eyes shut and whispered, "Why did I—"

"You fucking bitch!"

He stood her up quickly, keeping her trapped between him and the desk, then spun her around to face away.

"Your mouth is only good,"—he rummaged around on the desktop while holding her in place—"for one goddamn thing, and we'll get to that. Oh, yeah, we'll,"—he found the strap of cloth that he'd used to polish the sword—"we'll sure as fuck get to that."

He let her go to yank her hair down, aiming her face toward the ceiling and getting her mouth open.

While she whispered frantically, "Something, something is—" he hurried to stretch the cloth in front of her open mouth, then pulled it in and rushed a tight knot behind her head.

With her head still facing up and a tight cloth strung into her mouth, he grabbed her upper arms with both hands and spoke close to her ear.

"Just like that, you got yourself shut up, didn't you? Huh?"

She didn't kick or elbow him or move her arms at all.

She only moaned at a steady pitch and volume for a short time, starting and ending abruptly, and not conveying any identifiable emotion.

Archie tipped his head away from her and stared at the thick mass of black hair pinched tight by her gag. He let go with one hand and wiped all around his eyes for a few seconds.

"Shut up. Dammit, you need to shut the fuck up!"

He dragged her across the room, kept her facing away, and yanked open a drawer. The first rope he took out was short, so he groaned and tossed it to the floor. The next one was quite long.

"Yeah. This'll do, dammit."

He forced her up against the nearest wall and put a knee to the small of her back.

"Don't even think of—"

Another moan. Longer and louder. Still no identifiable feeling attached to it.

The rope swung from his hand as he held the end up near her head. A clock, if one were in there and made any sense in that world, would have clicked more than a few times.

"Dammit!"

He threaded it into her mouth near the rope's end, then laughed while winding it around her head and digging it in deep with every loop. While tying it tight behind her head, next to the knot from her first gag, he leaned enough to see what he'd done.

"Yeah. You look like you're screaming. I just kind of froze you like that, didn't I? You bitch."

She'd just started another moaning sound, and he hurried to shove her head into the wall, which stopped it.

"Goddammit! What's with you?"

Holding her against the wall and reaching back for the drawer, he found a wide roll of tape.

"Fucking mouth. That fucking mouth of yours!"

He pasted the tape over the other gags, then looped that around her head several times, almost covering every bit of rope, then he spun her around and tried to look into her eyes.

But she stared somewhere else, so he jammed her head backwards, smacking it into the wall.

She still didn't look at him, so he inspected his work.

"I remember that mouth under all that shit. You have a pretty mouth. Nice lips. Look what the fuck you made me do."

He checked that all of it was tight, then brushed her hair aside, off of her face.

"But don't you worry none. You have other warm, wet places for me to enjoy. And you can be damn sure I will."

He looked lower and smiled.

"I like the way you breathe. Oh, yeah, that's nice. I think you're finally ready for some fun. Shit, you're practically forcing them on me."

He reached out and got both hands on the top button again.

*　*　*

He never saw her hand as she slapped him hard enough to twist his head to the side.

"What the fuck?"

He grabbed both of her forearms and held her arms at her sides.

"Nobody does that. Nobody!"

He let go and backhanded her, and she swung her freed arm and caught him with a balled-up fist.

"Dammit!"

He spun her around, banged her head into the wall several times, then pressed between her shoulders to hold her there.

But he looked from one side to the other as Scarlet slowly raised both arms, then left them pointed up at an angle. Her fingers were spread, and the only other movement was the slight heaving of her chest.

"What the fuck is wrong with you?"

She tried her moaning again, but hardly any sound escaped past all of the stuff that he'd wound into her mouth.

"Yeah. 'Bout time you shut up. Stay the fuck right there."

He clunked her head into the wall, then took two steps back to the drawer and came back with a whole pile of rope.

"Goddamn bitch. No one hits me."

He pulled one arm down and tied the end of a short rope around her wrist. After yanking down her other arm, he crossed her wrists and wound that rope as many times as he could before tying a tight knot.

"Better. But you're an ornery bitch, aren't you?"

He found a much longer piece and, while keep her arms straight and as close together as possible, he wove it around both arms, starting near her wrists and pulling it tight with every loop until he could go no farther. He tied it off, then leaned close to her ear.

"Well, you're just a sweet little thing now, aren't you? What did that bug lady say she called you? Sugar? Yeah, Sugar. Well, Sugar, you're not just sweet—you're obedient for me now. Oh, yeah, just a sweet, obedient little thing."

He waited and didn't hear anything.

"Get over there!"

He walked her and sometimes dragged her boots toward the desk, and he got her standing up against it, then he leaned in to speak in her ear again.

"I think you want this as much as I do. You're just a horny little girl, aren't you? Can't get enough sex?"

He reached around and found the line of buttons, then slipped the fingers of both hands inside to hold the edges of the cloth.

"I'm sure this is all just a big turn-on for you, huh, Sugar? Yeah,"—he ripped her shirt open—"baby girl likes it rough."

Squeezing her thighs into the desk, he reached around and palmed both of her breasts, then rubbed them a few times.

"Nice. Real nice."

He got his fingers up under the cups of her bra, got a tight grip, and ripped that open too.

"Hmm," he said while rubbing her breasts and pinching her nipples, "little girl has some nice, big sexy breasts. Oh, those nipples feel good."

Scarlet stood still, let out no more moaning sounds, and only breathed.

"Yeah. Nice. You feel like you're excited to get a good fucking."

While still fondling her, he again spoke in her ear.

"What did I tell you before? Oh, yeah. I remember. About you having other sweet, wet places for me. They are for me, right? Yeah. Course they are."

He dropped his hands for her pants, unhooked her belt and popped the top button, then wiggled the zipper all the way down.

"Oh, yeah, here we go."

Holding the top band, he began shifting it around, working it down over her ass and hips, then partway down her thighs. He let the pants go to bunch up just above her knees.

"Ooh, nice ass. What the fuck is up with those panties, huh, Sugar? Don't think you're sexy enough for some lace? Damn, with a sweet ass like that?"

He held her shoulders and shifted her until she was squared away against the desk.

"You just hold nice and still for me."

He fluffed back her hair, taking his time.

"Yeah, just like that. Such a good girl for me now. Such a pretty little girl for me."

Watching her closely, he took the elastic band of her panties and chuckled while shifting the plain fabric from side to side, slipping it down over her ass cheeks.

"Oh, let's see that ass. I think you want me to."

He tugged it farther down along her thighs, then left the garment down by her knees with her work pants.

"Oh, that's a really nice ass. You're just about ready for what you want so bad, even if you won't admit it. I mean, if you could speak."

He laughed and pushed on her back, and she didn't resist as he bent her over onto his desk. A few gentle kicks to the inside of each scruffy work boot got her to spread them as far as the pants would allow. It wasn't enough, so he forced her to bend at the knees, then lie flat, facedown on his desk and sticking her ass back toward him.

"Good girl. This is the way you want a man to fuck you. You didn't want anything to do with that Betsy. I mean, before she got all bugged out. Oh, no. You need to feel a man deep inside you."

He gave her boots each another soft kick back, leaving her weight all on the desk.

"Just like this. You even like being so cooperative. Oh, yeah. Just a sweet little doll for me."

He snapped down his zipper and pulled out something long, thick, and ready for action.

"So sweet of you to offer your pussy for me. Bet you're as wet as can be."

With both hands, he spread her cheeks and laid it as far in as it would go, then squeezed her cheeks back together tightly.

"Ooh, that's tight. Nice smooth crack."

He slipped it forward and back a few times, riding the soft groove.

"Maybe I'll just fuck that ass, since you're offering it."

He lowered it and pressed it close to the target.

"Mm. Nice. Bet you'd like a hard cock deep in your ass, wouldn't you? Probably do that all the time."

He gave her a hard stab but not enough to penetrate.

"Uh-huh. You're kind of built to get your ass fucked. Bet you beg for it."

He pressed it in again, still not enough to get inside, and held it there.

"You'd probably beg anything in this goddamn world to fuck that hot ass. Oh yeah, you'd beg for it."

He gave it a push but not enough to break the surface.

"Bet that pussy is real nice too. You got a nice pussy, Sugar? Everyone else has probably had it, so why shouldn't I?"

While still poised to impale her, he slapped her ass with both hands, then backed his weapon away.

"Tell me now if you don't want it."

He waited a few seconds, then laughed.

"No, you want it. More than anything, you want a hard cock inside you. Just the kind of girl you are."

He lowered it, keeping it close and ready to strike.

"I'd loosen up all that shit in your pretty mouth if you'd promise to squeal for me."

He paused, grinning, then said, "No? Just as good. Just be a nice, very quiet, completely obedient little girl for me."

Just touching her, ready for the first push, he said, "Willing and obedient and so damn wet. And just the way you like it best—tied up and helpless."

Her only reaction was her slow, steady breathing.

*   *   *

"No," he said, then laughed. "This is too easy for both of us. No, little baby girl, you can't just zone out and stay comfy in shock somewhere."

He smacked her ass, and she didn't react.

"Come on. Get back to reality for that hard fuck you want so bad."

She got two more solid slaps on her other cheek, and he nodded at the sight of her shifting her hips to one side, then the other, causing him to lose contact.

"Yeah, there we go. Dance for me, baby girl."

He slapped her again, and she tried to kick one leg back.

"Whoa. You're coming back for it. Yeah, you don't want to miss any of it. Come on, baby girl."

With both hands at the same time, he gave her ass cheeks a few hard smacks, and she began to twist her body around, tipping her completely bound arms from one side to the other.

"Fight, little girl! You know what you're about to get—try to get away!"

She groaned through her heavy layers of gags, a dirty cloth pulled tight, stretching her cheeks back, then several layers of rope all crowded in her mouth. And the whole mess was taped over several times, locking it all inside and forcing her mouth into a silent scream.

Her work boots were jabbing back, one leg at a time, trying to find something to kick but still tangled in her work pants. He laughed, watching her futile attempts, and pushed down on her back to keep her from squirming away.

"Damn, you got some really nice, strong legs. So smooth. So powerful. But they can't do you any good, can they? Hell, no."

She kept kicking and trying to roll away, but he stayed close, holding her down and watching his target and how little her escape attempts did to keep him from it.

"You really don't want it, huh?"

She hesitated, then resumed her kicks and squirms.

"Okay. I can see that now," he said, his voice soothing.

He held her bare hips with both hands.

"There, there. It'll be okay. No means no, right? Even in a fucked up nightmare world?"

She snorted a breath out through her nose, then lay still, and he kept his hands on her hips, where he caressed her gently.

While he was leveling his tool, almost touching her.

"That's it. You just relax, stay still, and we'll get you out of this mess, alright?"

Her only reaction was to pick up her head, then lay it back down, facing the other direction.

He patted both ass cheeks, then rubbed them gently.

"Poor little baby girl. How did you get into so much trouble?"

It looked almost like she'd shrugged, just enough to slide both arms, lost in tight ropes, up and then back down.

"You just really want to get out of here. Is that what the baby girl wants?"

She offered a distinct nod, then lay still.

He tipped his head and shifted just enough to line up his stiff post, so close that it was almost touching her.

"Okay, okay. I see now what you really want. And I'll do the right thing—I'll give my sweet,"—he rammed himself halfway in—"obedient,"—he leaned in, driving himself deeper—"baby doll exactly what,"—he drove farther—"she,"—he thrust his hips forward, bottoming out—"wants more than anything."

He held himself there, buried inside her as far as he could go, then caressed her hips and ass cheeks softly, gently.

"That . . . is how we do things here. Mm, that's one tight, juicy pussy you have there."

With his stiff pole backed partway out, he grinned down at it and all of her wetness that he'd slid out of her. But only for a few seconds, then he wedged back in all the way and held it there.

"Now, you just lie nice and still for me. A pretty little thing like you needs it rough. Oh yeah, that's how a soft little baby wants it: hard and rough!"

He began pulling out almost all the way, to the point of freeing himself, then rammed it back in. Over and over, and quickly, he bounced the bound and helpless woman along the desktop, where her bared breasts were squeezed into the warm surface.

"Hard and rough. Yeah, just like that. You just keep being a sweet, obedient little girl and take it. Take your fucking."

With her silent and him sometimes laughing, sometimes grunting, he kept poking her, stabbing her, fighting like mad to dig into her deeper with each jab.

In between chuckles and groans, he heard a low sound coming from somewhere in Scarlet's throat, some odd sound muffled by layers of gags and tape.

"Is that you, baby girl? Trying to tell me how much you love it?"

He listened, heard only silence for a second as he pumped her mercilessly, then picked up another soft utterance, almost a moan but something with more shape to it. More purpose.

"What . . . what are you trying to say?"

Never slowing, he laughed and kept up his attack, but he stopped at hearing the sound again. And he stared down at the bound woman making no effort to escape.

She did nothing but make that sound—a sound that couldn't quite get past what he'd done into and over her mouth with any precise pronunciation.

But she was saying something anyway, from somewhere deep inside.

"Um, what?"

He slowed his vicious strikes at her soft, exposed flesh.

"You, uh . . ."

He stopped but at a time when the skin of his hips was smashed tightly against her soft, smooth ass.

"Shouldn't you be, um, trying to, uh . . ."

She could have been a lifeless doll and lay completely still, with his rod lodged deep inside her.

He stared, squinting down at her, as she made the sound again. A short note, then a second of quiet, then a long, slow, steady, droning tone.

"Stop that!"

He gave her a vicious smack and said, "I wouldn't mind cutting you, baby girl. Keep that shit up and you'll see just how much fucking worse it could get."

Scarlet stayed quiet, didn't move her head, and kept her legs still.

"All that soft skin. Mm. Be a shame to have to carve it up. Wouldn't be the first goddamn autograph I left."

He resumed some slow strokes, then picked it up until she was receiving a savage, flesh-covered piston.

"Yeah, baby girl. Just how you love it from a man. Hard and fast."

Chapter 13 – Mama, No! Don't Be a Bug!

Betsy's face was turned up, and her nearly blank eyes watched the ceiling racing past as all of her new legs waved and shifted in perfect time, speeding her through the dark hallway. Her hair sometimes scraped under her on the floor, and her boots dragged along, occasionally lurching up at hitting a defect in the tiles.

Several times, the bug legs teamed up and tried to climb the wall, but the weight of her human body always forced the whole mutated living thing back to the floor. She only grunted and sometimes laughed as tears leaked out and dripped off of her, mixing with the slime left behind by hundreds of pairs of tiny claws scraping with every step.

Just after her head flopped over to her left, she opened her mouth to scream but couldn't manage it, then shot out a human hand to grab a door jamb, stopping the whole scurrying mess.

Through the doorway, she watched a giant, rippling, sweaty monster of a young man standing near hungry flames in a metal box. In his hands, near his open mouth and sharp teeth, he held a dripping portion of an arm. A human arm.

He was about to take a bite, then he turned his eyes toward the hallway.

"Mama? Mama, no, what happened?"

He tossed the limb into the fire, where it bubbled and popped and began to smoke, then hurried over to the doorway. Towering over the prone woman elevated by a ring of restless legs, he leaned to get a better look into her eyes.

"Mama, this isn't funny! Stop that!"

She gurgled up at him through a generous cluster of appendages springing up and out and scraping at her face with little pointy claws.

"I can help! I'll help, Mama!"

He took her hand and dragged all of it back near the furnace, then looked her over, sometimes leaning, shaking his head, and seeing that her human body wasn't touching the floor.

"Mama, make yourself just Mama again!"

She gurgled, and a glob of goo got strained through the leg stalks in her mouth and began oozing down her cheek.

"Mama, no! I'll fix you!"

He reached under and picked her up with both arms, then stooped down, cradling her, and rested her across his thighs.

"You can get better, Mama! You can!"

Her eyes drifted around, only sometimes focusing on his, then they started rolling up.

"No! Mama!"

He winced while probing the deep gash in her head, then wrapped a massive, sweaty hand around the small forest of legs pointing up out of her mouth.

"Sorry, Mama! I'll help!"

He pulled them up, and they slipped out as a bunch, right up and out from wherever they'd grown. When they got tossed to the floor, they twitched and scratched themselves away in every direction.

"Mama, that helped! I'm helping! What happened to you?"

She tried to speak as many hundreds of growing legs, all around her perimeter, waved and frolicked.

"What?" he said, leaning his ear over her mouth. "What, Mama?"

"Scar . . . Scarlet."

"Scarlet? Somebody named Scarlet hurt your head? Scarlet made you a bug?"

Betsy's eyes rolled up higher and closed, and her torso and head and human arms and legs went limp.

"Mama, no! Don't be a bug! Don't!"

Seconds later, all of the jittery bug legs stuttered their last and hung toward the floor.

Crying, he curled her up close enough to kiss her. He touched his lips to hers, then kissed her cheek, then let her head flop over and kissed around her ear.

"Mama. Oh, Mama. Don't be a bug."

He gave her ear lobe a soft bite, held it with his teeth, and tugged at it gently.

His breathing got deeper, and his stomach growled loudly enough to carry over the crackling and snapping of the flesh that he'd just added to the fire.

Groaning softly, he bit through, then quickly swallowed that small bit of Betsy's ear.

"Mm. Mama."

He opened wide enough to get her entire ear in his mouth, then he chomped down quickly and decisively, removing all of it.

It took only a few seconds of eager chewing before he sent that all down to be digested.

With a free flow of tears mixing with the sweat on his cheeks and everywhere else, he kept feeding his relentless hunger, sometimes stopping only long enough to say, "Mm, Mama. Don't be a bug!"

* * *

"Dax, I can't see nothing!" Mikey strained to say through the mat of squirmy insect legs clinging to his face. "Where are we going?"

Dax ran through the dim hallway, holding his partner's hand and dragging him along.

"Shit, Mikey, we're just running! I don't care where!"

"These fuckers hurt! They got some kind of sharp little fingernails or something!"

"We'll fix you right up, okay?"

"What if you can't, Dax? What then?"

"If I still had my shovel, I'd chop your fucking insect head off."

"My head isn't an insect! Not yet, Dax!"

"Soon. Come on. We need to get back to—"

He skidded to a stop, forcing blind Mikey to collide with him.

"What? Are we there?"

"Holy fuck."

Dax looked in on a giant, sweated up monster of a man with no shirt to cover muscles packed onto him like thick ropes had been wound all around him. He cradled a thing with human arms and legs and a thousand more, and all of them shook around every time he took a bite.

"Good God," Dax whispered, "we have to go back. We have to—"

"Who are you?" Junior called to him, proving that his mouth was mostly packed with chewy, sinewy slop.

"Who am I? What the fuck are you?"

"Mama calls me Junior. She—"

He looked down and his bulky body jerked with one violent sob before he looked back up.

"She's been quiet. She's never this quiet. She—"

"She's a goddamn insect, you fucking freak!"

"Dax, what's going on? Who is that?"

"Shh. Wait."

"Don't you talk bad about Mama. No," Junior said, shaking his head. "Don't you do that."

"I, um . . ."

Dax started nudging Mikey to move back, out of Junior's sight.

"Don't you leave neither. I run fast. I run real fast."

"Oh, uh, okay. We're not going anywhere. That's your momma?"

"Uh-huh. My Mama."

"And you're . . . what? Eating her?"

"He's eating her?" said Mikey. "What, like licking her pussy? Even with bug parts, I still would have—"

"Shh."

"What did your friend say?"

"Nothing. He's insane from his bugs."

"I kiss Mama all the time," said Junior. "She likes when I nibble."

He took another sloppy bite, then stared at the two men in the hallway, one whose face was coated with a bristling bunch of slender bug legs and was constantly stretching them apart over his mouth so that he could speak.

"That's, um, that's not exactly nibbling. You, um, you're kind of devouring her."

"She tells me when to stop. She knows. Mama knows."

"Uh, dude, she isn't about to say anything. Not anymore."

"She will. Mama will say."

"Okay. Well, that's wonderful. Um, we're just going to—"

"Don't go. I run. Catch. Eat."

"Yeah, I don't fucking—"

"I run fast."

"Uh, yeah. I don't doubt that. Um, why don't you just keep chewing on your mother, and we'll—"

"Don't make fun of Mama."

"I wouldn't think of it. It's just that she, uh, she's part bug and—"

"Mama is not a bug! You're making me angry!"

"Whoa. That can't be good."

"Don't say Mama isn't good!"

"I didn't. But, dude, she—"

In one fast, violent motion, bug Betsy got dumped to the floor, and Junior was at the doorway, leaning to see out at Dax and Mikey.

"Holy fuck! How'd you get so goddamn—"

He slapped a sweaty vise on each of their throats, then dragged them back toward the oven. With their legs swinging and kicking, he held them near the fire.

"Scarlet is bad. Made Mama a bug. Hurt her head! Where is Scarlet?"

Dax held Junior's wrist with both hands, kicked around, and tried to choke out an answer, so the sweaty monster loosened his grip and let him fall.

He coughed a few times, then said, "Who's Scarlet? I don't know any Scarlet!"

"Huh."

Junior stared down at Dax and said, "Does this one know?" then shook Mikey around.

"No! Neither of us—"

Junior tossed Mikey into the flames, and the howling and screaming became only snapping and popping within a few seconds.

"Okay!" said Dax. "I, uh, Scarlet, huh? She, um—God, you freak, your mother's a goddamn—"

"Now, I'm angry!"

Junior heaved Dax onto the bubbling remains of Mikey, and the flames roared with their approval.

"Raw is better. But I like cooked too."

He stooped down and lifted Betsy's head off of the floor.

"I'll find Scarlet, Mama. I'll make her pay. It was bad to hurt your head and make you a bug."

He lifted her with one hand and slung her over his shoulder like a bag of oily dirt, then paused at the door, shaking his head.

"Don't be a bug, Mama. Not a bug."

Chapter 14 – Just Something to Fuck

"You're just a perfect little victim. What a sweet little doll."

Archie kept hammering Scarlet from behind, and she only lay there limp and unresponsive.

"A sweet, obedient little doll. A good fucking is what you want most."

The only sound in his office was skin slapping skin and a body dragging across the desk, sometimes squeaking the entire desk forward.

"Uh-oh. Mm, you're just too sweet. I'm about to give you a hot blast."

He pumped her a few more times, keeping his hands on her ass cheeks and keeping them pulled apart.

"You want that cum. You want that cum so far in there. Deeper than your husband could ever leave it."

He laughed, then rammed himself deep and said, "A fucking lot more of it too," and kept it there, then shifted his hips from side to side.

"I'm happy to be the one to stir things up for you. If I didn't do it, someone or something else would have."

He backed out, then shoved it back in.

"Everything out there is going to fuck you. It's all you're good for, and you know it. Before you get slaughtered, learn to love being only what you are: just something soft and sweet to fuck."

After a few more animal thrusts, he slapped her ass hard.

"Tell me now if you don't want me to unload in there."

He paused, listening and still pumping.

"It's a huge, hot, vile mess too. Last chance?"

Grinning, he nodded after a few seconds and a few more hard pumps.

"No? Of course not. It's all you really want. Ah, here we go . . ."

He squeezed her ass cheeks hard enough to dig in his nails and groaned with each deep, hard push into the helpless woman.

"Ah, yeah. Just like that. It's like you were made only for this."

He slipped himself out of her and got his trousers back in order.

"Huh. Just another day at work for me. Get your ass up."

Holding her shoulders, he helped her up onto her boots, then got her balanced on wobbly legs. He reached for the series of knots that he'd tied behind her head, then scoffed.

"No. We'll just leave that. Don't want you bitching to the next guy or mindless freak that enjoys that fine pussy of yours."

Instead of freeing her of her gags, he fluffed back her hair as well as could be done.

"We'll leave those arms all knotted up too. That's my favor to you. I think you like it."

He spun her around, and her slowly blinking eyes, more closed than open, tipped up high enough to look into his.

"Why? That's what you'd ask if you could? Because above all else, I can tell you love being nothing but a victim. You love having no choice but to let anyone fuck you."

He grinned at a single thick tear trying to travel down her cheek, then he reached out a fingertip to blot it up.

"What the fuck?" he said, holding it up to see it on his finger. "That, uh, what's going on with you?"

Scarlet only stared up at him, gagged and bound and with her clothing down by her knees.

"Huh. That feels kind of . . . funny."

A second tear leaked out of her other eye, and he reached for it, then stopped himself. He leaned to get a better look into her eyes, then he pointed at her face.

"You're changing. That's what it is. Into what, though? Who the fuck knows?"

He glanced down and saw what he'd deposited into her dripping down the inside of her thigh.

"Ooh. That's a mess. Hold on."

He stooped down, pulled her panties up into place, then her pants. He made quick work of zipping and buttoning and belting, then stood again.

"All packaged up for the next man or freak or beast to unwrap and fuck."

Still staring at him but not making any attempt to get away, she started a low moan from somewhere deep in her throat, and it came out as more of a vibration than anything else, being choked back by cloth and rope and tape.

"Hey. You fucking stop that. I'll hurt you real bad, dammit."

She stopped.

"Whatever the fuck is going on, that's part of it. Goddammit, that's part of it. You need to get you and your well-fucked pussy the hell away from me."

He held her with both hands, keeping the distance between them.

"Hey, maybe you can mutate into whatever the hell you want? Yeah. Why don't you try that? Think about it while you're getting fucked the next time."

He began walking her toward a door to the outside. Windows flanking it could have been black rectangles painted on the wall.

"Which should be in about a minute. If they ask why you're so goddamn sloppy, be sure to give me the credit. Tell them Archie just gave you the best fuck of your life."

* * *

He swung in the door, and they both stared out at a dark world with a black sky that contained no stars. Straight ahead, mostly just

146

a thick, darker line against the blackness behind it, barely visible pinpoints of light burned, sometimes flickered, and sometimes winked out.

"I'd like to keep you, you know. If you weren't lying, you have some skills I could use around this fucking reactor."

He nudged her, and she faced the city flat against whatever kind of horizon backed it up.

"God only knows what the hell you're turning into. But hey, you got fucked like a normal human kind of woman. Might be the last time for that. You're welcome."

He gave her a soft shove high on her back, and she took only one step.

"Go on. Run along, and I do mean run. All kinds of monsters are going to pick up your sweet scent real fucking quick."

She didn't move, but she shook once from a single, muted sob.

"Oh, I get it. You want me to sum up our special little relationship before you vanish into that nightmare night. Alright. Don't mind if I do."

He eased her around to face him, then took a step back, keeping himself inside the building. He looked left, then right at the desolate landscape, then made sure that he was completely inside.

"You and I, we—hey,"—he laughed—"I never did get your name."

He leaned both ways, grinning at all the stuff he'd used to pack away her mouth.

"Mm, I like even knowing that I gave you a proper, silent scream for your journey out here. And I'm not about to undo any of that just to hear whatever name you used to have."

He scoffed at a fresh tear trickling down each cheek.

"You probably think I'm suddenly going to be a nice guy. Say nice things. Wrong."

He started to reach out to wipe at her tears, then frowned and pulled his hand back.

"You're a sexy little doll that's good for not much but getting fucked. Oh yeah, you sure got all wet for it. Because that's the way you love it: tied up and helpless, no choice but to take it, and you don't care how rough it gets. Shit, you'd probably love it if I actually hurt you, just so long as you got a good fucking out of the deal."

He tapped one of her shoulders, forcing her to take a step back.

"You should change your name. I mean, if you survive long enough to get that mouth working again."

He nudged her other shoulder, and she shuffled back farther.

"Baby Doll would be a good name for you. Just a sweet little baby girl—something fun to play with. Just something to fuck."

With both hands, he gently turned her to face the black city almost lost in the endless night.

He fluffed her long black hair again and said, "And a little doll like you wants most just to be obedient. Go on, then. Go get another fucking."

He shoved her hard and got her walking.

"The next man or beast won't be such a nice guy. You'll be begging to be my fuck toy again."

She kept walking.

"But I'll never want you back. No way do I ever want to see what variety of goddamn freak you turn into."

She took one step, still faced the distant city, and shook lightly with muffled sobs.

"Aw, it isn't that far away. Here, I'll help you get started."

Archie stepped close enough, then gave her a solid kick and shove to the middle of her back, toppling her with no way to break the fall.

"See? You're closer. You're welcome. Now, get your ass back up."

Scarlet fought her way back up onto her feet, then turned enough to glare at him.

"Baby girl, this is as good as it's ever going to be for you. March your ass to town, and you'll find out. Go!"

He watched her turn, then walk until she was just another shadow that occasionally blocked one or more of the twinkling city lights.

Then, he scoffed, shut the door, and bolted it.

Chapter 15 – The Hottest, Sluttiest Ones

After bolting his door to the outside world, Archie swaggered back toward his desk but paused before sitting. With both palms flat on it, he leaned until his nose was close to the desktop, then inhaled deeply, so deeply that he choked and ended up laughing.

"She's lucky I'm such a nice guy. Cheap little doll. Helluva nice pussy, though."

He looked up at the sound of insect legs scratching at the door to the hallway.

"Oh, shit. Forgot about that. Too busy fucking."

From under his desk, he retrieved something like a fire extinguisher: a polished metal canister, some knobs and dials at the top, and a short flexible hose with a nozzle on the end.

"Damn freaks."

He got up, walked toward the door, then stopped to listen. The bug legs were still trying to get to him.

Standing near the door, where he'd come face to leg with them when he'd last cracked it open, he sparked his lighter, then pointed the nozzle away and turned a knob, causing a steady hissing.

"I hate freaks, even parts of them," he said, then twisted the knob, swung in the door, and touched the flame to the hiss.

He laughed as he swept fire at all of the wiggling legs clawing their way over the floor and up the walls and door.

"Die, motherfuckers!"

They didn't make a sound as they all curled and shriveled then lay there smoking.

"Someday, goddammit, I'm killing every goddamn freak in this dump."

He choked off the gas with a quick knob turn, and the flames died with a whoosh and a quick pop. Turning, then kicking the door hard enough that it didn't latch but bounced back open, he laughed as he walked back to his desk and set the flamethrower on the floor.

"There's time. Always time for the good stuff."

He leaned over and sniffed all around.

"Damn juicy. That was one juicy little doll."

He stepped around and sat back in his chair, spun a few times each way, then leaned forward and picked up a two-way radio.

After tapping a few times, he held it up and said, "Chubby, pick up."

The device gave him some static, so he tapped it against the desk.

"Chubby! Dammit, where the hell—"

"Sorry, Boss. I'm here. I was just—"

"Whackin' off again. Yeah. Like always. That's kind of why I'm calling."

"You want to know if I'm—"

"No! Forget that, and you'd better not be holding that soggy sausage of yours while you're talking to me."

"Oh, uh . . . hang on."

A few seconds passed, there were some zipper sounds, then Chubby said, "I'm not."

"Goddammit. You're disgusting."

They both laughed.

"It's all I got anymore. Hey, how are things at the reactor?"

"Eh. Just another day, or night, or who the fuck knows? Nothing unusual here—just the same old stuff that's getting boring. It's all the same all the time."

"Yeah, I get that. Not a lot of enjoyable shit around here. So, what's up?"

"Look, put those fucking bats on double shifts for a while. Send their sorry asses back up that earthquake crack and through that damn building more than what they've been doing. We need more bodies down here."

"Bodies? You mean, you want—"

"Yeah, that's right. Not just the sad fuckers that fuck and die at the same time and show up here, not knowing what the fuck is going on."

"Well, boss, how could they know? It's a fucked up thing."

"Yeah. Very. But tell those bats to grab some actual living women, alright? Fucking the ones that already died somewhere up there isn't all bad but shit, I'm kind of fucking dead women, right?"

"I, uh, guess so. Yeah. You got a problem with that?"

"Not really. I just need to upgrade. So, get those leathery bastards up there all night every night, and tell them to get me the hottest, sluttiest ones they can find."

"Sure, boss. I'll tell them. You want the hot, slutty women that—"

"Chubby. The important thing is that they're hot and slutty. You get me?"

"You mean, women and—"

"Hot and slutty. And not dead, goddammit. I'll fuck them all."

Laughing, Chubby said, "You're not a very nice man."

"Not any kind, you dumb shit."

Chapter 16 – A Slick Black Tomb

Scarlet's boots dragged more than they stepped as she aimed her mostly closed eyes at the dark city far enough away to be nothing more than a jagged part of the horizon.

Behind her, neat coils of rope remained tight around the entire length of her straight arms.

In her mouth, Archie's ambitious gags—a strip of cloth, then multiple winds of rope, then layers of sticky tape to hold it all in—had frozen her mouth in a soundless scream.

And her torn-open work shirt flapped with each step she took, sometimes showing her ripped bra and bare breasts, other times hiding it until the next footfall on the scraggly, often oily terrain.

With steady heat from a sea of flames nudging her along, working to sweat out of her the wetness that Archie had enjoyed and mocked, she trudged and struggled to get enough of the crude-scented air through her nostrils.

With a choked gasp, losing the battle for air, she stopped and waited for her breaths to slow. She tipped her head each way several times, trying to loosen her thick mane that Archie had trapped with the tight bindings wrapped around her head. And while fighting with that, and having some success, she kept her head angled back and stared straight up.

At a sky devoid of any feature other than blackness. It was the absolute absence of anything but night. No moon. No hint of sunrise or sunset. Not a single star.

Sighing as well as she could through the narrow channels of her nose, she froze, not even lowering her gaze, as a dog bark called out from far to her left, lost somewhere beyond the compound's floodlights.

It barked again, then another joined in, and Scarlet looked ahead and began a careful trek down a gentle slope toward a chain link fence.

The barking grew nearer, and sounds of laughter and polite conversation were mixed in.

She grunted and tried to hurry and almost fell.

More than one of the barking and laughing things were close and about to begin their descent of the low hill.

"Stop!" called one of them, and Scarlet stayed still, making only as much sound as she needed to keep an air supply flowing.

"Wait there!" yelled another.

Scarlet heard many light steps descending the slope and sometimes kicking loose small stones to tumble and rattle.

"Hey," said one, not calling to Scarlet, "we know that individual."

"Oh, yeah," said another. "That human was looking, uh, for . . . I don't remember. Something."

"Someone," said guard number three. "I think the search was for someone in particular."

"Probably not the boss."

"No. That wouldn't be wise."

Scarlet snorted and turned to face the three guard dogs with human faces.

"It looks different," said guard one.

"It's the same one. The clothing has been altered," said number two.

Guard one barked softly, got Scarlet to focus on it, then said, "You're dressed differently than when we first saw you."

When guard two spoke, saying, "It doesn't look very practical," Scarlet focused on that one instead.

Number three bounced on its front paws a few times, then circled around enough to see her tightly bound arms.

It looked up, caught her attention, and said, "If you fall, that could be problematic."

"Come back here. You're being silly."

The third guard panted and brushed past Scarlet's leg to join the others.

"We noticed that you're leaving. That's why we won't bite you."

"You might bite this one anyway."

"I might. Yes."

Scarlet was looking from one human face to another, fresh tears on her cheeks and taking breaths as deeply as she could.

Number one looked up at her.

"If you wished to have any of that removed, our teeth are very sharp."

"You'd have to jump. Now, who's being silly?"

"You. If this invader that's leaving would sit, no jumping from any of us would be needed."

"Oh."

Number one looked back up at Scarlet, who had begun squinting at all of them.

"No. We can't. We wouldn't dare."

"Because of the boss," said another.

"He'd be angry. That action isn't in our scope of operations."

"No. When he's angry, he'd fuck whoever bit through those hardware items."

"Yes. Perhaps all of us. Yes, he'd surely fuck all of us just to be sure."

Number three snickered, then yipped at the black sky, then said, "Again! He'd fuck us all again!"

All three yapped at the black, then number one gave it a rest and said to Scarlet, "Sorry. Your fate is in your hands. Your, um, tied hands."

"Give her some advice."

"Okay. Sure."

The first guard dog with a human face looked up at Scarlet's teary eyes and said, "That way,"—tipping its head to Scarlet's left—"the fencing is breached and hasn't yet been repaired. Be quick about it."

All three looked up at her, and she panted through her nose, staring at each of them for a second.

"Go! Before the boss has to fuck all of us!"

"Again!" said one of the other guards, followed by a chorus of raspy yips.

Scarlet groaned, turned to her left, and sobbed once as she looked in that direction.

Only a second had passed, and a roaring boom, like from an immense explosion, raced past them parallel with the shoreline of the sea of endless flames. All of them stared after its echo as it fled past them, leaving only silence.

She snapped her head toward the dog guards, two of which yipped only once each at the black sky and began running back toward the buildings.

"Lie down!" the remaining dog guard yelled at her. "There's no time! Lie down!"

Sobbing, still watching the human face staring back at her as the guard began a sideways walk after its companions, Scarlet only shook her head and sobbed while dropping to her knees.

"Really! Get down all the way, or you'll get knocked down!"

It squealed, turned, and raced after its fellow guards.

Scarlet looked all around, still on her knees, then winced as the sudden winds hit. Almost a hurricane force blast easily tipped her to her side and gave life to the smaller specks of gravel all around her. Groaning, she rolled over to face down as the storm of stones arose, many of them pelting her before rattling and swirling away with the rest.

And as quickly as it had started, it finished. Her hair lay calmly, the field of gravel beneath her stayed still, and the only sound was the sob that came when she again let herself breathe.

A human dog voice called to her from the safety of one of the reactor buildings.

"It's done for now! Go, or we'll come back and do our guard duty on you!"

With a tired groan, she fought her way up onto her reactor work boots, then angled herself toward the fence. She began with a cautious step, then a pause to look all around, then she continued down the slope and toward the fence.

"Run!" the guard called to her. "Get your ass running!"

Trying to run but still mostly dragging her boots, Scarlet approached a tear in the chain link fabric after only a short hike. She paused to look back and saw the shapes of the three guards near the building, all of them watching her silently. Only their tails were moving, pointing up and wagging lazily.

Grunting, she leaned and got her head and shoulders through, then got her arm ropes snagged on a cut wire.

Snorting and wrestling to free herself, she tumbled through the ripped opening and spun just in time to land on her side, then roll onto her back, pinning her arms to the warm, gravelly earth.

And she waited for her breathing to settle as tears flowed to each side, down to the oily dust, and she stared up at a sky that could have been nothing but more oil, all of it poised and eager to rain down and submerge her in a slick black tomb.

*   *   *

Closer to the city that still appeared built more of shadows than actual structures, Scarlet saw lines of dim lights that vanished behind tall, boxy shadows that carried their own few dim lights high above the ground.

High up, at the tops of those black boxes, thin strands of flickering light were casting strings of slender, twisting smoke upward, feeding it to the impenetrable night of the sky.

Snorting weakly, and with dried tear tracks on her cheeks and still a few sharp stones embedded in her hands that she wasn't able to pick loose, she resumed her walk, sometimes stumbling toward the city.

But the forceful but hushed whooshing of large wings, high above and lost in darkness, prompted her to crouch low, stop her breaths, and even close her eyes as the creature flapping those wings traveled above her, then past her and back toward the reactor.

After a few seconds, she staggered back up onto her boots, listened, turning her head to pick the whooshes out of the dead silence, then got walking again, tenderly, toward the streetlights.

Each step touched down softly, and she sometimes stopped to turn an ear toward the thing in the sky. She sobbed once when the thing showed its intent to return, perhaps to something it smelled on the ground below. Hearing the batting of its wings in increasing volume, Scarlet abandoned all efforts at quietude and sprinted toward the lights.

Whatever was flying in the sky approached quickly, and Scarlet's tired legs tried to match or exceed its speed as the buildings ahead took shape and the line of lights seemed more welcoming.

Looking down only enough to dodge and weave around low stacks of splintered pallets, machine parts all jumbled and stacked and forgotten, and ruts angling in every direction and deep enough to trip her and feed her to whatever was coming, Scarlet made a last mad dash for the nearest building.

Looking up at the streetlight, then down at her shirt, loosely draped and hardly covering her breasts, then down along her work pants, all lit up and inviting and advertising a meal for something, she hurried along the building wall, following the lights.

When the whooshing had drawn quite near, coming up rapidly behind her, she felt more than saw a recess in the wall—a doorway or an alley—and it housed a blackness to rival the sky.

She stumbled backwards into that void, shaking her head to cast away the tickling of fresh tears, and forced her breaths to slow until they made no sound. Which caused her chest to heave and her heart to pound as she watched the relative brightness of the street that she'd just fled.

The sounds from her pursuer had ceased, and the street, and especially the gripping of the darkness surrounding her, offered nothing to interrupt the steady, low buzzing coming from every direction.

She heard a squawk.

Somewhere close, just around the building's corner.

Something moved. Just a dark patch, moving up along the corner, then back down.

And again, something moved, just enough to trace a path against the weak light beyond it.

Scarlet's heart thumped, and her lungs refused to negotiate—they wanted air, even air heavy with crude oil—but she kept herself still, dying, as she watched the tiniest part of whatever was waiting for her.

And listening for her.

And sniffing around. Hunting.

Then, the streetlights flickered and died, the incessant soft buzzing halted, and the street looked like whatever sludgy blackness had gotten packed into the tight space around Scarlet had slithered out and suffocated every surface.

Chapter 17 – She Killed My Mama!

Archie let the radio tumble out of his hand and clatter onto the desk, just as something large took heavy steps past his door, blocking any view of the far wall. It stopped, something in the hallway clawed at the wall, then the bulky shape backed up and looked inside at him.

"What the fuck are you looking at, you stupid pile of meat?"

Junior wiped blood off of his chin with the back of a hand, then pointed at himself. He kept his other hand hidden behind him.

"Yeah, you. You really don't know you're a pile of meat?"

"Mama never said that."

"What? You know what, never mind. You're that freak that works at the furnace, right?"

"I burn things. Uh-huh. And I like to—"

"Eat the bodies too. Yeah, I've heard. See what I mean? That's not a healthy diet. That tells me you're stupid."

"I like to eat. Mama always told me that—"

"First, what the hell are you doing running loose? No, forget that for now. Let's see your hand."

He held up the visible hand, the one smeared with blood and guts and clenched in a massive fist.

"God, you're stupid. No. The other one."

Junior grinned and held up a fleshy fist strangling a stack of toasted insect legs.

"Nice. That's to . . . what? Eat?"

"I eat a lot."

"Yeah. Obvious. Go ahead, then. Eat that shit."

While grinning at Archie, he stuffed them into his stretched open mouth, then began crunching them, chewing and swallowing until it was all gone.

"Beautiful. Hey, shouldn't a stupid freak like you be chained to a stone wall somewhere?"

"I broke chains once. It was easy."

"Yeah. Sure. That's not the point. I can tell you're pissed about something. What's eating—oops, bad choice of words."

Still seated at his desk, Archie pointed at Junior and laughed.

"What I mean is, what's got you so pissed off, son?"

"Papa? Are you—"

"God, no. God, this is getting stupider by the second. Okay. Let's keep it simple for that brain that's been shrinking while your King Kong muscles have been growing. Here's the simple question. You ready to hear it?"

"Uh-huh. Okay."

"Why . . . are . . . you . . . so . . . angry?"

He bawled like a sweaty baby and yelled, "She killed my Mama!"

"So? Tell me something around here that doesn't get its ass killed."

"Uh . . ."

"Never mind that. Come on in. Let's have a chat, just you and me and no fucking bug legs."

Junior turned his head on a neck like a tree trunk and looked at some of those legs burnt into the open door.

"No. No bug legs. You could scarf those on your way out of here."

Junior turned sideways and leaned to get through the doorway without clunking his head.

"God damn."

Then, he stood inside Archie's office.

"You're a frightening son of a bitch, aren't you?"

"My Mama isn't a—"

"Oh God, just stop. So, let's keep this simple. You listening?"

"Uh-huh. Okay."

"Who is your mother?"

"She's the only Mama I have. And she got killed."

"Whoa. Hold up, bag of meat. Slow down. Let's try this: what is your mother's name?"

"I always called her Mama. She was beautiful. She's right out in the—"

"Was?"

"She was hurt. Hurt bad."

"That happens every micro-second around here to someone. Did she have a name?"

"Yeah. I think so."

"Enough. Already, I've lost interest. You need to get your sweaty ass back to the furnace. Of all the fucked up jobs in this place, that might be the worst."

"I like it."

"Sure you do. Go on. Get. Shovel those bodies in there."

"Mama had a friend."

"Wonderful. Skedaddle, freak."

"Mama was more beautiful than her lady friend."

"Wait. Your mother was with some other woman?"

"Uh-huh. I didn't eat her."

"Wait again. But you did eat your mother?"

"She wasn't really a bug. Mama could never be a—"

"Your mother was part bug? Tell me, you sweaty monster, what your mother's friend looked like."

"Like she worked here."

"Yeah, yeah. So? What else?"

"Her hair. It was long and black."

"Whoa, big man. Black?"

"Uh-huh. Like things that burn too much and get too crispy before I can—"

"Get back in here and close the goddamn door."

* * *

Junior stepped far enough into Archie's office that he could swing the door, but he did it so hard that it bounced back open.

"We're back to your mother's name. Let's have it."

"I never called her Betsy, but she—"

"Goddammit! Hey, cannibal Joe, you—"

"Mama called me Junior."

"You're still a goddamn cannibal. Look, I know who did that to your momma bug."

Junior swung both fists behind him, cracking the wall on one side and pounding the door on the other.

"Mama wasn't a bug!"

"She would have been if she didn't get attacked. She had a split skull, right?"

"It wasn't nice to do that to Mama."

"No. Not nice at all. I saw your mother just a while ago, back when she was normal."

"No one hurt her head yet?"

"No, but she was well on her way to joining the, uh, a special kingdom."

"I don't know what that means."

"Course you don't."

"Mama called her friend Scarlet."

"The one with the black hair? That's Scarlet?"

"Uh-huh. I wanted to eat her."

"I probably should have myself."

"You eat people too?"

"No like you, you hungry bastard monster."

"She was nice. Scarlet was nice."

"You wouldn't say so if you saw her swing this sword."

Archie held it out on both upturned palms, showing the congealing blood and streaks and globs of some mushy substance.

"It's hard to say saw and swing and . . . uh, sword."

"Right. Yeah. But that's the way it played out. Cleaved that skull like nobody's business."

Junior flexed every muscle he had as he held his vibrating fists tight against his hips.

"I'll eat Scarlet, then I'll kill her too."

"Sure. Maybe the other way around, for a guy like you. Hey, maybe you could fuck her too."

"What's that?"

Archie stared, squinting up at the young, shirtless man whose face was wet like he alone was out in the rain. If it would ever rain there.

"You've never, uh, fucked anyone? Never had sex?"

"Oh, sex. Me and Mama always—"

"God, sorry I asked. You're so sick and twisted I'm starting to like you."

"Thanks."

"Sure. That Scarlet, the black-haired bitch that clipped your mother's brain, headed out that way,"—he pointed at his back door—"not too long ago. Pack some arms and legs and kidneys and go hunt her down."

"Okay," he said, then turned enough to reach for the door to the hallway.

"Wrong way, hungry boy."

"I can't go without Mama."

"We don't have time for you to—"

Archie watched, grinning, as Junior dragged a chewed-up, insect-leg-infested body toward him, then picked it up and over a shoulder.

"Hold it. That was a joke. About the limbs and organs and stuff."

"I like that idea."

Archie scoffed and said, "Fine by me. Not like I want that shi— uh, your mother hanging around anyway. Here."

He tossed the sword to him, and Junior caught it by the blade. Both of them stared at it while blood began to drip.

"Try the handle."

"Okay."

"So, when you find her, you can—hey, wait a goddamn second."

Archie got up and walked over toward Junior, held out his hand, and took back his sword.

"You won't understand this, giant Junior, but you're departing on a mission from God. Especially since you're packing a kidney to nibble on the way."

"I don't know what a kidney—"

"You need to be properly knighted. Ceremony time. Get down on your knees."

While Junior was dropping to the floor, Archie scoffed and said, "That usually leads to something way better than this bullshit."

He scoffed again at seeing that, even kneeling, Junior's eyes were about level with his own.

"God, you're a scary monster. Alright, let's make this quick so you can get on that bitch's scent. Hold still. If I lop off an ear, you'll have to eat it—it's tradition."

"Okay."

"Well, fuck. Alright."

He tapped the flat of the sword blade on Junior's left shoulder.

"Heed this mission with your left side."

He tapped Junior's right shoulder.

"Pursue your goal with your right side."

Archie held the blade with both hands, edge down, high over Junior's head. The sweaty muscle boy looked up and waited.

"Wow. If there wouldn't be such a goddamn mess."

"Huh?"

"Nothing."

He turned the blade and rested the flat side of it on Junior's forehead.

"Keep your thoughts focused in whatever brain artifact might be rattling around in there. I dub thee The Fleshy Monstrous Hunter of the Wench Scarlet."

He lifted the sword, then gestured for Junior to stand.

"What's a wench?"

"Something to hack with a sword."

"Okay."

He put the handle back into one of Junior's hands, then pointed at his back door.

"She went thataway."

"I'll find her, and . . ."

"And?"

"And I'll kill her!"

"Good. Good. And then, what?"

"Then, I'll eat her!"

"Yeah! Good boy!"

Archie unbolted the back door and swung it in.

"Go get her, Junior!"

"Okay!"

He turned and leaned and squeezed through the doorway and started walking toward the city.

"Hey!" Archie called out, stopping him. "If there's anything left, bring it back and toss it in that oven, alright?"

"I could. I don't always eat skulls."

"Enchanting. And your job will be waiting for you."

"Okay."

Junior stared at him, a sword in his hand and sweat dripping off of him everywhere.

"Go, dammit! Go!"

Junior grinned, nodded, then turned and left for the city, while Archie swung shut the door and bolted it.

"Shit, most fun I've had in a while."

He walked back to his desk, leaned over, and sniffed all around.

"At least since I fucked old what's-her-name."

Chapter 18 – I Deserve to Lose My Mind

When the lights died and the buzzing stopped, so did Scarlet's breaths. What little air she'd allowed passage through the meager openings her nose offered, her only recourse with her mouth gagged so heavily, reduced to a trickle as she stared out at a scene that had been dim and gray and had become the deepest of blacks.

Absorbed somewhere in that thick muck of night, something was sniffing intently. Something near the corner that she'd been staring at before the streetlights quit, a thing that could be seen if there were any light at all, must have leaned around to sniff. And look into the dark for what it had smelled.

If she'd allowed herself to blink at all, she might have missed it: the lights flickered just once, for far less than a second, and she saw a shape blocking the entrance to her refuge, something large and backlit by the single, brief flash of light. Though greedily meager, the pop of light had endured long enough to show something wide and moving up—maybe a wing.

And Scarlet had also seen that the skin of her bare chest, from a shirt that had been ripped open for her rapist to get at her breasts, had invited some of that light over to bathe her skin, skin wet from the exertion of fleeing the reactor and from lungs starving for more air.

Refusing to breathe, Scarlet pivoted slowly and carefully to face the wall and pressed her breasts into the warm, somewhat oily brick surface.

The sniffing near the street became a single loud snort, then the whooshing resumed, up close—a mad scrambling of wings that carried the hunter off to the right, along the street flanked by blackened buildings.

Another followed from the left, unseen but heard as wind from its wing strokes reached into the alcove, tossing Scarlet's hair farther into the dark beyond her.

She took one short breath, and her chest heaved for more, but she didn't give in to that hunger as more whooshing passed from right to left, then another followed.

In the relative silence between wing traffic along the dead street, Scarlet stepped gingerly along the pavement, slipping skin against wall bricks, deeper in and farther from the things that sniffed and pumped powerful wings.

Something soft got a light kick from her, and she let escape a choked gasp as whatever it was retreated.

She waited, taking quick, short blasts of the warm air carrying the scent of crude oil. Until something squirmed against her ankle, and she felt sharp points trying to pierce her pants, squeezing and poking and stabbing.

Snorting out what little air she held inside, Scarlet took a step closer to the road, still keeping her chest and easily lit wet skin up against the rough bricks.

She didn't look toward the street when two sets of whooshing wings passed by again, but she groaned and took another step toward them when whatever was attacking her ankle tried again.

Away from its sharp pins or needles or claws, she looked toward the street when the wing sounds were approaching again, a hunting party of sorts swooping through the darkened city, sniffing and searching.

With a soft pop, the streetlights all lit, died, then stayed lit, renewing the life of the ambient buzzing as well. And the heavy black shapes that had just become visible in Scarlet's narrow view of the street screeched and sped straight up, large wings pounding the oily air and tossing around Scarlet's hair where it could—below her layers of gags.

Breathing again, her eyes wide, Scarlet looked down quickly and forgot about breathing, though her lungs were begging her for it.

Near her feet and on his back lay a boy, maybe ten years old, with ragged clothes and wild, oily blond hair. His big eyes stared up at her and his lips, pressed closed, offered a demented grin. His hands, close to Scarlet's legs, were opening and closing like mindless clockwork, sometimes scraping pointed fingernails along the alley floor.

Scarlet sagged, and fresh tears ventured down her cheeks slowly, then skidded over the wide tape over her mouth. She turned away from the street, not caring that her shirt had been pushed wide open and stayed there. And she stooped down and moaned and grunted at the lost child at her feet.

Until he opened his mouth, which still appeared grin-like but displayed rows of teeth sharpened to precise points. Still leering, he clapped them together, opened them again, then began chattering them non-stop.

And he began wiggling his way closer, fingers grasping to hold something for those saw-blade teeth to savor.

She tried kicking him away gently, but his hands were quick, and his nails were skillful and stubborn and snagged the cloth of her pants.

She groaned again while shaking him loose, then kicked him gently when he recovered and attacked again.

So, she kicked him hard, sending him backwards but still close, and he sat right back up, teeth chattering and hands reaching like some sort of mechanism.

Moaning and sobbing through cloth and ropes and tape, Scarlet met him halfway and pushed her reactor-issued work boot against his throat, then forced him down onto his back.

Shaking her head, she watched as his jaws never stopped, his claws had begun to find their way up under her pants, almost rending the skin of her ankles, and his desperate, demented eyes never blinked.

With a final sob, she put most of her weight down suddenly on his throat. His arms fell. His teeth locked open. And so did his eyes.

Staring down at what she'd just done, tears filled her eyes and sent the whole scene underwater. So, Scarlet kept her boot on its neck but leaned back, blinking hard and working the tears to each side where they could flow down her cheek, over Archie's tape, then drip away.

A quick glance toward the street and a short listen confirmed that the lighting was steady and the wings were gone. Or at least not close anymore. Only the barely noticeable buzzing disturbed the static world.

Scarlet looked down again and pulled up on her boot, watching closely for any remaining life there. The boy lay still.

She kicked him from one side, then the other, and his eyes never moved and his razor teeth were still exposed, like the lips wouldn't naturally cover them.

After one quick sob, she put half of her weight on the boy's neck, then leaned against the wall to engage in nothing but strained breathing and tears leaking from eyes clamped shut.

The lights stayed on, the buzzing kept going, and there was no movement from the dead child beneath her boot, so she pulled that back and looked down on him.

She grunted as she tried rubbing her arm bindings up against the brick wall, but its thin sheen of oil wouldn't permit even a slow abrasion of the ropes.

With a snort much like a scoff, she focused on the boy's teeth—two rows of them, perfectly aligned and locked apart, leaving a space.

Like a space between two saw blades.

Carefully, while also watching and listening for winged attackers, Scarlet stood near the dead boy's head, facing away, then stooped down and plopped down to sit.

She leaned back until she had to fall the rest of the way, and she'd gotten the coils of rope around her forearms to weigh down on the open mouth with uniform rows of sharp points. Teeth that could easily rip skin and muscle and tendons and would likely even more easily cut rope.

Groaning, sometimes sobbing, watching and listening for monsters in the street, Scarlet shifted herself around. With every movement, when she felt a tooth hook onto even just one of the rope's slender strands, she forced the issue, tried to make the snag worse, sometimes lifting the dead boy's head up from the warm, slick pavement, until his single tooth or a teaming of them cut through.

Severing every single strand was a battle that took some time, and her bare chest, with a flannel shirt and bra fallen to both sides, glistened with sweat. The boy's head sometimes flopped to one side or the other as she toiled, and she sometimes succumbed to a fresh sob at the feel of his head being ground into the rough bricks.

She grunted as she dragged his head across the alley floor, fighting to kill a snagged rope strand, then tried to laugh through her nose as the series of coiled loops around her arms, all the way from her wrists to high on her upper arms, went slack.

With a heaving chest, she rested, her weight smothering the dead boy beneath her, and did nothing but breathe.

Giving the stale air in her lungs a snort out, she sat up quickly and shook her arms, tried to pry them apart, and got the whole bundle to start to unwind. It all fell off behind her, some of it across the dangerous teeth that had saved her, and she moaned as she tried moving her arms forward.

But even that motion brought more tears, and she gently moved them to the front then back, over and over, restoring some life to them.

Watching the dead boy and scanning and listening for hunters on the street, she reached trembling hands up and felt around for the edge of the tape that Archie had used to seal up all of her gags.

Her breaths became violent, short bursts in and out when that tape end didn't reveal itself easily. Moaning, sobbing as well as she could, she found it all the way behind her head, and she picked at it, her arms and hands almost too shaky to be productive.

But she managed it and began to peel it off around her head, slowly at first to not rip it, then more quickly, in a near panic.

The tape fell away, and she hurried her cramping hands behind her and found the tight knot in the rope. Another battle ensued, with a willingness and need to rip it open and just breathe again competing with a need to use finesse, determine where to pull, and loosen and not tighten.

But she managed that, too, and got the knot loosened, then untied, and she hurriedly unwound all of it and tossed it down.

After the last two loops had been shed, revealing the strip of cloth that had been used to start it all—what had set her mouth in a silent scream—she paused and sucked deep breaths through above and below the cloth. Her breasts, wet with sweat, lifted and pointed across the alley with every gulp she took in.

Satisfied, primed with enough air for more work, she found the knot in the cloth behind her head. She almost laughed at how easily it came apart, like it hadn't mattered to Archie so much because he was already planning on more brutality, and that meager cloth had been just the start.

She was about to throw the cloth down, then she held it out to stare at it in the dim light. Instead of discarding it, she folded it and tucked it into a pants pocket.

"Oh, God," she said, and slid her back along the brick wall to stoop down where she could see the dead boy and the street. She focused on the boy for a moment and shook with a soft sob.

"I'm so sorry!" she whispered to him. "I didn't want to!"

While wiggling her lower jaw from side to side, stretching her mouth open and closed, and rubbing and massaging both sides of it, she groaned and stood.

"Oh, Daniel, I don't know about this. I just don't know."

She sighed, then began careful steps toward the street, which still possessed the relative cheeriness afforded by a string of dim, though burning faithfully, lights. Before leaning out to look each way, she tried buttoning up her shirt, but she had to scoff at all of the buttons having been ripped loose and scattered somewhere in Archie's office.

"It's never easy."

Shaking her head, she said, "Oh, wait."

She fished the cloth out of her pocket, unfolded it and stretched it out, then used it to tie her shirt like a robe, covering her breasts.

"A new shirt. On my shopping list."

She looked down and scoffed, mixing it with a high-pitched sob.

"I deserve to lose my mind."

She took a deep breath, puffed it back out, then stopped working her jaw around. Two steps got her almost to the edge of her alley and the sharp brick corners of the buildings.

Holding her breath, Scarlet was about to tip her head out and scout for danger on the street.

But the increasing clatter of a herd of hooves on the hard pavement got her back against the bricks and her lungs locked tight.

* * *

"I see the city, Mama. We'll find Scarlet and kill her."

He took a few steps, a butchered body held up on a shoulder and a blood- and brain-crusted sword in his free hand. Fluids were dripping down from Betsy and mingling with sweat across his bare chest and back.

"You'll help, Mama, won't you?"

He stopped and listened.

"Mama?"

He smiled when she barked her answer, then he turned and watched three dogs with human faces approaching.

He laughed and said, "I'm stupid, Mama. I should have known you wouldn't bark like that."

"Stop, there!"

Junior waited, grinning at the approaching mutant guards.

"You're beyond the approved radius of the work area to which you've been assigned. Explain yourself."

"Huh?"

The second dog guard said, "Too much? Okay. Start with that property you're removing without authorization."

"It's just Mama. I need her help, and I think her kidneys, but I don't know what that means."

"No," said the third human face. "Not the meat. The sword."

"Say," said the first dog, "isn't that the boss's sword?"

"He gave it to me."

"You didn't mangle him and take it?"

"No. I like the boss. He let me eat the bug legs I caught."

"He . . . what?"

"Yeah. They were on the wall. Cooked is good too."

Number two snickered and said, "So, it wasn't enough, and you packed a lunch?"

The other two joined in, laughing and yipping a few times.

"No. I packed Mama. She—"

Number three howled quickly, then laughed and said, "For her kidneys? Right?"

"I don't know what that is."

"Okay, alright," said the first dog. "Enough about lunches. Where are you going with the boss's sword?"

"There," Junior said, pointing toward the dark city compressed in the distance.

"Oh. A fun little trip to the city, huh?"

"Yeah. It'll be fun when I catch the wench, but I don't know what that means either."

The lead guard tipped its head each way, and the other two scurried to form a ring around the big, sweaty young man with his mutated, dead mother over his shoulder.

"We'll have to check your story with the boss."

"No. He said. He told me. He—"

"You eat bodies, right?"

"Uh-huh."

"And crispy bug legs, fresh and cooked and by the fistful?"

"Uh-huh. They're—"

"And we're supposed to believe that you wouldn't lie to take a scram with a kidney lunch away from your assigned duties?"

"What's a 'scram?' Why would I take it?"

Number two was tipping its head, ready to take a human-sized bite into Junior's leg, and it said, "Not like taking a dump, I can assure you. That must be a horrible sight when you do it. Veins and gristle and skulls and—"

"I don't always eat skulls."

"Look at me," said the number one dog's human face.

Junior leaned forward and held its gaze.

"Give us that meat, and you can stomp off and hunt that wench."

Junior straightened up, towering over them, and laughed.

"You funny dog people can't stop me anyway."

The three began circling, baring human teeth and beginning to snarl.

"We can slow you down," said number two.

"We like to bite. We'll bite you."

Junior offered a relaxed smile and said, "I'll bite you too."

Number one yipped loudly, and Junior and the other two stopped and stared at it.

"Wouldn't you rather hunt a wench without bleeding all over the place?"

Number three snickered and said, "And carrying a sloppy bag of meat?"

"Um, I—"

"You want to feed the dogs, don't you?"

Junior laughed and pointed at all of them.

"But you have people faces. That's funny."

Number one yipped again.

"But our bellies are still dog. Dog bellies like meat. Give us the meat."

"She's not just meat. She's Mama too."

The lead dog rolled its eyes and said, "Fine. Give us the momma meat."

"That's better. Okay. She doesn't talk much anymore anyway."

He slopped and splattered it down near his boots, then grinned at the guard dogs while smearing what had oozed out of her all around on his wet skin.

"Smart move, carnivore boy," said the first guard.

"I remember carnivals."

"Sure you do.

"Back away now."

Junior took a step back, and all three of them kept their eyes on him while tugging with sharp teeth and nibbling at bloody little chunks of his mother.

"The bug legs are good," Junior said, pointing.

"We'll get to those. Run along, oven boy."

"Okay. Are you all really hungry?"

"Like you wouldn't believe," said the second.

"Always," said the third, and it only began a sharp yip when the blade swung by a sweaty cannibal cleaved it into two pieces, each with two kicking legs.

"More meat!" Junior said, laughing and pointing with the bloody sword. "Want more?"

"No!" said the first just before chomping on the side of a frowning human face connected to half of a dog. "This is good! We're good!"

"Okay."

He looked toward the city while licking the sword and said, "You're good dogs. I like dogs."

The remaining two dog guards snarled and snapped at three piles of meat, their crazed eyes watching as Junior, resting the bloody sword over his shoulder, began the short hike down the gentle grade and toward the chain link fence.

Chapter 19 – No Goddamn Fingernails

The clattering of hooves on pavement stopped, and the city fell silent save for the pervasive buzzing again. Scarlet allowed herself a slow, deep breath, then let it out before sliding her back along the bricks, back toward the street.

Close enough, she leaned, looked, and stared at a group of giant boars, their bodies bloated and slick with oil, as they all rooted around on both sides of the road, along the curbs, and sometimes up the walls, reaching their snouts up almost to the height of the lifeless second-story windows.

One snorted and snapped its head around, bearing its beady eyes in her direction.

She held her breath.

The boar sniffed directly at her, then slightly left, then a little to the right. Then, again right at her.

It took a step, repeated sweeping with its snout, then stepped again.

One other boar looked but didn't move, then another. Many of them were looking toward Scarlet and sniffing, some snorting and stamping their hooves like bulls eager to charge.

Scarlet slipped out of sight behind the corner, scraping her back along the bricks, and took careful sideways steps into the depths of the alley.

She heard a single clop, then silence. Then, a few more stamps and some scrapes, all getting louder as the boars zeroed in on their prey.

With eyes on the alley's entrance, she surprised herself when her boot collided with the boy with razor teeth. She gave him a glance first, then shot one toward the street, then back down at the boy.

Who was starting to sit himself up, still not blinking even once, and straining out raspy sounds through his crushed throat.

The clopping of hooves was sporadic but getting closer, and Scarlet stared down at a mutant boy that was about to scream.

"No, no, no!" she whispered, but the boy didn't heed her request, keeping his non-blinking eyes locked on something in the distance.

Her chest began to heave, and she winced as thick tears fought their way out of both eyes.

Shaking her head at the boy, hyperventilating quietly, she wiped once across each of her cheeks, then stared across the narrow alley as she forced her face to calm, and her breaths began to slow

"No," she said softly, no longer whispering.

She looked down, saw the almost-dead mutant boy turn his head enough to point his blank eyes at her, then raised her boot high over his head.

He worked his jaws, teeth sometimes scraping, and started to choke out a pained shriek.

But her heavy work boot, driven by a powerful leg, fell with such force that the skull beneath it cracked like a muffled gunshot.

The clattering in the street increased, then stopped.

A fresh tear leaked from each eye.

She pounded his head again, saying, "No!" in time with each skull cracking gunshot.

A puddle was forming, and her kicks had to travel farther before meeting anything to crush.

Another pound and another crack to the sound of, "No!"

She gave her cheeks another quick swipe.

The next stomp was more squish than crack, and the sound of approaching hooves didn't slow and didn't stop.

She left her boot on the mushy slop of his head and turned her own head toward the street. A giant snout was angled across, partway in, and sniffing with each tip up.

A low growl came from deep inside it somewhere, and Scarlet held a hand over her mouth as she watched the beast turn its bulbous body to face the narrow space between the two brick walls where she cowered.

It leaned back, then rammed its body against the bricks, shattering some and sending more crashing down.

Scarlet took a step farther into the alley as the boar rammed the entrance again, gouging bricks loose and widening its path to her.

From one side along the street, another boar jumped its front hooves up onto the back of the one doing the ramming, sniffed all around, then wailed and snorted like a screechy trumpet.

"Dammit," she whispered to herself, "I had to stop that thing from screaming! I had to!"

She looked down at the mess that she'd made and gave the boy's deadly fingernails a long look.

"Hell," she said, followed by a sob cut short. "They already know I'm in here."

She took a measured breath, let it out slowly, and glared at the boy's hands. With her clean boot, she stomped the boys hands, mangling them, peeling back skin, and shattering the nails.

"Don't you ever!" she said, stomping each of his hands with its own boot as she marched in place.

The boars were pounding the buildings, snorting and screeching, and bricks and mortar were dropping with every hit.

"No nails! No goddamn fingernails!"

She gave each hand its own final brutal strike, then, while wiping again across her cheeks, she twisted her boots into them, leaving them mere stumps with only some of their fingers still attached.

Looking back at the attacking pigs, she whispered, "No fingernails, dammit."

Then, she backed away from the starving pack to the sound of squealing and falling bricks and was about to turn to run when she heard vigorous whooshing directly over her.

Only two stories above, on the unlighted rooftops, the streetlight was sufficient to give a hint of giant winged creatures flapping while their heads and arms were wedging between the walls. Black, leathery fingers like oily gloves were grasping, coming nearer to snagging her with every swipe.

"More fingernails. Goddammit!"

Chapter 20 – An Entirely Separate Head

Ducking to evade the swiping black claws, Scarlet froze when a halting, deep voice said right above her, "Human. Eat."

Another voice, similar but from a different angle, said, "Hate humans."

"Eat?"

"Yeah. Eat."

Scarlet crouched low, with her hands over her head, and heard the swiping fingers sweeping past, almost close enough to hook a clump of her black mane.

"No, no, no!" she whispered as she crept along.

Behind her, ravenous boars were demolishing the brick walls, snorting and screeching and clattering their hooves.

Above her, giant bats were sticking themselves deeper into the slot between the old buildings, swinging leather hands and still flapping long wings up in the darkness above the roofs.

"Human good to eat."

"To eat."

"Only."

"Yeah."

Something wet and mucky trapped the toe of her boot, and she fell to her hands and knees, which sank into and squirted out mush. Too little light had crept that far into the alley to identify any of it.

"Oh, God."

She crawled forward, and her knee contacted something solid that rocked away but didn't roll to the side. With one hand, she reached down, felt around, then pulled her hand back.

"A skull! Oh, God . . ."

She climbed over and past it, hands and knees sloshing through the thick puddle of gore until her head hit the very end of the alley.

She looked back and saw that the boars hadn't given up. If anything, they'd gotten hungrier and more determined. Bricks fell like a steady rain.

A quick breeze hit her from above. Then another.

She looked up and saw dark shapes tight between the walls above her, and there was just enough light to see the sweep of long arms, hands with claws trying to catch a human meal.

"Hurry."

"Entrails."

"Hot. Good."

She reached around blindly all over that end wall, found nothing close, then rose up higher, still searching until her hand rested on the warm, oily metal of a doorknob.

Breathing in choppy bursts, she turned the knob and pulled the door open, then ducked farther out of the reach of the monsters on the roofs.

Against the constant rumble of falling bricks, snorting, and stomping, and even with the whooshing of wings high above and from long, clawed arms closer to her head, she heard something inside.

A shuffling of feet.

A dragging of something across a floor.

And laughter. Brief blasts of cackling, maniacal laughter.

*　*　*

"Dammit!" she whispered.

Scarlet looked back, saw the boars still attacking the walls, widening the path to her and fighting each other to be the first to take a juicy bite.

Just when she was about to check if the monstrous bats had given up, even though the whooshing of wings and claws hadn't stopped, she gasped when something sharp snagged a few strands of her hair and snaked them up toward the absolute darkness of the sky.

"No!"

She ducked down and crawled through the doorway, stayed low, and pulled the door closed as quietly and as quickly as she could. Her back stayed against the wall where she sat, and she rested her face, wet from tears, in her hands.

Outside, through the rotting wood door, she still heard the crushing and scattering of bricks and the occasional hooting and snorting, but the whooshing of the flying creatures had been muted altogether.

Looking up from her wet hands, she studied her refuge, seeing that where she sat, near the door, was just another block of the night. But farther away, from somewhere around the nearby corner, a light burned.

And something sometimes laughed like a maniac.

Crawling on her hands and knees, which were soaked with slime that she still hadn't observed, she peeked around the corner for a view down a short corridor with two doors on each side of it.

The last door on the left housed the light. A dim light, but enough to see that the floor between her and it was clear.

Behind her, through the door that she'd just closed, a renewed ramming of the buildings that used to have sharp corners sent more bricks tumbling and rolling.

"Oh, God . . ."

She crawled again toward the light, holding her breath when she passed the first two closed doors, one on each side of the hallway.

A few more crawling steps, leaving only distinct splotchy patches after having had most of the gory slime scraped off onto the floor, got her close enough to lean and look into the room.

Where burned the only light that she'd seen in the old wrecked and abandoned building.

Where laughed someone or something, maybe even something incapable of language.

Scarlet closed her eyes, and her head shook softly, almost imperceptibly. After one deep breath, and then a silent expelling of it, she put one hand out for the door jamb.

And she caught her breath at the blood drying on the back of it and the tiny bits of rotting meat packed between her fingers.

She mouthed the words, "Oh, God!" then wiped that hand on her pants, then the other hand, then reached again for a hold at the open doorway.

Holding a deep breath, wincing in advance, she leaned enough to look inside the room.

Her eyes locked on a small man nearly up against the far wall and facing away from her. Between her and him was a small lamp on the seat of a chair, its bare, weak bulb unblocked by a shade.

The little man danced from side to side, sometimes kicking a leg, and shaking his head and odd, puffy jacket around.

His right hand was around front, and his left hand held the belt and top edge of his pants, which were partway down his thighs.

His bare ass picked up the light as he flexed it several times, thrusting his hips forward, toward the wall.

Scarlet covered her mouth, her eyes big, and watched his display. And she watched for only a few seconds more before whipping herself back around, hiding from his sight as he turned.

She'd seen that his right hand held a surprisingly rigid rod of flesh, and he'd begun to cackle at the sight of his stroking of it replayed as a shadow on that far wall.

"Oh, God!" she whispered.

The laughter stopped.

"What now?" she whispered again.

She leaned to look, and he was facing her, phallus in his hand also pointed right at her.

His small, close eyes stared right into hers.

And shrouded within the lumpy jacket, all mounded up above his shoulders, was an entirely separate head.

Its small, close eyes also stared straight into hers.

Chapter 21 – Stay With Igor

Scarlet had just begun a loud gasp, then the speedy little man with two heads was upon her. Even before she could pull her hand back from the door frame, his tiny but mighty grip took possession of her wrist and with more strength than he should have, he dragged her over to where his obscene shadow had been amusing him so greatly.

"Let me go!" she screamed as he flopped her across a floor littered with cardboard boxes and greasy, ripped pillows, through which she plowed, scattering some and flattening others.

"I will not! You're beautiful—so beautiful!"

He swung her like a doll toward the wall, and she fought enough to stand. But he had both of her wrists, clamped in greedy little hands, and he shoved her back into the wall.

"Stop! God, stop it!"

"I'm useless! Stupid! I don't know any better! I don't deserve anything this beautiful!"

His second head was nodding and grinning.

"Good, then let me go!"

"I can't! I'm stupid, but I can't!"

Head number two opened its mouth for a laugh, but stayed silent and only bounced from the attempt.

His meager stature was perfect for him to tip forward and kiss her navel, but he only looked up at her as she started trying to knee him. She caught his jaw with a solid hit, tipping back his head, but he re-righted it and grinned up at her.

"I deserve to be kicked! Nothing more! I'm just a stupid thing!"

The extra head nodded and bounced its eyebrows.

"What are you? Let me go!"

"No! I can't, and I won't!"

He lowered his eyes to see the loosening knot that she'd tied in the cloth band holding her buttonless shirt closed.

He cackled, released one of her wrists, then suffered her punches and slaps to both heads as he quickly pulled the knot, letting the strip fall to the floor and reveal her breasts, which were jostling all around while she tried to beat mostly his natural head.

"No! Don't you dare! Leave me alone!"

He secured her ineffective punching and slapping arm and pinned that to the wall like the other.

"Oh, so beautiful," he said, staring from one breast to the other. "Perfect! I don't deserve perfect!"

"No, you don't! Let me go!"

She tried kicking him, and both heads only grinned as he accepted the pummeling.

He began licking his lips and tried stretching up on his toes to get his mouth on Scarlet's nipples that were close but just out of his reach.

"I want them! I don't deserve them!"

He strained his tongue up, far out of his mouth, almost touching one of his prizes. Scarlet was trying to wrestle free her arms and kicking with her knees, but nothing worked, and even the surplus head had its tongue out.

"Oh, God, what is this? Stop it, you goddamn freak!"

"I'm a freak! A useless freak!"

The second head nodded and grinned, then aimed its tongue again at the closest of Scarlet's nipples.

"Oh, God, stop!"

As if she'd had a violent spasm, she used both arms and legs together and shoved the two-headed, lecherous thing back.

"Whoa! I deserved that!" he said as he fell backwards.

She ran past him toward the exit, but he grabbed an ankle, held it like a bear trap, and Scarlet tumbled to the floor. Before she could scramble to her feet, he cackled and toppled a heavy bookcase across her back, knocking the air from her lungs and leaving her squirming but unable to free herself.

"Stay! I don't deserve it—too beautiful! But stay with Igor!"

* * *

Calling back over his shoulder, Junior said, "You'll be okay, Mama. I'll come back for you. I'll fix you."

He slogged on through the darkness toward the city, sometimes swinging the stained sword around and sometimes etching a thin rut alongside his footprints.

He stopped and spoke over the other shoulder.

"Don't be a bug, Mama."

Walking again, he looked ahead toward tiny, twinkling points of light and tipped his head at the sight of them winking on and off, in a series from right to left.

Then, left to right.

"Huh."

He took a few more steps, then stopped to see how some of the lights in the faraway city were blocked out.

"Who's there? Mama? Did you run ahead of me?"

From the deep shadows walked two human forms, lit only meagerly by the weak glow of the burning ocean back beyond the reactor.

"Hi. I'm Junior."

He waved with his free hand and held the sword pointed down by his side.

Something in the shadows barked, then growled.

"Huh? Are you guards too?"

The bodies got close enough, and Junior laughed and pointed at a naked man and a naked woman with heads of dogs.

"That's funny! You're like those other fun guys!"

Both started snarling and growling and ran toward him like any human would.

"Wait! Can't you talk?"

Their growling continued as they dashed toward him.

"Those other guys could bark. How come you dog people can't talk?"

The male body was faster and was about ready to take a final leap at Junior.

"You're no fun," he said, and swung his sword like a baseball bat, slicing clean through the thing's torso.

"Huh. Like before. Kind of different too."

The two halves convulsed in the oily soil, one half kicking and the other half snapping its canine jaws and trying to grab him.

"Good dog."

He looked up at the female who had stopped itself before leaping at him.

"Can you talk?"

It looked down at the sectioned one on the ground, then yipped and stared at Junior.

"Oh, I'm sorry. Maybe I shouldn't have cut him in half?"

The female whined and stooped down, petting the dog head and rubbing around its ears. It only looked up at Junior, its eyes closing, staring at him through thin slits.

"Oh, okay. You can have half. Which one do you want?"

It yipped and scampered off into the shadows.

"Huh. Not hungry. How could that be?"

Junior hoisted the leg part of the thing up onto a shoulder and resumed his walk toward the city and a wench named Scarlet.

* * *

"Damn you, get this thing off of me!"

"No! You're beautiful—too beautiful for someone so stupid!"

"If I get out of here, I'm going to—"

"You won't! It's heavy. Useful. But I'm useless! I'm nobody!"

He pinned down her legs, held them together, and sat on them.

"Stop! Get off of me!"

"No! Can't!"

He reached up and grabbed her pants and tried pulling them down, but the belt was buckled, and he couldn't get any of it past her hips.

"Stop! Don't!"

"I won't stop! Too stupid!"

He reached around her hips and fumbled for the belt, and Scarlet groaned and tried to squirm anywhere, but he'd pinned her down with something far too heavy.

"I did it!" he said after unfastening her belt. "Stupid, but I did it!"

"Leave me alone!"

He jerked at her pants, easily sliding them down past her ass, and he stopped at the sight.

"Ooh, panties. Ooh, ooh, ooh! I don't deserve that! I don't!"

"No, you don't, so let me go!"

"No!"

He twisted around one way and yanked off one of her boots, then repeated it for her other leg.

"No! Please, don't!"

"Don't say please! Too stupid to understand!"

Sliding himself down along her legs, he peeled off her pants like opening a present. A quick tug sent them across the floor, and he sat himself back down.

"Stop. Please, just stop."

"No!"

She lay still when he got a grip on her panties and pulled them down just far enough to tuck the top band under her ass cheeks.

"Ooh. Ooh, so beautiful."

He leaned forward, still trapping her legs, and began licking her thighs and ass, moaning as he left tracks of slobber all over her.

"No, don't. Just don't!"

"So beautiful. Mm, so beautiful."

He held the outsides of her thighs, hugging her as he licked, then he tightened up his hold of her legs with his knees, reached under, then lifted her ass higher.

"Don't! Leave me alone, please!"

"Mm. Can't. Too beautiful. Such perfect skin. Mm."

He jammed a greasy pillow under her belly, then held her up and licked her ass all over.

"Taste so good. All over! Want to taste it all!"

He moaned and licked, and Scarlet almost whispered, "Please, just stop!"

"Mm, I'm so lucky. But I'm stupid and useless—I don't deserve it!"

* * *

"Igor doesn't deserve to fuck. But Igor wants. He wants to fuck!"

While still holding both of Scarlet's legs straight against the dirty wood floor, he pulled one as far as he could to the side, then tipped a heavy crate across her calf, locking it down.

"No. Please!"

"Mm. So tasty. Want to fuck! Igor's stick is ready!"

He fought with her other leg, spreading the two of them far apart, then leaned a heavy, thick piece of oily metal onto that leg, scratching up her smooth skin and squeezing it down into the floor.

"Mm, so good. I don't deserve it!"

He laid himself between her legs, with a pair of scissors in one hand, and moaned and humped the floor while licking the insides of her thighs.

"So soft. So beautiful. Not like me—I have no value!"

Scarlet tried to recoil at the touch of the warm metal against her thigh as Igor slipped a point under the twisted-up pantie material.

"So beautiful. Going to fuck! Have to!"

He gave the scissors a few hard squeezes and cut through near one of her ass cheeks, then the other. The scissors hit the floor somewhere across the room, and Scarlet yipped when he yanked the shredded cloth out from between her legs.

"Stop! Don't!"

"Igor's ready! His stick is so much a stick. It's ready!"

He got up on his hands and knees and almost climbed up onto the bookcase that was nearly crushing Scarlet into the floor. His stick was close, almost touching, when Scarlet, trapped and helpless, sighed loudly.

Igor tipped his head to listen, ready to laugh, and she said, with a voice calm and controlled and flowing like a river of thick syrup, "You don't want to do that."

He pushed himself up, both heads looked both ways, then at each other, then both looked down at his stick. It was still ready.

He strained quietly to push his hips forward to stab with that stick, but all he did was shake from the effort.

With his spare head rolling its eyes and scoffing silently, Igor said, "I . . . I don't want to do that."

A few moments of silence passed in the forgotten room of an abandoned building, where a mutant with two heads had been determined to ram his stick into Scarlet.

"What . . . what did you say?" she said, her voice still thick and drippy.

Igor hesitated, his face twisting in agony, and he said, "I said . . . I *say* . . . I say what you say I say."

She wheezed in a few breaths, then said with a shaky voice, "What just happened? How did—"

"Mm, Igor sees your pussy. It's so beautiful. It needs my hard—"

Scarlet snorted out a quick breath, then, in a voice like tumbling loaves of honey, she said, "You will not fuck me."

"I will not fuck you."

His second head shook silently while Igor stared straight ahead.

"You will just back away. You will not fuck me."

He tipped himself back, then stood between her spread legs.

"I . . . I'm away. I won't,"—he stared down, his eyes focused only on where the smooth skin inside her thighs tried to meet near the top but displayed something that got both heads of the mutant shaking in quick jerks, like spasms—"won't fuck your . . ."

"Say pussy," came from beneath the bookcase like bubbling warm sugar.

"Pussy."

"You can't have it."

"I can't have it."

"Free me."

"Right away!"

He tipped the heavy items off of Scarlet's legs first, then groaned as he lifted the bookcase from her back and stood it up.

She rolled over quickly and rose up, then hurried to pick up her pants. Two heads leveled their eyes at the sight of her pulling the stained and torn fabric up to cover each of her long legs.

And both heads salivated at the sight of her flapping open her shirt, showing her full, round breasts before she closed it up and tied it with the same cloth as before.

Only then did both pairs of eyes look into hers.

Speaking slowly and without any hesitation, like a warm dripping of the sweetest nectar, she said, "Go stand by the wall."

Both heads nodded, and he backed up until he was pressed into the dented and cracked paneling. He turned his eyes just enough to see his second head, and he pushed its forehead, clunking it into the wall.

"Please," he said, looking down and sobbing, "just kill me. I don't deserve to live!"

"No," she said, smiling and her voice still flowing. "You don't. But I won't kill you."

"Please! I'm begging you: if you won't kill me, I'll kill myself!"

"No. No one's killing you, not even you."

"Then . . . then, suck my stick! I don't deserve it, but I want to feel normal again!"

"You're far from normal."

"I know! We know! I want . . . I . . . please, just suck my stick for me!"

"No. Sit against the wall."

He did, without hesitation.

"Close all of your eyes."

The normal two closed first, then the extra ones.

"Sit quietly," she said, the sweet liquid of her voice invading him and leaving no room for a will of his own. "Don't move unless I tell you to."

Chapter 22 – No One Deserves Sexy Like This

"No way in hell am I going up in that damn thing."

Pauline picked at a few tangles almost lost in her wild, long red hair.

"Not dressed like that, you aren't," said Ham, a robust, meaty fellow with a long blond ponytail that he almost always looped around to hang past a shoulder and sway around on his thick chest.

"What, this little nothing?"

She looked down, grinning at the coarse and worn black men's button-down shirt that draped almost down to her knees but was unbuttoned up top to show a good portion of her breasts.

"You know this isn't my style. You're lucky I cater to your fetishes for teasing bullshit like this."

"Yes," he said, tipping his head back to laugh, "I'm damn lucky. You wear it well."

"Eh. Leather suits me better."

"How about something really soft and sexy sometime? Give an old dog a goddamn treat."

"You couldn't handle me in lingerie. No one could. Your fucking heart would seize up like an engine without any fucking oil."

"I could try. I'd try, dammit."

"Not a chance, Ham. This goddamn world is a savage nightmare, and all it wants is to kill anything soft."

"Like you? Hasn't killed you yet."

"Shit, it tries all the—I mean, it would if I ever let myself get soft. Like a goddamn machine, it'd kill me. You know it would."

"Can't argue with that. Yep. Alright, guard the fort while I'm gone."

They stood near the massive wooden door, bolted shut and barred with a thick crosswise post inside an abandoned command center high up on a mountain near the city, which was sometimes decorated with streetlights, other times as black as everything else around them.

"Sure. Just don't ask me to clean it. Especially if the power goes out again."

"That damn reactor. Someday soon, maybe when Risk comes back, we'll go down there and really kick some ass."

Pauline laughed and jabbed a finger toward him.

"First, you don't know when the hell Risk is coming back. And second, that place is a nightmare packed with every freak you can imagine."

"And some I can't."

"Yeah, Ham. Yeah, and hardly any sad bastard makes it out of there alive. Don't waste your time."

"And die and leave you all alone up here? Wouldn't want that."

"Damn right. Hey, while you're out hunting bats with that kook navigator of yours, why don't—"

"Ziggy isn't a kook. Ziggy's pretty cool and remember, fucking no one messes with him. I'd never get around out there without him."

"You ever try flying that balloon contraption yourself?"

Ham laughed and said, "Only once. That was enough. I tried controlling that blast thing that he rigged up, and all I did was spin the goddamn thing in circles."

"In the dark," she said, grinning.

"Yep. Not fun."

"No. What I was saying is that while you're out there, maybe touch down somewhere and get that crafter to make you some shirts that actually fit. You got some freak shit going on yourself."

He raised his right arm, drawing their attention to a flexing fist ten times the size of his other hand. His bare arm showed the muscles he'd developed to wield the weapon his hand had become before he'd fled the reactor, where he'd been shoveling dirt like all of the other slaves.

The left sleeve of his otherwise normal button-down shirt was typical, but the right one, plus most of the fabric around the shoulder, had been ripped and cut away.

"Well, yeah. Thanks for pointing that out. Again."

"It's why I'm here."

"No. Bullshit, like always. You're here because you did some crazy-ass fucking on a motorcycle before you road-rashed yourself here."

"Thanks for reminding me of that. Again. You must have had some wild sex and died right at that moment yourself."

"I wish I could remember it, but it's been a while. Hope the sex was good."

"Had to be. It's the only way that works. You were cumming like a maniac. We just don't know how you died."

"I still cum like a maniac."

"You're welcome. Look, all I'm saying is that if that crafter is still lurking around somewhere in that den of freaks and monsters, get yourself some clothes."

"Hey, why don't you take a fun little shopping trip through the town? Ziggy and I could swing low enough, and you could jump your ass down there. Need some cash?"

"You're funny as fuck. I'm not going anywhere near that city. You know that. Fuck no. I'll just keep hermitting my ass up here on your mountain."

Ham hefted up the heavy beam across the door and stood it up against the wall before looking back at Pauline, who had tipped her head and waited for his response.

"Huh. Hermit all you want, as long as I get a piece of that hermit ass once in a goddamn while."

She gave him a genuine smile and said, "Even hermits have to pay the damn landlord, right?"

"Damn right."

"Even if they don't dress their asses up all cutesy for the savage to fuck?"

"It would be preferred," he said, grinning. "Takes the edge off of all the death and misery in this goddamn world. So, yeah, that's how you pay."

"And I suppose I can't ever stop paying?"

"Either keep paying or feed yourself to the bats. They're always hungry."

"Oh, that reminds me—when you deliver a bat, see if—"

"Or parts of a bat. Sometimes it's just parts."

"Yeah. Fine. But when you get paid, see if you can get some actual food, alright? The pantry's running kind of lean."

"Sure. Would the lady prefer live lobsters or a pretty box of French pastry?"

"For fuck's sake. You're a crude asshole, Ham."

He rubbed at his clean-shaved chin, then pointed at her and said, "I'm working on it. Risk is a good influence."

She scoffed and said, "Right. When he's a man, at least."

Ham laughed and said, "Yeah. Only then. Be back soon."

"The fuck you will. Just make sure you eventually come back."

"I love you too."

"Lying fuck. Get out of here already."

Grinning, he slid several heavy iron bolts to the side, then swung in the door. Fires in barrels close to the entrance cast some dancing light into the dim living area of the house and beyond those, past the high iron fence with sharp points on every upright piece, the dark world waited far down the mountain's steep slope.

He puckered up while glancing back at Pauline, she showed him her middle finger, and he shut the door with a heavy boom.

* * *

His boots were quiet on the stone patio outside the residence, the flat surfaces bearing a perpetual sheen of crude oil that seemed to ooze right out of the air. The fires in the barrels crackled and waved around as he passed them, on his way past the spare vessel that he kept and maintained.

He stopped to rest his hands on the top edge of the wide, circular wicker basket and looked over the edge at the rough plank floor littered with ratty burlap blankets and pillows that had welcomed a dose of oil long before.

Before looking up, he grabbed a taut steel cable to each side of him along the basket's rim. He gave them both a pull and nodded at them not moving, then he followed their path upward with his eyes, seeing how they joined many others evenly spaced around the basket and routed up past a large iron pot suspended in the middle.

Below that pot, which revealed the presence of the fire it held as bits of it escaped around the edges of a flat metal lid, another small pot hung down, carrying its own fire and lighting the basket area.

"You're keeping the lines tight, Hawken. Good work."

"Ham. As long as anchors stay."

Ham leaned each way and confirmed that the hook lines were in place, holding onto thick iron rings embedded in the heaviest of the patio's stones.

"Yeah," he said, looking up again but not seeing clearly the extra balloon's navigator crouching in darkness on a small wooden platform near the main fire pot. "It's good. Ziggy and I are heading out. You want anything?"

"What I always want, Ham."

"Oh, Hawken, I don't know, my friend. I'm looking, all the time, but I don't know if I'll ever find a girl match for you."

A few quiet seconds passed before Hawken said, "I know. Thanks, Ham."

"I sure can bring you something to eat, though. That alright?"

"That's always alright. Yes."

"Okay, then. I'm off. Balloon up, lines tight, my friend."

"Always, Ham."

He tapped the rim with both hands, then continued on across the patio toward his regular ride, a similar basket with a similar balloon. At its side, he checked its lines, like he always did, then looked up.

"Ziggy, you ready to ride?"

"Yeah, Ham. Hop in."

"I'll cut us loose first. Don't leave without me."

"That's funny, Ham. I'll loosen it all up some so we don't sail with you hanging on the rim."

"Appreciate that."

Ham watched long enough, looking up at a similar pot of fire, hanging lantern pot, and a platform in the shadows above for his navigator, to see the thin rim of orange around the pot get snuffed by a tight lid.

All around him, the cables and ropes holding basket to balloon seemed to sigh as they relaxed. Ham hurried to one side, unhooked a thick rope from its mooring at the patio's bolt, then tossed the end into the basket. He repeated that for the other side, all the while monitoring the cables and ready to scream up at Ziggy if the lines ever got too loose.

But they were all fine, and Ham grinned and said to himself, "Damn Ziggy. You're the best."

He held the rim with his left hand, balled up a massive right fist and swung it to pick up enough momentum, and it assisted in his jump to scramble over the rim and inside.

Looking up, he said, "Using the real fire this time, Ziggy?"

"Yeah. Giving myself a rest."

"Alright, you've earned it," he called upward. "Let's ride."

"We ride!"

Ziggy tipped aside the fire pot lid and flames, eager to do their part, licked high up into the balloon, which stretched and groaned as it puffed out and whipped tight every rope and cable.

While the basket lifted silently off of the patio, Ham held the rim with both hands, one normal and one almost comically mutated, and looked down at his house on the side of a mountain.

"You're not missing much out here, Pauline. Stay safe inside."

*   *   *

Pauline stepped toward a shuttered window after Ham had closed the door and she'd bolted it and put back the stout beam. The inside shutter, too, had an array of heavy iron bolts at its swinging edge, each one slipped into several brawny loops welded to the window's thick metal frame.

She slid each one aside quietly, then pried the shutter open enough for a single eye to watch Ham board his basket and share some banter, which she couldn't hear, with his navigator above.

Even after the craft had been carried aloft, she leaned and watched it depart until it had fully merged with the oily night that choked the mountain from all sides.

"Huh. See ya, Ham."

She clunked the shutter closed, then snapped each bolt back into place.

Wiping her hands as she walked, she dodged the old furniture that had been there when Ham had first staked his claim to the place, and aimed her steps toward her bedroom. The door squealed in easily, and she paused to look first at the cracked glass block window, appearing to be painted black and trapped behind a tight array of steel rods.

Below that, a single fat candle tried its best to illuminate the small room, which contained a lived-in assortment of old, worn furnishings, cardboard boxes piled against walls, and a bed hidden beneath mismatched, scavenged pillows and dingy stuffed animals, all tossed about like an earthquake had shaken the whole room.

"Shit. This is my life, now that I'm dead?"

Scoffing, she focused on the dresser top, where the flickering candle streaked light across the top of a dusty jewelry box and gave a weak shine to stained and broken figurines, reminders of a life that had ended in her death, which then had continued there, with Ham on his mountain.

"Sex. Or death. Should have picked just one."

She grabbed a dresser drawer and pulled it out, then rummaged below the top layer. She laid on the dresser a black t-shirt and black pants that were made of some type of leather.

After bumping the drawer closed with her hip, she pulled open another, reached to the back and beneath the sloppily stacked clothing and retrieved two knives in sheaths.

A glance down, to the side of the dresser, reassured her that her scuffed black western boots were also ready.

She set the knives down next to the change of clothes, then looked at herself in the dusty mirror that showed patches where the incessant oil in the atmosphere had soaked in on the backside and refused to depart.

"Hmm."

She fumbled around with the shirt she wore as a nightgown, pinching it and pulling it up until she could take hold of the bottom hem, then she slipped both hands under it.

"Sure. You cum like a maniac, Ham, because you are one. A sky-faring rogue. But I need . . . more."

Holding the shabby fabric up with her right hand, she rubbed downward with the fingertips of her left hand, found a soft spot that got her fingers wet immediately, then inserted two, rubbing her way inside.

"Mm," she said and kept her eyes open only enough to reach through the garment with her other hand to fondle her breasts.

She let her eyes close and whispered, "So soft. Such a gentle touch—don't ever stop."

Her left hand had settled into a rhythm that it liked, and Pauline chuckled and said to her reflection, "Tramp Pauline. Mm-hmm. Oh, yeah."

Eyes closed, breaths short and choppy, Pauline gyrated gently in front of her old mirror, sometimes moaning, until she shuddered out a deep sigh, then opened her eyes to see her mirrored eyes.

"No. Oh, no, just not sexy enough. I have the goddamn place to myself."

She let the shirt drape itself back down over her thighs, scoffed, then picked up her wardrobe change and boots and knives. With all of it piled for one arm to tote, she left her bedroom and hurried across the living area to another door, one with an old-fashioned combination lock.

While spinning the dial each way, hitting the correct numbers, she said, "My room, Ham. You don't need to know why."

After spinning as needed, she pulled on the heavy latch and swung open the thick door made up of several alternating layers of wood planks. Light from behind her was enough that stairs leading down were visible, and she reached for the exact location of a switch, didn't miss it, and lit up the private bunker built apart from the house and dug into the mountain.

"Mm-hmm," she said, grinning, and ventured in far enough to close the door, clunk all of its bolts, then drop a heavy pipe across the door.

* * *

Taking slow steps down into her private space, Pauline looked around at the spacious but dim area with weak electric lights mounted on most of the walls of its irregular shape. Near the far wall sat a typical bed, wider than most and set up neatly but simply with a practical bedspread, a few pillows, and a wood headboard.

Scuffed and gouged wooden nightstands bordered it, each with a drawer and almost touching the wall.

Odd furniture pieces populated some of the bunker, and other areas contained stores and supplies in boxes on pallets, sacks piled on each other, and shelving for smaller items.

Pauline walked toward the bed and put one knee up on it, then looked up, past the rough-hewn timber framing. She focused with an overt smile at the shadows beyond them, up where the darkness concealed the cut mountain ceiling, and let her black, practical change of clothes tumble to the floor.

"Do it right, tramp. You have time."

She stepped back onto the floor and pulled open a drawer of one nightstand beside the bed. Out of there, she lifted a flimsy, silky emerald green babydoll with thin spaghetti straps and made entirely of only the sheerest fabrics.

"Hmm."

She cast aside Ham's black shirt and dropped the lingerie over her head, then fluffed her hair out to cascade over her bare shoulders and a lot of skin that was still exposed on her back. She leaned to each side, observing the bottom hem hanging low enough to almost cover her ass cheeks and only partially hiding her in front.

From farther back in the drawer, she took out two matching high-heeled shoes with ankle straps, then put those on and took a deep breath, watched her breasts rising with it, then let it out.

"No one deserves sexy like this. No one I've ever met."

Standing near the bed again, she lifted her knee up onto the bedspread, and the smooth material of her special wardrobe was short enough that it offered no resistance and left her entire thigh uncovered.

Looking down again, she caressed the smooth skin of her thigh on its inside, then its outside, then used both hands to caress it up and down.

"Hmm. So soft."

She climbed farther onto the bed, on her hands and knees, and arranged two of the pillows up against the headboard, then sat herself close and leaned back into them. With both hands, she hiked the hem of her lingerie higher, taking her time and watching so much more than just her thighs as she revealed herself just a bit at a time.

With the fabric pulled up high enough to advertise her lack of panties, she leaned to one side, toward a nightstand, then sat back up with a button-operated control unit connected with a flexible cable to something high above.

Looking up, smiling and breathing more deeply, she held one of the buttons. A soft whirring came from high up above the rafters, and a cable descended toward her with a loop at its end.

She stared with a calm smile at the sturdy velvet material of the loop, about three fingers wide and with the generous, comfortable nap facing inward.

When it had dropped to level with her face, she took hold of it and pressed the other button.

The motor whined, and the cable climbed back up at an agonizingly slow speed and tried to take the loop with it, and Pauline couldn't stop it easily. But she did stop it, having set the maximum tension the hoist could deliver, and the motor held it there, its ratcheting feature locking it in place, waiting.

Still holding the soft loop, she took her finger off of the button, and the mechanism disengaged, allowing even just the weight of the cable to pull itself and its loop all the way down to her lap, where the soft material lay against her bare thighs.

She tested it again, and it proved itself reliable, letting the slightest weight bring it back down the instant her finger stopped depressing the button.

Putting aside the controls for a moment, Pauline fluffed back her red mane with both hands, then tied a tight ponytail directly on one side. Almost holding her breath and grinning, she took the loop with both hands, placed it down over her head, then popped the tied hair up and over to hang outside of it.

She touched the loop gently with both hands, fingers gliding around its soft inner surface, and positioned it in a precise location around her neck. Then, she reclined against the pillows with the cable loose and running directly up behind her head and angled forward.

Before picking up again the control panel, she reached for both breasts and felt them through the flimsy fabric, squeezing them and pinching her nipples, stretching them forward repeatedly.

Only after she'd retrieved the switch box did she place the palm of her other hand on her belly. Her fingers appeared to slip down of their own volition, and they began a soft touch, barely even a caress, as she got her finger ready on the button.

Tipping her head forward, then shifting it to align the hoist cable properly, Pauline gazed first at her excited nipples, then past them, toward her hand between her thighs, touching herself in just the right ways.

At the same time, she kept a gentle touch of her finger on the hoist's button, and she rubbed it around, playing with the smooth surface. Caressing it too.

Watching her breasts rise and fall with every breath, she depressed the button and the hoist responded instantly. The cable began winding up, and the velvet noose tightened, touching her softly at first, then slowly sliding itself into an unyielding grip.

With the button still down, the cable began to force her head forward even more, and the soft touch around her throat became brutally obstinate. She watched the exact moment when her chest held completely still, no air able to pass in or out of her lungs and leaving her nipples pointing up toward the hoist, as if thanking it for its efforts. Or maybe teasing it and daring it to try for more.

Almost immediately, Pauline let the button pop back out, and she settled back onto the pillows, taking deep breaths and watching her chest heaving from the first brief ordeal.

"This damn world. So uncaring. So brutal."

Still rubbing between her thighs and smiling at the sight of her nipples straining even more against the sheer cloth, she gave herself a more ambitious touch, rubbing up, then down, going in, then back out.

Her breathing picked up its pace, and she fondled the noose button almost as vigorously as she fingered herself, but she didn't press it.

She began to force her wet fingers to move at a speed that was almost frenzied. Her breathing quickened.

"Mm . . . so soft."

She moaned and held the satisfied tone, drawing it out as she held down the button again with a decisive pressure, and the loop shortened itself around her throat, silencing her with a quick, high-pitched gag.

And the hoist complied, lifting her neck and upper back off of the pillows beneath her. When it had reached its set limit, it locked and held her there with her head lifted and tipped forward, her chest still, and her fingers dipping and rubbing.

In a room where nothing broke the silence, not even the slightest of breaths, a ponytailed woman wearing emerald green lingerie and heels held a button down in one hand and brought herself close to an orgasm with the other.

In that silence, unable to make a sound—not even a gasp as the patient motor above the rafters obediently strangled her—she stared at her skillful hand and fingers, rubbing and caressing and slipping in deep as her eyes began to close.

She gave herself the last vigorous strokes and rubs, and her mouth, snarling open in a soundless, ecstatic gasp, quivered as she licked at her lips. The helpful mechanism had tipped her head so far forward that she could have almost kissed her own breasts, sucked on them, licked them as her fingers gave her the final warm and wet strokes, then she pressed down hard, soft fingertips trapping her orgasm and holding it there.

She locked her hand in place, warm and wet high up between her thighs, and held the button with no sign that she entertained even the possibility of releasing it.

She shook gently, spasming and jiggling around her breasts in quick, sporadic gestures, and her eyes opened in only the thinnest of cracks. Her tongue made a feeble attempt to touch them right then, to lick them or suck them through the lingerie, at the moment her fingers had just finished their loving work.

But her tongue only came close, never touched what she'd wanted to taste, then she froze there. Her eyes locked into thin, unblinking slits, and her wet tongue fell out farther, forgetting where it had wanted to lead her eager lips.

Many long seconds passed in that quiet room hidden from the rest of that nightmare world and carved into a mountain.

Her finger's pressure on the control box button trembled, then slipped away, and her falling arm let it go.

The hoist motor's patient locking came to a quick end, and the soft velvet loop strangling the redhead relaxed and began a silent fall toward the bed. The back of Pauline's head rested easily against the propped-up pillows, and her eyes and mouth closed.

The hand between her thighs, fingers wet and glistening in the dim light, fell to one side and remained still.

A long, quiet moment passed, then Pauline's chest rose and fell with her easy, satisfied breathing.

* * *

Pauline's lungs emptied out a deep breath, and she reached up to rub her eyes before opening them. Without looking, she pushed aside the hoist controls and sent one hand to her breasts and the other back where it had been.

"Mm," she said, "that's the way."

She rubbed and played with herself halfheartedly for a few moments, then sighed and sat up. Careful to not snag her ponytail, she cast off the loop from around her neck, then held the button long enough to send it back up into the shadows.

After stretching, then swinging her legs over to sit on the edge of the bed, she said, almost laughing, "Like they say, if you want something done right . . ."

She stood up and got wobbly, which made her lean back onto the bed.

"Whoa. That was a good one."

She rested there, doing nothing but breathing, then stood cautiously and found that she'd regained enough balance. Stooping down to scoop up her clothes and gear, she rose back up and dumped it all on the bed.

The soft lingerie came off easily, then dropped to the floor. She flipped around the ordinary clothes, then scoffed.

"No panties. I always forget, don't I?"

She stretched on the thin leather pants, then worked her way into the t-shirt. Seated on the bed, she took the socks out of the boots, put them on, then the boots.

Standing again, she clipped one knife onto the boot at the inside of her calf, then wiggled the tight pants down over it. The other found an accessible location at her hip, clipping to the belt and waistband, and she dropped the t-shirt over it.

From the end table, she snatched up a black ball cap that hinted that it might have been a different color before exposure to the ubiquitous oil everywhere, even high on a mountain. She undid her hair, fluffed it all back, then donned the cap.

A quick walk got her to the far wall, the one deepest inside Ham's mountain, and she reached around above the top shelf of a bookcase until she found a small lever. She gave it a pull, then swung the bookcase out to reveal a square opening in the wall and a large wooden box just beyond the wall.

She left the bookcase as it was, crawled inside with enough room to sit comfortably, and said, "Like always, no fucking power failures, please."

To the side were several buttons, and she pressed one. The box lurched for an instant, then began to drop silently toward the base of the mountain far beneath Ham's house high in the dark sky.

Chapter 23 – You Can Survive this Shit

"I won't talk anymore!" Igor said, his back against the wall after his failed attempt to rape Scarlet.

"Not unless I tell you to," she said, her voice like sweet warm molasses, but her breaths were quickening.

"Okay."

Still staring at him, she shook her head and sneered while taking rapid shallow breaths, and she said, in a strained and grating voice no longer convincing and commanding, "I barely survived getting in this building."

She snapped her head to look all around, then squinted at a small boarded-over window.

Glaring at Igor again, she said, "Some kind of monster pigs were trying to kill me. Out there!"

She jabbed a finger toward the window, causing Igor's head to turn, but the other one stayed still and watched her indifferently.

Looking up quickly, she pointed and said, "And some kind of giant . . . I don't know, some kind of black monsters with wings. They tried to get me too! They almost did!"

Igor faced Scarlet again, his head leaning to one side and his eyes wincing closed. His eyelids fluttered like he was expecting a hard smack any second.

"Then . . . you. What you tried to do to me. Dammit, I've already been raped. The bastard tied me up and raped me."

Snarling, she scattered papers and trash around her, shuffling through it all, and found a wooden chair leg with the heavy end showing burn damage.

While stooping to get a grip on it, she said, "And you would have raped me too."

With a solid grip on the dense piece of wood, she stood slowly and turned to face him.

"Goddammit, I will not be raped again. Never again."

She raised her club and took the few steps needed to stand over the cowering mutant. Her left hand pointed at his regular head, and she raised the blunt instrument high with her right.

"Speak. Tell me why I shouldn't beat you to death right here."

Igor shook, and his eyes stared up at her through tiny crevasses.

"Speak, dammit. I've already killed once and dammit, I'll do it again."

"You should kill me! I don't deserve to live! Kill me!"

Scarlet aimed the stick for the head that was speaking and shook quietly, straining and ready to swing it. Then, she shifted just enough that her strike would crush the other one, which only gazed at her calmly.

She shook from holding back her clobbering, then gasped and threw the club across the room.

Igor sighed and let his heads hang forward.

"I . . . don't deserve mercy. I have no value."

Sobbing softly, Scarlet backed away from him until she could drop down into an old upholstered chair, sending puffs of dust into the stale air. She glared at him while her breaths slowed, and he covered his natural eyes with both hands.

Scarlet scoffed at the second head still watching her, then looked up at the ceiling.

After her breathing had regained some normalcy, she tipped her head, stared at him for a second, then spoke in a calmer voice.

"I'd rather see that nasty extra head growth than what you call your stick. Put that god-awful thing away."

He forced his lips to stay together, tucked the less eager appendage back inside his pants, and gave the zipper a forceful tug upward.

"Better. You will always tell me the truth. Got that?"

He nodded and said, "Okay."

"First, do you—no, I just can't."

She looked around the cluttered and dirty room until she saw a mostly intact plastic bag halfway under another chair. She looked back at him.

"Your buddy, there. Does he need to breath?"

He shook his head quickly, which jostled around the other head, too, sending its tiny pupils, that appeared to float in some kind of milk, in lazy circles until they could focus again on Scarlet.

"You can answer me out loud. Can he talk?"

"No. I don't even know if he's a he. He doesn't have a stick. And he can't use—"

"Stop."

He stopped, and Scarlet walked over, reached down for the plastic bag, then stood and returned to stand closer to Igor.

"Don't move."

He shook his head once and continued to look up at her as she slipped the bag over the second head and cinched up its drawstring.

"That helps."

Igor nodded.

She coughed, then calmed herself and spoke like sugary syrup dripping from her lips and into his ears.

"You will always do whatever I say, no matter what."

He nodded, and the plastic bag nodded too.

"From this moment forward, you are my slave."

Both heads agreed.

She coughed again, then talked in a normal, non-honey way.

"You will do what I say, when I say it."

A head and a plastic bag nodded.

"Sit."

He slid down the wall, not having far to go, and rested his back against it. Scarlet walked across the room, turned, and sat again in the dingy chair which coughed up a fresh cloud of dust.

"You're Igor?"

He nodded.

"Talk. Tell me your story. How did you get . . . like that?"

"I never deserved anything. I've always been useless ever since—"

"No, the, uh,"—she winced and pointed at the bagged head—"thing you got growing there."

"Oh, that's from when I worked at the reactor. There's—may I ask your name?"

"No."

"Okay. That place is scary. But it's still too good for me! Sorry, I yelled. Um, scary radiation all over, except where bosses hide."

"There are more than one boss?"

"I don't know! I made that up! Sorry!"

"Stop yelling. It's fine. Go on."

"Radiation blasted me. I started to itch. It started like a blister— a big one! It swelled up quick, and I had another head."

"And how did you get out of there?"

"They chased me out. My other eyes were scaring people. They made me walk to the city."

"And you found this building?"

"This one and the next one over. There are better bugs in this one. They're crunchy. Are you some kind of bug?"

"What? What a stupid thing to say! Stop talking!"

He slumped his head forward, looked down, and blinked his eyes like they were too heavy to hold open.

"But you're still my slave."

The heavy head and the bagged head both nodded.

* * *

"Does this open?"

Scarlet had left the dusty chair in Igor's lair to walk over to the window shuttered on the inside. Igor had barely tipped his head up enough to eyeball her as she'd walked across the room, then turned back toward him.

"Not a good idea. Too low. Close to the street."

"Pigs?" she said, running her fingers along the rough edge of the planks.

"Boars."

"What?"

"They're boars. Some say they're left over from farming long ago."

"Farming? In a place where it's always dark? I've been here a while, and I still haven't seen the sun."

"You won't. There isn't any. Not here."

"No moon or stars either?"

"Nothing but rock."

He pointed up.

"The sky is rock."

"We're in some kind of cave? Some horrible underground place with fires too?"

"Yes. Maybe the reactor gave light once and helped raise pigs. Then, they got loose and ate and ate and—"

"Okay. I get it. What about up there,"—she pointed toward the ceiling—"some kind ugly black things, with wings like—"

"Bats. Some kind of bats. Big and hungry."

"They started out normal, then kept eating?"

He shrugged, tipping his extra head to the side.

"No one knows anything about them."

She scoffed at the boards keeping the room hidden from massive, savage boars and facing away from Igor, she untied her cloth belt, repositioned her shirt, then gave it a fresh knot.

"Clothes. You need clothes?"

"I didn't bring my credit card. Not the way I got here."

"It's how we all got here."

She turned, facing the mutant again, and said, "You? Sex and death?"

"Um, I kind of . . . I never really, I mean, with any—"

She laughed and said, "Oh, don't tell me. You were still a virgin, playing with yourself, and somehow, you got yourself killed?"

He hung his head but managed a meager smile.

"Yes. I heard the first gunshot, but I was so close. Couldn't stop. The next one whizzed through the wall and got me, I guess. I don't remember."

"That's pathetic."

"Yes. Can I call you Mistress?"

"No. Don't call me anything. I still might kill you. Again."

"Okay. No credit needed for a crafter."

"What?"

"No money, no credit card, just a crafter to make clothes for you. She would come here. Would you like?"

"What, like a seamstress?"

"Uh-huh. Very skilled. In high demand."

"Sure. Call her."

"Can't. I'll go. I know where lots of things hide."

"Wait. She's a thing?"

"Uh, maybe not. Looks normal."

"No extra heads?"

Igor laughed, bouncing both heads, and said, "No! Just one!"

"Fine. Go."

"Don't wait here."

"I'll wait wherever I damn well—"

"Yes! You can! I only meant—"

"Stop yelling."

"Okay. I meant that you'd like it better in the next building. It's connected—a hole in the wall at the end of the hallway. Then, upstairs. Higher up."

"Why?"

"Safer. No one knows about it."

"Alright. Where?"

"Take the stairs. Last door—"

"No elevator?"

"Cables cut long ago. Last door before the roof. May I go?"

"No. Show me the room. Then, you can bring the crafter, as you call her, up there when you return."

"Okay."

He rose and began shuffling toward the door to the hallway, and Scarlet followed closely behind him. She exited the room after him, then slipped to one side to watch him lock the door. He led her down the low building's hallway, through a hole gouged into the connecting wall, then to the stairwell of the much taller building.

The small man with two heads exerted himself climbing up, but Scarlet gracefully took two steps at a time, placing her boots without looking and barely making a sound as they traveled up many flights of serrated metal stair treads, each flight divided in two and hosting a narrow landing.

With several flights of stairs waiting in shadows above them, Igor pointed toward the darkness of the hallway high above the streets of the city.

"There."

"Go."

He began his tired walk toward the far end, and Scarlet took long strides, her legs strong and sure, to follow several steps behind him.

"Here," he said, pointing at a wide and scraped up metal door.

"Open it."

He leaned in close to see the dial, gave it several turns in alternating directions, then was about to reach for the doorknob. But Scarlet grabbed his wrist.

"Sorry!"

"Don't yell. You will tell me the combination."

"I will. Inside? Safer."

She said, "Sure," and followed him into the room.

* * *

Scarlet's eyes adjusted quickly to the room that had only weak traces of the hallway's feeble light slipping in.

Across the room sat two high-backed chairs fitted with a dark blue fabric, and a narrow, high wooden table rested between them. On it sat a once-fancy candelabra with a collection of slender tapers with white wicks ready for a match.

Directly above the chairs and table, a large, dusty painted portrait of a grim older woman stared back toward the doorway. And to the right of her sullen visage, a tall and wide section of the wall bore a neat array of thick and wide wooden planks, all but one bolted to the wall and spaced closely enough to allow only thin slivers of firelight from the next roof over, across the street, to slice into the dark.

The one unbolted plank was hinged at one end and was held tightly closed by a heavy draw bolt.

Igor looked first at Scarlet's eyes, then in the direction she looked.

"Keeps things out."

"Good."

The rest of the room housed a variety of tasteful furniture whose time had passed and had been busy gathering dust. Many of the other tables held vases and other items, and everything appeared to have remained untouched since the room had been abandoned.

When Scarlet looked at the wall on each side of the doorway, tipping her head, Igor said, "Each has its own."

He looked up, then she did, too, and they both studied the orderly pattern of large squares, decorative and once fashionable, and the single light fixture in the middle of each. Thin, dusty chains hung from each, their ends just low enough to be reached.

Scarlet took a step inside, and Igor backed himself out to the hallway, saying, "I go. Spinning the dial, either side, locks it."

"Wait."

"I'll wait."

She walked to the closest overhead light and pulled the chain, blinking it on and casting enough light to see better what she'd already seen.

She turned and said, using her warm, thick, syrupy voice, "Now, go. You will return."

"I will. Yes."

"With the crafter for me."

"With the crafter for you."

He bowed and shuffled backwards toward the stairs, and Scarlet closed the door quietly, then gave the dial a spin and sighed at the sound of the lock mechanism engaging.

She turned and gave the dusty floor its first set of footprints as she walked toward the shutter. The bolt slid open easily, and a gentle tug squealed the hinges to give her a view outside the building.

Straight across the street and higher up, above the roofs, two shifting orange glows tried and failed to break the black sky's grip.

The windows of the buildings showed either nothing but darkness inside or just the street side of makeshift shutters like in her room.

Many levels down, the tops of a line of streetlights were tiny dark pupils set in the centers of dim circles, showing spotted and littered sidewalks and curbs alongside the street pavement. On the far sides of the lighted areas, the circles appeared folded up onto the bottoms of the brick buildings.

Minutes passed as Scarlet studied not just the street below but the tops of the buildings and many of the windows facing the street. Farther to the left, several squares stuck to the sides of the blocky structures advertised by their weak, slightly bright coloring that something, perhaps with only candles like she had in her room, was eking out some sort of existence there.

To the right, the building faces were unbroken black, but several more fires burned above, behind parapets, and sent up thin snakes of smoke which stretched straight and true up toward whatever ceiling covered that world, fading and merging into the night in the still air.

A slight motion caused Scarlet to look down, where a small shape was hobbling on her side of the street, ambling hurriedly from one light circle to the next, dwelling longer in the shade between them.

"Huh. Igor."

After he'd blended himself into the black beyond the last dim glow that she could see, she pivoted around and studied her room.

To her right sat the two blue chairs and a grim painting on the wall above them. She stepped out far enough to scrutinize it, then approached it for a better look.

The woman wore clothing that gave hints of a uniform, perhaps military, and her hair could have been gray, but the entire thing was mostly gray from the accumulated dust. Scarlet reached up and dragged a finger across the bottom while holding a gaze that seemed to reach out from another time, another century.

Holding up her finger, she saw a thick cake of the dust, but she looked past it after a second and focused on a box of strike-anywhere matches, its label showing some sort of words and pictures that had long ago faded.

Picking it up caused the sagging box to pull itself apart without any sound, and the matches fell and scattered across the table.

"Please, still work," she said, pausing before picking one up. "For when the reactor goes out."

She dragged the match head across what was left of the thin strip of abrasive material from the box, but she'd held it too far from the head, and the stick bent, then quietly folded.

"Dammit."

She picked up another, held it close but stopped to look back at the single ceiling light working to fill the spacious room, then snapped her head toward the shutter planks over the window.

Where she'd left one open.

"Oh, God. No!"

She dropped the match, scurried the few steps needed, then pushed the plank back into its place.

"Oh God, think, Scarlet! You have to think!"

With the ceiling fixture glowing only for the room and not as a beacon to whatever might be hunting outside, she dragged the small table closer while holding the candelabra and matches in her other hand. She arranged all of it near the plank end that could be swung into the room, successfully lit one of the matches, then walked to the light pull chain and switched it off.

Walking in her own circle of light across the dusty floor, scoffing at the footprints that she'd just left, she retraced her path and again stood near the shuttered window.

A quick shake snuffed the tiny flame, and she tossed it to the floor. Creaking open the plank door with nothing but night behind her, she again studied her neighborhood, with most of her surveillance aimed at the street and sidewalk.

Far to the right, a subtle movement was gaining some shape in the gloom, and Scarlet fixed her eyes on it. It shifted around as it approached, moving from one streetlight circle to the next.

When it was closer, she saw that the figure kept itself near the buildings and lingered in the shade between lights, much like Igor had done. But whatever it was made steady progress and would pass Scarlet's window soon.

"Oh, no. What is this? Can't be Igor already."

She saw another shape, moving much more quickly, coming from the same direction. The first shape had moved into one of the nearby circles of light, and its stride caused a bunch of hair behind it to sway with every step.

"A woman? Out there?"

But the other shape, the one moving in more quickly, seemed content with hurrying through shade as well as light, and it was getting closer to the woman with swaying hair.

"No. Oh, no . . ."

She leaned her head out where glass had long ago been broken out, but she froze there and never screamed a warning.

Instead, she got her hand on the matches, then swung closed the plank. A quick strike gave her some fire, and she started walking toward the door to the hallway.

"Good. You're learning, Scarlet. You can survive this shit."

Chapter 24 – This Place Is Just Too Brutal

Scarlet dropped the lit match in the hall and rushed to quietly close the door and give the dial a quick spin, then sprinted through the dark hallway toward the stairs. Each of the landings leading down to street level had a light fixture in the ceiling above, and many of them were functioning. Some flickered, and even the ones that burned steadily gave off only enough light to hint at the metal stairs and railings.

She started with one step at a time, sometimes jumping the last few to the landing or to the hallway floor. After a couple of flights, she began skipping steps, and her boots landed heavily with each jolting placement.

After a few more flights, she still skipped every other step, but every movement had become strong and sure, almost gliding her along, and her work boots made barely any sound as she whisked herself down and down and finally jumped the last six steps to the floor.

Running through the wrecked lobby toward the building entrance, she passed the hole in the wall leading toward Igor's lair without giving it a glance. Ahead, through the building's glass doors, only the faintest of light from high up on the lampposts kept the panes from looking like they'd been painted black.

Scarlet checked behind her and saw that there was even less light there, then she eased open one of the doors and leaned her head clear of it. Her eyes immediately fixed on the lone traveler with bouncing hair who was just then almost even with her but across the street. With a closer view, she noticed that the long hair hung down from under a dark cap.

The door's opening caused that stranger to stop, half in shadow and half in light, and stare directly at Scarlet, who waved her hand up and down, then pointed repeatedly down the street, toward the right at whatever was also out there and coming their way.

The figure half in shadow looked, then turned back to Scarlet and nodded. She held up a finger for a second, and Scarlet nodded and slipped quietly back inside. From there, she watched the woman on the sidewalk keep walking as she had been until she was too far for Scarlet to see from the recessed entrance way.

A few seconds later, Scarlet gasped and spun herself around, placing her back against the wall next to the door. She checked the backlighting again, then leaned just enough to view the lone hunter on the trail of someone with long hair.

Moving in a deliberate way, swaying slightly to its left then its right, the shape fled through a patch of light and let the darkness in between swallow it up.

Scarlet held her breath and watched.

It emerged in the next lit region, then came to an abrupt stop, and Scarlet covered her mouth and spun herself back out of sight. She'd seen something like a tall, fit man striding along on his thick legs and wearing only ratty pants that had one leg longer than the other.

Before he had stopped to look her way and sniff all around, he'd turned quickly to look ahead, then behind himself, each time whipping his long and rigid, nearly horizontal tail from side to side.

She let her breath out slowly, then pulled in another, but a rapid series of loud snorts outside made her jerk herself back out of sight.

A few seconds passed, and Scarlet leaned for another look, just in time to see the pointy end of the man's stiff tail, straight out behind him, as he crept into the next shadow, still moving in the direction of the long-haired traveler who had opted to lead the man with a tail away from Scarlet.

Again out of sight with her back to the wall, Scarlet squatted down, leaning against the wall, and let her breaths slow to a normal pace.

But a minute later, her heart began a fresh thumping at a rapid, subdued rapping on the glass door.

She tipped enough to peek around the corner and saw first a head with long hair trapped against the glass, then a shapely body with tight black pants squeezing against the door. The woman didn't look inside—just turned her head from one side to the other, watching the street.

Scarlet walked closer, then tapped on her side of the glass, causing Pauline to turn enough to see her and smile. She kept holding Scarlet's gaze as she grasped the door handle and swung it out just enough to talk to her.

"Permission to get my ass in there?"

Scarlet said, "Of course, get in here. Who was that?"

Swinging the door wider, Pauline entered, saying, "None of them have names. They can barely talk."

"What are you talking about? That man, you mean?"

With her back against the wall on one side of the doorway and Scarlet on the other side, Pauline looked from Scarlet's eyes, down along her makeshift robe that didn't hide her figure well, and past her khaki work pants to her boots. She looked back up top and tipped her head to smile at Scarlet's thick black hair.

Scarlet said, "You done?"

Pauline got her eyes to look again at Scarlet's and said, "You've been through some shit."

Scarlet looked down, then scoffed at the blood and gore drying on her pants. She only nodded, then looked up when Pauline spoke again.

"Keeping things clean is a fucking challenge. Not the best fashion you got there but about right for this scary fucked up place."

"Thanks. Scary is right. Why didn't you just run inside? I would have."

Pauline scoffed and said, "Good way to get dead. I mean, deader. Shit, I don't know. Hey, just trying to be polite. I'm Pauline."

"Hi. I'm Scarlet."

"A genuine pleasure to meet you."

Scarlet chuckled, stayed against her wall, and said, "Because a man wearing only pants was chasing you."

"Wasn't totally a man."

"What? Oh, that tail."

"That's part of it, sure. This place is full of freaks. Some way worse than that one."

"Oh. Yeah, I know. That's not good."

"No," Pauline said, and her eyes roamed for another complete scan of Scarlet from top to bottom to top. "No, I mean it. Even without something chasing me, it's nice to meet you."

She looked around while saying, "This your place?"

Scarlet hung her head and sighed, then said, "I wouldn't know where else to go. I'm kind of new."

"Oh, I kind of figured. Well, looks like a damn nice hideout. Show me around?"

"Um . . ."

Scarlet looked up at Pauline, then scanned all around inside the building, everywhere she could see.

She snapped her eyes back to Pauline when she said, "Before some goddamn monkey man tries to fuck me in the ass, please?"

"Why are you calling him a monkey man? Because of that tail?"

"Huh. It isn't just that. And I'm not kidding. All of them will fuck anyone's ass if they get half a chance."

A laugh slipped out of Scarlet, and she said, "Can't have that. Sure, come on in. You're the only reason I've had to laugh since I got here."

*　*　*

They walked side by side farther into the building, and each of them glanced over her shoulder a few times, watching the doorway and street beyond.

"You're new, huh?"

"Yeah. I haven't been here long, but it's been an absolute nightmare already."

"This place doesn't waste much time. It gets right the fuck to it. How bad of a nightmare? You been alright?"

Scarlet glanced quickly at Pauline, then fixed her eyes straight ahead again.

"Uh, just bad. You know. But I'm alright."

"Well, good. I can't even remember how long I've been here, but I can sure as fuck say that it's been too fucking long."

"How do you survive this place? It's just one nightmare after another."

"You've noticed. Yeah, it's—"

They were passing the ripped open passageway to Igor's other building, and Scarlet stopped and stared at it. Only a few stray stabs of their light reached through, and it looked like nothing but a dark cave.

Pauline saw it and said, "That your place? Through there?"

Scarlet scoffed and said, "No. That's where a, um, kind of a strange little—"

"A freak? A goddamn freak? Don't be shy, Scarlet. Just say it."

"Alright. Yeah, a freak named Igor. He spends time there in that next building."

"What's his deal?"

They'd stopped and faced each other, both looking to their sides repeatedly.

"He has an extra head."

"Could be worse. At least he didn't have two dicks."

Scarlet's eyes stretched wide, and she said, "That can happen? Oh God, just that one was bad enough."

She reached for Scarlet's shoulders, but she flinched back, then took a step backwards.

"Ooh, yeah. Sorry. Trust is in short supply in this fucking dump. For good reason. Yes, Scarlet, it can happen. How is it that you know for sure this freak had at least one?"

Scarlet rolled her eyes and resumed walking toward the stairwell, and Pauline hurried to walk beside her.

"He tried to rape me."

"Better than killing you, I suppose. But he probably would have done that too."

"Nice."

They stopped at the bottom of the first flight of stairs.

"Up there? That's where you've dug yourself in?"

Shaking her head, still looking up, Scarlet said, "No, not really. I haven't had time to. I just was checking it out when I saw you out there and that man that was—"

"Horny for my ass?"

She turned toward Pauline, grinning, and said, "Yeah. That man with a tail."

"Huh. Looking for my tail. Better than a boar trying that."

"You've seen them too? They're huge!"

"And smart and mean. And always so fucking hungry. Stay the fuck out of their path, Scarlet."

"I plan to. Those bats too. They're as big as the boars."

"Ah, yeah, those fucking bats. The stories I could tell. Why don't we get up to your place before the boars and bats chew on us while some goddamn monkey is fucking me in the ass?"

Scarlet almost doubled over with laughter, then looked at Pauline while shaking her head and smiling.

"God, I needed to hear something like that. Thanks, Pauline."

"You're very welcome, Scarlet. Humor. Takes the edge off of the total fucked uppedness of this place."

She winked at Scarlet, then began a steady climb, but Scarlet easily and smoothly took two steps at a time and passed her by.

"Some damn strong legs you got there, hiding away under that shitty reactor issued khaki."

"You're right. I don't know why, but they feel stronger lately too. Huh."

Scarlet stopped at one of the landings to let Pauline catch up.

Taking those few steps to join her, Pauline said, "Those pants aren't very flattering but Scarlet, I have to say, your figure is quite stunning."

"How can you tell? These pants are so—"

"Hey, what do you think I've been checking out while following you up the stairs?"

"Oh. Um, well, thanks. Anyway, Igor, the little guy with—"

"Two heads. He's little?"

"Oh, yeah. Weird too. But I sent him out for—"

"Wait. Just stop."

Breathing more heavily than Scarlet, she stood facing her on a dimly lit landing, almost high enough in the stairwell to find Scarlet's door.

"He tried to rape you, then you sent him out shopping for you? You bossed his rapist ass around after that?"

"Somehow, yeah. It was weird. He just, uh, started listening to me. I wasn't going to complain."

"Weird is right. So, what fool's errand did you send him on?"

"A crafter? That's what he called her. He said she could make clothes for me."

"I've heard of crafters in the city. Sure. Well, that's nice. I'd say, don't compromise. Boss that crafty bitch around like you do that two-headed, one-dicked little rapist freak, and get her to—"

Scarlet was holding Pauline's gaze and laughing too hard for her to finish her thought.

She grinned back at Scarlet and said, "I get a little carried away sometimes. Sorry."

"Don't be. You were saying I should get the crafter to make whatever clothes I want?"

"Oh, damn right, Scarlet."

They began walking again, and Scarlet kept herself to one step at a time, matching Pauline's pace.

"The only kind of honesty around here that matters is brutal honesty. So, what I'm saying is that none of us can expect to survive even another goddamn minute. I say you should get extreme and get some clothes that are just fun."

"But if I have to go out for food, and run from boars and bats, and—"

"Butt fucking monkeys. Don't forget them 'cause they sure as fuck won't forget you."

She laughed and said, "How could I forget them? But I need practical clothes, Pauline, don't I?"

"Not if you hardly ever leave your building."

"So, I'll just keep sending Igor out for whatever I need?"

"Yeah. Shit, let him get fucked by a monkey. Freaks probably like that kind of stuff."

"You might be right. Here's my door."

They stopped, and Scarlet spent a few seconds dialing the combination. She pushed it in, and they waited there, looking into a cavernous room that swallowed the tiny bits of light leaking in from the hallway.

* * *

"This is promising," Pauline said, then led the way in.

She fumbled around on the walls, like Scarlet had done.

"Uh-uh. The ceiling lights all have their own switches."

"Oh, that's kind of nice."

She stretched up and switched on the nearest one, giving the room a dull warmth.

"I don't know how many work."

"When the reactor craps out, which it always does, none of them will work. You'll need—"

She saw the candelabra on the table near the shuttered window.

"That," she said, pointing. "That's where you saw me? There's a window behind all that wood?"

"Yeah. Well, there's no glass. One of the boards is hinged, and I opened it to check out the outside."

Scarlet had followed Pauline inside and eased the door closed. They both heard the lock click into place when Scarlet spun the dial. Pauline scoffed at the sight of the setup.

"I'm a prisoner. Unless I can overpower you or sweet talk that combination out of you."

Scarlet laughed and said, "Oh, no, Pauline. I'm not interested in trapping anyone. Still, though, I hope you can stay at least a few minutes."

"Sure. Only because I don't want—"

"A monkey man fucking your ass."

Pauline pointed and said, "You're catching on. I'd recommend using the F-word every fucking chance you fucking get."

"Like that?"

"Fucking right."

Scarlet let a deep breath leak out, then walked over to the pair of dusty blue chairs guarding a flat, brooding woman also covered in dust.

"You alright?"

"Yeah. Yeah, I'm fine."

"Good. Keep a positive attitude. Monkeys be damned."

She watched and waited for Scarlet to smile, but she didn't, so she took a walk around the room, investigating what she could.

"This is good, Scarlet. You can secure this room pretty well. There's only that one door and when you reinforce that, your ass is safe enough in here."

Scarlet looked around and said, "Some cleaning would help. It could be move livable."

"Sure. And send that little mutant rapist fucker of yours out for whatever else you need. Set yourself up."

"I think he would do it, Pauline. I don't know why, but he seems like he'll do anything I tell him to do."

"Even with you just in that outfit?"

Scarlet looked down and smiled.

"Yeah. But he liked me better when I had nothing on."

"Oh, don't say it. You stripped for the freak with two heads? That's what got the fucker fired up and—"

"No! I'd never do that. I'm married, Pauline, but I, um, don't know if I'll ever see my husband again."

"Did he come here with you?"

"I think so but not at the same time. I think he ended up working at the reactor."

"Scarlet, I say this as someone who already cares about you: try to not think about him too much. This place is just too . . . brutal."

She hung her head and stared at her lap, but she didn't sob, and no tears made a dash for her cheeks.

Pauline sat in the other chair, then held its arms with both hands and scraped it across the floor closer to Scarlet's.

"Hey, you might still find him. What the fuck do I know?"

"You knew enough to get away from that man."

"Told you. Not completely a man. A mix."

"Oh."

Pauline smiled, still looking at Scarlet's tipped head, and said, "It'd be different if he at least bought me some fucking dinner."

Scarlet shook with a quiet laugh, then looked up and held Pauline's steady gaze.

"I shouldn't even laugh, Pauline. I don't know what any of this is."

"No one does. Try not to dwell on it."

Scarlet sighed noisily while leaning back into the old cushion, then put her forearms on the chair's arms.

"What am I going to do, Pauline? I can't stay here. I just can't. How am I going to survive here?"

Pauline placed her hand over Scarlet's, and they kept looking into each other's eyes before they both focused on her hand on Scarlet's.

"You survive by staying inside as much as you can."

At the same time, they looked at each other again.

"And Scarlet?"

"Yeah, Pauline?"

She rubbed Scarlet's hand gently a few times, then reached her fingers around to hold it lightly.

"When you find a friend, you keep that friend, and you hold that friend just as close as you can. Like your fucking life depends on it."

Chapter 25 – You Need a Practical Fucker

"That city," Junior said, turning his head to one side to chew off a piece of the half-animal he carried on his shoulder. "It's so far."

His thighs like tree trunks stretched and were about to rip open his blood-stained khakis as he stomped his boots on the dry but sometimes oily and spongy ground.

A few pinpoint lights twinkled among the jagged shapes planted in the mostly flat ground against a backdrop even blacker. The burning sea was too far behind him to light his path but when he turned enough, he could still see a crescent of orange glow on the horizon.

"Huh. That's far away too."

The heat, though, never respected any amount of distance, and none of his steps brought him anywhere cooler. Bare from his belt up, his muscles rippled in the dark and shed streams of sweat down, soaking all around his pants, some of it shaking off to wet the scrabble beneath his boots.

A low growl up ahead got his attention, and he stopped, but he didn't stop chewing. Waiting to hear more, he gnawed off another bloody bite and packed his cheeks, then waited quietly.

Out of the gloom emerged a humongous shape that blocked most of the city's lights. As it drew nearer, Junior, holding the meat on his left shoulder and the sword in his right, blinked and tipped his head around as he watched its progress toward him.

Close enough to pick up traces of the burning ocean's orange light, a giant pig head stared at him, its jaws working and guttural grunts vibrating its throat.

"You're big."

The boar didn't answer, just kept approaching, and Junior pointed the sword at it, which made it stop.

"You're a lot of meat."

With a sound like iron machinery digging into the ground, it stomped one of its front hooves, then scraped it front to back repeatedly.

Junior frowned at the beast, then turned his head to look at the half body heaved onto his shoulder, then back at the boar.

"You're hungry? Me too. I'm always hungry."

The monstrous pig lowered its snout and snorted, scattering anything dry enough to not stick to the patches of oil everywhere.

"Oh, okay. You want to play? Bad idea, pig."

He cocked back his sword, ready to swing it, and waited.

"I cut things all the time. I bite them."

The boar charged, and Junior wasn't quick enough for the thing's blinding dash. But he did duck low to evade its snapping jaws, only to get pummeled by its burly front leg. It hit him hard enough that he lost his meat and his sword, but he was quick enough to reach around it like he was hugging a tree.

"Hey! Put me down!"

The unwieldy, ravenous animal reared up on its hind legs, snapping its front legs high into the night air.

"This is isn't fun! Stop playing!"

The leg Junior was riding jerked upward hard enough that he lost his grip around the meaty post coated with short bristle and oil.

"Whoa!"

He found himself hanging from one of the boar's ears, which was also slick with crude. But he hung on and got jostled around enough that he flipped up and onto its back. He saw the beast's other ear and grabbed it, leaving him riding on its back with a desperate grip on each of its ears.

"Hey! Wait till I tell Mama!"

The boar raised itself up again, squealing, and tried to shake loose the sweaty monster man from his back, but Junior held on tight.

"I bite Mama! I'll bite you too!"

Holding the ears of a bucking, squealing, gigantic pig, Junior got his jaws close enough to bite and came back with only a smattering of stiff, oily fur on his lips and tongue.

He coughed and tried spitting it out, and he began to reprimand the beast.

"That's not good! Stop being oily and furry!"

The thing shook and snorted, stamping its hooves into the ground and kicking stones and soil up into clouds.

"I'm going to eat you! All of you!"

He tried biting again and drove his face into the thing's back, scraping his teeth on mostly oily fur but sometimes able to bite into and stretch up a thick layer of flesh.

But it slipped right back out, leaving him spitting and coughing.

"Bad pig! You're a bad pig!"

It snorted and bucked.

"I'm telling Mama!"

It tried shaking him loose, then crashed down on its side, quaking the rough land around them. And just as it began to roll over and onto its attacker, Junior screamed while letting go and tumbling off to the side.

"Hey! That would hurt!"

He scrambled farther away from it, and it kept rolling until all four legs were close and pointed at him.

Then, it squealed and kicked all of them, the ones closest to the ground digging trenches and flinging stones at Junior.

"Hey! Stop that!"

He kept backing away, and the boar stayed on its side, squirming and squealing as its sharp hooves jabbed and swiped at him.

"Okay!" Junior laughed, "Okay, you win!"

He kept laughing and backing away, and the bloated body kept kicking its way closer to him.

"Stop! I won't eat you!"

The boar stopped and turned its snout toward him. Eyes that glowed with dim, orange reflected light stared at him, and air whistled in and out of its nostrils, holes in its snout big enough for Junior to jam his head inside.

"Okay, I won't tell Mama either."

The pig rolled away, crushing stones and flattening everything beneath it, then stood and looked at Junior for only a second.

Then, it turned and ran, giving Junior the final sight of a spindly, curly little tail high above the ground as it got carried along by thundering hooves toward a black horizon.

"I still have meat," he said and picked up the body part with bites removed randomly all over it.

Heaving that over his shoulder, he leaned and picked up his sword.

"And I still have my sword."

He blew out one sharp breath, then the rest that followed were calm and steady, showing no sign of the battle that he'd just fought.

"And there's still a Scarlet there. In the city. Scarlet killed Mama. She's a wench."

Dragging the sword's point and leaving a meandering rut, he continued on toward the dark buildings with a few points of light.

"Don't be a bug, Mama."

* * *

As the large round wicker basket swayed easily every time Ziggy gave the burning pot's spout a quick blast, Ham stared out into the darkness trapped beneath the thick layer of rock high above them.

To his left, the burning sea that stretched to the horizon with no sign of anything not aflame, kissed his cheek with barely noticeable heat. To his right, too far away to even approximate its size, another fire burned. Black dots circling it in stuttering paths made no sounds, or they were too distant to hear.

"Damn city," he said, looking down, then spat over the basket's rim.

Far below, what few lights drew power from the reactor could have been pinholes in a pattern of black shapes and gray shapes and thin black lines running everywhere through them.

Some of the buildings hinted at the presence of life there, evidenced by the flickering orange lights—fires in barrels—that sent up, in straight, largely undisturbed lines, thin strings of white smoke.

As Ziggy piloted them silently above the cityscape, they sometimes passed the smoke as it sought the jagged ceiling above, quiet columns that accepted the occasional accidental severing by a basket or a balloon, then quickly resumed their steady lengthening upward.

"Ziggy," Ham called, tipping his head to one side while still scanning all around, ever alert.

"Yeah?"

"I'd leave this shithole in a heartbeat."

"Can't. You know that."

"I know. I'd just find my sorry ass dead up there again. Do you suppose anyone up there even knows about this place?"

"No. Unless Risk told them."

"Yeah, that bastard. I don't know anyone besides him that can travel there and get his ass back here. It's weird shit."

"Yeah. He's different."

"Pauline's kind of—uh-oh. Silent running, Ziggy. Traffic."

"I see it."

The navigator slipped the lid over the steady flames inside the pot, then reached down to snap shut the pot lantern too. They became a silent, invisible vessel drifting with whatever thrust Ziggy had aimed for them before the call for going dark.

Directly ahead, a small round shape drifted from right to left, backlit by an ocean of fire. If the navigator of that craft had been using their own fire, giving sideways blasts from its horizontal spout, that fire would have been lost against the endless burning beyond it.

They drifted in silence until the unidentified vessel had traversed far enough that Ziggy's resumption of tooting the spout, sending them along, wouldn't be seen.

"Okay. We're good."

"Alright."

Ziggy opened the lantern, giving the basket below only the dimmest of light, and he shot a few blasts into the night, swaying the basket and keeping them on course.

"You'd miss her," Ziggy said, high above on his platform near the hot controls.

"Pauline?"

"Yeah."

"I would. Yeah. She's right about what she just told me, though."

"What's that?"

"That she can't let herself be soft. She's damn right. I'd like it, and I'd treat her nice enough, but—"

"You're a savage."

Ham held the basket's rim and shook with his quiet laughter.

"That I am. Especially this."

He held his right arm back toward the center of the basket, where most of the light shined down, and flexed his beefy, mutated fist.

"Yeah. Especially that."

"But still, I wouldn't hurt her. But this goddamn world . . . she's right. It's like a machine that would fucking kill her. It takes anything soft and just kills it."

"How soft you want her?"

"Maybe stop swearing so much. Maybe some lingerie. I remember shit like that."

"Does she have any?"

Ham laughed and said, "No fucking way. Here? She's more likely to find a goddamn symphony orchestra playing on a rooftop."

"Not likely."

"Fuck no, Ziggy. You know what? I think she's just bullshitting anyway. There's nothing about her that I'd call soft. She's just talking shit."

"Probably. Good-looking, though."

"Yeah, you've seen her. That body of hers . . . damn. Maybe she's right: fucking around with her while she's dressed like that? I'd lose my ever-loving fucking mind."

"Don't, then. You need it."

"You're a practical fucker, Ziggy. I like that."

"You need a practical fucker."

"Yeah. Hey, take us over closer to that wide crack where so many goddamn bats roost."

"Not good. Could get swarmed."

"True. How about just close enough to snag one that's fucking around on the outskirts of their flock? All we need is one."

"Today."

Ham shook his head and spat over the side.

"Yeah. Then tomorrow, another. And on and fucking on."

Chapter 26 – Bet It's the Sweetest Ever

Scarlet had looked away from Pauline's eyes after her advice to find a friend and keep that friend close. She watched instead her own right hand, on the arm of the chair, as Pauline lifted hers up enough to lose contact.

Scarlet's hand started shaking lightly and when she got a grip on the chair's arm, her own arm did the shaking instead.

They both looked at her left hand, resting with her entire forearm on the chair and also shaking.

"You're scared," Pauline said, then tapped her hand gently, then left it down. "Can't blame you."

Looking up at the ceiling, Scarlet said, "It's just been too much. No one would believe what I've been through already. And it's still just the first—oh, I was going to say it was the first day."

Pauline laughed knowingly and said, "No such thing here. No night and no day. Just one thing after another."

"I thought it was just the longest night ever."

"No. We're underground somewhere, Scarlet. You'll never see a sunrise."

Scarlet sighed, then shook her head and turned it toward the redheaded woman seated in the chair close beside her.

"I can't even tell you everything that happened to me already."

"The fuck you can't. What are friends for?"

Scarlet laughed softly and said, "To keep their friends safe from oversexed monkeys."

"I do so appreciate that, Scarlet. That alone makes you just about my best friend here."

"Really? You hardly even know me. And if I told you even half of the shit I've been through, you'd—"

"I'd keeping holding your hand,"—she gave Scarlet's hand a firm squeeze—"and listen to as much as you want to tell me."

"You're sweet, Pauline. Thank you."

"I'm pretty damn sure no one has ever called me sweet before. Thank you, Scarlet. So, go on. Tell me some stuff."

"Well, I woke up here, and right after—"

"How you got here is probably one of the better stories, right? Want to start there?"

"Oh, um, no. Maybe some other time."

"Sure. So, you just got here, then what?"

Scarlet scoffed and gazed across the room.

"Pauline, I can't. It's just—"

Without letting go of Scarlet's hand, Pauline spun out of her chair to kneel in front of her, and she took her other hand. Scarlet looked at that first, then into Pauline's eyes.

"Listen, Scarlet. It's okay. You can tell me."

Scarlet's eyelids were drooping, and she kept them closed more than open as her head tipped until she caught it.

"Oh, God, I'm just so tired too."

"Whether it's day or night. Yeah. We all sleep just whenever."

Pauline looked around the room and saw a couch across the room, up against a wall with more paintings and other odd furnishings.

Standing, and still holding Scarlet's hands, she said, "Come on. You need a nap."

"I don't think I'll ever be able to sleep. Pauline, this is all a nightmare."

"Yeah. No way in fuck to argue with that. Even some sleep will help, though. Come on."

She helped her up, and Scarlet stood, wobbly, until Pauline held one of her hands and put the other around her waist. She got her walking slowly toward the couch.

"Even just lying down will help."

"Okay. It's either that, I think, or just collapse. Might as well be on a couch."

"Exactly. Here," she said, turning Scarlet and nudging her to sit, "park yourself right there."

After she sat, Pauline coaxed her lie on her side, then helped her get her legs up on the cushions and curled to fit.

"It's never really cold here," she said as she reached for a dusty blanket folded over the couch's back, "but getting all cozy is still pretty nice."

"I think I'm too messy. This blood and stuff will just get all over that."

"Then, we'll find you another one. Now's the time to not give a fuck."

She unfolded it and laid it over Scarlet, leaving her top arm free and her head on a pillow.

"See? Bet you feel better already."

"You're right. Even just lying down helps."

Pauline stooped down, then sat back on her heels and found Scarlet's hand with both of hers.

She kissed it quickly and said, "When you're rested, you can tell me more. If you want."

"I had to kill a boy."

"Oh my God. Why?"

"Because he was going to scream and tell these giant bat things where I was hiding."

"Oh, the bats. Yeah. They're fucking nasty. So, they didn't find you. Good."

"He had teeth like razors. Pointy little things. I used those to cut the ropes, then I—"

"What ropes?"

"Oh. Uh, I got tied up by this horrible man that raped me."

"Not Igor?"

"No. Someone else."

"Sounds like everyone wants to rape you, Scarlet. Sorry."

"Almost everyone. That man did it, though, not like Igor. Oh, he finished, too, and he was so mean about it. Then, he kicked me out, still tied up. And gagged."

"He gagged you too? Why? Were you screaming for help or—"

"No. That was strange. I don't know what happened. Something about my voice bothered him."

"Men. They sure can be horrible."

"They really can, and the monsters are even worse."

She started shaking and pulled her hand free, then worked the blanket up close to her chin.

"No place is safe here. Pauline, so many things can—"

"Shh. It's okay, Scarlet. You'll feel better if you just get some rest. Tell you what: you want me to watch over you while you take a nap?"

Scarlet was close to sobbing as she looked up at Pauline.

"You would? Just for a minute or two, I promise."

Her eyes were sinking closed, and she said in a softening voice, "I'm just so tired."

"Sure. Happy to. Hey, scoot forward real quick."

"Huh?"

Pauline reached behind Scarlet, to the small of her back, and gave her a gentle push out away from the couch back.

"Um, Pauline, I don't know if—"

"I'm tired too. And it's either this or the hard floor. Come on, Scarlet, it's no big deal."

"Uh, sure."

Scarlet shifted her hips to move forward, and Pauline laid herself between Scarlet and the couch back.

"Um, I guess this will work, Pauline. Thanks for—"

"Shh," she said as she sneaked her arm under Scarlet's waist while pulling the blanket over both of them. "I'm just trying to keep the monkeys off your ass."

Scarlet laughed and held the blanket close up under her chin.

Almost in Scarlet's ear, Pauline whispered, "You don't want a monkey . . . fucking you . . . in the ass, do you?"

Scarlet laughed again, her eyes closed, then she said, "No, please not that."

"See? You're safer already."

"I am. Thanks, Pauline."

"You're welcome. Now, keep those beautiful eyes shut and get some sleep."

She gave her a kiss on her cheek, then leaned her head back but still close enough to rest her cheek on Scarlet's hair.

"Okay. I'm so . . . so . . ."

Her head sank more into the pillow, and Pauline whispered, "Yes, you certainly are."

* * *

Pauline had been awake for a while, and she'd managed to carefully get her left arm under the blanket too. She hugged Scarlet with both arms as she slept, every curve of their bodies nesting together, and she'd kept them close enough to let her breasts stay pressed against Scarlet's back, allowing them a slow squeeze with every breath she took.

From Pauline gently moving her fingers around, touching Scarlet's belly through her work shirt that was held on like a robe, she got Scarlet to begin to stir. So, she slipped her left arm out from under their shared blanket and carefully brushed strands of black hair back, off of her face and neck.

She stopped her gentle caressing only when Scarlet yawned, and she stretched her arms and legs, then curled them back to where they were, snug against Pauline.

"Hey," said Pauline, "I bet you feel better."

"Yes, I—"

She turned her head quickly, just long enough to see Pauline smiling from very close, then tried to squirm herself off of the couch.

"Hey, easy. I won't bite. You're not even awake yet."

She'd never released Scarlet from her hug under the blanket, and she added her other arm over the blanket, holding her close.

"Oh," she said, relaxing in Pauline's arms again, "you're right. I'm still so sleepy. But I, um, I should probably—"

She tried getting away again, but Pauline tightened her grip.

"No, don't. Not yet. While you were sleeping, I thought I heard someone on the floor below us. They might hear us if we started walking around."

"Oh. No, I don't want that. And I'm still so tired."

"You should be. You've had some experiences."

"I never finished telling you about them, Pauline. Nice of you to listen."

"You can tell me more now, if you want."

"Well, we are kind of trapped here by—"

"Lecherous butt fuckers on the floor below."

Scarlet shook with a soft laugh and said, "There are worse things."

"Yeah, and the worse fucking things already found you. That's so sad that you got tied up and, well, you know."

"And gagged. Yeah. You really want to hear my stories?"

"Sure. Who else you going to tell?"

"Not the monkeys."

"Not while they're fucking you, no."

Scarlet laughed softly again, and Pauline reached up to brush more of her hair back, then whispered in her ear, "Monkeys, men . . . not much difference."

She paused a moment, then added, "Shit, there's a lot in between too."

"What does that mean?"

"Experiments gone bad, maybe. Some are just a trace of monkey, and I've heard that some are as much as ten-percent monkey. Hell, there might even be fifteens and twenties, but I don't know anyone that's ever seen one. The tens are probably the worst we'd ever meet, and they still look mostly like human men, just harrier. Oh, and they have long tails and can barely talk. But all of them seem to have been bred for sex."

"I suppose that's not all bad, huh?"

"Think again. From what I've heard, they get wilder and almost uncontrollable right after they have sex."

"Why?"

"Because sex makes them want more sex. I hear they get even crazier after they cum."

"Who would breed things like that?"

"Some kind of sick fun maybe? Crazy live party favors? Another mystery in this fucking place. No one knows. Just saying that men and monkeys are kind of all the same here. It's easier to just call all of them monkeys."

Scarlet scoffed and said, "Especially when they want sex?"

"Exactly. Try to make the best of it."

"I don't see how. Pauline, I haven't had a single good experience since I got here. Except . . ."

"Yeah?"

"Except this. You're being so nice to me."

"I'm nice compared to boars and bats and sex-starved monkey men?"

"Way nicer. You're just nice. Thanks."

"You're welcome. So, what was the last good experience you had, then?"

"I miss my husband. I tried to find him at the reactor, but I don't think I'll ever see him again."

"Uh, no. You probably won't. So, what's the good memory? With him, you mean?"

"I'd be embarrassed telling you. I can't."

"Huh. I can't see you if you blush. It's like I'm not even here. You know, forget I'm here. Just tell it to the room."

"All of it?"

"Well, yeah. All the details."

"Alright, here goes. Don't laugh."

"Promise. If anything, I'll just be jealous."

"Okay. Well, we were having an anniversary dinner at a nice Chinese restaurant on the roof of a tall building in Chinatown. He was being silly. Daniel's his name. He wanted us to sneak out on the roof and, uh, mess around."

"Sounds like fun."

"It started out fun, but oh, Pauline, he surprised me with what he wanted."

"And what was that?"

Pauline waited, holding her breath and tipping her head up enough to watch Scarlet's lips form every word as she gazed across the dim room.

"He, um, wanted to watch me masturbate."

Pauline let her breath out slowly, controlled, and wasn't able to stop her arm from squeezing Scarlet closer.

"The dirty man," she said. "Did you? Did you make his day?"

"Well, yeah, but then, these bat things came, and I fell over the side, and they took Daniel and—"

"Whoa. Back up. Don't even get to that part about the bats."

"You really want to hear all of that?"

"Look around, Scarlet. How the hell else are we going to amuse ourselves around here?"

"Monkeys?"

"Hey, might not be all that bad."

"Stop, Pauline. You're silly. Okay. He watched me like an insane man as I lifted the hem of my dress. He asked me about my thighs and if I liked touching them, crazy things like that."

"Yeah, crazy. What did you tell him?"

"I, um, played along. I said everything I knew he wanted me to say."

"Tell me that. What else did he make you say?"

"You sure you want to hear this?"

"Yeah, I really do. Go on."

"Okay. I was, um, touching myself and God, Pauline, I was getting so wet. It was just such a weird experience. He asked me if I liked that. I told him that I did like all that pussy juice."

"And did you?"

"Well, yeah, I guess. Then, he told me I was using too many words, and I knew what he meant. So, I told him that I loved my pussy, and I love to cum."

"And you do, right?"

"Pauline! You're being silly. And then, oh my, I was just starting to cum. And he kept prodding me, making me say more."

"Like what?"

"Just when I started to cum, probably nicer than ever before, I told him, um . . ."

"What? What did you tell him?"

Scarlet turned her head again, enough to look into Pauline's eyes, and they held that gaze for a few seconds, their bodies molded together under the blanket.

"Tell me!"

"I told him . . . that I love pussy. I told him that I absolutely love pussy, but he'd just never asked me before."

"Scarlet. You weren't just talking about your own?"

"Not right then, I wasn't. No, I remember that feeling. It felt like I was finally admitting something that I should keep secret. Or maybe it was just the cumming and wanting to tell him what I thought he wanted to hear. I don't know."

"What feeling? Tell me more."

"Oh, I was cumming so hard, and I knew that what I wanted most, more even than him, was to be touching a woman. I was touching myself, and it felt so good. And since I knew so well just how to, um, you know. I just started thinking about, well . . .”

“Touching another woman like that?”

“Uh-huh. I remember feeling like getting a woman all wet like that was like earning a passing grade. A sign that what I was doing was accepted and welcomed.”

“Uh, yeah. That’s all true. And you meant that, right?”

“Oh, I don’t know, Pauline. I thought so at the time anyway.”

“Can I, um . . .”

Pauline kept watching Scarlet’s eyes as she rubbed her hand around on her belly, then began to slip her fingertips between the robe parts of the shirt, but she stopped there, waiting.

Scarlet did nothing but breathe deeply, so she went in farther until she dragged her fingers lightly across Scarlet’s breast, then held it in a gentle squeeze.

“You’re gorgeous, Scarlet.”

“Pauline, maybe you—”

“Mm, you’re so soft, Scarlet. Nothing in this fucking world is so nice and soft.”

Scarlet gazed back at her, her eyes blinking slowly, and Pauline felt around until she could pinch her nipple, and she gave it gentle pulls away, letting it go, then squeezing it again.

“But I don’t—”

“Mm, you feel so good. Let’s you and I forget that world out there for a while and just—”

Scarlet tipped her head back just a small amount and sighed, and Pauline froze—her hand, her eyes, her voice . . . everything.

She saw in Scarlet’s mouth, descending down from her perfect upper teeth, two gently curving fangs with points as sharp as pins.

While slipping her hand back out from Scarlet’s shirt, she said, “Scarlet? What the . . . what do you—”

“Mm, I’m feeling so much better now, just from talking.”

“But your teeth, you’re—”

In a voice only somewhat like warm honey, Scarlet nodded and said, "Touch me more, Pauline. You're right about this world."

Pauline choked back what she was about to say and resumed her gentle fondling under the blanket. With her outside hand, she pulled back more of Scarlet's hair, her eyes focused only on the fangs.

"I, uh, sure. But Scarlet, you have, um, you—"

"What?"

Pauline coughed softly, then said, "Have you always had fangs?"

In a totally normal voice, Scarlet said, "What?"

Scarlet's eyes stretched open, and she wrestled her hand out into the open and touched around inside her mouth.

"What is this? What's happening to me?"

With her hand still close to Scarlet's breast, outside the shirt robe and under the blanket, Pauline reached her other hand close to Scarlet's mouth.

"May I? Let me see."

Scarlet tried to get her lips out of the way, exposing all of her teeth along with the fangs, and Pauline said, "Well, damn."

She touched the side of one, then touched all around the sides of the other one.

"You have fangs, Scarlet."

Scarlet's breaths had become more urgent, and she stared into Pauline's eyes as the examination continued.

"Those are some serious kind of—ow!"

She pulled her hand out and displayed a finger for both of them to see. A drop of blood was taking its time, collecting where the sharp point had caught Pauline's finger.

"They're sharp."

"Mm-hmm," Scarlet said, more moan than words, then reached out slowly for Pauline's hand.

She brought it close and touched her tongue to just the growing droplet of blood, and the small volume of it lost its form and flooded down onto her tongue.

"Mm."

She pushed Pauline's hand away and said, "Oh, I'm so sorry. I don't know what's going on!"

"It's okay. Really. Just a tiny little nick."

"You must think I'm a monster, Pauline. Don't I look horrible now? Pauline, I have fangs!"

Pauline laughed once and said, "No self-respecting monkey will ever fuck you. Not even in your ass."

"Pauline, this is serious! Do I look like a monster?"

Pauline tipped her eyes down to study again Scarlet's open mouth, where the fangs were only modestly longer than the rest of the teeth, and one of them had just a dot of red at the very end of it.

"No. Um, not at all. Scarlet, it looks good."

"Really?"

"It's, uh, kind of sexy. Can I, um . . . I want to kiss you."

"Now? You want to kiss me with fangs in there?"

Pauline nodded, never taking her eyes off of Scarlet's wet lips, parted enough to reveal two very sharp, slender, curving but not very long teeth.

"Oh, yeah. Uh-huh. Um, may I?"

Scarlet reached back but could get only a few strands of Pauline's red hair, and she gave that a gentle tug. Pauline's head followed the pull on her hair and leaned closer and closer until she pressed her lips against Scarlet's.

"Mm," said Scarlet, more sound from deep inside than her voice.

The kiss continued, and Pauline swept her tongue around, touching the base of the two long teeth, up near where they merged with all of the rest.

When Scarlet moaned again, Pauline slid her tongue down the length of one of the fangs, then dragged her tongue across the point of it.

"Oh, I, um, I think I—"

"Give it to me," Scarlet said with a voice that would allow no resistance.

Pauline, breathing quickly and with the softest possible squeals, held her tongue out.

And Scarlet, looking into her eyes, sucked it much more than was needed for the trace amount of blood that her fang had drawn from it.

Pauline tipped her head away, grinning, and Scarlet said, "Again. The other one," honey swirling in every word she spoke.

"Can't say no to that."

Pauline smiled and leaned in, still looking into Scarlet's eyes, then a soft, tentative knocking at the door locked them in place.

Pauline rolled herself back more completely behind Scarlet and hugged her with both arms, then whispered in her ear, "Monkeys. They want your ass."

Scarlet whispered, "Hmm. I think maybe not just them."

Pauline's reply had to wait until she had sighed, rested her hand on Scarlet's belly, then nuzzled into her neck and thick black hair.

"Bet it's the sweetest ever."

Chapter 27 – Sexiest Goddamn Thing

Pauline had returned her other arm to under the blanket, and she kept both palms against Scarlet's belly, over the closed flannel shirt.

"Pauline, who do you really think that is? It can't be a monkey."

"No, it can't. Monkeys don't knock. They just take what they want."

"Hmm. My ass, I suppose."

"Hey, have you ever?"

"Oh, you mean have I—no! Pauline, stop it," she said, her voice back to normal.

"Alright. Maybe they left. It's all quiet out there."

"I hope so."

Scarlet searched around and found one of Pauline's hands, then placed it over a breast with only the flannel in between.

"Oh," said Pauline. "Nice."

"It's, um, kind of a hug. I know what you mean about this world—it's horrible."

"Mm-hmm. I'll behave."

She kept her hand still, not even squeezing Scarlet's breast.

"I should tell you more about Daniel. I think that helps keep the memories."

"Probably. You talked about what you like, at least at that wild time, and you might never forget that now. Whether you really meant it or not."

"You might be right."

Pauline held her breath as she carefully moved her other hand to cover Scarlet's other breast, then she kept both of them completely still. Scarlet had just begun to say something about that, and Pauline hurried to continue with a story.

"I don't remember much of anything from when I was alive. I have a story that I tell, but that's just made-up stuff."

"Tell me."

"Sure. It's not like I talk to anyone, really, but I've told Ham and Risk that—"

"Who?"

"Ham. I live with Ham. He's got this nice, safe place. And Risk, well, I'm not sure what to say about him. He's kind of hard to describe, but he's not always around."

"Sounds fun. You have people, at least."

"Sure. But I tell them that I died while having sex on a rolling motorcycle."

"That's not true?"

"Nope. And don't ask me for the truth. Maybe someday, I'll tell you."

"Okay."

"Hey, um, I'm not trying to be mean or anything but seriously, your husband, uh, if he got taken here, then he—"

"He's probably dead. I know. Oh, Pauline, I really can't hardly remember him already."

"Maybe that's a blessing. Kind of. I mean, we're stuck here anyway. Have you thought about changing your name?"

"Why would I?"

"Like, a fresh start?"

"No. I never thought about that. I suppose you have a suggestion? Don't make it anything about monkeys, please."

"No, nothing about the monkeys that want your ass more than anything."

"Hmm. That's kind of going around."

She turned enough that Pauline could kiss just the edge of her lips, and they held it there before Scarlet relaxed again.

"So, anyway, I was thinking," she leaned in until her lips were touching Scarlet's ear—"Widow."

"What? Why Widow?"

"Well, I don't know. It's kind of like remembering your husband. Sort of like he's not completely gone."

"Oh, I don't know about—"

Pauline gave both breasts a quick, gentle squeeze, then spoke in her ear.

"Oh, come on. It's just one little suggestion from me, then you can boss me around to do probably anything at all."

"What? Why would you—"

"You just have this . . . something about you, Scarlet. I mean, Widow."

"Tell me it's not the fangs."

"Oh, the fangs."

Pauline slipped one hand inside Scarlet's shirt and rubbed a fingertip across a nipple, getting a sigh from her.

"Pauline. Maybe—"

"This, uh,"—she gave her nipple a light squeeze and a soft twist—"kind of got those sexy teeth going, didn't it?"

Widow sighed and said, "Mm-hmm. I think you like those fangs. You do, don't you?"

She gazed across the room, comfortable and getting fondled under the blanket, and waited.

But seconds had gone by without an answer.

"Pauline?"

"Oh, uh, yeah. Widow, don't take it personally, but it has at least something to do with your fangs."

"That's kind of personal."

"Well, sure. It's just that . . . when that sharp little thing got me, I felt . . . something. I must be imagining things. This has just been such a good experience, and hearing your stories, and—"

"Pauline, what did you feel?"

Pauline hesitated while getting her other hand involved, and she was giving gentle squeezes with both.

"Uh, kind of like a, um, a trace of an orgasm. Like the start of one, maybe."

"Just from that?"

"Weird, huh? Maybe I'm just all agitated from everything else. But Widow, it felt like that even more when I dragged my tongue across it. I swear, all I wanted was to feel those sharp little fangs of yours."

Widow laughed, shaking her head, and said, "Wait. You're saying you want me to bite you?"

She waited again for an answer, and the silent seconds slipped past.

"Pauline?"

"Well, Widow, what if just a bite from you could give me an orgasm? What the hell? You like orgasms, right?"

"Well, sure, but—"

"Oh, and just think of it: what if I was having a real orgasm the usual way, too, while your gorgeous little fangs were giving me another one? Would they add up somehow? I think I'd lose my mind."

"Pauline, you're being silly. How could biting you do anything like that?"

"Once again, Widow, look around at this world we're in. How can you doubt anything?"

Widow only said, "Hmm . . ." and kept looking away from the couch and their warm embrace under the blanket.

She stared across the room for a few seconds, then giggled and shimmied herself around, with Pauline holding the blanket up, until she was facing her.

Gazing into Pauline's eyes from so close that they could kiss, she said, "What would a monkey go for first?"

Pauline reached under her again, then held her ass cheeks with both hands.

"Good girl."

"You just called me a good girl."

"I did, didn't I? I didn't plan that."

"Well, that's what you said."

"I should just stop. I don't know what's—"

"No, Widow, just go with it. Really. Just for fun, alright?"

Widow scoffed, then cleared her throat, kept looking into Pauline's eyes, and kept her voice normal.

"You're a very good girl. So, the little girl wants to try a little bite, huh?"

"Sure. It's like an experiment. Oh, and I do like orgasms, too, so there's always that."

Widow giggled for a second, then said, "Somewhere soft?"

"Uh, my neck, right? Is that a good place?"

"Yeah, I think so."

She kissed Pauline's lips, then backed away just enough to whisper.

"You're a soft little girl for me?"

Pauline was breathing deeply, and no smile marred her serious gaze into Scarlet's eyes. She nodded.

"Mm-hmm. I'll be your soft little girl."

"Mm. Soft and juicy? You're my soft and juicy little girl?"

Pauline stared for a second, then laughed and looked away.

Widow laughed, too, and said, "God, I don't know why I'm saying things like that. I'm just—"

Pauline turned back to her, almost rubbing noses.

"Oh, yeah, this really is kind of silly. But still, I don't mind. I kind of like it. Keep going."

With a voice slower and thick with heated honey, Widow said, "You're my soft girl that needs a bite. You can't say no."

Pauline lost her smile and again held Widow's intense gaze. She nodded.

"Good girl. So good. So soft."

Widow bared her fangs and began to tip her head, and Pauline stared past her, holding her breath.

"So soft. You're just as juicy as you can be."

"Mm, like you wouldn't believe."

But something—human or monkey or something altogether different—rapped on their door again.

* * *

Widow was close to sinking her fangs into the soft skin of Pauline's neck, and she kept her eyes locked on her target.

"It's really not a monkey, Widow. But someone or something wants in."

Pauline watched closely as Widow said, in a completely normal voice, "Maybe they'll just go away."

"Hey, Widow. Your fangs are way smaller than before. You feel different?"

Widow reached around with her tongue, her eyes big and staring at Pauline's.

"I don't know. I guess. All I could think about before was biting you, then that knock kind of got me off-track."

"Oh, you know what? Maybe it's like an erection."

"Hmm. In my mouth? You're bad, Pauline."

Pauline laughed quietly, gave the door a glance, then said, "No, not that. I mean, like if you're getting into it. Maybe some kind of mood comes first."

"Oh, okay. I see. That makes sense."

"Let's test it."

They were still lying face to face on the couch, and Pauline slipped both hands under Widow's shirt that she wore like a robe, then wiggled them until she got just her fingers under the tight waistband and belt of her work khakis.

Widow sighed and used one hand to unbuckle her belt, pop the top button, then get the zipper going in a helpful direction.

"Mm, good idea, Widow."

"Hmm. We'll see."

"Like this, alright?"

Widow nodded, and Pauline easily slipped in both hands until she got a palm on each of Widow's ass cheeks, then she squeezed them gently and kept her hands there.

"Ooh, no panties, huh?"

"Oh, that. Igor took them when he, um, was trying to rape me."

Pauline giggled and said, "Bet he ate them."

"Pauline!"

"Couldn't blame him."

"Hmm."

"Mm, you are so soft and smooth," Pauline said, "Strong."

"I do feel kind of strong."

"I mean, God, what an ass you have."

"Hmm."

"Anything with the fangs?"

"You tell me," Widow said, and bared her teeth.

"No change. They're sharp, but they're still tiny. You'd never suck the juice out of—"

Widow groaned and tipped her head back, her warm breath rolling out between her lips and past two sharp teeth that had grown longer.

"Damn, Widow. We're onto something."

Widow panted softly for a few seconds, then said, "I got hungry too. I feel it. All I can think about is how . . ."

"How what?"

Smiling around her still-growing fangs, Widow said, "How . . . juicy you are. Pauline, you're kind of all . . . juice."

"Uh, that's a compliment. I know part of me sure is."

"No, I mean, all of you. Pauline, this hunger, it's, um . . ."

"Go on. Let's figure this out."

"This hunger is sexual too. It's like a resonance frequency that's forcing—"

"Whoa. English, alright?"

"Okay. Um, you touching my ass—"

"Before a monkey defiles it."

Widow giggled, then said, "Yeah. No monkeys, please. Um, it started sexual, and it still is, but that, I think, made me hungry too. And feeling hungry made me feel, uh, closer to . . . an orgasm."

"Damn, Widow. You're the sexiest goddamn thing ever."

"And you're juicy. God, Pauline, you're so soft and juicy. I'm going to bite you. I have to."

She started to lean toward Pauline's neck, but she put her lips in the way instead, and Widow sighed when their lips met.

"Wait," said Pauline. "Here's a plan. Another experiment. Go answer the door and if it's even close to human, then—"

"How close? I mean, how far from human?"

"In this world? No one can even guess. But here's the plan, kind of a test: while you're walking over to answer the door, you just—"

"What? No. I'm not going anywhere near it."

"Listen. It'll be alright. Just keep thinking about whatever's outside that door being almost as juicy as me."

"Almost?"

"Huh. I'm the juiciest. You'll see."

"Oh, Pauline. You're too much. So, what are you talking about?"

"You think about him or her being juicy, and that should keep your fangs out. Your erection."

"Stop. Then, I do what?"

"Well, you just lure in here whoever it is, then try that bite on them first."

"You're scared of my bite?"

"Uh, a little. Yeah. I still want my turn, though."

Widow gave the door a look for a few seconds, then turned back to Pauline, who was still tight up against her where they lay on the couch.

"What if it is that monkey, Pauline?"

"Let's get those pants down now, then," she said and started rubbing her hands all over Widow's ass, "so he doesn't just rip it all open."

"No, stop," she said in a forceful whisper. "Let me up."

Pauline slipped her hands back out and said, "You're going to do it?"

Widow stood, still close to the couch, and looked toward the door while fixing her pants.

"I don't want to. I just want to hide."

"Widow, you have to. Whatever's going on with you might be your best survival tool, but you have to figure it out. Seriously, this world will burn you down really fucking quick."

She faced the door and took a quick step away when Pauline slapped her ass.

"Hey. Alright, I'll go take a look and if it's that monkey, you're in big trouble."

"No, Widow. Your ass is. That was probably a ten that was after me. A goddamn sex machine."

"Almost completely monkey?"

"Well, ten-percent. Not totally human anymore. They're all brutal, even though they all kind of look like ordinary men."

"Except for their tails."

"That's another thing. If you see the tail stiff, pointing straight back, you can be fucking sure it's the same on the other side."

"Oh my God. That's how it was with the one following you."

"Shit. He sure was zeroed in on my ass, wasn't he?"

"No, he couldn't have been just as big with his, um, in front."

"Not that much, no. Really, though . . . seriously big."

"Really?"

"I mean, that's what I heard. It's kind of what they're made for."

Widow scoffed then smiled at her, then turned and began walking toward the door.

"Widow, wait."

She stopped.

"When that crafter gets to stitching stuff for you, I say it should match those fangs. Something that fits with that."

"Uh, maybe. Like what?"

She tipped her eyes down, locked them on Widow's legs, then said, "Your legs are incredible. I'm kind of dying to see them. You should show them off."

"My hus—I mean, someone told me that before. You mean, like a skirt?"

Pauline nodded and said, "Yep. Short. A really short one. Sexy fangs and sexy clothes. God, that's irresistible."

Widow sighed, amused, and said, "I'll think about it. Anything else?"

"I'll be right there with you when you're getting fitted. You'll just have to trust my fashion sense. Show me those fangs?"

Widow grinned, keeping her lips apart, and Pauline scoffed.

"They're gone. Remember the plan? Come here."

Widow walked closer.

"No, like right here. Stoop down."

Widow sank herself lower, then dropped to her knees.

"My pussy is so wet, Widow."

Widow drew in a quick breath, then pulled her lips back.

"There we go. Sexy little fangs you got there."

"Yeah?"

While Widow kept them out for inspection, Pauline added, "My pussy isn't just wet. Mm, it's juicy. So juicy."

Keeping her fangs bared, Widow held her belly when it growled.

"Nice fangs. Longest yet."

Widow didn't smile, and she kept her sharp teeth bared as she kept leaning closer to Pauline's lips.

"No, no, no! Those are for the ass-fucker monkey! Go!"

* * *

"Work on that walk too."

Widow turned her head, smiled, and said, "Shh!"

But she began taking longer, more graceful strides, and Pauline moved the couch from the wall enough that she could hide behind it.

With her hand on the doorknob and the other spinning for the numbers, Widow touched her tongue all around and felt that her fangs were still there but not as long as she and Pauline had seen them earlier.

She hit the final number, heard the unlocking clunk, then turned the knob. She pulled in the door and peered into a hallway dimmer than her room.

A young man, barely twenty and not as tall as her, tipped his head to look inside. He quickly got his eyes to focus on Widow's, and he squinted at her, then jerked his head to look each way along the hall, then back at her.

"Can you help me? I don't know where I am."

"You're knocking on my door."

"I know. Sorry. I saw you. Before. I saw a light in your window, then I watched you let someone into the building. I'm sorry. I'm so scared."

She pulled the door open enough that he could see her entirely, then said, "Let me guess: you just woke up somewhere around here, and you don't remember how you got here, right?"

He nodded quickly, then looked each way again.

"Please, can I come in? I'll just sit in the corner. Honest. I've seen horrible things outside. Please."

"You're alone?"

He nodded.

"Sure. For a while."

She moved along with the door as she swung it wide enough for him to step inside, then he put his back right up against the wall. Widow closed the door and locked it, all with him staring at her turning the dial.

"You're not trapped, so don't worry. I just don't want any scary things in here either."

"Okay."

He looked all around the room, which still held the light from only one ceiling fixture.

"You live here?"

"I just got this place. It'll need some work. Have you been to the reactor?"

"What? What reactor?"

"Nothing. Good. Why are you sweating?"

He rubbed at one cheek, then the other, and said, "I ran up the stairs. I'm not sick or anything."

"Good. But you're tired," she said, tipping her head toward the couch with Pauline behind it. "Rest while you can. I just did."

"Sorry. I woke you."

"Hey," she said as they walked, "you're just trying to survive. Everyone has that right, you know?"

"Yeah."

They both sat, and he closed his eyes as he fell back into the cushions.

"Here," Widow said as she rose back up, "why don't you lie down?"

He almost fell over onto the pillow, then tugged at the blanket enough to partially cover himself. Widow stooped down near him.

His eyes popped open, and he said, "I can't. I can't rest. I don't know where this is, or what I'm doing here, or—"

"Shh," she said and touched his lips. "You need to rest before you can figure anything out. Rest."

"Oh . . . okay."

With his eyes closed but his face still wet with sweat, he said, "I'm Lucas."

"Hi, Lucas. You can call me Widow."

He looked up at her, about to speak, and she smoothed down the hair around his ear and said, "Shh. Just rest."

He sighed and closed his eyes, and Widow pulled her hand back but kept staring at the wetness of his skin. Even after Pauline had picked her head up high enough, quietly, to glance down at him, the moisture of the young man drew her attention the most.

She finally gave Pauline a glance and saw her tipping her head down toward Lucas, who had already lapsed into soft snoring.

Widow shrugged, peeled back her lips, and showed that her fangs were pointy but not nearly long enough for a serious bite. Pauline bounced her eyebrows once, then puckered up like she'd give Widow a kiss. Then, she slipped out her tongue, which she'd gotten quite wet, and swept it across her upper lip, then back along her lower, getting them slick enough to pick up the room's dim light.

They both heard Widow's stomach growl.

With Widow still watching her lips, Pauline put her tongue straight out, then curled it repeatedly, like she was trying to lick something.

Widow shook her head slightly, then looked to Pauline's eyes, which were focused on Widow's breasts. Her shirt robe wasn't fastened as well as it could be, and parts of her breasts and a lot of skin were visible.

When she looked higher again, she saw Pauline nodding and still licking—almost laughing at her attempt to make it clear exactly what she wanted to lick.

Her stomach growled again more loudly.

Widow groaned, just enough for her and Pauline to hear, and reached both hands for her breasts, which she squeezed then held underneath, offering them. Her own tongue had come out and was coating her lips, rubbing them all over.

Pauline again tipped her head toward the sleeping man on their couch, and Widow, still holding her breasts and licking her lips, parted them and made no effort to check for herself—the view of her fangs, the longest yet, was only for Pauline.

Lucas had left one of his hands visible, up near his face, and the sweat from his cheek had given it a distinct shine from the overhead light. Widow reached for it but stopped short and looked again at Pauline, who only smiled and nodded.

Widow got a gentle hold of the sleeping man's wrist, lifted it up, and brought it close to her mouth. She'd kept her lips pulled back, and the length of her fangs was enough to wipe away any trace of a smile from Pauline's face.

Pauline mouthed the words, "Do it!" and chomped her teeth quietly a few quick times.

Widow stared at the wet skin for only a moment, then she opened wider, took his wrist in under the fangs, and snapped her jaws shut.

Both of them watched the man, and both listened to Widow's deep, very low moan as his eyes popped wide open and he tried to sit up. While he fumbled to get free of the blanket over him, he pulled back on his arm, trying to yank it loose, but Widow's fangs were in as deep as they could go.

"What . . . what are you doing? Stop that!"

He'd made hardly any progress at getting out from under the blanket to sit up, and Pauline, reaching over the couch back, easily pushed against his forehead and held him on the pillow.

"Hey! Don't! Just let me go!"

Pauline used her other hand to hold the one Lucas was using to reach for Widow, and she held that down too.

"Please! What are you—"

Widow covered his mouth with her free hand, and she and Pauline watched him closely, all while the fangs stayed deep and the moaning from Widow paused only for her to inhale.

Pauline gasped at the sight of the young victim showing the beginning of a smile around Widow's fingers and when his eyes started to roll up, he slumped more comfortably into the cushions. Pauline tested it by raising her hand from his forehead, and he lay still. Widow let go of his wrist, and his arm lay still too.

"Widow, what is this?"

She kept her teeth deep and only stretched back her lips. A soft hiss joined the glare that she shot up at Pauline.

"Whoa. Okay. You just, uh . . . yeah."

After half a minute, Widow backed her bloody lips and tongue away from Lucas's wrist but still held it close. Looking up at Pauline, she licked across her lips and gave a sigh mixed with a higher-pitched moan.

"Uh, Widow? You okay?"

Widow nodded, then licked at the man's wrist, cleaning it all up.

"God, that felt like taking a . . . first breath."

"Right. Uh-huh. You, uh, you sure got him to settle down."

"Mm, so sweet. Such sweet juices."

Her stomach growled.

"You, uh . . . what? You sucked out his blood?"

"Mm-hmm. Not just that. Everything wet inside."

"Oh, my. Um . . ."

Lucas formed thin slits with his eyes, and his grin was just as thin.

"You're smiling?" Widow said. "Why?"

"I, I don't know," he said. "It felt . . . good. It still does."

Widow's honey voice dripped down from almost directly over his mouth.

She didn't look up when Pauline said, "Like I was saying . . ."

To Lucas, Widow said, "You want more. Another nice little bite."

He closed his eyes and nodded.

Widow got her fangs out, and her stomach growled more as she looked up at Pauline, who was only staring from one to the other. She finally shrugged and nodded.

Holding his wrist in one hand and pushing up his long shirt sleeve with the other, Widow got her fangs close to a meaty section of his forearm.

She paused to look up at Pauline, a soft moan mixing with a gentle hiss.

Pauline swallowed hard and kept a tight grip on the couch back with both hands.

Still holding Pauline's blank look, she sank her sharp points easily through his sweat-moistened skin, down into whatever other fluids were inside and keeping him alive.

And while moaning and looking up at Pauline, who stared and didn't move, not even to blink, Widow closed her lips over her bite and began to suck.

And if Pauline was able to see Widow's steady swallowing, she didn't say a word about it. But her eyes drifted away from the sight of Widow feeding, and she let them stop somewhere else.

Seeing something that got her eyes stretched wide open again.

"Oh my God. Will you look at that?"

Chapter 28 – Loving and Consuming–All the Same

Widow kept sucking the life out of Lucas, the lost fellow who had strayed into her room in the dilapidated building, but she let her eyes follow Pauline's pointing finger.

"Widow. You see that? No, wait—don't stop!"

Widow managed to utter, "Mm-hmm" and kept her fangs and lips at their task, to the sound of a happily grumbling stomach.

The man was mostly covered by the blanket as he lay flat on his back on the couch. Near the middle of him, though, a fairly significant bulge was growing, even as they watched.

Pauline snapped another look at his face and said, "He's not even fighting you, and that's going on too?"

Widow shrugged, her eyes on what both of them knew was enlarging under the blanket.

"How could that be? Whatever you're doing, keep doing it."

She hurried around the couch and knelt beside Widow, then slapped Lucas's cheeks a few times. She got him to open his eyes, but he only grinned and let them close again as his head flopped over toward the couch back.

"Are you still sucking?"

"Mm-hmm."

"The more you suck, the more,"—she pointed—"that grows?"

Widow shrugged, and Pauline scooted around her to kneel on her other side. When she threw back the blanket, then started to unfasten the man's pants, Widow backed out her fangs and quickly licked her lips clean.

"Hey, what are you doing?"

"This is just too much, Widow. It's like we're in the bonus round here."

"Huh? Oh, wait. No. You want me to bite . . ."

Pauline pulled out something long and hard and held it to point straight up at the ceiling.

". . . that?"

"Hmm. Maybe later. You got me all horny with those teeth and every other delicious part of you."

"No, you're not really going to?"

"I sure as hell am."

She let the man go, then stood, kicked off her boots, which rattled loose the knife that she'd clipped there back on the mountain.

"Oh," said Widow. "A weapon."

"Yep."

Before she began unbuckling her belt, she removed the knife there and set it by her boots.

"Hmm. Armed to the teeth."

Pauline smirked and said, while looking down at Widow, who'd kept her fangs out and ready for more, "Talking about teeth . . ."

Widow managed a grin without hiding her fangs.

"You know what?" Pauline said as she shimmied her pants down to her ankles. "It's, uh, time for another experiment."

"Like how? Pauline, you—"

"Let's see if we can get those darling fangs of yours even longer. What do you say?"

Wearing only her t-shirt and socks and a ball cap, Pauline stood close enough to Widow to touch her, so she did. She rested a hand on her head, then stroked fingertips through her hair.

"You don't know how dangerous those can get, do you?"

"Uh-uh. No idea."

"So, it's worth a try, right?"

"I guess. What kind of a try?"

Pauline nodded, then took on a more serious look.

"You like juicy, remember? Remember that, Widow?"

"Uh-huh. I remember."

Pauline turned just enough to face her directly, and Widow let her gaze drop to level, focusing on a part of Pauline that she hadn't seen till then and that the t-shirt wasn't long enough to conceal.

"Keep those lips apart for me. I'm watching your fangs."

Widow pulled them back, and a soft hiss escaped. She turned her head up to gaze at Pauline, giving her a clear view of them.

"Ooh. Longer already, I think. Good start."

Still caressing the thick black hair as Widow knelt beside the passive man, Pauline said, "You see what your bite is doing to him."

"I'm doing that to him?"

"Seems like it. I mean, he's kind of letting you bite him, and that thing of his is getting outrageous."

She reached for and found Widow's free hand, then placed the palm against her hip before touching her hair again.

"Not as outrageous as those monkey men, though."

Widow looked up, smiling and showing her growing fangs, and said, "Hmm. So you've heard."

"Yeah, that's right. What else do you like, Widow?"

"Um . . ."

"Not just monkeys, right?"

"Who said I like monkeys?"

"Alright. But they sure as fuck would like getting you alone somewhere."

"Hmm."

"So, you said you like something that can get all juicy real quick?"

"Oh. I did say, um, something like that."

Keeping her eyes turned up to Pauline, Widow let go of Lucas's arm and placed her other palm on Pauline's other hip. Pauline eased herself closer and used both hands to twirl around Widow's hair.

"So, tell me what else you like. Ooh, and at the same time, tell me what this boy's hard cock is itching for."

Widow giggled softly past her fangs, the longest ones yet, then looked straight ahead and said, almost in a whisper, "Um, before, I said a woman."

"Mm," Pauline said, rubbing across her hair, brushing it back. "Yes. That's the exact answer to both questions."

Widow stared straight ahead, her eyes sometimes scanning Pauline's thighs, and she didn't fight Pauline's gentle pull, drawing her nearer.

"Now, show me," she said while touching her chin lightly, tipping her head back.

Widow looked up, so close that her chin was touching both of Pauline's thighs.

"Mm, nice. Nice and long. The longest yet."

Still close and still looking up at her, Widow covered her fangs and held her lips together.

"Ooh, just as sexy as the fangs. Just a kiss."

She sighed loudly and said, "Oh God, Widow," then pulled her face in as close as it could go, and Widow didn't fight at all—she only reached both hands around to the backs of Pauline's thighs.

But it lasted only a few seconds before Pauline giggled and separated them.

"Damn, Widow."

"Hmm. That was nice."

"Doesn't always have to be sharp teeth."

"Uh-uh."

Pauline let her go and leaned over enough to get a grip on the man's solid shaft, then began slow strokes on it.

Widow gazed at the sight, again showing her lengthening teeth, and her stomach responded loudly.

Both giggled, and Pauline said, while tousling her hair gently, "Hmm, I hope we can pick this back up soon."

Widow smiled and said, "Oh, but you have some other urgent business. That's right."

"Yeah. I'm fucking this young stud while the getting is good."

Still holding him straight up, Pauline swung a leg over, straddled him, and kept her left foot on the warm floor.

"Watch, Widow. Watch me fuck this lucky boy."

Widow stared at the sight of it and saw the exact moment Pauline got him to penetrate her.

"Oh, he's in," she said and placed both palms on his chest.

She wiggled herself lower, taking in more of his shaft, then bottomed out and said, "Ah. Just like that."

She ground into him at the bottom for a few seconds.

"This view is for you, Widow."

She slid herself up slowly, and Widow gazed at how wet that shaft had become. It seemed to pick up the ceiling light's modest efforts from any and every angle.

"It's . . . it's wet. It's so, so wet."

"Mm-hmm. Juicy. It's got pussy juice all over it. Oh my God, your fangs! Widow!"

She checked them with her tongue and found that Pauline's scheme had had the planned effect—they were longer, curved more and from the gentle touch of her tongue, they seemed sharper than ever too.

"Mm. They feel good. I like them."

"Me too. They're sexy as hell."

Pauline began a steady bounce with her hands still resting on Lucas's chest. She watched Widow's fangs but mostly her eyes, which stared every time she hesitated at the top.

"Bite him, Widow. It obviously gets him all sexed up. Something about your kisses."

"Hmm. My bites, you mean?"

"Oh, both. Yeah, both. Mm, you got him so worked up for me. Bite him more."

Widow tugged up on his shirt, pulling it free of his trousers, then bunched it up to reveal the soft skin near his waist.

"Yeah," said Pauline. "Right there is good."

"So that I can—"

"Watch my juicy . . . what?"

Widow didn't smile when she whispered, "Pussy."

"That's right. Bite him close, and watch my pussy getting all juicy with him."

Widow hissed softly as she dug her much longer points into the man's soft, pale flesh, and she kept her eyes turned to watch how Pauline was taking advantage of the man that she'd aroused with her modest bites.

Her focus didn't change even when she felt Pauline again toying with her hair, fussing with it and tucking it behind her ear.

"I, I think, Widow . . . we're figuring this out."

Pauline's breaths were getting more urgent, and her bouncing on the man's pole had sped up. She no longer seemed capable of pausing on the upstroke to give Widow a prolonged view.

With her lips tight around her bite, Widow could only say, "Mm?"

"It's like . . . this: your fangs . . . your sweet bites, they . . . go with sex. Widow, they . . . the two go together. Don't you see?"

She withdrew her sharp teeth and looked up at Pauline with bloody lips and a trickle from one corner of her mouth. She nodded.

"I see. Oh, I see now. And I don't want to stop."

Her stomach growled, and she plunged her points back in at a different, fresher region of his side.

Pauline kept bouncing, sometimes groaning, and Widow kept sucking, constantly moaning and watching the action from very close, and the man got more pale by the second.

With a gentle touch to Widow's cheek, Pauline said, "Wait. I have an idea."

* * *

"When I was snooping around your place," Pauline said while humping Lucas steadily, "I saw something we should try. Over there,"—she tipped her head toward a pile of crates and supplies— "I saw rope. Why don't you go get some?"

Widow's lips smeared around the thin trickles of blood from her bite into his side when she shook her head but didn't let go.

"Why not?"

With a sigh mixed with a faint hiss, Widow released him, drawing her fangs out from deep beneath his skin.

"Bad experiences."

She shivered quickly, then added, "Remember what I told you. About what happened."

"And that's exactly why. Widow, it's payback time."

Widow looked down at the nearly unconscious man, whose eyes were contented slits gazing back at her.

Still looking at him, she said, "You don't think he'd mind if we—"

They both saw him nod just once before his weak grin grew.

"There's your answer," Pauline said. "We're experimenting, right? Maybe it'll be like some kind of therapy for you. Help you get past all that."

Widow licked her lips clean, then looked up at Pauline.

"Okay. But I'm not sure I like this idea."

Pauline scoffed and said, "You didn't think you wanted to bite the monkey or whatever was begging to get in here and get bitten."

Widow laughed and covered her mouth with one hand.

"Oh, Pauline. You do make me laugh."

"Told you that having a friend is what you need. Go on. Even just a short little piece."

"Okay."

Pauline kept riding the weakened but enormously aroused man and watched every sway of Widow's hips as she snatched up several pieces of rope, some short and some long, and returned with it all.

"That's a lot of rope."

"Maybe some of it's for you."

"Ooh, I wish."

Pauline gathered the man's arms together, then crossed his wrists.

"No," said Widow. "No, not like that."

She held Pauline's waist with both hands and coaxed her up, slipping her along then off of the man, then guided her to sit on the arm of the couch. She proceeded, then, to wrestle Lucas over and pulled his hands behind him.

"Oh, nice."

"Mm-hmm. Therapy? This is what I had to endure."

She tied his wrists tightly with several loops of the cord, and Pauline said, "You got him now, Widow. Tied up just like—"

"You deserve it, too," she said to Pauline. "Oh, I think maybe you're next."

"Um . . ."

She watched, suddenly quiet, as Widow began winding tight loops with a longer rope, starting near his tied wrists and packing all of the coils together all the way up his arms before tying a secure knot.

"Well, um, that ought to do it. You sure have—"

"No sound from you," she leaned close and said in Lucas's ear. "I don't want to hear you!"

"Oh, my . . ." Pauline said to herself.

Widow had brought back long strips of dusty cloth, and she held one with both hands to wedge it under his face. She found his closed mouth and pulled it tighter, jerking it from side to side until he opened his mouth and accepted it.

"That'll certainly keep him—"

"There we go. Nice and tight in that mouth. It's exactly what you deserve."

Widow circled his head twice with each of the ends that she held, then paused to listen to his strained attempts at breathing before she used all that remained of the strips to tie as many knots as possible.

She touched her fingertips to his taut lips, tapping them then rubbing them. She poked one finger against the cloth wound tightly between his lips and tipped her ear close.

"Pauline, he's barely breathing."

"Well, he can't, Widow, you—"

"He didn't resist at all. I think he likes it."

"Huh?"

"Help me roll him over. He'll tell us."

Together, they got Lucas onto his back, and both marveled at the length of his exposed appendage jutting out of his unzipped pants and lying up across his belt.

"Oh, wow, Widow. Look at that."

"It only gets him more excited. All of it—the ropes, the gags, the—"

"For you, though, back when you were, I mean, that didn't—"

She hissed and glared at Pauline and said, "No! I didn't enjoy it, so don't even ask. Just don't."

"Fine. Sure. Hey, now that you got our boy all helpless, let's tag-team him. You bite, and I'll fuck."

Widow was already clearing an unbitten space on his side, bunching his shirt high up, and said, "Don't I get to fuck him too?"

Pauline shimmied herself down onto him, grunting softly with every push, and said, after she'd hit bottom, "Sure. But . . ."

Widow held her lips back, fangs long and close to his soft skin, and said, "But what?"

"Mm, maybe you like something else more."

She hissed her response, not as a question: "Biting."

"Mm-hmm. And sucking. You like the sucking part."

"He's a juicy baby boy for me. He's so juicy."

"Mm-hmm. You like juicy things. Not just biting things."

Pauline grinned, eyes mostly closed, as she watched Widow hold her fangs ready but turned her eyes to the juicy part of her that was swallowing part of the young man.

Her stomach growled, and she said, "Yes. Yes, I do."

"Do you feel your fangs, Widow? Do you feel how long they've grown?"

"Mm-hmm. It feels so good."

"Mm, I'd bet. Keep watching and suck, Widow. Suck."

Widow moaned and drove in her points. The two punctures sprung out tiny red leaks before she'd closed her lips around them, then her throat moved with her steady, relentless swallowing.

"I think even that word is good for you. Suck, Widow. Mm-hmm, suck."

When Pauline moaned and fussed around with her hair, she didn't look away from what Pauline was doing to the part of Lucas that the biting and sucking and tying had excited, engorged, and given endless vigor.

Pauline watched Lucas's chest taking short, jerky attempts at breathing and said, "Don't stop, Widow. I think he wants you to suck everything he has out of him."

She backed her fangs out, showing the smeared blood and the trickles that she'd set free to leak down onto the couch.

Shifting enough to hold her face near his, she said, her voice dripping like the sweetest of nectars, "Is this true? You wish for me to enjoy all that you have?"

Even Pauline held herself still as both women watched the thin cracks of his eyes, focused only on Widow, and they saw him nod.

"Oh, such a good boy. Such a very good boy for me."

After a quick glance up at Pauline, with her lips peeled back to show blood all over her fangs and other teeth, she tipped Lucas's head back and snarled as she bit deep into his neck.

Sometimes tipping her head, with her stomach growling and her throat swallowing at regular intervals, she kept going as Pauline spoke behind her and shifted around with every bounce Pauline was giving the man.

"Don't . . . don't stop, Widow. It's like . . . an experiment. And you're so, so . . . hungry. Keep . . . sucking. Suck, Widow."

Widow moaned and sucked, and Pauline said, "Oh God, I think I'm cumming. I'm going to cum, Widow."

"Mm-hmm."

She slipped out her bloody fangs and said, "Mm, me too."

"You . . . you too? Just from that?"

"Oh, God yeah. More than just the bite—I love him, Pauline. I . . . I . . ."

"Widow, but you're . . . you're consuming him."

She looked from Pauline to the man's throat, then hissed out a soft sigh.

Rushing the words, Widow said, "There's no difference. Same. All the same."

She attacked his neck in a fresh place, her fangs longer than before, and Pauline, moaning, leaned forward on the man. Her face pressed against Widow, and she kissed her hair and ear and shoulder and anywhere she could.

With her face buried in thick black hair, Pauline moaned and said, "Oh God. Oh, I'm sure cumming, Widow."

Pauline had slowed herself only long enough to draw out her orgasm, and she smiled when she heard Widow moaning almost as loudly as she continued her deep bite into Lucas's neck.

Then, smiling, Pauline renewed her pumping on the still stiffening post. But she tipped herself up enough to watch Widow and sometimes the man's chest.

Moaning and rocking her head from side to side, Widow kept sucking and swallowing and she only stopped when Pauline said, "Uh, Widow. I think he's dead."

"Mm?"

"No, really. His breathing stopped."

Widow snapped her fangs free, leaving a dripping trail across him and leaned back to watch his chest, which wasn't moving at all.

After a single sob, which bore no taste of honey or any kind of nectar, Widow said, "Oh, God. I killed him? Pauline, I was just so hungry. I went crazy!"

"Widow, it's okay," Pauline said, pausing her amorous ride. "He was probably close to begin with, and something around here would have finished him soon enough anyway."

Widow still looked down on the unmoving man, sobbing as quietly as she could.

"Or that monkey would have . . ."

Widow wiped at her tears and chuckled softly.

"Fucked him in the ass."

"Yeah. Then killed him too."

"Thanks, Pauline. I hope it wasn't my biting that—"

Lucas's chest expanded from halting, choppy inhales until it was swollen and full. Then, it all wheezed out, and he resumed his strained breathing.

"Oh my God. He really was dead, wasn't he?"

"What is this, Widow? He was . . . what? Just sort of dead?"

"Was it from my bites? Oh, you know what? Maybe I'm not just sucking. Maybe—"

"I like you talking about sucking."

"Pauline, this is serious!"

She grinned and added, "I like talking about sucking too. Words can be fun. But no, I'm saying that maybe my bites are doing something else too."

"Oh. Oh! Like, poison?"

"I'm sucking his juices and feeding him poisons? What the hell is this?"

"No questions why, Widow. Not in this nightmare world. Bite him again. Suck, Widow. See if you can 'sort of' kill him again."

"What if he really stays dead?"

"Like you said: loving and—"

"Yeah. Loving and consuming—all the same. Oh, damn, it sure is."

She bared her fangs with a determined hissing, then started to lean for Lucas's throat.

But all three of them, even nearly-dead Lucas, held still and listened as someone else or something else rapped on their door.

Chapter 29 – The Crafter Named Marie

Widow hissed softly, her fangs almost grazing Lucas's smooth neck skin, and said, "Again with the door?"

Pauline chuckled and said, "Someone else for you to bite, Widow?"

"Hmm. Maybe for you to fuck, too, Pauline."

"Good. Keep the F-word coming."

"It feels, I don't know, crude."

"No. Everything you do is sexy."

"Because I have fangs?"

"Hmm. Definitely part of it. So, you want to watch me fuck whoever is knocking this time?"

Widow giggled and nodded.

"Maybe I will," Pauline said. "It's the only real thing I remember about myself from when I was alive: goddamn sex addict."

Widow sat back on her heels, then rubbed a fingertip around on the bloody mess of the young man's neck.

"Well, I wasn't, um, anything like this."

"No biting and sucking and getting all fangy like that?"

"No. Never. I still remember playing with myself for someone, though. I remember telling him things too."

"Uh-huh. And not just because you were lost in an orgasm."

"Hmm. Maybe not."

Widow coughed, looked toward the door, and then added, "Oh, you know what? I did send Igor out. Maybe that's him."

"Go look," Pauline said as she slid herself up, very slowly so that Widow could watch, then dismounted. "But from what I heard, no way in hell I'm fucking him."

She threw the blanket back over the bound and gagged man, covering even his face.

"Hey, um," Widow said. "Maybe make a little . . ."

"Good idea."

Pauline reached under, pointed the spear toward the ceiling, and let the blanket hold it upright.

"Yes. Just like that."

"You did that, Widow. Somehow, you and those sweet little bites of yours."

Widow's stomach whined out a low rumble.

"It wasn't enough," she said while standing and tidying up her makeshift robe. "I didn't want to stop."

"I felt the same. For something else, though."

"Addict."

Pauline scoffed, then smiled and said, "You too."

Widow smirked but gave Pauline a smile before turning and beginning a walk toward the door. With her hand on the knob, she spun the dial around, then pulled in the door.

Igor grinned up at her. Around his wrist was the looped end of a narrow black band of some stout material, and Widow followed it with her eyes. It ended in a bent, rusty metal clasp attached to a collar fashioned of a wide, oil-stained blue strapping.

Around the neck of a pretty woman younger than Widow.

One cheek showed moderate bruising, and a bloody smear at the corner of her pursed lips suggested that she'd tried to wipe it clean.

She wore simple clothes—stained and ripped jeans, a dark blue t-shirt, a dingy ball cap—and her curly and unruly brown hair barely touched her shoulders.

Widow looked again at the second man who'd tried to rape her.

"Igor. You're back. And you . . . who's this?"

"She's the crafter! I told you about—"

"No yelling."

"Sorry. Alright. I found her real quick—I know how to find hiding places. But she didn't want to come. I, uh, convinced her. I did good?"

Widow studied the woman's injuries, then looked her in the eye.

"Are you okay? I didn't send this, this man to hurt you. Only to ask for your help."

"Well, he did hurt me. Said he'd hurt me more if I didn't come along. With a goddamn leash!"

"Look. No yelling from you either, okay? What's your name?"

"Marie."

She leaned enough to look each way inside Widow's large room.

"Do you have food? Water? I'll help if you—"

Igor had jerked on the leash, tightening up the choking collar, and eliciting a bitter frown.

"Igor. Don't," Widow said without a trace of dripping sweetness. "Be nice."

The leash relaxed.

"No. I don't have anything. I just got here. You should come inside, though, before something comes along that wants to—"

She looked back toward the couch and smiled at Pauline, who covered her laugh with one hand.

"Hurt you. You probably know all about this world by now. Come on inside."

Marie waited, bulky tote bags hanging from each hand, until Igor had come inside first, tugging the leash to get her to move.

With all of them clear of the doorway, Widow locked it up again. She turned around to see that Pauline had walked over and stood nearby.

"Hi," she said, looking at both Igor and Marie. "I'm Pauline. I'm, uh, a friend of Widow's."

Igor stared up at Widow, his eyes big and round.

"That's my name now, Igor."

"Okay. Yes. It's a good name."

"You and me, Igor," Pauline said. "Let's scout around and see what we can find."

"Like what?"

"Well, food would be nice. Water. All kinds of stuff."

He listened, then looked up again at Widow.

"Widow?"

"Yes. Go with her. You might see something useful."

"As you wish."

"Yes. Always. You're my slave, remember."

"I remember!"

"Don't yell."

"Sorry."

"He's your slave? That's pretty cool."

"Thanks, Pauline. He's happy enough."

Widow spun the right numbers, let them out, then said, "Pauline, just three knocks, okay? Then, I'll know it's you."

"Sure."

She closed the door, spun to lock it, then turned and leaned her back into it while she took a better, longer look at the crafter named Marie.

*   *   *

"So," Marie said as she set both bags on the floor, "your slave said you need clothes made."

"Yes," Widow said, her voice normal. "I'm glad it took him a while to find you and—oh, I didn't tell him to force you to come. My apologies."

"So, I can get rid of this?"

She held up the leash, and Widow quickly took it and pulled just enough to take up the slack.

Smiling, she said, "Unless you think I need it," then bounced her eyebrows.

287

"No," Marie said, looking down and smiling, then back up. "I'll help you out. I've helped a lot of people here. I used to be a seamstress, before—well, before I got here."

"Hmm. We were all something else, I suppose. No, I'm sure we won't need this."

She let the leash drop from her hand and watched Marie's fingers, so near her neck, as she unhooked it from her collar, then looked around for somewhere to put it.

"Anywhere. There's no organization in here yet."

Marie was about to toss it when her eyes rested on the couch and what was obviously a covered-up body.

"Hey, um, that's not—"

"No, he's not dead. And it's obvious, as you can see, what he has on his mind."

Marie laughed and said, "Wow. Uh-huh. Um, so . . ."

"Just drop it. And the collar too. There's no need to, uh, clutter up your neck like that."

"Okay, I will."

She quickly let both items clatter to the floor.

"Grab your bags. Let's talk."

She snatched them up and followed Widow to the two blue high-backed chairs guarded by a brooding stare from a grim woman spread thin on the wall. They each took a seat.

"So, I decided just moments ago that I don't care about practicality. Not like this stuff."

She pinched the oily fabric of her pants, which also carried drying blood spots and a few shreds where the boy with razor teeth and nails had tried to get to the skin of her legs.

"So, not reactor work clothes."

"Oh, it's that recognizable? You can tell?"

"Yeah. I think they have a warehouse full of that. Everyone that gets out of there is wearing that stuff."

"Good. You understand why I'm done with it."

"Sure. So, what did you have in mind?"

"First, what kinds of materials do you have?"

"Honey, there's not much to—"

"It's Widow. Try that."

"Sure. Um, Widow, any material that was nice is mostly used and spongy with crude oil. There's only—"

"I saw a lot of oil on my way here from the reactor. That stuff is everywhere."

"You actually got yourself out of there? Well, shit. Good for you. So, don't get grossed out, but the best stuff I have came from the bats. The big ones."

"I hate them."

"We all do. So, you won't mind that they get harvested for all kinds of stuff."

"Not at all. Show me."

She lifted out of a bag a small swatch of flexible black material that felt and acted much like leather.

"Your friend that just left with—hey, what was going on with his back?"

"Oh, that. He has an extra head. I ordered him to keep that covered."

"Good. It's gross. I hate this place. So, your friend, Pauline, was wearing pants probably made from this. It's got some decent stretch to it."

She handed it to Widow, who caressed it, then tried pulling it apart each way, then held it up to sniff.

"This is good. Mostly, I want a couple of skirts, but at least one pair of pants would be good."

"Sure. We can do that. What else?"

"What else you got?"

She pulled out a strip of white cloth and held it out to Widow.

"It's real cloth. Someone ran out of that reactor place with a bundle of something, no one's sure, but maybe it was parachutes or something."

"Uh, I heard there's no sky. Just rock way up there. You have planes down here, too, or what?"

"I've seen giant balloons up there sometimes. It's rare. Maybe it was for that. Or maybe people used to jump from them. God, I don't know."

"Can you make blouses out of that?"

"Sure."

"Anything, um, thinner?"

Marie grinned and pointed at her.

"You're thinking underwear, right?"

Widow laughed and said, "Yeah, and you won't need much material."

"I kind of like your style. Yeah. We can get you all of that."

"Good. Thank you."

Marie sat forward, then looked carefully all around the room before sitting back.

"So, this seems private. I hope you're not shy. I need some measurements."

"Oh, I didn't even think of that. Of course."

Widow stood, stayed near her chair, and rested her hands on her hips. Marie scooted herself to the edge of her seat, shaking her head while looking up at her.

"No, um. I'll be quick, but your clothes are too baggy."

"Oh, of course."

While Marie dug around inside her bags and laid items beside her and on the table with the candelabra, Widow unbuttoned her shirt, slipped it back over her shoulders, then tossed it onto her chair just as Marie looked up.

"Good. You still have a bra."

"It got damaged. The clasp is all messed up, but it still sort of works."

"If you threatened to kill me if I didn't make one of those, I'd say, have at it."

Widow laughed and said, "I'll try not to let it get ruined any worse. This is good?"

"Well, maybe lose the bra too. I can probably rig up a new clasp for it. If you want."

Widow was already slipping the straps down off of her shoulders when she said, "Thanks. I might not wear it much, though."

Marie only stared straight ahead at Widow's bared breasts and didn't look where she'd dropped the bra. She coughed and looked away.

"Uh, you wanted pants, too, right? I can't get a good inseam or anything else through those khakis. I'm guessing you want a tight fit on the pants?"

"Yes,"—Widow kicked off her boots then let the pants drop and stepped out of them—"everything else too."

"Sure. We can do that."

She stood with a measuring tape, then took one step to stand in front of Widow, who held her arms out to her sides.

"I, uh, I could just eyeball it if you—"

"No. I want a snug fit for the blouses."

"Gotcha."

With Widow watching Marie's eyes and hands, the crafter looped the tape first around her waist, nodded and mumbled a number, then slipped it up higher and did it again.

"You're not writing anything down?"

"Nope. Good memory from doing this so much."

She paused to hold Widow's gaze, then brought the tape up across Widow's back, then pulled both ends across her breasts and held it together between them.

"Okay, that should—"

"Hold it. I think a little bit tighter would be good."

"Uh, sure."

Still looking into Widow's eyes, she tightened it up, squeezing her breasts, and she held it there.

Widow sighed and said, "Mm-hmm. That's nice."

"You, uh, you're quite attractive for a widow."

"I'm not. My name is Widow."

"Oh, sure. Okay. So, this is about right? Squeezing just about that much?"

"Mm-hmm. That should do."

"Um, sure. Let's just fit you for the pants and skirts, alright?" Widow nodded.

Marie let the fabric tape slip down behind Widow, then knelt in front of her. She spun her hat around, pointing the bill behind her, then tipped her head back to see Widow looking down at her.

"I already got your waist. Just need the hips . . ."

She got the tape snug around Widow's cheeks, nodding as she mumbled the numbers to herself, then looked up again.

"Uh, that inseam. You'll, uh, need to . . ."

Widow stepped her bare feet farther apart, then held Marie's shoulders.

"For balance."

"Oh, uh, sure. Okay."

Marie played the tape out, pinching the very end of it, and tried to hold that high up between Widow's thighs.

"Okay, got it. That's—"

"Maybe double check that. I'm not sure you got the full length."

"Uh, sure."

Marie pushed the end of the tape, held tight in her fingers, higher up, pressing it into Widow, who moved her hands to the sides of Marie, touching her cheeks.

She looked up and said, "Uh, um, I think I got that."

"The thighs too."

With Widow holding her face with both hands, palms against her skin, she looped it around one of her thighs and mumbled.

Marie looked up, grinning, and said, "You have some really strong legs. You an athlete?"

Widow said, "Only if you count running from monsters. Would you run from monsters?"

Marie's eyes got big and round, and she said, "Oh, for sure I would!"

She still held the tape around the smooth, bare skin of Widow's thigh, and both hands were touching her. Widow let just a little bit of honey blend smoothly into her voice.

"Even if I was the monster?"

"I . . . I, um . . . don't think I'd even think—"

Widow smiled and fluffed her hair gently, then said with a completely normal voice, "I'm not a monster."

Marie sighed, still touching her thigh, kneeling, and looking up into Widow's eyes.

"Besides," said Widow, "you haven't finished my wardrobe yet."

Marie let out a single nervous laugh, and Widow helped her up, then placed a hand on each of her arms.

"Boots. I have some ideas for boots too. Can you make some?"

"Yeah, sure. The only difficult thing is the soles. But I can do it. I can scrounge up materials, probably even in this building."

"And after you're done?"

"Yeah?"

Marie waited, holding her breath.

"They, you can try to run. Or . . . maybe you won't."

Marie tipped her head to one side and stared for a second, then she let her deep breath out, and they both laughed.

"I'll get started right away."

"Good. Thanks."

Chapter 30 – Nauseating Ball of Bait

"Hey, hold up a second," Pauline said before she and Igor reached the stairwell.

He'd been leading the way, and she'd checked out the lump under his jacket from every angle. He stopped and waited for her to get beside him.

"What's wrong?"

"Your back. That's what's wrong. What's the fucking deal?"

He grinned and said, "You want to see? I'll show you!"

"Don't start that yelling again. I swear."

"Sorry. Okay, no show. It's an extra head. I got it at the reactor."

"Oh my God, it's true. That's so gross."

He looked down and started up the steps. She followed.

"Hey, sorry. It's not your fault. Does it talk?"

"No, but it can look around. Uh, sort of. It's not normal."

"You think?" she said, shaking her head and grinning.

He looked down again but kept ascending.

"Sorry again. Fine, just keep it all packaged up. I don't think anyone wants to see it."

"Okay. Sure. I think it likes Scarlet."

"Widow."

"Yeah. Her. When I, um . . ."

Pauline grabbed his arm and pushed his back into the wall on a landing halfway up to the next level.

"You tried to rape her, you shitty little freak."

"I'm sorry. I'm stupid, and I don't deserve to live. I asked her to kill me, and I meant it. I meant it!"

"Maybe I will."

"She's beautiful. I saw her naked."

Pauline's eyebrows perked up.

She let him go and said, "Hmm. How'd she look?"

"Mm, like a dream. A dream! You'd rape her too! You'd—"

"Stop yelling. Dammit, Igor, you might as well be phoning in the goddamn monkeys."

"Huh?"

"Too goddamn loud. No, I'd never have to rape her. She'd volunteer."

"I wish I was you. I wish!"

She gave him a smile and said, "You'd miss having that spare head."

"Yeah, but I'd play with myself all the time if I had your body. All the time!"

"Of course. I do with this body. Mm, it all feels so good."

"You're making me—"

"Too loud."

"—crazy!" he whispered.

"Don't blame that on me. Come on. Let's keep going."

They resumed the trek, and he said, "What are we looking for?"

"Nothing special. Just scoping out the place. Anything Widow could use or should know about this place."

They were approaching the floor directly above Widow's, and they saw no door leading out of the stairwell.

"Come on," Pauline said. "Keep moving."

The next floor up was the same, as was the one above that.

"To the roof."

"We should go back," said Igor. "It's just a roof. Fucking bats flying around."

"No, we have to figure this out. Something isn't right. There are three levels above Widow's lair that—"

"I like that: Widow's lair!"

"Wonderful. Come on, loudmouth."

She kicked open the rusted metal door that swung out onto the gravel roof from a small metal shed.

"See? It's just a roof," the man with two heads said as he twisted his hands together and frowned at the black sky all around.

"There," Pauline said as she pointed to the roof's edge at the front of the building, and she started walking toward it.

There was just enough glow from the distant burning sea that they could make out the building's edge.

But Igor stayed back, and he said, "If I go close enough, I'll jump. I'll jump! I want to die! And I—"

"Shh. You can be a slimy piece of bait for the goddamn bats if you want, but I have better things to do. So shut your mouth, whichever one was yapping."

"It's only this one. Sorry."

"Fine. Come on."

He followed her to the low parapet, where she leaned over enough to look straight down.

"Fuck, this is high."

"Let's go back. I miss Widow."

"Oh, shut up. Hey, there's a ledge there. Climb down this pipe and see what you can see?"

"What? No!"

"When Widow isn't around, you're my slave. Got that?"

"No, I'm not! I don't have to—"

She pulled the knife out of the sheath clipped inside her waistband and aimed the point toward him.

"I already said I want to die. Go ahead. I'm not your slave."

"What? Kill you? That's too easy. How about if I chop off sloppy little pieces of that head and feed them to you? How about that, huh?"

"You wouldn't."

"Yuck. I sure don't want to touch it, but I'll do it. Maybe the eyeballs first. Squishy little appetizers. Then, some of its brain, if it has one. Maybe you don't even have one. Bone chips from the skull. I'll laugh when a sharp piece gets snagged up in your throat and—"

"Okay! Dammit. But after this, I'm not your slave anymore."

"We'll see. Shimmy your sorry ass down that pipe. Tell me what you find."

"Dammit."

He looked over, then sucked in a quick breath and shook his head.

"Fine."

He leaned over onto the low wall, then rolled up onto it and grabbed the slender vent pipe running up alongside the building before bending and running off somewhere into the darkness on the roof.

Reaching around with his oily sneakers, he hooked one on a support brace, then began feeling around for the next one down. With the streetlights far below giving Pauline a silhouette view of his slow progress, he shifted from side to side, stepping lower each time, until he could spin his back against the wall and stand on the ledge.

He tipped his head back and looked up at Pauline.

"Fine, dammit. I'm here. I'm almost dead. I know I'm going to—"

"Shh. You're easy pickings for the bats. Just a nauseating ball of bait on a wall. Look around."

Holding the pipe, he leaned out and looked each way, then back up.

"Windows. Boarded up."

"Widows? A few levels down?"

"No. One level down. Then, the next. And the next. All boarded up."

"Huh. There are rooms above Widow's. But no way to get in them. Weird. See what else you can see."

She waited, watching his shape dark against the dim street far below, and saw him lock in place, then slowly turn his head to face up at her again.

"I want to come back up!" he said in a strained whisper.

"Why?" she said, her voice at a normal level. "You're not done. Keep—"

"Shh! There's a monster down there, on the street!"

"So what? There are monsters every—"

"Not like this! He's—"

"Even when you're whispering, you're yelling."

"Sorry! He's gigantic, and I can see him because he doesn't have a shirt. And, and—"

"Spit it out already."

"He's carrying a sword!"

"You're a pussy, Igor. Both of you. Fine. Come on up."

She sat on the roof, her back against the parapet, and listened to him scraping his way to the top.

"Huh. Not the kind Widow likes."

She heard a raspy whisper from over the side.

"I'm going to fall!"

She didn't move—she only scoffed and said, "No, probably like Widow loves."

* * *

After running down four flights of stairs, Pauline leading and Igor holding his other head as still as he could, they soon stood outside Widow's door.

"What did she say? How many knocks?"

"Three," said Igor. "Shall I?"

"I command you to knock."

"We're done with that. I belong to Widow. Only to Widow!"

"Fine. Who wants a screaming slave anyway? Go the fuck ahead and knock."

He knocked three times, and they waited.

They saw the doorknob rotating, then the door began to swing in, and Marie was there to greet them.

"She told me to let you in. She's, um, kind of—"

"Persuasive," Pauline said, then gave Igor a shove into the room.

Marie closed the door, gave the mechanism a spin, then walked quickly back to Widow, who was still standing naked near her chair.

"Uh, having some fun?" said Pauline.

Widow shook her head and said, "Only taking measurements for the wardrobe. Crafter Marie is quite thorough."

"I'd bet. Sure. Um, we—"

Pauline stopped and tipped her head at the sight of Marie again kneeling right up against Widow and playing with a tape measure around one of her thighs.

Widow looked down and said, her voice thick and sweet, "Good crafter," and played with her hair with both hands before looking again at Pauline.

But Pauline was still looking lower, watching as Widow turned the crafter's head and rested her cheek on her thigh.

"You what?"

"Uh, we have news. We went upstairs—thought we'd check the rooms up above first. It's weird, but there aren't any . . . any . . ."

She squinted at Marie reaching one arm around Widow's legs, then using both hands to test the size of Widow's other thigh.

She looked back up when Widow shrugged and said, "Thorough. Told you. There aren't any what?"

Pauline coughed, smiling, and said, "There aren't any doors for the next three floors. No access from the stairs. And Igor climbed down the front of the building to—"

"She made me!"

"Stop yelling," Widow said calmly, giving her eyes a quick roll.

"So, he climbed down and saw that there are windows to those floors, but they're all boarded up. Widow, something's up there."

"Something good?"

"Hell if I know. We should try to figure it out."

"Good. We will. Somehow. What else?"

"I didn't see it, but he said he saw—"

"A giant! He was walking on the street, and he was nothing but muscle. Gigantic! And he carried a sword that—"

"Wait," said Widow. "Pauline, Igor, how many swords have you ever seen in this shitty place?"

"None," said Pauline.

"Me neither, Widow. I have good eyes, and—"

"Yeah, extras," Pauline said with a snicker.

"And I think the sword was bloody. It was long!"

"Hmm . . ."

While Pauline and Igor stared and waited, Widow looked down at a crafter girl who was looking up at her. She let the words drip out, not at their sweetest level but still with an undeniable sticky feel.

"Are they the same size?"

"Oh boy," Pauline whispered, not hiding a grin, as she and Igor watched the crafter, still on her knees, hold both of Widow's thighs, moving her palms slowly around behind them.

Just to Igor, she added, "Addict."

When Widow started to pull Marie's face closer, Pauline blurted out, "But we didn't find any food. Widow, we need food."

Widow didn't look over. Neither did Marie.

"I want food too!"

Widow scoffed, then reached lower to nudge Marie's shoulders, aiming her back toward the other chair before she focused again on Igor.

"You're just a screaming little thing, aren't you?"

"Sorry. Hungry, though."

"Well, I'm kind of hungry too. For, um, real food."

Pauline covered her mouth and snickered.

"What do you suggest, Pauline?"

"I can get you some. Back where I live."

"Where in this city would that be?"

"It wouldn't be. It's almost impossible to find any real food here. It's just freaks eating freaks."

She glanced down and said, "Sorry, Igor. Face the facts."

Looking at Widow again, Pauline said, "It's a house up on a mountain just past the outskirts of town."

"Why would you even be here, then? Why were you running along the street?"

"Well, if you must know, one reason is that if you know where to look, you can find small stashes of truly bizarre drugs. You never know when you might need them."

"Huh. Alright, and what's the other reason?"

"I have a friend that hides himself away around here. He's, um, kind of special."

"Special, how?"

"You want the plain, simple answer?"

"Always."

"Alright. He's a vampire."

"No. You're kidding, right?"

"It's no joke. He's real, they're real, and his ass ended up here too."

"So, aren't you afraid of him?"

"No, he's alright. I sometimes let him nibble, and I've actually begged him to convert me. But he won't. Says he doesn't even like biting women. He just takes a little blood, which I don't mind, and we're good. Like visiting a friend for a spot of tea."

"A spot?"

"He's British."

"This place is weird."

"Yep. So, I suggest you and I take a hike over to my place, which really isn't my place. I just rent a room."

"How does that even work? There's no money here, is there?"

"Trade," said Igor. "Even if you have nothing, you have something to trade."

"Just need a pulse, huh?" said Pauline.

"Nope," he said with a big grin.

Pauline scoffed at him, then looked back at Widow.

"He's right. I just don't pay all that often. So, you want to check it out?"

Widow turned toward Marie and said, "I'd like it if you could stay and craft those things for me. Will you?"

"If you want me to. Sure. Just bring back some food for me, alright?"

Widow pointed at her and said, "It's a deal."

She focused on Igor and said, "There's a whole lot I need from you."

"Finally! Yes! I—"

"Stop shouting and no. No. You stay here and keep an eye on Marie. Protect her with your life if you have to."

"I will. I want to die anyway."

Pauline scoffed and said, "You could have just jumped, you lying coward fuckhead. Fuck *heads*."

"I, uh, want to die quick. Jumping takes time."

Pauline rolled her eyes up for Widow to see.

"Okay, good," Widow said. "You help her out. And figure out that attic or whatever is above us. You don't know what this building was before, do you?"

"No. No one does. No one survives long here."

"I will."

Chapter 31 – Me and You and a Monkey

Walking through the trashed and filthy lobby toward the building's entrance, Pauline scoffed and said, "This is where we first met. Sort of. I was out on the street."

"Yeah. With a monkey on your tail."

"A monkey with a stiff tail sniffing around for my sweet tail."

"Pauline, I do believe he wanted more than a sniff. No matter how sweet."

"True. Hey, you hear that?"

They both listened to a clamor outside, and Widow started walking toward the door. Pauline grabbed her arm and stopped her.

"No, wait."

She looked each way, then pointed to one side of the doorway.

"There. Let's look out that broken shutter."

"Okay."

They hurried over and got their eyes aligned with a cracked opening in one of the planks shuttered over a tall and wide window area. Close together, they listened in silence as the raucous laughter and multitude of footfalls and an occasional yelling voice approached from the right.

Widow gasped, then said, "Oh my—"

"Shh!" Pauline said in an urgent whisper.

She covered Widow's mouth with a hand, kept it there, then moved to stand behind her and watch over her shoulder.

In her ear, she whispered, "Stay quiet. We don't want them to know anything is alive in here."

Widow pried her fingers away and said, "They, who? Who's out there?"

"No one you want to meet, Widow. There are far stranger things than butt-fucking monkeys."

Widow started to choke on a laugh, and Pauline covered it again, choking it even more.

A crowd came into view, all of them appearing to be calm and rational humans. Their clothing was tattered and oil-stained and hanging, and the hair of a lot of them was raggedy and clumped with globs of crude oil. But most were smiling, some holding hands and chatting as they wandered along the street, sometimes pointing at the buildings or up at the roofs.

And in the middle of the throng, taller than everyone around him, walked a shirtless man with muscles enough for ten men. His short brown hair was matted and clumped, and the skin of his torso, most of which was visible above the bobbing heads of those walking around him, was slick with sweat and oil and blood, all of it picking up and reflecting the paltry light from fixtures on poles lining the far side of the street.

Widow's body stiffened at the sight of him, and all she did was stare and jab her finger silently at the crack and the giant, sweaty man beyond.

"Yeah, he's big. He—"

"No, Pauline, I know him. I mean, I saw him before. Back at the reactor. He's an outright horror show."

"Hell of a body, though. Will you look at all those muscles?"

"Pauline! Don't even think about it. You want to know how he grew all of that?"

"I'd guess that before he died and got his sweaty ass thrown in this goddamn pit, he was a bodybuilder, so he probably took—"

"No! Pauline, he's been eating bodies at the reactor. His job is to toss them into some ugly oven, but he mostly just eats them."

"No way. No one gets that big just by—"

"He's eating mutants, so who knows what the hell he's ingesting?"

"Oh, yeah, mutant stuff. Twisted DNA. No telling what the fuck that would do."

"There's your telling of what it will do. Right there. His mother called him Junior. He—"

"You knew his mother? How? How did they both get here?"

"Take a wild guess."

"Oh, that's disgusting. Together, you mean."

"Uh-huh."

"Hold up," said Pauline. "Oh no, they're stopping. Right in front of the building."

They heard the calm voices and sometimes laughter from the crowd around Junior, who glared down at all of them.

"Who are those people, Pauline? They all live here?"

"Oh, where to begin? First, they're not people. Second, they're not alive. Third, they—"

"What are you talking about? They look pretty normal."

"Sure. But don't let—"

"Oh, I met that one," Widow said, pointing. "His name's Mortimer."

"Yeah, it is. I know him too. He—look! That muscle freak really has a sword!"

Junior was looking above their heads in every direction with his bloody sword held high and pointing wherever he looked.

"I know that sword, too, Pauline. It belonged to Archie, the—"

"I heard of him. The reactor boss of some kind? That Archie?"

"Yeah. And we killed Junior's mother with it. I mean, well, I didn't actually—"

Through the glass and shutter boards, they heard Junior scream, "Scarlet! Where are you?"

"Uh-oh. You killed his mom, Widow, now he—"

"No, I didn't. Not really. Archie made me hold the sword with him, then he chopped into her. She was still alive, but she was turning into some kind of insect."

"That happens around that reactor."

"Yeah, well, she must have told him my name somehow. He thinks it's my fault, Pauline."

"Terrific. Now, he's out hunting you with that goddamn sword."

"Shh. He's looking right at us."

"He can't see us, Widow. These buildings all look like they've been abandoned forever."

Mortimer stepped farther out in front of the mob and beckoned with his arms for the rest to follow. They complied, some jostling past Junior and his sword sweeping around before he joined them.

As the crowd moved past, out of sight, the street outside grew quiet again.

"Betsy," said Widow. "That was her name."

"Who? That guy's mother?"

"Yeah. Pauline, she was growing bug legs all over her."

"That's horrible. Was she a friend?"

Widow scoffed and said, "In a way, she was raping me as much as she could too. I was so scared and lost, and she took advantage of that."

"And now, she's a dead bug. Good."

"But Junior isn't dead. And he wants to kill me."

"He'll never find you. We should go before they come back."

"You think they might?"

"Probably not—this city's like a maze. They could wander around forever and never backtrack over anything. Let's get up on my mountain. Get you some actual food."

"Okay. And bring some back for my crafter."

"Huh. Your crafter. She's cute."

"Can't argue with you on that."

* * *

Outside the building, Pauline started off walking, and Widow whispered, "No, Pauline. That's the direction they all took."

Pauline turned back to her and said, "I just want to make sure they're leaving. Come on."

She extended her hand, Widow took it and followed along, both staying up close to the brick walls of the buildings they passed, until they could spy around the corner after the mob and Junior.

"Good," Pauline said before hiding herself again. "They're really hiking away from us. Can't be too sure around here."

"No, I guess not. So, we're going the other way?"

"Yeah."

She looked the other way along the street, squinting at the building tops that blocked the view of anything beyond the city.

"There," she said, pointing above the skyline. "See how it's kind of lighter but blacker all around?"

Widow stared for a while, then shook her head.

"No, I don't see it. It's just all black."

"Well, maybe it's just because I know it's there. That's Ham's mountain, and he staked his claim to some kind of official compound up there before I ever got here."

"Sounds safe. Who exactly is Ham?"

"Ham Sledger. Not a bad guy but pretty crude. You won't find any sophisticated types here."

"Just Junior types. Oh, and vampires."

"Yep, and Archies. Place is fucking full of them. You ready?"

"Sure."

They'd hiked for more than a block toward Pauline's mountain home when they heard a chorus of chattering and playful shrieking coming from up ahead.

"Oh, it's always something, Widow. I hate to say it, but I know that sound."

"Should I even ask?"

"No, you should hide. Me too. Like, really soon."

They took backwards steps, eyes watching for the first sign of what was coming toward them, and Pauline took quick glances at every boarded-up window as they passed.

She grabbed at the end of a split plank and pried it away from the window frame enough to look in.

"Oh, good. No glass to break. Give me a hand."

Together, they loosened enough of the boards to climb in, then swung closed all but one to cover the opening. The last one could only close far enough to leave room for the fingers pulling it closed, and they waited quietly, again side by side and watching the life forms roaming the city.

"Oh my God," Widow said in a hushed whisper. "It's a monkey man like the one that was following you."

"Shit. They never should have brought those things here. Just look how that turned out."

"What?"

"Some of us think they had research labs here long ago, before whatever happened, happened. The monkeys got all kinds of sex experiments done to them, mixing them with human men. They got loose, got themselves mutated even more, and they've been roaming in packs, eating anything they can catch."

"Oh," Widow said, giggling softly, "that's not all they're doing."

Pauline turned her head enough to hold Widow's gaze from up close.

"Yeah. Right. They're genuine ass-fucking freaks."

"Aside from his tail, he's kind of an impressive looking guy."

"Yeah. Kind of built. Fuck, try talking to one, though. You'll find out right quick he isn't no fucking guy, no matter what he looks like."

They could hear the scraping and sounds like insane laughter as they got closer.

"You're making that up. About what you said they do."

"No, really, they're known for that. I mean, I've heard that."

Widow squinted at her and said, "You say that like it's kind of a cool thing. Don't tell me one got you."

"Well, no. I mean, not yet. Maybe today's the day."

"Oh, just stop, Pauline. You don't want a man who's part monkey . . ."

Grinning, Pauline said, "Say it, Widow. Go on. You started this conversation, so just say it."

"Fine. You don't really want a monkey man fucking you in the ass."

Pauline had no reaction for a second, so Widow hurried to add, "You have to think about it? This is crazy. You can't possibly—"

"No, Widow. It's just . . . I get so horny all the time. I mean, all the time."

"But Pauline . . . a monkey man?"

"Crazy, huh? Maybe you'd want a monkey fucking your ass, Widow."

"What? No!"

"You're a bit of an addict yourself."

"Hmm. Not like that."

"What if you were all hot and horny, like while you're biting someone? Right then?"

"Oh, I don't think so."

Pauline pointed and said, "What if it was only a one or a two percent, maybe not an all-out ten, huh?"

Widow pointed back, smiling, and said, "Hmm, maybe for a one or a two. I don't know about my ass, though."

"What if you saw his tail out like a stiff fucking two-by-four?"

"Hmm. I guess that would be a sight."

The first monkey men were squawking and passing by, sometimes through the cones of struggling light but mostly in the shade between. Their tails weren't two-by-fours and waved around lazily.

"If you were biting me, I probably wouldn't complain if one nailed me right then. Your bites are so sexy."

"My bites can't be that sexy, Pauline."

"Remember that guy on the couch that you—hey, he's still up there?"

"Yeah. He should be fine with Igor and the crafter. I hope he's okay."

"Shit, Widow, he was still stiff like a flagpole when we left. That's what your bites do. That's all I'm saying: I'd probably be so goddamn horny that I wouldn't care what was fucking my ass."

"I feel that, too, when I'm biting. God, Pauline, it's an orgasm that just keeps cruising along. But I don't think I'd ever—"

Pauline gently squeezed one of Widow's ass cheeks through her baggy khaki pants, then leaned close enough to whisper in her ear.

"Alright. Picture this. The crafter did her thing, and you're wearing a sweet, short little skirt. That's what you ordered, right?"

"Uh-huh."

"Alright, and you're on your hands and knees, and I'm—"

"Wait. How'd I get like that? Who—"

"You mean 'what.' The monkeys made you get down on the floor, and I'm down there too. We're side by side, Widow, and the monkeys forced me to wiggle your tight skirt up over your ass. And they don't take no for an answer. So, your skirt is up and my pants are down, and—"

"Pauline, this is crazy!"

Pauline laughed softly in Widow's ear and whispered, "Oh, I know. We have to pass the time till all those perverted monkeys are gone, right?"

"I suppose."

"Good. So, we're both ready. I mean, those monkeys are lining up at the sight of the two finest asses they'd ever seen."

"Lining up? How many are there?"

"They travel in packs. They're too wild to just hang back and tell their buddies to have all the fun."

"Fun fucking our asses."

"Exactly. So, we're ready for all of them, but you're still not sure. You kind of want them to go wild on you, but it's a little scary too. So, I kiss you then offer you my neck."

"Ooh, your neck. Go on."

"You're still not convinced, then you look at the crowd of them, and you gasp at the sight of every goddamn tail totally stiff. Then, you grin because you know exactly what the fuck that means."

"Hmm, I guess I do."

"So, that gets you ready, and you bite. You suck. And the monkeys start shrieking and jumping around while the first two—"

"What? The *first* two? You were serious? All of them?"

"Yeah, exactly. The whole fucking tribe of them. And they're tens or worse. The first two of them get going on our asses, and we both want to scream because those guys are—"

"They're guys now? Pauline!"

"You know what I mean. So, they're pounding us, really stabbing in there, and we don't even care because we're both having crazy orgasms from whatever's going on with your bite."

"You've given this some serious thought."

"This world is insane, Widow. We have to laugh or we'll get just as crazy."

"But do we have to let monkeys fuck us?"

"In the ass. Maybe you'd want everything else with them too."

"What, like . . ."

"Say it."

"Um, like in my pussy too?"

"Yep. Maybe. What else?"

"Pauline, you're terrible. You're joking about me giving oral to a monkey?"

"No one talks like that here. Try it again."

"Pauline . . ."

"Say it. Go on."

Widow coughed, then said, "You're saying that I'd actually want to . . . suck a monkey's cock?"

"I don't know . . . maybe? Maybe you'd be so crazy that it would be your idea. I think you liked even just saying it."

"Oh, Pauline, you're just too—"

"Say it again. Come on. Just for fun, say you want to do that."

"Huh. Fun for you."

"Yep. Maybe you too. Go on."

Widow coughed, then smiled and said, "I'd want to . . . suck a monkey's cock."

Pauline patted her ass and said, "Yeah, I think you would."

"Pauline, there's no way that—"

"Anyway, they're all gone. See? We had some fun and stayed the fuck out of their way. Let's go find that mountain."

Widow started pushing the boards out over the sidewalk, then saw that Pauline was waiting, just watching her.

"Unless," she added, grinning at Widow, "you want me to call them back?"

"Pauline, you're too much."

"I'll take that as a yes. Alright, it's on the schedule."

"What is? You don't—"

"Me and you and at least one monkey man. Me and you and a monkey. A wild fucker too."

Widow rolled her eyes but smiled.

"And remember what you said you'd want to do."

"Hmm. I remember. Maybe I'll even say it again."

She leaned in and whispered in Pauline's ear, then backed away just enough to look into her eyes.

"I'd love to watch that."

"Hmm."

Pauline let out a deep sigh, then said, without a smile, "Damn, that's so sexy, Widow."

"Mm-hmm. I guess it is."

They both continued out of the building.

* * *

"See it now?"

Widow and Pauline had passed between the last of the buildings on the edge of the city with as much silence and stealth as they could muster. They'd heard the hoard surrounding Junior two blocks over at one point, but none from that group had wandered anywhere near enough to intersect their travels.

After a steady, mostly quiet hike away from the city, Widow stopped and looked behind them.

"I can hardly see the orange sky from that burning ocean or whatever that is."

"That's what it is."

"Okay, but everything's mostly just all black all around us. There's barely enough light to see anything at all."

She looked ahead again, squinting up, then left, then right.

"We're there? It's up with those stars?"

"Yeah, we're just about there, and those aren't stars. I left some fires burning out on the patio."

"God, that's high up. I can barely see them."

"Yep. It's a regular goddamn mountain."

They began to weave through and around natural rocks and cut slabs which had been discarded and stacked and provided space for even darker shadows. Sometimes, they could see enough that they could aim themselves around small fields of crude—perfectly flat areas that cast dull reflections of the fires high on the mountain. Other times, they walked through them, carefully placing each step, and found them to be more just a film than actual pools of it.

Widow stopped while again looking at fires twinkling so high above that they were barely visible, and she stopped Pauline with her.

"My legs feel good," she said. "Even the crafter thought so."

"Anyone would. That was quite a sight, her kneeling for you like that. She sure was feeling you up."

"Mm-hmm. She was. Thanks for the compliment. I know they're strong, but there's no way I can climb up this mountain. How the hell do you do that?"

"I don't. Come on."

She took Widow's hand and led her through an area where the rocks gave way to boulders, and there were places where they had to turn sideways just to fit between them. After rounding a particularly large one, Pauline stopped Widow.

Ahead of them, at the end of a path that was part tunnel and low enough that they'd have to stoop to get through, there was light.

"What's this?"

"A secret. Don't tell anyone. Really, Widow—no one."

"I won't. But what is—"

"Let's just get through. You'll see."

Holding Widow's hand, Pauline shepherded her along a narrow walkway that sometimes appeared carved out more than natural, and they soon stood in a modest clearing surrounded completely by jagged rock walls three times their height. On the far side, maybe twenty steps distant, a single bulb glowed where it hung from a loose wire above a dark pocket in the wall.

"No hiking for us, Widow. I'd never make it up or down this goddamn mountain either."

"Who could?"

"No human. Come on."

She took Widow's hand, and they began an easy walk in the dim light toward the other side, but they both kept their boots in the oil and dust when a rumbling boom raced toward them, then over the rock bowl where they stood, collided with the mountain, then echoed off into the distance.

"Dammit," said Pauline. "We have to—"

"Hurry! Let's get in that little cave!"

"There's no time, Widow."

She pointed to one side and said, "Over there! Go!"

Still holding hands, they got to the closest wall of rock, and Widow tried to back into it.

"No! The other way! Turn around!"

Widow didn't argue or question the command, and they both faced the jagged surface, then stooped low and put their arms around each other.

A second later, a hurricane howled over the tops of the rocks surrounding them, whistling and shaking loose the smaller stones that fell without any sound that could outdo the roar racing above them through the black air.

Only a second later, it all died.

"I hate that," said Pauline, then she brushed small stone chips off of Widow's shoulders.

"What the hell is that? That happened at the reactor too."

"Happens all the fucking time. No goddamn warning either. Ham said it's something to do with the air in this fucked up world."

"What about the air? It explodes?"

"No. He says it refills the oxygen or some goddamn thing like that."

She reached for Widow's hand, and they both stood.

"Now, maybe we can get the fuck up onto the goddamn mountain already?"

"Is it safe up there? From that?"

"So far. Yeah, we'll be fine. Come on."

Holding hands, they walked over to the dark alcove beneath the single dim bulb. Pauline fumbled around in a crack in the wall, then snorted out a quick laugh when she pulled something and made a click. And something in that alcove started to lower, a flat horizontal piece first, then sturdy sides, then a top—an open box big enough for far more than the two of them.

"An elevator?"

"Uh-huh. You'd never catch me prowling the goddamn city looking for drugs or any other—"

"And monkeys."

"Yeah, maybe. I was seriously getting fucking hot with all that monkey talk."

"I, um, kind of was too."

"Yeah, I could tell. I'm kind of sure you would want to—"

"Pauline, stop!"

"Alright. Really, though, I'd be trapped on that mountain and waiting on Ham to float me around with his balloon."

"Well, I can tell you're not the type to be dependent on anyone."

She brushed Widow's dark hair back over her shoulder, causing her to look.

"Maybe I'm already dependent on those little bites you love dishing out."

"Hmm. I do love dishing them out. Or I did back in my lair. Should I call it my lair?"

"Why not? That could be a sweet little hideout."

"Yeah. It'll need work, though."

"You do have a slave, remember?"

"Ugh. Igor. The freak with two heads that tried to rape me."

"Eh. Can't blame anyone here for anything they do. This place will make anyone nuts. You're not thinking about biting anymore?"

"I think maybe I'm just too tired. That's all confusing and now seems like I was just playing some kind of game. Pauline, I don't know what's happening to me. And right now, all I want most is to rest somewhere."

"Then, all rested up, you'll be planning out all your future bites?"

"Oh, Pauline, they're not that nice. You'll never get addicted to them."

"Huh. Says you. So, you ready?"

"Is it safe?"

"Safer than the city. Or anywhere else in this goddamn place. Come on."

Chapter 32 – Show Me Your Dungeon

Pauline bent over to get inside the elevator cab, and Widow followed. There was no door to be closed, and one side of the cab had a row of cabinets. Pauline pointed at them.

"I put food and other stuff in there. Weapons. Water. If I'm ever in the middle when the reactor kicks out, at least I'd be able to hang out a while."

"That sounds horrible. You could be trapped for a long time."

"I wouldn't have to be. That,"—she pointed up, where a square panel was distinct from the rest of the ceiling—"leads up top, and there are rungs built into the wall of the shaft. I've looked up out of here and seen them. There's supposed to be an exit to the side of the mountain somewhere, like a tunnel, but I'm not about to climb around and look for it."

"Unless you have to."

"Yep. Brace yourself. It isn't slow."

"Wait. You said there's food in here?"

"Sure. Some canned stuff. You want a bite? Ooh, I didn't mean that. You want something to snack on?"

"And bite. Later," she said, giving Pauline a grin. "Food sounds good, too, though."

"Well, let's see," Pauline said and opened a cabinet. "Crackers in a can. How tempting. If you want to—"

"I'll take those. Really."

"Sure."

She tossed a can with a pull tab toward Widow, who caught it, opened it quickly, and stuffed a handful of them into her mouth.

"Mm," she said, her cheeks swollen, "that's good."

"Not as good, maybe, as—"

Mumbling around the mushed-up crackers, Widow nodded and said, "Mm-hmm. But real food's good too."

"Enjoy. There's better stuff up top. Go ahead and ruin your appetite, though."

"I plan to."

Pauline sat with her back to a wall, and Widow had followed suit. Pauline hit a button, and they began to travel upward, slowly at first, then accelerating. In seconds, the box slowed, then came to a stop.

"And just like that, you're high up on Ham's mountain."

"That's quick."

"Uh-huh."

Widow leaned to look out of the elevator box, and all she saw was a dark room with only enough light to show that there was furniture and other things in there.

"My room. Come on."

She took Widow's hand and led her, sure of the way, toward her bed.

"I'm exhausted, Widow. How about you?"

"Like you can't imagine. This is all really just too much."

"Sleep will help."

"I feel bad about Lucas too."

"Don't. It's not your fault. Not really. Sleep will help that too."

She nudged Widow to sit, then lifted her legs up, laying her out without asking first.

"Comfy?"

"Mm-hmm. I'm almost asleep already."

"Here," she said, unfolding a blanket over her. "Getting all cozy is the best."

"Oh, that's nice. I'm so . . . I'm just . . ."

"Yes," Pauline whispered before lying down behind her and getting her arms around her waist, "you certainly are."

"Wha . . . what?"

"Nothing, Widow. Just sleep. This is the one place where both of us can relax because no one even knows we're here."

* * *

Pauline woke before Widow, the two of them keeping warm under a blanket in Ham's house on the mountain in the room that Pauline had claimed for herself.

With her face partially covered by Widow's thick black hair, Pauline only inhaled the scent, felt her every breath, and cautiously, slowly repositioned her arms around her as needed. Sometimes even when there was no actual need of it.

Widow stretched both arms straight out in front of her as she lay on her side, yawning the entire time, then licking her lips and sighing once, letting the air seep out slowly.

Pauline tightened her embrace for a quick squeeze, then said, "Good morning. Even though that doesn't make sense."

"Oh my God, I needed that. How long was I out?"

"There's no way of knowing. I've never seen a clock here."

Widow sighed again and said, "Maybe that's better. It probably doesn't matter anymore what time it is."

"Or day. Or month. Or—"

"Or year. Yeah. This is still so weird, but I feel better. Stronger. Like, a different kind of strong."

She rolled over to face Pauline and propped herself up on an elbow. She saw that Pauline was lying close, looking up at her, but she looked around the dark room first.

"What is this? This is your house?"

"Uh, just part of it. It's kind of my hiding place. No one else is allowed in."

"I'm in."

"Hmm. Almost no one. I mean, Ham never gets to come in here. And Risk, when he's around, isn't allowed in either. They don't even ask anymore. I even changed the combination."

"My lair's going to be the same way: invitation only."

"Good plan. I'd say keep Igor around long enough to extract some useful work from him. What else are slaves good for?"

"Nothing at all."

Widow sat up, still mostly covered by the blanket, and stretched and yawned, then said, "Where's the light switch? Show me your dungeon."

"Who said it was a dungeon?"

"No one. It's a secret room high up on some mountain, and no one's allowed inside. Could be a dungeon."

"Hmm. Maybe I'll rename it. Pauline's Dungeon. Nice."

"Is it always so dark?"

"Oh, you wanted the switch. Nope. Uh-uh. You get a tour of the house first. We'll save this for last."

"Is that elevator a secret too?"

"I've never said anything about it, and I'm not sure Ham or Risk know it's there. I found it hidden after I'd claimed it all as my, um, dungeon."

"I like it. You can lock yourself in and—"

"Or me and someone else."

"Ooh, you got me locked in. I might have to bite you yet."

"Promises, promises. Alright, you ready to check out the main house?"

"Sure."

They got off of the bed on opposite sides, and Pauline hurried around to guide Widow toward the few steps up to the door to the house.

"Steps."

"Okay."

In the near darkness, Pauline removed the pipe across the door, stood it up against the wall, then turned a heavy locking lever. When she pulled in the thick wooden door, the dim light of the living area greeted them.

"There's not much to see, but let's check it out."

"Okay."

Pauline closed the door behind them, didn't lock it, then led the way.

"That's the hallway to the bedrooms. I have one. Ham has one. There are others, but Risk sometimes just sleeps outside in his basket."

"His what?"

"Balloons, remember? He's got one, and Ham's got one. They have these big wicker baskets and stuff. We can look out there later. Anyway, Ham is gone with his. This here is the living area, just a big open mess where whoever's here hangs out. Over that way,"—she pointed toward a wide opening that led to a dark room—"there's a kitchen. It isn't much, but it functions."

"Ooh, a fire. Not a giant ocean of it."

"No, just a nice one there. We keep that going with a pot of water, which is good for all kinds of things."

"Water. I haven't seen any since I've been here."

"You won't. Ham says it all evaporates and floats up to the sky, which is just rock."

"So, where do you get it?"

"There are places where it trickles down from the world we died in. You have to know where to look, though. Ham knows. He's got a reservoir of it saved up just above the house."

"Ham sounds pretty resourceful."

"Yeah, he's a good man. He'd be better except for the time he spent at that damn reactor."

"How so?"

"Oh, never mind. You'll see eventually."

She reached out to brush back Widow's hair on one side, then the other, leaving it all falling down over her back. Then, she dabbed and wiped at her cheek, grinning about it.

"What?"

"Blood. Dried blood. Kind of tells us you're something just a little different. A sexy, dangerous kind of different."

Widow looked down and said, "Whatever it is, I didn't ask for it."

"Hey. Whatever it is is fantastic. Don't ever doubt it. I'll get you a fairly clean towel if you want to scrub some of that. There's a mirror right there too."

"Thanks, I think I will."

"Have a seat."

Widow sat in a dingy, worn upholstered chair near the fire and pot of hot water and watched Pauline walking toward the kitchen, swaying her hips in tight bat leather pants.

She returned with a few towels and handed them to her. In the pile was also a change of clothes, not much different than what she was already wearing but cleaner.

"Take your time," she said. "We have nothing but time, even though we can't tell it."

"Okay."

"And besides, we need to give that freak with two heads—"

Widow giggled and said, "My slave."

"Yeah, your two-headed slave. Give him time to figure out your attic. Oh, and your new wardrobe is probably getting stitched together right at this moment. Skirts and who knows what else."

"Marie knows. I know too. She's even going to make me some boots. I'm taking your advice and saying what the hell, make me some sexy clothes."

"Well, damn, I can't wait to see it all. I'll expect a regular fashion show from you."

"Plan on it."

Widow's head tipped forward, and she lost her smile.

"What? What's wrong?"

"It's not just new clothing that's back at my lair, Pauline. Remember Lucas? I think I killed him."

"No, I don't think so. You just, um, nibbled a little. He'll be fine."

"What if he's not?" she said, her eyes getting wet.

"Widow, he's okay. You'll see. And besides, like I said before, something in this god-awful world probably would have killed him if he'd left your building anyway."

"So, why not me? That's what you mean?"

"I didn't mean it like that. It's just a fucked up world. That pack of monkeys probably would have worked him over good. Try not to think about things too much."

On the verge of sobbing, Widow said, "How can I not?"

"I'll tell you exactly how—with a question: do you deserve to live? Do you deserve to survive?"

Widow still stared but also began shaking her head.

"Really, Widow. Do you? Once you answer that question, whether you say it out loud or not, your life here will make more sense. You won't have to beat yourself up about stuff."

Widow again looked down at her hands in her lap.

"You go ahead and enjoy that heated water, and I'll go on ahead and make sure my dungeon is presentable."

* * *

Before beginning to wash up, Widow watched Pauline again, who was giving her hips permission to sway even more as she walked toward her hideout.

"Hmm."

She kept her eyes focused back on her hands in her lap, let a few minutes pass, then sighed deeply and stretched out one of the small towels.

"You might be right, Pauline," she whispered.

She held her fingers close to the water for a second, then dipped them in and swirled the water around. Holding a towel, she soaked just part of it, then touched her face and neck all over, sometimes holding it away and studying it.

With her face cleaned, she wiped all of the exposed parts of one arm, then the other before laying the towel over the edge of the pot.

After a quick glance toward the doorway to Pauline's dungeon, she began to untie the knot in the belt that she still wore, let that drop, then pushed the buttonless flannel shirt back over each shoulder before removing it altogether and leaving herself bare.

Before reaching for the towel again, she kept a steady gaze at Pauline's door, then retrieved the towel, then looked again toward the door. Still watching for Pauline, she rubbed the hot wet towel all over, trying to get her back too.

Giving some attention to her breasts led to a soft moan, and she laughed quietly when it happened.

But she warmed the towel back up, barely wrung it out, and held it with both hands. She pressed it into her breasts, covering them, letting the warmth and wetness surround them, hold them, caress them.

And she rubbed the towel around, letting the coarse cloth drag across her nipples from every direction, many times. Holding the towel up under them with both hands, lifting them, she looked down and scoffed but with a smile.

"Hmm. They're bigger. It's not just the teeth—those fangs. What is going on with me?"

She gave the doorway a quick check, then looked at the pile of clothes, shrugged, then stood and started unfastening her pants. Before undoing them completely, she stooped down to untie her boots and kicked those to the side.

Free of the footwear, she wiggled her hips and got the pants to drop. All of it got nudged off to the side with the reactor-issued work boots.

"Crafter, I need you," she whispered, smiling about it, then added, "And not to bite."

She drew in a deep breath and sent it back out as a sigh.

"Well, maybe when you're done with your work."

While dipping the towel in the hot water pot, she grinned and said, "Hmm."

With fresh heat and wet enough to be softer than before, she wiped all around her bare thighs, front and back, then stretched out one leg at a time, wiping all the way down.

She hesitated, then scoffed and said, "Hmm, why not?"

She dipped for more warmth, then leaned back, angled her legs out straight, then let her knees spread as far apart as the chair would permit.

The first touch caused a gasp and got the hot towel pulled away quickly. She tried again, touching lightly and keeping it in motion. She crunched herself forward and got a better view, then proceeded to do a very thorough, very meticulous, and very dedicated job of cleaning.

Although she'd already spent a lot of time, she leaned back, closed her eyes, and made sure that she hadn't missed anything.

Not a single detail.

And she found that her fingertips had become as warm and wet as the towel, but they were smoother—so much smoother.

The towel found a place to bunch itself up on her belly, out of the way, and the cleaning continued.

Not just on the outside.

She began a soft moan, kept it low enough to not alert the dungeon dweller, and watched the door for any unexpected company.

And the fingers soon achieved so much more than a simple towel ever could.

She kept wiping and rubbing, fingertips warm and wet, while a soft moan drifted out with every breath.

With a smile and a sigh, she curtailed her thorough washing beside a sedately flickering fire.

"Alright," Pauline called from her room, "Looks good. Come on in whenever you're ready."

Widow kept her eyes closed but smiled, then made extra sure that she hadn't missed anything.

"Hmm. That's never quite done, is it?"

She giggled softly and laid the towel over the pot's rim, then took her time in getting dressed, but she left off the old work boots.

Tiptoeing barefoot, clean enough for any kind of inspection, she entered the dim confines of Pauline's dungeon, mostly unknown, off-limits to anyone else, and high up on Ham's mountain.

Chapter 33 – Kill Whoever You Want!

The crowd of not-alive people on the street kept shuffling along, chatting and laughing and following Mortimer as he led them through the streets with a barely noticeable buzzing from every direction.

Junior had stopped and become like an unmovable stone in their path, and the bodies were channeled and crowding together as they flowed around him like water in a stream. He looked up at the dark squares pasted to the street sides of the buildings, most covered over with planks or tarps, and some were just black and devoid of any inside lighting.

Pointing the sword at the windows on one side of the street, he called out, "Scarlet? Are you in there?"

The river of bodies kept flowing around him, and he looked at more of the boarded windows before scanning the other side of the street and pointing the blood-streaked tip of his sword at them.

"Scarlet? Why did you kill Mama?"

Most of the chattering folks dodged the mass of flesh in their way, but some collided and slipped off of his oiled skin to one side or the other.

He jabbed the sword again and said, "Did you make Mama a bug too?"

He looked down when Mortimer, who had fought his way upstream to get beside him, reached up and tapped him on his shoulder.

"Young man, I'm Mortimer."

"Hi, Mortimer. Do you know—"

"Well, what's your name, young fellow?"

"Mama always calls me Junior."

"Junior? Wonderful! What are you doing yelling and waving that sharp and delightfully bloody sword around?"

"I'm calling Scarlet. I want to find her."

"Oh, um, someone named Scarlet, huh? Hmm. It's a big city, young man. You could be searching for a long time. Why do you want to find this Scarlet character?"

"She killed my Mama."

"Oh, I don't think she'd—I mean, no one with such a pleasant name like Scarlet would do something so horrible. Would you like to come with us?"

Junior lowered his sword, then looked over the crowd in the direction they were migrating.

"Why? Do you know Scarlet? I want to find Scarlet."

Mortimer stepped himself into the calm waters downstream from Junior, then laughed and pointed.

"She might be that way, right? Why not take a little walk with all of us and we'll see, okay?"

Junior looked at the higher windows on each side, standing solidly and deflecting bodies, which kept Mortimer from being swamped. He pointed the sword toward one side and grunted, then let the blade fall.

And the sharp edge hit one of Mortimer's pack on a shoulder, digging it in.

The cut woman stopped and turned her head toward Junior.

"I'm sorry," Junior said. "I just want to—"

"Oh, it's okay. It takes more than that to dismember me."

"Huh? What does that word—"

She let the currents carry her along.

"See how friendly we all are?" said Mortimer. "You'd be very happy to spend some time with us."

"I would?"

"Well, sure. Of course! We're just about the friendliest, uh, people you'll ever meet."

"Uh, okay. And you'll help find Scarlet?"

"Why, yes. You'll never find her on your own, big boy. Oh, no. You need us."

"I do?"

"Sure! Let's just go with the flow. We're all heading back to our home. You'll be very comfortable there."

Mortimer gently nudged Junior's arm and got both of them walking along with the crowd.

"I will?"

"I'll see to it personally. Say, how did you get so, uh, beefy?"

"I like beef. But I never get beef. Everything else is good too."

"A young man after my own heart. Hey, I don't mean that literally!"

"Huh?"

"Nothing. Oh, just to be sure,"—he grabbed with both hands the sword handle in Junior's hand—"let's just unburden you of this—whoa!"

Junior, still walking, lifted the sword high over his head, and Mortimer's legs dangled high above the street.

"I like my sword."

"Yes, of course, you do. You, uh, can keep it. Yeah, keep it!"

The sweaty, oily arm thick with muscles lowered Mortimer back to the slick bricks of the street.

"My, but you're a strong one, aren't you?"

"I eat a lot. Mama likes me strong."

"Is that momma of yours really, uh, not quite living anymore?"

"Huh? She's kind of a bug."

He looked up and around and shouted to the dark sky, "Don't be a bug, Mama!"

"A bug, huh?"

He held Mortimer's gaze for just a second, then looked ahead as they continued hiking.

"I eat bugs too. Mama was a bug."

"Oh, you're just wonderful. I do believe you might be the King we've been looking for!"

"King? I can be King?"

"Sure! You only have to come with us, and we'll take good care of you."

"I'll be King?"

"Yes! And every King needs a sword, right?"

"I have a sword. See?"

He held it out for Mortimer to see.

"Well, look at that. You already have one!"

"Can the King kill Scarlet?"

"My boy, as King, you can kill whoever you want! Whenever you want!"

"I like being King."

* * *

"No, no," Mortimer said as he turned in one door of the double door set that led from the dimly-lit street to the darker building interior, "let most of them pass. They know the way."

"I don't know the way," said Junior.

"Not yet, no. But when you're King? You'll know everything."

"That's a lot."

"Yes!"

The talkative, smiling throng passed them, with Mortimer holding one door and a young blond woman holding the other.

"That's Janey," said Mortimer. "She's helpful with all kinds of things around here."

"Okay. Hi, Janey."

He waved at her, and she smiled and waved back.

Before the last two of the flock came inside, they stopped, grinning at Mortimer, who pointed at them and smiled.

"I didn't forget—you two have such very important work to do. The new King and I will—"

"He's our King? You found him?"

"Why, yes, Rousseau. He will be our splendid King very soon. Isn't he magnificent?"

"I'll say. He's big."

"I'm big," said Junior.

"Junior," said Mortimer, "these are Rousseau and Tanya. They have the critical task of seeing that we leave only darkness behind us when we return to our, oh, let's call it a hideaway."

"I don't hide."

"No, of course not—Kings don't hide from anybody. But we sometimes do. And we're happy to have you as our guest. Shall we?"

He gestured while starting off to follow the crowd that had passed, and Junior and Janey joined him. But Junior spun his head around enough to watch Rousseau and Tanya gently close both doors, slide in place a series of heavy bolts, then set across them a heavy timber in the iron brackets to each side.

He scratched at his head as he listened to the low buzzing and watched the two walking toward him.

"Huh," Junior said as he stopped walking. "They locked it. I could still break it."

Mortimer stopped, and Janey stopped with him.

"Well, of course, you could. That's just to keep out the things that don't belong in here."

"I'm King."

"Yes, you are. So, you most certainly belong in here with us."

They watched as Rousseau blew out the wall-mounted candle on his side of the wide, brick-lined hallway, and Tanya did the same on her side.

"I could do that. I know how."

"Well, sure you could. But Kings don't do any actual work. Come on. Let's get you to our hideaway where you won't be hiding because you don't hide. Kings don't hide from anyone!"

"Uh, okay."

They continued along as the hallway became a narrower tunnel that sloped downward, gradually at first, then increasing its steepness. Junior often turned to look and saw the two behind them snuffing out wall candles.

Beyond them, where all of the candles had been extinguished, was the blackest of night.

"Janey likes sex, you know," said Mortimer. "Well, that's just silly. We all do. Do you like sex, King? May I call you King?"

"I'm King. Okay."

"But what about sex? You like that?"

"I like Mama."

"Well, everyone likes their momma, King. So, tell me: is every part of you as fleshy and overdeveloped as these delectable muscles that we can see?"

"Huh?"

Mortimer coughed and said, "Janey, ask him."

She grinned up at Junior's neutral stare and said, "Do you have a giant cock, big like your other muscles?"

"I'm big."

"Yeah, but do you get a gigantic, screaming boner?"

"It never screamed."

She smirked at Mortimer and said, "This isn't easy."

"No, it isn't. Keep trying, though."

"We want to know," she said to Junior, "if your boner gets really big."

"I guess so. I could show you."

"You have a boner right now, even just walking with us?"

"You're pretty. I have a boner. It's big."

Mortimer snickered, leaned toward Janey, and said, "That's why he's King."

Addressing Junior, he said, "When we get home, and we're all gathered around, we'll make a wild, obscene spectacle of it. How does that sound?"

"Okay. What's a spectacle?"

"Your giant boner, King! That's what!"

"Okay."

They walked a little farther, and Mortimer continued.

"You know, King, that Scarlet that you mentioned—maybe she'd like that boner of yours too."

"She would?"

"Well, not if you kill her."

Janey giggled and said, "Oh, Mortimer. She still would, whoever she is."

"She's right," he said to Junior. "You can kill her and give her your boner, in whatever order you want. You're our King!"

"Okay. I'll eat her too."

"Oh my goodness," said Janey. "Mortimer, how did you find such a perfect King for us?"

"Well, I wasn't sniffing around and checking boners."

"Not this time?"

"No! That would have worked just fine, though. No, I could tell by his muscles."

"And his sword."

"Yes, Janey. His boner, his muscles, and his sword."

"In any order."

The three stopped and turned back when they heard Rousseau laugh and say, "Boner first!"

Tanya laughed and said, "Our King needs big muscles too!"

"And the sword," Janey said, "makes him even more dangerous. He could hack any of us to pieces in a second. That's sexy as fuck!"

"It's all just too perfect!" Mortimer said as they followed the hoard through another set of double doors, into a rapidly sloping tunnel with similar candles burning but farther apart.

"Almost there," he added and pointed above the throng leading the way. "Just through those big doors up ahead."

Behind them, Rousseau and Tanya bolted and braced those doors, too, and pinched out the closest candles.

* * *

By the time Mortimer and Junior and the rest had gotten to the opened doors, the crowd leading the way had swarmed inside and taken up positions where they, and the many more who were already in there, could watch the entrance of their king.

Junior leaned to get through the doorway, then stood towering over all of them. Mortimer, grinning and getting his back slapped, walked in far enough to stand in front of him, facing the new king's welcoming subjects.

"Attention!" he yelled and clapped his hands a few times. "Everyone, listen up!"

The crowd hushed except for a few giggles, some gentle elbowing followed by low cussing, and a few breaking the relative silence with their own contributions of pungent wind. It got quiet enough that a low, humming buzz could be heard.

"I told you all that we'd find our King if we tried hard enough."

"Hard is the best!" shouted a female.

"I'm here when you're ready," yelled a male nearby to her.

More snickering moved through the room like a wave.

"Quiet, all of you! Yes, we all love hard. And some of us are always hard."

"Talk dirtier, Mortimer," someone a few rows back yelled.

"Yeah, always dirty!" said another. "You know that!"

"Well, okay," Mortimer said, grinning and looking around the room. "We all love hard cocks, and our new King, here, has what we believe is the biggest, hardest, and most ferocious cock ever!"

The cheering exploded, and Mortimer encouraged them with vigorous waving of his arms. Junior's face remained blank before he bent forward and stared at the source of their fascination, then looked out over his subjects again.

"And he loves to eat! Just look at him! We were even talking about him eating my heart on the way here!"

Applause thundered, and cheering erupted throughout the cavernous room.

"Janey, here, even offered to suck his Kingly cock in the tunnels!"

"I did?"

Everyone hushed again and listened closely. Mortimer grinned at her as his eyes darted around.

"Well, sure. I mean, I think you said you would if he'd just, um, go into his temporary throne room. Remember that? Huh?"

"Oh, now I remember. Yes, I offered to suck our King's cock!"

Everyone murmured and whispered and watched.

Janie stood in front of Junior, facing him, and started taking backwards steps while unbuttoning her flannel shirt. The sea of staring eyes parted behind her.

"Come on, King," she said, flapping her shirt open and showing him two perfect breasts. "Want that mean and nasty King cock sucked? Huh?"

"Uh, Mama won't be mad?"

Mortimer reached up for Junior's shoulder and rubbed it, then patted it.

"Your momma would want you to let Janey suck it. Yes, she would. But she'd want you to get the Kingly treatment in your temporary throne room."

"Uh, where's that?"

"Just follow those tits!"

Laughter bounced off of the walls and high ceiling.

Junior's eyes locked onto them.

But he looked down at Mortimer's hand on his sword, trying to remove it from his grasp. He jerked it loose.

"I like my sword."

"Well, of course, you do, King! It's just, um, that it needs to be polished up. The King should have a bright, shiny sword, shouldn't he?"

"Um, I don't—"

"Then, the King can have fun getting it all bloody again. Doesn't that sound fun?"

"I suppose. Okay."

Mortimer tugged it away from Junior's hand and passed it to others in the crowd.

"When you get that back, it'll be the fucking cleanest and goddamn shiniest sword ever!"

"Okay."

He started walking, keeping his eyes on the perky, generous bare breasts being offered by Janey as she backed away from him.

Mortimer followed closely, then looked each way, snapped his fingers and pointed at two volunteers, then at Junior's kingly crotch.

The drafted members of the congregation soon walked closely on each side of Junior, and each fumbled around with his belt, then his zipper, yanking it down all the way.

Junior stopped and looked down, and a calm silence filled the room. All eyes were focused on one hand pulling part of his pants aside and the other reaching in.

That hand pulled Junior's bulbous, mutant-fueled phallus out of his pants, then let it go. It bounced a few times before locking in, pointed slightly up and directly at Janey.

"Oh, I can't! It's too big!" Janey said.

"I'll help!" a woman said.

"All of us will!" said the man beside her.

"You can do it, Janey," said Mortimer. "Or die trying!"

Everyone laughed except for Janey and Junior. She stared at Mortimer, her face an anguished mask.

"Oh, come on," he said, smiling at the young woman. "It's either that or he rips part of you open."

"I'd like to see that!" someone shouted.

"Do me! I'd love to be ripped open!"

"I've never ripped anyone," said Junior. "I bite, though."

"He bites!" said Mortimer. "He's just too good to be true!"

Janey kept backing, and the crowd formed a pathway behind her. Junior followed, his very erect part leading the way, pointing at Janey's mouth like it had some kind of radar to guide it.

"Go get her, King," said Mortimer. "She'll be just the first to suck off our King."

"Uh, okay."

"You're almost there, Janey!" yelled Mortimer. "Is your mouth ready? Are you ready to suck his deadly, murderous King cock?"

"Now, he's talking dirty," someone said from one side of the procession.

"About time. Always talk dirty," said another. "Fucking always!"

Janey had reached the open door of a prison cell attached to the far wall. Its vertical bars were thick and slick with oil, spaced closely, and allowed for the king's admirers to view the kingly ceremony from three sides.

She leaned forward, laughed, and said, "I'd get on my knees, but that cock would be too high!"

"Just open your mouth," said Mortimer. "That's good. Open that sucking mouth of yours!"

She did, and Junior took a step closer, almost close enough.

"God, that's huge!"

"She can do it! She can suck it!"

Mortimer scoffed with a smile at everyone close enough to see it, then gave Junior a gentle push from behind.

And just part of the throbbing end of it stretched apart Janey's lips.

"Hooray!"

"She's got her lips on it now!"

Few could hear her groaning as she fought to spread her jaws wider.

Mortimer shoved Junior again.

More of the king's thick kingly pole got jammed into her mouth.

"To the throne room, Janey!" shouted Mortimer. "Carefully, though!"

She backed away enough to lose him, then wiggled her lower jaw sideways rapidly.

"That can't be easy!" said someone.

"I'd try! I'd make it fit somewhere!" said someone else.

Mortimer nudged, Junior stepped forward, and it was enough of a thrust to jam the head of it entirely into her mouth.

"Look at that! She did it!"

"She sure can suck! We love that about you, Janey!"

Janey leaned her head each way a couple of times, swirling her lips around the thing, then backed herself away again and let it pop out. And she used two hands to jam her lower jaw left, then right, to the cheers of the crowd.

"It's too big! Even for her!"

"That's why he's the King!"

She'd backed herself completely into the jail cell and when Mortimer again gave him a shove, Junior didn't budge. Only his kingly member bounced like a recently used diving board.

He looked around at the cell's doorway, then touched the warm metal, then tried the door, swinging it with a low squeal.

No one in the expansive room made a sound. Except for Janey.

"Mm, I love King cocks. I'll suck that monster till it explodes."

Junior started to take a step closer, and his thick post swayed from side to side, brushing across Janey's parted lips.

"Go on, King," said Mortimer. "No one sucks like Janey. We all know that. She's the best for getting any cock sucked. Not just a King's!"

But Junior didn't budge.

"Um. I don't know."

"What don't you know?" said Mortimer. "You don't know if you want your Kingly cock to blow up in the pretty girl's mouth? You must want that!"

"I, uh, I do. But . . ."

Someone from behind Mortimer yelled, "Oh, come on, King! Get that fucking monster cock sucked!" and gave Junior a shove.

But Junior didn't move at all except for turning around, grabbing the man's throat with one mighty hand, and crushing it like a paper cup. Goo splattered and dripped, and the sloppily removed head cracked when it hit the concrete floor.

"Don't push," he said without emotion.

Mortimer backed away, out of Junior's reach, and said, "Oh, he meant well, King. Everyone just wants your Kingly cock sucked."

"Uh, I do too."

"Well, lookey there," said Mortimer. "There's a pretty little thing with her mouth open, just waiting for it. Why don't you just put that fleshy beast in her mouth? She'll suck it. She wants to suck it!"

"I want it sucked. But . . ."

"But nothing," said a woman behind Junior, who had turned back and was staring at Janey's mouth. "Unless you want my butt instead. My ass, I mean! Go get your vengeful King cock sucked already!"

Her push with both hands moved him only enough to get his boner close to Janey, and she leaned forward more, just enough to capture it and hold on tight with her lips.

But Junior was already turning, and that dragged Janey with him. He got one hand on the pushy woman's throat, shook her around, which also shook Janey as her lips stayed clamped on him, and everyone in the quiet room heard her neck snap.

"Well, you just killed another one, King," said Mortimer. "And that's just fine. You're the fucking King!"

"This isn't fun," Junior said.

He looked down, and Janey looked up at him, unable to grin with her lips stretched so far apart.

"That's nice, though. I like that."

He turned his head to see the woman that he'd just killed, then lifted her off of the floor. Still holding her neck, with her head flopping around and with staring eyes, he pulled her close enough to bite a chunk loose from her shoulder.

"And I'm hungry," he said, garbled with his mouth packed. "Always hungry."

"You go right ahead and eat," said Mortimer. "You're a fabulous growing boy of a King! In fact, take that little snack right into your throne room, and you can enjoy that tasty meal while Janey sucks that swollen cock of yours."

"You all are so nice," Junior said while chewing and watching Janey's eyes popping out from the exertion of trying to swallow a tree trunk. "But I, I don't like my throne room."

"Well," said Mortimer, "if you want to be our official King, the King that can kill and get his cock sucked and fuck anyone anytime—"

"Mortimer's really getting it now!"

"I love it when he gets rolling with the dirty talk!"

"—you'll have to eat and get your granite boner sucked in your throne room. Go on, King. Let Janey suck like we all know she can!"

"We all sure know it!"

"More than once! A lot!"

"She practices," said Mortimer. "All the time. Everything with everyone, all the time—she's a goddamn sex maniac!"

Everyone listened quietly, with all eyes on Junior.

"Okay. But, um . . ."

The buzzing stopped.

Mortimer's face twisted into a drooling scowl. Everyone around them started growling.

Junior snapped his eyes down to the mouth around his shaft, a mouth that was once warm and wet and soft but had become an angry hole full of sharp teeth.

"I don't want to be King!"

He jerked his hips back, popping himself out of a mouth that hissed and chased after what's she'd been sucking with a blur of clacking teeth.

"Mama!"

Chapter 34 – You, Pauline, Are Edible

Pauline saw Widow first and said softly, "All cleaned up?"

"Mm-hmm. It felt good."

"I heard."

"You what?"

Pauline smiled and said, "I heard the hot water sloshing and kind of knew you were enjoying it. Even in a hot world, hot water is nice. Come on down."

Widow took the handrail and started to tread carefully down the few stairs in the dark, but Pauline called out to her again.

"Oh, wait. While you're there, there's a light switch. Next to the door."

Widow found it, and the room brightened but still remained dim and sultry like a lounge.

"Better," said Widow. "Don't want too much light in a dungeon, huh?"

"Exactly."

She began the short walk toward the bed. Before she got there, Pauline threw aside her cover, revealing that she was dressed, then sat on the edge.

Standing, then stretching, Pauline yawned before speaking.

"Before you decide you need another nap, which is fine, of course, we should finish the tour."

"There's more?"

"Well, there's an upstairs, but hardly anyone ever goes up there. Nothing worth seeing."

"Oh, okay."

"But there's something down here that might interest you. I'm thinking about your lair. You know, you might need all kinds of stuff for fixing that. Things for security, too, not just comfort."

"Well, you're right. I haven't thought ahead too far yet, but security is important."

"Especially with that muscle giant hunting you down."

"Hmm. Thanks for reminding me."

"Sorry. I don't think he'll be much of a problem, though."

"I hope you're right."

Widow looked around, taking a few seconds with each wall, then looked to Pauline again.

"What else is there? I mean, it's a nice dungeon, but I've seen it."

Pauline took her hand, then began walking her toward the wall that was most lost in shadows.

"You haven't seen this."

She slid a floor-length curtain aside and revealed a square hatch door secured with a closed padlock. Its lower edge was about knee-high, and its top was about chin-high.

"What's in here?"

"Everything."

"Huh?"

"Well, a lot of stuff. I don't even know what most of it is. We think this used to be kind of a command center, and in there's a storeroom full of all kinds of hardware, tools, just a lot of stuff. I haven't even explored the whole thing, so I don't know how far into the mountain it goes."

"Can I see?"

"Sure."

Pauline spun the wheel, unclasped the lock, then swung open the door.

"Ooh, it's so dark."

"Watch. Like magic."

She reached inside, flicked a switch, and an orderly pattern of ceiling lights came on. Leading directly away from them was a concrete walkway wide enough for two, and tables and shelves and pallets were arranged neatly on both sides.

The lights, a row on each side of the path, went as far as they could see.

"Wow. They got all that stuff through this little door?"

"I doubt it. No. No way. There must be another entrance somewhere. Maybe around the mountain. No one I know has ever even looked for it."

"You'd see it from inside here, though, right?"

"Maybe not. There's so much crap piled everywhere. Stacks of pallets of stuff. There are probably even, uh, those things that, um—"

"Forklifts?"

"Yeah, those. Anyway, I'm pretty sure even Ham doesn't know about this warehouse."

"You haven't told him? Why not?"

"Girl's got to have some secrets, right?"

Widow laughed and said, "Of course. Like my fangs."

"Widow, that's a way cooler secret than most. You want to go in there and check it out?"

"Sure."

Pauline kicked closer a small cushioned ottoman, then used it to step over the low section of wall and into the secret warehouse. Widow followed, and they stood side by side and gazed all around.

"It smells like oil," said Widow. "Like machinery."

"There's a lot of that in here. All kinds of hardware and machine parts. I barely know what a hammer is for, and I sure wouldn't know what to do with any of this."

"I would," Widow said, then stepped closer to the nearest rack of supplies. "I'm an—I mean, I was an engineer, even though I'm not sure how much I remember."

"You probably remember enough. Go build what you need."

"Like what? And how would I get any of this back to my lair?"

Pauline walked closer and faced Widow, then reached out and held both of her arms gently.

"Think about that: you have a lair, and I have a dungeon."

Widow giggled and said, "We should team up sometime."

"Hmm. Yeah. My thoughts exactly."

She let her arms go, then said, "Hey, your slave can make as many trips as you need. Would he rat out this place? Or the elevator?"

Widow swirled some honey into her words, which came out steady, calm, and a bit deeper than she'd been speaking.

"Not if I tell him not to. I'd tell him: 'You do only what I tell you.'"

Pauline had begun staring at her first word, and she'd swooned and almost crumpled in a swaying heap, but Widow giggled and helped her stay standing.

"Like that," she said in her normal voice.

"What the hell is that? You're like a hypnotist or something?"

"Hmm. Something. You okay?"

"Uh, maybe not. That doesn't wear off quick—I already wanted to do only what you tell me to, but that was by choice before anyway."

"And now?"

"Now . . . I have no choice."

"Hmm. I like that. That rest did me some good. I feel good."

"Yeah, I can tell. You even look stronger."

A thicker sample of nectar tagged along with Widow's voice when she said, "I'll always be stronger than you, is that not true?"

"I . . . uh, yeah. Always. Stronger than—"

Widow laughed and snapped her fingers close to Pauline's staring eyes, and they didn't blink.

"Pauline. Hey."

She shook her with both hands, then said, "How about that, huh?"

Widow turned away, studying the wide variety of stores, and said, "Don't ever doubt that my two-headed slave will always—"

Something shrieked, something not Pauline, and Widow spun herself back around to see on Pauline's back a child with the flat face of an owl and the long blond hair of a girl. It had human hands, one of them covering Pauline's mouth and the other groping around for her throat.

"Dammit!"

Widow jumped toward them and hissed roughly as she grabbed the thing, pried it from Pauline's back, then held it down against the warm stone floor.

With it kicking and snapping and pecking, Widow was quicker and lunged her open mouth toward its neck. With a satisfied moan, she bit her fangs in deep, then shook her head and the owl girl from side to side. The thing struggled for only a few seconds, then went limp.

Pauline stared and held her breath as she watched Widow, hunched over the thing and sucking the life out of it.

Widow began rising up before releasing her bite, and the incapacitated creature got lifted off of the floor. She withdrew her fangs and let it drop, and it slumped, flattened out, and appeared to be asleep.

"Did you kill it? What the hell is that?"

"Oh my God, I didn't even really look at it until now. I don't know what that is, Pauline, but it was trying to kill you."

"Yeah, but you got it. How did you know to bite it? You knew you had fangs right then?"

"I didn't even think about it. I just bit it."

"Wait a second, Widow. That was enough to grow your fangs? Not some kind of sexy thing going on?"

"Huh. Wow, I guess. I'll tell you, though, that that felt sexy. Having to bite it. I still feel sexy. I don't think I can just snap back from that."

She faced Pauline and peeled back her lips, showing long fangs and the blood and fluids she'd sucked out of the thing's neck.

"You, uh, you look sexy," Pauline said. "Damn."

Widow's chest was heaving gently as her eyes roamed around on Pauline, then lingered on her throat before focusing on her eyes.

"I still feel like biting."

"Uh, are you in a killing mood or . . . something, um, sexy?"

Widow let her eyes close to thin slits as she stared at Pauline, then hissed softly as she spoke.

"I don't know. I think . . . they're the same."

Pauline tipped her head toward the hatch opening that led to the dungeon bedroom.

"I'll take that as a—"

"Yes," Widow said, her voice thick and sweet, "you will."

* * *

Back in the room, Widow stood close and watched as Pauline relocked the hatch door.

"Okay, I won't keep doing that, whatever that is. With my voice."

"You don't know what that is?"

"Uh-uh. It just kind of happens. I mean, I want it to, then it happens."

"I kind of like it."

"You do? Why?"

"Mm, I don't know. Um, there's something exciting about knowing I can't stop whatever you might want to do."

"You really don't think you could stop yourself?"

"It sure as fuck doesn't feel like it."

"Oh, but maybe if you tried, you could—"

"That's just it—I don't even want to try. So, if you're ever, you know, feeling like you want that voice, just do it."

"Okay, I will."

"Maybe you can't stop yourself from using it."

"Hmm. I won't argue. What the hell was that thing in there?"

"Some god-awful mutant. They're everywhere, Widow."

"How'd it get in? Through that other door you mentioned?"

"Probably. Maybe it'll get itself back out the same way. You really bit the fuck out of that thing."

"Mm, I could barely stop. Pauline, it was like an orgasm from the moment my teeth broke its skin. I kind of felt that before, with you first, then that Lucas guy. I hope he's okay. But it's so much stronger now. I'm still tingling from it."

"Incredible. You're incredible."

Widow laughed and said, "No, I'm not going to say it."

"What? Tell me."

"Okay, I was going to anyway. You, Pauline, are edible."

"Um, alright. You're getting a little scary now."

Widow reached out both hands, and Pauline only moved her eyes to watch them as she lifted off her cap, then put it on her own head.

"Oh, scary. Uh-huh."

She grabbed both of Pauline's wrists and held her arms down against her sides. Pauline struggled to pull them free, but she couldn't.

"Dammit, Widow."

"Told you I was stronger. Are you afraid?"

"Yes. Alright, I get it. Let me go."

"No."

Still holding her wrists, Widow forced Pauline toward the bed, backed her into it, and snapped her arms down, making her sit.

"Widow, come on."

She nudged Pauline's knees apart, knelt there, and still had her arms locked at her sides.

"Tell me what I want you to be."

"What? Come on, Widow, you—"

"Soft," Widow said, adding just a trace of honey.

Pauline still struggled, but Widow wouldn't let her go.

"What else are you?"

"Widow," she said, her voice showing a bit less resolve, "just stop—"

"Mm, juicy."

"Hey, enough, alright? I'm not going to fight if—"

With a heavier dose of syrup mixed in, Widow said, "No, you're not going to fight."

She lifted one of Pauline's arms, held it across, close to her mouth, then looked into her eyes.

"You're edible," she said, then let it trail away with a soft hiss before biting her fangs deep into Pauline's soft and juicy skin.

And she held it there, looking into Pauline's unblinking eyes as she sucked quietly and also gave something in return, feeding her something.

Pauline relaxed in her hold, and her breathing slowed.

"Yes, that's better. So much better for me now, aren't you?"

"Yes, I feel something, Widow, but—"

"Tell me what else you are for me."

"No, you should let me . . . let me . . ."

"Say it. You know you want to."

"I'm . . . I'm your little girl?"

"Mm, yes. Yes, you are. What kind?"

Pauline's head was tipping to one side, then the other, and her eyes were almost closed. But she was still smiling.

"I'm a . . . soft, juicy, um . . . little girl."

"Yes. So sweet now."

Widow watched Pauline closely as she let go of her wrists, and Pauline let them drop, making no effort to fight or get away. Smiling, scoffing softly, Widow unfastened Pauline's belt and slipped it out of the loops of her black leather pants.

"Are you having an orgasm?"

Pauline, smiling and watching her, nodded and said, "Mm-hmm. I'm soft and . . . juicy and having . . . an . . ."

"Shh, now, little one. Me too, just from biting you. It feels too good to even think of stopping."

After turning around the hat she was wearing, Widow tucked one of Pauline's arms behind her, then the other. Reaching around, she crossed her wrists and cinched the belt tight around them.

"Hmm. Just like that."

Using a gentle touch under Pauline's chin, she tipped her head up enough to hold her gaze.

"Such soft lips," she said, and raised herself up enough to kiss the captive woman in her own dungeon.

"Mm," she said after a minute, "so sweet. Even sweeter with another tiny bite. You don't mind, do you?"

"Uh-uh. Maybe just a . . . a little one."

"Hmm."

Widow leaned one way, then the other, trying to get a good angle on either of Pauline's arms, but she scoffed and straightened up, still on her knees.

"Well, let's just see."

She took the bottom hem of Pauline's t-shirt and began lifting it, bunching it up, using the backs of her hands to pry it away as her fingertips led the way. She got it high enough that she could bounce her breasts a few times, then rolled it up tight enough to rest it above her exposed breasts.

"No," Pauline said, "not the . . . um, not . . ."

"You sure helped yourself to mine back at my lair."

"I, um, I was just—"

"Shh, soft little thing. Shh, now."

"But—"

"Shh."

She reached around with both hands to hold Pauline's bound wrists, which brought her lips and fangs quite close to her breasts, but she looked up from there, into the helpless eyes looking down at her.

"No, please not . . . not . . ."

"You know you want it, sweet little girl. You do, don't you?"

She waited, smiling with her long fangs out and already streaked with blood.

And when Pauline smiled and nodded, Widow said, "Of course, you do, precious little girl."

Then, she opened her jaws farther, showing fangs longer than they'd ever been before.

But she hid them away behind wet lips, which she pressed into and held against the soft skin that she found at the side of one of Pauline's smooth, round breasts.

Looking up into Pauline's eyes, she kissed her lightly, each kiss bringing her lips closer to the nipple that was poking straight out for her.

"Mm," Widow said, laughing with her lips still closed. "This would be even better."

With a soft hiss, she opened her mouth wide, causing Pauline to flinch from seeing how long the fangs had become. That flinch shook her breasts, but they settled quickly, and Widow moaned as she leaned enough to move her open jaws, and the waiting fangs, close enough to bite Pauline right there.

"You want this even more, little girl. You'd tell me if you didn't."

Pauline's steady, deep breaths were silent but they moved the nipple deeper under the fangs, then back out with each rise and fall. But she didn't speak.

"Mm, I knew it. You want that sweet little bite right there, on your tempting, delicious nipple. And we'll both enjoy the feelings that will give us."

Holding her gaze, Widow said, "Mm, I do believe I'd love giving a sweet bite to a little girl's nipples. Lots and lots of bites."

Chapter 35 – So Soft and Quiet for Me

Widow held herself there, ready to sink her fangs into a sensitive and excited part of her captive, then giggled softly, puckered her lips, and gave Pauline's nipple a quick suck, then a few slow, wet licks.

"Mm, sucking is so good too. Maybe no piercings for now."

Pauline's breaths had become choppy as she watched with her head tipped forward and with Widow still holding her bound wrists behind her.

In a normal voice, Widow said, "Oh God, I shouldn't. But I can't, I mean, it just feels—"

"Don't stop."

With her lips still bumping into Pauline's breast, Widow said, "You mean that?"

"Mm-hmm," Pauline said, her voice weak. "It's . . . an experiment, remember?"

"Uh, sure. But how far?"

"Like I said: don't stop."

"You feel it too?"

"Oh my God. Yeah."

"Hmm. Okay, then."

She gave Pauline's other breast a few seconds of gentle sucking, then backed away to hold her tired gaze.

"Soon, little girl. I want you even more helpless when I give you the bites you're beginning to crave so much."

Widow closed her eyes, shivered, and said, "Just saying 'helpless.' Mm, I felt that too."

She released Pauline and stood, then tipped her back onto the bed. Pauline flopped around under Widow's arranging of her, offering no resistance until she'd been placed facedown on the thick quilt.

Still wearing her black western boots, black leather pants, and a black t-shirt rolled up to allow her breasts to press into the soft blanket, she stayed very quiet, even when Widow climbed up and sat on the backs of her thighs.

As if she were speaking only for herself, Widow said, "So helpless. Just a tied-up little girl."

She took her thick and long red hair with both hands, pulled it up and back, then let it all fall off to one side.

"Ooh, someone has a very smooth neck. And she's offering it to me so nicely."

Pauline didn't speak and only kept taking slow, deep breaths.

"I believe I want my little girl even more helpless. The bites are so much tastier when the juicy thing is tied-up tightly and has no hope of escape."

She gave Pauline's ass a two-handed squeeze, then used them to get her own belt unfastened then out of its loops.

"You want that, too, don't you, little one? To be more helpless for me?"

"Mm-hmm. Yes."

"Mm, of course."

She'd just started tying it around Pauline's upper arms when Pauline moaned and said, "My . . . my throat?"

"Oh, you're a dirty little girl, aren't you? You know what that will do to you, don't you?"

Pauline nodded but didn't say another word.

Widow fed the end of the belt under Pauline's neck, then through the buckle but didn't fasten it. She sat back with a leash in her hand that led to a leather choke collar around Pauline's neck.

"Just like that. So helpless for me and maybe in real trouble too. Hmm."

Holding the collar but not cinching it up, Widow looked down and saw that Pauline's fingers were reaching up, trying to touch her.

"Oh, so sweet," she said, then scooted forward until she sat on them.

She held the leash and kept one hand on Pauline's back as she lifted and lowered her hips, giving Pauline a chance to finger her, even if only through the flimsy pants that she'd put on after her bathing with the hot water and towels.

"Oh, that's nice. Yes, I know what you're feeling because I feel it too. Touch me. Touch me, soft little girl."

Widow leaned forward, still holding the leash and placing her other hand on Pauline's back. From there, she squirmed and rubbed herself over Pauline's busy fingers.

Pauline's hair was still pulled to one side, fluffed out on the bed, and Widow leaned forward more, positioning her lips to touch her ear.

"We both know what you're so desperate to touch, don't we?" she whispered in her ear.

Pauline nodded.

"Hmm. Such a good girl. You like how I'm playing with you, don't you?"

She nodded again.

Widow laughed just once, softly, then said, in her normal voice, "I don't even know where this is all coming from. But I like it, and I'm not stopping. Not for anything."

Pauline's fingers kept probing and rubbing, touching as well as she could through Widow's pants.

"And no one else is going to stop me. We're locked together in a dungeon high on a mountain. No one can save you from whatever I wish to do to you. Isn't that right?"

Pauline nodded, and Widow leaned to the side and saw the best smile that Pauline could manage.

"That's part of the orgasm you feel—knowing that you're helpless for me. And Pauline?"

With Widow lying on her back, pressing her into the blankets, Pauline stopped her breathing and held still.

"I love having my pussy touched."

Pauline let out her held breath and resumed a steady pace.

"Oh, you like me talking about that, don't you?"

Pauline's head barely nodded, and she whispered, "Yes."

Widow kissed her ear, then whispered, "My pussy, Pauline."

Pauline moaned softly.

"Such a good little girl to touch my pussy."

Pauline's moaning got slightly louder.

"A soft, helpless little girl that has to play with my wet pussy."

Pauline groaned and worked her fingers even more.

Widow kissed her ear, then raised herself back up with one hand on Pauline's back and the leash in the other.

Pauline's moaning had become constant and drawn out every time she exhaled.

"Enjoy my pussy, and remember that no one, no one at all, will save you. This is what happens to soft little girls that become so helpless for me."

Widow pulled the leash, the makeshift collar tightened around Pauline's neck, and her moaning came to an abrupt end.

"Oh, poor baby. All the sweet little girl can do is keep rubbing my pussy. Rub my pussy while I strangle you in this forgotten dungeon."

She leaned forward and found it easier to kiss Pauline's ear with the leash and collar tipping her head up and off of the blanket. And she smiled at seeing Pauline staring straight ahead.

"Such a good girl for me now."

Widow leaned in closer, kissing and licking Pauline's neck, and she pulled the noose just a bit tighter.

"So soft and quiet for me."

*　　*　　*

Widow kept enough tension on Pauline's tight leash to force her mouth open, and the tip of her tongue ventured out as her eyes, unblinking, stared straight ahead.

Leaning out just enough to see, Widow smiled and sighed, then nuzzled around her ear before giving it a long kiss.

Whispering, she said, "Such a perfect, beautiful little girl now. So quiet for me while the orgasm I gave you with my bite flows everywhere inside you."

She pulled more, keeping it snug around Pauline's neck while she kissed all around her ear and neck.

"I know what you're feeling, little girl, because I feel it too. You should be trying to save yourself, but you don't care. No, you just want to feel it even more."

She sat back up but supported herself, leaving Pauline room to keep her fingers touching and caressing through the thin fabric. From there, she pulled back yet more on the leash, arching Pauline's back and lifting her farther off of the bed.

"Oh, it feels so good to be cruel. Mm . . ."

Then, she let her down and allowed the noose to loosen.

"There, there, little one. That might be enough cruelty for the moment."

Pauline's head slumped on its side, facing away from her mane, and her lungs took in generous quantities of the dungeon's air. Widow brushed her hair aside, fussing with it and tucking it behind her ear.

"But only for a moment. I know what my sweet girl likes now. Oh, she's a dirty, naughty little thing."

She leaned forward and kissed her cheek, and Pauline didn't open her eyes.

"So soft. Just a soft little thing and captured by such a cruel woman."

While shifting herself around, seeking the best positions to enjoy Pauline's fingers, which had never stopped, she began to unbutton the shirt that Pauline had given her.

"Oh, no, we'll give the little one more of what she wants as soon as I'm more comfortable."

Widow slipped the shirt back over her shoulders, let it drop, then tossed it to the floor. Wearing only long pants and Pauline's cap, her hands immediately went to her breasts, which she squeezed then held up while pinching gently.

"Mm, I'm soft, too, not just cruel," she said while rubbing the rough leather across one breast, then the other. "Mm, so soft."

She leaned forward and gave Pauline a quick kiss on her cheek.

"Just lie still for me, sweet little one."

Widow stood herself up on the bed, watched Pauline taking easy breaths, and unfastened then removed her own pants.

"Oh, no panties for me. Hmm. Naughty, naughty that you didn't give me any at my bath time."

She tossed the pants aside with the shirt and sighed, looking down at Pauline's legs and ass in tight leather and the bare skin of her back from her t-shirt being rolled up above her breasts.

And at the ends of her crossed and tied wrists, all of her fingers were reaching up for her.

"Oh, so sweet. Okay, my soft little girl. You may touch me."

Widow sank down onto her knees, kept them tight against Pauline's sides, then lowered herself down to where Pauline's fingers could find her.

Right after Pauline's fingertips made contact, she tipped her head back and gasped softly.

"Yes, precious girl, I'm very wet already."

Pauline moaned and shook her head softly just a few times.

"What, then?"

"I . . . I feel this too. Almost like . . . the bite."

"Just touching my pussy feels like that?"

Widow watched as Pauline panted and worked her lips, trying to form a word. She tossed the cap she was wearing off of the bed and leaned closer.

"Tell me."

"It's the . . . juice. Your juice."

Widow kissed her cheek and sat upright but held herself away from Pauline's fingers.

"Oh, I see. Yes, of course. Whatever is in my bite is in my pussy juice too."

Pauline sighed and lay there waiting, taking easy breaths.

"Well, let's give my little girl a better dose of my juices. My little girl wants to touch my pussy."

She lowered herself, and Pauline used one set of fingers outside and the other set inside.

"Aw, there we go."

She brushed her hair again, then leaned close and kissed her cheek.

"Such a sweet little thing to touch my pussy. Mm-hmm, little girl. Let that juice soak right into you."

Widow tipped her head and grinned at seeing a weak smile across Pauline's face, her lips sometimes twitching as her fingers got busier.

"Yes, that's it. Touch my pussy before I tighten up your pretty noose."

Pauline moaned, softly and only briefly.

"Oh, you even like the sound of that, too, don't you? You like knowing you'll get more of it. Hmm, you're quite the pretty little victim."

Pauline nodded, never opened her eyes, and said softly, "Yes."

Widow leaned forward again to whisper in Pauline's ear.

"Poor soft little girl has a dangerous noose around her throat. Mm, and it's going to get tight again. Oh, so very tight."

She kissed around her ear and neck, her hissing soft and barely noticeable. Then, she began whispering in her ear.

"When you touch me, make sure you . . ."

She kept whispering, and Pauline smiled, nodded, and complied.

"Oh, yes, just like that. Slowly, now, little victim girl. So soft and slow for me, my precious little victim."

She kissed Pauline's ear while she did exactly as she'd been instructed, her fingers steadily touching and caressing between Widow's thighs.

"Mm, no pants in the way now. Just soft fingertips. So soft for me. Mm-hmm, no sharp fingernails on this one."

Widow watched and listened and when Pauline started a low, protracted moan, she said, "Oh, but I like my little girl quiet while she's touching me," then jerked the noose tight, lifting her head off of the bed.

"Oh, such a poor little victim," Widow told her, still kissing her while Pauline stared straight ahead, her mouth open and the tip of her tongue visible. "So much cruelty."

Pauline kept touching Widow, using soft fingertips, and Widow laid herself on top, pressing her breasts against her exposed skin and feeling not even the slightest breath from Pauline moving them.

She kissed her neck, then whispered to her, "Good girl. So soft with such a cruel, tight noose around her throat. So nice and quiet for me."

Relaxing her hold, Widow let the noose loosen, and Pauline fell to the blanket, breathing deeply and not trying to escape.

"Hmm. You're just about ready for a very special bite."

She kissed her neck.

"You know where. Tell me now if you're afraid."

Pauline grinned and in a hoarse whisper, said, "I'm afraid."

"Hmm, even better. You must know, soft little girl, that the bite along with a very tight noose could be the end of you?"

Pauline kept breathing, slow and easy, and showed a small grin. And Widow saw the slightest of nods.

Widow laughed and said, "Oh, that orgasm. It's really something. You don't care what happens to you, do you?"

Pauline shook her head just once.

"Be a very good little girl and keep touching my pussy. So slow and soft. Yes, just like that. And I'll just tighten up this lovely noose,"—she jerked it tight, snapping Pauline's head back—"and strangle you while you're so soft and helpless for me. Hmm, such cruel fangs for your very soft skin."

Holding the noose tight, getting fondled and stroked by her captive, Widow leaned forward, bared her fangs with a hiss, then bit them deep into the soft skin of Pauline's neck.

Chapter 36 – A Required Quantity of Ejaculation

"Mama!" Junior cried out. "They're not being nice!"

A snarling male was closest, his mouth open and his teeth chattering, and he was the first one that Junior grabbed. He wrapped a meaty hand around his throat and lifted him high overhead.

"Mama, they're bad!"

He spun himself around, lowering his captive, and swept his head into the iron bars of the cage that they'd called his throne room. The skull got crushed, and a lot of the slop inside got flung across the bed in there.

But Janey had gotten both of her hands locked onto something very large and thick and unrelentingly hard, holding it at its base. Her teeth were a blur as she tried to pull it closer, like feeding it into a wood chipper.

"No, you're bad! Don't bite that thing!"

He took both of her wrists, lifted her, and kept swinging her body up and over and behind him, and she crashed into the crowd ten bodies back.

Another jumped on his back, his clacking teeth close to biting loose an ear. Junior turned his back to the prison bars, then rammed himself into them with the biting attacker hitting first. Blood and organs and coils of squishy ropes splattered through the bars and dripped to the floor like Junior had blasted apart a balloon made of skin.

"Stop! I don't want to hurt you!"

They didn't stop, and their growling and snapping jaws increased, all of them moving in for a bite.

"You were so nice before!"

He clapped both hands to one head, sending a red geyser toward the ceiling.

"Stop being bad!"

He punched one in the gut and wiggled his fingers around in the open air on the other side before pulling the twisted spine out the front.

Janey was coming back for more, crawling across the heads and shoulders of the mob, her eyes blank and her teeth chomping.

"No! Not you again!"

He backed himself just past the cell's doorway and fought them one or two at a time, and the mangled bodies began to pile up. If he took a step, it would be in a puddle of slime and slop and in a field of grabbing hands, some connected to arms.

Holding a cage bar with one hand, Junior saw Mortimer closing in, trying to push bodies aside to get at him.

"Mortimer! Why?"

Mortimer didn't answer, but his jaws were flying, angry teeth snapping and grinding.

Junior disemboweled several more and removed heads from others, tossing them out across the throng, hitting Janey with one, and Mortimer was close, just about to reach him when . . .

. . . the buzzing started up again.

Mortimer straightened up and held Junior's gaze while brushing liquid and paste off of his chest and belly.

"Oh, my. That was unfortunate."

"Why did everyone get so mad at me?"

"Well, they weren't exactly mad, like angry kind of mad. They just—"

"You wanted me to be King!"

"Well, yeah, we did. I mean, we still do. We just, well, we're a bit unpredictable, that's all. No hard feelings, I hope?"

Junior looked around at the bodies and body parts and body filling that he'd spilled everywhere.

"I hurt your friends, Mortimer."

"And you should have. That's what Kings do, my boy!"

"I, uh, don't know if I still want to be King."

"Well, of course, you do! Enough of that silly talk. We'll get some mops going, maybe a few buckets, and everything will be just fine."

"I, um, think I just want to find Scarlet. Then, go home to Mama."

"Uh, isn't your mother a bug?"

He stared out above the sea of friendly faces.

"Don't be a bug, Mama."

"Well," said Mortimer, "we'll have you on your way soon. And the next best thing to your momma is this fine young lady,"—Janey had gotten close, and he put his arm around her—"and she's still so eager to suck your monstrous Kingly cock."

"He's talking dirty again!"

"He only stopped when the fucking buzzer stopped!"

Mortimer pushed Janey toward Junior, but he placed a meaty hand against her forehead, holding her at a distance. Still, he grinned at the sight of her licking her lips, pretending to be sucking something.

"See? Your Kingly cock belongs right there in her sucking mouth."

"That was a good one," said someone nearby.

"Yeah. And all of us know all about her sucking mouth."

"I, uh, I don't know," Junior said, but he'd begun tipping his head, looking from her mouth to the head of his impressive king tool, seeing how close together they were.

"Well, she needs to suck someone," Mortimer said, laughing. "Maybe me? Yeah, you can watch her work. She's a champ at sucking cocks!"

"Woo-hoo!" shouted a woman to one side. "Janey always sucks someone!"

"She sucked me just the other day! She's good!"

Mortimer whipped out his own flesh post, letting it point straight out. He spun around, threatening all of them with it.

"Get her, Mortimer!"

"She can't say no! She never does!"

Janey had just turned toward Mortimer and his tool and dropped to her knees, then the buzzing clicked a few times and died.

She turned right back around and began crawling toward Junior, her smacking jaws leading the way.

"Hey! I don't like this game!"

Hundreds of snapping jaws were zeroing in on Junior, and he backed himself farther into his prison throne room. When the first biting body got close enough, he lifted it by its throat, then . . .

. . . the buzzing snapped and crackled, then evened out into a steady drone.

"Oh my goodness!" said Mortimer.

He looked down, saw that he was still pointing at Junior, then looked to one side.

"I'd say, leave it out," said one of them over there.

He grinned while looking the other way.

"It's too big to put away!" said someone on that side.

He gave that one a thumbs-up sign, then looked again at Junior.

"I do apologize, King. We just—"

"I'm not King yet. Janie didn't suck my thing."

"Oh, that's right. That's very right. She can do that right now if—"

"No, no, no. I don't want to be King. But I sure am hungry from the games you all play."

"Well, that's no surprise. And lookie there! You're holding a very nice snack right now!"

"Tell him to fuck it," said someone behind Mortimer.

"Yeah! Yeah!" said the one that Junior was holding up. "Tell him to fuck it!"

"Or," said Mortimer, "Junior, you could just fill that hungry belly of yours."

"Okay."

The snared male member of that hoard screamed and cackled as Junior held him up by one arm, caught the other arm that was trying to slap him, and took a healthy, sloppy bite out of it.

"He could have fucked him," said someone, sounding disappointed.

"Eating him is good, too, though," said another. "And he can still fuck him."

"Either way," said Mortimer, "he'd be a perfect King. Hey, everyone! Is he our perfect King, or what?"

Everyone hooted and hollered, and Junior grinned with gore dripping down his chin as he chewed. He looked around the vast room at all of his approving subjects as he took another bite and packed his cheeks.

But he frowned and stopped chewing.

And the entire room went quiet.

Junior reached into his bloody, oozing mouth and pulled out a piece of circuit board that dripped blood and shot out weak sparks that fizzled in the sloppy red puddle at his feet.

* * *

"Huh? I never ate stuff like this before."

"Oh, but you eat all kinds of stuff, right?" said Mortimer.

"Uh, yeah. Squishy stuff. This isn't squishy."

He held it up and squinted at it, then held it inside his mouth and chattered his teeth against it.

"What is this, Mortimer?"

"We truly don't know, King. It's just—"

"I'm not King yet. Janie hasn't—"

"Sucked your cock. I know. She wants to, though."

"Uh, maybe in a while. I want to, um, fig . . . fig . . ."

"Figure it out?"

"Yeah. That."

"Oh, but you're still hungry, aren't you, big boy?"

Junior still held the bitten one above the ground, having forgotten about him in his confusion. Blood dripped as the soft cackling from the limp body continued.

"Take another bite! Go on!"

"Okay."

He pulled the chewed-up body closer and bit into the skull, and everyone in the room said, "Ooh," or, "Ah," at the sound of the bones crunching and splintering.

"Such a King!"

"Such a fucking King!"

Junior began chewing, and he frowned and looked around, his head tipping, then he swallowed hard.

"Uh-oh. That's not meat."

"You swallowed some of that weird stuff we all have in us? Is that right, King?"

"Not yet I'm not because—"

"Oh, for fuck's sake! Just let her suck your cock already!"

"Maybe in a—"

Junior started twitching and convulsing, and he sloshed the lunch body to the floor of his throne room. The would-be king's eyes were fluttering, sometimes rolling up, sometimes snapping to one side or the other, and sparks were flying out of his ears and nose.

"Well, I'll be royally fucked," said someone in the crowd.

"You would be if the King fucked you. Yep."

"Wait, everybody!" yelled Mortimer. "Wait!"

The fireworks from Junior's visible orifices halted, and he slowly opened his eyes and focused them on Mortimer.

"Well? How was that?"

In a calm voice, Junior said, "It wasn't quite as delicious as the fresh body on which I dined."

Mortimer stared. The crowd behind him didn't make a sound. The room contained only a steady buzzing sound.

"Uh, tell us more?"

"I could. Very well. I don't sense that the nutritional value of that electronic circuitry is sufficient to meet my caloric intake goals."

Mortimer grinned but waved at everyone behind him to stay hushed.

"Do you, uh, feel any different?"

Junior smiled pleasantly and said, "I notice that you didn't refer to me as King just now. Thank you because that wouldn't be entirely accurate. I believe we've already discussed why. Now, back to your question about how I—"

His face froze in a grimace, and blood leaked and sparks flew out of his ears. He hit one side of his head, then the other, tipping it each way and shooting out lightning that gradually lessened, then stopped.

"Well," said Junior. "That's moderately embarrassing. I'd wager that it's related to the electronic components that I so greedily consumed."

"Yes," said Mortimer. "I agree. I think they're kind of, I don't know, burning themselves in. Banging your head seems to have locked them in place."

"Very astute observation. I believe you are correct. If my mother was alive, and if she wasn't an odd hybrid variety of insect, she'd likely be quite proud of my unexpected new growth and development."

"Speaking of growth," Mortimer said, snickering and pointing.

Junior looked down at himself and scoffed.

"My, but I do have a resolute and likely lethal, some may say, erection. And it doesn't appear that it will ever experience any fatigue or even the slightest unflattering effects from gravity."

"I think what you're saying is," said Mortimer, "that you're ready for Janey? Now that you're all electrified?"

"If that offer is still good, yes. I believe the plan for Miss Janey was to . . . suck my cock? A crude phrase, to be sure, but it's accurate and hints at the satisfyingly vulgar nature of such activity, which only adds to the anticipation."

"What he said!" called out someone far back.

"That's why he's the fucking King!"

Mortimer shushed them with his hand gestures, then said, "Well, soon, he'll be King. Janey?"

"I'm ready!"

"Yes, of course, you are, darling," said Mortimer. "Aren't you always? Dear Janey, the future King would like his Kingly rod sucked. So, get going with the sucking!"

She dropped to her hands and knees and started crawling past Mortimer and toward the horizontal fence post, staring at it and giggling and licking her lips.

"Yes," Junior said to Janey as she opened her mouth and focused on her target, "I'm more than ready for you to siphon off some of the hazardous pressure in that rigid physiology."

"He talks dirty, but he uses funny words too," said someone watching the action closely.

"As long as it's dirty," said another, "he gets my vote for King."

"Mm," Janey moaned as she got her lips around the head almost as big as a baseball.

"There you go," said Mortimer. "How is that, King?"

"It's quite pleasant. Would you please instruct her to use her hands too? I fear that not too much of that punishing length and jaw-spreading diameter will fit inside her mouth."

"Well, King, you can just tell her your—"

"Oh, no, no, no. I haven't seen the written decree, and you haven't conveyed the details in our conversation, but I must believe that there should be a required quantity of ejaculation before I can wear the crown as your—"

The buzzing stopped.

Small rockets of sparks flew from Junior's ears.

Janey's sucking became biting.

"Ow! Mama!"

He grabbed the back of her neck and dragged her loose, saving himself from the impending decapitation. Holding her up, he pointed at her snarling and snapping face.

"That's not nice!"

He looked around at all of the savage faces, teeth chattering and eyes blank, as they approached while raking their hands like claws through the air.

"You guys! Not again! I don't want to be King!"

Still holding Janey as she snapped and convulsed high above the floor, he twisted one head loose, then crushed a throat, then strangled another with his free arm, then . . .

. . . the buzzing crackled, steadied out, then hummed like it had before.

Janey stopped flailing and kicking, and she covered her smile and giggled before saying, "Oops! Sorry!"

Junior angled her closer, their faces near each other, and said, "It will take some research and investigation before I fully understand the dynamics of the buzzing and its relationship to your behavior. But even without that knowledge, it might be good for you to resume the Kingly initiation rites. Does that sound reasonable to you?"

"I don't know what kind of dirty talk that is," said someone behind Mortimer.

"If you're asking if I want to keep sucking your cock, my answer is—"

"Now, that's some dirty talk!" said another. "That's our Janey!"

"My answer would sure as fuck be yes!" said someone else.

"Very well, Miss Janey," said Junior. "And please recall that a request was tendered that you use your hands as well."

"I'll do it! I will fucking do it!"

Junior set her down, she got as much as she could in her mouth, to the hoots and hollers of everyone in the room, then she began giving the timber of flesh vigorous strokes with both hands.

"Isn't she something?" said Mortimer.

"She's quite adept," said Junior. "I believe we'll soon come to—"

"Yeah! That's our King!"

"It'll be buckets full! Watch and see!"

"—to some sort of finality on my ascension to the throne. But Mortimer, I do still have some nagging hunger that should be addressed."

Mortimer kicked the body that Junior had bitten many times already. It giggled but didn't move around.

"Well, there's no reason you can't eat and get sucked at the same time."

"I suppose not," Junior said, then leaned for the body, never prying anything out of Janey's mouth or hands. "It's an odd time to pursue multitasking, to be sure, but I'll give it the old college try just the same."

Standing again, he took another bite, chewed for a few seconds, then packed it off to the side in a bulging cheek.

"There's still the issue of a wench named Scarlet, too, esteemed colleague Mortimer."

"Ah, yes. The wench that killed your mother, right?"

"That's only about forty-percent correct, I'm afraid, if you'll tolerate my being somewhat persnickety."

"Huh?"

Junior chewed what he already had and swallowed it all.

"By my estimates, she was already approximately sixty-percent insect at that time."

"Ah," said Mortimer, nodding. "Yes. Odd things sometimes happen in that world out there."

Chapter 37 – Upside Down for a Cruel Woman

Widow held her fangs deep under the soft skin of Pauline's neck, lying atop the facedown and bound redhead whose fingers were still touching and stroking, pleasuring her as she'd been instructed.

Holding the leash back with one hand, Widow kept the noose tight around Pauline's neck, too, forcing her to remain very quiet and only staring straight ahead as they lay on the dungeon bed, in a hideout on a mountain where no one would come to intervene.

After just a few seconds of strangulating her, Widow moaned softly and relaxed the grip on Pauline's throat, which allowed her head to settle and roll to the side.

And the moment the noose loosened, Widow groaned and began swallowing quickly with her lips covering the bite, never letting even a drop escape.

A half a minute after that, she slipped her pointy teeth back out, then licked the wounds several times, sometimes sliding her tongue on more of Pauline's neck and her ear too.

"Mm, that was so sweet. Oh, it all rushed out for me so happily. So much urgent juice you gave me, little girl."

Pauline's breaths were deeper and more rapid than normal, but she managed to say, "Oh my God, Widow. Whatever is in your bite and, I think, your . . ."

"Say it, precious girl."

Like speaking in a dream, from a far distance, Pauline said, "Your pussy. Your pussy juice too."

"My pussy is still so wet."

"Yeah, and whatever it is, it's getting stronger."

"Stronger orgasm, you mean?"

"Yeah, but not just that. It feels like, I don't know, like it could kill me too. I know you don't want to—"

"Hmm, I'm not so sure. Whatever it is, it's making me hungrier too. Hungry and orgasming, and I don't ever want to stop feeding off of you."

"I'm edible?"

"Mm-hmm. Oh, Pauline, and I don't want to just consume you—I feel my orgasm even more when I'm talking to you. Even when I'm being cruel. I love tormenting you."

"You, uh, yeah. You're cruel. Sexy cruel."

"Mm-hmm."

Widow shifted off of her, then smiled at the sight of Pauline still working her fingers.

"They're cramping up?"

"I guess. But Widow, I don't want to stop either. I felt it even in my fingers—something you're giving me."

"And you think it could kill you?"

"Uh-huh. I'm not sure it's strong enough, though. But oh my God, that orgasm just doesn't stop. I still feel it."

"Hmm," Widow said, then rolled Pauline onto her side and laid herself facing her.

"Mm. That's so nice. Tell me how this feels."

Lying face to face, with Pauline's arms still bound behind her and her t-shirt pulled up to let their breasts press together, Widow touched her tongue to Pauline's ear.

And she shivered.

"Oh. Oh, that was nice. I felt that all through me."

"Just the touch?"

"Mostly. Maybe something else too."

"Pauline, even just through my skin?"

"Mm-hmm. Saliva?"

Widow got an arm under Pauline's waist and laid the other over her. She grabbed her bound wrists with both hands.

"Oh, you are so trapped and helpless and now, you're asking for a kiss too?"

"Mm-hmm. Not like I could stop you."

"No, and no one else will either, my soft, helpless little girl."

"And I'd bet that turns you on?"

"Like you can't imagine. If anything would make my . . . what should we call it? Poisons?"

Pauline laughed softly and said, "Uh-huh. They sure are."

"Mm. Poison kisses."

Pauline giggled once, then said, "A poison kiss. Oh my God, what's going on with you, Widow?"

"I don't know, but I think I like it. I think all of this, everything I'm doing to you, is making the poisons stronger."

"How come you knocked out that sucker Lucas so quick?"

"Hmm. It was urgent? I just felt like pouncing on him. My whole thing right now is to take my time with you. Maybe that controls it somehow."

"Mm. Probably."

Widow gazed into Pauline's eye from up close, waiting until all traces of a smile left her face. Then, she turned her eyes down to Pauline's lips.

"Kiss me, my helpless little girl. Take more of my poisons."

Pauline gasped softly, parted her lips, then closed her eyes as Widow moved in closer and began their kiss. While Pauline moaned softly, Widow felt around with one hand, behind Pauline, until she found the leash.

Still kissing and sharing her saliva's poisons, Widow tugged on the leash, tightening it just enough to hear a quick gagging sound. She backed away from her lips only enough to speak.

"And just like that, my sweet girl is very quiet for me. Hmm, I think I'll keep her quiet for as long as I want her to kiss me. Such soft lips. Such soft, wet lips my helpless little one offers me."

Pauline's chest had stopped moving, and Widow tightened the noose but not enough to tip back her head. And she took her time, kissing with open mouths, seeking Pauline's tongue and playing with it, then licking both of her lips many times.

She backed away just enough to smile, and she kept the noose tight.

"Mm, so beautiful now."

Again with her mouth open and lips against Pauline's, she kissed her and squeezed with her lips Pauline's upper lip, then the lower, then the upper again before resuming a deep, wet kiss.

And she pulled the leash harder, almost tipping back Pauline's head.

But Widow ended the kiss, then turned to place an ear close to Pauline's lips, which were still apart.

"Mm, so very quiet for me. I do love soft, helpless, quiet little—"

She saw Pauline's eyes roll up, then close, and she let go of the leash and reached up to force open the noose.

"Pauline! Hey, wake up!"

Pauline didn't move, so Widow leaned back and watched her chest but saw no sign of her breathing.

"Hmm," she said at the sight of Pauline's nipples having become quite stiff. "Maybe don't wake up just yet, little girl. Maybe never. You're an adorable little doll to be so quiet and so excited for me. Mm."

Just then, Pauline sucked in a deep breath, and Widow saw her attempting a weak smile.

"Pauline? I'm sorry about—"

She shook her head and said in a whisper, "Don't be. Oh my God, Widow. That was the best ever."

"Really? Because of my poisons, you mean?"

"That and your noose. Oh my God, I love that. I love that you did that to me."

"I, uh, almost couldn't stop. Pauline, I almost didn't."

"I know. Maybe that was part of it."

Widow still had her arms around her, so she rushed to unfasten her arms, then helped her lift them up and move them around.

"There. You're free again."

"And I'm still in that orgasm."

"Me too."

Widow shimmied herself up toward the pillows, then turned onto her back.

"Do I need that special voice to get you to do something?"

"Uh-uh. Not right now."

"Okay. Get those pants and everything else off."

"I will."

Pauline sat up, undressed herself of everything, and threw it all onto the clothes that Widow had discarded earlier. Then, she got an arm around Widow's waist and placed her hand on her abdomen, high up near her breasts. She sighed deeply with her head on Widow's shoulder and under an arm that was holding her in close.

"I think I almost killed you, Pauline."

"Yeah. You almost did."

"You hate me?"

"What? No, Widow. No, I loved that."

"I loved it too."

"You were kind of consuming me, I think."

"Mm-hmm. I love consuming you."

Pauline rubbed around Widow's belly and said, "Probably every touch, even like this, is giving me more of your poisons, right?"

"I think so. Maybe more when I'm really orgasming."

"Oh. That makes sense."

"I realized something else, too, Pauline. I had a quick memory, then it was gone."

"What about?"

"I . . . I had a baby girl, um, before. But we lost her."

"Oh my God, Widow. That's horrible."

Widow sobbed softly and hugged Pauline more tightly.

"I can't remember what she looked like. I can't even remember her name."

Pauline got up on an elbow, still close, and said, "Widow, I'm so sorry. I'm kind of sorry you even remembered that."

Widow's wet eyes looked up into Pauline's, and she said, "I'm already losing that memory. Even the feeling of it is just about gone again."

"Maybe that's good. That won't help you here."

She blinked and squeezed a tear from each eye.

"No, you're right."

With her free hand she wiped her cheeks, then dabbed around her eyes. She managed a smile.

"That feeling is gone now. I remember only . . . the words of it. I'm glad I got to tell you, though."

"I'm never going to remind you of it."

"Good. Don't. I just want to . . . be whatever I am."

"You're gorgeous. Scary but absolutely gorgeous."

"Thanks, Pauline. Don't worry about me. Already, I mostly just feel what's left of that orgasm."

"From consuming me."

"Mm-hmm. You were such a—oh my God. I want to call you my baby girl."

"Why not just let yourself?"

"Maybe I should. You know, I don't even care about that fading memory."

She gently guided Pauline's head back onto her shoulder, then brushed all of her hair back and to the side.

"You know why?"

"Why?"

She nudged Pauline's head down, slipping her cheek across the skin of her shoulder, then her chest. Without looking away, she reached for a thin blanket and pulled it to cover them both.

"Oh," said Pauline. "I think I know. I can be your baby girl for you."

"Mm-hmm. Be a soft, sweet little baby for me. Right now."

Widow sighed when Pauline shifted herself farther down, and she turned a bit onto her side. She fluffed out Pauline's thick red hair, getting it out of the way as Pauline moved again to place her lips where they needed to be.

"Mm, good girl," Widow said while playing with Pauline's hair. "Such a good, soft little baby girl."

* * *

Widow stretched her arms out to her sides before opening her eyes, then she saw and felt Pauline sleeping with her head on her shoulder and under her arm. She eased herself out from under her, then covered her with the blanket.

Seated on the bed's edge, Widow stretched again and yawned, then stood and rubbed around her scalp, bouncing around her long black hair.

She retrieved her clothes, got dressed, then walked first toward the door and saw the heavy pipe that sat in stout brackets to either side. She took a leisurely walk around the perimeter of the room, examining and touching almost all of the furnishings, opening drawers and cabinets.

In one cabinet, she found shallow cardboard boxes containing neat arrays of small glass bottles. Most of the places held a bottle, but some of them had been removed.

She tried to open the hatch to the vast storeroom where she'd bitten the odd mutant, but Pauline had locked it up tight.

She ended her travels by standing near the bed and looking down on Pauline, who stretched and squirmed around, then rolled onto her back on a substantial pillow. Her head tipped back, exposing her throat, and she didn't awaken.

Window stared at Pauline's throat and didn't look away, not for a while.

To herself, she said, softly, "Widow, no. She's your friend."

Scoffing but smiling, she bent to gather up Pauline's clothes, then held them over the bed, ready to set it all down.

But she bit her lip and stared at the exposed throat, the smooth skin of it.

"She's edible, too, though," she whispered for only herself to hear.

Bending again, she quietly set all of the clothing back on the floor, then stood to gaze at the bare neck tipped back over the edge of a pillow.

"Huh."

She shook her head, not smiling.

"More edible or more friend? Hmm."

She lifted a knee up on the bed and gingerly let her weight sink into the soft blankets. The other knee came up, too, and Widow crawled forward just enough to look directly down at Pauline's throat.

With her lips back but not allowing even the softest of hisses, Widow touched her growing fangs with her tongue, just testing the points.

"Hmm . . ."

She leaned closer, then held herself very still, with no breathing, and slipped the fangs in easily, like two of the sharpest possible needles.

Her lips were already wet, and she made a warm, snug seal all around, then began a very slow sucking and swallowing, not in any rush, just a little at a—

Pauline opened her eyes, and Widow stopped. But she left her fangs just barely piercing the soft skin.

"Breakfast?" Pauline said, and she smiled but didn't move anything other than that.

Widow withdrew her points and nodded, then said, "I couldn't resist."

"Don't, then."

"It's so much better, so much more urgent with you tipped back like this. It's hotter."

"Huh. I'm more edible this way?"

"Mm-hmm. Sorry, but yes. Oh, God, yes."

Pauline blinked a few times, then rolled her neck away before the next bite could land. She sat up and held the blanket around herself.

"Hey, that's an idea. Oh, you're going to like this, Widow."

"What?"

She grinned and pointed up, and Widow, for the first time, looked above the bed.

Almost lost in the shadows between the beams, a soft strap, shaped in a loop, hung down. Beyond that, a dark device appeared locked onto a narrow metal beam running parallel with the ceiling beams.

"What is it?"

"My little friend."

"Huh?"

"In the heat of the moment, you called me, I think, a dirty, naughty girl. Remember that?"

"Oh, I sure do."

"Well, that's because I am. I use that to, um, get more of a thrill when I, uh, you know."

"No, I don't know."

"What you said you did on that roof. How you got here."

"Oh, really? How does it work? What do you do?"

Pauline reached behind her and found the hardwired control box where it stayed hidden behind the nightstand.

"Watch."

She held a button, and the motor clicked then whined and sent the loop down toward the two women on the bed.

Pauline let it stop, then tugged downward on the strap.

"This goes around my neck. And when I'm cumming, right at the sweetest time, I hit this button,"—she pointed at it—"and this wonderful little thing lifts the loop, which is around my throat, and I black out right at the peak. Oh, Widow, it's amazing."

"So, you really are a dirty girl, aren't you?"

Pauline nodded and bounced her eyebrows.

"See why I'm so hooked on what you're figuring out you love to do?"

"I do love doing that. God, you're just perfect for that. But . . . I don't get it. Doesn't it just lift you up to the ceiling and murder you?"

"No, and that's the beautiful part. It has a setting where it can only lift so much weight—it's set to pull just enough to lift me up some. And it only stays there as long as I'm holding down the button. So, when—"

"You black out, then your finger comes off of the button, then—"

"Then, I don't get murdered. Yeah. It's kind of sweet."

"And if the reactor quits? What then?"

"Then, it unlocks and falls too. No real danger at all."

Widow crawled the short distance and held Pauline's gaze.

"There is with me."

"Uh, yeah. Uh-huh. You're even scarier now. That rest did you some—"

"Stronger too. Feel."

She moved Pauline's hands to hold one of her thighs.

"Damn. Is it from—"

"Consuming. Yeah, I think so."

Pauline held her leg and said, "Uh, scary."

"I'm soft, too, though?"

Pauline rubbed Widow's thigh with both hands, as far up as she could reach, and said, "Oh, yeah. Soft and scary and so damn sexy."

Widow kept her serious expression for only a few seconds, then giggled and sat back.

"Oh, Pauline, I do have my moments. The heat of the moment, I guess. But this is all so crazy. This whole place. How I'm changing into who knows what, and how—"

"Hey, Widow, try not to think about it too much. This world is nothing but a mess of deep, crazy cracks that any of us can fall into. All we can do is become some narrow form of our own kind of crazy. Maybe then, we can fit in. Somehow."

"Like offering to hang upside down for a cruel woman to suck the life out of you more easily? Crazy like that?"

"Uh, maybe not all of my life."

"Hmm."

"Widow?"

"Mm, doing that, going all the way, might someday be my narrow form of crazy, Pauline."

"Oh. Um . . ."

She took one of Pauline's hands and put it back on her thigh.

"Still, I'm soft."

"Mm-hmm. Soft and strong. Scary, though, too."

"Hmm. What else?"

Pauline turned her eyes to watch as she rubbed her hand slowly up and down Widow's thigh, then she looked up again.

"Sexy. So damn sexy."

Chapter 38 – Nails Hammered into My Spine

Janey hadn't finished granting a royal initiation to Junior, which would officially make him King, and he still talked intelligently with Mortimer. Almost everyone in the room fought to hear their words and to watch Janey almost choking on a thick pole and rubbing it like crazy with both hands.

"Perhaps I will be a very beneficent King for all of you," said Junior.

"Because Janey sucks cock so good?"

"Well, there's that, of course. She's quite skillful, and her enthusiasm is compelling. But I was referring to the unidentified electro-mechanical components that—"

There was a loud pop, and the buzzing vanished.

Junior's eyes fluttered while multi-colored sparks danced out of his ears.

"I know what happens now," Junior yelled as he threw Janey over many of the heads before she could gnaw on his kingly rod. "You won't be nice anymore!"

Mortimer was closest to him and gripped his shirt with both hands, but Junior easily lifted him up and held him away, where his snarling face and snapping jaws couldn't rend into his flesh.

"Mama! I don't like this!"

Mortimer was kicking him, and several others had gotten hold of his clothing and were moving in for deep bites.

"I'm coming, Mama! Don't be a—"

Another loud pop led to a steady buzzing.

"—insect. *An* insect."

From high above Junior's head, Mortimer said, "I really need to fix that sometime. I'm not sure I can, though."

Junior set him down gently, then helped him straighten out his clothing.

"It would seem that some sort of remedy is needed," Junior said. "That occurrence, which seems to trouble your fine community often, doesn't cast any of you in a favorable light."

Mortimer pointed at him and said, "No, it surely doesn't."

"It's based, would you say, mostly on a power interruption of some sort?"

"I believe so. Yes. Those buzzers that are everywhere were created by yours truly and installed by a dedicated team under my direct supervision. The problem is, King, that the—"

"Not yet because—"

"Make it dirty, Mortimer!" shouted someone. "Fucking dirty!"

"Now's your fucked up fucking chance!"

Mortimer grinned and looked back at the commentators, then turned the other way when someone else shouted, "Use a lot of fucking dirty words, dammit! We love it!"

Looking up at Junior, Mortimer shrugged and said, "Have to keep them happy."

Junior nodded knowingly and said, "Of course. It's little enough for the common folk."

"You ready?"

"Yes. Proceed. You have no recourse but to deliver a dense dose of expletives."

"Alright. You, Junior, will soon be King when you shoot gobs of thick, creamy cum from that giant, hard-as-a-rock cock, right into Janey's mouth, so much of it that she'll fucking drown if she can't swallow it quick enough. But she's so good at sucking cocks, all kinds of cocks, and swallowing cum almost as often as she inhales, that she'll just lick and suck and swallow everything your obese horror-show dick can pump out!"

The room blew up in cheering and clapping, and everyone close enough slapped Mortimer's back. Even Junior was clapping and smiling.

"Well said, Mortimer. It sure is still hard as a rock too."

"Janey will surely suck that thing until it droops down to the floor like a noodle that got drowned in a bucket of spit."

"I'd like that, even though the expectation that it will resemble any sort of pasta is misguided," Junior said. "But tell me, Mortimer: what are all of these electronic components that I've ingested? I can also feel some sort of mechanisms moving around, latching onto things, little gears spinning, pistons pumping . . . odd sensations like that."

"We truly don't know, big boy with a big cock."

"He really snuck one in there!"

"Mortimer is the best! The fucking best!"

Looking around the room, Junior said, "So, all of you have at least some of those items incorporated into your physical form?"

"Soon-to-be King—when you finally blast out that immense reservoir of cum—we're fucking packed with the stuff. We don't know what the hell we are!"

"That's interesting. I could easily devote some study time to—"

A loud pop stopped the buzzing, and Junior's face twisted into a knot. Hot sparks blew out of his ears, some of them burning into faces all around him, and a low roar and snarling rose up throughout a sea of ravenous faces.

Then, before anyone could bite, the buzzing resumed.

"That's kind of distracting," Junior said, rubbing his chin.

"Tell you what, you cum cannon King, you."

"Nice one!" said someone nearby.

"I'd bet it'll really shoot like that. What Mortimer said!"

Mortimer continued, saying, "I have a unit that I can install that might help. It's kind of experimental, though, but I think it might sustain your electronic and mechanical features."

"Where would this experimental unit be attached? Like, to the wall there?"

"Well, no, dick-like-an-iron-pipe King. It would—"

"Mortimer's only speaking truth."

"Sure, but it's dirty. Always talk dirty."

"—it would be installed right on you! Ideally, it would become part of you. You'd probably quickly forget that it's even there."

"And it would offer an uninterruptible power supply?"

"Exactly! Much like the hardness of your massive cock could never be interrupted!"

"That was a good tie-in. Mortimer's got a way with words."

"Except that Janey would love to suck some of that hardness away."

"Guys!" Mortimer said, smiling at the folks behind him. "She'll get her chance again. We just need to power up—"

"His cock!"

"I, uh, was going to say, 'the King,' but your idea is so much more tantalizing!"

"Look," said Junior, "I'll give it a test run. I have so many things that I need to think about, and I see now that I would benefit from a more reliable buzzing."

"Yes, you surely would."

"Mortimer's talking about the King's wood!"

"He's putting the entire fucking forest to shame with all that wood!"

"For instance," said Junior, "my dear mother quite often, seemingly warranted by a blinding obsession, would compel me to participate in unseemly acts of such perversion and depravity that my only recourse was to abandon all notions of right and wrong and simply perform as directed."

"Uh, what?"

"We can discuss it more later. Right now, let's see about that newfangled power source of yours."

"Right!"

He reached behind him, and someone placed something in his hand, which he held up for Junior to see.

"Check it out. It's a crude first effort at this, but it just might work. You see, there's a little reservoir right here—just keep that filled with crude oil. That's the fuel. You'll hear it right away, but the important thing is that it shoots that buzzing—"

"Like he shoots his cum!"

"I bet he could shoot it across this goddamn room!"

"—that buzzing right into you. It's packed with all kinds of odd circuit things that will keep evolving, and it'll keep all of your new electronics and mechanical gizmos sparking and firing and—"

"Cumming!"

"—and mechanicalizing all over in that big, muscle-packed, and—"

"Cum-filled!"

"—body of yours."

"Well, okay. Let's give it a try. Do I strap it on?"

"Oh, he's really setting us up!" someone said with a snorting laugh.

"It's like he's already got a gigantic strap-on ready to shoot like a damn fire hose!" said another.

"Well, no," Mortimer said to Junior, shaking his head. "See this?"

He flipped it over and showed a tight array of short needles, all of them about as long as a single joint on a non-Junior-sized adult's finger, none as long as the deadly appendage of the would-be king that just wouldn't relax.

"We just hammer this thing into your back."

"Um . . ."

"Oh, it'll be fine. It all connects inside automatically, and our goddamn King will be an even more fucking kingly King!"

* * *

Junior rubbed at his chin while saying, "That marvelous contraption will operate as you have outlined?"

"Who the fuck knows?"

"That Mortimer's an honest fucker, isn't he?"

"He sure is a fucker. That much is true. Ask me how I know."

"Does it hurt?" Junior said, his eyebrows up as he looked down at Mortimer.

"Won't hurt me a bit. If you're ready, we can set you up."

"Sure, I'm up for it."

"I can't," said someone. "Fuck, I just can't!"

"Me neither! He's making it too fucking easy!"

Mortimer reached behind himself again, and someone handed him a giant mallet, which he held out for Junior to see.

"Might I make a suggestion to ensure a comfortable experience for you?"

"Well, sure," said Junior. "I appreciate your concern. Thank you. I truly welcome your recommendations."

"I say we get Janey to work on that King-sized post that defies gravity. If we time things just right, you probably won't even notice the vicious pounding it will take to get those needles and spikes into your spine and expendable organs."

"I do believe you mean 'vital?'"

"Let's hope for the best!"

"He didn't say anything dirty," a woman said, sounding dejected.

"It's kind of violent, though. That's always nice."

"Well, okay," Junior said, nodding. "This might not be an entirely pleasant experience, but I do so wish to have my very own buzzer unit."

"Did he say eunuch?"

"No, not the King! Never!"

"Janey!" yelled Mortimer. "Get your sucking mouth busy on the future King's cock!"

"Pretty standard language from Mortimer, but quite good."

"Agreed. I mean, fucking agreed."

"Okay!" yelled Janey, and she hurried over to Junior, stooped down, and took the sizable swollen end into her mouth.

"Hands, too, Janey! Strangle that prehistoric serpent!"

"Mm," she said, almost gagging, and got both hands busy on the thick shaft.

"Now," said Mortimer, heavy hammer in his hand, "I just need to get around behind you."

"Please be sure to find enough room for a forceful swing. This likely isn't a time for timidity and needless concern for my comfort."

"Yes! I'll do that! Fucking all of that!"

While he was offering his back, Mortimer said, "It's quite helpful that you aren't wearing a shirt. Do you even own one, you sweaty, Kingly beast?"

"Oh," Junior said over his shoulder, "I did have one not long ago, but I outgrew it."

"Not surprised," said Mortimer. "Your heavy monster pole has already outgrown almost every mouth here, but we—"

"Mine's big!" someone shouted.

"I'd tear off my lower jaw for a shot at that!"

"You mean a shot *from* that!" yelled the first one.

"—but we at least have Janey, who's still quite proficient."

"She's doing an admirable job," said Junior.

"She always does," Mortimer said, grinning as he leaned around to view the action. "Now, Janey, I want to time my pounds to your strokes. And both of us need to make every one of them count. Sound good?"

She nodded, her eyes rolling back from lack of oxygen.

"Perfect. Now, King in the making, we just—"

"He means King in the sucking!"

"Or cumming. He might mean cumming!"

"—we just need to line this up,"—he held the box-like power unit high up against Junior's back—"and just get the needles and spikes poked in enough that it doesn't move. Yes, like that. Just like starting a nail, huh?"

"Okay. I feel it. Are you sure that it's aligned with my spine and whatever other sacrificial components of my anatomy are needed?"

"Well, it's not all that critical. As long as we get a few in your spine, this baby should fire right up and power all of those devices that are anchoring themselves everywhere inside you."

"Sounds very technical. You're a gentleman and obviously a scholar too."

"Well, sure, King, it's technical, but all that stuff knows what to do. We sure don't!"

Janey kept stroking his thick shaft, looking at him whenever her eyes weren't rolled back, and Junior grinned while looking up at the ceiling.

"Get that hammer ready, Mortimer. Finally, after so much aggravating foreplay and priming the pump, I think I'm about to—"

"That's a monster pump that Janey is priming!"

"Fuck, it's more volcano than pump!"

"—I think I'm just about to . . . one more good . . . stroke will . . . now, Mortimer!"

Janey pulled with both hands, trying to choke a petrified tree trunk, and couldn't contain the first gigantic blast. At the same time, Mortimer swung his mighty mallet, driving the power supply's array of points deep into Junior's back.

"That's a first! Janey's letting some leak out!"

"I'm going to help!" someone else yelled, ran over, and stooped down to lick up the thick sludge that dripped down on her chin.

Janey groaned, throttled the rigid post again, and sloshed another wave of it out and into her mouth, just as Mortimer cackled and beat the spikes deeper into Junior's back.

"It's in!" said Mortimer. "See the light come on? We did it!"

He leaned around to yell to Janey, "Empty that fucking thing, Janey!"

She tried, and more leaked out.

Looking around at the excited faces, Mortimer yelled, "More of you—help them! Lap that Kingly shit up!"

Junior watched Janey calmly as the red light on his built-in buzzer blinked and she wrestled with his kingly staff, wringing out every thick drop and feeding the slurping lips and tongues of the scavengers gathered around the geyser overflowing her mouth with every long drag.

"I'm so proud of all of you fuckers!" Mortimer yelled above the hooting and hollering of the crowd. "All of your sucking and licking and lapping is finally giving us the fucking King we've wanted for so long!"

Several of the starving slop suckers had fallen to the floor, holding their bellies and groaning. The others were doing their best, trying to not miss a sticky drop while also holding up Janey, who had long before gotten knocked unconscious from the thundering trauma to the back of her throat.

"Okay," said Mortimer, "okay! I think you all have finally squeezed it all out of there. Nice work!"

"Call them fuckers," someone nearby said to Mortimer.

Mortimer coughed and said, "Nice work, you fuckers!"

A team worked together to lay Janey down on her back, some snickering and pointing at her belly.

"Hey, you fuckers," Mortimer said to them, "she only looks pregnant. She'll digest all of that sludge soon enough."

"Kingly sludge," one of them said.

"Yes, Drake," said Mortimer. "That's correct. You fucker."

He nudged Junior's arm and got him to turn to face him.

"So, do you feel like a King?"

"I truly do. It's well worth the excruciating distress of having nails hammered into my spine. Overall, I'd rate the experience as positive."

"Very good! Now that you're powered up, in a self-contained way, and your massive Kingly cock has been drained of every sinister drop, you can just take a step or two backwards,"—Junior looked behind him at the open door to the prison cell—"and reside in regal elegance in your very own—"

"No!" roared King Junior. "Oh, sorry if that frightened you. It's just a personal preference about which I have a fair amount of passion. What I mean is that that will have to wait. There's still a wench named—"

A short, shrill squeal led to the buzzing all around stopping.

But Junior's spine-piercing buzz unit kept flashing its tiny red light.

"Oh," said Junior. "I see that I'm in for another round of being assaulted by everyone, and none of you will remain coherent enough to—"

Mortimer hissed and snapped and swiped at Junior, who leaned away and said, "Whoa," then laughed calmly. "You again, huh? Shame on you."

He pointed at Janey, who was trying to sit up with a bloated belly, and said, "Hey, maybe reconsider such elementary gymnastics. Not while you're pregnant, hmm?"

Choking one attacker and lifting his boots off of the floor, Junior took a civilized bite out of his neck, then swung a kingly backhand to sever the head of another.

"Well, I suppose I could do this all day. But I'd rather you would all show a little more etiquette and—"

There was a quick shriek, then a loud pop, then steady buzzing.

Everyone calmed down, and Janey lay back again, holding her belly.

"So, uh, Mortimer?" said Junior. "Have you truly returned to your previous level of sanity?"

"Yes. So sorry about that, King. How did you fair during that episode?"

"Oh, I was fine. The device on and in my back, about which I'd love to scream—if that wouldn't be outright unkingly behavior—operated within its intended parameters."

"Huh. That's fucking remarkable."

"Yes, Mortimer, and it's a testament to your ingenuity and design capabilities. Oh, and during that tragic interlude, I even took the time to enjoy another snack."

He took another bite, causing a mix of gurgling and insane cackling from the convulsing one being bitten.

"And you were saying?" said Mortimer. "About that wench?"

"Oh, yes, thanks for the reminder. Yes, I still intend to scour the streets and rooftops of the wretched city for that wench."

"If you must," said Mortimer. "Why not take that snack along for the journey?"

"Thank you. I'd like that."

"Oh, King, and don't forget your exquisitely polished and ready for slaughter sword."

"A useful reminder. Thank you, Mortimer. Alright, well, I'm off to find the wench named Scarlet that killed my mother."

"But she was already mostly—"

"By my estimates, she'd already become nearly sixty-percent insect. A centipede, by my reckoning."

He shook his head and grinned at Mortimer, then struck a regal pose and looked out above all of the heads of the silent crowd. They all fell silent and not a single pair of eyes looked anywhere else.

"Like I always say: make a better effort, Mama, to not allow a complete transformation from the mother I knew and loved to a scurrying member of a loathsome branch of the insect kingdom."

Chapter 39 – It's Bath Time, Baby Girl

Pauline stood near the bed and got dressed while Widow lay back against the pillows, sometimes watching her and other times looking up at the hoist above the beams.

"Well," Pauline said after pulling her t-shirt over her head, "I'm definitely perverted, and I can't blame this fucked up world entirely for that. But I'm sure not suicidal either."

"Not even for—"

"Not even for a gorgeous monster that's giving me the orgasm of my life."

Widow laughed and said, "Hmm, the way you describe it makes it sound kind of nice, doesn't it?"

Pauline tugged down the hem of her shirt, then said, "There are worse ways, for sure."

She matched Widow's steady gaze for a second, then scoffed at Widow's raised eyebrows.

"Alright, yeah. I'd tell a whole fucking different story when you have me all—"

"Helpless and orgasming?"

"Hmm. Hey, I just thought of something: let's see if there's any useful stuff in that storeroom that would help out back at your lair."

"Like what?"

She pointed above Widow and said, "Like that. You could have one of your own."

Widow looked up and said, "There's no way you or I could—"

"You have a slave, remember? Make him do it."

"How would I make him?"

"Tease him. Give him a treat once in a while."

"No, Pauline, I don't think I'd want—"

"I bet for a suck on your nipples, he'd work himself to death."

"Pauline, that's gross! He has two heads!"

She grinned and said, "You already know what I'm going to say, don't you?"

Widow scoffed and said, "What, one head for each? Even more gross."

"Alright. Yeah, it is. But I think he's kind of in love with you, and not just from that sticky smooth voice you sometimes have. He'd do whatever you want."

Getting up from the bed, Widow said, "Alright, maybe he would. I am curious about what kind of cool stuff is in there. Let's go take a look."

Pauline led the way with Widow close behind, and she said, "You have an excellent ass, Pauline. I see that, the way you walk, and almost all I can think about is juicy."

Pauline said over her shoulder, "I think my entire body is juicy for you and those sexy fangs."

"Hmm. I think you're right."

Pauline unlocked the hatch, swung it open, and leaned while stepping herself inside. Widow followed and looked around when Pauline flipped the light switch.

"Oh my God, there's a lot of stuff. This is incredible."

"Told you. You were an engineer, huh? Think of all the wild stuff you could build—or make Igor build—out of the junk that's in here."

"After he dies trying to drag it all back to my lair."

"As long as he gets the important stuff back, then, who cares? One less two-headed guy trying to suck your nipples."

"You like talking about that, don't you?"

"Huh. I like doing it. I mean, I think I would."

Dripping honey with every word, Widow said, "Yes, you would enjoy sucking my nipples."

Pauline took in a quick breath, her eyes locked on Widow's breasts, and she said, "I would. I would enjoy that."

Back to her normal voice, Widow laughed and said, "Hmm, how about later? Right now, let's go shopping."

"Let's."

They walked past and around tables piled high with crates and boxes, and many larger ones were stacked on the floor. All of them were labeled, advertising that they contained machine parts, computer components, electronics and communications parts and supplies, and every tool imaginable.

"No guns?" Widow said after they'd seen most of the inventory.

"Yeah, never have seen one here. Not sure why."

"There must be a reason. Maybe Ham knows where some are?"

"No way. He'd be carrying five or ten of them with him all the time. If there were any here, he would have gotten them already."

On the way back to the hatch, they passed another group of stacked crates that they hadn't seen before.

"Oh, like it's meant to be," said Pauline. "Electric hoists."

"All packaged up and ready for Igor to take to my lair too. Yeah, it's meant to be. If I'm going to set that up, I'd also want . . ."

She kept walking, leaving Pauline hurrying to catch up with her.

"You'd want what?"

"Generators. Or at least one. I'm already thinking up some sweet schemes, and I wouldn't want the reactor to cut out and ruin everything."

"Smart. Get that two-headed boy of yours busy."

"I will. Hey, there's more of those," Widow said, pointing at a stack of cardboard boxes.

"What do you mean?" said Pauline. "You were snooping around, weren't you? While I was sleeping?"

"Sorry. Yeah. I saw a box of those in one of your cabinets."

"And you wondered what I use them for, I suppose."

"Uh, no, but I do now."

"I'll tell you. It's no big secret. Remember that vampire I told you about?"

"Yeah, but I still kind of doubt that—"

"No, Widow. Believe it. He's here. Probably a lot more of them too."

"Okay, so what's the deal with the bottles?"

"When I met him, he was in all kinds of trouble. Someone had roped him to a chair, but there was no one around. He later told me that something else came around and—"

"Some thing?"

"Yeah. Thing. So, something else came around and killed and dragged away the thing that was about to start torturing him."

"But the new thing didn't want the vampire too?"

"Ugh, no. Most things won't eat them. Something sick tasting about them. So, he was looking at me with those vampire eyes, which are kind of hypnotic, you know, kind of—hey, sort of like that sexy voice of yours."

"It is kind of hypnotic, isn't it? That's why that creepy rapist gagged me, I think."

"Yeah, I'd bet. Anyway, I was about to run off before his eyes did that shit to me, and he begged for me to stay. He tipped his head toward some garbage on a table, and I found a pair of welding goggles."

"Oh, I've used those."

"Is there anything all engineering-like that you haven't done?"

"No, I've kind of done it all."

"Alright, so he said those would filter out a lot of whatever shit is going on with his eyes. I put them on and what the hell, he wasn't lying. But here's the thing: he was so weak from being trapped like that for God knows how long, and he begged for some of my blood."

"He wanted to bite you?"

"Yeah. And later, he did. He said—"

"You just go around getting bit by everyone, don't you?"

"Jealous?"

"A little."

"I could be, too, you know."

"How?"

"You had that sweet little crafter girl on her knees, making her feel you up. If I hadn't walked back in . . ."

"Hmm. Okay. Let's both agree to never be jealous about anything, alright?"

"Hmm, I'll try. So, that vampire, he told me he hates women and had no interest in biting me in a real vampire way. So, he bit me, not much either, and took just enough to get his strength back. That's when we made a deal."

"A deal with a vampire. Nice."

"Yeah. So, the deal was that I come around sometime and let him have my blood, which isn't too messed up from the radiation everywhere in this nightmare."

"Because you live high up on this mountain?"

"Yeah, that's probably it. And for me doing that, he agreed that he'd consider someday biting me for real."

"No. To make you a vampire?"

"Yeah. Crazy, huh? I figured what the hell. It's not like any of us have any career plans here."

"I kind of do. My mind is already planning out all kinds of stuff."

"I'd bet."

"Alright, but what about the bottles?"

"That city is damn scary, right? I don't always want to spend all kinds of time there. And sometimes, I don't want to go out there at all. Times like that, I open a small cut, fill a bottle, and send it down the elevator. He—"

"How does he know when to come get it?"

"Two-way radio. I think he and I and maybe a couple others are the only ones that have them. Maybe people at the reactor too. I don't know. But I tell him, and he comes out and gets it. We have a system."

"I see that."

Pauline scoffed and said, "And that system is about to get a giant fucking upgrade."

"Huh? Like what?"

"Well, Widow, no more self-cutting to feed blood to a vampire. Oh, no. You do it. You bite, suck out some blood, then—"

"Spit it into a bottle? For the vampire?"

"Too crazy for you?"

"I'm getting crazier by the second, Pauline. Sure, I'll do it."

"Like, now?"

"Um, we could. Right here? Or—"

"No. Remember how you woke me up before?"

"Yeah, your head was hanging off of the pillow and when I bit you, I found that—"

"You found that you liked that. All hot and squirty, wasn't it?"

"Well, yeah. So, you'll get back on that pillow and—"

"Uh-uh. Nope. My little friend will get me just where you want me."

"The hoist above your bed?"

Pauline nodded and said, "Mm-hmm. You just can't say no, Widow."

"Biting you and sucking out your juices while you're hanging upside down for me? Hmm, no way I'm going to say no to that."

When she saw Pauline nodding, smiling and relaxed, she mixed some nectar in, warm and smooth, and said, "Neither are you."

Pauline lost her smile, then gave Widow just one more nod as she stared at her.

* * *

Without reverting back to her normal tone of voice, Widow picked up a large coil of smooth nylon rope, packaged up neatly, and said, "Hmm."

"That's, uh, that's a lot of—"

"Shh. Back to the dungeon."

She followed Pauline out through the hatchway, watched her locking the door, then grabbed all of her red hair in a tight grip and caused her to gasp.

Tipping her head back and leaning close, her breath hot on Pauline's neck, Widow said, thick and sweet, "Fetch the hot water. It's bath time, baby girl."

Pauline took short, quick breaths but managed to say, "Okay."

Widow didn't release her, just kissed her neck and said, "Mm, soft. Good girl."

Then, she relaxed the hold on her hair and fluffed it back with both hands, then smoothed it down over her back.

"Such a pretty little girl."

She let her go, and Pauline started to turn to look at her, stopped herself, then began the short walk to the several steps leading up to the doorway to the living space.

Widow watched her every movement, every little sway of her hips, every step of her legs, and even the rough, crude boots that she wore. And when Pauline lifted aside the pipe that barred the door, she watched her arms working, holding the pipe. And when she turned, she saw her breasts already approving of what was coming, the soft fabric of her t-shirt not able to hide every detail.

And the last that she saw was Pauline's hair, long and red and swaying behind her as she left to fetch hot water for her bath, just as she'd been instructed to do.

Chapter 40 – She's Almost Inviting Cruelty

After Pauline had gone and quietly closed the door behind her, Widow found the hoist's control box where it was kept hidden behind the nightstand. She held it up, played with the buttons a few times—lowering and raising the velvet loop—then sent it back up into the shadows again.

She put the controls down on the table, then glanced across the bed to an identical piece of furniture on the other side. Crawling across the bed on her hands and knees got her close enough to drag her hand around behind it, and she found a similar control panel.

"Huh."

Sitting back on her heels, she tapped a button, heard the whining up above in the shadows, and another cable descended, one with only a shiny metal hook on its end.

"Oh, nice. Huh."

She gave the door a glance, and it was still closed, so she stood on the nightstand, then put one foot on the highest part of the bed's headboard, and got her hands high enough to reach the hoists.

Minutes passed as she gave her attention to the machinery between more quick looks at the closed door.

Back on the bed, she tugged at a loop made of cloth, then hit the button to send it back up, out of sight, then hid away the control box.

Just then, the door swung in, and Pauline walked in with a large wooden pail and a jumble of towels in her arm.

"Good girl. Bring them to the bed."

"Okay."

Pauline carried the bucket carefully, not allowing any to splash out, and set it next to the bed. Widow took the towels from her and made a neat stack beside her where she sat on the edge of the bed.

She looked up at Pauline, who was barely breathing and not smiling.

Widow laced her words with warmed honey, so much so that every word after would be soaked in it as well.

"Bar the door."

Pauline hesitated, held her breath, then nodded and started to walk that way.

But Widow said, "Stop. Come back."

She turned slowly and walked back, then stood facing Widow.

Widow said, "Take off your boots, then turn around."

Pauline started to speak, then stopped herself. She bent over, tugged the boots and socks free and tossed it all to one side, then stood straight again. Watching Widow's eyes, she turned to face away.

Widow moved her knees apart and said, "A step back for me."

Pauline complied and was close enough that she could have sat down on Widow's lap.

When she felt Widow's hands on her waist, she looked down and watched as Widow reached farther, found the button, then the zipper, and loosened it all.

Looking ahead again, her breaths quickening, she heard Widow say, "Let's have a look at you, little girl," and Widow held the waistband of her black leather pants, tugged it around, and began to slide it down over her hips.

When her ass cheeks had just begun to be bared, Widow said, "Mm, so nice. So soft and smooth."

She kept going, uncovering Pauline's entire ass, then said, "Oh, such a soft and smooth baby."

When the pants had hit the floor, Widow held one of Pauline's thighs with both hands, guiding her to lift her leg up and out, then she did the same with her other leg.

And the room was completely silent as Pauline faced the door, her eyes locked on it, as she stood with nothing but a t-shirt and Widow's hands on her hips, rubbing them up and down gently.

"Hmm, so soft. Now, you may go bar the door, my soft little girl. And I will enjoy the view of your soft, naked ass. Mm."

Pauline shivered once, then began a slow walk and took the stairs up, then used the pipe to keep any intruders from getting through, and she paused there.

"Turn for me."

Pauline spun around slowly, and Widow remained seated on the bed, her eyes scanning all that she could see.

"Come back to me. As you were before, little girl."

She walked back toward Widow, then turned herself around, standing close again.

"Yes, just like that."

She held Pauline by her hip with her left hand and dunked a towel into the hot water bucket. Pauline remained still as Widow raised the dripping towel up and rubbed it up and down her right leg. Then, she changed hands and repeated it for Pauline's left.

"Good girl. Hold very still while we get you all washed up."

With the towel again in her right hand, Widow soaked up more hot water, then reached it around, washing Pauline's thighs, both sides, and letting it drip and run down off of her skin.

"So much cleaner already. Such a good girl."

Leaving the towel in the bucket, Widow stood up, kept close enough to rub herself into Pauline, then lifted her t-shirt with both hands.

"Up, now, little girl. Arms up for me."

Pauline held her arms straight up, and Widow pulled the shirt past the red mane, then up and off of her arms. She tossed it onto the bed behind her and when Pauline started to lower her arms, she touched both of them gently.

"Oh, no, no, no, little one. Not yet."

Pauline kept them up, and Widow leaned over, got her hot, dripping towel, then stood again behind her.

"Hmm, just like this," she said as she slid the wet cloth all around on Pauline's arms, then her throat and neck, then high on her chest.

"Oh, we'll need just a bit more water now," she said, and leaned again to soak the towel.

Reaching around and holding the towel with both hands, Widow first unfolded it and held it flat over Pauline's breasts, causing her to gasp.

"Mm, it's hot. Yes. Such a soft, sensitive baby girl."

Holding her breasts through the towel, she began to rub them, squeeze them, and gently pinch the nipples while whispering in her ear.

"Such a good girl to take a hot bath when she's told. Mm, such a good little girl."

Pauline swooned, her legs getting wobbly, and Widow chuckled softly and helped her stay on her feet.

"Almost there, little one."

She gave both breasts a long squeeze, then a dragging of the cloth across her nipples, then leaned to get it soaked again. She reached around Pauline again to hold it with both hands.

"Just a little bit more, precious little girl."

With her fingertips, Widow nudged the flattened towel deep between Pauline's thighs, causing her to look up and gasp.

"Yes, right there for my girl. It's already so warm and wet, but little girls have to bathe when they're told to."

A quick shiver went through Pauline, and Widow continued, dabbing it around, sometimes rubbing softly, and not stopping any of the hot water from trickling down the smooth skin of her thighs.

"Hmm, so nice. So nice and wet."

She fed just one end of the towel between her thighs, about halfway to her knees, then held that end from behind her. Slipping it through, to the front and back, and lifting it slowly, too, Widow found that she couldn't go any higher with the hot wet towel between Pauline's thighs.

"Oh, right there, little girl. Mm, let's wash you up real nice."

Pauline's breathing had become quicker, and she sometimes leaned before recovering as Widow slipped it through while keeping a firm upward hold on the towel.

"So nice when a little girl is all washed up."

She gave both ends of the towel a stronger lift upward and held it. When she saw that Pauline had risen up onto her toes, she gave it a stronger pull upward, causing a short, high-pitched gasp, then let it relax.

With her left hand on Pauline's back, right above her cheeks, she wiggled the cloth through and out, then let it drop into the bucket.

Again holding both of Pauline's hips, Widow leaned forward and kissed one ass cheek, then the other.

"Such a sweet little girl, all washed up for me."

* * *

"You can let your arms down, sweet girl. You're such a very clean little girl now."

Standing behind Pauline again, Widow reached both of her arms around, up high enough to squeeze her breasts, and held one of Pauline's shiny knives for her to see.

"Such a useful thing to have around. A good little girl would never need to worry about such things, though, would she?"

Pauline shook her head and said, "Uh-uh."

"Hmm. Not as long as she stays a good girl."

She sat back down and used the knife to cut a short length of rope off of the coil on the bed.

"Be a good little thing and cross your wrists, back here where I can see them."

Pauline took a deep breath, let it out, then did what Widow had told her.

"Good girl."

She took her time and tied a snug loop around one of Pauline's wrists, crossed the other one over, then found that she'd cut enough rope to make several loops around both wrists. She finished it with a secure knot.

"Oh, that's nice. Just lovely."

She stood, then, and gathered up all of Pauline's hair, then used a shorter piece of the same rope to tie a ponytail with a nice bow.

"Good girl. Such lovely hair you have."

Pauline didn't look when she felt Widow leaning toward the bucket, then heard light splashing of the water. But she did look down at the thin strip of cloth that Widow held horizontal in front of her face.

"Little girls are so much prettier when they stay quiet, don't you agree?"

Pauline hesitated, then nodded quickly and stopped quickly too.

"Hmm. You're not sure. And that doesn't change a thing. Open. Open that pretty mouth."

"Widow, maybe you should just, um, do the usual—"

"Oh, a troublesome little girl."

Widow leaned enough to get her fangs close to her shoulder.

"Hmm, let's see if this helps. Hold very still for me, Precious."

She sank in her fangs just enough to pierce Pauline's skin, sucked for just a second, then slipped them back out.

Pauline opened her mouth, and Widow said, while moving the taut cloth between her lips, "There we go. So much more cooperative now. Yes, just like that. Good girl."

She pulled it in far enough to touch Pauline's lips, then said, "Oh, a little tighter is always nice."

She applied more force, pulling it hard enough to tip back her head, and she leaned her own forehead into Pauline's hair to hold her in place.

"Hmm, maybe a little more. It's such a delight."

Widow pulled back hard, causing Pauline to gasp around the wet cloth, then she kept the tension in it as she tied a tight knot behind her head.

"And just like that, the little girl is helpless and so very quiet for me."

With a hand on each of her shoulders, Widow nudged and tugged at her to turn and face her.

"Mm, a very beautiful little girl now."

Pauline stared at her, with no sign of attempting a smile. And Widow, seated with her face level with Pauline's breasts, gave an obvious smile as she looked up at her.

Then, Widow stretched back her lips, showing her long fangs to the woman that she'd just bound and gagged, and Pauline flinched. But Widow held her in place.

"Ooh, they're so sharp."

She glanced ahead at one of Pauline's breasts, then the other, then back up to her eyes.

"And this little girl acts scared, but I see that she's excited too. Perhaps she'd like a little nibble where's she's such a sensitive little thing?"

Pauline shook her head softly, almost like a twitch.

"Oh, such a sweet little girl. I could be very careful and bite right here,"—she touched a fingertip to the soft skin just above a nipple—"then the little girl would feel those very sharp fangs sink in so deep, all while my wet tongue held her nipple still, keeping it safe from those bad teeth."

Pauline shook her head again.

"Hmm. We should find time for that later. Right now, my sweet little girl wants to get all trussed up nice and tight. Don't you?"

Pauline only stared for a few seconds, then nodded.

"Oh, such a good girl. So sweet to want to be even more helpless for me."

She stood, rubbing up against Pauline as she rose, then held her face with both hands.

"Hmm. A nice little silent scream," she said as she touched the pulled-back corners of her mouth. "Poor little thing."

She kissed her tight lips, then said, "And that nice little binding in your pretty mouth will only get tighter as it dries. Poor little girl."

She then guided Pauline to lift one knee onto the bed, then the other. She kept nudging and got her to lie facedown in the middle.

"There we go. Just like that. Just lie very still now, little one."

Widow got herself seated on Pauline's thighs, facing toward her ankles, and cut another length of rope.

"A little girl isn't completely helpless if she could somehow run away. No, we can't have that."

She lifted one leg, bending it toward her, and knotted a loop around the ankle. With the other up, too, she wound the rope around as many times as she could, then tied a tight knot.

"Hmm. So much better already."

She shifted back farther, seated on Pauline's bare ass, then tied another set of coils around her thighs, just above her knees.

"Oh, my. My little girl is becoming so much more helpless all the time."

Widow rose up onto her knees, turned herself around, then sat again on the backs of Pauline's thighs.

"You'll have to be a very patient and quiet little girl now. Shh, little one."

Pauline lay still, with only her chest moving from her breathing, and Widow used a long piece of rope to loop all around her arms from her wrists to the very top, leaving no skin visible, then tied several knots.

"So much better now. I do adore a completely helpless little girl."

After whisking Pauline's tied hair to the right side, Widow laid herself down atop her, letting her lips touch the left side of her neck.

She giggled softly, then kissed her ear.

"Oh, Pauline. I know you're not really a little girl."

She kissed her again and let her hot breath touch her too.

"But I'm falling into that crack that you mentioned, the one where I have to just be myself, whatever that is. It truly feels like I'm falling."

She brushed aside a few stray red hairs.

"The dungeon door is barred, and no one from out there can stop me."

She kissed her neck, then licked it softly.

"And you've become so perfectly helpless. You can't stop me either."

A soft giggle ended abruptly, and Widow whispered in her ear.

"You've become nothing but my soft, juicy little baby girl."

She paused, feeling Pauline's deeper, quicker breaths lifting her.

"And you're the most . . . edible . . . little treat I can imagine."

*　*　*

Widow let a deep breath rush out, almost with a soft laugh.

"But even a delightful little treat tastes so much better if packaged up nice and pretty."

She pushed herself enough to lean up, keeping her legs rubbing all over Pauline's. From the drawer in the end table, she retrieved one of several rolls of gauze, then tore off a length.

"And little girls want to stay very quiet, don't they? Yes, they do."

She grabbed Pauline's ponytail, gave it a gentle pull, and said, "Up now, little one."

She let go, and Pauline kept her head up off of the blankets.

"Yes, just like that."

After arranging the thick hair to extend straight down her back, Widow held the band of gauze in front of Pauline, distant enough that she could easily examine it.

"Let's just cover up that cloth that is so cruelly forcing you to scream silently. Yes, let's make that our little secret."

Pulling the strip back, with it pressed against and completely blocking any view of Pauline's anguished, gagged mouth, Widow wrapped both ends around her head, then held them off to the sides.

"Oh, it is long enough, isn't it? Yes, let's do that too."

She wound first one end over Pauline's eyes, then the other, then tied a tight knot behind her head.

"Mm, I like that. The little girl will have to be surprised at the things that happen to her. Hmm. Cruel things, perhaps."

With Pauline's head laid on its side on the bed, Widow sat on the backs of her thighs, playing with her hair.

"Yes, packaging is so important. I see now that sticky gauze would be so much better. I'd love to just wrap it around and stick it all together. Oh, you poor, helpless little thing."

She giggled when she saw Pauline's fingers reaching, trying to touch her.

"Oh, so sweet. Soon, precious little girl."

Holding her hands, she said, her voice normal and serious, "God, the sight of you is making me so hungry. So hungry. I want to wrap you completely, just cover everything except where you want to feel my fangs. Yes, you want that—to offer me your sweet juices."

While letting out a deep sigh, Widow rose up to her knees, leaned across the bed, and found Pauline's control box. Sitting back again, she held a button, causing a low whining high above.

When she saw Pauline's head turn at the sound, she laughed softly and said, "You know what that is. Of course, you do."

Watching Pauline's chest working harder, she grinned while snaking the loop over her head, then arranged the soft strap to fit well against her throat.

"Oh, my," she said to her captive, allowing the heated honey to blend in with each word. "The little girl has never let anyone else play with her like this. She was always in control. Certainly never tied up so tightly. If someone were to hold . . . this button."

She pressed the right button, and the noose tightened around Pauline's neck, gagging her.

"Oh, that could be bad."

She stopped pressing it, and Pauline's chest showed that she welcomed access to the warm dungeon air again.

"There's no need to be that cruel with such a sweet little girl. Still, though, it's just so tempting to touch a simple button . . ."

She held it again, which raised the loop and began to strangle her, and she didn't let it go while she leaned forward and kissed around Pauline's ear.

"Mm, such a sweet little girl. So soft. I do believe the baby girl's softness is almost inviting cruelty."

She gave the bound and gagging woman a few more kisses around her ear, taking her time, letting her feel her hot breath.

Then, she released the button and let her lie flat and breathe deeply.

"Hmm. Perhaps we'll finish that fun bit of cruelty someday. Maybe when I have you wrapped completely, hiding away all that juicy skin. Keeping it hidden for me to enjoy at my leisure. Mm, all soft and juicy."

Still smiling and running her fingertips over the smooth skin that she'd left uncovered, Widow pivoted off of her, then held one of her shoulders to roll her onto her back.

With her arms bound behind her and under her, Pauline's breasts were forced higher, and her identity was mostly blocked by the gauze straps that Widow had wrapped over her mouth and eyes.

Touching her again tenderly, Widow paused to observe how the arms beneath her also raised her hips and the soft skin of her thighs. She touched all along Pauline's legs, past the coils of rope just above her knees, then across her lower legs until she reached the tight bindings around her ankles.

"Mm, such a tender little treat. Oh, little girl, I just can't help myself."

She slipped the loop up off of her head, then installed it around her ankles. She tugged it once, found that it was stable, then guided the cable as she held the button, and it began to raise her legs off of the bed.

"Yes, little one, I made some adjustments to your little toy. It's quite strong. Strong enough for what I want from it. And from you."

The motor whined steadily, lifting Pauline's legs, and Widow didn't release the button when it lifted her hips, too, up off of the bed.

"Oh, the little girl is in so much trouble. And no one will save her."

Still holding the button, Widow caressed Pauline softly as the motor lifted her high enough that only her upper back and shoulders were touching and forcing her bound face toward her chest.

"Oh," said Widow, "hmm, that's kind of nice."

She lay facedown on the bed, up on her forearms with her face looking down at Pauline's.

"Mm, the little girl is so close to kissing her own breasts. Would you kiss them for me, little one? Yes, you would. You'd suck them for me if I'd only unbind you."

She gave the gauzy lips a kiss, then each of the breasts that were close and almost touching the gauze too.

"So nice when the little girl is hanging like this. Hmm, just adorable."

She sat back up and held the hoist control button again and within a few short seconds, Pauline's red ponytail was the only part of her touching the blankets.

But Widow didn't let the motor stop, and even her hair left the bed to hang down beneath her.

"Mm, and just like that, my tasty little treat is right where I want her."

Widow knelt close and used both hands to spin Pauline slowly, kissing her all over. She held her still when her ass cheeks were near her mouth, and she gave each a kiss.

"Hmm, such a juicy little thing."

She got a more determined hold on her hips, reaching around, then spoke close to Pauline's bare ass.

"The roundness of it, like a luscious piece of fruit, is tempting me, telling me how full of juice you are. Mm."

She gave each cheek a slow lick, then spun her halfway around, gave her a longer kiss, then said, "Oh, my. That's such a sweet and juicy part of you. Mm, so very juicy for me."

She backed away and smiled, then licked a thin trail up from Pauline's navel.

"So juicy. And we have nothing but time."

She gave her another kiss there for a few seconds, then backed away, smiling.

"A part of my little girl where her juices just bubble right up for me. Hmm, perhaps to convince me that I don't need to bite? Hmm, I'll take these delightful juices you offer, and I'll still bite. Oh, I'll still bite you."

She burrowed in between Pauline's thighs and reached around to hold both of her ass cheeks.

And in the silent dungeon high on a mountain, behind a barred door and with no one anywhere that could interrupt them, one of the only movements in the quiet room was Widow's head moving gently, rhythmically, as she moaned and kept her captive close.

The other movement was Pauline's breasts, excited and resting upside down, as her stiff nipples tried to rub against Widow with every breath she took.

Chapter 41 – Fuck Them Then Kill Them

"Shh, shh, shh," Archie said, then laughed. "No screaming on your first day of whatever the hell you're becoming."

The woman he'd bent over his desk tried to kick back at him, but he'd left her pants down around her knees, tangling her up. He held both of her wrists with one hand and tried slapping her bared ass, only sometimes connecting with a loud smack.

"Hey, this isn't easy," he said as he rammed his tool into her repeatedly.

She jerked her hips each way, trying to evade his attack, but had no success. He only slowed down once.

When the puffy fur at the end of her long tail slapped his cheek.

"Hey! Get that fucking thing under control!"

He choked it with his free hand, then spun it in circles, winding it around his hand like a coil of rope.

"You're a goddamn freak. A damn sexy one, though."

"Please, just let me go!"

"I don't think so! I'm the boss. I fuck everyone and everything. You, little cutie, are one of the things."

"But it hurts! It's too tight!"

"I hear that all the fucking time!" he said, then rammed it in, fighting the friction. "I can feel that all shrinking in there. Probably from you growing a goddamn tail. Ha!"

"Please, stop!"

"Oh, you're still sweet enough for me, even with that shrink wrap you got going on there. Hey, you got yourself a shrink wrap pussy!"

"Where the hell am I? I just want to go home!"

He winced as he thrust his hips again, then said, "Huh. Getting a little fucking tight. Yeah, maybe too tight. Shit, I'll just fight my way through it. Like a goddamn boss."

Renewing his hold on her wrists and tail, he said, "Honey, even if you could get home, they wouldn't take a freak like you even at the goddamn zoo. Oh, no. Circus sideshow, sure. But, you tight little bitch, there's no way for you to go back anyway."

"Just stop! It's too big!"

"That's what they all say, shrinking pussy or not. Shit, human or not."

Someone rapped on his office door.

"Not now! I'm in the middle of a goddamn interview!"

The laughter was enough to carry through the dilapidated door.

"When are you not, uh, interviewing someone?"

Archie stopped mid-stroke and let the tail go. Then, he gave her ass a hard smack.

"You raise a good point. Come on in."

The door swung in, the operations foreman walked in, then stopped and stared.

"Uh, maybe this is a bad time."

"For her, yeah. Don't mind me. What's the problem?"

"I, uh, the sight of your bare ass while I'm trying to tell you that—"

"Well, shit, come around the desk, then, Sammy."

Sammy walked around, then leaned to get a better look at the young mutant woman with sloppily cropped blond hair that wove around her tall, pointed ears, tears on her cheeks, and big eyes staring back.

"Huh. Kind of cute."

"Here," Archie said, then grabbed both of her wrists, one in each hand, and passed them to him. "New job description. Hold that."

Sammy took them and held them, and her fighting to free herself had no effect.

"She, uh, she's got a—"

"A tail. Yeah. Oh, and a shrink wrap pussy."

"A what?"

"Never mind that. Tell me what you think is so fucking urgent."

"Uh, sure."

He moved her arms so that he could hold both wrists on the desk, then flapped around and unfolded a piece of paper almost as big as the desk, and he covered Archie's victim with it.

"A map of the fucking reactor? So?"

"I've circled areas here and here that are backing up. I mean, Archie, the bodies are piling up."

Archie kept thrusting, shaking the map all around.

"Hold the fucking thing up. This darling mutant doesn't have the sense to hold still and take her fucking."

He rammed it in, struggling against the tight fit, and she screamed.

Sammy grabbed one edge of the paper and held it up.

"Oh," said Archie, "I see it. Yeah. The logjam starts at that goddamn oven, doesn't it?"

"It's like this, Boss: we need Junior back."

"Fuck no, Sammy. He took my sword and went to hunt down that scary freak. The muscle-brain dope thinks she killed his mother."

"What scary freak?"

"He said her name is Scarlet. Sexy as fuck but dammit, she was already changing into some scary kind of freaky bitch."

The tail slipped out from under the paper when Junior gave her another hard poke, and it flapped around before Sammy could drop the paper and grab it.

"Like this one," he said, shaking his head and laughing.

"What? No, this one's just fun and sexy. Like in some bizarre beast kind of way."

Sammy pointed and said, "You like that, don't you?"

"Sammy, I fuck them all. The fucking around here is equal opportunity."

"Decent of you."

"Thanks. So, no, that Scarlet bitch was getting scary in some sick way. I had to get her out of here fast."

Sammy kept a grip on the tail and used it to hold the paper down over the struggling woman.

"They always think they can fight."

Sammy grinned and pointed again.

"You like that too."

"Won't deny it! It's good to be the boss. So, alright, we need that body-chewing, mutant-digesting giant muscle stooge to come back and work the oven."

"I think that would help. I tried putting backup slaves there, and they just couldn't handle it. I had to toss most of them into the fire myself."

Archie pointed, smiled, and said, "You kind of like *that*, don't you?"

"I kind of do, yeah. But the bodies are piling up. Straight humans, freaks . . . all of them."

"We can't have that."

Archie kept thrusting and scratched at his chin, the young woman with a tail and covered with a map of the reactor kept squirming, and Sammy waited for his orders.

Finally, Archie lunged in deep, let out a sharp scream, then said, "Ooh, I think I'll switch to a blow job. This is getting ridiculous with all that shrinking going on."

"Smart. That's why you're the boss."

"Damn right. Okay, Sammy, gather up a posse. Tell them all to bring their favorite weapons, things they particularly like killing with."

"We're going after that scary Scarlet bitch?"

"Mostly for that son of a bug, Junior, but we should probably finish off the Scarlet wench too," he said, then grimaced as he thrust himself in deep again. "Not just them, goddammit, Sammy. We're going on a goddamn freak killing expedition through that fucking city."

"To kill freaks?"

"I hate freaks. Let's kill them all."

"Uh," Sammy said, then lifted the paper to see the same teary eyes looking up at him before he let it drop. "You, uh, you're—"

"Oh, fine. You got me, there. Let's fuck them *then* kill them!"

* * *

Widow gave suspended and bound Pauline a gentle nudge, and she spun back around to face her. Down on her hands and knees, she got herself close to speak to her captive, and she paused to lick her lips.

"You're right where you want to be, you naughty little girl. You love more than anything being stripped down, bound up, fondled and licked, and never knowing when your captor might decide to tighten a cruel noose around your neck.

"Or even if she'll ever loosen it again. Hmm, that could be so delicious. God, my orgasm is growing just from talking about it."

She waited and didn't see any response from Pauline, just her steady breathing giving life to her breasts.

"Do you like what has happened to you so far, naughty little girl that plays with nooses?"

Pauline's head, with a cloth pulling her lips into a tight scream, then covered with gauze, and with her eyes banded over, too, nodded.

"Oh, of course. Hmm, before I hang myself up with you, maybe—oh, I didn't explain that to you, did I? I found the second hoist, and I'll use that to hang beside you. We could have shared just this one cable, but I might want to leave you like this for a long time. A very long time."

She gave her a kiss where Pauline's lips would have received it if she hadn't been wrapped to cover her mouth.

"Where was I? Oh, yes, I remember."

She checked under the blanket, then under the pillows and found Pauline's belt, which she threaded through the buckle to make a choke collar again.

"You're so very quiet for me, little girl. But all that talk about your soft neck, how you're so helpless, and how a cruel woman could easily strangle you has gotten me so excited."

She slipped the loop around Pauline's hair, past her head, then cinched it up enough to stay around her throat.

"And I'm feeling so delightfully cruel."

She gave it a quick tug but not enough to choke her.

"And you're such a delightful little victim. A helpless little victim girl."

She kissed the gauze on Pauline's lips, held her lips there, then pulled the noose tight.

Pauline gagged softly until it got cut off completely, then she only hung silently.

Widow backed away, then caressed what could still be seen of her cheeks.

"And we're never in any real hurry, are we, precious little one?"

She kept it tight, then held one of Pauline's arms, pushing and pulling, making her captive's breasts sway one way, then the other.

"Oh, that's a sight. My little girl has such soft, tender breasts."

She kept rotating her, watching them react to the motions.

"And her nipples are so stiff and teasing, almost begging to be given a sharp bite."

"Hmm," she said as she parted her lips and covered one of them, letting the sharp tips of her fangs drag across but not pierce Pauline's skin.

She backed away, giggling, then licked her nipple several times, then loosened the noose.

From up close, she watched as Pauline's deep breaths drove her breasts toward and away from her, over and over.

"Oh, so sweet. My little girl wants more. Okay, little one."

She snapped the leash, stopping Pauline's breathing instantly.

"Such delightful nipples you offer me. And there's no doubt that they like what I'm doing to you. Oh, they sure do, you soft little orgasm girl."

Widow used only her lips and tongue, squeezing, pulling, and sometimes licking. She gave one of them one last pull, stretching it out, then let it snap back and bounce the breast a few times.

"Oh, okay, little one. Here you go."

She loosened her collar and played at licking one nipple, then the other, as Pauline's breaths brought them closer then took them away, and they settled within a few seconds.

Whispering in her ear, Widow said, "You must know that I'm delaying what we both know is coming: a very good and deep bite. Oh, I'm going to suck so much of your tasty juices, and I'm wondering if I'll be able to stop myself."

Pauline shook weakly and moaned softly, but she couldn't free her arms or legs at all.

"Shh, now, sweet little girl. I know you're excited. I am too."

She kissed her, then spun her enough to whisper in her other ear.

"I might not stop. I don't believe I'll want to."

Around the tight cloth in her mouth and through the gauze covering it, Pauline groaned softly and tried to move her arms and legs.

"Yes, it's very exciting. You like even hearing about it."

She backed her around enough to kiss the bindings over her mouth.

"But you, my sweet, juicy little baby girl, don't want me to stop either. Even without yet having a serious bite, you already don't want me to stop. Mm, you want me to take all of your hot juices."

Pauline took a deep breath, drawing Widow's appreciative look from very close, then let it out slowly, carrying a groan with it.

"I'm so glad you're offering all of your sweet juices to me. I see now that that's why you encouraged me to just be myself. You want more than anything to be just a sweet, juicy little baby for me."

Widow took hold of the other hoist's controls and lowered the loop that she'd attached to the shiny metal hook. She pulled it close and held it while tying a length of rope around her own waist.

"Soon, little one, we'll be so close."

She attached the loop around her ankles, lay back, then held the button. The mechanism whined softly and began to lift her legs, then her hips, then she was hanging above the bed, her face even with Pauline's gagged and blindfolded face.

After hooking the controls to her makeshift belt, Widow reached behind Pauline and held both of her ass cheeks.

"Oh, so soft everywhere. So much soft skin."

Pauline groaned and shifted around enough to sway them together.

"Shh, now, little girl. Be patient."

The bound woman settled and held still, and Widow reached down for one of the bottles that she'd set on the pillow.

"This won't be easy, but I did say that I'd do it. I'll give up the first warm trickles from your neck to fill that bottle."

She spoke over Pauline's soft groaning and said, "But I may just keep it as a reminder of all that we've shared. No need to waste any of it on some silly vampire man."

Pauline trembled enough to vibrate her hanging mane, and Widow pulled her in closer, squeezing their breasts together.

"Oh, you feel so nice. Such a soft little thing."

She slid her hands to Pauline's back, her fingertips caressing her all the way, then squeezed their breasts together more.

"Mm, so stiff. Such an excited little girl. Me too."

She reached farther and placed her hands on the tight gauze and red hair, then turned Pauline's head to one side.

"This is just to be sure we both have a wonderful orgasm, one like you've never had before. Here, little one. Feel my cruel fangs."

With a low hiss, Widow sank her fangs into Pauline's neck but not as deep as she could have. She moaned softly for a minute and swallowed many times before backing the sharp teeth out.

"Mm, such hot juices when a little girl is hanging like this! And the soft little girl is so relaxed now, happy with her sweet orgasm. Such a good little baby for me."

She licked the punctures several times, then said, "Now, let's fill that bottle together. It will take several sweet bites and a lot of sucking. Doesn't that sound wonderful, baby girl?"

Pauline nodded, her head still in Widow's hands.

"Such a more cooperative little girl already. So sweet."

She turned her head, exposing the other side of her neck.

"Even the words I say will only increase your orgasm. Listen closely."

With more honey in her voice than she'd been using right from the start, Widow said, "I love sucking out your sweet juices. You are only hot juice for me to suck. You're nothing but hot juices."

She hissed and bit and sucked, and Pauline didn't make a single groan or moan or anything else. Widow stayed there, her fangs poking into the soft skin, and used her cheeks to siphon out the juice that she'd need for the bottle, and she didn't swallow any of it.

"Mm," she said after withdrawing her fangs and bending around to let it dribble over her lips and into the bottle.

"We need more. You want another bite, don't you? Even deeper this time?"

Pauline stayed quiet and nodded.

"Oh, such an orgasm you're having now, you sweet little thing. If you insist."

She bit in again, sucked, then moaned while letting a mouthful of Pauline's hot juices drip down into the bottle.

"Well, that should be enough," she said, then capped the bottle and let it fall to the bed.

Holding Pauline's ass cheeks again, she pulled their hips tight together, then kissed the bindings over her mouth.

"That wonderful orgasm is flowing all through you, little girl. You know that I can't help myself—I am sure to take more than I should. You're just too soft and sweet, and I can't stop."

She kissed her again and said, "And you don't even care. Oh, such a cruel little game I play with pretty little babies."

Nudging Pauline gently, she rotated her to face away, then tapped the hoist button a few times, making minor adjustments until Pauline was at the right position for her fingers, and she got those busy immediately.

"Oh, just like that. Yes, baby girl. So soft and slow for me while I suck out so much of your hot juices."

She reached down for the roll of gauze, then played out several loops around their hips, trapping Pauline's fingers, leaving them nowhere else to go except to touch her, just the way Widow had instructed her.

"Slowly, baby girl. Ooh, just like that. Soft and slow."

She dropped the roll onto the bed, near the bottle of Pauline's blood, then found the leash and tugged it just enough to take the slack out of it.

From close to Pauline's ear, with her mouth rubbing on her neck, she said, "It'll be like turning on a faucet. You know what I'm going to do. You want that, too, don't you, sweet baby girl?"

When Pauline nodded, Widow laughed softly and said, "Mm, of course. You can't imagine being anything besides just a juicy little treat for me."

Holding the leash with her right and fondling Pauline's breasts with her left, Widow said, "Aw, here we go now. Such a sweet little girl," and jerked the leash, tightening the noose around her throat.

As the seconds passed, Widow kissed the soft skin where she would soon sink in her fangs and rubbed and pinched Pauline's breasts.

After many quiet moments had passed, while Widow and Pauline hung upside down in a dungeon on a mountain, Widow said,

"Nothing but a juicy little doll girl for me. Just a juicy doll of a baby girl."

She bit her fangs in as far they would go, made a tight seal with her lips, and she paused to feel Pauline's fingers still wanting only to please her, to feel their hips bound tightly and holding all of their skin against each other, and to fondle the breasts, tugging at the nipples gently, stretching them out.

Then, she let the noose loosen, and Pauline drew in a deep breath.

"Mm," Widow moaned as the hot flow hit her, and the only sounds in the otherwise dead silent room were from Widow's eager sucking at Pauline's neck and sometimes a loud, urgent swallow.

Chapter 42 – A Sexy, Curvy Bottle of Poison

Sammy had assembled the group to hunt down and bring back Junior and had them lined up in the hallway for inspection outside of Archie's office. They waited patiently, each bearing a weapon of their own choosing.

The office door swung in, and Archie stood there, looking out into the hall while zipping up, then buckling his belt. He belched, then looked each way until he saw Sammy.

"Boss, we have a damn good posse, just like you wanted."

Archie scoffed, stepped out of his office, and pulled closed the door.

"We'll see."

He looked the other way, squinted at the two men on the end, then said, "The Spencer twins? They're still alive?"

"Yeah, somehow. They're good fighters, boss. We might need them."

"But they're mutants themselves, dammit. What the hell are you thinking?"

"Uh, yeah. They do have some non-standard body parts on them, but you want Junior back, right?"

"Only to keep the fucking oven burning bodies on time. I have no fondness for that mountain of stupid, sweaty flesh."

"No, of course not. But we need them. The Spencer boys will be—"

"They have their bows and arrows. Good."

"Yeah, Boss."

Archie looked the other way, tipped his head, then walked toward a tall, lanky character in ragged clothes.

"What's your story?" he said, looking up at him.

"I, uh, don't have a story. Sir."

"You should fucking make one up, then. What's your name?"

"Most folks just call me Blade. And I'm stronger than I look. I swear."

"Why Blade, Blade?" Archie said, then snickered.

Blade held up his long, shiny sword and kept it pointed down.

"Because I always carry this around. I found it at a shop in the city, and I'm never going to—"

"Gimme that," Archie said and swiped it out of his hand. "I gave mine to that flesh-eating stink pile of stupid flesh, Junior."

He hefted it around, took a few swings.

"Hey, not bad."

"But, Sir, I won't have anything to—"

Archie jabbed a hard finger into his chest and said, "I have something else for you to carry. You said you're strong, right? You going to let me down, Blade? Huh?"

"Uh, no, Sir. Nope."

"Fucking right. There's a crate in my office. That's your job. Carry that fucking crate with us."

"Uh, sure, Boss. What's in the crate?"

Archie grinned and pushed in the door, and he and Sammy and Blade and as many others as could fit gazed into his office.

On his desk was a crude crate made of oil-stained, splintered boards. It covered only about half of the desktop, and one end had a small hinged door that was shut and latched.

Near that end, on the top surface, there was a hole about the size of a man's wrist.

And sticking up through that hole was a tail.

"Don't tell me," Sammy said, unable to hold back his chuckling.

"Alright, I fucking won't. Let's just say that nasty little mutant babe was a downright good fuck. I'm taking her with us."

"Can't you just, you know, fuck whatever you—"

Without turning to look, Archie sailed the business edge of his new sword up to Sammy's throat and held it there.

"I plan ahead, Sammy. That's why I'm the fucking boss and you're about to go chasing your head when I roll it down the hallway."

"Uh, sure. I get it. Smart."

"Thanks."

"Um, what's the door for?"

"I'm not stupid enough to let that ever-evolving freak show out just to get a little fucking when I need it."

"So, you . . . what? Just open that up, and her pussy is right there, and—"

"Could be her pussy. Sure. No way to aim perfectly."

"So, you just fuck whatever is closest to the—"

"It's either that or I go up and down this shitty posse line and fuck all of the posse fuckheads."

Everyone heard Sammy swallow hard.

"We, uh, we don't want that. Blade, grab that fucking crate. And you take fucking good care of it!"

* * *

Pointing with his new sword toward the dark city that seemed lodged between the black land and the black sky, Archie said, "She went that way."

"She?"

"Yeah, Sammy, that scary freak that I fucked, then kicked out. That she."

"Oh, and Junior went that way too. Got it."

"Glad you fucking got it."

The exit door from Archie's office to the gravel lot had just slammed shut behind them, and they all stood, weapons and freak crate ready, and looked past the chain-link fence and over the barren, bleak lands leading to the city.

"Might we be of service?"

The ten of them turned to see two guard dogs with human faces, both panting quietly and waiting for a response.

"Oh, it's the boss," said one.

His partner bumped him and said, "We should still offer our protection or tracking or—"

Archie pointed and said, "Tracking. Yeah. Both of you, lead the way."

Two human faces turned toward the black landscape, then back to Archie.

"Uh, sure. Lead where?"

Archie sneered at the mutant reactor guards and said, "You're still kind of dogs, right? So, you should remember the scent of—"

Blade groaned, and everyone watched him trying take the crate from his shoulder.

"What the fuck you think you're doing?"

"Uh, sorry, Boss. This thing's pretty goddamn heavy. Just taking a break. I swear, I'll pick it back up when we're leaving."

"Okay, fine. Set her down."

He dropped the box from knee height, causing a squeal then a sob inside.

"Alright," Archie said, turning back to the guards, "not that long ago, you—"

He stopped and watched both guards trot over to the crate, then sniff all around it with their tails happy about it. One pawed at the door.

"Well, fuck," said Archie.

"Uh-huh," said Sammy. "That's exactly what they want."

"Well, shit, open it up, then. That's their year-end bonus. Like we have any fucking years in this shitty place."

"Seriously, Boss?" said Blade. "You want these dogs to—"

Archie pointed and said, "With human faces."

"Uh, sure, but you want them to just take turns with their dog cocks and—"

"Hey, wait. Maybe they have human cocks?"

"I'm not checking," said Sammy.

"Fuck it, then," said Archie. "Nobody's checking and nobody's fucking her but me."

He grinned at the sound of someone sighing loudly inside the crate.

"Now, you guard dogs with unidentified cocks of some kind, remember that scary freak Scarlet that hiked out of here?"

"Sure."

"Fantastic. And you must know the smell of a freak human that eats humans and freaks, doesn't care which? Remember that guy?"

One human face scrunched up its nose and nodded.

"That one had quite a distinctive scent to him."

"Distinctive? That's what you call it?"

"Like a days' old autopsy left out in the desert sun."

"That's goddamn poetic. Exactly. Why don't you two lead the way, and take us to whichever of those fuckers you can find first? How's that?"

"After a successful hunt," said one, "can we fuck the treat in the box?"

Archie looked up at the total black above them and grinned.

"Treat in a box. I like that."

One guard dog snickered and said, "Alright! So, we can fuck—"

"No! I fuck the treat in a box. Only me. Take us to the city. Find that flesh-eating, furnace-feeding psycho-beast and maybe that sexy scary monster that Scarlet sure has become by now. Go!"

* * *

After the dogs had led the way and they'd all gotten through the fence, Archie barked an order.

"Hold up. Let's get those torches fired up. It's only going to get darker the farther we get from the fucking ocean."

Some of them looked up at the dim orange glow clinging to the tops of the buildings, a few others struck matches and got torches burning, and two dogs sniffed around Blade and his cargo, up on their hind legs.

Archie scoffed and said, "Oh, no. No fucking my treat, you goddamn freaks."

A few laughed, then Archie pointed Blade's sword and said, "Onward, you fuckers!"

The torch bearers followed closely behind the dogs, lighting their way. Sammy and the Spencer twins were next, then Blade and his crate, then Archie, who waved his sword around like a child with a new toy.

He glanced up at the crate on Blade's shoulders and said, "Hey, turn that shit around. At least let her see where we're going."

"She's got eye holes?"

"Yeah. Not just a fuck hole. I want the fuck hole facing me."

"Aw, and you want her to see," said Sammy. "You're going to get a reputation for being kind-hearted. Be careful."

"I could end that real quick."

"How?"

"Cut your throat and leave you for the fucking boars."

Sammy swallowed hard and looked into the darkness all around them.

"Uh, I forgot about those. Are you sure they're still alive?"

Archie laughed and said, "I haven't yet seen a fucking thing that can kill them. If you think you can, you hotshot son of a bitch, get the fuck on ahead and lead the way."

"Uh," Sammy said, wincing and looking ahead, "I think, um, I'll just hang back here. You know, in case you want to share that fuck hole."

"I might. Yeah, I just fucking might. It'll be fucking sloppy as fuck for you, though."

"Well, shit, fine by me," said Sammy, "I'd step right up, whip it right out, and jam it right—"

"Shh. Hold it," Archie said, and he and Sammy watched as the dogs lowered their heads and growled at the dense blackness ahead. Everyone behind them stopped in their tracks.

"Mutants?" Sammy whispered.

"Maybe. We should be so fucking lucky."

They heard nothing except the occasional swat on a crate from the agitated tail of the treat in a box.

"Hey," Archie whispered. "Somebody stop that."

The nearest posse member held back his short sword, ready to swing it.

"No, not that. Dammit, you fucker, be nice."

He grinned, put away his sword, then held the tail straight up.

"I need that," Archie said. "Something to hold onto when I fuck her."

"Did you ever think of stuffing the fluffy end of it in her ass while you're fucking her? Huh? How about that?"

"Sammy, you're a fucking genius. A furry tail jammed into her sexy tail end, deep, too, and probably twitching all around to get her all squirmy and—"

There was a low snort somewhere out in the night.

They waited and listened, with only low growling from the guards to break the silence.

"You hear that?" said Sammy. "Tell me that wasn't a—"

"Snort. It was a goddamn snort."

"Fuck. At least, it's just one of—"

"Wait!"

They listened as another snorting joined the first one, then another and another.

"Goddammit," said Archie. "The fuckers are probably coming this way too."

"By the looks of the guard dogs, yeah. Uh-huh. What do we do?"

Archie looked all around before answering, then addressed all of them.

"Ready your bows, boys, not that they'll do any fucking good. Knives too. Whatever you got. We make a stand right here."

"Uh, why don't we, um, just run back?"

"Hey, shit-for-brains, these aren't dumb fucking barnyard pigs. We heard their snorting only because they wanted us to. This is mostly where they hunt—out in the open fucking wastelands."

"Still, Boss, if we just—"

"They're already set up behind us for the big fucking ambush. Those,"—he pointed ahead, toward the chorus of snorts—"want us to run. No, we fight right the fuck here."

He left Sammy and walked quietly to the front row, the best fighters, who were just in front of the torches but behind the snarling dogs.

"Relax your hold on those arrows, boys. You can't hold that shit all day then expect a true aim. Just be ready."

"Yeah, Boss."

"You two. With the torches. One of you throw your fire as goddamn far ahead as you can. Do it now."

They gave each other a glance and nodded, then one extended the burning stick far behind him, then let it fly in a graceful arc through air thick with crude oil.

Before it landed, they already saw them.

A line of fat boars, each a story-and-a-half high and standing close, their bloated bodies forming a blubbery wall.

"Oh, shit," said Sammy. "Maybe we just do some fast, really fast running back to—"

Archie snapped his finger, then pointed behind them while glaring at the other torch guy, who wound up and heaved it over all of their heads.

"Oh, fuck," Archie said when they all saw two lines of boars behind them, a group on each side, all of them ready to rush together and crush then devour them.

"Boss? What the fuck?"

Blade started to shift the crate from his shoulder, but he froze when Archie said, in a hoarse whisper, "Don't even fucking think about it. We're not leaving my treat in a box."

All around them, boars were snorting softly and hoofing at the slick ground. A Spencer twin raised his bow and drew back.

"No, don't fucking bother. That shit won't work unless you hit them just right, like in a goddamn eye socket. They're just too fucking oiled up. Smart fuckers."

"Boss, think of something. Quick!"

Archie scoffed, then walked ahead, past the best fighters, past the two torchless torch carriers, and up behind the guard dogs.

"You two fuckers," he said, and they stopped their growling to listen. "You pick up any scent other than fucking monster pigs?"

"Yes," said one. "The flesh-eater is directly ahead. We just need to follow the path we're on."

The other said, "And the scary female that you mentioned. Her path is the same, but it's not as strong."

"Straight ahead, huh?"

"Yes."

"Yes."

"Good."

With a quick downward slice, he cleaved one of them in two, leaving two twitching legs for each segment.

The other guard spun around and leaped for an escape, but Archie caught him with a quick lateral cut, unfairly leaving one meaty chunk with only a human head and the other with four twitching dog legs.

"That's why he's the boss," said Sammy, and the rest murmured their agreement.

"Easy now, boys," said Archie, and he led them off to the side, on a path to get around the line of fat blocking their path.

The boars barely noticed them as they all stomped confident steps toward the warm food that was already cut up for them.

"They're just letting us go?" Sammy whispered.

"Look at those blimp bellies of theirs. It's hard for them to think of anything else with a fucking hot meal waiting."

Archie stopped to watch as all of the boars descended on the dog parts and let the others pass him, on their way clear of the giant pigs.

"Huh. Maybe no one's ever fed those fuckers before. I'm a real kind fucker."

* * *

"Oh my God! Pauline!"

Widow reached down to hold Pauline's gagged and wrapped head with both hands on her cheeks. She gave quick glances at her chest, but she was causing a lot of commotion, and it wasn't clear whether Pauline was even breathing.

"I'm so sorry!"

She attacked the gauze, groaning as she struggled to loosen the knot, then quickly unwound it and saw that Pauline's eyes were still closed. And the gag, from a wet cloth that had cruelly dried, tightening itself even more, was still forcing her into a silent, unconscious scream.

"Oh, Pauline, no, no, no!"

She quickly untied the gag, pulled it free, and threw it blindly to the side, then she slapped her cheeks softly with both hands.

"Pauline, wake up! You have to wake up!"

"Hmm . . ."

Pauline licked her lips while trying to tip her head up, then she let it shake back down. She'd never even cracked open her eyes.

"Pauline!"

The smile appeared first, then thin slits let her watering eyes look from side to side, then focus on Widow's as they both still hung upside down in the dungeon on the mountain.

"Are you okay? Say something!"

"I did," she said, then her eyes closed again.

"Pauline," Widow said, then shook her lightly. "What do you think you said?"

She laughed weakly, then said, "I said 'hmm.'"

"Oh. So, that means that—"

With eyes still closed, Pauline said, "Means that I'm still . . . orgasming. Oh, yeah . . ."

Widow let out a deep sigh, then laughed for a second.

"Oh my God. I thought it was only me. And I thought you were dead."

"Hmm. I wouldn't have cared. Damn, Widow. Mm."

"How come you're not dead? I don't think I sucked out all that much of your blood before my orgasm kind of knocked me out. But didn't I give you that, whatever it is, some kind of poison?"

Before answering, Pauline struggled weakly against her bindings, then said, "How about my arms too?"

"Oh, just a second," Widow said, then untied the binding holding the two of them together at their waists.

Then, Widow spun her around while saying, "Even though I don't want to untie you."

"Goes against your nature, huh?"

"Mm-hmm. My nature now."

She undid the knots, pulled it all loose, and let it drop to the bed before spinning her back around.

Pauline stretched her arms to both sides, then held Widow around her waist. Before speaking, she gave her lips a gentle kiss.

"About that poison. I think it's like you said, how it knows what you want. I felt it, though. If you'd wanted to kill me, God, it probably would have been plenty strong enough."

"Oh, that's good."

"For when you want to kill me? You might want to kill me next time?"

Widow laughed and said, "No, I don't really want to kill you. No matter how tempting it is."

"Alright. That's only a little scary."

"Not scary enough to keep you from doing this again?"

"Um, maybe not falling asleep hanging like this."

"Oh. Yeah, let's fix that."

Widow found her control panel, then got the hoist motor to whine softly and began to lower herself.

"Oops. Wrong controls."

"Stop there."

She stopped as soon as Pauline said it—when Widow's breasts were even with her mouth. Using both arms, she embraced Widow and held her close.

"Told you I was still orgasming. Damn, Widow."

"Oh, me too."

Pauline began to suckle quietly, sometimes moaning.

"Mm, uh-huh. Me too."

Widow let her arms drop, then held Pauline's red ponytail with both hands, rubbing the hair around her face and inhaling deeply.

Pauline paused her affections and said, "Oh, wow. Here too."

"No. Poisons? Even from my breasts?"

"Uh-huh. You're just a sexy, curvy bottle of poison, aren't you?"

"I guess."

She reached higher, for Pauline's head, and made it difficult for her to not continue.

"And you'll just have to see if my poisons are stronger. I think maybe they are."

They hung in near silence, and Pauline held Widow by her ass cheeks as she sucked and licked and gently nibbled.

Pauline tipped her head away, gave one a final kiss, then said, "I really need to get myself upright again. Don't you?"

"Huh. I'm pretty comfortable like this. Feels natural."

Widow hit the button and lowered herself past Pauline, who fondled and kissed what she could reach as it all slipped past her to the tune of a softly whining hoist motor.

Lying on the bed, Widow quickly freed her ankles from her loop, then found the controls for Pauline. She let her down slowly, laying her on her back with a whine up high near the ceiling, then slipped the loop off of her ankles.

She waited, naked and on her knees, and looked along the length of the bound woman.

"Well?"

"I'm thinking about it," Widow said, grinning and still examining her.

"What, exactly?"

"How to do it better next time. Oh, Pauline, I'm getting some wonderful ideas."

"Huh. Cruel ideas, right?"

"Mm-hmm. Oh, yeah. But I'll untie you, since you're such a sweet, juicy little thing. Mm, you're still so—"

"No. Don't start that again, Widow. You'll never turn me loose if you get to saying things like that again."

In a normal voice, Widow said, "You're right. Okay, let's free you from your cruel bindings."

She began undoing the loops around Pauline's legs, while Pauline said, "You even like saying that, don't you?"

"Cruel bindings. God, Pauline, like you can't imagine. I don't know what's going on with me."

"It's sexy as hell, whatever it is. Oh, uh, kind of scary too. Sexy scary."

"I like that."

She finished Pauline's legs, then laid herself down next to her. After a quick kiss, they relaxed, with Pauline's head on Widow's shoulder, an arm around her, her top leg bent up and resting on Widow's thighs.

"You really didn't care if you died?"

"Uh-uh. I wasn't stupid—I knew your sucking or your poisons or both could kill me—but I just didn't care. All I wanted was to be what you were calling me: your sweet, juicy baby girl. All I wanted was to be juicy for you. Weird, huh?"

"You sure were juicy for me. Mm, all over. But I'm glad I didn't kill you."

Pauline quickly said, "So that we can do it again? That's why?"

Widow laughed softly and said, "Yes. Oh, yes."

"Good. That should keep me alive for a while. It wasn't just the orgasm, Widow. No orgasm is going to make me okay with getting murdered. It was that other stuff."

"I like that. I captured a juicy little thing and made her not even want to get free."

"Yeah. That's it exactly."

"I should probably go, though, Pauline. Are you coming back to my lair?"

"If you don't mind, I'm just going to sleep and see how long that tingling keeps going. It's not a full-blown orgasm, but it's still damn good."

"Me too. It's still humming along quite nicely."

"You're unbelievable. Oh, and besides, I should be here when Ham gets back."

"Yes, you should. Have to keep your secrets. I'll take that bottle of your blood with me."

"Oh, I forgot about that. Yeah, it's for that vampire named Bentley. He's around. Ask your slave."

"Okay. He might know."

Widow sat up then stayed seated on the end of the bed.

"What's wrong?"

Widow shook her head, didn't look back at Pauline, and said, "I don't know what's happening to me, Pauline. It's fun and sexy and exciting but there are moments, like right now, where it just kind of scares me."

Pauline reached out and played with Widow's hair.

"Hey. It's alright. Focus on those things you like about it and forget the rest. It's all any of us can do here."

Widow sighed and said, "You're right. I know you are. I'll feel better, I think, when I get my new clothes."

"Oh, God, I forgot about that. You know what I think?"

"What?"

"When you dress yourself up in your sexy new clothes, that alone will boost the power of your poison to some crazy level, whether you want it to or not."

"You think so?"

Widow turned to look down at her.

Pauline smiled and said, "I volunteer to be the first to test that out."

"Really? You'd seriously want to be—"

"Juicy. Juicy for you. God, more than you'd believe."

"I like that. I don't remember why anymore, but I'm starving in such a strange way for a juicy baby. A baby girl."

"Don't even try to remember, Widow."

"Okay. Hey, Pauline?"

"Yeah?"

"Next time, could you, um, if you have any sexy clothes somehow, could you—"

"Dress like a soft little baby girl for you?"

"I know it's silly, and nobody in this world has anything like that anyway."

Pauline gave the drawer of her nightstand a quick glance, then smiled at Widow.

"Plan on it. Would you like it if I was so soft and sexy that you absolutely couldn't stop yourself?"

"Oh, God. Yes."

Pauline sighed and said, "Hmm. Me too."

Chapter 43 – Name Is Rodney

Back within the depths of the dark city, after leaving Pauline satisfied and exhausted in her bed and then riding the elevator to ground level, Widow kept to the shadows between streetlights and walked close up against the buildings when she could.

Backing two steps into a recess between buildings, she looked out and up at the building fronts, all looking mostly the same in nearly total darkness.

"Dammit. Around this block maybe?"

She looked both ways along the street, listened for a few seconds, then crept toward the left, the sack of food and supplies on her back sometimes grazing a dingy brick wall. Placing each step carefully and quietly, glancing each way repeatedly, and listening for boars or bats or—

A heavy plank door swung out and if she'd have taken the next step, she would have collided with it. Instead, she took a quick step back, then raised her hands and stared into the absolute blackness inside.

And at Igor. Igor appeared from out of the interior night, just enough that the pale streetlight illumination gave him some shape.

"Igor!" Widow whispered. "What are you doing?"

"I scared you! I'm so—"

"Shh! Stop yelling!" she said with a strained whisper. "Especially out here in the city. What's wrong with you?"

He stepped farther into the light, then turned to show his hump, then bounced his eyebrows a few times.

"Do you want a list of my obvious failures? Or would you like—"

"I don't want to hear any of it. It's tragic enough that I have to see it. Why are you jumping out at me like that?"

"Two reasons."

"Try one, and see if I let you live long enough for the second one."

"Uh, yes, Scarlet."

"Try to remember that I'm Widow and by either name, I'd kill you real quick."

Igor stared up at her, holding her cold gaze, and shook his head.

"You're even scarier after, well, whatever you did when you were gone. I'll be a good slave, but I want to die too. I could die, but then I'd—"

"Make up your mind."

He tipped his functional head toward the extra one and said, "I won't even make a joke out of that."

"Thank you."

"Okay, Widow, I'll just be your slave. You decide when I'm allowed to die."

"Fair enough. Now, your first reason for jumping out at me?"

"Because I want you to have a secret entrance to your building. This is it! This is—"

"Shh."

"Sorry," he whispered. "Through here, you can follow a path back to your place. It's secret."

"I might need that. Sure. Why else?"

"I can—"

"Shh."

"Sorry, Widow," he whispered. "I can fetch things for you, things you really want."

"Sure. Food and water. Supplies. Maybe even—"

"Men."

"Men?"

"Women too. Like that crafter that I like too. That very sexy young—"

"Hey. You get only what I allow you to have. You're offering to bring me . . . victims?"

"I'd call them lucky fools!"

"That's good. You whispered that. Well, we can talk about that later. I'm not sure I want anyone roaming the city and dragging back men and—"

"Women."

"Thank you. Yes. We'll see."

She reached into her pocket and took out the bottle of Pauline's blood.

"You sneak around out here a lot, don't you?"

"If I have to, yeah. I hide a lot too."

"Have you ever heard of a character named Bentley?"

"The vampire? Sure, everybody has."

"This is so weird. This whole place. There really are vampires here?"

"Yes, and this one is actually quite dashing and polite."

"Huh. Probably only because he can't make himself bite you."

Igor looked down and kicked at the bricks.

"Oh, forget that, Igor. He probably just hasn't been hungry enough when you've seen him. Here. Take this to him."

He took the bottle, then held it up to study it in the faint light. When he started licking it, Widow scoffed and forced his arm down.

"Oh, come on. Stop that. You're disgusting."

"Me? You somehow have a bottle of blood to deliver to a vampire, yet you say that—"

"Okay. Never mind. You have a good point. He'll know who it's from."

Looking at it again and licking his lips, Igor said, "Is it your blood, Widow? Huh? Is it?"

"No. And don't even think of sampling it. Now, how do I get—"

They both held still and listened to heavy footfalls from far down the road.

"Show me how to get back to my room."

He nodded and pulled open the door.

"Nothing to say? Quiet when danger is on its way?"

He only shrugged and grinned and led the way into a sea of black.

*   *   *

After Igor had pulled the door closed, there was no sign that anything at all existed.

Igor said, "Don't be afraid of the dark! I'll light a match, and we can—"

"Shh! Whoever that was is right outside. Be quiet and first, take a look."

"As you wish," he whispered, then he cracked open the door only enough to take a brief look, then he closed it quickly and quietly.

"I saw him before!" he whispered. "When I was on your roof, he was down there on the street, waving around a sword, and he—"

"A sword. No. It can't be."

She shoved him aside and peeked, then closed the door again.

"Not that guy again," she said. "He was out there screaming that he wanted to find Scarlet."

"But there is no Scarlet. Just Widow."

Widow scoffed and said, "He doesn't know that. Let him move along, then go follow him and see what he's up to. Tell him that there's no one anywhere around here like that."

"I don't want to, but I will. He's very large."

"Yeah, and you don't want to know why. Try not to get yourself killed, okay? I have all kinds of slave labor for you."

"Oh! Oh, Widow! When you get back to your room, look at the ceiling panel in the middle. I found it! I found—"

"Shh! Igor, you have to stop yelling."

"I'll try, but this is important!" he whispered. "That square of ceiling is rigged so that if you push on one end, it tips up. Widow, it leads up into that attic!"

"That's good. That's really good. Anything else? What's up there?"

"I only poked my head up to—"

Widow laughed softly.

"That's a stupid thing for a man with two heads to say. I know. But I looked and saw all kinds of equipment, machinery, stuff like that. It's big and dark and has lots of stuff."

"Speaking of dark . . ."

He struck a long match and cast a weak, flickering light around the room.

"Oh, put that on your list. Can you find more of those?"

"Yes, Widow. I will!"

"Settle down. Alright, which way . . ."

She looked around and saw that they stood in a large room that had a dozen closed doors distributed along the interior walls. Between the doors sat all kinds of clutter: moving equipment, boxes and sacks, and shelves with smaller junk.

"What is this place?"

"No one knows. Should I ask around?"

"No, don't bother. It doesn't matter."

Looking around again, Widow said, "That's a lot of doors. You're saying one of them will lead to my room?"

"One will give the shortest and safest path. Two others could get you there, but it'll take longer and there are more risks. The rest of them? No one will ever see you again."

"By all means, then, show me the right one."

"I will!"

He led the way to the door third from the right and yanked it open. Colder, darker air leaked into the room.

Widow leaned in and sniffed all around.

"It smells like something died in there."

"Yes, many things. Not you, though. Not you!"

"I just walk through here, and I'll get there? Are you sure?"

"If you follow the directions. Don't mess up!"

"I won't. I'll go only where—"

"And be careful of the snake. The one that isn't entirely a snake."

He let the door quietly swing itself shut.

"What? Come on, you said this was a safe path back to my room."

"Ah, no, I did not. I said it was the safest. And it is. Sort of."

"Fine. What kind of snake? Where?"

"Huh. Could be anywhere. It must have been a troll before it got here because it's not happy to let anyone past."

"Vampires and now, trolls too?"

"All kinds of things. Yes. Just remember the directions, and don't waste too much time with the snake."

"Why would I? What are you talking about?"

"I don't know! I'm just a slave and don't know what I'm saying!"

"Yet, you tend to shout it," she said, scoffing.

"Sorry. I just heard that about the snake. I've never met him. He doesn't—"

"It's a 'he?'"

"Yes, Widow. Name is Rodney."

"This is just stupid. Look, tell me the directions, then you go convince Junior to—"

"Junior?"

"Yeah. The muscle guy with the sword. Convince him to hunt for Scarlet somewhere else."

"Okay. I can try."

"Directions?"

"Easy: left, right, left, right. Then, up."

"What? What kind of directions are those?"

"The kind that will get you back to our home."

She glared at him, and he saw enough in the almost total blackness to recoil and wince.

"It's my home. You're just a slave. Until I decide you can die."

He relaxed and said, "That sounds fair. Widow, when you start out, keep up against the left side until you come to a corner."

"Won't I just see it? Hey, I need some matches."

"Sure," he said and handed her a small bundle.

"But it gets windy in there. Maybe—"

"How could it get windy?"

"No one knows. From somewhere underground maybe. The tunnels go on forever."

"Nice. Okay, up against the left side, then, go left?"

"Yeah. Then get yourself up against the right side until—"

"Okay. Got it. Left, right, left, right. What about up?"

"After you turn right the last time, stay on the right. There's a ladder on that wall."

"How high do I have to climb?"

"Only three levels. That will get you to the ground floor."

"And the stairway."

"Well, it's close. You'll see. Easy, huh?"

"So you say. I think maybe out on the sidewalk would be—"

A polite voice on the sidewalk outside called out, "Scarlet? I'm attempting to locate you so that we might converse!"

Igor snickered and said, "You were saying?"

"He sounds smarter than before. Huh."

"He wasn't smart before?"

"Never mind that. Go talk to the monster with the sword. Slave."

"I'm going! I'll just—"

"Just for fun, try yelling at him too. God, that's annoying."

She struck one of her matches, then turned to the third door from the right, placed her hand on the knob, and looked back.

"Well?"

"I'm going!"

He peeked out at the street first, then slipped himself through the crack and closed the door, taking his burning match with him.

"Slaves," Widow said, scoffing. "He'd better do some useful work. Good that he had matches, though."

She opened the third door, and a cold, rotting breeze greeted her and snuffed out her flame.

"Dammit."

*   *   *

Widow turned her back to the light wind and struck another match. Backing through the doorway, she turned enough each way to get a look but not enough to lose her light.

There was no way to travel to the right. It was a dead end and to the left, a narrow hallway sloped down. The far wall and the near wall were built of brick, and stout timbers supported wide, flat stones up above.

Holding the match with her left hand, she pulled closed the door, then took a step backwards in the only direction possible. She took another step, and her heel scraped up against a protruding brick, causing her to stumble.

"Dammit."

She glanced down behind her but turned too far and let the stale breeze blow out her match.

"Oh, this place. Maybe I should just go outside and deal with Junior."

She scoffed, then turned to face the direction of travel. After stowing away the stack of matches, she touched the brick wall to her left with her left hand.

"Easy. Says the slave."

It took several minutes of careful steps, left hand on the wall, before that hand felt a sharp corner. Then, a wall angling to the left.

"Hmm."

In total darkness, she took the turn, walked only two paces, then reached out to her right. But the tunnel had widened, and she couldn't touch the far wall.

So, she took more careful sideways steps, moving away from one wall to try to find the other one. She took another step. Then, another, but she'd placed her reactor-issued work boot up against a thick rope.

Before she could step over it, it rolled up against her ankle, then slipped away to the left.

And she heard a voice, deep and brassy, like melted copper.

"Careful. Watch your step."

"Who said that?" she said, her voice a raspy whisper.

"I'll tell you. Yes, I will. Just promise to not step on—"

"Who's in here? Dammit!"

She fumbled around in a pocket, found a match, and reached the head of it toward the stone floor to strike it.

But a rope, possibly the same rope, coiled around her wrist.

"Hey!"

She reached down her other hand, and another rope wrapped around that wrist, too, then shook it until she lost her shoulder bag, then it got a winding grip.

"What is this?"

"I don't like light. Please, no light."

Widow fought against the ropes trying to hold her down and managed to stand before saying, "Get these ropes off of me!"

Rodney chuckled, with a voice metallic and gravelly, and said, "Uh . . . no! I'm blind, so you're blind. We're all blind."

"It's not my fault if you're blind!"

"It's my fault," said Rodney. "Living underground. Eating rats, even the mutated ones. Not a good life. No, not good."

Wrestling against the ropes, Widow slipped another match out of her pocket, then struck that one against the other still in her hand. Both sparked and then burned steadily.

And she stared, in the dancing light, at a human head and torso with two snakes for each human arm that wasn't there. One from each side remained out, coiled around her wrists.

Below, supporting him, was the thick snake body that his body became, which branched into four snakes, each as thick as a human leg. All four were curved up, the snake heads watching her while the body sections propped him up like bent table legs.

"Oh, God! You're the worst thing yet!"

Rodney tipped his head, his milky white eyes blank and rarely blinking.

"Well, that's hurtful. Must you be so mean?"

"Yes! I can't be mean enough! Let me go!"

The unused two gently twisting snake arms coiled neatly near their roots, where there was more light, and each had the head of a snake. Their eyes appeared to be functional as they studied Widow, and their slimy forked tongues waved hello.

"Oh, you're worse than I thought! What happened to you?"

"I was kind of okay until—"

"The reactor?"

"Uh . . . yes! Now, I'm not sure if I started as one snake, or several snakes, or maybe a human male. Can you tell me? You can see, so tell me: what was I before the reactor?"

"You were disgusting! Let me go!"

"Stop yelling. You'll only summon something worse."

Widow held her breath and looked each way.

"Sorry!" she whispered. "You're Rodney?"

"In the flesh and scale. And you are?"

"Widow. Let me go, Rodney. I tried being nice about it, but I see that's not going to work."

"It hasn't worked yet. No, it sure hasn't."

Widow took a deep breath, then let it out slowly. Her matches still burned, and she dripped some warm nectar into her voice.

"You want to let me go. Do it now."

Rodney grinned and said, "No! Uh . . . no!"

Widow scoffed and ramped it up immediately to full nectar, not attempting any weaker blends.

"Get your snakes off of me."

"I . . . I, um . . . no!"

In a normal voice, one blended only with panic, she said, "Hey, what's going on with—"

"Whatever that is, that thing with your voice, it isn't working either. No!"

"God, what do you want? Are you the troll?"

"Oh. Oh, maybe that's how I started. I was a troll, then I became part—"

"Just stop your stupid theorizing and tell me what you want. I need to get out of this tunnel."

"Okay. Okay, listen closely."

Widow calmed her breathing and turned her head, pointing an ear at him.

And the snake table legs worked together to tip his human torso forward, where he blew out a short, sharp breath at each match and let the night flow over them from every direction.

"Hey!" she whispered. "Why did—"

"Blind again. Blind like me!"

The snake arms started tugging and pulling, rotating her until she faced away from him.

"Stop! Let me go!"

"Oh, not just yet. Uh, I think . . . no!"

Widow got pulled until her back was against Rodney, and the two snake arms holding her wrists had crossed her arms in front of her, locking her in a slithery embrace.

"Dammit!"

She started kicking, trying to stomp on any part of the four leg snakes that she could, but two of them wiggled up and around her thighs, then squeezed them back against the other two snake legs.

"Stop! Don't!"

"I, uh . . . well, you must know the answer by now. It's 'no!'"

"What do you want?"

"I can't see, but I hear quite well. And my sense of touch more than makes up for the loss of those useless human eyes. Way more!"

Widow struggled but was held too tightly by a thick snake clamping down each thigh and more slender snakes around her wrists like ropes.

"Hey!"

All of the snakes worked together and began lifting her off of the warm stone floor of the tunnel.

"Stop! Put me down!"

"Soon! Or . . . not!"

The two other snake arms, so far unused and only watching in the dark, hissed softly and wiggled their heads under her shirt in back.

"Oh, get those off of me!"

"Uh . . . no!"

Their tongues were poking her gently, licking and caressing her as they slipped over her skin, their scales rough. They paused only enough to open their jaws and bite her, just tiny nibbles.

"God, no!"

"God, uh . . . yes!"

Widow sobbed and fought, flexing arms and legs but to no avail.

"Your skin feels so nice. It's kind of . . . moist. Mm, no scales!"

"Oh, uh, you like moist, huh?"

"Yes! I think maybe I was a water snake. Yeah, that's it. A water snake. Or a human swimmer? So confounding!"

Widow groaned out a deep breath, then winced and relaxed as she spoke in a pleasant voice.

"Are you human enough to remember where, oh where, I might be very moist?"

"Huh?"

"Mm, I'm so very moist."

The two snake heads bit gently, licked with quick tongue jabs, and circled around until both were rubbing around on her belly.

"I, uh, don't remember. Or maybe I never knew. Where?"

Widow snarled quietly, then shook her head before speaking in a calm voice.

"Why, between by legs, that's where."

"Oh. Oh, I think I know. Maybe I was human."

The snakes swept from side to side, sneaking their heads under the waistband of her khakis much like thick fingers.

Widow sucked in a quick breath, then groaned and let it out slowly.

In a calm, controlled voice, she said, "That's so close. You're— they're very close now."

"What . . . what am I looking for?"

With a slow, deeper voice, Widow said, "My pussy. My pussy is right there between my thighs. It's very wet too."

The snake heads were trying to push between her thighs, then the two bigger ones started to pull Widow's legs to each side.

"Oh, God," she whispered.

"Huh?"

"Nothing. I mean, yes, they're very close now."

One of them began rubbing its head up and down on one side, then the other matched that on the other side. She and Rodney both heard the hissing as they fought each other for room.

"Maybe one should—"

She caught her breath when one of the snakes slipped its head back up, then around her waist, then wiggled its head between her ass cheeks until it found an opening.

In a frantic whisper, Widow said, "I was saying maybe one should just stop! That's all!'

"Huh? Why?"

"Fine," she said, her chest showing her heavier breaths. "They'll both get something. Damn, I hope they—"

"Shh! Quiet! I want to listen!"

They both listened to hissing from both snakes.

Widow said, "Oh!" as the one from behind wiggled its head inside.

And then, there was only the hissing of one snake.

She said, "Oh, no!" as the one in front wiggled its way just inside, just enough to silence its hissing too.

"I feel it!" Rodney whispered, almost cackling with his glee. "You have much wetness! It's good!"

"Well, okay, but they've had their little—"

"Uh-uh. More!"

"Oh, God!" Widow said as both snakes wiggled in deeper.

"Yes! This is good!"

"Hey, tell them they've had—"

Each snake began twisting its head around inside her. In different places.

"Oh my God!" she whispered. "This had better work!"

"It's working for me! I, uh . . . wait a second. Something is . . . something . . ."

The snake that sneaked in from behind shuddered, causing Widow to gasp, then snapped itself out in a rush.

"Oh, that's not something I ever want to—"

The snake in front dove in deeper, then tried to back out. And it almost made it before ramming back inside.

"Oh, God!"

It wiggled like it was powered up with batteries then popped out, left a wet trail up her belly and around her waist, then coiled back up near Rodney.

"I don't feel so good," Rodney said, his voice tired.

"No? Huh."

"I feel . . . kind of, uh . . . sick."

"That's what you get. Hey, let me go. You've all had your fun."

All of the snakes released her at once, and Widow fell to her hands and knees. Standing quickly, she slung her pack over a shoulder and got out two more matches, then struck them together.

"You're pathetic," she said to Rodney as he lay on the stone floor, twitching as all of his snakes tried to scurry him away into the darkness.

Almost wailing, he said, "I am! I am truly a pathetic thing!"

"Have you learned something, Rodney?"

His human head nodded.

"Yes. Oh, yes!"

"To never again mess with a human woman?"

Most of the snake heads held their mouths open as he muttered, "Not . . . this one!"

"Git. Go catch some rats."

"I'm going! I'm, uh . . . gone!"

The last snake wiggled on the fringes of the light from Scarlet's matches, then all of Rodney and his squirming snake parts sunk into the impenetrable night.

"At least there's no—"

A sudden breeze dumped her back into the darkness.

"Oh, shit."

Chapter 44 – Run, Little Two-headed Man!

Igor never stopped scanning the dark street in both directions as he closed the door and leaned his back into it.

"You hear anything?"

His second head didn't answer.

"Punk. Even if you could talk, you probably wouldn't tell me."

He snapped his original head to one side and said, "Shh. Listen."

Far off to his left, someone was tapping something metal against something brick.

"A sword. A brick wall."

He listened for a moment as the sounds began to fade.

"Come on."

He started walking toward the sound of sword against bricks, dwelling longer in the darkness between streetlights than in their cones of light. A few steps before an intersection and the corner of a drab brick building, he stopped, then leaned to look around.

Junior was leaning against the building front, not ten paces from him and facing him. He was tapping the handle of the sword against the bricks gently.

Igor whipped himself around and glued his back to the wall.

"I didn't want to talk to him, that monster!" he whispered. "But I'm just a slave, so I have to. Just a slave!"

He looked again and saw Junior smiling and looking back until he hid himself out of sight again.

"That makes you a slave too! We're both slaves!"

His second head had no comment.

After coughing softly, Igor straightened up his clothing and pulled his ratty jacket high enough to cover the other head.

"Stay quiet," he whispered, then stepped out where he could be seen.

Junior stopped his tapping and laid the flat of the sword's blade up over a shoulder, then pointed with his free hand.

"My hearing is quite good," he said, "and you are not as quiet as you might believe."

"We—I heard someone tapping, so I just thought I'd introduce myself."

"That's very polite. We can exchange some niceties and then, I have a question or two for you. Come closer."

Igor approached the towering man without a shirt whose skin was slick with blood, sweat, and oil.

"Closer."

Igor grimaced but took another step.

"This is good!" he said. "Right here!"

"Do you always yell?"

Igor leaked out a raspy breath mixed with a laugh and let his heads hang.

"Yeah. I'm a stupid slave. Just a slave."

"Well, a slave might not have much, but he probably has a name, hmm?"

Igor looked up, grinning, and said, "I'm . . . Bob."

"Good day to you, Bob, even though there's no such thing as day here. I'm Junior."

"Hello, Junior. I haven't seen you around this part of town before."

"That's not entirely correct, is it?"

"Um . . ."

Junior pointed again and laughed before saying, "My vision is quite good too. I saw you on a roof not long ago. In this part of town."

"Oh. Oh! That was you? I didn't recognize—"

"Tsk, tsk. Come now. Few, if any, others have an appearance such as this."

"Uh, yeah. That's true. I'm just out scavenging for things like I always—"

"A redhead too. Up on that roof."

"Uh, sure. That was, um, Pauline."

"Pauline. What a lovely name. Okay, so, you are out scavenging, you claim?"

"Yes, all the time. You too? You were walking that way, weren't you?"

He pointed past Junior, then added, "Scavenging for something that way?"

Junior turned to look back where Igor was pointing and made his remote, built-in buzzer power supply visible where it had been nailed into his spine and nearby organs. He stayed facing away long enough to display several flashes from the tiny red light.

He turned back and said, "Well, all over this general locale, really."

Junior tipped his head and squinted, then pointed at Igor's hump under his jacket.

"Say, Mortimer gave you one too? You're one of them?"

Igor scoffed and uncovered his head.

"Uh-uh. This is just—say, that's not an extra head there on your back. And it's buzzing. What the hell you got there, Junior?"

"It's a very convenient little device that—"

Junior danced in place as the convenient device popped and crackled and sparks flew from his ears.

"Hoo, boy! Woo-hoo! Run, little two-headed man! Run!"

Igor's eyes almost popped out, and he turned and started to run. But the fireworks behind him fell silent with a quick blast of static, then a whistle.

"Wait," Junior called to him. "I find that somewhat distressful myself. Please, come back so that we can finish our conversation."

Igor aborted his sprint abruptly and turned enough to see that Junior had stopped his violent jig on the concrete sidewalk. He took a few steps closer.

"That's rather inconvenient, but the overall advantages outweigh such infrequent malfunctions. So, tell me what you're scavenging for, and I'll tell you what I seek."

"Uh, sure. Um, just the usual stuff. Food is good, and maybe—"

"Food is always good. Yes, that's true. I do believe I could eat non-stop."

He took a step closer to Igor and said, "I'm actually quite hungry right now."

Igor took a step back and said, "Uh, I believe it. Looks like you eat a lot. So, water is good to find. You know, just stuff like that. Widow said to—"

"Widow? Who might that be?"

"Oh, uh, nobody. Just, um, somebody I met. You don't know her. She doesn't know you. Neither of you could possibly know—"

"You've launched into a strange spell of erratic babbling that has me convinced that you're nervous from my rather simple inquiry."

"Huh?"

Junior leaned forward, smiling, and said, "Relax! Just curious who Widow might be."

"Who else could she be? Widow is Widow, and she was never, ever anyone else. She's just—"

Junior pointed the sword toward Igor's face.

"Shh. If you were taller and more muscular and sweaty and bloody like me, you might get away with such inane theatrics. But you?"

He looked him down then up, then scoffed and lowered the sword.

"I'd endeavor to project intelligence if I were you."

"Good advice! Thanks! So, uh, if you don't mind me asking: who are you looking for?"

Junior took another step closer.

"Well, that's interesting. I think I'd recall if I'd said I was touring this part of town in pursuit of someone in particular. How exactly did you choose those words?"

Igor let out a string of choppy laughs while nodding and grinning.

"I told you I was stupid! A stupid slave!"

"Yes. I'm inclined to believe you. Very well. I'll tell you. I'm out here in this perpetual night to—"

A loud pop fired roman candles from Junior's ears.

"Wow, wow, wow!" Junior screamed as he jumped in place. "Woo-hoo!"

He closed the distance quickly and lifted Igor by his throat and held him close.

Igor held on, trying to shriek but unable to.

Junior heard the pop, turned his head, and bathed Igor's faces in a sprinkle of sparks, causing all four eyes to clamp shut.

"Hoo, boy! Yi-yi-yi-yi—"

Igor opened his eyes just enough to reach over Junior's shoulder and aim a hard slap against the box fused into his back.

The sparks stopped with a dull pop, and the unit resumed a steady buzzing.

"Better?" he said, straining to get the words past the giant paw wrapped around his neck.

Junior set him down, then brushed off his clothing, straightening it up, and said, "Quite. I'm thankful."

"Shit. Me too."

* * *

"You seem like an altogether reasonable little fellow," Junior said after taking a step back from the mutant man that he'd almost strangled to death.

"I try to be. But I'm just a slave!"

"Shh. Let's not attract any of those massive pork repositories."

"Huh?"

"The boars. I had a difficult time with one of them on the outskirts of town. Either they're collectively a combative bunch, or the one I met was a particularly quarrelsome representative."

"Huh?"

"We fought, and our battle served mostly to stoke my appetite."

"So, you're looking for lunch?"

"Without any timekeeping devices, it would be folly to call it lunch. Something to eat. That states it plainly enough. But no, that isn't my main objective at the moment."

"Sure. What is, then?"

"A wench. A wench that goes by the name Scarlet."

"Huh. Goes by the name Scarlet. Nope. No one around here that goes by the name Scarlet."

Junior tipped his head and stared for a few seconds.

"At certain specific times in our dialogue, you exhibit a peculiar discomfort. It's quite noticeable, so please don't offer a lame defense that I'll reject outright."

"Huh?"

"You know something, little man. Yes, I'm eloquent and well-mannered, in contrast to my exaggerated comic book malevolent super hero appearance. But don't for a moment doubt that I would bludgeon you and trim you into lunch-sized slices while your four eyes are—say, can those extra eyes see too?"

"How would I know?"

"You could politely ask."

"I have. It doesn't talk."

"You've reached no conclusion on it being a male or female head?"

"Nope. Oh, uh, head from a female sounds good, though."

"Yes, decidedly so. I miss my Mama."

"Huh?"

"It's a matter best kept private. So, back to my conjecture from just a moment ago: you project a distinct nervousness at certain lines of questioning. Which leads me to believe that you are perhaps withholding valuable information that would aid in my search."

"Uh . . . what?"

He stepped closer to the cowering man with two heads.

"My politeness has been depleted sufficiently that I will, while speaking quite clearly and coherently, dismember you until one of your heads delivers the info I believe you are hoarding."

"Dis . . . dismember?'

"Yes. I won't even use the sword."

He let it clatter near their feet.

"There's a certain satisfaction at feeling living things squish in one's hands."

"Uh, that's not good."

"For you? No, surely not. So, I've reached an adequate level of certainty that you know the wench Scarlet and where she can be found."

"I told you! I don't know a wench that goes by—"

Junior again lifted Igor high off of the sidewalk, this time with a grip on both arms.

"Let me demonstrate that I can be quite barbaric even if the marvelous contrivance on my—"

It whistled and popped, and a liquid alive with sparks oozed out of his ears and nose.

"Yi, yi, yi!"

He let go with one hand and started slapping Igor with the other.

"I'm just a slave! Stop it! Just a slave!"

"Tell me! Woo-hoo, wow! Tell me! The—hoot, hoot—wench!"

With a sound like a belch, a streamer of sparks left one ear, then another belch sent more from the other ear.

"She's not a wench! I mean, I don't know anyone that—"

Junior stopped slapping him and rested his massive fleshy hand on the top of Igor's second head.

"Wow, wow, wow!" he said as he shook his own head rapidly, sending trails of sparks out. "You tell me, then! You! You with eyes number three and, and—"

Igor cowered, still hanging high above the sidewalk and was about to speak, when the second head cried out, "The Webber Building!"

Igor screamed, "Good golly, it can talk!"

A final trail of sparks puffed out of his ears, each with the sound of a round stone plopping into a pool, and Junior's buzzer stuttered, then delivered a steady buzz.

"Not for long, I'd wager," he said, then punched Igor's extra head.

Its eyes drifted around a few times, then the entire thing became a sack of gelatin slumped on its side.

"No," said Igor. "Not anymore."

Junior set him down and let him go.

"You're not going to kill my real head too?"

"Why, no, little man. I have the valuable data I seek. The Webber Building."

"There's no such thing! A slave would know if—"

Junior raised his fist, shaking his head and grinning.

"I'll just go now," Igor said and began slow backwards steps.

The big sweaty and bloody man picked up his sword, then smiled pleasantly at the retreating man with a dead extra head.

"Run along. I'll find that building without your assistance. And besides . . ."

"Yeah?"

"You don't look like a very appealing meal."

"I'm not! I'm just a slave!"

Igor stopped and grinned, then bounced his eyebrows.

"That head, though, might have just been pureed into some very tasty and nutritious pudding."

"Uh . . . huh?"

Pointing, Junior laughed and said, "I'll eat your bag of pudding if you don't—"

Igor began a quick sprint with his companion head sloshing around on his shoulder and back.

"—run along home."

Chapter 45 – My Little Crafter Girl's Ass

Widow stood outside the door to her room, breathing easily after navigating the dark tunnels to Igor's directions, climbing three levels on a ladder, then almost running all the way up the steps.

"New clothes!" she whispered to herself, then dialed the combination and pushed in the door.

Across the room, the crafter, Marie, stood up quickly from her chair. She'd placed a larger table nearby, and it was covered with neatly folded cloth items.

"You're back! Please, tell me you found food."

Widow held out her pack and said, while Marie was almost sprinting toward her, "Yes. Have some."

The crafter sat with the bag, dug around inside, found a small package, ripped it open and stuffed the contents in her mouth, then looked up at Widow while chewing.

"Enjoy. I've had quite the adventures too."

"What kind?"

"The first one was satisfying and well, educational. The second one, just a minute ago? I guess you could call it sexual, but I wouldn't call it satisfying."

She came inside, let the door swing closed, then reached back and gave the dial a quick spin.

"So, one good and one not so good. I have good news for you: I got all of your new clothes done."

Widow was walking with her toward the chairs, mostly scanning the wardrobe laid out on the table, and said, "That was quick. Did Igor help any?"

She got close enough to look down at and touch all of the freshly tailored garments.

"If you call—sorry, I'll just say it: if you call begging to fuck me 'helpful,' then sure. Yeah."

Widow scoffed and said, "He tried to rape me when I first met him."

"He wanted to rape that guy on the couch too. I told him that you'd really be mad, and that scared him enough. He didn't go near him."

"That little freak. I probably should have killed him already."

"Uh, maybe not. He didn't help with the clothes, but he did some good things around here."

Widow turned and studied the ceiling, checking out all of the identical large square architectural features, each with its own suspended lighting fixture. Her eyes fixed on one near the middle.

"He told me about the ceiling."

Widow pointed and said, "That one, right?"

"Yeah," said Marie. "He stood on some furniture and found out how to tip it open. He didn't go up there, though. He just kind of looked around."

"You didn't go up, did you?"

"No way! I've seen enough darkness already. That's just too creepy up there for me."

"I'll investigate that soon. Right now, I'm so excited to have new clothes! I'm not waiting another minute to ditch this reactor outfit."

"I don't blame you. Your new stuff is really, uh, sexy. I think it's the nicest stuff I ever made."

"You sound proud of it."

"I am. Let me show you."

She moved to stand beside Widow, close enough that they were touching, and both looked down at the neatly arranged assortment.

Pointing, Marie said, "Those two are the—"

"Wait. You made the boots too?"

She picked one up and held it close, rotating it and nodding. It was short, like Widow had requested, and high enough only to reach her ankle. The entire front of it was packed with crossing black laces that reached all the way to the very top. And beneath it, a durable material made up the small portion of sole that would actually touch the floor. The rest of it curved up and was supported by a high, gracefully curved and deadly sharp heel.

"Nice. Like fangs."

"Huh?"

"Nothing," she said and set the boot back on the table.

"You like them?"

"These are perfect. I'll keep the reactor boots for when I'm not being sexy, and I'll—"

"Sorry, but you'll still be sexy. You are now anyway."

Widow turned to her, and she turned toward Widow.

"Marie, would you volunteer to be my servant for a short while?"

"Your slave? Like Igor, you mean?"

Widow laughed and said, while touching Marie's hair, "Hmm. Not a bad idea. Perhaps later. Right now, I just need my expert seamstress to lend her skilled hands to dressing me in my new outfit."

Marie said, "Um . . ." and glanced at the clothes on the table.

Widow kept her voice calm and normal and said, "I insist. Help me get dressed."

Marie locked onto Widow's steady gaze and nodded, saying, "Look, I made the clothes, so you—"

"Are you sure I'm not one of the monsters?"

She swallowed hard and said, "Uh, no, I'm not."

"Think you'd be able to run out of this room quick enough? Or at all?"

Looking again at the table, Marie sighed and said, "What's first? The pants or—"

In a sweet voice but one devoid of honey, Widow said, "Silly crafter girl. I need to be undressed first."

"Oh, of course."

They turned to face each other, and Widow watched Marie's eyes as she unbuttoned her unfashionable shirt that she'd received at the reactor. She got to the last one, popped it open, then slipped the soiled flannel fabric back over Widow's shoulders. She caught it before it could fall to the floor and set it on her chair.

"So, tell me if you still think I might be a monster."

Marie grinned and said, "Uh . . ."

"Hmm, do I resemble a monster in any way?"

"Uh, you're probably not a monster. Those are . . . quite nice."

"Hmm."

When Widow saw Marie look down, she said, "Yes, crafter girl. The pants, too, of course."

"Uh, of course."

"Maybe the boots first?"

"Uh, yeah. Uh-huh."

She leaned over and reached toward the boots, but Widow held both of her shoulders and gently guided her to kneel on the floor.

"Yes, like that."

She backed her hands away, then Marie quickly untied her practical work boots, pried them off, and set them to the side. She then unfastened Widow's khakis, and they were loose enough to slip down and bunch around her ankles.

"Let me help," Widow said, and she held Marie's shoulders again while lifting one leg up and out, then the other.

"Oh. There's no, um, you're not—"

"No. No panties this time. Probably hardly ever."

"Uh, of course."

Still kneeling, Marie looked up at Widow and waited.

"Huh," said Widow. "You've offered to be my servant for an unspecified period of time. I suppose that means for however long I want. Does that sound right?"

Still looking up but not returning Widow's smile, Marie said, "Uh, I suppose. Uh-huh."

"And my servant is kneeling before me after having removed all of my clothes. Can you guess what your next task might be?"

"Uh, I, um . . ."

Widow smiled and fluffed out Marie's hair on one side and kept her other hand on her shoulder.

"Yes?"

"Uh, get you dressed? That's what you said."

Widow laughed and shook her lightly by both shoulders.

"Yes, that's exactly right. Let's get me dressed in my new things."

Marie sighed, then, still on her knees, reached for the new panties.

Widow said, "Uh-uh. Maybe next time."

"Pants?"

"No. A skirt. Let's see if you followed my instructions."

"Tight, you mean?"

"Yes."

Marie changed directions and picked up a black skirt that she'd fashioned from the thinnest, most flexible bat leather she had. She held it low, and Widow picked up one foot, then the other, and Marie wiggled it up over her calves, then past her knees, then found that it was already snug as she tried to pull it along Widow's thighs.

"That's tight. Good so far."

"Thanks."

She had to fight with it, stretching it each way while lifting and sliding it up. Widow reached down with both hands, over Marie's, and helped her pull the waistband over her ass until they could let it rest around her waist.

"This is good," Widow said as she leaned each way to see and felt all around. "Very good work."

"Thanks. I'm glad it fits the way you like."

"I do like it. Blouse?"

"Oh, right away."

Marie stood and got behind Widow to hold the shirt. Widow poked her arms into the sleeves, held all of her hair up as the girl slipped it up onto her shoulders, then brushed her hair back while Marie reached around to button it.

She started at the bottom and said, "Ooh, kind of tight already."

"Yes. Nice."

She continued up with the buttons and had to force the material together to button it over any part of Widow's breasts.

Looking down at the pair, Widow said, "They've grown."

"I'll say. Just since I measured you."

Marie's wrists were squeezing Widow's breasts as she fastened the button just below them.

"That's good. That's high enough. Let's see about those boots now."

Widow walked to her chair and sat, and Marie picked up both boots and stood close.

Marie showed her the socks that she'd made too.

"Oh, nice. I didn't even remember to ask for new socks."

"They were easy enough."

She dropped to her knees without being told and slipped the socks onto Widow's feet. It took more effort to get the boots on and even more effort to lace them snugly all the way up. After she'd finished, she stayed kneeling and looked up.

"Do you remember that special voice I used before?"

Marie nodded and said, "Yeah. That was, um, something."

"Yes, it's something. When I got back, I told you I had a sexual encounter that wasn't at all satisfying. Do you remember me saying that?"

"Uh-huh. Yeah."

Widow kept her new, very high heels on the floor and moved her knees apart. The tight skirt didn't allow much of a spread.

"Come a little closer."

Marie gave a glance at the insides of Widow's thighs and the quickest of looks at how the skirt had slipped up higher from her making room for her.

"Uh, I don't know."

"I might be a monster."

Marie swallowed hard, looked Widow in the eye, and said, "Uh, you might. Yeah. But I should probably just—"

"Touch my thighs," Widow said, dosing her words with thick, sweet nectar. "Both hands."

Still kneeling, Marie took a sharp breath, then leaned forward enough to put her palms on the outsides of Widow's thighs.

"I specified that my skirts should be stretchy, didn't I?"

Marie only nodded, her breaths quickening.

"Let's just see. Slip those soft hands up, just a little at a time and always touching my skin, until your fingertips are up under my new skirt."

"Uh, okay."

Marie started rubbing her fingers higher along Widow's thighs but paused when Widow said, with a sticky sweet voice, "Look at me while you do as I say."

"Yes. Okay."

Holding Widow's gaze, Marie resumed sliding her hands up, her fingertips on the soft skin of Widow's legs, and began to push the skirt up, stretching it to go around the increasing curves.

"Mm, just like that," Widow said and repeatedly lifted Marie's hair to one side and let it fall back.

"How, um, how far?"

"Hmm, if it's as stretchy as I requested, it should all go quite nicely around my waist, shouldn't it?"

"Yes. Uh, it should."

"Let's find out."

Still looking up, Marie needed more force to stretch the thin black leather, and she was able to leave the entire skirt bunched up around Widow's waist.

"Mm, that's nice," Widow said, then moved her knees apart as far as the arms of the chair would allow. It was obviously far enough.

Marie waited with her hands high up on Widow's bare hips, and she kept her eyes on Widow's.

"Now, touch my cheek. Just one hand," Widow said, smiling.

"Uh, what?"

Widow scoffed, still smiling, and took one of Marie's hands, held it close, and kissed it. Then, she opened her mouth, showing Marie the fangs. Still holding her gaze, Widow casually drew her hand into her mouth, hesitated, saw not the slightest sign of reluctance or resistance, and gave her a gentle bite.

"Mm."

She held the fangs in her, sucking quietly, only until Marie's eyes fluttered but remained open.

Marie took a breath and was about to speak, then the door to the hallway swung in.

* * *

Igor stepped inside the room, didn't look around, but faced the door as he closed it hard enough that the latching sound carried through the room. He began to speak even before he'd turned all the way around and had just given the dial a turn.

"I saw him! He's even crazier than—"

His open mouth locked, too, and he blinked rapidly, then kept them open as he stared at the two woman busy with something near the chair across the room.

"Shh," Widow said to him, her voice calm as she held Marie's hand close to her lips and fangs. "You're quite the little screamer."

"Sorry!" he whispered.

Widow scoffed at the intense stare he was giving the scene, then laughed softly at him rubbing around his crotch with one hand.

"Oh, why not just get yourself closer? Come on."

"Really?"

Widow nodded and offered him a pleasant smile.

"Uh, yeah!" he said, his voice rising.

Then, he whispered, "I mean, yeah. Yes."

He walked over quickly and stood to one side. Marie was still breathing quickly, and she turned her head only once to see the little mutant man with a burlap sack over his spare head.

Widow shook her head at the sight of him and his head sack, then turned again to Marie.

"Maybe just another tiny little bite. Just another tiny nibble in your pretty little hand."

Marie didn't fight to escape when Widow again showed her fangs, then hissed softly and bit again, only enough to barely break the skin.

The bitten crafter's head swayed a few times but didn't flop over.

"Yes, just like that," Widow said, then placed Marie's palm back on her thigh. "Touch my skin. Feel how soft."

"Uh-huh."

Marie rubbed Widow's thighs, inside and outside, and Widow looked again at Igor beside them.

"You've done well, slave man. This is mostly for my enjoyment, but I believe you'll find it worth watching too. You've earned it."

"Okay. Okay!"

"Shh."

She touched Marie's hair with both hands and said, "Mm, I want to give you a real bite. Doesn't that sound nice?"

Marie nodded and said, "Okay," and started to raise one of her hands.

Widow scoffed and said, "Oh, no. Not like that."

Marie resumed her rubbing of Widow's legs, and Widow held Marie's hair away from her neck on one side.

"There. The very soft and tasty skin of your neck. You don't mind, do you?"

She smiled and showed the length of her fangs.

"Whoa," Igor whispered and took a step back.

Marie's eyes got bigger, but she didn't say anything, and Igor picked up the pace with his crotch rubbing from a safer distance.

With a whimper so soft that it barely made a sound, Marie began to lean closer and turn to offer her neck, but Widow's hands on her shoulders stopped her.

"Oh, not yet. Let's make this more special."

She only nodded and waited.

"Good. I want your pants down when I bite you. Will you do that for me?"

"Yes."

Marie unfastened her pants and shifted around until it all fell down around her knees. Her bare ass angled out and away from Widow, who reclined in the chair with her legs spread.

"Yes, just like that. Slave? Is that a pleasant sight?"

"Yeah, yeah, yeah!" he whispered, using both hands on himself.

"Is my little crafter girl's ass round and smooth, like a sweet little piece of fruit?"

"Yeah! Oh God, yeah!"

"Marie," Widow said, "roll up your t-shirt so that it stays up. You'll feel better, too, that you're not selfishly keeping those to yourself."

"Uh, okay."

Kneeling straight up for the moment, Marie did as she was told and left the t-shirt up above her breasts.

"Unhook that too," Widow said.

She felt around between her breasts, unclasped her bra, and let it fall open to reveal two plump breasts with pointy nipples.

"Mm, so sweet. I see that even that little bite has you feeling an orgasm like you've never felt before. Isn't that right?"

Marie nodded. Igor leaned from side to side, unable to stifle his giggling as he tried to see the bare ass and bare breasts all at the same time.

"Good girl. Now, I want that bite. And you want it too. Oh, yes, a serious, deep bite for my sweet little crafter girl."

Marie sighed and leaned forward while Widow slumped back into the chair, spreading her legs farther. She held back the crafter's hair and looked past her at Igor, one hand down his pants and the other almost touching the bare ass.

Widow spread her jaws open and hissed, then buried the points deep in Marie's neck. The girl became a loose and floppy rag doll lying atop Widow, who was sucking loudly and keeping her lips in a tight seal around the bite.

Only Widow's eyes moved when she heard Igor's strained, desperate whisper.

"Widow! Widow, please! May I touch?"

After a silent scoff that didn't interrupt her bite, Widow nodded.

"Thank you! I don't deserve it! I'm just a slave!" he whispered, and he knelt behind Marie and felt all over her ass with both hands.

The minutes passed in Widow's silent room as she sucked at Marie's neck and got her looser and collapsed across her.

She paused only long enough to withdraw her fangs, flop Marie's head to the other side, then bare her long, sharp teeth for a fresh bite.

But before biting, she said, "She has very nice breasts, too, slave. They feel so perky pressed into me."

"I want them! I want to touch them!"

"Yes, you'd like to reach around with both hands, then squeeze them and rub them and pinch them."

"They're too nice! Too nice for a slave!"

Widow grinned, shook her head, then pierced the soft skin on the other side of Marie's neck. She sucked and swallowed, seemingly melting Marie as she lay atop her.

"Widow," Igor whispered after many minutes had passed and he'd used every second to fondle Marie's ass in every possible way. "Widow!"

She looked up, kept sucking, and watched as Igor moved one of his hands down behind Marie, near his pants, then shifted himself around.

With that hand back on an ass cheek, he grinned and said, "Can I? Huh? Can I? I know I don't deserve it!"

With her bloody fangs out but still close, she said, "What, exactly?"

Grinning and bouncing his eyebrows, he turned sideways, pointed his mighty mutant tool straight out where Widow could see it, and said again, "Can I?"

"Oh my God. Igor, you're disgusting."

"I know!"

Chapter 46 – The Orgasm Keeps Going

"That's quite impressive equipment you have, slave."

"Radiation isn't all bad!"

"Yes, well, this sweet little thing doesn't deserve that."

"Aw . . ."

"Tell you what: you can lick and suck whatever you can reach. How's that?"

"I don't deserve that! But I will!"

Widow hissed and said, "At least it will stop that yelling."

She pushed against Marie's shoulders, tipping her up and away and giving the mutant access to her breasts. But her head hung forward, sending her hair down to mostly cover her face.

"Go ahead," said Widow. "Just for a second. I just don't want to stop sucking on this sweet little thing."

"She's sweet! She's very sweet!"

He started trying to get his functioning head and his other one, hidden in a burlap sack, between Marie and Widow.

"Hold it," she said. "I just can't. Sorry. Go see what else you can find."

"I will! Yeah, I will!"

He crawled back around behind Marie, and Widow let the unconscious crafter slump back down onto her. She was still fussing with her hair, clearing room to bite again, when she heard the moaning and slurping.

"So disgusting," Widow said to herself. "Way more than a slave deserves."

She got all of Marie's hair off to one side, then held her head and turned her bared fangs toward her neck. But she stopped and bounced the young woman's head a few times.

"Hey," she said. "I, um, think maybe I knocked her out."

She looked over Marie's shoulder, across her back, and saw only Igor's eyes above the gentle curves of Marie's ass. His head was moving methodically, and all he did was bounce his eyebrows.

"Did you hear me?"

He nodded and kept licking, sometimes taking such long strokes that Widow saw his tongue before he ducked it back down for more.

"Well?"

He moved his head up high enough that Widow could see his lips, which were wet with slobber.

"Now, then? Can I? Huh?"

"What?"

"She won't care! I can fuck her now, right?"

"Oh, you're something else. You'd really do that when she's unconscious?"

"Yeah, yeah, yeah! I'm just a slave! A disgusting slave!"

"Well, you're right about that."

Widow pushed the limp woman back up, held her there, and watched her closely.

"Can I? Huh? Can I please just—"

"Shh. Wait a second."

Widow held her as still as she could and watched her chest. After a few seconds, she groaned and let her unroll back onto her.

"She's dead. She's not breathing. I can't believe I killed her."

"Why did you kill her? Why?"

Close to sobbing, Widow said, "I didn't mean to. I'm just so hungry, and she's so soft and sweet and juicy and dammit, it's so hard to stop!"

"Whoa. Um, maybe I should—"

"Stop licking the dead girl?"

"Uh, yeah. That. And maybe—"

"Forget about fucking her?"

"Yes, Widow, all of that! But mostly, maybe I should get the hell out of here before you kill me too!"

Still looking over the limp body's shoulder, Widow said, "No way I'd bite you. Sorry. There are other fun ways to dispose of you, though."

"I shouldn't yell anymore."

"Yes. That would help. Just your yelling is enough to make me want to—"

Widow snapped her head to the side and stared at Marie's tongue as she poked it around, reaching for whatever it could find.

"Oh, what is this?"

"What?"

"Shh!"

She pushed the crafter's body back up and held it there, watching her chest closely.

"What, Widow?"

"She's, uh, kind of dead. I mean, she's not breathing. But oh, what the hell—she's trying to lick me?"

"I would! I'd love to—"

"Shh. Enough."

Widow looked away from the wet, slowly twisting tongue and again at the crafter's chest.

"Well, that's something. Her nipples are—"

"Nipples? I want them! I'm going to—"

"Stop. You just stay back there, and stop licking this poor girl."

She let the crafter slump back onto her, and Igor grumbled while standing and keeping himself behind her.

Almost whispering and holding Igor's gaze, she said, "She's doing it. I think she's dead, but she's licking me."

"Maybe she's not all the way dead?"

"What, like a zombie?"

"Oh, no, not like them. Uh-uh. They act more like—"

"Hush. I don't even want to hear that there are zombies here too. So, she's not a zombie. But . . . God, I still feel her nipples poking me. She's—"

"Having an orgasm! Because of me. I did some really good licking back here, and she—"

"No, you didn't. You probably fumbled around back there, you and that extra—hey, why is that gross thing covered up?"

"Like I was trying to tell you, Junior—"

"Not now. I need to figure this out. You've been a mutant for a long time. What do you think is going on?"

"It's not from me licking her very tasty pussy?"

"No. God, no. Can't be. I'm sure she's still orgasming, though."

Igor slumped, then shrugged.

"You're right—can't be. I don't deserve to make her cum. I'm just a slave!"

"Yeah. One that likes to yell even when whispering. So, what do you think, slave?"

"Mutants sometimes have poisons that—"

"Oh! Yeah, my poisons. God, they must have gotten so much stronger since I, um . . . never mind. This is amazing: my poisons kind of kill, but the orgasm keeps going?"

"Looks like it, Widow."

"And my tasty victim keeps licking me?"

"I would. I sure would, Widow, even if I was dead."

"You might be soon."

"Right. I know. I don't deserve to have an orgasm, do I?'

"No. But I do, and I sure am having one. Biting does it, and it gives it too. But it really does kind of almost kill? I didn't want to believe it with Lucas."

Igor sobbed and looked down, then wiped at his cheek.

"If that's what killed him,"—he paused to glance toward the dead young man on the couch—"he was a lucky man. I'd die, too, for a Widow orgasm."

"Be a good slave, and we'll see. Right now, I need to sleep and let this sweet little orgasm carry me away."

"Um, can I just, you know, keep—"

"Leave the girl alone, slave. Go find a corner somewhere and sleep or at least stay quiet."

Widow turned Marie's head so that her tongue could swipe tiny wet paths over her neck and watched Igor grumble and retreat into the shadows at the far side of the room.

*　　*　　*

Widow shifted around under the almost-dead weight of the crafter at the steadily increasing volume of Igor's snoring. Despite him being far across the large room, there were no other sounds, allowing his hacking and snorting to waft over like a soiled mist.

But she was able to continue sleeping until the mutant's loudest snort sent him into a violent twitch that banged his real head into a wall with a hollow clunk.

She opened her eyes, then brushed aside some of Marie's hair to glare at the vague movement in the shadows against the far wall. She almost yelled, then turned her eyes toward the woman who still seemed dead on top of her but who had suspended her eager licking of Widow's neck.

But Marie awoke, too, and started with a deep sigh.

"Oh, good," Widow said, then brushed more of the crafter's hair aside. "It's good to hear you breathing again."

Marie groaned and turned her head to face the other way, then laid it back down on Widow's shoulder.

"Huh," she said.

Widow scoffed, smiling, and said, "What, that orgasm wore off?"

"Uh-huh. Damn, that was something."

"Any more, I think, would have killed you. Maybe you should get up and get dressed."

Marie didn't move.

Widow smiled and said, "Or get bit until you're for real dead."

Marie hesitated, then said, "Okay."

"Huh?"

The crafter turned toward her, held her with a steady gaze, then pushed herself back. Widow squeezed her thighs into her where she still knelt between her legs.

Looking down at her bare breasts, where her t-shirt had remained rolled-up and secure up above her breasts, Marie said, "I was the, uh, entertainment, huh?"

"Mm-hmm. Could have been worse."

She scoffed, then stood and rolled back down her shirt, then scoffed again before pulling up her pants.

"You could have killed me," she said.

"True, but I meant that I could have let that little—oh, never mind. You'll just throw up."

Marie crossed her arms, glanced down at Widow's skirt, which she'd nudged up around her waist before getting bit, then back into her eyes.

Widow said, smiling while blending warm honey into her voice, "I love the skirt you made for me. Straighten that out."

Marie sighed, stepped closer, then knelt again between Widow's spread legs. With both hands, she reached for the skirt, then stopped, leaving her hands on Widow's thighs when she spoke.

"Lean closer."

Marie leaned herself farther in, laying her forearms on Widow's thighs and close enough for Widow to fluff up her hair with both hands. She kept playing with it as she looked up at the sound of Igor walking toward them.

"You never stop!" he said, whispering loudly.

"Oh, I really can't," Widow said, her voice normal. "My hungers are growing and getting to where I can barely control them."

"Sorry I interrupted."

Widow nodded to him quickly, then looked down at the woman kneeling between her legs.

With a calm, sugary voice, Widow said, "Tell me, crafter girl, what you want."

"I, um, want you to bite me. I mean, really bite me."

"Hmm. For the orgasm."

Marie shook her head and didn't smile when she said, "Not just that."

"You meant that?"

She nodded and said, "I'm ready to get out of this place. I can't imagine any better way to go."

"Me too," Igor whispered, "I want to—"

"Shh."

Widow raked her fingers into Marie's hair and held her head with both hands. She added a small amount of nectar as she began to slowly guide Marie, pulling her closer.

"Soon, little one. You'll need to be a pretty little slave girl for me."

"I will," she whispered, her eyes pleading.

"Yes, you will. Here, then. Be a sweet, obedient slave girl."

Widow drew Marie's head closer, smiling at the girl's eyes staring at her destination and her tongue already out. She giggled softly as she stopped her progress, keeping her tongue just barely touching her, just the very tip of it.

Looking at Igor's bulging eyes and pants, Widow sighed and let go of Marie's head, and Marie moaned and closed the distance, then began steady, rhythmic licking, starting low and lingering higher up.

Widow touched the girl's hair lightly, caressing and playing with it, sometimes tucking strands behind her ears.

She tipped the crafter's head away and said, "Are you my baby girl? Tell me you are."

"Mm-hmm. I'm your baby girl. I'm your baby."

Widow sighed and let her continue, with a good view of her wet tongue lapping up along the sides and sometimes hiding most of it away with a deep stroke up the middle.

"Yes, just like that. Slow for me, baby girl. Mm."

Widow scoffed softly at the sight of Igor taking out his swollen tool and stroking it, much like when she'd first met him.

"Mm, I'm so juicy for you, little girl. Such sweet juice for you. Be sure to swallow all you can."

Igor kept fondling himself but moved around behind the crafter, who was still fully dressed but on her knees, leaning forward and showing the graceful curves of her ass through her thin pants. He tipped his head toward her ass, then bounced his eyebrows toward Widow.

She scoffed again and shook her head, then mouthed the word, "Slave."

He nodded, smiling about it, and said softly, "I don't deserve it!"

Widow smiled and shook her head, then her eyelids fluttered and her breaths got deeper.

"Slow, now, baby girl. So slow for me. The more juice you bring out and swallow, the greater your own pleasure."

Marie slowed her tongue strokes, taking time for unhurried passage up on each side, then so deep in the middle that her soft lips were sliding along, then dwelling with her lips on what stopped her tongue from going higher.

Widow played with her hair and said, "It feels so good to lick my pussy, doesn't it?"

Marie never slowed, only turned her eyes up and nodded.

"Good girl. Such a nice baby to lick me. Slow, baby girl. Don't stop."

She didn't appear that she'd ever stop, and Widow looked up at Igor.

"You wanted to tell me about something."

"Huh? Now?"

"Mm-hmm. So that I don't kill this sweet thing right now like she wants. Distract me like your life depends on it."

"Eh," he said, pumping harder and leaning to see Marie's curvy ass from every angle. "I want to die anyway."

"Mm, I know. But how much suffering to you want before?"

"Uh, oh. Okay. Um, I talked to that guy. That big guy."

"Junior?"

"Yeah, him. There's something weird—"

"Slowly now, baby girl," Widow said, looking down and holding the crafter's head as it looked like she was slowly nodding in an exaggerated way. "So slow with that sweet tongue."

Widow looked up and sighed, then raised her eyebrows at Igor.

"Uh, he's got this thing on his back. It buzzes. But when it stops, he has all kind of fireworks. And he—"

He knotted up his face as he stared at the crafter's ass and gave himself blinding strokes.

"Can I? Can I just—"

"No. Finish the story. What happens?"

"It's like he loses his mind. He's very intelligent and polite, then he goes crazy."

"How crazy?"

"He should be chained to a rock somewhere. When my other head spoke, which I never knew it could do, he—"

"It spoke?"

"Yeah. Surprised me."

"What did it say?"

"Um, it, uh . . . maybe I don't remember."

"I'll torture you in ways you can't imagine. Tell me."

"This is already torture!" he said, leaning so close that he could have licked Marie's ass.

"Very well. As soon as there's time, I'll carefully and systematically remove parts of you that—"

"Okay! I wasn't going to tell him, Widow."

"What did your extra head tell him?"

"The name of this building. I'm sorry!"

Chapter 47 – The Fucker's Begging for It

With fresh fire on fresh torches, Archie and his pack had veered widely around the feasting pigs and had gotten back on the trail called out by the guard dogs, the ones that he'd diced up to distract the attacking monster boars.

"We're back on course, Sammy. I hope you learned a fucking lesson back there."

"Uh, that giant pigs like butchered dog people?"

"You dumb fucker. No. Well, okay, that's true too. No, the point is that if you can prove you have some valuable function, that might be the only thing that keeps your ass alive."

"Oh, I see it. Yeah. Those loser dog things did their job, so we didn't need them anymore."

"You figured it out. Good for you."

"Hey, uh, Boss. What exactly is my, uh, valuable function?"

"Lesson two: The boss will never tell your sorry ass. You have to figure that shit out on your own."

They continued walking, the fire bearers in the lead—a tight band in a dim bubble of light amidst fields of black.

"Hey, uh, Boss? Could someone have more than one valuable function?"

"Sure, Sammy. But you know what? The boss still might stab the fucking life out of you just for kicks."

"Oh. Uh, yeah."

Many pairs of reactor-issued work boots stomped softly and sometimes dragged through the rough scrabble, staying the most quiet when traversing patches slick with crude. A fire carrier stopped in his tracks and held up a hand, palm forward.

None of the boots took another step.

"What?" Archie whispered.

"Voices. Ahead."

"Count?"

"Too many to count."

"Fuck. Coming or going?"

"Coming."

"You got some good fucking ears, there. Valuable."

"Yeah."

Archie leaned closer to Sammy and whispered, "Guess what might happen if someone was to slice off those good fucking ears."

Sammy doubled over, keeping his laughs quiet.

Archie grinned and said, "Well, shit, let's go meet them. Everyone, stay sharp. Your goddamn blades too."

The crowd of boots resumed their hike, more slowly and more quietly.

A human shape drifted into the dim light.

Then, another and another, and dozens of smiling faces, both male and female, kept approaching. Archie elbowed his way to the front of his pack and held a palm in their direction.

"Close enough," he said, and they all stopped.

"We're happy to stop right here," said a smiling man in ragged clothing, then he held his hand up too. "Let's all stop!"

"We're already stopped, you freak. What are you doing out here in the middle of the goddamn night?"

Archie turned each way, smiling at the laughing men behind him before again focusing on the roaming mob.

"It does seem that we're always in the middle of the night. Very true. Why, we're just out for some exercise, like we always do. Keeps things . . . fresh."

Many of his companions giggled and snickered, and the woman next to him said, "Well, fresher," which caused outright laughter from most of them.

Archie grabbed one of the torches, took a few steps closer, and waved the fire side to side, studying their faces.

"Oh, of course. Fucking zombies. Mortimer's tribe."

"Ah, yes, dear Mortimer. Our informal but much revered leader. Oh, but we don't really find the term 'zombie' acceptable. In fact, it's—"

"Yeah, yeah, yeah. I've heard that bullshit. Listen, freaks, I'll call you whatever the fuck I want. Who's your fastest runner?"

He looked behind him at the pleasant faces, then pointed at one young man.

"Trent. Trent is quite the speedy fellow."

Looking at Trent, Archie said, "Go tell Mortimer that Archie is looking for a hungry monster named Junior and a sly wench named Scarlet. I know that he knows every nook and crack in the goddamn city. He'd know where they are."

Trent grinned and nodded but didn't move.

"Go, dammit! Run!"

Archie scoffed at the sight of him vanishing into the darkness, en route to the city.

"Alright. Tell me what you're doing this far from the city."

"Well, if you must know, we—oh, how callous of me. I'm Murray. This sort-of-fresh beauty is—"

She caught him in the ribs with a sharp elbow.

"I mean, this beauty is Henrietta. And who might you be?"

"The fucker with the sword."

He pointed it at Murray's face while his band cheered and a few slapped his back.

"It's Blade's blade, actually."

"Well, that's a bit of a riddle."

"The fuck it is. Fucking answer me."

"And it's a very nice sword! Or blade! Just lovely! Well, to answer your question, we're testing the limits of a new installation of sanity beacons. We—"

"Huh?" said Archie. "What the fuck is that?"

"Oh, come on. Surely you can hear them. We're still within range."

Archie lowered his sword, then he and his gang pointed their ears toward the city.

"That buzzing?"

"Precisely!"

"A buzzer is a, what the fuck did you say, a sanity beacon? Start making sense."

Murray pointed at Archie, kept his finger aimed, and turned and licked Henrietta's cheek.

"He's catching on," he told her. "I won't even have to explain. He already—"

"No, no, no. You'd better explain."

"If you insist. It truly is all about making sense. We do when there's buzzing."

"And, uh, when there isn't?" Archie said while scratching at his chin.

"Party time!" someone back in the crowd yelled, and the rest of them hooted and hollered.

"Here's an idea for your party," Archie said, then raised his sword again. "It's called feeding the goddamn free-range livestock. Ever hear of that kind of party?"

"Well, no, can't say that I have. How does one play?"

Archie held up one finger and said, "Just a second."

He turned his back to Murray and his hoard, and Sammy turned with him.

"I get it! I get it!" Sammy whispered.

"Do you, now? Explain so even a boss can fucking understand."

"We'll do some boar feeding, but only after they stop having any kind of valuable function."

"Good. You got yourself a fucking brain, there, Sammy. Go for the extra credit. I insist."

"Uh . . . hmm. Oh! Like the dogs, right? Get whatever info they have first? That's their function?"

"I just might not cut that fucking head off of your body, Sammy."

"Uh, thanks."

They both turned around.

"Murray, before we commence with any kind of party, tell us: do you swear none of you know of a wench named Scarlet? We have reason to believe she took her sexy evil wench ass to the city."

"Hmm," said Murray, then he looked all around at his compatriots, who all just shrugged, shook their heads, and murmured.

Facing Archie again, he said, "Well, what would they know? They're a brainless lot."

"I have a brain!" shouted one.

"I just had one before we left!" yelled another, and Murray only grinned and held up a hand, silencing their proclamations.

"They really do have brains. I know because I've checked so many of them."

"He has!" said Henrietta.

"I tend to goad them just for fun. So, back to the wench question. I've heard of her. Long black hair, right?"

"Yeah," said Archie. "Oh, yeah."

"That must be the wench of which you speak. I've heard that Mortimer and his pack encountered her in the city while on a routine expedition."

"About where in that fucking hellhole of a city?"

Murray turned himself around and pointed.

"I believe it was in that area, there. Kind of on the outskirts nearest to that impossible to climb mountain.

Archie bumped his shoulder into Sammy, causing him to snort out a giggle.

"You're sure?"

Murray kept pointing, and most of the rest were looking toward the city too.

"Why, yes, I'm fairly sure. Right about there."

He kept looking and pointing and said, "I'm sorry, but that's really all I know."

"Ha!" yelled Sammy.

Archie laid his sword up over his shoulder and held it with both hands.

"The fucker's begging for it, Sammy."

"Yeah. Oh yeah, he sure is."

Murray began to turn, saying, "I'm practically—"

With one well-aimed, whizzing swing of his sword, Archie encouraged Murray's severed head to tumble away and rest facing up, where it continued to talk as his body folded over and collapsed.

"—begging for what?"

Archie pointed his sword, grinning, and said, "That. That fun fucking slice. See, the goddamn boars are following us, and they—"

"They are?" said Sammy.

"Fuck, yeah, Sammy. And they,"—he said to the head—"need a tasty little distraction to keep them off our goddamn asses. Boys, it's party time!"

Archie swung his sword straight down, cleaving Murray's face neatly and symmetrically, and neither half had any more to say.

The Spencer twins let loose their arrows, each zipping through a squishy skull, then nocked fresh ones.

Blade started lowering Archie's treat in a box, then caught sight of his shaking head and heard him say, "Uh-uh. Not my treat, dammit."

So, he kept it high up on a shoulder and drove his heavy boot through the closest chest he could kick.

The torch carriers each created a dancing, whooping torch, then another.

"Whoa!" said Archie. "That's enough!"

Half of Murray's entourage lay in sticky puddles, some twitching and some burning.

"Leave some alive. Ish."

"For the boars?" said Sammy.

"Fucking right. They kind of love the sport of it."

"You're becoming quite the enabler of those things, Boss."

"I kind of am. Damn. Maybe someday, they'll offer one to us out of fucking gratitude. Then, it'll be fucking bacon till the cows come home."

"That's funny," said Henrietta's head. "Till the—"

Archie ran two steps and kicked it into the darkness, and its laughter spiked with each bounce until it was lost and silent.

"Why, Boss?"

"Eh. Never liked the name Henrietta."

*   *   *

Junior paused under a dim streetlight and looked up at it while wiping sweat and blood from his brow. After flicking heavy drops of it toward the closest brick wall, he waited and listened. The city street was silent except for a low buzzing from the box on his back.

Walking again, sometimes tapping the pavement with the tip of the sword that Archie had given him, he said to himself, "A fairly charming little man, that Igor gent."

He laughed and added, "Almost two little men. Until I punched one of them. Perhaps I should have displayed more compassion and restraint."

He passed through the gloom between light cones and came to a building entrance.

"What did the little man say? The Webber Building?"

He squinted in the near total darkness and said softly, "Brick . . . Building . . . One. Huh. That name isn't very imagina—"

Sparks popped out of both ears as the buzzing staggered and stuttered.

"Whoo-hoo! Here I go, here I go!"

He spun twice, up on one leg and stabbing the sword out for balance as his cheeks ballooned like he'd swallowed a leaking helium tank. With a scratchy boom, he blew out sparks and bits of charred metal like a sweaty volcano, spraying a smoldering pattern on the building's front.

"Oh boy, oh boy! Hot! Hot!" he said as he banged his forehead into the splatter, embedding steamy bits of metal in his skin and adding more blood to the gory mess.

He twisted himself around and tried to rub Mortimer's device loose against the bricks, but it wouldn't let go, even though he was slapping the sword against the wall and yelling, "Yi, yi, yi!"

Still spitting red hot shrapnel, he scraped his mobile buzzer unit along the craggy brick surface until he was seated.

"Hoo, hoo, hoo! That's really—"

Like a gramophone finding reserve electricity and winding up to resume its tune, the buzzing returned and steadied out.

"—annoying," he finished with a calm voice.

After one belch of sparking fluid, he slumped over onto this side and managed to get his arm positioned to keep his head from cracking on the concrete.

"Mama, I . . . don't like when the buzzing stops."

Fluttering his lips, then spitting out a few bits of cooler circuitry, he let his eyes close with a deep sigh.

And he lay there only a moment before he felt something lick his cheek, then start to climb onto him. He opened one eye and saw one eye looking back. An eye in the head of a monkey man. A big one.

He sat up quickly, causing the tall, hairy man to jump back and tip his head and study him.

Junior pointed his sword and said, "You have no cause to take such liberties. Maintain some respectful distance."

The man stretched back his lips and chattered his teeth while Junior grunted and groaned and got his own body to stand.

"What do you want of me? Can't you see that I'm facing several troubling and incendiary personal issues at the moment?"

The man grinned, showing clamped teeth, then nodded and pointed. Junior looked first at the long, hairy finger, then to where it was pointing.

"Huh. You've helpfully alerted me to another troubling personal issue."

Something under the skin of his left forearm, about the size of a small coin, was pulsing with orange light and throbbing the skin up and down. When the man squealed, Junior looked away from whatever was alive inside his arm.

"What? This unique and likely dire predicament amuses you?"

The man shrugged and said, "Huh. Some."

"You have the power of speech, yet you mostly screech like a monkey? Explain yourself."

"Part monkey. So, screech."

"Hmm. You delivered a lot of logic with a minimum investment of your paltry language skills. Good for you."

Junior saw the man tip his eyes toward his arm, so he looked, too, and they both watched the steady, pulsing light for a few seconds.

"Huh. A peculiar phenomenon to be sure."

He reached his sword far to the right, then turned the point until it was almost touching the throbbing orange invader.

Without looking up, he said, "Please consider watching. It's unlikely that you'll be able to assist in any way, but—"

"Because I'm monkey."

Junior looked up and said, "I suppose that could have been construed as an insult. I assure you that I did not mean to slight you."

"Sure."

"Don't be a smartass. I could, you know, allow this sharp blade to deliver some quick and fatal insults that would definitely slight you."

"Got it."

"That was a fun little play on words. It was close to saying that it would 'slice' you. Get it?"

"Got it. Still."

Looking down again, Junior mumbled, "Goddamn monkeys."

"Hey."

"Apologies."

He twisted the sword, driving the point under the glowing intrusion, which allowed a steady stream of hot blood to trickle out. He drove it in farther, then pried up the pointy end.

The skin ripped enough to expose a black metal disk at the center of a dozen filaments jutting out radially and embedded under the skin that he hadn't torn open.

While he and the monkey man watched, it swelled up and glowed orange, then returned to its original state.

"That can't be good."

"Not good."

Junior looked up, then the man ignored the glowing object to look into his eyes.

"What would you do?"

The man shrugged and said, "Look for food."

"That's wise and always a good objective. I meant about this foreign object."

"Look for sex."

"Huh. Again, I can't fault your logic. Do you care about anything except food and sex?"

The monkey man squinted back at him, then tipped its head and squinted some more.

"There's more?"

Junior laughed and said, "Not for me there wasn't until I met Mortimer and his kind friends. I seem to have expanded my view of the multitude of possibilities in this world since—"

Sparks and smoke puffed out of the hole that he'd just put in his arm.

"Woo-hoo! Damn!"

He kicked the wall behind him, several times with each boot, then started banging the back of his head into the bricks too. The man-monkey stepped farther away.

"Ha, ha, ha, hoo! Mama, I just—"

A drawn-out fizzling led to a steady buzzing.

His arm calmed down, and he let out a monstrous sigh.

"Quite inconvenient. I was about to say that vengeance is good too. I happen to be looking for someone that killed my mother. If I could only locate her building, I'd—"

"Building? Monkey knows buildings."

"You're displaying your comedic skills, aren't you? Calling yourself 'monkey?'"

The man giggled and nodded, and Junior pointed at him with his sword.

"I knew there was a good reason to not dice you up. So, you know buildings?"

"Monkey knows."

"Monkey knows them by name?"

"Monkey knows names."

"It's called The Webber Building."

"Know it."

"Could I persuade you, without threat of violent swordplay, to offer directions to that particular building?"

"Show you."

"Even better. Lead on, my wise and charitable simian friend."

"Tired."

"Oh. Yes, no doubt, what with gallivanting about incessantly along dark and deserted lanes and avenues. You need to rest?"

"Carry?"

"I could. Sure. Like, how?"

The man tried pointing around toward Junior's back.

"Well, sure. Why not? All aboard, helpful but weary monkey."

He turned, and the monkey man jumped up, wrapping his legs around his waist and his arms around his neck. One hand, in front of Junior's face, pointed out a direction.

"March."

"You're amusing, Mr. Monkey. Very well. I'll march."

Chapter 48 – My Shaggy, Horny Friend

Widow was about to speak but instead, she tipped her head back and moaned toward the ceiling.

"Such a sweet slave girl. My pussy likes it just like that. Mm."

She leveled her gaze at Igor and said, "These buildings have names? What the hell is this place?"

"Yes. And no one knows what this is. It's only a matter of time before Junior finds us."

Stroking Marie's hair, Widow scoffed and said, "You speak like this is your home."

"It's not?"

"It's where you will die."

"Okay."

Still pumping with his right, he groaned and reached for the crafter's pants with his left.

"No, slave."

"Dammit. How about just her ass, then?"

Marie whimpered and tried to move her head, but Widow held it where she wanted it to stay.

"Shh, little girl. I won't let the horrible little man do that to you."

"Like a monkey," Igor said.

"What did you say?"

"There are monkeys running wild out there."

"Yes, I've seen. So?"

"That's what they like. They're sneaky. They can jab it in before you even know what's happening."

"That's preposterous. But Pauline and I were joking about that. What a weird coincidence."

"Who started that joke?"

"Uh, Pauline."

"She knows. She probably got it. Maybe more than once."

"No, she would have said so."

"Doubtful. You wouldn't, would you?"

"Let it happen or talk about it?"

"Either?"

"No. Neither."

"You might like it, Widow."

"You're a disgusting slave with a dead extra head."

"Yes! All true! But even if you're tempted someday, Widow, be very careful."

"Oh, I already heard from Pauline. Sex makes them want more sex. It's what they were made for, apparently."

"It's not just that, Widow. It's worse."

"Explain."

"The sex makes them crazy, like really crazy, and they try to kill whoever they're fucking."

"Are you sure? Why would they make them like that?"

"No one planned it. Fucked up DNA. So, even if you ever want to—"

"Do not be concerned—I won't. I'm not sure I believe that story anyway. Dim the light, slave, then open that shutter just enough to look down at the street."

"Yes, Widow. I, uh, might explode before I can—"

"Oh, you're so gross. Can't you just empty it somewhere?"

"I have to! It'll pop soon!"

"Hmm. Take it back in the corner, drain it, then do as you were ordered."

"How about the dead guy on the couch?"

Widow turned her head enough to see. He still lay under the blanket, but the rigid center pole of his tent had evaporated.

"God, he really is dead."

"I don't care."

"You can't fuck the dead guy. No, slave."

"Dammit."

He shuffled off toward the far corner, where thick shadows congregated. Widow moaned softly and touched Marie's hair as she continued her slow, steady licking.

But they both stopped at Igor yelling, "Wow!" then cackling softly.

"Oh my goodness," Widow said to herself and chuckled for a second.

Using both hands, she tipped back the crafter's head to look into her eyes.

"Do you love the orgasm?"

Marie nodded, and her eyes blinked slowly.

"It's from licking my pussy. Do you love licking my pussy?"

Before Marie could nod twice, Widow said, "Tell me, then," and tipped her head back just enough.

The crafter licked her lips, then said, "I love licking your pussy."

"Mm, I knew you would, and I love hearing it. You want only to please me, don't you?"

Marie nodded again and began quicker strokes with her tongue.

"Oh, slowly, my little one. There you go. Just like that. We're having such sweet orgasms together."

She looked up enough to see Igor, walking funny, as he ambled to where he could switch off the light. With a match that he'd just lit, he kept up his odd gate, sometimes stopping to kick a leg to one side, over toward the shuttered window.

"You haven't moved in a while," Widow said to Marie. "Except for that lovely tongue of yours."

Marie's head didn't move, and she didn't answer.

"Hey. You okay, there, sweet little thing?"

There still wasn't an answer.

"Hmm. Those poisons. And you're still doing such a wonderful job."

She played with the crafter's hair for a moment, then said, "I'd rather hear you say it, but I'll say it for you. You're a sweet little crafter girl, and all you want to do is lick my pussy when I tell you to. Isn't that right?"

Using both hands, she got the girl's head to nod.

"Mm. So sweet."

At the sliding of the metal bolt, Widow turned her eyes from the head between her thighs and watched Igor drop the match, stomp it out, then swing open the hinged board.

Peering out, he whispered, "No, no, no!"

"What? A pig? A bat?"

"Worse, Widow! It's Junior, and he—"

"First, no yelling. And he, what?"

"Sorry! You won't believe me! Why would you? I'm just a slave and can't be trusted to—"

"Quiet! Tell me."

"One of those monkeys? Remember them? He has one on his back!"

Widow giggled and fussed with the crafter's hair while saying, "And we know what those monkeys like to do. Is that what's going on?"

"Too high up, Widow. Can't see. Junior sure has a big sword, though."

"Sword, huh? Is that what you call it?"

"No, but that's probably gigantic too."

"Let's hope we never find out. Okay, so,"—she tipped Marie's head back and like a rag doll, she slumped over, then flowed onto the floor—"we probably have time before he gets this far. There are a lot of rooms to check first. Close that up."

"I, uh, only unzipped it to—"

"You're really some kind of mutant. I meant that shutter. And just why did you unzip again?"

He closed the swinging plank and while locking it up, said, "Well, he, he's so big and sweaty, and he's got a horny ass-fucking monkey on him, probably about to fuck him, and I—"

"Stop."

Widow stood up on her pointy heels and shimmied around to get her skirt over her hips.

"Didn't you just empty your vile stuff in the corner?"

Walking toward her, his grin lit by the burning match in his hand, he said, "Radiation. I charge up so damn fast."

"You get more disgusting every second."

"I'm sorry, Widow. But part of the charging was from you telling that crafter what she liked to do. I could hear it! I heard her tongue! And then, your voice got all sexy and demanding, and I saw a bloody, sweaty monster without a shirt, about to get his—"

"Look, if he makes it this far, and if the monkey's still with him, they can both fuck you wherever you want it. But right now, we have to hide."

She looked around at the dusty room that still mostly appeared abandoned and unused. Only the crafter's bags were conspicuous, as well as Widow's old clothes.

And the dead body under a blanket on the couch.

And an unconscious crafter who moved only her tongue.

Widow sighed, then looked up at the ceiling.

"You think we can get up there?"

"All of us? Even the dead guy?"

"Maybe not him. Maybe not even you. I'm keeping Marie, though."

"You can't leave me! He'll make me talk! You can't leave me for that monster!"

"It was you that brought that monster here."

"Not me! Not me!"

"Right. Your other head blabbed the building name. Alright. Watch out the window for when Junior goes into the building. You watch, slave, to make sure Junior has been in the building for a while, then throw the body out."

"What if Junior's monkey is still out there?"

"Try to hit it with the body. We can't leave it in here."

"Then, what do we do?"

"We go up there," she said, pointing at the hatch to the attic.

"While you're following my commands, I might have this sweet girl lick me just a little bit more."

"You're torturing me! I don't deserve any better!"

With her short black boot, Widow nudged the unconscious crafter onto her back, then placed a sharp heel on each side of her head.

"Mm, she has such a delightful tongue."

Moaning, Widow shifted around as she wiggled the skirt back up around her waist.

The short mutant started struggling with his zipper.

"Tell her what she likes to do. Tell her again!"

"Go to the window and watch. And don't get distracted by playing with yourself."

Widow lowered herself gracefully onto her knees, then glanced at a mutant staring and fumbling around again with his zipper.

"Go. Don't even think of looking back again."

He bowed, grumbling, then said, "As you wish, Widow."

With Widow watching him, Igor quickly scurried over to the couch, heaved the stiffening body up over his shoulder, and then stumbled back to the window. Standing still and ready, he snuffed out his match, then opened the shutter.

With his face angled to watch Junior and his monkey man companion on the street below, and the body ready to be thrown out, Igor didn't see Widow slowly sit herself down, just a little at a time, then shift her hips until she smiled in the darkness.

But he did hear her say, "Mm, such a good, obedient baby girl. Mm-hmm, just like that. Lick, baby girl."

He whipped around, one hand on his crotch and a pained smile on his face.

And the body tumbled out and fell toward the street.

* * *

Junior still had a tired monkey man clinging to his back, hairy legs wrapped around his waist, and only a few drops of blood still sputtered from the gouged area of his forearm where the skin was already growing back over the embedded metal disk.

Both stood in a struggling cone of light beneath a streetlight and looked across the street at a building, one with the name Webber chiseled into the heavy stone lintel above the doorway.

Squeezed tight between giant and monkey, a box continued its steady buzzing.

"See?"

"You're a remarkable example of a monkey and quite helpful. I could easily have wandered for an extended interval of time before happening upon this building."

"Owe me?"

"Why, yes, I believe I do. How can I repay you?"

"Not hungry."

"No? Surely, you must be in need of something while roaming throughout this grim wasteland. Name it. You've proved yourself to be a valuable asset."

The man chattered his big teeth up at the streetlight's dim glow, then chomped them together rapidly.

He snorted out what could have been a laugh and said, "Not hungry!"

"You're lack of precision in your response, and the noticeable repetition in your words, suggests that you believe that I should be able to come to my own—"

His hairy arms squeezed Junior more tightly as he snickered up at the lamp.

"—own conclusion. Let's see . . . you've probably already offered sufficient clues, hence you're feeling no urgency to restate your case. Hmm. Oh. Oh, my first solution can't be correct."

The man chattered hot breath into Junior's ear.

"You stated clearly that you care about only two things: food and sex. Then, in response to my query about—"

The hairy monkey man on his back howled past the glowing bulb and up toward the absolute black of the sky.

"Query. That word elicited a distinct response. As did the word 'asset.' Am I coming close to—"

Thick, hot monkey breath bathed Junior's ear.

"That word agitates you further as well."

"Agitates!"

"I feel confident that I can solve the riddle of what you want with a simple, three-letter word: sex."

"Bingo."

"Ah, finally, your pressing need is—speaking of pressing, I didn't notice that you were carrying a club earlier. Yet, you've stowed it tightly between us. It's quite a large club too. One might dare to call it a war club."

"Not hungry!"

"Huh. Likely not a club at all, then."

"Not a club!"

"So, I should help you find a female monkey to—"

"Club can't wait!"

"Why don't I just set you down, then you—"

"No! Set pants down!"

Rough, hairy hands grabbed at the waistband of Junior's pants and began jerking it around, trying to force it down past his hips and ass.

"Whoa! Wait just one minute, my fine hairy friend who knows building names and wants only—"

"Sex!"

"You know that I'm not a female, don't you?"

"Ya, ya, ya!"

"So, just exactly what did you think you'd—"

"Ass! Sweaty ass!"

"Oh, I see. Yes. Mama often enjoyed such unconventional copulation too."

"Momma!"

Junior kept his sword pointed out to one side as he unbuckled.

"I did offer you recompense for your valuable and timely assistance."

"Yeah!"

"Very well, my hairy, over-sexed ape-like friend. Sure your club is ready?"

"Hardly!"

"With so few words at your command, you're still remarkably clever."

Junior grinned at the mad chattering and stale monkey breath in his ear as he worked his pants down. At the same time, a bulbous monkey club, hotter even than the skin of his back, was slipping down along the streaks and smears of sticky sweat and blood.

At the sound of a splat and a clatter, like a bag of viscous fluid mixed with brittle sticks had itself slammed against an obstinate obstacle, the body from Widow's window high above them landed and sprayed out jagged lines of slop on the sidewalk across the street.

"Wait just one second," Junior said, then began pulling up his pants.

"Like momma!"

"No, wait. Kindly dismount, good fellow."

The hairy man held on more tightly and resumed his clawing at Junior's pants.

"No, really, this sudden, tragic development might indicate that the wench Scarlet is indeed in The Webber Building."

"Don't care. Ass!"

"Perhaps another time."

Junior leaned his sword against the nearest wall, used both hands to wrestle the obscenely excited man off of his back, then pushed him back a step.

He laughed, looking down, and said, "You could hang a rather large flag on that pole of yours."

"Flag? Close."

"You're a rather comical monkey but a cunning linguist too."

"Nope!"

Laughing, Junior said, "Ha. Sarcasm, my sinewy, hairy friend."

He retrieved his sword while pressing a meaty hand into the man's shoulder, pressing his other shoulder into the wall. Then, he leaned and looked behind the grinning monkey.

"Huh. That's a fair indicator of your intentions. One could hang out a day's worth of laundry on that horizontal tail of yours."

"Ya!"

Then, Junior looked up.

Even in near total darkness, there was enough light reflected back up off of the roadway surface to make clear that not all of the windows were shuttered and blockaded. The lowest of them with any access to the interior were about halfway up, and there was a staggered assortment of them going higher toward the roof.

"I'm going inside. Careful with that war club of yours, Mr. Monkey."

"Monkey come?"

"You'll just get in the way. I need to go alone and focus on—"

The man giggled and snorted and chopped his teeth for a few seconds.

"Stay outside," he said. "Monkey come."

Junior shook his head and grinned, then pointed at the man's war club.

"Yes, it's time to take matters in hand, my shaggy, horny friend."

* * *

Igor spun himself around and ducked below the edge of the open shutter.

"Sorry!" he whispered.

"Why did you throw that out? You were told to wait!"

"I heard you and the crafter, and she was licking, and you were—"

"You should have focused on my commands!"

"But you were telling her she was obedient, and she was licking you, and—"

"She's still licking me."

"God, that's making me—"

"Mm, she's still so obedient too. Such a sweet little—"

"Widow! Pardon my rudeness. I'm just a slave and don't know anything, but won't that monster come looking for us?"

Widow said, "Are there other windows where a careless mutant slave could have tossed out a body?"

"Yes. There are others."

"So, the monster with a sword will—"

"And a monkey on his back."

"This is getting too complicated. Stick your good head out there and see what's going on. And don't you make a sound, you inept slave."

"I'm inept! And a slave!" he whispered.

He slowly leaned out to look, then whipped himself back around.

"Widow! He—"

"Close the shutter, slave. Then, strike a match."

He locked it up, then added some light to the room.

"Speak."

"He's gone. He must be in your building."

"And the monkey?"

"He's across the street."

"How do you know it's a he?"

"Because his boner's as big as his arm!"

"Oh, those sex-crazy monkeys. There's no way Pauline ever—"

"I'd bet she did! I would!"

"We can't debate that now. How did you get up there to look into the attic?"

"Easy. I piled furniture. There's no ladder."

"Very well. Light a candle, then gather—"

"Um, Widow. Perhaps Marie should, uh, save her tongue for later?"

Widow sighed and tousled Marie's hair around.

"Mm, perhaps."

She rose to her knees and nodded at seeing Marie's tongue still seeking her and her poisons.

While Igor was bumping and nudging a table to get it under the hatch to the attic, he said, "Will she wake up? Will she yell or anything?"

Widow held his gaze, causing him to stop and stare back at her.

"If she yells, slave, it'll be for my . . . pussy."

He groaned but smiled and said, "You're torturing me! I don't deserve any better!"

"You don't. After you get everything stacked, find some sturdy rope."

"Yes, Widow. Um, this would get done quicker if you, uh, helped."

"Oh, I have something else I need to do. I'm going to give my little sleeping beauty a nice little bite."

"To kill her! Good idea!"

"No, slave. Just to be sure she doesn't wake up while we're hiding from the monster with a sword."

"Easier just to kill her and throw her out too."

"Well, then, who would lick my . . . pussy?"

Igor hung his functioning head forward and grinned, saying, "I'm not allowed to volunteer, am I? I'm just a slave?"

"No, you're not allowed. But I outright command you to think about . . ."

He looked up, shaking his head and about to sob.

". . . my pussy."

* * *

In the littered, oil-stained lobby of The Webber Building, Junior paused to study in every direction. Straight ahead, the stairway waited. Off to the right of that were the bent and gouged open elevator doors, which left a clear view of the cracked and soiled back wall of the shaft.

To his left, he saw a long desk backed up by cracked mirrors, and he walked over and tapped lightly on a bell, which didn't ring.

"Perhaps I should just check the directory," he said, then laughed. "Why yes, kind sir, Ms. Scarlet is waiting for you in suite number—"

His left arm sparked, hot bits of a rainbow burst out, and his right hand raised the sword high.

"Oh, wow! Oh, that, that—"

With a deflating whistle, the sparks sputtered and stopped, and he lowered the blade.

"Whew. That's always a jarring surprise."

He let the sharp edge clunk the dusty counter next to the bell.

"Huh. It is rather exhilarating, though."

With a quick snap of the blade, the bell got flung across the room, and it dinged each time it bounced.

"That's amusing, too, how it rings only at a time of its own choosing."

With a contented sigh, he turned and began walking toward the stairway, saying, "I believe you're up there, somewhere, you wench that killed Mama."

With his sword up and over his shoulder, he climbed the first flight and was about to step onto the small landing area, but a whistle led to a pop of sparks from one ear, then another pop and sparks from the other.

"Woo-hoo! Damn, damn, damn!"

He spun around twice, then halfway again, and his boots slipped out from under him. He landed on his ass on the landing, then hit each step on the way down, each impact blowing wet sparks from both ears.

"Wow, wow, wow!"

A whistle ramped up, then faded, then ended with a sloppy pop as he sat at the bottom of the steps.

He shook his head and said, "I dare say, this miserable situation isn't improving. I might need to have a conversation with that Mortimer character if I—"

His next word was a fireworks display, followed by a series of gags and coughs that sent out the last of the sparks.

"Hoo, boy," he said while standing up and turning to look back up the stairs. "Better hurry before I detonate altogether."

He stomped two steps at a time and stopped at a floor about midway between ground level and the roof.

Before kicking open the door closest to the stairs, he paused and looked down at his hands, one holding the sword and the other flexing into a fist at the end of an oily, bloody, sweaty but very muscular arm that was dotted with small burns.

"Hmm. Barehanded or the sword? Slowly or one quick partitioning?"

He kicked in the door, sending hardware flying into the room and leaving it hanging on only its top hinge.

"Either way, the wench must pay for killing Mama."

He bellowed up at the ceiling, "I miss you Mama!"

Stepping into the room, he chuckled and muttered, "Don't devolve into an insect, Mama."

With the unhinged door still creaking as it swung slowly, light from the hallway lit a path to the far wall, which faced the street. Junior saw a wide unshuttered window and hurried toward it, keeping his sword raised high.

Leaning out and looking down, he scoffed at the sight of a horny monkey man standing where he'd left him, masturbating with both hairy hands.

"Disgusting," he said, shaking his head. "Understandable, though. Even a monkey has to do what a monkey has to—"

"Whoo-hoo!"

Burning balls of sparks shot straight out of his mouth, five in a fast series like a roman candle, and they sizzled and popped as they fizzled out before reaching the street and the hairy masturbating man far below.

Swallowing rapidly, hacking, and dragging his free hand across his face, he looked down again and yelled, "Hey, monkey! Be a decent fellow and spray your toxic fluids onto that wall! No one wants to step in that—"

He jumped straight up and screamed, "God, God, God!" when his ears popped and whistled, shot out flaming streamers, then seemed content to just burn, each with a tiny, twisting flame.

"Ow! Woo-hoo! Dammit, dammit, dammit!"

He danced around, spun in circles, then lost his grip on the sword. It landed on the window ledge and started tipping, ready to fall, so he lunged for it.

"Ow, ow, ow!" he said while tamping down the flames on each side of his head with his free hand.

And he started to fall out himself as the sword evaded his grasp and clattered against the building once as it fell toward ground level.

"Whoa! Whoa!"

He'd just gotten the flames reduced to smoldering irritations and hooked both hands on the window frame.

With only thin wisps of smoke rising from the sides of his head, he hung there, high above the street and its wanton monkey man, and said, "I did say that that was inconvenient, didn't I?"

He looked down at the man when he heard bemused chattering from the street.

"Yes. I'm sure that I did."

* * *

"Shh!" said Widow. "Listen."

She and Igor, along with the still unconscious crafter, were up in the attic and looking down at the unlit room. The candelabra that Igor had brought up there held enough burning candles to light their vicinity and let them see the stack of odd items below—a table, a chair, a light wooden crate—that had served as a makeshift stairway.

They both heard Junior's screams and exclamations as different parts of his body succumbed to malfunctioning electronics. His last yelling got the two of them to lean enough to look toward the shuttered window.

"That came from over there," whispered Igor.

"How? He's outside?"

"Who knows? Maybe he fell?"

"No. We would hear him screaming all the way down."

"Or laughing. Widow, you should have seen him. He had sparks shooting out everywhere, and there was—"

"Sparks? That can't be any kind of mutation."

"Not a mutation. It's probably from that box on his back, making weird noises."

"As if he wasn't dangerous enough after eating tons of mutants."

"I believe he's quite insane."

"Says the insane mutant slave."

When she didn't hear a response, Widow turned and saw the small man mumbling silently with his head hanging.

"I take that back. You're not insane."

His grin spread even before he tipped his head back up.

"But I'm still your slave?"

"You'll be a dead slave if you don't stay quieter."

"Sorry!" he said in an almost silent whisper.

"Good. Now, lift up all that junk."

"You're smart to make me to tie it all together."

"I like things being tied. I'm learning just how much."

"You can tie me! I'd love to be tied and have to—"

"You're not licking anything. Pull that garbage up here, and do it quietly. I'm not totally against feeding you to the monster."

"As you wish, Widow."

"We'll have to close it up. The monster's next stop is probably this room."

"Yes, Widow. There's a port in the hatch, though. A hidden one. We can listen to him if he comes in this room."

"Was that meant to be funny?"

"No. But he probably will. Even without his monkey."

"True."

The little man with a burlap sack covering his second head hunched himself over and began pulling the rope, lifting their stairs. He stopped when he heard Widow.

"Now for you, my sweet little one."

But all he did was grimace quietly and focus again on his assigned task. Until he heard her continue, then he squinted and winced as he turned his head just enough to watch.

"This is where you want me, little girl," Widow said as she straddled the poisoned woman lying on her back.

She'd arranged her arms straight along her sides, and she knelt, facing toward the crafter's worn sneakers, with her knees squeezing her tight.

"Let's just find a very soft, smooth place. That's where you want to feel my sharp little teeth, don't you? Of course, you do."

Igor watched in the flickering candlelight as Widow gently unbuckled Marie's belt, unzipped her pants, then spread the fabric open enough to reveal the girl's skin above the thin elastic line of her panties.

"Mm, so soft for me."

She grabbed near the pockets and pulled down, first one side then the other, until she'd bared part of the crafter's thighs.

"Oh, such soft skin. Mm, and my fangs are so cruel. So sharp and cruel."

Igor held the rope and slowly rotating suspended items with one hand and his crotch with the other.

Upright again, Widow sighed and raised her skirt up above her hips and ass and left it like a tight black leather belt around her waist.

"This will help with all the cruelty I'll inflict on you, there where your skin is so soft and smooth."

She turned her head just enough to catch Igor's staring eyes.

"Here," she said to Marie while gazing at Igor, "my sweet little crafter girl. Forget the cruelty by tasting my very wet, very sweet . . . pussy."

When Igor swallowed loudly, she only grinned at him.

Then, she looked down, placed her hands to each side of the crafter's hips, and lowered herself onto Marie's waiting tongue and didn't need to shift around to improve her aim.

"Oh, mm, just like that. Such a sweet, obedient little girl."

Widow again looked at Igor's eyes, then down at the eager rod that he held out in the open, then back into his eyes.

"So obedient for such a cruel, cruel woman."

She bared her fangs and hissed at the mutant pleasuring himself, then tipped her head toward the cargo still waiting to be lifted up and out of sight of the monster that would soon crash into their room.

But Igor hesitated just long enough to watch Widow lean forward, mouth open wide, and sink her sharp teeth into the waiting skin of the already poisoned crafter girl.

Chapter 49 – A Hot, Sticky Mess Hung On

Junior tried opening Widow's door politely, but it refused his modest efforts. So, he kicked it, leaving it destroyed like the one on the floor below. As the twisted, dented metal slab twisted silently on a single hinge, it remained open enough to provide adequate dim light to most of the room.

He gave his smoking ears a few more hard slaps, snuffing them out completely, then walked in. His eyes locked on the room's boarded-up window, and he strode over to it. Seeing that the shutter was still closed and bolted, he looked around until he located the stubs of used matches scattered around hear his boots.

"Aha!"

Holding a few of them long enough to smell that they were fresh, he tossed them aside and looked next toward the table and two chairs. After scowling at the woman in the portrait and saying, "You're not my Mama," he saw a clean spot on the table where the candelabra had remained for so long before its journey into the attic.

"Uh-huh. Yes. This is real evidence of something. Perhaps not a launching point of a body, whether living or dead as it began its accelerating descent. But something suspicious is going on here."

Staying close to the wall, he began to circumvent the room and not many steps later, he saw the weak reflection bounced up from the coagulating squirts that the mutant had left there.

"Hmm, more evidence. Of something nefarious."

He stooped down and reached for it, but he scowled and arrested his investigation.

Standing again, he said, "Inconclusive and not deserving of any hands-on scrutiny. That could be from a monkey."

Laughing, he continued his tour and said, "They can't always find a willing or even just an overpowered ass for that. Must be heartbreaking for such insistent creatures with obviously mutated libidos."

Before passing the couch, he stopped to lift the blanket, then sniffed the air.

"Huh. Smells like recent sexual activity. But what kind? That is the pertinent question, King: was it—hey, I almost forgot that I'm King! But about the sex on this furniture: was it human or monkey? Or both?"

He took two steps, continuing his inspection, then turned to face the couch again.

"If both, would it ever be with the unforced consent of both participants? Hmm."

Walking again, he got himself all the way back to the entry door, having traversed the entire room. Taking one last look, he smiled at the bits of light reflecting off of the chain hanging from the movable hatch.

He walked over to stand under it, then looked up and pulled the chain, then all around at the brighter room again.

"Sadly, even though I believe this room could be the origin of the high-diving body, the perpetrators appear to have—"

The soft buzzing from his back unit sputtered then stopped altogether.

A quick jet like from a blow torch shot out of each nostril, then ended with two loud pops.

"Ah . . . ha!"

Two more quick flamethrower blasts sent sparking bits to the floor.

"Hurts! Ha, ha, ha, hurts!"

Another two burning streams like rocket exhaust snapped his head back and landed him on his back.

And a robotic voice from the mobile unit nailed into his back said, "Please stand by. Compulsory software upgrade in progress. Please stand by."

* * *

Widow had suspended her gyrating and grinding, but the poisoned young crafter girl beneath her, with her face nestled between Widow's strong thighs, continued her steady licking.

Igor crept closer to the listening port, held his ear nearby, and left enough room for Widow to hear too.

When he looked her way, she shook her head, then held out a hand, palm up.

Mouthing the words, "I don't know!" only got a frown from Widow and a finger to her lips.

He nodded quickly with a grin, and they both listened for a second.

But his eyes had drifted to the plain view he had of the top of Marie's head, which didn't move at all. Widow scoffed silently at him squinting and licking his lips, then looking into her eyes again.

"Me too?" he said silently. "Me too?"

She scoffed again and shook her head.

She mouthed the word, "No," then added, "slave."

He winced and mouthed the word, "Torture!"

* * *

Junior lay still, eyes locked open and focused on the overhead light, as many quiet seconds passed.

"Software upgrade complete," said Mortimer's box on Junior's back. "Current release of 'Talk Dirty/Be Dirty' language and behavior module operable."

No buzzing came from his mobile control box.

"Yi, yi, yi! Wow, that, that, that—"

516

A sputtering and burst of static led to a sustained buzzing from the box on his back.

"Fuck that," Junior said calmly while sitting up. "All that fire and fucking flame bullshit could have burned my goddamn ass into a lump of fucking charcoal. It's not a fucking proposition that I fucking welcome, to be sure."

He stood up and rubbed around his crotch while looking around the room again.

"Scarlet," he called out, his voice loud but steady. "I remember you! I had an undeniable inclination to fuck you when I saw you with Mama!"

He stomped over to where he could gaze into the eyes of the dusty portrait above the table.

"Given sufficient fucking time, I surely will locate you, you sexy fucking wench!" he yelled over his shoulder to the empty room. "And I'm going to fuck you senseless!"

He kept rubbing his crotch.

"And then, I'm going to fuck some sense into you! Take a moment and consider the fucking ridiculousness of that!"

Grinning up at the portrait woman's eyes, he said, "You're not even a reasonable caricature of Mama. But you're fucking close enough."

He yanked down his zipper, wrestled out into the open his swollen kingly tool, and began a steady, brutal stroking.

"You have my perspiring, engorged, and fucking at-attention attention, Mama!"

The only sound in the dim room was the deep breathing and hard pounding from a king's mighty hand.

"Please feel free to go the fuck ahead and transform into a bug, Mama. Be a goddamn bug."

He grunted and stroked.

"I'd sign up for intercourse with a bug, Mama. Oh, yes. Yes, I fucking would!"

Looking up at the portrait, he still didn't see Widow's old clothes folded up on a chair.

"Don't cry, Mama, with your face flat on that fucking goddamn wall, in a well-done fucking portrait that resembles you not a fucking bit. No, don't shed a fucking tear—your fucking eyes are too goddamn dusty. Ha!"

Showing his teeth, straining as more rivers of sweat mixed with the blood and oil, he pumped his majestic meat with a kingly urgency.

"Scarlet! This hot stream is for you until I can fucking deliver it in person!"

He groaned as he gave it a long yank, aiming the splatter for the candelabra's circle.

"I'll fill you up with it! Your sexy fucking pussy will be overflowing!"

He tugged it hard, adding to the hot puddle.

"Then, your sexy smartass mouth will get disgusting gobs of King cum! My persuasive skills will compel you to swallow all of it! You'll look pregnant when all my King slop is burning and churning in your goddamn belly!"

He pulled it again, spraying most of it against the wall.

"And the whole goddamn time—"

He gave it a hard squirt.

"—while my glorious, regal cock is shooting into your goddamn pussy and hungry fucking mouth—"

All of it hit the wall and was too thick and sticky to drip.

"—my best new fucking friend, that goddamn horny son-of-a-bitch monkey hybrid fellow, will—"

Another jerk, another splat on the wall.

"—will be ramming his goddamn monkey—"

Higher on the wall, a hot sticky mess hung on.

"—cock so deep in your posterior fucking orifice! You're going to get fucked in an unapologetically brutal way by—"

Junior's final violent pull worked the last thick blob up and out and sounded like a bean bag hitting the wall.

"—me and my—"

He sighed and grinned at all that he had accomplished.

"Monkey," he said calmly. "My goodness, it's alarming but quite exhilarating to pepper one's speech with such crude expletives. Oh, and Scarlet, if you're listening? I'll eat you too. Not just your pussy, as the term 'eat' is so often fucking employed. You. All the tasty parts first. Mm, yeah, so tasty. My monkey might want a few nibbles too. He seems kind enough, but you should see his fucking teeth. My fucking goodness. Their primitive, ravenous lust is haunting, dammit!"

Breathing deeply and grinning, he zipped up, scoffed at the mess he'd made, then walked with his typical heavy footfalls past the broken door, along the short bit of hallway, then down the stairs, buzzing all the way.

* * *

The sound of bludgeoning footsteps and evenly powered buzzing diminished steadily, bringing a grin to the two-headed mutant's frothy lips.

"I think he's—"

He stared as Widow ground her hips into the helpless crafter, rocking her head from side to side on the gritty attic floor. With first her right hand, then her left, she fought with the girl's trousers, frantically working the waistband down over the gentle curves of her hips to expose the soft flesh of her thighs.

"Widow?"

With her fangs bared, she snapped her head to face her slave and said, "What?"

"You, uh, hmm. Tell me you didn't get turned on by the, I mean, the monster guy and—"

She hissed but didn't look away.

519

"All that stuff he said he'd do to you?"

"What is your question, slave?"

"He said he'd gush gobs of cum in your pussy, and—"

Widow hissed and peeled her lips back farther.

"And in your mouth? He said you'd swallow so much you'd look pregnant, and . . ."

He shrank back at seeing her longest fangs ever.

"And? Speak, slave!"

"You liked hearing that his monkey would—"

"He's lying. Monkeys belong to no one."

"Okay, well, any monkey, then. Some random monkey would be fucking you in the ass while he's doing all—"

Widow growled and pierced the crafter's smooth thigh, sinking her fangs in deep. Her lips closed around the bite, and she moaned as she began to suck and swallow.

"Oh my goodness!" Igor said, his voice shaking.

Widow backed away from her deep bite, licked two red punctures in the white skin, then growled and bit Marie's other thigh.

"Um, Widow, could I . . ."

Her fangs were dripping and barely out as she hissed at him.

"What?

"Can I, um, get a closer look?"

She snarled and nodded, then said, "No touching. You're just—"

"A slave! Yes!"

He sealed up the eavesdropping port and scurried close enough that he could almost kiss the crafter girl's forehead and so much more.

Staring at a view of Widow that got him smiling, he said, "He said the monkey would be fucking you in your—"

Widow growled and shook her hips around as she jabbed her sharp teeth in even deeper.

"God," Igor whispered, "I wish I was a monkey. That monkey!"

* * *

Widow withdrew her fangs, licked both of Marie's thighs, then turned her head and said, "You see something a monkey would like, huh?"

"Oh, God, yeah."

"Hmm . . ."

She raised her hips and shifted them from side to side, leaving the young crafter with her motionless tongue out and pointing up.

"You're torturing me! I don't deserve any better! I'm just—uh, Widow, I think maybe she's, uh, dead. Like, really dead."

Widow scoffed, then shook her thick black hair back, keeping it all on her back.

"No, slave. I'm learning. I can sense how close she is."

"She's close?"

"Oh, so very close, and she tastes so, so sweet for me now."

"You're going to kill her?"

"Hmm. I'd love to, but no. I don't want to kill."

"You killed that other guy."

"Lucas."

She coughed and swung her leg over to one side, then sat back on her heels and fussed with Marie's hair.

"I didn't mean that. I didn't know he would die."

She scoffed when Igor tipped his head forward and left it there.

"Hey, uh, let's forget about Lucas," she said. "Something else would have killed him anyway. Open the hatch. Quietly."

"As you wish, Widow."

He worked the counterbalanced mechanism and silently, the heavy concrete square tipped up, letting its single light fixture shine into the attic. Widow looked past the cowering man and his burlap sack.

"Wow. There's a lot of stuff up here."

He looked first at her, then around the room.

Pointing, he said, "There are all kinds of machine parts over that way. And there, those crates have all kinds of chemicals or something. Jars and bottles of stuff. Along that wall, there are tools, wires and ropes, electrical stuff. Over there, there are jugs of water too. Plenty of food, too, like for a long time. This is some kind of warehouse."

"That's all good. Anything else?"

He pointed up and said, "It's hard to see, but there are a couple of hoists high up there near the roof. They're on trolleys to move from side to side. They—"

"You have good eyes, slave."

"No, there's nothing good about me! But I climbed up there and looked. They probably used those to lift all this stuff up here and move it around."

"Soon, you'll take an inventory of all of it. I want to know everything that's now at my disposal."

"Yes, Widow."

She stood up and worked her short skirt back down over her hips, then looked up.

"How did you get up there? Show me."

"Yes, Widow. Follow me."

He picked up the candles and led the way to the farthest corner, distant enough that the ceiling light fixture had to leave it to its shadows. Widow walked closely behind him, staying in the bouncing candle glow.

"There," he said. "A ladder. Hard to see it. Just metal rungs on the wall."

"Here's your first task up here in my hidden retreat. Get both of those hoists lowered for our use. Be quick about it."

"Yes! I will!"

* * *

Igor began the climb in the dark, and Widow carried the candles back to the open hatch, where she knelt beside the poisoned girl, whose tongue had slipped back inside.

"Hmm. So helpless and in so much trouble. Mm, and still so soft and juicy."

She brushed aside some of her hair, then tapped her cheek lightly.

"Marie. Wake up."

There was no response, and Widow placed a palm on the girl's chest between her breasts.

"Hmm. No breathing."

She leaned closer, then whispered in her ear.

"Is my little girl lost in a continuous orgasm? Is that where you are, little one?"

She shifted just enough to kiss her lips.

"Oh, did I just feel your tongue? You're still giving me your tongue?"

There was no more sign of the crafter's tongue, so Widow smiled and said, "Let's just see what happens while the vile little slave is performing his duties."

With both hands, she rolled up the girl's t-shirt and left it above her breasts.

"Oh, your nipples! You are still lost in a sweet orgasm, aren't you?"

Marie didn't answer, even when Widow pinched one stiff nipple and wiggled it.

"Mm, so sweet. Such a sweet, obedient little thing now."

She gave the other one a gentle pinch, then stretched it up high and held it there.

"You feel that, don't you? You feel every little touch now."

She tipped her head down and moaned while closing her lips on one nipple, sucking it for a few seconds, then enjoying the other one before sitting back and rubbing both breasts.

"Such a good little girl. Just a soft little doll, lost in an orgasm."

At the sound of two clicks high above, then a low, steady whining, a blend of two slightly different pitches, Widow looked up but saw only blackness that the candles and light couldn't dispel. So, she looked down again.

"Even a cruel touch? Would my little girl like some cruelty? Yes, I believe she would. My little one is orgasming like she never has before, and she craves any touch. Even a cruel touch from a cruel woman."

She heard the whining three stories above her as she stared down at the helpless woman, a helpful crafter that had dutifully created new clothes for her. But now, she lay helpless, not breathing but with excited nipples pointing straight up.

"Mm, so sweet that you're asking for cruelty. Your orgasm compels you to beg for any touch, even if it's cruel. I just know this to be true."

She swung a leg over the girl and sat back lightly on her thighs.

With a light pinch to each of Marie's nipples, she gave them a very light twist.

"Just a little at first. I know you want more cruelty than that. Shh, be patient, little one."

She twisted and lifted, watching for signs of breathing, or a tongue, or anything to suggest that the girl was still alive.

"Oh, I have an idea."

Widow unbuttoned her blouse while looking up, hearing the motor near the roof but seeing only dense shadows.

She flapped the material aside, baring her breasts, then took one in one hand, letting her fingers get her own stiff nipple in a gentle pinch. Her other hand reached again for one of the crafter's breasts, and her fingers got a firm grip on her too.

"Slowly, now, little one. I have cruelty for both of us. If you could speak, you'd be begging me, promising to do anything for any touch I could give you."

She tightened her grip on both of their nipples, letting out a soft gasp as she watched the girl closely.

"Mm, so sweet. So helpless and just lying there for me to enjoy."

With her mouth open, licking her fangs carefully, Widow gave each of their nipples a hard pinch, then stretched them as far as she could, hers out and the crafter's up.

"Oh, that's a little bit cruel, isn't it? What? It's not enough? Hmm. Okay."

She let go of her own breast and took Marie's other nipple, then stretched it up to match the other.

"More? Mm, good idea."

She pulled harder, trying to take the crafter's nipples up to meet the hoist that was approaching steadily.

"Aw, just like that. Now, a good, hard, cruel pinch for my helpless little girl."

Widow squinted from the effort as she squeezed the nearly-dead girl's nipples as hard as she could and held them like that, watching.

And she saw Marie's wet tongue trace a cautious path between her lips, then vanish back inside.

"Oh, I knew it. Mm-hmm, yes, little one. It seems that the orgasm I'm giving you loves cruelty more than anything. Oh, such a sweet little helpless doll you are."

Still twisting and stretching, Widow looked up and saw two shiny metal hooks approaching, each attached to its own thick rope, coming out of the shadows above them. Slightly higher, another similar pair followed.

"Hmm," she said, then released the crafter and smiled at the girl's breasts bouncing gently then resting on a chest undisturbed by even a weak breath.

Leaning forward, she paused with her lips close to Marie's breasts, and said, "Such a good little girl. Oh, what a cruel woman I'm becoming."

She sucked in one of her nipples and moaned while working it in and out between her wet lips before letting it pop back out.

"Such a cruel woman has captured you. And you're so helpless and soft and juicy. Such a juicy little girl."

Sucking on the crafter's other nipple, Widow moaned and tugged it from side to side, then let it go and giggled.

"Mm, just a sweet and juicy baby girl."

She'd just taken in another nipple and was sucking it gently, a moan blended with a hiss, when she looked ahead, past the crafter's lips with her slowly sweeping tongue, and saw Igor on his hands and knees, close and watching her. And licking his lips too.

"Torture!" he whispered, and his eyes never met Widow's.

She grinned and let the girl's stiff nipple slip from between her lips, then opened her mouth enough to show both a smile and a pair of fangs.

"It's all you deserve."

Chapter 50 – Suck the Girl's Nipples, Slave

"That's enough for now for this captured little thing," Widow said, then gave each of Marie's nipples another wet lick. "Let's get out of this attic."

"Yes, Widow," Igor said then reached for the rope connecting the furniture that they'd used to climb up there.

"No, wait. Let's use the hoist. Show me how."

Igor gave the unconscious crafter girl's breasts another stare, wincing at the sight of Widow's saliva picking up bits of candlelight.

She scoffed at the sound of him moaning, then said, "Keep looking at her luscious breasts, slave."

"I will! Yes!"

He did.

"I need a lot of productive work from you. It won't be easy."

He rose up to his knees, then sat back close to Marie.

"I'll do it! All of it!"

"You may touch her breasts."

He looked up with his mouth stuck open.

"I can? I don't deserve it!"

"Stop yelling. No, you don't deserve it. And don't expect such a treat again."

"I won't," he said softly, grinning and reaching one hand toward her.

"Both hands."

He groaned and got a hand on each of the girl's breasts. He held them without moving and grinned at Widow.

"Play with them. Now's your chance."

He started squeezing them and pinching her nipples while mumbling, "I'm just a slave! I don't deserve a treat!"

"You don't."

He kept fondling her and drooling, staring at them when Widow added, "You will never question any command you're given?"

Without looking up, he said, "Uh-uh. No, Widow. Never!"

"Look up."

His hands stayed busy, and he looked into Widow's eyes.

"Lower," she said, then started unbuttoning her blouse, starting at the top and pulling it open with each one she unfastened.

The mutant's hands got rougher, grabbing the breasts and squeezing to point them straight up, and he held them that way when Widow finished, pulled the thin cloth aside, and bared her own breasts.

"You will never hesitate to fulfill my commands."

"Yeah, yeah!"

"Watch my fingers," she said and started fondling her own breasts, "while you suck that poor little girl's nipples. Obey the order."

He kept his eyes on Widow's fingers gracefully rubbing, pinching, and stretching out her own nipples as he leaned forward and found one of Marie's nipples.

"Suck the girl's nipples, slave. Suck them."

In the quiet room, the sound of his wet lips slobbering and nibbling competed only with his moaning.

"And imagine that you're sucking these."

She held both of them up, pointing her nipples toward him. He groaned and kept sucking.

"Oh, these are so much tastier. If you're a very good slave, who knows?"

He moaned and snorted, never letting his lips rest and kept watching Widow touch her own breasts, rubbing them softly for several minutes.

"Stop sucking," she said and kept toying with her own.

Igor backed away, then wiped his lips with the back of his hand.

"Yes. Obey immediately. Now, just watch."

Holding both of her breasts up, she tipped her head forward and let saliva trickle first onto one, then the other. She let them go, then used just one fingertip to swirl the wetness around on her nipples.

"Mm, they feel so good when I'm excited. Mm-hmm. Perfect for sucking."

Igor groaned and began to whimper.

She pinched them both, rubbing her saliva around to coat them everywhere.

"Stand up, you disgusting slave."

He jumped up and held his arms straight down at his sides, and his eyes never left Widow's gentle fingering.

"You're imagining the ecstasy, but you feel the torture."

Almost crying, he said softly, "Yes, Widow."

Smiling, shaking her head at him, she let go of her breasts and began to button her blouse.

"Enough torment for now. Let's get out of this attic."

* * *

Pauline crept along a dark street near Widow's building, oftentimes brushing her ass, covered in tight black bat leather, along the coarse brick walls. She paused in the darkness between two streetlight cones of light and scoffed at the sound of low buzzing coming from every direction.

"Huh. At least I have that."

She held the knife in her left hand up toward the lighted area ahead, a pattern of relative brightness on the sidewalk, then turned only her head at a soft scraping sound coming up from behind. Still looking that way, into a mix of alternating dark and light that persisted until the road had curved too far to the right, she took careful backwards steps.

But she froze at the sight of a large humanoid shape darting across a narrow region of light while scraping along the wall, just like she had done.

"God," she whispered, "what now?"

Her hip bumping along the wall sensed a recess, so she kept watching as she turned the sharp corner and waited just out of sight.

Her pursuer rushed through another light cone, then vanished again in the dark space between light posts.

"A goddamn monkey?" she whispered, scoffing.

She reached the knife behind her, deeper into the alcove, and felt the point strike another wall about an arm's length in.

"Fuck."

The monkey man advanced, rushing through light and hiding in dark.

Jabbing the knife around, Pauline felt the wrecked condition of the brick walls, where many pieces were missing, and she didn't hesitate. She withdrew into the darkness of the narrow space and found a foothold on one side. Stepping up on that, she quickly and quietly found another on the other side, higher than the first.

"Nobody's fucking this ass," she said softly and climbed another step.

From there, she leaned out and saw the would-be attacker hurrying, barely lingering in the darker regions.

She climbed higher, until she was teetering at a place where the hairy man, if he didn't see her, could walk right under her.

"Well," she said, smiling in the dark, "maybe Widow will want to somehow. God . . ."

She leaned out, then whipped her head back inside—the man was close, his back pressed into the warm bricks.

They both listened to the clattering of hooves coming from the same direction, about to make the gentle sweep and come into view.

The man squawked softly to himself, then shimmied farther along the wall just as a pack of oily boars, each a story and a half tall, came around the bend, their snouts either near the pavement or in the air but all of them sniffing.

Pauline held her breath as the monkey man repeated her escape moves, easing himself around the corner, then peeking at the pigs while standing directly under her.

If he was breathing, he did it quietly as he watched the advancing beasts, and Pauline pointed her knife down at him.

The man watched the pigs, and Pauline kept looking down, not seeing anything in the night packed into their tight space.

She heard the pigs getting closer, almost in view, and their snorting got more angry. Their hooves clattered as they walked, and they sometimes dragged them, trying to dig.

Then, all of them stopped. No sounds at all.

She heard one sniff loudly, then a brief rapping of hooves.

Another sniffed then snorted. The scraping and clapping of hooves was coming closer.

Holding her breath and holding her knife, point down, she heard a raspy, humorless voice whisper, "Fuck."

Without a sound, she squatted down, letting the knife lead the way, and felt the minimal resistance as the sharp point found some part of the man's shoulder.

He squealed even before Pauline could rise back up, and he rushed out into the street, yelling, "Fuck!"

She fought her laughter as he looked to the right, at the pigs, then shrieked and ran to the left. A thunder of hooves commenced as the boars roared and squealed and sent mountains of oily, fleshy bodies past Pauline's hideaway.

After the last one had passed and the stomping and monkey-man screeching had dwindled into the night, she climbed back down, then leaned to look out to the left.

There was no sight of any of them and a second later, she heard a raspy, humorless voice scream, then go silent.

"Fuck," she said to herself. "This place really sucks."

She followed after them, again creeping with her back to the bricks until she came to a rough wooden door made up of thick planks.

"Ah, the shortcut. Thanks, Bentley, for wandering your vampire ass around so much. Don't mind if I do."

* * *

Igor reached for the rope that connected the furniture pieces that he'd stacked for them to get up into the attic.

"Yes, Widow. I'll—"

"No. Not the rope. I already said the hoists."

"Sorry, Widow. I'm a stupid slave."

She crawled forward, knelt beside the crafter, then pulled her t-shirt down over her breasts and fluffed up her hair. Igor tied a loop in the furniture's rope, then guided it onto one of the hoist's metal hooks.

"The controls are here," he said. "I lowered those two! For both of the—"

"Too loud."

"Sorry!" he whispered.

He reached up for a pair of small boxes, each hanging by its own electrical cable.

He turned it to show her the buttons on one but when she reached up for it, from where she still knelt on the attic floor beside Marie, he said, "It can't. It's—"

"You'll lengthen those control cables for both hoists. Make it so that the controls can be near the room floor even when the hooks are above the hatch."

"Yes, Widow. There's—"

"Better yet, make it so that both hoists are controlled with one unit."

"Yes, Widow, I will. There's more cable in the attic. I'll just go and—"

"Not now. First, find something to make comfortable loops to go around this tasty girl's ankles."

"Her ankles, Widow?"

"Yes. I want her to hang like that, even while we just lower her out of the attic."

"Why, may I ask?"

"I just . . . want to. I have to."

"As you wish."

He ambled off toward the shadows all around them, and Widow examined the bites that she'd given Marie, pairs of red dots all over her thighs.

"Hmm. A tasty treat for later too. So sweet that she wants it as much as I."

Igor returned with sheets that looked like cotton, small blankets that could have been burlap, more lengths of rope, and strips of thick leather similar to Widow's skirt.

"That," she said, pointing at the leather. "Be quick about it. Make loops and secure them to both hooks of one hoist."

"Yes, Widow. Right away."

He showed an uncanny ability to rig things quickly and pulled tight knots over two hooks.

When he tried placing one of the loops around the crafter's ankles, Widow said, "No. I'll do it."

"Yes. Yes, Widow."

She stood and looked down at the girl lying on her back, studied her for a few seconds, then stooped and rolled her over. Resting herself lightly, almost seated on the girl, she bent one leg, removed her sneaker, then dropped a loop over her foot and gave Igor a thumbs-up sign.

Igor tapped a button, one of the motors whined softly up near the ceiling, and it pulled enough to take out all of the slack as both ropes were lifted higher.

"Hmm. I like this."

She took Marie's other leg, bent it, removed the shoe, and got that one through the other loop.

"Oh, just wait a second."

With both hands, she rubbed up and down on Marie's calves, working her pants down as far as she could on each leg. She gave Igor another signal, he nudged the hooks higher, lifting Marie's legs more, then Widow made him stop with the girl's knees above the attic floor.

"Mm. That's so nice."

One leg at a time, she tugged the pant leg down farther, around the knee, and showed as much of the girl's thighs as she could.

"Cut that?" said Igor. "I can go get—"

"Hmm. Not yet."

Widow rummaged around at the materials that Igor had brought over and found a length of lightweight rope. With a steady smile, she crossed the girl's wrists behind her, then looped the cord around and tied a knot.

Then, she tugged at the pair of taut ropes and said, "Loosen these."

"Yes, Widow."

Igor buzzed the motor enough to relax the crafter's legs, and Widow rolled her back onto her back.

"Now, cut?"

"No."

"Up?

"Yes."

Igor held the button, coaxing a continuous hum high above them and a few seconds later, the crafter girl's legs were straight up. Widow sat back behind her and worked the pants down farther along her thighs.

Then, she wrapped her arms around the girl's legs and pulled herself in close. After a deep sigh, she kissed and licked each of her calves.

"Hmm, so sweet like this. Up, slave. Slowly."

"Yes, Widow," he said, then tapped the button in short bursts, nudging the crafter's legs higher and higher until only her shoulders and head were still on the floor, and Widow stopped him.

"Hold there," she said, then scooted closer.

Reaching around again, with her face pressed into the girl's ass, she unbuckled her belt, slipped it out, then held it while unzipping her pants. She worked the waistband up over the crafter's hips until it was halfway up her thighs.

She handed the belt to Igor and said, "Tie that."

While she held the pants in place, Igor looped the belt around her thighs and tightened it all up.

"Oh, this is so nice," Widow said as she kissed each ass cheek through the thin cloth of her panties. "So sweet, all bound up like this."

Holding the elastic band of the panties with both hands, Widow moaned as she started pushing the flimsy material up, a little at a time, then left it up where it would stay on its own.

"Aw, there we go. What a sweet little thing for me. She's undressed so nicely now."

With her breathing quickening, Widow hissed softly and opened her mouth wide, and Igor held still at the sight of her fangs.

And he made no sound at all as she moaned again while biting into one of Marie's cheeks, just enough to get the points in.

She backed away and licked the two red dots, then giggled softly.

"Oh, just too sweet. Another little bite for my girl."

She bit Marie's other cheek, gave it a soft lick, then backed away.

"Up."

"Yes, Widow."

The motor whined agreeably, and Marie lost contact with the attic floor. Widow stood and took a step back, smiling at the progress she'd made.

"There. That's good."

The motor stopped lifting, and Marie's hair hung down, almost touching the floor.

"Lower this junk so I can get to the floor."

"Yes, Widow."

He quickly got the stack hooked up to one of the other hoist's ropes, then lowered it all down, and Widow held that rope for balance, then the one tying together the items until she was safely standing on the floor.

"Lower the girl," she said after unhooking the pile of items.

"Yes, Widow."

He first started motoring the other hooks back up, but Widow said, "No, leave that. Just bring her down to me."

"Yes. Yes."

Widow watched as her tied-up girl was lowered toward her head first, and she signaled for Igor to stop when their faces were at the same level.

"Oh, you wish to kiss your captor? Aren't you just the sweetest thing."

She began kissing the crafter on her lips and didn't look up at the sound of Igor fighting to get his zipper down.

"Oh, you are a sweet little kisser. So soft and quiet for me now."

She gave her another quick kiss, then said, "Lower. Just a little."

"Yes," he whispered and nudged the girl lower, stopping her when her breasts were even with Widow's face.

"And you want me to notice these again? You must know how much I love tasting them."

Igor's vigorous thrashing got louder, but Widow still didn't look up. Grinning at the sound, she took her time and folded down the crafter girl's t-shirt until she'd bared her breasts.

"Those hang so nicely when I have you captured like this. And I see you're still a very excited little girl. Mm, such a sweet orgasm you're having."

Widow spun her around halfway, then reached around to hold her breasts while she kissed her bare back.

"Mm, and all you can think of is that orgasm. You want cruelty from a cruel woman, don't you? Yes, of course, you do."

She pinched both of her nipples and stretched them forward, swaying the upside-down girl away from her kisses.

Holding her out just by the force of the hard pinching, she said, "Yes, just like that, little one. So much cruelty for such a soft little thing."

To the sound of Igor pounding himself up in the attic, Widow chuckled, pulled the girl farther, and said, "Mm, I do love being cruel. Enjoy that sweet orgasm, little one."

She kissed her back, then relaxed and spun her around to face her.

Looking up, grinning at the sight, she said, "A smart slave would save that just a few more seconds. Lower my little treat."

Still working his oversize irradiated post, he fumbled until he could squeeze the button and get Marie lowering. He watched Widow kissing the crafter's breasts, then her belly as it moved past, then Widow held up a hand, and he stopped her downward journey.

Widow looked up at the furious, desperate stroking from her mutant slave as she unhooked the belt holding the crafter's pants up. After shifting around to raise up her skirt, she moved the belt lower, holding it to both sides with the flat strap across her own ass. Then, still looking up and grinning, she clasped the buckle behind Marie's head and began to tighten it, drawing the girl's face tight between her thighs.

"Oh," Widow said, "the sweet little thing is so, so eager to please the cruel woman who has captured her."

She scoffed at Igor turning himself to not spray her or her captive, then focused on what Marie was offering so close to her own lips.

After a quick kiss, and keeping her lips brushing the girl's soft skin, Widow looked up at Igor, who was still looking down and stroking like a maniac.

"But I'm not always a cruel woman, slave."

Igor panted and shook.

Widow licked her lips, then said, "Sometimes, I'm just a woman, one who loves to love . . ."

Igor groaned and flogged himself.

". . . a soft little girl's very wet . . . pussy."

Still watching the stunned slave, Widow got busy with her tongue and lips, and Igor staggered and almost fell through the hatch before turning away and groaning as he finished himself off.

*   *   *

Pauline pulled shut the heavy wooden door but not before getting her eyes locked on the third door from the right. She walked directly to it, opened it, then slipped into the tunnel that had long before gorged itself on more than its share of the night.

"Damn wind," she said softly as she tread carefully along the wall, touching it continuously with her left hand.

After a few more steps, she scoffed at noticing that the air had calmed, then she reached into her pocket and took out a match. It took a few seconds to find a place on the warm brick wall that wasn't slick with oil, then she struck it there.

And even while it did its momentary flaring dance, she saw the head of a snake level with her face, eyes on hers, and close enough for its snapping tongue to tickle the tip of her nose.

"What the—"

"Shh," someone said, with a voice like cold molten metal.

Pauline tried to take the first step back, away from the snake, but another one quickly coiled around her ankle, startling her enough that she dropped the match and it fizzled out.

"Dammit!"

She tried stepping with her other leg, and that one got snagged too.

"Why you little—"

She'd almost gotten both hands around the snake that was tipping its head from side to side and kissing her nose, but two more of them coiled around her wrists and wasted no time in pulling them around behind her.

"What is this? Snakes?"

"Snakes. Yeah."

"Let me the fuck go!"

"Go where?"

"Dammit! Who's talking?"

"I am. I'm Rodney."

"Dammit, Rodney, get your goddamn snakes off of me!"

"Uh . . . no! Go where?"

"What the fuck is it to you?"

"I'm blind. I eat mutant rats. Bugs if I'm lucky. Oh, and I'm more snake than man. How about that, huh? Reason enough? Shit, give me a fucking break."

"Fine! God! I have a friend named Widow. I was going to—"

"Widow! Yes!"

"You know her?"

"Do you?"

"Uh, yeah. She's incredible. I think I'm kind of in love with her."

"No! Really?"

"I think I am—like, a crazy amount. And I want to be just like her."

"Damn you!"

The snakes began stretching out all of Pauline's limbs and lifting her off of the cave floor.

"Hey, stop that!"

"Uh . . . no!"

"Let me go! What do you want from me?"

"What I wanted from your Widow friend."

"What, for God's sake, is that?"

The snakes all worked together to spin Pauline around and pull her into the mostly human torso, so close that Rodney could whisper in her ear.

"Moisture. Mm-hmm. Oh, yeah."

"What? No, you can't—"

"Shh, now. Yes, I really can."

She twisted and turned, never touching the floor, and the coiled snake limbs Rodney had accepted as his own instead of human arms and legs pulled harder, spreading her legs and forcing her arms straight out to the sides.

"I'm quite strong."

"Yeah, I see! Dammit!"

"I don't see. I told you."

"Goddammit!"

She stopped fighting and said, "Hey. What are you doing?"

"Oh, wait and see!"

"You're not funny, dammit!"

She felt a scaly snake head, then the solid flesh of its body as it circled around her waist, under her t-shirt, then started feeding itself down inside her pants.

"Oh, no you don't!"

"Shh. Uh . . . yes, I do! You, uh, might want to hold still."

Pauline whimpered, then kept herself still as the snake head tickled around with its tongue, probing, sliding around, then found an opening and began to slip itself inside.

Not moving, Pauline whispered, "Don't!"

"Don't what?"

"Don't put that snake in . . . there!"

"In where?"

The snake dove in deeper, and Pauline sobbed and said, "Do I really have to say it?"

"Oh, come on," said Rodney. "I'm blind, I eat rats, I eat bugs, I—"

"Fine! Don't put that snake in my pussy!"

"There, was that so hard?"

"Hard? Dammit!"

"Oh, I feel that. It's like I have a finger way up inside your pussy. I'm going for more."

"Don't!"

"Shh."

Pauline sobbed quietly as the snake wiggled around until it couldn't go any deeper.

"There. Just like that," he said. "A good start."

"Huh? No way are you—"

"Uh . . . yes, I am! It's already begun."

"Oh, God."

She felt another snake under her shirt, slipping around, then finding the very beginning of her ass crack. It slithered down, working its way between her cheeks.

"No! Not in my ass too!"

"Oh, be nice. I promise not to go as far as is possible. Know what I mean?"

"God!" she whimpered.

"Not here today. Haven't seen him."

"Dammit!"

The snake head found a tight, puckered-up part deep between her cheeks and started to twist and push.

"Best to hold still!"

"Oh, God . . ."

"The head's kind of big. Yeah. Sorry. It'll get better after that."

Pauline stifled a scream as Rodney sent the snake head in completely, and she sighed at feeling less stretching from the snake's narrower body.

"See?"

"Damn you."

"Oh, but it gets thicker again real quick. Watch. In the dark."

He laughed while the snake twisted each way, wedging itself deeper and deeper, bringing even thicker parts of itself through the tight opening.

"I wanted to do this to Widow, but I didn't get a chance."

"Huh?"

Rodney spat, then said, "Ugh, her poison. She's toxic, you know."

Pauline felt another snake sliding around her waist, on the other side, then poking around right above the one in front that had already bottomed out.

"Oh, no. Don't you—"

That thinner snake found just enough space to begin diving in, too, riding along atop the other one.

"This is what I wanted to do! Just like this!"

Pauline groaned as the smaller snake, coasting along the very top of the one already inside her, jabbed in, then twisted itself slowly back out. Then, in again and out again. And again. It got itself into a steady rhythm.

"Please. Please, just stop!" she whispered, suspended and penetrated up above the tunnel floor.

"Do you always talk so much on a date?"

"What? You're an insane son of a bitch that—"

A spare snake raced around Pauline's neck and squeezed.

"There! Just like that! Too much yacking!"

Pauline couldn't even gag as four snakes held her by her wrists and ankles, one had penetrated her from behind, very ambitiously, and another had bottomed out in front, with its eager companion sliding along above it, giving steady strokes in and out.

"I might be blind but damn, I sure treat my dates good!"

He loosened the snake noose, and Pauline coughed and sucked in a lot of air.

"Again!" he said and tightened it back up around her neck.

All of the snakes conspired to pull her closer to him and never backed out or relaxed.

He said in her ear, "You just might die here in the dark. Hmm, I do like strangling."

He relaxed the serpent around her throat, gave her only a second to breathe once, then tightened it again.

"Yes. Nice and tight. I don't think I'll loosen that again. You just feel that snake in your tight ass—oh, it just got in there deeper! And that thick one in your pussy. Oh, yeah. And that clever little one is rubbing you just right. That's a quick one!"

Pauline hung there in total darkness, suffocating in silence as the snakes all tried for just a little bit more depth. And they got it.

"So tight around your neck."

All of her limbs went limp.

"Yep. Time to die. Time for you to—hey, what's going on? No, that can't be. It just can't!"

He loosened the hold on her throat, but she was unconscious and her head only hung forward. Listening closely, he smiled at the sound of her weak breathing. The strangler snake slapped her cheeks lightly until she coughed and shook her head.

"Did you just . . . um, no, it can't be."

She nodded and pulled in a few more deep breaths.

"You, uh, you—"

"Hand an unbelievable orgasm. Mm, I still am."

"I felt it! You flooded my snakes!"

He withdrew everything and unwound everything and nudged her to lean up against the wall.

"I can't believe I actually got you to climax! How is that possible? Maybe I'm not as gross as I think?"

She struck a match, waited for it to flash then even out, and looked him over. The thicker snakes were supporting a human torso, and two more, smaller, waved lazily from their anchor points near each of his shoulders.

"No, Rodney. You're gross as hell."

The snakes slowed, he sighed, and his head tipped forward.

"Not your fault, though. It's that snake fuckery you got going on. It's fucked up."

He sighed but didn't look up.

"Rodney."

He looked up, unseeing eyes wet with tears.

"Thanks for the date. You sure know how to treat a lady."

Chapter 51 – The Right Amount of Poison

Pauline walked quietly, almost limping up the stairs then toward the door to Widow's room. Seeing the severe damage it had sustained, she leaned to look in before entering.

The first thing she saw was a woman that she recognized as Marie, the crafter, hanging upside-down in the middle of the room.

"Oh, Widow," she said for herself, then smirked. "Not surprised."

Leaning farther, she looked toward the couch and saw Widow reclining and writing something in a notebook.

"Huh."

She looked up along the thick ropes which held the crafter just above the floor and saw that they passed through a large opening where part of the ceiling had been rotated out of the way.

"Well, the lair is shaping up."

Scoffing while creaking the wrecked door farther open, she took a step inside and met Widow's gaze, who looked up from her work without a smile.

But the smile grew, and Pauline said, "Hey, it's me. Can I come in?"

Widow said, "Yes, of course. Especially with that door being beat to hell."

"Yeah, it really is."

Pauline ambled over toward the couch, sometimes groaning but laughing about it too.

"You okay, Pauline?"

"Sure," she said, then sat when Widow swung her legs off of the couch and sat too. "If being sore from crude sexual abuse, embarrassed from enjoying it, and still tingling from an orgasm counts. Yeah."

Widow grinned and said, "You can't be talking about me. I wasn't that rough."

Pauline tipped her head toward the hanging girl and said, "Uh, I think you're getting close. Is she alive?"

"Yes, she's alive, and she'll be fine. I brought her close to it for my enjoyment, but I didn't push her over that line."

"Uh, you sound pretty sure of yourself."

"I am. I'm learning how my poisons work and how much my victim can—"

"Victim?"

"Well, lover is a better word. Good point."

"Um, that's not exactly what I was thinking, Widow, but sure."

"You know what else I'm finding out? Oh, this is a fascinating thing too. I think I'm instinctively giving just the right amount of poison, just enough so that my, uh, lover isn't completely swamped from it. They can still protest and resist, and they feel like they have a chance."

"But they don't?"

"No. There's no chance of escape. It worked on you."

"Oh my God. Yeah, you're right. There were times that I tried to talk you out of it when it got scary. I remember that."

"It didn't work."

Pauline laughed and said, "God, no."

"You didn't really want it to. It's like a game."

Pauline shook her head and said, "Some game," then smiled at the crafter.

Pointing, she said, "I'd love that too."

"Yes, you did. And you will again. Hmm, maybe right alongside her."

"If that's what you want."

"Mm-hmm. I think I might. I could tie you two together. Oh, maybe one of you not upside-down too."

"Damn. Uh-huh. Then, we could—"

"Have to."

"Yeah, uh, then we'd have to, um, to each other for—"

"For my amusement. Heads tied so nicely in place. Mm-hmm. So, Pauline, tell me about the abuse, embarrassment, and tingling."

"Ugh. It was from someone you know. He—I mean, it—caught me when I—"

"Widow?"

Both women looked at the functioning head of Igor hanging down through the hatchway just enough to be seen.

"Hey," said Pauline, "you have a slave in your attic."

"Yes. You saw me writing? That's his list of chores."

Widow turned to face Igor and said, "Yes?"

"I wasn't listening, I promise!"

"Stop yelling. What is it?"

"I heard your guest arrive, and I suggest you order me to repair your door first."

Widow nodded for a moment, then said, "That hoist is fine? And what of the other one?"

"Yes, Widow, that one is—"

"Damn, you have two hoists? I thought you strung her up from ropes."

"Oh, no, Pauline, this is high-tech. Igor, I accept your suggestion. Delay your activities in the attic and see to the door."

"Yes, Widow. As you wish."

His head zipped up and out of sight, and Pauline said, "You, uh, sound like more of a boss—already, and I just saw you a short while ago."

Widow turned toward her, scoffed softly, then said, "I'm finding that if I welcome whatever changes are coming for me, it progresses much more quickly."

"Yeah. I see that. It's, uh, a little scary."

Widow grinned and said, "You feel fear, little one?"

"Oh, God, I could just melt when you talk like that."

"Or hang upside-down for my amusement."

"Both."

"So, who abused you so expertly that you had yourself an orgasm?"

"He said he met you too. Rodney. Some god-awful mutant snake thing."

Widow laughed and said, "He abused me too! Two snakes for me: one in front, one in back."

"He said you poisoned him."

"My juice. My—"

"I'm melting again . . ."

"Hmm. My juice didn't sit well with him. His loss. He got you with two snakes too?"

Pauline grinned and held up four fingers.

"What? How?"

"One in back."

"He seems a little obsessed with that."

"Yeah, Widow. Uh-uh. Then, a thick one way up in my pussy. Then, a thinner one riding along on top of that one, just jamming in and out."

"So, if my poison hadn't gotten to him so soon, he—"

"Would have jammed your pussy up good too."

"Huh. And the fourth? Down your throat?"

"Oh, no. He strangled me with that one. Told me I was going to die down there in the dark, with snakes in my pussy and ass."

"So, even with Rodney strangling you, you still climaxed?"

"Huh? No, Widow, I think it was because he was strangling me. I seriously didn't think I'd survive. Maybe I'm more of a freak than—"

They both looked at the suddenly silent, two-headed freak hanging enough from the attic to look their way.

"Um," said Pauline, "more than that Junior guy."

They watched as Igor flashed them a grin, then got busy again.

"Worse ways to go," said Widow.

"Huh. I suppose. Like a monkey fucking my ass."

"You don't know, Pauline. You might like it."

"Okay, you're right. I really don't know."

"Are you just claiming you don't know?"

Pauline laughed and said, "I'll never tell. So, Rodney was choking me and jamming snakes everywhere, and he felt it: he felt me orgasming. And you know what? That made his day. Kind of made him feel like he wasn't so gross."

"He really is gross."

"Oh, yeah. But he let me go after that. Shit, I can barely walk."

They turned their heads to watch Igor first lower a box of tools stacked along with a box of metal pieces, then shimmy down the rope himself. Not once looking their way, he picked up his supplies and walked toward the door.

"I can't believe you already have two hoists. That was kind of fun, back up on that mountain."

"Yeah. But this isn't for fun anymore. Pauline, it's some kind of hunger. It's all I could do to stop myself from killing that poor girl."

Pauline looked around and said, "Hey, what about that guy that was here, Lucas? He left?"

Widow looked down and said, "Sort of. He died."

"Oh."

"Yeah. I'm trying not to feel bad about it. I didn't understand about my poisons and gave him too much."

"You can control it?"

"Mm-hmm. It just feels natural. I know just how much to give my, um, someone like Marie," she said and pointed toward the hanging crafter.

"You said he left? What does that—"

"Out the window. Igor tossed him."

"For the bats? Or boars?"

Widow shook her head and said, "Not exactly. That Junior character was coming up here. Remember that muscle freak? Igor and I and Marie hid in the attic. We just wanted to get rid of the body."

"Well, out the window would do it."

"Yeah, and that's not all. Junior is even worse than before. He's got some kind of electrical box stuck on his back. When it's buzzing, he's smart. But when it stops, damn, what a freak show."

"I don't know what that is, but I know someone who probably does."

While Pauline was taking out her small two-way radio, Widow said, "Who?"

Tapping the device, Pauline said, "Mortimer."

* * *

"I met Mortimer," said Widow. "When I first got to the city."

"Alone?"

"Yeah, I was."

"No, him. I'd bet he wasn't. They always travel in packs."

"You're right. First, I met some others, a couple named Isabella and Jonas and a bunch of others. Later, Mortimer came around with even more."

"Creepy?"

"Yes. They seemed like really odd people."

"That's because they're not."

"Not people? What the hell are they, then?"

"I have no idea. Part machine maybe. Or clones or something. As long as you hear that buzzing, they're just weird and not so dangerous. When that buzzing stops, though, you'd better—"

"Run," said Widow. "Yeah, that happened, and I got the hell away from them."

Pauline looked at her radio and scoffed.

"He's not answering."

She stowed the radio in a pocket of her tight leather pants, saying, "He'll see that I called and probably call back. We have an arrangement."

"What kind?"

"They, uh, look for things. People. They have their favorites."

"Go on."

"Mortimer said they're looking for someone to lead them. He talked like they'd be some kind of royalty. I think they're all nuts."

They were sitting close enough together, and Widow reached out to brush some of Pauline's red hair back over her shoulder, then gave her a steady stare.

"You didn't think of offering me to them, did you?"

"No way. Uh-uh, I knew right away you were way too special. And even now, I want to see—"

"Dammit!"

Igor was leaning to look out into the hallway when he cussed, then he hurried back inside and shut the door.

"What, slave?"

Pauline whispered, "Even that's a turn-on. You bossing around your slave."

Widow smiled but kept looking toward Igor.

"Something's coming!" he whispered.

"What?"

"I don't know, Widow! Something on the stairs!"

"Peek your head out there and—"

"Better tell him which one," Pauline said, snickering softly.

"—and see what it it is, slave."

"Yes, Widow," he said, then opened the door just enough to look around and down the hall toward the stairs.

"You're bad," Widow said softly, shaking her head at the red-haired woman close to her on the couch.

Pauline said, "It's only because I'm scared. So many scary things out there."

Widow placed her arm around her and pulled her closer.

"There, there, little one. There are scary things in here too."

Pauline only sighed, and they both kept a watch on the mutant slave at the door, who'd begun waving his hand at them while monitoring the approaching thing on the stairs.

After shaking noticeably for a few seconds, he ducked back inside and closed the door quietly.

"Well?"

"It was a monkey, Widow. A big one."

"How much of a monkey?"

"Probably a five. Big and hairy but looked mostly like a man. Except for that tail."

"He's gone?"

"Sort of. He kept going up the stairs to the roof."

"Not the attic?"

"No, Widow. There are no entries above this."

"Alright. Good. Proceed with the door. Do as much as you can do quietly."

"Yes, Widow."

Something in Pauline's pocket buzzed twice, then went silent.

"That has to be Mortimer."

She took it out and didn't try to free herself from Widow's embrace.

"Yep, Mortimer," she said, then hit a button.

"Thanks for calling back," said Pauline.

A second later, she said, "Wait. I'm putting you on speaker."

She tapped the unit again, then laid it on her thigh, which was pressed up against Widow's, which was bare and almost completely exposed from her short skirt getting hiked up high.

"Alright," said Pauline. "I'm here with Widow, and we—"

"Who's Widow?"

"I meant Scarlet. Widow's just a fun name for her. We—"

"You're where with Scarlet?"

Widow touched a fingertip to Pauline's lips, and she giggled softly and kissed it.

"Nowhere. Just out on the streets. We need to—"

"Which street?"

"Dammit, Mortimer, you don't need to know every little detail, alright?"

"Fine. I'm, uh, asking for a friend."

"A friend, huh?"

"Well, our King, actually."

"You have a king? Since when?"

"Oh, not long ago. King Junior. He's quite a specimen, a real—"

"Wait a second. I've seen that guy. Monster muscles, all sweaty and bloody and oily. That Junior?"

"He's truly magnificent! Yes!"

"Sure. Right. Why the hell would you want to know about Scarlet for that guy?"

"King Junior is of the belief that Scarlet killed his mother. He's not at all happy about that. He'd like to, uh, talk with her about it."

"Talk? Yeah, I believe that," Pauline said, laughing. "We need to ask you—"

"We? You really are with Scarlet? Hello, Scarlet!"

"Hello, Mortimer. Pauline is correct. We'd like to ask—"

"And I'd like to know—"

"Don't interrupt me again," Widow said, with no honey and no expectation of being challenged.

Pauline slipped out from under her arm and backed away, staring at her.

"I need to know what is going on with Junior. He's been modified?"

"Uh, yes. He, uh, he—"

Pauline said, not smiling but still staring, "You scared him. Not easy to do."

"Pauline? Is that you again?"

"Answer me, Mortimer. Forget about Pauline."

"Yeah, uh, okay. Um, he, when we first met him, was just a big simpleton kind of guy. But he bit into one of our community, and that—"

"He was biting you, and you still made him your king?"

"So, it's okay for you to interrupt me?"

"Yes."

A few seconds of silence passed, with Pauline shaking her head and Widow offering her only a brief smile.

"Okay. Alright, then. Uh, when he bit, he swallowed some circuitry things, those things that we, uh, that make us who we are."

"Go on."

"Okay. He, uh, got some of them inside him, and those things, from that guy in particular, are kind of uh, self-replicating."

"They're growing in him?"

"Yes. And multiplying. We can't predict what will happen with him because he was already mutated in some horrible way. No telling what all that stuff will do to him."

"I think I have some idea."

"You've seen him? He's alive?"

"You could call it that. What is that thing on his back?"

"Oh," Mortimer said, then paused to laugh. "That's just a little experimental thing I whipped up. It's a mobile continuity module. We watched the King go insane when the buzzing stopped, and he agreed to have that installed. I'm not sure that was a good idea, though."

"It wasn't. He's part human, part whatever the hell you are, and part fireworks show too."

"Oh, that's not good. Not good at all, even though this dark world could benefit from some fireworks. Anyway, I'm afraid I might have created a monster."

"He already was a monster."

"Not like this, Scarlet. He might be about the most dangerous thing around now, whether his back buzzer is buzzing or not."

"And he's determined to find me?"

"He's kind of mindless, but he has a one-track mind too. Yeah, he wants you bad. The best thing you can do is find him, let him kill you, then he can return to reign as our magnificent King."

"And if I kill your king first?"

She held Pauline's gaze as Mortimer's laughter came through the small radio for several long seconds.

"Good luck with that. Because when that back-mounted buzzer of his stops? The slaughter begins."

* * *

Pauline saw that Mortimer had signed off, so she stashed her phone in a pocket while watching Widow, who only stared straight ahead and took measured breaths.

"All I want . . ."

Pauline waited, and even Igor stopped working to listen.

". . . is to be left alone. In a quiet corner. To feed."

Softly, from the other end of the couch, Pauline said, "Mortimer's probably exaggerating. Junior can't be that bad."

Widow turned to hold her gaze.

"Oh, no? I saw him and heard him. I don't know what it would take to stop him."

"Even just your voice, Widow. Maybe that would—"

"And if I learn that it has no effect on whatever he's become, then what?"

Pauline shook her head but didn't answer, and Widow turned to again look across the dimly lit room.

"And even if I manage to bite him, would my poisons have any effect?"

"Um . . ."

Widow scoffed, then looked at the crafter, still hanging by her ankles. She'd begun taking slow, deep breaths, and her nipples were still obvious against the thin t-shirt material from it being pulled tight and tucked into her work pants again.

She turned her head to address Igor.

"Let that rest for now, slave."

"It's almost done, Widow. I just need to get the lock installed and working."

"It will have to wait."

"Uh, okay, Widow. What about the monkey? He's going to come back down sometime."

"Maybe a bat will devour him."

"Could be. Sure. Okay."

He closed the door, and it clicked shut, but he couldn't lock it. Leaving his tools and materials, he began walking back toward the couch.

"Stop. The crafter is awakening. Lower her and leave her there on the floor."

"Yes, Widow."

He turned and began to fulfill her command, but she halted him again.

"First, take these couch cushions and arrange them near the hatch."

She turned enough to see Pauline staring at her, then tipped her head up, and they both stood. Igor gathered up the cushions and pillows, and the two women sat back on what was left of the couch.

They watched as Igor arranged the cushions, then hurried up into the attic, got the motor whining high above near the attic's roof, and lowered the crafter gently beside them. He rushed back down, unhooked the girl, and left her on her back.

Caught up on his assignments, Igor stood and waited for Widow to give more orders.

"You have a list of tasks. Go up in the attic and get started."

"Yes, Widow. If the monkey—"

"Never mind about the monkey. Raise the cable and close the hatch."

She turned toward Pauline and said, "I do not wish to be disturbed, slave. Wait for my call."

"Yes, Widow."

He bowed, then started climbing the rope, but Widow stopped him midway up.

"This is not on your list, but you must do this first: prepare two more leather loops for the other hoist."

He bowed his head, still hanging onto the rope, and said, "As you wish, Widow."

She and Pauline watched him shimmy the rest of the way, up and out of sight. A soft click got the motor humming, and the ropes and their hooks were soon out of sight too. With a soft thump, the thick and heavy concrete hatch closed.

"You're getting better at giving orders," Pauline said, smiling. "You probably scared that little freak."

"Fear is a good motivator," Widow said, then turned to look at Pauline. "I have some fear of Junior."

"You can handle him."

Widow shook her head and said, "I'm not so sure. But even a trace of fear about him is . . . making me hungrier."

Pauline waited, looking from one eye to the other.

"Perhaps you should be afraid, little girl."

Pauline choked a soft giggle before it grew, then said, "Um, of you? Uh, maybe a little."

Widow kept a steady gaze into Pauline's eyes and said, "You have never seen me this hungry. All I want is to satisfy my hunger."

Pauline tried laughing again, but it ended quickly with a short cough.

"Uh, which one?"

Widow smiled and said, "There is only one. And you will satisfy it."

"Um," Pauline said and squirmed back as far as she could go, "you really are starting to scare me."

"Oh?"

"Uh, yeah. Like before, on the mountain, you do all kinds of fun stuff, but it's just for fun, right?"

There was no change of expression on Widow's face.

Pauline added, "Maybe I'll just leave before that monkey can—"

"Go to the cushions," Widow said in a serious but ordinary voice.

"Uh, how about later? I should probably just—"

Widow's next words rolled out like thick, simmering honey.

"Go to the cushions, little one. Play along or I'll bite so deep you'll have no choice."

Pauline instantly rose from the couch, took one step as directed, then paused with her eyes focused on the couch cushions and the slowly breathing crafter girl.

"Um . . ."

A streak of sweet syrup bubbled along with the honey.

"Hmm. Crawl to the cushions, little girl."

Pauline whimpered softly and dropped to her knees.

"And, for now, think only of tempting me with every move of your ass."

She crawled quietly as ordered, and Widow smiled and watched her ass shifting gently, wrapped in tight leather, as she obeyed the order.

Chapter 52 – No Matter How Cruel and Uncaring

While Pauline was crawling toward the couch cushions and the prone crafter, she managed a smile, but Widow couldn't see it. She'd gotten up from the couch and was following closely, watching every curve and the slow, teasing crawl Pauline was performing for her.

Walking, she struck her sharp heel into the floor with every step, and she added a hint of honey to every word.

"Lie down on the cushions, close to the girl."

Pauline laid herself down, then stayed on her back next to Marie.

"On your side. Face her."

Keeping her breaths quiet and hiding away any trace of a smile, Pauline got herself nearly touching the crafter, who was off of the cushions and on the wooden floor.

Widow knelt on a folded cloth on the other side of Marie, then sat back on her heels. She brushed the girl's hair aside to reveal her pretty face and lips that were sometimes moving as she began to awaken from the poisons Widow had given her.

"I know her name," Widow said, watching Pauline closely. "But she is no one anymore. Just a girl."

Pauline looked up and met Widow's gaze.

"I have captured her. She is mine now."

Pauline nodded and didn't look away.

"I'm letting her rest and recover, but I'm not done with her. And do you know why?"

Her red hair barely moved when Pauline shook her head lightly.

"Hunger, little Pauline. It's as simple as that. Touch her hair."

Pauline looked first, then raised herself up onto her forearm. She reached out and touched, then brushed back some of the girl's hair.

"Soft. Even her hair."

Pauline nodded and kept fussing with it.

"So soft everywhere. Untuck her shirt."

Pauline coughed softly, then pinched the thin material and tugged it out from behind the waistband of the pants.

"Her belly is soft too. Touch it. Keep your hand there."

Pauline looked up at Widow while sneaking her hand under Marie's t-shirt, then she kept her palm flat against her belly.

"Soft?"

"Uh-huh. Yes."

"You see her breasts, how they show the excitement she still feels from what I've already done with her?"

Pauline kept her hand on the crafter's belly but looked at her breasts. The girl's nipples were two sharp points under the thin cloth, up above the soft curves of her breasts.

"She, uh, yes. I see."

"Keep touching her, keep enjoying the sight of her breasts, and listen to not just what I say but the voice I use. Can you do that, little one?"

Pauline started to grin but lost it quickly, then she nodded and said, "Yes."

"Good. I'm going to roll her over and bind her wrists but not yet. I want her awake and knowing clearly what is happening to her. With her wrists tied tightly and her arms straight, I'll wrap her arms all the way up and tie a tight knot. Can you see how that will be?"

Pauline nodded and didn't look at Widow.

"She'll be more helpless like that. She might suspect that she'll be bitten again, but it will still be a shock to her when my soft kisses on her neck become a sharp, quick, deep bite."

Widow smiled at Pauline breathing more rapidly.

"Can you imagine the feeling of a soft kiss becoming a sharp bite?"

Pauline only nodded.

"Yes, it's not hard to imagine. That bite will settle her down nicely for me. I do love a little girl that has had some of her defiance taken away. She might protest when I remove her pants, but her voice will already be so much weaker. It will only be amusing for me."

Widow used both hands to slip Marie's pants farther up along her calves, then she caressed each leg for a moment.

"Mm, so soft."

She got a solid hold on one of her ankles and said, "I'll tie this ankle to the other one, then perhaps add more bindings just beneath the girl's knees. Can you imagine that? The girl will already be feeling my poisons in her, and she might have a vague thought of wanting to run for her life. But her captor has just bound her legs. All that soft skin of her legs and only her very thin panties to cover her soft ass. Hmm, so soft and smooth. And she'll start to fear that no escape is likely."

Widow released the girl's ankle, then caressed her way up her leg, giving extra attention to the inside of her thigh, all the while noting that Pauline's eyes remained on the girl's breasts.

"I'll bend her legs, tied together so nicely, then fasten them to the bindings around her wrists. I'll pull that tight. With each tug, she'll feel the trap becoming inescapable, and she'll start to wonder why even that realization—that she's becoming hopelessly ensnared—adds to the very gentle orgasm that's just getting started for her."

Widow's hand caressed higher, and she dragged her fingers across the girl as high up as she could between her thighs, then let her hand rest on Pauline's.

"She'll be lying very still for me, and she won't struggle much when I hold a thick binding across her lips. When I command her to open her mouth and accept it, she will. And I'll pull it in tight. Oh, so tight in the pretty mouth."

She paused to enjoy the sight of Pauline's quickening breaths.

"And do you know why I want it so tight?"

Pauline only shook her head and rarely blinked.

"Because my soft little girl will be locked into a scream. A very silent scream. Mm, a silent scream and an orgasm at the same time for my soft little thing."

She patted Pauline's hand, then rubbed it lightly while saying, "Before I lie beside her, I'll add another binding in her pretty mouth. She'll be struggling to breathe with so much between her lips, and I'll pull back on that new one, tipping her head up, and tie that to her wrists too."

Pauline didn't see it, but Widow grinned at the sight of her staring at the girl's breasts and nodding.

"And just like that, the little girl is completely helpless. She can't even move. I'll lie beside her, then, and kiss the soft skin of her neck. I'll tell her to be a good girl and stay very still, and the only sound in my room will be my captive fighting to breathe. That's when I'll slip my fangs into her. They're so sharp that there can't be any resistance. The points will sink in so deep, and we'll lie there together as if we're sharing just one orgasm."

Widow gently nudged Pauline's hand up farther under Marie's t-shirt, over the smooth skin of her belly, and smiled at Pauline's hand covering one of the girl's breasts.

"Yes, she's so soft. Isn't she a soft little thing?"

Pauline mumbled, "She's soft. A soft . . . little thing."

"Like two lovers, we'll lie here together as I enjoy all of the sweet juices she's giving me. And she is giving them to me. By then, she's starting to wonder why she wants nothing more than to be sweet and juicy for me. And she'll find that the more she thinks that way, the stronger her orgasm becomes."

Pauline rubbed and squeezed the breast, then the other.

"Mm, so sweet and juicy. With enough bites, she won't even think of breathing. She'll be such a quiet little girl for me. I'll roll her over onto her side, and she'll offer me her very soft breasts too. I'll see that her nipples are quite stiff, even though the soft little thing isn't breathing anymore."

Pauline's breaths were quiet but getting choppier.

"Can you see how wonderful my little girl will be for me? She'll be offering me her soft breasts for whatever I want of them. Without even the slightest breath to disturb them, she'll hold them so still for me. And she'll be surprised by her desire that I be a cruel captor. She'll know that cruelty will only add to the uncommon orgasm that she's feeling, one that she suspects will never end."

Pauline kept rubbing the girl's breasts, and Widow reached for the t-shirt's hem, then peeled it up and out of the way. Pauline stopped rubbing and held one of the girl's breasts, squeezing just enough to help the nipple point straight up at the closed hatch to the attic.

"But even a gentle kiss would fuel her orgasm."

Widow brushed back Pauline's hair on one side, then the other.

"Mm, just a gentle sucking would feel so good to such a soft, juicy little thing that has become oh so helpless."

Pauline let one deep choppy breath out, and Widow moved her hand to the back of Pauline's head, then began coaxing her to lean forward.

The red-haired woman didn't resist. When her lips were close, Widow released her.

"Such a soft, helpless little girl. She wants so bad to feel lips gently sucking on her."

Pauline groaned and leaned enough to part her lips, then squeeze them tight around the crafter's nipple.

"Aw, there we go. Such a good girl for me now."

Pauline nodded softly and kept suckling.

"All that I described just now—I could do all of that to you."

She only let out a soft groan and kept her lips on the crafter.

"But I feel so desperate and in danger that I might not be able to stop. Once I get you helpless and start biting, I might not want to stop."

Pauline moaned and shifted over to the girl's other breast.

Widow played with her thick red hair and said, "Yes, you wouldn't mind. You wouldn't mind at all. Such a good girl."

* * *

While Pauline was busy sucking Marie's nipples, Widow got behind her and brushed her hair back, exposing her neck.

"Yes," she whispered to her. "You feel how soft she is, and it reminds you of how soft you are too."

She kissed her neck, then said, "Such a very soft little thing. So soft and warm."

She let her hot breath touch the skin of her neck, then said in her ear, "You do need a gentle little bite, don't you?"

Pauline only nodded and didn't stop.

"Of course, you do. Just a tiny one for you now."

She eased her fangs in, and Pauline didn't make a move to escape. A quiet few seconds passed, and Pauline sighed and slumped forward a small amount, almost lying atop the prone crafter girl.

After removing her wet fangs, Widow grinned and said, "Mm, just like that. You might have thought this was just for fun, but you feel what I just gave you, don't you? Yes, you do. Just the right amount. You'll be so much more cooperative with even a modest orgasm that just won't stop."

Kneeling, she coaxed Pauline around until she was seated and got herself close behind her. She reached around and held the hem of her t-shirt.

"Let's start with this," she said and began lifting up the shirt.

She rubbed the hem several times across Pauline's breasts before taking it up higher, and Pauline raised her arms to help.

"Oh, such a good girl for me."

She lifted it more, got it out of the way, and let Pauline's hair fall onto her bare back, where she fluffed it out and arranged it, then touched her skin gently all over.

"Just lovely. Lean back, now, little one."

"I like when you call me that."

"Hmm. I like calling you that. You see how I've allowed you to speak?"

"Mm-hmm. And I can still say no."

Widow laughed and shook her head.

"I have allowed that, too, little one. Even while saying it, though, you know that you have no hope of stopping me."

Holding Pauline's shoulders, Widow guided her to lie back into her, then reached around for her pants. With Pauline's hands gently riding along on top of Widow's, Widow unfastened the black leather pants, then unzipped, then began working the tight material down.

"Help, little one. Even though you might fear what's coming."

"Yes."

Pauline moaned softly and shifted her hips up and around, and Widow was able to strip the pants down along her thighs. A few kicks from Pauline and help from Widow got the pants loose and tossed aside.

"Mm, just panties now. And soon, so very helpless for me."

She leaned Pauline back into her and again moved aside her hair.

"Mm, just so sweet to bite. Another little bite for my girl."

"You can make it a bigger bite if you want. I know you can't hardly help yourself."

"Hmm. It's so sweet how I'm keeping you right where I want you. Any thoughts of fleeing this danger have faded, and you can barely even consider that."

Pauline groaned softly as Widow sank in her fangs and held her in the quiet room. Both pairs of eyes were focused on Marie's breasts, still wet from Pauline's sucking and licking.

After ending the bite and with Pauline relaxed and calm in her arms, Widow said, "Aw, we're getting there. Such nice little bites. But my girl wants to be helpless for me, doesn't she?"

Pauline nodded.

"How helpless?"

"Mm. Completely."

"Good girl. Lie down for me, precious girl."

Pauline tipped then laid herself flat on the cushions, and Widow helped to get her completely on them and lying facedown. She reached into a nearby bag and took out a large roll of narrow gauze, then tore off a long piece.

"Just enjoy the beginning of that special orgasm you're already feeling. You must wonder by now if I'd ever be able to stop myself. I'm becoming so cruel and heartless."

"You should be cruel. You have to."

"Hmm. You don't want me to stop, and maybe I won't this time."

She jerked Pauline's arms behind her, causing her to gasp, then crossed her wrists, then wrapped them tightly and tied a secure knot. Before continuing, Widow sat back on her heels and observed what she'd done.

"That is such a tempting sight: wrists tied together and so much soft, vulnerable skin. You're so soft everywhere. Mm, only those tiny panties to hide the rest. Let's make sure those arms never again come loose."

"Um, never?"

"You can just wonder about that, little one."

Widow waited and watched for a few seconds, then said, "And still, no attempt to get away. So cooperative for me."

Using many pieces of gauze, she looped around Pauline's arms all the way from her wrists to the very top, then tied it tightly.

"Do you remember what's next, precious little one?"

Pauline only moaned softly and said, "My legs?"

"Yes, let's get those soft legs tied up nicely too."

She tore off more gauze, then paused with the long strands hanging from her hand.

"While I'm binding your legs, you'll start to accept that their only real use is to move around your tastiest parts, the juiciest, and bring them to me. All that matters about you is that you're tasty and juicy."

She nodded at the sound of Pauline sighing but not disagreeing.

"Oh, your arms, too, precious little girl. They're so unnecessary."

She rolled Pauline onto her back, hiding her bound arms underneath and leaving her breasts and hips highest above the cushions.

"See?" she said, then rubbed both of her breasts, one after the other, jiggling them around and giggling. "So soft. No need for arms and legs anymore."

She ran her fingertips down over her belly, then caressed the insides of her thighs.

"Hmm, nothing but soft and juicy, all ready and offered for a cruel woman's hungers."

Pauline's breaths were becoming more rapid, raising and lowering her breasts.

"Such soft things to offer. So sweet," she said, then promptly rolled her over to face down and put a hand on one of her ass cheeks. "So soft and luscious on this side too. Hmm, such a soft, juicy little treat."

Then, she tipped up both of her calves and bound her ankles together with many loops before reaching for more strips.

"Hmm, so sweet. Let's just tie my little girl up like a nice little farm animal."

She was about to tie her ankles to her wrists, but she stopped and looked toward the door.

"Hmm, I wonder . . ."

Pauline turned her head on the cushion and said weakly, "About what?"

"We'll just have to see. If it's meant to be, little one . . ."

After letting Pauline's legs down, she rolled her onto her side, facing Marie.

"Let's try this instead, little girl."

She looped the length of gauze around her thighs, just above her knees, then fed it around as many times as possible before tying a knot.

"Oh, such soft skin. And getting so helpless for whatever amusement a cruel woman wants."

She smiled at seeing Pauline nodding softly.

"Mm-hmm, such a good girl. Okay, let's just,"—she began nudging Pauline's knees close, squeezing then up against her breasts as she lay on her side—"set you up so nicely. Yes, good girl."

"Not like a, uh, hog?"

"Mm, something better for . . . what might soon happen."

"Huh?"

"Shh, little one."

Using a much longer piece of gauze, Widow worked it under Pauline many times, each time pulling her thighs in closer and pressed against her body. She finished the last two loops to include Pauline's shins, folding her up tightly. She tied a snug knot and rolled her onto her back, trapping her bound arms beneath her and leaving her hips raised up above the cushion.

"Yes, just like this."

While she brushed Pauline's hair away from her face, she said, "Think about how helpless and vulnerable you've become."

"You like that," the completely bound redhead whispered, her voice barely loud enough to be heard.

"Mm, like you can't imagine. I'm so hungry to have a sweet, juicy little thing as helpless as she can be."

"I . . . I sure am."

"Should you really trust such a cruel woman?"

Pauline shook her head softly and kept a steady gaze up at Widow.

"No, it's not wise at all. Yet, here you are, all packaged up so nicely for absolutely anything, no matter how cruel and uncaring."

She leaned forward and kissed her on her lips, then stayed close and said, "Because you already know that no matter what happens now, all you'll keep feeling is that sweet, unfamiliar orgasm. I feel it, too, little one."

With one hand, she caressed her captive's ass through the thin material of her panties while kissing her for thirty seconds.

"Mm-hmm. We're feeling it together. And I don't want to stop. I want to bite you and never stop. Not until you're—"

The doorknob cranked, and the door creaked in.

Pauline couldn't see, but Widow looked, then leaned close to her to say, "Hmm, ready for some fun, little one?"

She looked down at Pauline's eyes and grinned at the confused expression.

"Yes, I do think you want some fun. And even if you don't,"— she reached out and tested her taut bindings, rocking her gently— "you're just too helpless to stop anything."

She looked back toward the door.

"No, you can't stop anything at all."

"Hey, uh, Widow," she said, soft and breathless. "Maybe you—"

"Shh, precious little girl."

Pauline groaned softly, causing Widow to look down at her again, and she said, "Whatever you're thinking, Widow, you—"

"Shh, pretty thing. When you offered to be my soft, helpless little girl, you agreed to whatever I wanted from you."

Widow smiled toward the doorway while leaning forward and kissing Pauline's forehead.

"Hmm. You helpless, soft little thing. You're just a juicy little baby girl. And there are so many ways for me to enjoy you."

Chapter 53 – Oh! So Much!

Widow kept kissing Pauline's forehead and sometimes smiled at the occasional soft whimper that came from her. She gave her another kiss, then backed away enough to speak close to her ear.

"I won't even bind your pretty mouth, sweet girl. I'm just sure you'll want to kiss someone, and I'll kiss you. Mm-hmm, I'll kiss those pretty lips of yours—while something exciting is happening."

Pauline began a weak effort to speak, but Widow covered her mouth with her hand. She looked up again at another hand on the doorknob and a face with a curious expression.

"It's okay," Widow said, sending warm honey in that direction too. "Come closer."

The hand stayed on the doorknob, and the head tipped, eyes staring.

Widow coughed to clear her throat, then poured into her voice a substantial measure of melted sugar.

"Come closer, but do only as I say."

The hand remained on the entrance door's knob even as the figure crouched, not coming closer, and the head tipped the other way, eyes staring.

Grinning, Widow leaned down and kissed Pauline's forehead, still watching as the intruder rose up to its full height, then began slow, hesitant steps toward them.

With her lips warm against Pauline's ear and a hand still stifling her feeble attempts at speech, she whispered, "You feel how completely helpless you are, and you're desperate to know what's going on. Soon enough, pretty girl."

She gave her a kiss on the lips, then licked them a few times before returning to her ear and covering her mouth again.

"You feel how vulnerable you are, all tied up like a scrumptious little treat. And you're wondering who's being invited inside. Hmm, you can't even see."

Pauline groaned softly into Widow's hand but couldn't get free enough to speak.

"Oh, so sweet. Yes, let's be sure to keep you quiet for now. So soft and helpless and quiet for me."

She looked up, smiling as the invader took a few steps closer, stopped, crouched and stood up quickly several times, then paused with a tipped head.

Widow shifted around to one side of her bound redhead captive and leaned enough to keep her face over Pauline's.

"I'll tell you, then I'll kiss you. And even if you had some dream of protesting, my kiss, just my kiss alone, will give you more poisons. You'll forget any silly hopes of stopping this. No, little one, I'm going to make you want it and believe it's your true desire."

She closed the distance and kissed her open mouth, then, after a few seconds, giggled softly and backed away.

"Mm, a tongue for me still. Such a cooperative little girl. Have some more of my delightful poisons."

She extended her tongue, and Pauline whimpered softly and sucked on it for several seconds while Widow caressed her hair.

"There you go. Yes, even my kisses are sweet and juicy with my poisons."

She gave her another kiss, then stayed close.

"You," she said, grinning, "are a helpless little girl that's about to get fucked . . ."

She kissed her again, then rubbed their noses together.

". . . by a very, very horny . . . monkey man."

Pauline's soft groaning got smothered by Widow's wet lips, and she kept the captive woman's mouth covered until she became quiet again.

"It's okay, little one. Oh, except I think he's a five. A big, wild, horny five."

Pauline started to whimper, and Widow's kiss stifled it again. She held their lips together until Pauline had quieted again.

"There. That's better. Such a quiet little thing now. Do you see how cruel and uncaring I'm becoming? Oh, little girl, it only adds to my orgasm. It's already stronger than it's ever been, and I'm losing my mind."

She looked toward the approaching man, whose member was rigid and obvious where it lay to one side inside his baggy trousers. As he walked, his horizontal tail swayed enough with each step that Widow scoffed before looking into his eyes.

"Come closer," she said, her voice dripping with hot sugar. "See what she offers you?"

The tall man-monkey took a few steps closer, snarled at Widow, showing big stained teeth, then stopped and said, "Sex."

"Mm-hmm. Isn't she beautiful?"

The man looked Pauline over while licking his lips, then looked back into Widow's eyes.

"Sex. Me."

"Mm-hmm. She's offering you her very soft and tight pussy."

"Wet."

"Mm, yes. It's very wet for you too."

The man took two more steps and stood close enough to kick his bare feet into Pauline's ass, which was pointing toward him and covered by only a thin layer of stretchy cloth.

He dropped to his knees and touched her ass with one hand, keeping his mouth open and his teeth together but chattering softly.

Widow blended in some molasses and said, "Oh, but do stop those teeth. They're too—"

He snapped his eyes to her and snarled with his lips peeled back.

"Oh, um, that's fine."

He growled once, then looked again at Pauline's ass. With both hands, he pulled the top edge of his filthy pants down just enough to let his hard tool flop out, and he rested it in the warm line where Pauline's thighs met.

Widow smiled at the sight of it and said, "Mm, such a big one you have. She feels it there. She knows now how big it is."

"Big."

"Mm-hmm. Yes."

"Widow," Pauline said softly, "it's too danger—"

"Shh, little one. I'm too hungry to care."

He looked up when Widow moved her arms, and he watched for only a second as she quickly unbuttoned her blouse. But after that quick look, he snarled again, reached up for her blouse with both hands, and jerked it down over her shoulders, sending her breasts bouncing out into the open.

"Hey," she said, sugar coating the words, "there's no need to—"

He snarled and grabbed a fistful of her black hair and shook her head around.

"Hey!" she yelled, her voice back to normal. "Stop that!"

He snarled loudly and gave her head another rough shake before letting go.

Widow inhaled deeply, jutting the pair out, and said, "Do you like the sight of them?"

"Yeah. Like."

Widow looked down as Pauline's lips moved slowly, mouthing the word, "No!"

"Shh, now, pretty little girl, he's only a five. Maybe."

She looked up when the man shrieked and began jabbing his stiff rod at Pauline.

"Hey," Widow said, her voice dripping molasses again, "patience."

He stopped but stared at her with his face twisting in a silent snarl.

"Yes, patience. Good monkey."

"Good."

She leaned closer to Pauline and said, "Let's just call him a monkey for fun. Mm-hmm, he's just a monkey."

Then, she leaned over her, swaying her breasts above Pauline's face, and bit into the soft skin on the side of her calf.

She sucked for a moment, and Pauline relaxed more in her bindings. Widow backed out her pointy teeth, licked the two punctures, then sat back on her heels.

From there, she leaned to speak in her ear.

"Better?"

"Mm-hmm," she said weakly. "Oh, I feel that. Mm . . ."

"Hmm. This is the question I want you to answer, you sweet, vulnerable little girl, who's been poisoned just the right amount. Would you like a very hard, savage monkey cock in your soft wet pussy?"

Pauline hesitated.

Widow giggled once and said, "My voice is barely working on him. I don't think I can stop him now anyway. You want to get fucked by a monkey, don't you?"

Pauline didn't smile, but she nodded just once, then frowned and said, "But he . . . he won't stop."

"Nonsense."

"Widow, it's only your hunger that—"

"Shh. Play along, or I'll bite really deep next time."

Pauline stayed quiet and nodded.

Widow giggled and said, "Mm, this is a fun game, how I'm giving just the right poisons. Yes, little one. You just have to play along."

She kissed her, then moved back to speak in her ear.

"Are you sure, precious one? It's quite a large . . . monkey cock."

Pauline held her eyes shut, then smiled, nodded, and whispered, "Um, yes."

"Aw, such a dirty little girl. I knew by the way you talked about it before that you might want to give yourself to a monkey. You just couldn't admit it to me. Oh, sweet little thing, you're right where you want to be."

Pauline sighed but didn't agree.

"Mm-hmm. You're a naughty girl, but you're not completely sure. Oh, I see that your panties are very stretchy, so let's keep those on. He can push against that cloth, right into your pussy, and it won't be like he put his hard cock in you at all. You'll never have to tell anyone that you gave your pussy to a monkey. Okay?"

The bound redhead nodded and licked her lips.

Widow looked up and saw that the man was already stabbing at her, stretching the cloth into her.

Widow scoffed, looked up at him, and said, "She's all yours. Like I could stop you anyway."

He looked at the ceiling, chattered his big teeth a few times, then began jerking his hips forward, driving in deeper.

Widow, leaning around to watch, smiled at the sight and said, "Yes, just like that. Oh, you're really getting in there. Good boy."

She didn't look up at him when his teeth chattered again. She only watched as he kept stretching the sheer pantie material, forcing it in farther with every push. A few times, when he backed away far enough, she saw how the wet cloth had stayed tucked in tight, waiting for the man's next penetration, which always arrived quickly.

"Mm-hmm," she said, "just like that. Such a helpless human pussy for you."

The man lunged his hips forward, driving it in deeper and stretching the panties to the point of ripping.

"Yes, you like it even more because she's so helpless for you."

He groaned and drove in farther.

Widow moved back around and whispered in Pauline's ear, "You have a hard monkey cock in you, little girl. Such a brutal monkey cock in your soft pussy. You've wanted this so bad."

Pauline managed a very weak smile, nodded, then said, "Mm-hmm. I didn't know until now. But you knew."

Widow said, "Yes, I did know. It's something you've wanted for a long time. And I also know this: you wish that cloth wasn't in the way, don't you?"

She watched as Pauline lay quite still, not nodding or smiling.

Slowly and weakly, she said, "You won't tell?"

"Tell the man you live with that you let a wild monkey fuck you? Hmm, I might. Yes, I almost certainly will. In fact, I promise that I will tell him. You still want it, don't you?"

Pauline nodded weakly, then said, "Yes."

"Oh, such a good girl that's lost in my poisons. You want to get your wet panties out of the way, even if I plan to tell on you?"

"Mm-hmm. Yes."

"Of course, you do. Let's let you feel what you've wanted so badly. I could tell that you've wanted a monkey to fuck you and not just in your ass. Oh, no, you've wanted a hard monkey cock right there in your pussy."

Reaching around with both hands, Widow got a good grip on Pauline's panties, then said to the man-monkey, "Back that dangerous thing out for just a second."

He did, but he held it close, snarling and sometimes swiping a hairy hand, trying to grab Widow's hair.

She backed out of his reach, dodging his grasp, and said, "Oh, you're just too wild, aren't you?"

"Sex."

Holding his intense gaze, she leaned closer and got a grip on Pauline's panties.

"Mm, here we go," she said, then wiggled the flimsy wet garment up and left it as a thin, tight strap around her thighs.

"Oh, so much softness. So helpless."

The hairy man didn't wait for the go-ahead from Widow, his eyes frantic and breaths quick as he stared at what Pauline had waiting for him tight between the smooth skin of her thighs. Not even a second after Widow had bared Pauline for him, he drove himself halfway in.

"Get ready," Widow said with a chuckle.

Grinning with big teeth, he pushed himself all the way inside, and Pauline opened her mouth in a silent gasp. Widow gestured for him to pause there, which he did.

"Sex!" he bellowed.

Back over Pauline, she said, "Aw, feel that? You have a monkey cock packed in there tight, sweet little girl. Oh, he's in there so deep. And you don't care who knows about it. Kiss me while he rams that monkey cock into you."

Pauline had just started a soft whimper, and Widow smothered it with a wet kiss, moaning herself. They both felt each hard thrust as he leaned into his work, pounding her hard.

"Was man," Widow heard and looked up.

"You were? Really?"

"Long. Ago."

"Well, you're a sex-starved monkey man now."

"Angry!"

"Yes, of course, you are. And you sure are fucking this sweet human woman."

Back near Pauline's ear, she said, "You do want that monkey to cum in you, don't you? Be a good girl for me, precious one. Say you want the wild monkey man to pump his cum into you."

Breathing slowly but not smiling, Pauline nodded and said, "Okay. Yes."

"You're such a naughty tramp."

Pauline nodded, then said softly, "What about you? You're . . . you're hungry, aren't you?"

Widow lost her smile, stared down at her captive, and moved her lips silently for a few seconds as they both bounced and shook from the man's brutal thrusting.

"I'm so hungry I'm going insane. And my orgasm feels like an explosion."

"So?" she said with a low giggle that shook from a hard pounding. "I can always find . . . my own . . . monkey."

Widow backed away, still looking into Pauline's eyes as they both bounced to the monkey's steady rhythm.

"Really. For you. Your monkey."

Seconds passed as the man kept going, then Widow nodded but didn't smile.

"For whatever I want?"

"Yes. Anything."

Widow bit her lip, then focused on the monkey's thick shaft as it slid in and out.

"God, I really didn't think I'd ever want to do something like this, but I'm so hungry, Pauline."

Smiling, Pauline said, "Let go. You can't stop . . . what's happening to you."

"It's like I'm falling off a cliff. I might never come back."

"Jump, then. Just . . . jump."

"My voice is barely working on him. But my saliva is strong."

"Yes. Give it to him. Everywhere."

"Everywhere?"

"Mm-hmm. If you don't, he might kill both of us."

"He might. Damn, Igor might be right."

"Remember what you told me . . . you'd do?"

"Oh, yeah. I remember."

"What?"

"I said . . . that I'd want to suck a monkey cock."

"Well?"

"Pauline, I'm so hungry."

"You have to . . . let go."

"Oh God, you're right. Okay. I'm going to jump. I have no idea how crazy I might get."

"Mm-hmm. Go as crazy as you can. Crazier. You have no choice."

"Mm," Widow moaned as she gave her captive another wet kiss, then backed away enough to speak. "Okay, then."

She snorted out a quick breath, then found her smile again.

"I have something very juicy for you to keep busy with."

Up on her knees, she turned to get one on each side of Pauline, then looked down at her and saw that her tongue was already out.

"Time to be a very obedient little girl for me."

"Mm-hmm. Yes."

Widow lowered herself down onto her face.

"Oh, just like that. Oh, such nice, slow licks. Just like that, little one."

Even with Pauline mostly holding still, unable to move, the man's vicious lunges were forcing her face to slide across Widow every time.

Widow looked up toward the man-monkey and said to Pauline, "Nice little licks while I lose my mind."

Holding onto the bound woman's legs for balance, Widow leaned forward, locked her eyes on the man's, then opened her mouth. She'd managed to retract her fangs, and she showed him only an open mouth with wet lips.

"Sex," said the man. "Mouth."

Widow leaned down onto Pauline's taped and bound legs, placing her mouth as close as she could to where he'd been ramming it into Pauline, making the switch effortless for him.

"Mm-hmm," she said. "Try this warm, wet hole instead."

He backed himself out of Pauline, grunting softly with each tight tug as he slipped it out, then stood.

"Fangs."

"Uh-uh. No fangs. Just warm, wet sucking. Very wet for you."

He screeched quickly at the ceiling, then looked down at her open mouth as she waited with her palms flat on Pauline's thighs.

"Wet. Mouth."

"This mouth wants something hard to suck."

"Yeah," he said, grunting, then grabbed clumps of her hair into both of his tight fists, causing her to gasp. "Suck."

She looked down at the head of his erect member almost touching her lips, puckered those lips to form a tight circle, and said with her sweetest voice, "Mm-hmm. When I tell you, you can—"

With his lips peeled way back, showing filthy, chomping teeth, he growled and took a hard step forward. The swollen head spread her lips and stabbed deep into her mouth, snapping her head back.

She moaned and held it tight with her lips, and she leaned forward as he drew back. And when he jammed it back in, he again jerked her head back and shook all around her thick black mane.

"Mm. Mouth," he said, snarling as he kept thrusting his hips, sending her head back roughly each time.

"Mm-hmm," Widow said with her lips tight around his shaft and trying to hold on.

His next backstroke got him outside of her mouth completely, and she said, "Maybe slower would—" and he pounded it back in, gagging her.

Keeping her lips tight, she drenched him with her saliva, leaving more on him with every violent stab into her mouth.

She shifted her hips, grinding into the captive woman as she leaned away from his attack. The man pulled it out of her mouth but kept it so close that it rested on Widow's outstretched tongue.

"Wet. Tongue."

She gave it a long lick up, then said, "Mm. Perfect for licking a monkey cock."

"Wet. Good."

"Mm-hmm. This human woman's wet tongue loves monkey cock."

She gave it another long, slow lick.

"Love."

"Mm-hmm. Mm . . . loves licking monkey cock."

She licked it more, raising it slightly each time, then extending her tongue under it and as far along the shaft as she could before licking it again.

"Does the monkey like a human woman licking his big cock?"

"Like."

With one of his rough hands, he held it almost straight up and stood himself closer.

"Mm, okay. Mm-hmm, so much for me to lick."

After he'd stepped himself closer, she reached both hands around to hold his thick tail at its base. With a solid hold on the rigid thing behind him, and with her lips almost touching the rigid thing in front of him, she paused to look up at his crazed eyes.

Then, she moaned as she started at the very base of his shaft, near the bulge right under the waistband of his pants, and dragged her wet tongue all the way up. Near the top, she bubbled out as much saliva as she could and let it trickle down.

After many slow licks, leaving him soaked, she added some hot syrup to her voice and said, "Mm, human woman loves to lick. Monkey will hold still now until—"

With an impatient snort, he jammed the hard post into her lips, spreading them and going in deep to pound her head backwards.

Widow groaned and tightened her lips around it. She snorted out short breaths as he pounded it into her mouth a few more times, then she fought to back away from it.

While he squawked and grabbed at her hair, thrusting his hips and trying to stab it back into her mouth, Widow rushed to say to the side, to Pauline, "I know what I have to do, little girl. Even my spit isn't—"

He screeched and pulled at her head with his hard fingers tangled in with her hair, and he quickly slid them around back and allowed no escape from his brutal thrusting.

Widow let go of his tail and tried prying loose his strong hands.

Her thick black hair shook around like from hot blasts of wind with every hard pump. Each brutal attack snapped Widow's bare breasts up, and she let out a high-pitched whimper with every thrust that she couldn't escape.

* * *

The man-monkey gave Widow's mouth a vicious jab, knocking her back, then pulled out and stooped down, aiming for Pauline.

"No, monkey! Up here! Up here!"

He shrieked at the ceiling and slapped one side of her head, then the other, causing Widow to rise up just enough for Pauline to plead with her.

"Widow, this isn't going right. It's not fun anymore!"

He'd already found Pauline's spot, and it welcomed him halfway in.

"Widow!"

"Monkey!" she yelled. "Mouth is better! Fuck the mouth!"

He grunted, pulled himself back out and stood, his pole horizontal and close to Widow's lips.

"Mm-hmm. Fuck the wet mouth, monkey. Fuck my—"

He jammed it in like a fleshy battering ram, almost choking her.

"Monkey cock. Suck."

"Mm-hmm," she said when she had a chance. "Make me suck the—"

"Like," he said with it hard against the back of her throat.

She gasped when he pulled it out, then said, "Mm-hmm. I love to suck the—"

He chattered his teeth, then drove it back in, snapping her head back, and resumed his steady, urgent penetrations through her tightly held lips.

Pauline squirmed her head to one side, enough that Widow rose up, and she said, "Don't let him . . . cum . . . in your mouth."

The man kept pumping, and Widow felt all around Pauline's exposed ass cheeks and thighs and probed everything in between while looking up into his wild eyes. A half minute passed as his thick shaft slid in and out, rubbing across her wet lips.

"Widow?"

She groaned and managed to pry his hands off of her, then pivoted around on her knees until she was facing the other way. All the while, the monkey man had kept a fistful of her hair but only stared at her, confused. She looked down at Pauline's eyes as she lowered herself heavily onto her waiting mouth.

"Even my spit isn't working, Pauline! But I . . . I don't want to stop anyway."

Pauline moaned and blinked while licking her again.

"No reason to stop myself. Not with what I'll have to do soon."

She turned her head to look back at the befuddled man.

"Monkey," Widow said, "find the wet hole. Fill the human woman's wet mouth. Remember what she loves?"

"Monkey cock."

"Mm-hmm. Oh, yes."

The man groaned and hurried around, then aimed the big head for Widow's open mouth.

"Like you said, little girl."

She gave the very tip a slow kiss and held it, then backed away only enough to speak while looking down again at Pauline.

"Might as well jump off that cliff. He sure is cumming in my mouth."

"But . . . even just a five . . . you shouldn't—"

"Shh, now, precious one."

She groaned and fought against his hands pulling at her hair and his hips lunging, stabbing mostly her lips but all over her face too.

"I'd do all this if he was a ten."

"Widow, no! We're in real—"

Pauline got smothered, but she was still able to look up past Widow's bare breasts at a monkey man attacking her mouth, ramming it.

"Or even a twenty, Pauline. Oh, mm, I should find a twenty. See how rough a savage like that would be with me."

"Widow, don't!"

"Hush, now. I could do this over and over, with every monkey man I can find. All of them, sweet little girl. I know what I'll have to do, but I don't want to. God, I'm just going crazy . . ."

She quit fighting enough and opened just enough that the man could push the head inside her mouth, and then kept her lips squeezing it as he got back to his steady, violent pumping.

"Going," he said after thirty seconds of harder pumping, each thrust knocking her head back like a callous slap and shaking around her long, thick black mane.

"Mm-hmm."

"Want."

"Mm,"—she held him away, still touching it to her lips—"yeah. Be a good, juicy monkey boy for me. Fill my mouth with your monkey cum."

"Cum. Mouth."

"Hmm. I love hot monkey cum. Make me suck it all."

Widow held him with both hands and looked up at him as he stopped thrusting, tensing up and keeping the head of it well past her lips.

"Mm," she moaned and held the moan for many seconds.

Then, half smiling, she gave his shaft a long, very fast stroke with both hands, causing him to groan as he shot his first hot stream.

"Oh!" she said, parting her lips just enough to speak. "So much!"

Then, her lips squeezed it again, making a tight wet seal, and she said, "Mm . . ." while giving his wet shaft another strong stroke.

"Mm-hmm, even more!" she said, struggling to speak clearly with so much already in her mouth, then readied her hands for another tug.

Just as she was starting to pull his shaft with both hands, he snapped his hips back, pulling himself out of her mouth. She'd been squeezing it with her lips and without that thick shaft between them, they'd closed into a tight pucker. And with her strong tug, at just that moment, the heavy blast sloppily covered both lips and one side of her nose.

"Mm!" she laughed, smacking her coated lips together. "Oh, mm-hmm."

Then, she parted her lips not nearly wide enough, made no effort to cover the firing hose with her mouth, and pulled his shaft again.

Only some of it squirted inside on her tongue, and the rest added to what was already clinging to her lips and chin.

"Mm-hmm . . ."

With her head tipped back, the thick fluid sagged onto both cheeks.

"Mm, mouth."

She spoke quickly then kept her mouth open again, tongue far out, aimed it there, and gave it a hard pull. Most of it sprayed onto her upper lip, a thick mass of it on her nose, and she swiped around with her tongue while saying, "Oh, mm . . ."

Still pulling, giving it the longest strokes she could, he kept dosing her from a supply without any apparent end. Some shot deep into her mouth, some to one side or the other.

Most stayed where it had hit, but some of it had run down to the bottom of her chin. The drippings there increased with every pull and weighty squirt, and Widow didn't stop until she'd wrung it all out of him.

She'd let her mouth collect what it had caught, thick and hot and sticky, then backed away and tipped her head up, with an open mouth to show him.

"Cum," he said. "Mouth."

She kept looking up at him with lips mostly hidden by the thick goo and random splashes and drips across her cheeks.

"Mm, bad monkey, spraying cum on my face. Such a messy monkey man."

Holding him with one hand, she wiped around with the other, feeding what she could into her mouth, then sucking her fingers.

"Mm, sticky monkey cum," she said, gargling out the words. "So much wild monkey cum on my face."

His teeth chattered a few times, then she needed several ambitious swallows to get it all down. And even with that effort, more of it leaked out from between her lips, adding to the thick mess of it covering her chin. The first heavy bead of it dangled then fell onto one of her breasts and stayed stuck on the soft skin.

"Mm, such a juicy boy monkey for me," she said while using one hand to smear it around on her breast. "So much hot monkey cum."

They all heard her stomach growling.

"Ooh, mm. Maybe there's more."

She lifted it up and held it close, poised to get it back inside her mouth.

"Mm, good monkey. All done. Monkey can rest now."

He screeched at the ceiling and grabbed her head with both leathery hands. His hips rocked toward her as he held her head in place, but his thrusts were so violent that each pound jerked her head back, causing a high-pitched whimper with each brutal hit.

Still whimpering, she grasped at his hands, trying to free herself, and the monkey got a tight fistful of her hair in each hand and pulled her forward with each push.

After howling and yanking her head from side to side, still thrusting roughly, he began backing all the way out, then ramming it deep into her mouth, snapping her head back each time.

Groaning, still fighting to free herself from his determined hold of her hair, he backed out enough that she could say just one word.

"Sorry!"

He roared and jammed it back in, and she closed her lips around it. With the thick shaft between her lips, she opened her mouth with a hiss. Then, she moaned and clamped down on him and gave him two quick piercings when her fangs sprang out, longer than ever before.

He locked up and moved only his mouth, saying, "Fang! No!"

"Mm," she said, then pulled her lips farther back to show him how the two white teeth had only their points in him. Most of their gracefully curving lengths were still out, ready to be driven in.

He stayed frozen except for his slowly shaking head.

"No! No!"

"Ah, such a good boy," she mumbled, her teeth embedded enough to keep him from moving while she laughed at her inability to speak clearly.

"Little baby girl," Widow said, her voice again calm and drenched in thick honey. "You know what to do."

Pauline moaned then began hard, steady licks at just the right place, and Widow tensed for a second, gasping around the pole in her mouth, then bit into the man's still hard member. He shrieked and chattered his teeth and grabbed at her hair, then got quiet and started to sway from side to side.

She barely had time to pull out her fangs as he backed out of her mouth and toppled to the floor, and her long hair slipped through his fingers all the way down.

Raising her hips up off of Pauline's face, she heard her captive woman say, "What just happened? Did you really let him, uh, you know?"

"Oh, yeah. More than I expected. I wanted it so bad."

"Where is it? Tell me you didn't . . ."

With only her fingertips, she rubbed her belly, sometimes also touching Pauline's lips as she was so close.

With Pauline watching from below as she continued to caress her belly, she said, "Mm. Yes, I sure did. Oh, there's so much of it in my belly now. It's all hot and sticky in there."

"Oh, sure. Why the hell not?"

"And I learned that I can retract my fangs if I try hard enough."

"Good to know. Because with those things ready to bite, you'd—"

"I wouldn't be ready to suck. That's right."

She looked down, and Pauline saw the remains of the monkey's efforts thickening all over Widow's face.

"A little messy there, Widow."

"Such a bad monkey."

"You didn't want him spraying you like that?"

"I didn't think so at first. Then, God yeah. Uh-huh. It was some kind of mad celebration. Mm."

"Huh? Celebration of what?"

"Juice, Pauline. Oh my God. So much juice."

"He collapsed?"

"I bit him, Pauline. Even after he came like a fire hose, he only wanted more. Damn rough too. I bit right when you gave me such a powerful orgasm. I think that worked up more poisons than normal. I think he's, um . . ."

"Dead? You killed him?"

"Uh, yeah. I think so."

She spun around off of Pauline, saying, "Let's get you out of all this trouble you're in."

"What trouble? Getting fucked by a monkey and licking you?"

Widow laughed and said, "Yeah. Just another day."

"Okay. Deal. Another day, same thing."

"No, that's not what . . . oh, we'll see."

She quickly cut away all of the gauze, and Pauline groaned while stretching her arms and legs.

"Damn, Widow. That was scary but so good. In the beginning, I really didn't care if you were going to kill me."

Widow scoffed and rolled Pauline to face Marie, who was almost conscious, then she lay down behind her.

"I still might."

"Huh. I still feel the orgasm, but it kind of got too scary for a while."

"Yes, for me too. But I won't tell on you."

Pauline grinned and said, "Hmm. Maybe you will the next time?"

"So many monkeys running loose, huh?"

They both tipped Marie toward them, then shifted around until Marie's lips were near Pauline's breasts. Widow pulled the crafter's head closer, and she sighed and began sucking on one of Pauline's nipples.

"She's a good little girl," Widow said, then brushed Pauline's hair out of the way. "She's still lost in the sweetest of feelings. Nothing scary could get to her."

She reached between Pauline and Marie and got her fingertips up between Pauline's thighs.

"Oh, you're a very wet little girl, aren't you?"

With widow rubbing her, Pauline tipped her head back, gasping, and said, "Mm-hmm. All I want is to be a good, wet little girl for you."

"Mm-hmm. Maybe from watching me suck a hard monkey cock."

"Mm, maybe," she said, then laughed. "I can't believe you wanted him to cum in your mouth. He sure was sloppy about it, though."

"Oh, Pauline," Widow said, giggling. "That was my doing. It was fun."

"Widow, that's—"

"You'll do that sometime too. I insist."

"Huh. You always get your way."

When Pauline turned to see her, Widow said, "Hmm. Such a sloppy monkey man," then kissed her, leaving a few traces of sticky stuff on her face too.

The long, open-mouthed kiss lasted half a minute, then Pauline ended the kiss and Widow tipped her head enough that Pauline could lick her face clean.

Then, she giggled and offered her face to Widow, and she lapped up every trace of it too.

"Oh, little one. My breasts too."

"Hmm, of course."

Pauline finished licking her breasts clean, then said, "Mm. Still warm too."

"Recognize that taste?" Widow said.

"Huh. I'll never tell."

"Maybe you won't live long enough."

"I'm not afraid of your very sharp teeth."

"Even if I bite and maybe never stop?"

"You . . . you wouldn't want to—"

She sank her fangs into Pauline's neck and began sucking out her juices.

Pauline nodded and said, as her eyes were closing, "Yes. Don't stop. It feels so . . . so . . ."

Chapter 54 – I Didn't Ask for This

Widow's fangs had slipped out of Pauline's neck long before, but they still lay embracing with the sleeping crafter's lips close to Pauline's bare breasts.

The monkey man lay dead nearby, and the warm, quiet room was lit by only the single weak fixture attached to the movable heavy concrete hatch above them, which was still closed.

Widow's right hand, which had been eagerly probing and caressing Pauline between her thighs, was now draped across her and Marie too. She'd lost her blouse during her romp with the monkey man, and that left her bare breasts pressing up against the warm skin of Pauline's back.

But her short black leather skirt was still in place, as were her short black boots with very high, sharp heels.

Pauline had been mostly stripped naked—her panties were still tight around her thighs from when she'd agreed for the man-monkey to have unobstructed access to her. She lay squeezed between Widow and the crafter girl, who still wore her khaki work pants and a t-shirt.

After a slow, lazy yawn, Widow licked her lips, then nuzzled in closer to Pauline's neck. She licked her skin a few times, then sighed, which caused Pauline to flex her legs and try to arch her back.

Tight between the other two women, Pauline didn't stretch well enough and opened her eyes, then squirmed around until she was lying on her back. She reached her arms around the other two, and they both settled in, cheeks against her breasts, and continued to sleep.

"My God," Pauline whispered, barely forming the words. "This world . . ."

She tipped her head up just enough to see where Widow and Marie were, then looked back at the ceiling and whispered, "Oh, why the hell not?"

Moving both arms gently, she coaxed the sleeping women around, getting their faces to press more into her breasts. And she kept making slow, careful adjustments while looking up with a smile.

She let her left arm rest when she felt Marie's lips find her nipple and begin a quiet, gentle sucking.

Seconds later, she nodded just once and let her right arm rest too. Widow's tongue had begun investigating what had been touching her lips. She lapped gently a few times, then closed her lips over it, sighed, and gently sucked it in and out, taking her time like keeping her lips on it was all she'd ever want to do.

Pauline arched her back slightly and held it, forcing them to readjust and find what they wanted, and they both did.

Smiling at them passing that test, she relaxed and lay back into the cushions, and the eager lips found her nipples and continued their quiet sucking.

"Oh God," she whispered again, "I feel it. From Widow. Even just this."

Glancing down at them again, she carefully brushed first Widow's hair around and over, leaving it all cascading and almost covering her own belly. Marie's hair was shorter, but she moved that over, too, and together, the women's hair mostly covered all of her skin except for her breasts. She'd arranged it like a nest of soft hair, with two eager pairs of lips contained and content, sucking without a sound.

"Mm," she said, leaning her head back again, but then she tipped her head back up to watch.

Marie was first. Pauline began nudging the back of her arm, sometimes reaching farther for her forearm, all the while guiding her hand up. She sighed when the crafter's hand found a place where she could hold the breast that she was sucking, and she squeezed it gently in her sleep.

"You too, Widow," she whispered, then encouraged her arm up, too, until Widow held the breast as she sucked it.

Before Pauline let her head back down, she watched Widow yawn, use her index finger to rub around on the wet nipple, then sigh and place her lips on it again.

"Damn . . ."

She kept herself still, held them close, and let the two keep sucking, neither one making a sound to disturb the quiet of the room. Many long minutes passed before the sound of the concrete hatch opened right above them, and Pauline was already looking at it.

Igor's head appeared first, backlit by the candelabra behind him. His face twisted into a scowl at what he saw.

He saw that only Pauline was awake, so, to her, he mouthed the word, "Torture!"

She only smiled, bounced her eyebrows, then said silently, "Slave!"

He grimaced, then looked just past them at the dead man-monkey, collapsed in a heap with his trousers down. He pointed at him.

Pauline rolled her eyes, then nodded.

"Widow," she whispered and touched her hair softly.

"Mm . . ." she said, still asleep and still sucking.

Pauline looked up to see Igor grinning and shaking his head.

"Widow, really, we should all wake up. You're making me cum, but still . . ."

Widow let the nipple slip out from between her wet lips, then picked up her head and blinked a few times.

She and Pauline watched as Marie let go of hers, too, when she yawned, then licked her lips and opened her eyes.

"Oh, why not?" Pauline said and used her arms to nudge their heads closer together.

She smiled at the sight of the still sleepy women's lips meeting, each with a warm cheek resting on her breasts. Then, she looked back up at Igor and bounced her eyebrows again.

He'd lost his grin and only stared with his mouth hanging open.

Widow ended the kiss but stayed close, then said to Marie, "Mm, sweet girl. And just a touch more of my, um, stuff for you."

She leaned back enough to look into Pauline's eyes.

"Hmm, just a bit more for you too," then kissed her and didn't stop.

After half of a minute, Igor said, "Widow, sorry to interrupt. But there are things to do."

Widow ended the kiss, gave her another quick one, then turned enough to see her mutant slave above the ceiling.

"Yes, the dead monkey."

"Sort of. Yes. And the door. A lock would be good."

"All important. Come on down and get started."

All three watched him shimmy down the rope, then walk toward the hairy dead man.

"Out the window again, Widow?"

"No. Take it to the roof."

Before Igor could answer, Pauline snickered, nuzzled in close, and whispered in Widow's ear.

"An it. Not a he?"

"Well, just trying to be accurate."

Pauline kissed her ear, then whispered, her breath hot in Widow's ear, "And you sucked all the cum out of its cock. *Its* cock."

"You didn't mind a little taste yourself."

"Hmm. No."

Widow didn't laugh or even smile when she said, "It's a hunger, little one. So much hunger."

Focusing again on Igor, she said, "The roof is a better long-term solution. Let the bats have . . . it."

"As you wish, Widow."

He reached for the body, but Widow stopped him when she said, "Get the blanket first. Cover us."

"Yes, Widow."

He hurried to what was left of the couch, retrieved the blanket, and covered the three women on the cushions on the floor.

"Mm, better," Widow said.

"Yes, Widow. I'll dispose of it."

Pauline snickered again quietly near Widow's ear, then whispered, "You sucked an it. You sucked cum from an it."

"Well, you got fucked by an it."

"Hmm. Yeah, but he didn't come anywhere in me."

"Careful, little one, or I'll suck out everything you have. You won't even be juicy when I'm done with you. Just a beautiful, dry shell."

Pauline only nuzzled in deeper and said, "I don't even care."

They both looked when Marie said, "Me neither. Do me like that."

Widow raised her brows, looking at the crafter still resting her cheek on the blanket over Pauline's breasts.

"I accept your offer. And you wish for me to do it my way, don't you?"

She hesitated, made and lost a quick frown, then nodded.

"Very well. Soon, juicy little one."

They all watched as Igor staggered past them, toward the door, with the dead body over the shoulder that didn't have an extra dead head.

Widow said softly, "That was all so satisfying. Yes, even the it. Maybe especially the it."

"You thought your voice would work on it?"

"Yeah, at first. It had hardly any effect. Then, I thought my saliva would do it."

"Oh. That's why you volunteered for that?"

"Hmm. It started out as the why. I kind of went crazy. Then, I remembered what you said—how they get even crazier after sex. I had to."

"You really did, Widow. He probably would have gone nuts and killed us all."

"Yeah, Pauline. And then, fucked our asses."

"Just like a monkey."

"Yep. God, I'm so hungry sometimes. But I still have to deal with Junior."

"King Junior," Pauline said. "With a body full of electronics."

"Yeah. I need to figure out a way to keep his buzzer buzzing. Then, he's more of a man, and I might have a chance."

"Oh. Maybe Mortimer has some advice? Should I call him again?"

Widow called out to Igor, "Hold it, slave. Before you leave it on the roof, fetch the radio from the black leather pants over there."

"Yes, Widow. Can I take a second to sniff the pants before I—"

"No."

He kept the dead man draped over himself as he stooped, got the radio, then handed it to Widow. She quickly brought it and her arm back under the blanket.

"You may proceed. Leave it on the roof."

She smiled at Pauline giggling softly in her ear.

"As you wish."

While he was walking away with the limp body, Pauline whispered to Widow, "You killed its tail too."

* * *

Widow set the small radio unit on Pauline's belly, left her hand over it, then slid her fingertips lower.

"Hey, uh," said Pauline. "Ooh. Hmm. I'm supposed to call Mortimer like this?"

"No, not like this," said Widow.

Looking at Marie, she tipped her head down toward the blanket bouncing softly between Pauline's thighs. The crafter girl nodded, and her hand soon joined Widow's.

"Like this," Widow said.

"Damn. You never stop."

"Hmm. I'm not sure I can. It's like breathing. Call him. See if he has any advice."

Pauline sneaked both of her arms out from under the blanket, tapped the radio a few times, then laid it back on her belly above the blanket.

"Pauline? This is Mortimer."

"Mortimer, that king of yours might be a huge, nasty problem."

"Yes, yes, he sure is huge and nasty. Anyone can see that. Have you seen his Kingly cock? It's so—"

"What?" said Pauline. "No, we haven't seen his cock. Stop talking so dirty, Mortimer."

"Hmm. Can't do that, Pauline. You know better than that. Now, why have you called? We were just about to go out on another transmitter installation mission."

"Well, it can wait. Widow wants to know about—"

"Who's Widow? The one that—"

"You forgot already? You might need a tune-up. She used to be Scarlet. Now, she's Widow, and that freak Junior is—"

"Hey, that's the King you're talking about."

"Ooh, a king. He's got some weird thing on his back, and when—"

Widow had slipped her hand out from under the blanket, and she plunged her wet fingers into Pauline's mouth, silencing her and eliciting a quick giggle.

"This is Widow."

"Yes, I recognize the voice, even though it's, um, deeper maybe? Anyway, when you find some time, be sure to visit with a gentleman named Archie from the reactor. He—"

"What? Archie?"

"Yes, that's the name. I got word from one of our expeditionary team that he wishes to speak with you. He's roaming the city somewhere."

"Huh. Nice. Thanks for the tip."

"You're very welcome. Now, what do you need?"

"How do we keep that unit on your king's back from stopping? I've witnessed how deranged he becomes when the buzzing stops."

Looking across at Marie, Widow tipped her head toward Pauline. The crafter girl grinned, took her hand out, and slipped her wet fingers into Pauline's mouth too.

"Well," Mortimer said through the radio, "I'm not exactly sure. It's experimental."

"How is it powered?"

"Crude oil. I'm proud of that invention. It has a reservoir, kind of like a battery, one could say, and it gets its power from that."

"Ingenious. So, what would make it malfunction?"

"Huh. Good question. It didn't run dry if you hear it starting up its buzzing again on its own. So, maybe the flow of oil got interrupted? There's a very fine tube that leads from the reservoir to where it converts to energy."

Pauline had begun squirming around, turning her head to get the fingers out of her mouth.

"Hold on," said Widow.

She withdrew her fingers, got her arm back under the blanket, then it was obvious through the blanket that her legs were spread and she was rubbing herself.

Both Pauline and Marie held still and watched until Widow took her fingers, wet with her own poisons, and put them deep into Pauline's mouth.

She whispered, "Good baby girl. Suck the juice, little one."

Again, she tipped her head while looking at Marie, mouthed the words, "You too," and the crafter reached under and began fingering Widow under the blanket. Seconds later, she relaxed on Pauline's chest and sucked the poison from each of her own fingers.

And seconds after that, Pauline and Marie both calmed down and stopped moving altogether. After both sighed deeply, Widow nodded and picked up the radio.

"So, it's an oil feed problem? That's your best guess?"

"Sorry, Widow, yeah. That's all I can figure. Do you have time? I want to tell you about King Junior's kingly cock and all that he—"

Widow tapped the button, scoffed, then dropped the unit on Pauline's belly.

Pauline grinned and, sounding intoxicated, said, "Hmm. Maybe he should tempt you with a different kind."

Widow grinned, shrugged, and said, "Hmm, not kingly, you mean. Let's blame it on heat of the moment. My hunger isn't too picky."

"Yeah. And it got that one horny monkey dead and dragged to the roof for the bats."

"He died happy. I think I'm only going to get worse. Really, Pauline, every living thing seems mostly like juice sometimes."

They all turned their heads when Igor returned and closed the door. He looked at them for a second, bowed to Widow, then started messing with his tools and the parts for the lock.

"You seem okay. You were out of control before, though."

"I'm only okay now, Pauline, because I got some satisfaction for my hunger."

"The only thing you ate was, um . . ."

"Hmm, I sure did. But real food and sex and even—"

"Cum?"

Widow giggled and said, "Yes, that too. It's just all consuming. I don't see a lot of difference anymore."

Widow rolled out from under the blanket and stood, smoothing down her short black leather skirt while looking down at Pauline and Marie. She shifted her gaze to her blouse, still lying where she'd had it stripped off by a sex-crazed monkey man, then picked it up and put it on.

While fluffing her thick hair back, she said, "You should leave, Pauline. I feel it. The change is moving quickly. I don't know if I might really kill you soon."

Pauline gave the crafter a quick glance, then looked up again at Widow.

"Uh, sure. You don't think you could, uh, control yourself?"

Standing with her hands on her hips, appearing to the prone women as mostly long legs, Widow said, "I can't promise anything."

"Well, what about her?"

Widow turned her eyes to the crafter, then said, "She stays."

Marie started tossing aside the blanket, saying, "Uh, maybe I changed my—"

Like a blur of skin, black boots, and wild black hair, Widow was on her, crouching and holding her shoulders and keeping her down.

"She stays," she said, holding Pauline's gaze, then she leaned into her, bared her fangs, and sank them into the girl's neck.

Looking past the crafter and into Pauline's wide eyes, Widow sucked at her neck and didn't stop until the girl had collapsed in her arms. She laid her down on her back, then peeled the blanket aside.

"Good. She's still breathing."

"See? You didn't kill her."

"I will later."

"Oh. You can control it if you try, Widow."

She scoffed lightly and said, "Maybe. Anyway, she volunteered. She said she's ready."

"That might be some kind of turning point for you. The point of no return."

Widow sighed and closed her eyes.

"I'm starving for her, though, Pauline. Why can't I just do what's natural?"

"What's natural now, you mean?"

"Yeah. It would be so much easier to just be me."

She held Pauline's stare for a few seconds, then added, "I didn't ask for this."

She effortlessly rose to stand above them both again, straightened her skirt again, and said, "Even if you trust me, remember that King Junior,"—she paused to scoff and shake her head—"could show up anytime."

She turned and walked toward the mutant working on the door locks, with her boots' sharp heels striking the wood floor in an otherwise silent room.

*   *   *

Igor turned and looked up at Widow, then smirked and pushed aside the flopping extra head still hidden in a loose burlap sack.

"Damn head is just in the way now."

Widow squinted at him and said, "And before, it had some value?"

He scoffed and said, "I'm a stupid slave, Widow. That's all I am. No, it never had any value."

She locked her hands on her hips, looming over the small man, and said, "You still have some measurable value, though. You will have that lock repaired soon?"

"Yes, Widow. I'm installing another with a combination for inside and outside."

"Good. Like it was."

"Yes, and you can share the combination with me, and then—"

"I don't intend to."

"Oh. Yes, of course. So,"—his smile took hold and he struggled for a second to keep his eyes only on hers—"I can just keep knocking—"

"Three times. That's correct. Remember, too, that I might grant you entrance only to kill you."

"Yes, Widow, my life is yours. I'm just a slave!"

"Stop yelling."

"Sorry."

They both looked toward the sound of Pauline's western boots thumping on the floor as she approached them.

"Maybe I will leave, Widow."

"Back to your mountain home."

Pauline grinned and said, "Uh-huh. Back to my dungeon."

"I might wish to visit that dungeon again."

"Anytime no one is around, yeah. Or I could, maybe, visit here again?"

"You, Pauline,"—she paused to smirk at Igor—"will know the combination. But you might walk in on things that prompt you to walk back out."

"You really don't think you'll ever control it?"

Widow sighed, looked down, then back up at Pauline.

"Before that monkey escapade, which I find rather unsettling at this moment, I felt something spreading inside me. Taking over. Changing me."

"Yeah, and I encouraged it. I kind of pushed you."

"What happened?" Igor said, bouncing his eyes at each of them. "What did I miss?"

Widow scoffed and said, "Just a monkey living a dream before crashing out of this hellish place."

"Huh?"

Pauline said, "Can I tell him?"

Widow rolled her eyes and said, "Oh, why not? Let's torture the pathetic man further."

"I am pathetic! I'm just a—"

"No yelling."

He looked toward the crafter, prone under the blanket.

"Because I might wake her up?"

"No. Even your yelling wouldn't do it."

"Alright," Pauline said, stooping down to more closely look into the mutant man's eyes. "First, she stripped me down to my panties and tied me up."

"Just, just panties?"

"Yep. I didn't know why at the time, but she made it so my pussy, and my ass, too, I guess, were out in the open and I couldn't stop anyone from—"

"Or anything," Widow said, laughing softly.

"Oh, yeah. Any *thing*. Well, you get the picture."

"I do! I really—"

"Stop yelling," Pauline said.

Then, to Widow, she said, "That really is kind of annoying."

"You think?"

"Uh-huh. So then, that monkey man that hiked up to the roof invited himself into the room."

Igor was staring, and Pauline held him by his shoulders.

"And Widow? She invited that monkey to fuck me."

He tipped his head, trying to see between her thighs.

"He, he—"

"Yep. He fucked me, Igor, and not in my ass. Oh, no. I got the real treatment, and he got something way sweeter than the usual monkey man gets."

He whined softly, and both hands covered his crotch.

"While I was getting fucked, I told Widow she deserved to have some fun too. And she said that she was hungry. Hungry like no one could imagine."

He turned his shaking head toward Widow.

"She speaks truth. A hunger I couldn't fight."

Pauline shook him, got him to focus on her again, and said, "So, she did what a hungry Widow would do—she . . ."

Igor shook lightly on his own and said, "She, she what? What?"

Grinning, Pauline said, "She sucked that monkey's cock. Oh, damn, Igor, she sure knew that he was part monkey too."

One of his hands got jammed down into his pants, and he was fighting and wrestling with what he found there.

"Yep. And she loved sucking it. Her lips and tongue were all over that thing."

"Yeah? Yeah?"

"Yep. You know what else?"

"What? What?"

"She sucked him so good that he was going absolutely crazy. He was pulling her hair, slapping her, and being so brutal that—"

"I didn't mind as much as you might think."

Pauline stared at her for a second, then said, "Seriously?"

"Mm-hmm. Such a wild monkey man."

Pauline scoffed, smiled, and focused again on Igor.

"So, he was practically spearing her with his super hard cock. I'm surprised she didn't get a concussion. He was going out of his crazy monkey mind."

"I'm going crazy! I *am* crazy!"

"I kind of was too! And I had to keep licking her pussy—no way would she allow me to stop. But then, she had his big cock in her mouth, and he was about ready to explode. She held it with both hands, gave it a yank, and that monkey shot that muck right into her mouth."

"Muck?" said Widow.

"I don't know. Was it mucky?"

"You tasted it. You tell me."

"You tasted it too?" Igor said, almost hyperventilating. "You too?"

"Yeah, little man. Widow swallowed most of it, but the damn monkey was sloppy and sprayed a lot of it all over her face. Then, she wanted me to lick that up, so I did."

He had both hands in his pants, working furiously.

"He shot it on her face! Monkey cum!"

"Yep. The rest of it,"—she pointed at Widow's belly—"ended up right in there."

Igor's knees buckled, and he barely stopped himself from collapsing.

"Oh, Pauline," Widow said softly, scoffing, "you're killing my slave. You should stop."

She didn't stop, and she didn't even acknowledge Widow.

"Every hot sticky squirt, gobs of it, all shooting out of that monkey's—"

"Ah!"

"You're truly killing him, Pauline."

"I know. It's fun. Oh, Igor? Then, she bit her fangs right into him. That monkey hit the floor like the zoo was taking out the trash."

Igor's hands stopped, and he looked up at Widow.

"It's true. Made bat food out of him just like that," she said and snapped her fingers.

"That . . . that quick?"

Widow grinned and said, "Mm, so quick. No possible escape."

Turning to Pauline, she said, "I learned from that bizarre experience that a strong orgasm, like you so expertly gave me, leads to insane poison. But I made the choice to kill him. I could have just bit him. But at that moment, I was starving to kill too."

She looked down, shaking her head.

"Hey, Widow. He probably wanted to die at that point. I know I would."

"Me too!" Igor whispered. "Me too!"

"You can't die yet. Soon, perhaps. Right now, I need—hey, leave yourself alone. You can finish that later, in a dark corner somewhere."

Pauline giggled, and Igor slipped his hands back out.

"Yes, Widow. Where no one has to see."

"Exactly. I need you to gather up some crude oil. Find some kind of container for it. And locate a spray bottle too."

"Yes, Widow."

"What's that for?" said Pauline.

"It's an idea I have about that box on Junior's back. Mortimer said that it malfunctions from a lack of oil, some kind of interruption. I think that if that box were coated with oil, it might keep it running just long enough."

"For what, Widow? For what?"

"For me to kill him. I think he needs to keep that buzzer going for me to have a chance. Then, I'll kill him."

"You haven't killed anyone on purpose yet, Widow. Lucas was an accident. And the monkey man doesn't count. Not really because he probably would have killed us."

"Well, I guess. With Junior, though, he'll kill me if I don't kill him too."

"Yeah. True."

Pauline looked toward the girl on the cushions, then back at Widow.

"You're really going to kill her?"

Widow sighed, then said, "I don't know. Maybe."

"Hey, uh, that's a turning point," said Pauline. "Just to kill someone outright like that."

She watched Widow gazing at the sleeping woman.

"Widow, it matters. Maybe you, uh, shouldn't?"

"I went insane for sex, Pauline. I didn't care about anything else."

"I saw. With a monkey. Shit."

"Yeah, even with a monkey. Only a five, though. I'm not sure I can stop myself with Marie."

"Can you try? See if you can stop it?"

"Radiation got me, too, little one. I don't think anything stops it."

"Uh, no. Probably not. Alright, I'm leaving. You'll come visit sometime?"

"Yes, of course. I find your dungeon pretty exciting."

"You have a dungeon?"

Widow and Pauline both said, "Shh."

Pauline continued.

"You, uh, promise you won't really kill me, right?"

Widow stepped closer and held Pauline's shoulders, then she let go with one hand to brush back her red hair.

Smiling, she said, "Oh, little girl. You don't want to hear that."

"I don't?"

"Uh-uh. What you want—what you need—is to stay on that edge when I have you. When you're my captive."

Pauline sighed, then it eased into a smile.

"When I'm your baby girl."

"Mm-hmm."

They both looked down at Igor, who had both hands working vigorously inside his trousers.

Widow and Pauline shared another smile, embraced, shared a quick kiss, then Pauline left the room.

Chapter 55 – God, I'm Losing My Mind

From her seat on the stripped-down couch, where she was working again on a list of chores for Igor, Widow looked up at the sound of some commotion in the attic near the open hatch.

Two thick ropes quickly fell through, and the leather loops on the end of each thumped softly on the couch cushions still on the floor. A second later, two more fell, not even an arm's length from the first two.

Igor hung his head down, looked around until he'd found Widow, then said, "Like that, Widow? That's good?"

"Yes, like that. How long before you extend the controls just as far down?"

"I'll be quick! I have everything I need."

"Good. Do it now, then."

"Yes, Widow! Yes!"

After he'd vanished back up into the attic, Widow scoffed and said softly, "And stop yelling. Slave."

She let the notepad drop onto her lap and said loudly, "Igor!"

The sound of his shuffling steps carried through the hatchway and a second later, his head hung down again.

"Yes, Widow?"

"Did you gather the crude oil and sprayer?"

"Sorry, Widow! I couldn't—"

"No yelling."

"Sorry!" he whispered.

Then, in a strained normal voice, he said, "I found bottles of oil up here. Maybe it was used as a lubricant for the equipment."

"What equipment?"

"Generators. Motors. Power tools. Things to move heavy things around. All kinds of things."

"And what of the bottle?"

"No, Widow. I don't think so."

"A sponge, then?"

"I saw sponges. You want that down there with you?"

"Yes, slave. A small bottle of oil and a sponge."

"Right away, Widow."

She left her notes on the couch, stretched her arms out when she stood, then walked toward the cushions and the crafter. She paused there, looking down at the unconscious woman mostly covered with the blanket.

"Hmm. Soon, little one."

She stooped down enough to brush her hair aside, then touched her cheek gently.

"I know you're a real person. A real, actual, living young woman. As much as anything can be called alive here."

She stood, her long legs straight and her hands on her hips.

"But all I can see is a juicy little thing that I want to . . . consume. That's the only word for all of it."

"Me too," Igor said from the attic as he leaned down to see.

Widow spun around and said, "How long have you been spying, slave?"

"Um, sorry. Just a minute. Not even a minute. More like just—"

"Shh. What do you want?"

He made it clear that he was adjusting his head to focus on the crafter girl.

"To fuck her! Now, while she's asleep! No one will know! I can just—"

"No. She's mine. I don't want you getting her all fouled up."

"I would love to foul her up! I'm foul! If I were able to—"

"When I'm done with her, if there's anything left, you can have that."

"I'll take it!"

"Even just a dried-out little doll of a girl?"

"Yes, please! She'll still be the prettiest I'll ever have. I'm not picky, Widow!"

"No. You just yell a lot. Get those controls fixed as you were ordered."

"Yes!"

She watched him duck back up into the attic, then listened to his crusty sneakers on the rough concrete attic floor as he hurried away.

Looking down again, she blew a kiss toward the girl, then walked to the shuttered window and almost swung open the hinged plank. But she stopped herself and looked back at the light coming into the room from the attic.

"Igor."

A few moments later, his head hung down again, and he said, "Yes, Widow?"

"I'm going to look out the window. It must be darker."

"Yes, it must. I should close the hatch?"

"Yes. Or cover the opening."

"There's a big canvas tarp. That's okay?"

"Yes. Go ahead."

"As you wish."

She leaned back into the shutter and watched the crafter on the cushions until the room had gotten too dark.

The bolt slid easily and quietly, and she eased the plank open and looked down.

"Camping out, huh? Waiting for me?"

Junior, still bare-chested and showing black streaks across his chest, sat in a ratty recliner on the sidewalk across the street, right in the middle of a streetlight's cone. He held the sword with one hand, and the blade lay across his thighs, which were too thick to allow it to touch the chair's arms.

His other hand was holding his chin, maybe rubbing it, but he was too far below for Widow to make out too many details.

"Well, you do look like some kind of king. Pondering things."

Widow didn't hear anything, but she saw Junior snap his head to his left and stare off into the darkness. She held her breath and watched.

Seconds later, a monkey man came into view. Tall and strong, walking perfectly upright, and snapping his curving tail from side to side.

Widow's stomach growled.

"Oh, God. Really?"

The hairy man vanished in the nearby dark region, then strode into the next light cone.

"I think that one just might be a ten. Maybe more. Hmm, might be a lot more. He looks quite savage."

And her stomach growled again.

Barely aware that she was speaking, she said, "Oh, I'm so hungry."

The monkey man went dark again, then stood in the light, the next lit area before the one occupied by Junior.

"Hmm," she said softly, staring at the large creature whose tail was snapping around forcefully. "Could he be a very horny ten? Not much of a man left there. Still, man enough that he could be tempted by a woman. A human woman could probably get him . . . interested."

Junior rose from his seat and faced him, but he stayed next to the chair.

Widow laughed softly, shaking her head.

"I do like talking dirty now. Did I always? I don't think I ever did . . . before. Whatever was before."

Junior appeared to be speaking calmly with the man, who kept his distance and seemed to be listening.

"I talked dirty to Pauline, when I barely knew her. She pushed me, but I liked saying it. What I'd do to a monkey man."

She gave a glance toward the crafter, but it was too dark to see her. She resumed monitoring Junior.

"And she told me to jump off that cliff when that monkey was . . . fucking her. With his big monkey . . . cock."

A soft scoff went along with her shaking head.

"I like that word. I like saying it. She likes me saying it."

Junior sat back down, but the man-monkey didn't go any nearer.

"What was I saying to that monkey? I wasn't even thinking, but I remember what I wanted. Pauline pushed me to jump off that cliff, then I wanted to. And that got me so much hungrier. I remember wanting so bad to have his hard cock in my mouth—such a deadly place for my poisons. And I sure knew he was part monkey. I knew he was probably a five—couldn't be called human—and I still wanted his cock."

She gave a glance toward the crafter, but it was too dark to see her. She resumed monitoring Junior.

"Hmm. Was it really just about the poisons? What if I had nothing like that? Would I still have wanted his . . . cock?"

She smiled down at the conversing giant sweaty man and monkey man bred for sex.

"Mm, I sure did have a five's cock in my mouth. I should never be sucking a monkey's cock. I knew that. It felt bad. Wrong. But maybe that's why I wanted it so much."

Widow balanced herself with one hand on the shutter plank, mumbled, "Hmm, in my mouth," and she slipped the other hand down over her belly, stretching the flimsy fabric of her skirt.

"Oh, just like that. Yes, a little crafter girl's job. Soon, she'll be doing this for me. So soft and slow with that sweet, eager little tongue of hers. Mm . . ."

She got herself into a steady rhythm, rubbing herself gently.

With her eyes mostly closed, touching herself and gazing down at the street, she said, "So, could that one be a ten? Hmm. Would

I? Would I do it? Would I suck a ten monkey's cock? Ten percent monkey, kind of far from being a man, and his cock is in my mouth. Hmm."

She kept fingering and said, "My mind lately. What the hell is this? Sex and feeding is all I can think of. Fantasize about. Hmm, Pauline would goad me, push me to go crazy in my imagination too. I know she would."

Her left hand came out and up to her mouth, and she sucked a few fingers for a second, then got it right back to work.

"Hmm, I didn't even need to do that," she said, then giggled. "Okay, Pauline. Little one. You want me to fantasize? Here we go."

She got herself into a steady rhythm while focusing mostly on the solid, strong man-monkey on the street below.

"We're in your dungeon, and I've used my voice on you. My poisons from kissing you and from everywhere that you've kissed me. You're tied up. Oh, you're so hopelessly bound up, and we're hanging upside down above your bed. I give you a good bite. Just enough that every word from me feeds your orgasm. You don't ever want me to stop telling you my fantasy.

"It starts with me and my sweet little crafter girl. I know all the things I'm going to do with her, and she's going to satisfy all of my hungers. All of them.

"Then, the door opens and a monkey joins us. Yes, I invited him. Teased him. Led him into my lair. And he's a ten, Pauline. So savage. An animal.

"I'm lying with the crafter, embracing her with my fangs near her neck. Then, I remember just how much I liked that I was kneeling for that monkey that was fucking you. Something so wrong about a human woman on her knees to suck a monkey's cock, even just a part monkey.

"And I'm not just kneeling for the monkey, Pauline. No, I'm wearing just a tiny skirt and those sexy boots. I'm not wearing a blouse because I don't want to. I want my breasts bared for him. It's like I'd dressed myself sexy just to get on my knees and suck a monkey's cock. A ten monkey. Mm, yes. A ten would be so . . . I don't know."

She groaned and picked up speed, still watching the calm conversation far below on the sidewalk.

"And once I'm on my knees to suck his cock, I forget all about that little girl. That sweet, juicy little girl is forgotten entirely when the second monkey struts into my lair. Yes, two monkeys. Mm-hmm, two very horny monkeys. I'd kneel for one and suck his hard cock. My poisons make the cock even harder. I slobber all over that stiff thing because I wonder how hard I can make it."

She gasped and kept rubbing.

"And the other ten, he starts fucking me from behind. I'd stay very still while two thick monkey cocks pump me at the same time. That would be so . . . seductive?"

The only change outside was Junior standing and stretching out his arms, but Widow's hand was making more decisive motions.

"Or maybe Junior? Maybe just Junior before I kill him. I'll make him fuck me everywhere that he can. Over and over. And I'll suck that kingly cock. I'm sure I have enough poisons even for such a massive beast of a man."

She kept rubbing, and she kept watching.

"I'll make that king fuck me in the ass. I'll make him screech like a monkey would. Then, I'll make him—"

She paused with two fingers deep inside, then she smiled and rubbed again.

"No. Not him. I'll just kill him. I must be losing my mind because I know it would be so much better with just two monkeys. So wild. That's what it's about—the contrast. Me, so soft and smooth, and the monkeys, so rough and wild. So smooth and . . . seductive? Is that what it's about?"

Her skirt stretched more as she wiggled fingers in deeper, then kept rubbing too.

"No, that's not it. Soft and smooth and holding myself still for them? No, that's not seductive—that's submissive. Letting them be rough and take whatever they want, that's the way."

She slipped her fingers in deeper and said, "Ooh, lingerie, Pauline. While you're orgasming, think of me in lingerie just special for a pair of wild monkey men."

Rubbing again, she said, "Mm-hmm. So soft and sexy for the savage monkeys. Didn't I think I should dress sexier for someone? Was that for a monkey man? Or two? Hmm, must have been."

Still rubbing, she took a few deep breaths.

"I'd be dressed sexy and alone in a locked room with them. And they'd get so much rougher and demanding even after I've satisfied them. So dangerous. I'd have to try like hell to control them. What a dangerous, sexy game."

She kept rubbing herself and said, "No, that monkey before with you liked helpless. I'd have to stay as helpless as I can, making them even crazier. I want to look so pretty when I kneel for one and suck his cock. Mm-hmm, just delicate lingerie and heels when I'm on my knees. I'll stick my ass out for— oh, no,"—she gasped and took a deep breath—"ooh, Pauline, this is even better.

"I could make the slave bind me for them, then hide himself. Or better yet, leave the building altogether. After he'd bound me up like I did to you. Yes, soft and sexy and helpless in a locked room for the vile monkeys."

She closed the plank and leaned her back into it.

"Hmm, but they'd only get wilder after they both cum. In me and on me. They'd be ready, and they'd want to fuck me again. I'd be tied up so tight I couldn't stop them. Yes, they'd fuck me again, make me suck them again, getting crazier each time. And I'd just be so soft and delicate, in pretty lingerie, tied up and unable to stop them. God, how many times would they force me to satisfy them?"

She groaned and rubbed herself harder.

"And I think I could bite each one, give them just enough poisons, that their brutal nature would compel them to satisfy me.

My fantasy. But then? Hmm. No possible escape for them, and they wouldn't even know until it killed them. And I'd just enjoy my orgasm until the slave returns to unbind me."

She sighed and laughed once.

"Yes, tens wouldn't stop. Oh, but neither would a fifteen. Would I suck a fifteen monkey's cock? Maybe even a sixteen or seventeen . . . very much a beast of some kind. Mm, I could hardly kid myself that he's still a man.

"I'd tell you all of that, Pauline, while we're hanging together, in a dungeon lit only by candles. You're tied up and bitten. And we're both lost in orgasms better than we could ever imagine. Hmm."

She rubbed for a second, then laughed once. With her eyes wide open again, she gazed blindly into the dark room.

"Just say it, Widow. Say what you know is true: you would suck the hard, savage cock of a . . . fifty. Mm, a fifty. I'd kneel in lingerie and beg for a fifty's hard cock in my mouth. Just as much monkey as man, and his hard cock in my mouth, and I'd suck and swallow and suck and . . ."

She moaned as she climaxed and slid down the wall until she was seated.

"Oh! Oh, that sure did it. A fifty. Mm, two fifties . . . yes. Yes, I would. I will. Someday. I promise that to myself right here and now."

She clunked her head back into the wall, eyes closed, smiling and letting her breaths calm.

Laughing, she said, "All that savage monkey cum. All for me. And they'd never stop until my wonderful poisons drop them. The slave will find them for me somehow."

She shook herself once, then sighed and let her hand rest.

"A fifty? Two of them at the same time? Lingerie? God, I'm losing my mind. Whatever else is going on with me, it's that too."

She sighed and slipped her wet fingers out, then sucked one.

"Maybe it's just . . . a different mind. Just . . . different now."

She sucked two more, then paused, touching her tongue to one for a second.

"That different mind knows that seduction, even fake submission, tempts them. No, it traps them. And traps lead to feeding. It's not just sex. It's sex and . . . feeding."

She gave the last finger a strong suck, then scoffed at the darkness.

"Mm. Taking all of their juices should be fun too. Hmm, yes, I'll have to keep that promise to myself. Two."

She giggled softly, then slipped her fingers back where they were.

"Oh, I have to do it all, don't I? The lingerie, the getting tied up for them, and ordering the slave to leave the building? All of that? Leaving me helpless and alone with the horny savages?"

She sighed, giggled softly, and said, "A promise is a promise."

* * *

Standing again and straightening out her clothing, Widow remained near the window in the room without any noticeable light.

"Igor. Light it up."

The edge of the tarp snapped to one side, revealing a dim sliver of the lighted area above the ceiling.

"Yes, Widow."

He quickly dragged the tarp off to one side, and the room returned to its usual meager light level.

With his head hanging down again, he said, "Anything out there, Widow?"

"Yeah. Junior, sitting in a chair. With his sword."

"Not good. Anything else?"

"Oh, not really. Just, uh, a monkey."

"Is he, um, will he—"

"He's not invited in. You won't need to feed his carcass to the bats on the roof."

"I could, though. So, maybe you should."

"Come down here, slave."

"Widow?"

"Now, you're hesitating? Do as I say."

"Yes, Widow."

He shimmied down the rope and stood holding it.

She began walking toward the couch cushions on the floor and said, "Stay."

She got to where she could stand beside the crafter, then she sat and lifted the girl's head onto her lap, facing her.

"I'm just about at the point where I could kill her without any remorse. Without any reason."

"Yes, Widow."

"You as well. No one would care."

"Yes. I know."

"Likely, some would rejoice."

"Even truer. Yes."

"Come closer."

He ambled toward her, then stood a few steps away.

"You seem to be forgetting that you're my slave."

"No, Widow, I'd never—"

"You are not to disagree with me. Ever. You only obey."

"Sorry! I just—"

"Don't yell."

"Sorry!" he whispered.

"I will soon lure into this room a formidable once-human thing called Junior. He carries a sword. He's charged up with hazardous electronics that make him even more dangerous. He thinks I killed his mother."

She waited, watching the mutant man with a head in a sack.

"Good. You questioned nothing of what I just said. The monstrous thing that Mortimer has called a king will seek to subdue me and kill me. I will require you to obey instantly if there's a need."

He nodded but didn't speak.

Widow scoffed softly and nodded, then wedged a small pillow under the crafter's head and shifted her around until satisfied with her position.

She looked up at the mutant slave standing and watching silently and started to unbutton her blouse.

"I must have this pretty thing sucking at my breast. I know that she craves my sweet poisons, and she gets them even this way."

His lower jaw trembled, but he still didn't speak.

"She is quite beautiful, and it's enjoyable to watch her delicate, soft lips closed around my nipple as she sucks."

Igor let out a very quick, quiet whine.

She finished unbuttoning and pulled open her blouse on the crafter's side, exposing her breast and revealing that her nipple wouldn't be difficult for the crafter to get a hold of.

A few minor adjustments touched it to the girl's lips, and she didn't make a sound as she opened up for it, held it with her lips, then began a rhythmic sucking of it.

Widow stared into Igor's eyes as she opened the other side, baring her other breast.

"This one is for you. Do not speak. Suck."

He dropped to his hands and knees and crawled until his lips could almost touch it, but he paused to look up at her. He saw that she'd turned her eyes toward the young girl busy with the other, and she kept her eyes there.

He sucked. He moaned and stayed on his hands and knees and sucked, and he had no reaction to Widow's next statements.

"You're a grotesque little slave, but I need you to suck in more of my poisons. Yes, you're enjoying it—you'll likely crawl to some dark place and masturbate after—but more importantly, you're cementing your fate as my slave."

She brushed back Marie's hair, then caressed her cheek.

"And I will try like hell to think only of this fair thing, this juicy little girl, as she suckles. Even as she already has so much that she's not even aware of what she's doing."

She kept caressing the girl's soft cheek, never looked at Igor as his wet lips fumbled around and his rough sucking left her juices dripping down both sides of her breast.

After looking up at the ceiling and frowning, Widow groaned and pushed him away.

"Enough."

"Enough. Yes."

"Back to work."

"Yes, Widow. Back to work."

Without being told, he crawled back to the rope, never looked back at her, then climbed back up and out of sight in the attic.

She scoffed, then looked down at the girl that she was still gently touching. She carefully coaxed her head to lean it away, giving her a better view of the wet lips contentedly working.

"Hmm. Gentle is nice too."

She laughed softly and said to the girl, "No damn monkey would ever be nice like this."

Another few minutes of quiet sucking passed, then Widow stopped touching her altogether.

Looking straight ahead, she said, "Oh, no. They're savage. So savage and hard."

She glanced back down and scoffed.

"Which I think I love too. Hell, I did tell that monkey that I loved it."

With her eyes pointed up, she said, "Then, I killed him. And had him fed to the bats on the roof."

She sighed and pushed the crafter away, smiling at her nipple popping out from between her lips. After buttoning up and laying her flat on her back, she crawled over nearer to her feet and grabbed one of the leather loops at the end of a stout rope hanging down from the attic.

"Let's just store you away for later."

She giggled and added, "In my pantry."

She slipped it over the girl's sneaker and left it around her ankle.

"Stay nice and fresh for me? Hmm. Of course, you will."

She added the second leather loop to the girl's other ankle, then lifted one rope, then the other.

"Good. Just like that."

She stood and smoothed down her skirt, then looked up into the attic.

"Igor."

His functioning head appeared.

"Yes, Widow?"

"Where is the control unit for this hoist?"

"I'm sorry, Widow. I should have corrected that by now."

"Soon. Alright, lift her up. Get her up there in the dark."

"Yes, Widow."

His head slid out of sight and seconds later, the control button clicked, the motor high up near the roof whined, and the ropes and loops began to lift the crafter's legs.

"Good. Keep going."

"Yes, Widow."

Her hips left the cushion, then only her hair touched, then she was completely up in the air and rising.

The motor worked steadily, lifting her at a constant pace, and Widow called out, "Hold."

A click stopped the whining and the lifting.

Widow scoffed at the girl's arms hanging down.

"That will never do."

She found the roll of gauze that she'd used on Pauline and tied the girl's wrists behind her back.

"Not very artistic. Hmm. I'll have fun fixing that later. Igor. Up."

"Yes, Widow."

A button clicked, a motor hummed, and the crafter girl, sloppily bound and hanging upside down, rose above the ceiling.

"Good."

She stopped.

"Close everything up, and stay quiet up there. I'm inviting in something much more dangerous than a simple horny monkey."

"Yes, Widow."

"You would ask if you weren't such a complete slave. You'd ask if I'm inviting Junior in for sex."

Igor waited quietly.

"Good slave. The answer is perhaps. Perhaps he will be used for sex before I kill him."

She grinned at Igor nodding.

"Or while I'm killing him. Yes, that would be better. Either way, I'm killing him."

Chapter 56 – A Noteworthy Variety of Arachnid

Widow stood inside the closed front door of her building, looking out at the oily, sweaty, bloody monster of a man sitting in a recliner and holding a sword. She leaned each way to check and saw no monkey man.

"Good," she said to herself, laughing softly. "Monkeys are too distracting. I'd want to, well, I'll think about that later. Hmm, maybe fantasize is a better word."

She started to give the glass door a push out, then stopped quickly at the sight of a fireworks display and a giant man screaming strings of obscenities.

"Oh, this is stupid. What a freak."

Multi-colored ribbons of sparks were flying through the night air in random directions, creating a confetti cloud, and Junior, still holding his sword, was dancing around and cackling loud enough to be heard through the door.

It came to an abrupt end, and he fell back into his seat. Widow coughed once, pushed the door open, and began walking toward him.

He was still brushing at his skin, where small burning bits of circuits had landed and were sizzling, and he snapped his head up to see.

"Hello! I need a big strong man!"

He stood and said, "I'm certainly a large and capable fucker. But what is this goddamn need of yours?"

"My, do you always curse so much?"

"Only fucking recently did my speech become laced with such vile terminology. Please proceed to describe this fucking need to which you alluded."

She stood in the street, several steps from him, and said, "Um, sure. Okay. Just minutes ago, I thought I'd hide out in this building,"—she hooked a thumb over her shoulder—"and I did find a cozy little place to hide. That's all I want to do is hide. But there's this one big heavy thing that really needs to be lifted up, then everything will be fine."

He looked above her at the name of the building carved into the thick stonework above the doorway, then back at her.

"You live in that goddamn building, right the fuck there? The Webber?"

Widow spun around and looked quickly.

"Huh. What an appealing name. Well, I'd like to live here. I hope nobody else already claims it. Am I intruding on someone else's building?"

"Yes, I believe that's a possibility. I have reason to suspect that a sexy, whore-like wench named—"

"A wench? What's that?"

"Huh. I'm not totally sure. That's a fair question and deserves some fucking research. Anyway, the damn wench is a woman named Scarlet who, or so I've fucking heard, now prefers to be addressed as Widow."

"How peculiar! Is she a widow? I've never known a widow myself."

"It's possible that she is, indeed, a goddamn widow. I've never known any myself either. Fuck—unless one were to count the spider type."

"Well, whatever do you mean?"

"Black fucking widow. It's a noteworthy variety of arachnid. They're considerably entrenched in folklore, and the term is often also applied to—"

His buzzer sputtered, one soft thump sent just a few sparks out of one ear, and he raised his sword and screamed, "Don't be a bug, Mama! Fuck, fuck, fuck! Don't, don't, don't you fucking dare—"

With a whistle and a click, the buzzing started up again. Junior slapped the side of his head and laughed.

"My apologies for behaving as such an outright fuckhead. I think I might need a tune-up or a goddamn upgrade or some other remedial attention."

"Yes, you probably need something, a big boy like you."

"Fuck yeah, I'm definitely a big boy. A King, actually."

"Oh, a king. How intriguing. Kings are kind of sexy."

"We are?"

"Well, sure. You want to know what's so sexy about them?"

"Yes. Please elaborate."

"Well, big king, it's because all kinds of women, the sexiest ones you can imagine, want so, so bad to have wild, screaming sex with them."

"They do?"

"Uh-huh. They just can't help themselves. They'd do anything at all for a king. Anything."

"Hmm. That's an interesting and attractive reason for one to strive to be a veritable goddamn King."

"I've been told that I'm a little bit sexy."

She turned herself around, taking small, cute steps with her very high heels, then shook her ass a few times while giggling, then faced him again.

"What do you think?"

"Why, yes. Even in this piss-poor light, you look quite nice."

"Nice? Only nice?"

"I endeavor to be a fucking gentleman. It sort of goes with the King job. Yes, you're quite sexy and arguably quite fuckable."

"Oh, the king job. Yes. What other kinds of jobs do you like?"

"Oh," he said, looking down and laughing, then he pointed at her, jabbing a giant finger in her direction. "I get it. Yes, you're referencing blow jobs, cock sucking, those kinds of so-called jobs. I kind of miss how—"

His left ear popped out sparks, then a whistling from the right sent a single flaming piece to bounce away into the night.

He jabbed the point of his sword toward the black sky and said, "How Mama used to, how she, fuck, fuck, fuck, how she, wow!"

The buzzer ramped up to a comfortable level and even in the dark, the increased sweat coating his thick body welcomed the few traces of light falling from the streetlight.

He lowered his sword and said, "I apologize for my intolerable fuckheadedness again. I really do need some timely fucking repairs."

"Sure. I can see that. What was that about your momma?"

"Oh, nothing. I was about to make a fucked up joke at my dear mother's expense, that's all. I tend to act kind of, um, like a fuckhead when—"

"When you're exploding?"

"Yes. Exactly that."

"You remain quite profane too."

"Oh, fuck yeah, there's that. My goddamn mobile generator got a recent fucking software upgrade, and I'm fucking swamped with goddamn curse words, even in those fuckhead times of flaming distress. I truly did not volunteer to issue such vulgarities, especially when I'm—"

"Exploding?"

"Precisely. You're nice, and you're sexy as fuck too. I'll help you with the heavy lifting that you need to make yourself a comfortable home in this damn building."

"Thank you! Do you carry that scary sword everywhere you go?"

"Oh, that. Some fucker named Archie gave me that when he sent me after the slutty wench, Scarlet, who goes by—"

"Widow. I like that name. It's a good name."

"Well, I suppose it is. Fuck yeah. Um, no, I don't need this silly goddamn sword. But I kind of like having—"

"Why don't you just leave it on the chair? It'll only take a second to get that heavy thing lifted up, and I'd bet that sword will still be there."

He laid the long blade across both arms of the chair, then turned back to Widow and took a few steps closer.

"You know? Your recommendation is likely the prudent goddamn course of action. All I need is—"

"Your friend? Weren't you talking to someone?"

"I'd say that he was more of a thing than an actual goddamn he."

"Oh, my. Um, more than a ten?"

"If I understand your damn terminology correctly, I'd estimate he's more like a fifty. So, maybe fucking half and half."

"Oh. Goodness. Um . . . wow. Too bad he left because—"

Pointing to his right, Junior said, "He heard someone approaching and went to hide his fuckface in the shadows. It's rather odd, but he seems somewhat shy compared with others of that kind."

"Well, that was unnecessary. I kind of, um, like monkeys."

"They're more than a bit savage, you know. Fuck, especially one with that concentration of goddamn contamination from possibly even a hybrid genome."

"Mm-hmm. Oh, yes, I know. Savage and strong too. Perhaps we'll need his help?"

"Maybe. It's a heavy thing you need lifted?"

"Yes, quite."

Junior turned his head and whistled, then gestured with one hand.

The large man-monkey emerged from the shadows, walking mostly upright with only tattered khakis stretched over his strong legs and leaving his hairy body exposed everywhere else. Behind him, a thick tail stuck straight back and snapped one way then the other, drawing Widow's intent stare.

"Oh my. He sure, um, he—"

"I'm not sure why he chose to pose his tail out like a goddamn erection from somewhere near his monkey ass. It had an overall relaxed appearance just a moment ago—just looked lazy as fuck."

"Oh, um, that probably doesn't mean anything. But I'd say that he's a fifty. At least."

"Hmm," said Junior. "Perhaps more. It would behoove a curious onlooker to perform a more detailed inspection."

"Oh my!"

The monkey-man showed his teeth to both of them and covered his crotch with one hand.

"Oh, he, uh, he—"

"Lead on, miss, uh, what is your name?"

"I plan to call you King, so why don't you just call me Queen?"

He laughed and said, "That's a brilliant fucking idea. Yes, I'll call you Queen. Have we met before, Queen? You remind me of someone."

"Oh, I don't think so, King. I just got here. And I'd certainly remember a big, sexy boy king like you. Watch closely so you don't get lost. Both of you."

Before turning all the way to begin her walk back to the building, Widow grinned at the fifty monkey showing his big teeth to her, but his eyes, wild and savage, were locked on her ass. And his tail could have been a long, hairy metal rod.

Sighing, she turned and began a slow strut back toward the building, shifting her hips gracefully with each step and saying softly to herself, "My God, what am I doing?"

* * *

Just a few steps from the building's door, Junior said, "Fucking wait. Allow me to behave as a damn gentleman."

Widow stopped, said, "By all means, King," then turned her head enough to watch Junior walk past, towering over her, then reach for the door.

As he was opening it, she felt a hot body pressed up against her, then felt two strong hands reach around and squeeze both breasts.

"Hey!"

Junior had the door open, and he turned to look.

"Monkey! Strive to be a goddamn gentleman too!"

The man chattered his teeth and let go of Widow's breasts, but he only held her belly instead and started driving his hips into her.

Junior laughed and hurried behind him, then pried them apart.

The monkey man grinned, and Junior said, "I've become educated on monkeys just recently, the dirty fuckers. Apparently, they are quite the enthusiasts of sexual activity—anything to satisfy their goddamn cocks."

Widow had turned to face them, pointed at the wild man, and said, "Hmm, such a naughty monkey!"

The man tipped his head, and Junior said, "Oh, he's not really a bad sort. This fucker, like the fucker that I met earlier, is just—hey, I'm a bit curious where the fuck that other hairy scalawag has meandered off to."

Widow pulled open the door and said, "It's a dangerous world. Perhaps the bats got him?"

"Yes, that's very likely. And it would be wise as fuck to stay prepared for such eventualities. Just a goddamn moment, please, Queen."

He jogged back across the street and returned just as quickly with his sword.

Widow frowned at the long blade extending from his hand to the sidewalk, then turned and reached for the door.

"Allow me," she said, and bowed while holding it open.

"Thank you."

With his arms around the monkey man, and holding his wrists and jamming his tail to one side, Junior walked the two of them toward the door but stopped when they were even with Widow.

"Are you sure we've never fucking met?"

"Like I said, I just got here."

"Did you arrive at the reactor?"

"Why would I drive a tractor?"

Junior tipped his head and squinted at her for a second.

"Hmm. Okay."

He walked the fifty monkey through the door, and Widow followed.

"We need to take the stairs," she told them, and Junior let go of the shaggy, savage man.

Both of them stopped and looked ahead, and Widow passed them, saying, "Just follow me, boys."

"We'll be happy to," Junior said. "As you've already learned, our hairy friend will surely enjoy the view of your tight ass."

Widow said over her shoulder, "Not you?"

"I only wished to not be so crude. Yes, of course, I appreciate a fine ass as much as the next son of a bitch."

"You might as well. It's the least I can do for your generous help."

"We are both happy as fuck to help. My friend's motives might be rather self-serving, though, the fucker."

Widow was two steps up when she said, "Oh, not you, though."

Junior didn't see it, but she smiled at the sound of his deep sigh.

And she made sure to give her hips a lot of action with every step.

And midway up the next flight, she kept her hands out of their sight and tugged at the waistband of her skirt, raising it up a bit at a time.

"If I may be so bold," Junior said, coming up behind her, "your legs are rather magnificent in a decidedly sexual way."

She stopped and turned to face him, a few steps above, at a level where he had direct line of sight at her bare thighs. She held one leg out and rotated her short black boot a couple of times.

"Oh, you think so?"

"Yes, without a fucking doubt. So does . . ."

He was looking behind him, and Widow was looking past him, and they saw the monkey man squatted down on the landing several steps lower.

"Hey, Monkey. We have pledged our service to the Queen. Up on your fucking monkey feet."

"Tired."

"Come on, Mr. Monkey. At least try."

The monkey man sighed deeply but didn't get up.

"Hey," said Widow, "we need him to save his strength anyway. Um, to lift that heavy thing, remember? For that. Why don't you carry him, King?"

"Well, that's a wise solution, Queen. Yes. I shall."

He traveled back to the landing, while Widow muttered to herself, "Save his strength? God."

Junior stopped beside the monkey and said, "What the fuck was that, Queen?"

"Oh, just, um, clearing my throat. Better get that monkey!"

"I fully intend to," he said, then turned back to the reclining monkey man.

He'd completed only his first step before burning cinders flew from his ears, and he fell back into a corner, yelling "Yi, yi, yi! Ow, that fucking—"

He shivered like hit by lightning, gagged on his next words, and listened with Widow and the monkey to the unit on his back announcing, "Updated software terminated pending release of new version. Thank you for your patience."

Shaking his head, then wiping away his frothy spit, Junior said, "Well, perhaps that's a blessing. Cursing so much casts me in a poor light, and it's unexpectedly tiring as well."

"I wouldn't have guessed."

"Pray that you never find yourself in such a predicament."

Junior helped the man-monkey to his feet, then turned and stooped a little. The tired monkey man jumped up and held onto him.

While climbing the stairs again toward Widow, he said over his shoulder, "Just don't try any sexual pranks with me in my anal regions. I've become quite knowledgeable about the natural proclivities of monkeys."

Junior couldn't see the monkey man's big grin, but Widow did, and she said, "Yeah, don't bug the King while he's carrying you."

She turned from them and began swaying her hips, climbing steps, and keeping her skirt high, but she heard Junior's heavy boots go silent on the stairs.

"Bug? Bug."

Widow stopped but didn't turn around.

"Mama was becoming—back when Mama . . ."

Widow held her breath, raised her leg and tapped the sharp heel on the next step, then didn't keep climbing.

"What about your momma, King?"

She took a slow, quiet breath as a few silent seconds passed.

"Oh, nothing . . . Queen. Let's all just get up to your room."

Widow hesitated, scoffed without a sound, and said quietly, only for herself, "Well, this should be fun."

* * *

"Here's my room," Widow said as she held the doorknob. "Well, I mean, maybe someday. It seems like it could be nice someday."

She swung in the door, and her eyes were drawn first to the sponge and small bowl of oil on the table across the room. She took a few steps inside, and Junior and the fifty followed.

Before turning to face them, she tipped only her eyes up to confirm that the hatch was closed. It was and looked like every other square pattern covering the entire ceiling. Its single light fixture was glowing, keeping the room dim but with enough light to see.

She turned and gestured with both arms, saying, "What do you think?"

Junior said, "I think I've carried this monkey long enough."

He tapped his strong, hairy arms a few times, and the monkey man unwrapped his legs from around Junior's waist, then stood and let go of him.

"Thanks," he said. "Better."

"You should be rested up. You're rather a lazy type of monkey, aren't you?"

The hairy man only grinned.

"You're very kind, King," Widow said, then turned and aimed for the table between the high-backed blue chairs and its emergency supplies of crude oil.

Behind her, Junior said, "Yes, I've been thinking about Mama and the unfortunate turn her life took."

Widow kept walking.

"It was bad enough that she was becoming—"

A loud pop got Widow to turn in time to see sparks shooting from both of his ears as he danced in a circle, stabbing the wood floor with the point of his sword.

"Whoa! Wow, fucking goddamn—I remember Mama! She's a fucking bug! A fucking, fucking bug!"

Widow froze, watching the scene.

"Yi, yi, yi! Fuck it, fuck it, fuck—"

He hacked and spat a hot sparkling puddle onto the floor.

"Then—then—some goddamn fucker killed her!"

Hacking again, coughing out multi-colored sparks, he rushed toward Widow and grabbed her hair in a meaty fist.

"You killed her! You—"

He shook when something popped and whistled, then a steady buzzing resumed.

In a calm and rational voice, he said, "That's such an unfortunate and challenging malignancy. But as I was attempting to state, I know that it's you that killed my mother."

"I didn't kill your mother," she said, with streaks of desperate honey mixed in. "Let me go."

"Not just yet."

He held his sword up high, ready to drop it through her skull.

"Yes, I knew her, King!" she said, honeyless. "But why would I kill her? It was Archie!"

Junior chuckled and shook his head.

"Oh, nice try. It's a sure sign of guilt to try and blame our noble reactor boss. Shame on you."

"No, really!" she said, her eyes big and pointed at the blade poised above her head. "It wasn't me!"

"You might think that such histrionics will lead to the sparing of your life. I assure you that it will not."

"But I—"

"Shh."

Widow stood within striking distance of his heavy metal blade, looking mostly at Junior, but she also scoffed at seeing the fifty monkey leering at her and sporting a stiff tail.

"The King demands silence to ponder the circumstances."

A few seconds later, he said, "A King is sometimes tasked with finding solutions that are fair and just to all involved."

"What? Have you totally lost your—"

"Shh."

He looked around the room, then at the monkey man beside him. After taking a step back, he rubbed at his chin and surveyed the hairy man's entire height from his feet, up along his hair-coated legs partially hidden under ragged work pants, then across the hairier torso, then at the face that displayed distinct hints of a monkey.

"I have arrived at that solution. I decree that you, Scarlet, will satisfy the sexual needs of my good friend, who I'll refer to simply as the monkey."

"What? You're out of your mind."

"No, that's inaccurate and a faulty, unqualified diagnosis. I am only the King."

"I see how that might seem fair to the damn monkey, but you?"

"Oh, I'll just enjoy the spectacle. This humble room will have to suffice in lieu of a royal ballroom."

"How does it help me?"

"It delays your inevitable demise."

Widow squinted at him and shook her head.

"As an added incentive," Junior continued, "if you surpass my expectations and provide a compelling, if somewhat crude and disturbing spectacle for my entertainment, it might merit the indefinite postponement of your well-deserved slaying."

"This is crazy."

Junior shrugged and said, "Yet, it's what I have decreed."

Widow snarled at him, then looked at the man-monkey, who was watching her from several steps back and already rubbing his crotch.

Looking at the blade of his raised sword, she said, "I guess the oil doesn't matter anymore, huh?"

Junior looked down at his bare chest and rippling abs, then smeared around some of the oil.

"Why would it ever?"

"Um . . . exactly."

"You may begin with that shirt, which is quite pretty, by the way."

Widow stared at him and scoffed, then reached both hands for the highest button.

"Oh," Junior said with a relaxed chuckle, "no, no, no. Look at him. Your goal is to reveal your nakedness to him."

She shot a quick snarl at Junior, then turned her gaze to the hairy man that was at least as much monkey, who kept grinning as he watched only her hands.

She reached quickly for the top button, but she stopped when Junior said, "Oh, do it right. You know you want to seduce him."

She scoffed and said, "Like he needs it."

"It's more about you, Scarlet. You want to be seductive. For a monkey."

"I do?"

"Only you know for sure. But rest assured that I certainly want you to seduce the monkey."

Taking her time, she unbuttoned all the way down, then stopped and looked at Junior. He only tipped his head toward the monkey and raised his sword higher, so she scoffed and looked at the hairy man again.

One shoulder at a time, she pushed the thin blouse over and down her arms, revealing her breasts and their prominent nipples. She let it fall to the floor, then fluffed back her thick mane of black hair.

"Those are very good. The monkey will enjoy those. The skirt now."

"This is enough for—"

"Shh. The skirt. Leave on the boots, though. Your legs are already uncommonly long and curiously shapely, and the provocative height of those heels will surely magnify the appearance of you advertising yourself for sex."

"I'm what?"

He grinned and said, "You deny it? Plead your case. I entreat you."

She scoffed at his smiling face and was about to speak again, when he pointed toward the waiting man.

"Fine," she said, again looking where she'd been told, locking her eyes on wild eyes that were all over her.

The waistband of the skirt was tight but elastic enough that she could stretch it down over her hips, and she let it fall to the floor to bunch up around the very high heels of her short black boots.

She looked down at it, then scoffed while kicking it to the side.

"Now, what?"

"You ask for permission to crawl to him."

"You're really out of—"

He drew back his sword and said, "Shh. We could end this very quickly. Remember that entertaining me is important to both of us."

She took in a deep breath, expanding her chest, then let it out.

"Fine. May I please crawl to the monkey?"

"I will answer you when you kneel."

Widow scoffed silently and lowered herself to her knees.

"Your answer is yes, you may, if you state what you want to do when you get there."

Widow shook her head once, then said, "I, um, want to, uh, give him oral."

Junior laughed and said, "No one employs such clinical and sanitized language here. Come on. Say it right. Say it like you mean it."

"Okay. Um, I want to crawl to him so—"

"Just call him the monkey. More fun for me."

"Okay. Uh, I, uh, want permission to crawl to the monkey so I can—hey, he's really a fifty?"

Junior shrugged and said, "Probably not. I mean, look at his face and his tail."

"Good. That's a re—"

"He might be an eighty."

Widow swallowed hard, then said, "An eighty?"

"Yes, at least. But it's hard to estimate with any reliable level of accuracy with his DNA all puzzled up like that."

"Oh, God. An eighty," she mumbled to herself.

"Proceed."

"Alright. I'm asking for permission to crawl to the monkey to, um, suck his . . . cock."

"And you're not being forced, are you?"

"Oh, uh, no. I really want to. I, um, really want to suck that eighty monkey's cock."

"By all means, then, go ahead."

Chapter 57 – Doing Something So Degrading

Widow leaned forward to place her palms on the floor, and she kept her head up to look at the grinning monkey man. With her bared breasts hanging down, she crawled across the dusty wood floor until her head was near his legs, then she sat back on her heels.

"So, uh, I should just—"

"Yes, your assignment is to service him. He shouldn't be bothered with offering you any assistance. Go on."

She turned her head enough to look up at Junior, kept her lips hiding her fangs, and said, "Maybe I should do you first, big boy. What do you say?"

"I say you tend to my uncivilized friend. Perhaps later? Yes, I might just require that from you. First, though, suck the . . . what?"

She turned enough to look up into the monkey's eyes and said, "The monkey cock," which got him to display a gigantic grin.

She rose up onto her knees, then reached for the top of his stretchy, torn pants. She'd kept her hands out at his sides, and that was barely enough distance to not touch the thick pole behind the cloth and pointing to one side.

Before going any further, she reached both hands around, held the stout tail for a second, then paused when Junior spoke.

"That's a nice touch. Some odd form of jungle foreplay, I'd wager."

She scoffed and returned her hands to the sides of his waistband.

Pulling down, it took hardly any effort before his large, hard post rolled out and pointed straight at her. She left the waistband right up under his shaft, then rushed her hands down by her sides.

With the head of it close to her lips, she looked up into his wild eyes.

"The only reason he's not violently raping you already, Scarlet, is the threat of a sword in the hand of a King. You should thank me, as I'm sure you would not relish a rape by a monkey."

"Um . . ."

"I think it might be nice," said Junior, "if you cross your arms behind you."

"Why?"

"In my estimation, it's a sign of submission."

"Oh. Submission."

"Yes. You're making yourself available to him and kind of promising that you have no wish to interfere."

"You've given this some thought."

"Kings devote much time to careful thought. So, be submissive for the monkey."

She crossed her arms behind her, keeping her forearms together. And she shot a quick glance at her breasts, which she'd just displayed so much more prominently.

"There, see? You're being very submissive and tempting him with those very nice breasts. You're sticking them out there, hoping to get his approval."

She looked up at his big grin and said, "He approves."

"He's a horny monkey. You seem to be at just the right height for what you just requested permission. Do you recall what that was?"

"I, uh, wanted to suck his cock."

"Oh. Past tense. Not anymore, you're saying?"

Widow smirked, then said, "I want to suck his cock."

"Correct. Open your mouth and wait. Both his man and monkey instincts will provide the guidance he needs."

She stared ahead, her lips together, and shifted her lower jaw from side to side a few times. After a quick groan, she looked up again.

Widow parted her lips some, enough for anyone to see that there weren't any fangs in there but not wide enough for what was aimed at her, and waited. The monkey man kept grinning and took a step closer, just enough to touch her lips, then he pushed the entire head inside. Her lips were a flexible ring that conformed to it, then closed around it.

"Bravo. A very good start."

She waited, not breathing, and he took another step, driving the large head deeper into her mouth.

"And there you go. You're a wench on your knees with a nearly one-hundred percent monkey cock in your mouth. I'm enjoying this!"

Widow resumed her breathing, keeping it steady, and waited with the head and part of the thick shaft squeezed between her lips.

Junior said, "Hold his cock with both hands, then keep it close to answer."

She held it as instructed, both hands around the stout base of it, and backed it out to where it was almost still touching her lips.

"Are you enjoying this, Scarlet? Tell me what you're enjoying. Make me believe it, too, for your own sake."

"Yes, I'm enjoying it. I'm enjoying sucking a monkey cock."

"Again."

"Okay. I'm enjoying this. I love sucking monkey cocks."

"Oh, you said love? And cocks? Plural?"

"Oh, what the hell," she said softly to herself. "I'd better just be honest."

"What was that?"

"Nothing. Yes, I love sucking monkey cocks. Mm, I really do love it."

"Well, go ahead and suck, then."

"Mm-hmm," she said, "I sure will," then pulled it back into her mouth.

She squeezed it with her lips and began bobbing her head on it, sliding her wet lips all along the shaft.

"Mm," she moaned, and the monkey man touched her hair softly with a big hand that was hairy and kind of leathery.

She popped it out just long enough to say, "God, I love monkey cocks in my mouth. Mm-hmm."

Her lips again spread her saliva all up and down his hard shaft as she bounced her head on it.

She didn't slow when Junior said, "Monkey, if you cum, I'll remove your head real quick."

All the monkey did was grunt.

"You, Scarlet, beg for his cum. Beg for it as if it's the only sustenance you require."

"Mm-hmm," she said as she slid the stiff post back out.

"I think his name is Igor," she added.

"Splendid! A good name for the brigand from the bush!" said Junior. "Beg Igor for his cum."

Not speaking loudly, she said, "Mm, cum in my mouth, monkey. I want your cum. I beg you to shoot all your hot cum in my mouth."

Then, more loudly, she said, "Igor, I need you! I really need you!"

"To cum in your mouth, you mean."

In a normal voice, she said, "Uh, yep. I'm begging him to cum in my mouth."

She took it back in, squeezed it tight, and pumped it with both hands. She heard the monkey man gasp, but she didn't stop.

"Don't you dare cum," Junior said. "Even though the wench is desperate for a disgusting, sticky delivery."

Junior stepped closer and leaned over, and Scarlet turned her eyes to his as she held the thick monkey cock in her mouth and pumped it steadily.

"You truly do love that, don't you?"

"Mm-hmm."

"You look good like that. That's a good look for you."

"Mm. Mm-hmm."

He brushed aside some of her black hair and said, "Yep. A monkey cock in your mouth for you to suck. That's how you look your best."

"Mm."

"Yes, just like that. Stay still. Huh, look at you now. One minute, you're killing my Mama. And just like that, you're kneeling for a monkey and happily slobbering all over his cock. Life's twists and turns are indeed mysterious at times."

He didn't tell her to moan, but she did anyway.

"He's at least an eighty. Mostly just a wild animal. And you stripped yourself naked, got down on your knees, begged for him to cum in your mouth, and now, you're sucking that giant monkey cock of his. Quite a sight."

She turned her eyes from Junior and his big grin up to the monkey's eyes and even bigger grin.

"I haven't yet consulted a dictionary, but I believe this, what I'm witnessing, is my own personal definition for a wench from this moment forthwith."

"Mm-hmm."

Junior leaned in to get a better look and said, "It's fun for me to watch as you're doing something so degrading that you'd never, ever do it on your own."

She paused her moaning to scoff softly.

"What was that?"

"Mm-mm."

Junior got behind her, knelt, and reached around to fondle her breasts.

"Oh, these are quite nice. A bit small for a King's hands, but I do accept that they are quite large by ordinary standards. Quite large and soft."

In her ear, he said, "Keep sucking that monkey boner, wench. It's where you belong."

He stretched out both of her nipples and held them.

"This is exactly what you should be doing every chance you get. But you know what?"

She shook her head but kept the monkey post snug inside her mouth.

"You need a good fucking too. Yes. A solid fuck from a monkey."

Widow groaned and shook her head, letting the big rod slip back out.

"Oh, God. By an eighty?"

"Yes! Oh, yes, you're getting fucked by this charming fellow who's far more monkey than man."

"Igor, I really need you!"

"I like that," said Junior. "You're really warming up to our jungle friend. It's the kind of degrading sex you've always wanted."

"Mm-hmm. Igor!"

"Stand up and show Igor your ass. Don't let go of that stiff protuberance of his, though."

"Okay," she said, then stood with one hand still on his shaft and turned her back to him.

She reached back with her other hand and held the monkey man with both.

"Oh, just pause like that for a second," Junior said, shaking his head and chuckling. "My, oh my, that's a sight. You're a supreme example of an obscene and indiscriminately lusty goddess, Scarlet. You're standing there naked, just in those delightful little boots, with shamelessly high heels, and aiming a savage monkey's cock at your ass. Or your pussy. My guess is you don't care which."

Widow groaned softly.

"And Igor the lecherous monkey doesn't care either."

"Igor! I really need you!"

"Bend over, wench, and tell him what you want. I'm feeling generous today, so it really is your choice where to accept his brutal penetration."

Widow leaned forward, still holding it so close that the head of it was rubbing up between her ass cheeks.

"I, um, I'm really letting an eighty fuck me?"

"No," said Junior. "No, that's not correct. You're *begging* an eighty to fuck you. Go on, wench. Beg Igor the jungle dweller who's doomed to roam this desolate city."

"Please, I'm begging you," she said softly. "Please fuck me."

"Tell him where. His mind reading skills might be disappointing."

"I'm begging you to fuck my pussy. I want that hard monkey cock in my pussy."

Then, loudly, she called out, "Igor! Please, I need you!"

"Nice touch. I like the pretend desperation in your voice. But everyone here knows that you can't wait to feel that monkey meat inside you. On with the show, already!"

She used one hand on her thigh as she leaned forward, and she guided the hard tool with her other hand.

"Oh my God," she said softly as the monkey gave it a push, slipping inside just the big head.

"Yes, here we go," said Junior. "Tell Igor the wanton monkey man that you want more. You want it all."

"Mm," she said, still leaning forward, "I'm begging for all of it. Come on. Fuck the human woman's pussy."

"Nice ad lib," said Junior. "Extra points for that. Even though it almost, for some unfathomable reason, sounds rehearsed."

The man-monkey chattered his teeth, then gave a violent thrust with his hips. Widow groaned as his stab succeeded in only pushing her forward a step.

"Don't run from it," Junior said, "Yes, he has a mightily thick shaft, but you do want it, don't you?"

"Mm-hmm. Oh, yeah. I'm begging you to get that stiff cock in me."

A half second later, she yelled, "Igor! Now!"

The monkey man growled and pushed, and Widow groaned and took another step.

"Keep trying," Junior said, laughing and holding his sword over her head. "My goodness, what a sexual mutation he has there. It's downright devastating. He could batter to splinters locked doors with that thing."

The eighty kept thrusting, and that kept Widow stepping away, a sharp click on the wood floor with each step. But the violent shoving was never enough to lose contact—he continuously remained at some level of depth inside her.

Several thrusts and steps later, she was at the windowsill, and she held it with both hands, still leaning forward.

"Nowhere to go," Junior said with a laugh. "Bury that monster!"

The hairy eighty lunged with his hips, driving it in deep, and Widow tipped her head back with a silent gasp, her mouth wide open.

"There we go! Hold it right there, both of you! No, wait. Igor, grab her hair, and hold her head back. I like that!"

The monkey laughed with his hairy hips rough against the soft, smooth skin of Widow's ass, and he pulled back on her black hair, keeping her looking up, her mouth open wide in a frozen gasp.

"Perfect! Damn, what a promiscuous, non-species-specific wench you are!"

He laughed, then added, "I didn't think you'd really let a nearly total monkey fuck you. But look! Damn!"

"Igor!" she yelled.

"He's right there," Junior said. "Oh, I get it. You want to get on with the fucking. Beg him. Beg him real nice."

Widow took a few slow breaths, then wiggled her hips a few times, but she couldn't free her hair from his monkey fist.

"Please, Igor," she said softly to the ceiling. "I need a good monkey fucking. Fuck me good, monkey."

She didn't try to see his teeth chattering, but she started bouncing along with every thrust as he began long, steady pumps deep into her.

"What a wench," Junior said. "If there was another monkey here, you'd probably be sucking him."

Widow gave her voice a heavy dose of honey, concentrated and strong from her approaching orgasm.

"You're here, big boy."

"I, um . . . me?"

"Mm-hmm. I sure do want to suck someone. Doesn't have to be a monkey."

"You mean—"

"Mm-hmm."

She looked away and hissed softly, checking the length of her fangs with the tip of her tongue.

"I, uh, I suppose you're right. Doesn't have to be a monkey."

Widow groaned and let her hiss trail off into silence as her fangs withdrew, then she turned to show Junior her mouth.

"Look. Imagine these wet lips squeezing that kingly cock of yours."

"I've been told that. Yes, it's quite Kingly."

"Mm-hmm. Bring it closer."

She turned herself and the monkey so that the window was to the side of them, and Junior took a step closer.

"Closer. Think of it in my mouth. Think of having a wench suck your cock while she's being fucked by an eighty."

"That, uh, that's a unique proposition."

"See if you like it," she said, sugar mixing with each word. "We could do it all the time."

Standing in front of her, tugging down his zipper and holding the sharp blade over her, he said, "You mean, we could—"

"Mm, all the time. Or you could switch with the monkey. Mm, think of it."

"I . . . I . . ."

"Oh, yes. You could fuck me and watch a savage monkey jamming his cock in my mouth. Mm, you could grab my hair."

"I . . . I'd do that. I have a strong grip too. A Kingly—"

"Yes, and you could spank me. While you're fucking me."

"Ooh. Oh, God. Spank you until your ass is—"

"Red. Uh-huh. Oh, yeah."

He reached in his trousers, wiggled to get a grip, and let his stiff pole point straight out. It was bigger than the eighty's, and the swollen head almost touched her lips.

"Mm-hmm, big boy. A little closer."

The monkey kept ramming her, but she mostly held herself still with one hand on the windowsill. With her other hand, she reached out and tried to get a grip on the thick trunk where it grew out of him.

"I . . . you, um . . ."

"Yes, put it in my mouth. I sure know what to do with it. Mm-hmm, oh, I sure do know what do once it's in there."

With a hard monkey tool forcefully and wetly sliding in and out of her from behind, Widow tried pulling the kingly post close enough to get it into her mouth.

"So close now," she said.

"So . . . so close . . ."

"Mm, let me suck."

"I, uh, okay. You can—"

A loud rattle came from his back, his buzzer died, and Junior spasmed a step back as sparks dripped out of both ears and the end of his kingly staff too.

"I, yi, yi, yi! Damn! Sweet fucking goddamn shit!"

Widow hissed, and Junior would have seen her fangs if he hadn't started dancing in circles, cutting the sword through the air above her and the monkey man.

"Wow, Mama! Don't be a fucked up bug! Not a fucking bug! Not, not, not, fuck, fuck—"

He kept staggering in circles, sparks dripping and shooting out of him.

"Woo-hoo! Fucking wow!" he said as his sword clattered out of his hand and across the floor.

He'd twitched himself up onto the cushions and Widow, still getting a monkey planted deep in her, watched, hissing and not hiding her fangs.

She looked up and gasped at the sight of the hatch above Junior opening slowly and quietly, revealing only a dark attic.

"Hoo, boy! Yi, yi, yi . . . fuck!"

A final beat on a bass drum sent sparks everywhere, the buzzer stuttered then evened out, and Junior leaned over, breathing deeply.

"The timing," he said, fighting to breathe but chuckling too. "Such undeniably unfortunate—"

And from somewhere high above in the attic, a thick, wet-looking tarp fell and covered him, pulling him to the cushions.

* * *

Widow stared at the shape of the wheezing, bulky man struggling to move beneath a tarp heavy with some viscous liquid and already trying to lock the thing onto the floor. She looked up when Igor hung his head out.

"I heard you calling, Widow! I—"

"What took you so long? He was making me fuck an eighty!"

"Uh, Widow," he said, pointing. "You're, um . . ."

Widow hadn't moved. She was still naked except for her spike-heeled boots, leaning forward, one hand on her knee and the other holding the windowsill.

Behind her, the nearly total monkey man was grinning at Igor, holding Widow's hips, and treating her to a steady slipping and sliding that had never missed a beat.

Widow grinned and said, "Yeah, well, um . . ."

She took a couple more hard pounds, rough enough to shake around her black hair.

"How trapped is Junior?"

"Who knows? Not long, Widow! Maybe you should—"

"Stop yelling."

"Sorry!" he whispered.

"No, you're right."

She turned just enough to address the man-monkey, but she closed her eyes and let her hair get bounced a few more times.

"Monkey," she said with her eyes still closed.

He grunted and kept pumping, and a few seconds passed with only the sound of him slapping his hips into her ass.

Widow scoffed, then turned back to look up at Igor.

"He's been through a lot, this poor monkey."

"Yeah, and he's fucking a lot too."

"He, uh, he's kind of wild. I mean, you want to talk about stiff? This monkey is—"

Junior had risen to his hands and knees, groaning, and was trying to punch straight up through the thick, wet material.

"Um, Widow."

"I see him."

The monkey kept pounding. And grinning.

Widow sighed and closed her eyes.

More seconds passed.

"Widow! Really!"

"Oh, alright. Monkey, this has to stop."

The monkey didn't stop.

"No, really. You've had your fun. Get that monkey cock out of there."

The monkey didn't get his monkey cock out of there.

She turned and bared her fangs and hissed loudly.

The eighty shrieked softly and slipped it out, causing Widow to groan, then giggle.

She hissed again, and the hairy man-monkey took quick steps backwards.

Widow stood and pointed, saying, "You just stay over there. I'll deal with you later."

"Want."

"Well, so do—oh, just get over there and stay quiet."

He sulked away and crouched in the shadowy corner.

Widow grinned toward him, then walked over to the tarp and the king trapped underneath.

"What is this?"

"I found all kinds of chemicals up here, Widow. That's some kind of paste or adhesive or something. I don't know. I heard you calling, but I had to paint the tarp with it. I hurried! I really—"

"No yelling. You did good. You're a good slave."

"Thank you!" he whispered hoarsely.

She stood over the hidden, struggling man, then circled him slowly.

"What are you going to do, Widow?"

"I don't know. He can't get free of that, or I'm in trouble. My voice barely works on him."

"It worked on the monkey?"

"That and my saliva. Oh my God, I sure had enough time."

"I like your voice and your saliva. I always want to do what you say."

"Yes, you'd better. No, I'll have to think of—"

Junior stabbed a fist up through the fabric, mixing in some of the paste with the copious amounts of sweat he'd worked up and yelled, his voice rational, "Wench Scarlet!"

He hurried up most of his arm, and the sneaky component beneath his skin, surrounded by dried blood, blinked a steady orange rhythm.

"Your amateur parlor tricks cannot—"

Window didn't think, and she didn't speak. She only hissed and lunged for the king's hand.

With a moan mixing with a louder hiss, she sank her fangs into the fleshy back side of his hand. And when he tried to get it free, she hissed more loudly and didn't let it go.

Beneath the tarp, a raucous melody of whistles and small explosions erupted.

"Mama!" he yelled as a few sparks sprayed out through the punch hole in the tarp.

She sucked his blood and juices and shot poisons into him until his fist unclenched. And she still didn't let her fangs out until her bite was supporting the weight of his limp arm, an arm with a much dimmer orange blinker.

Hissing softly, showing fangs with blood filmy on them and dripping from their points, she grinned at the sight of his arm, bent at the elbow, lying still across the fabric.

"Wow," said Igor. "You, uh . . . wow."

"Yes. He's big, but he's not big enough."

"Is he, uh, is he—"

"Dead? Oh, no. Not yet."

A second later, the arm twitched, then flexed weakly into a fist.

"Mama, I'm dying! Mama, don't be a—"

Widow pounced again, hissing as she sank her fangs in deep.

After a minute of moaning, sucking, and swallowing, Widow backed out her fangs and licked the newest pair of red punctures.

"Mm."

"You sounded like you were having sex."

"I did because I was."

"No, I don't mean with the monkey. I mean—"

"That's what I mean too. Biting is sex. Sex is biting. It's all the same."

More than a few seconds passed in silence, then Widow looked up at Igor, who was only staring down at her.

"All the same," he said. "Um, scary."

"Don't forget it," she said, then wiped her lips with the back of her hand.

They both watched Junior's exposed arm for a while, and it didn't move again. The light blinked, but more slowly and less enthusiastically.

"Hmm. The king has fallen."

"I helped!"

"Yes, you did," Widow said, then she stood and picked up her blouse, slipped in on, then put on her skirt too.

"You didn't have to do that, Widow."

"Shush."

It took some effort, but she pulled the tarp aside enough to reveal Junior crumpled, mostly facedown from the weight of it and the poisons flowing through him.

"Hmm. Let's see."

"See what?"

"My poisons, slave. They're kind of amazing."

She got the tarp off to one side, exposing Junior completely. Stooping down, she moved one of his arms, the one out in the open, as close to his back as she could. But his muscles were too large and packed too tightly to get his wrist anywhere near his lower back.

His other arm was trapped under his chest. She tried to drag it out, then roll him enough to get at it, but nothing worked.

"Slave, climb down and help."

"Yes, Widow."

He shimmied down the rope and hurried to her side.

"Together," she said. "Ready?"

He looked toward the monkey and said, "He could help too."

Widow looked and saw the monkey stroking his shaft and said, her voice dripping with nectar, "Don't you cum, monkey. You just stay all tense and uncomfortable."

He groaned and said, "Yes."

Again ready to attempt rolling Junior over, she said, "Ready?"

"Yes, Widow."

Both groaned from the effort, and they tipped him just enough that Igor was able to pry his arm loose. Widow tried moving that one behind Junior and met the same difficulties.

"Well, close enough. Go find some—"

She'd leaned back to support herself, and her hand had rested on the tarp. But she quickly pulled her hand back and studied it.

"What did you say this stuff was?"

"Some kind of sticky paste. I don't know, Widow. I just wanted to make the tarp heavier."

"And it did. It was wetter before. See?"

She rubbed her fingers together.

"It's setting. There's more up there?"

"Yes, Widow. Lots of it. Thicker than this. Different types."

"Hmm."

"It's good? I found a good thing?"

"Could be. We'll see. Hand me a rope."

He hurried over to the shadows and returned with a long piece.

"He's strong, but he's not that strong," she said as she tied the rope first to one of his wrists, then looped and knotted it around the other.

"And if he is?"

"Good point."

She hissed softly at first, then it got louder, and Igor backed away.

A quick snap got her fangs into the sweaty skin of one of Junior's arms, and she hung on as she sucked and swallowed and the bulky, bloated monster man seemed to melt.

Chapter 58 – Quiet Now, Juicy King

Igor kept quiet and only stared and a minute later, Widow took her fangs out of Junior's arm, then licked the fresh pair of red dots.

"Mm, just like that. Sleep, King."

"He, uh, he's not dead?"

Widow stayed close by his back, watching for a minute, then laughed.

"Maybe. He's not breathing. That doesn't mean he's dead, though."

"No? What, then?"

"He's so full of my sweet poisons that he's barely functioning anymore. Oh, maybe just one thing. Let's check."

"Check what?"

"Help me roll him over."

It took some groaning and straining, but they tipped him then let him fall over onto his back. And his kingly rod, still out in the open air from when Widow had tried to seduce it into her mouth, flopped up onto his belly. It was thicker and harder than when he was completely alive.

"Wow," said Igor. "Long live the king."

"Hmm. Probably not."

"He's not breathing, but that thing is still . . ."

"Mm-hmm. I know you can't understand it, being a male. But he's feeling a constant, steady orgasm that just won't stop."

"How? From your bite?"

"Yes, from my bite. That's about all he can manage anymore. He's almost dead, and everything he has left is propping up a truly regal erection."

"But Widow, more bites will kill him?"

"Yes. I just don't know how many. I feel it getting stronger all the time."

"How do you know?"

"Call it instinct. I know the poison so well."

She turned to hold the mutant slave's gaze and said, without a smile, "I am the poison."

She only scoffed at his hard swallow, then she reached out and nudged the stiff pole one way, then the other.

"Well? Kill him before he kills us!"

"Why such a hurry? And stop yelling."

"I'll try. But maybe Archie will find you too? We should just—"

"Shh."

"Sorry! But if you leave him alone, he might recover? Could he?"

"Hmm. Maybe. Yes, I think he might. He's quite large."

"So? Either bite him or—"

"Mount his royal staff? Hmm, you're a wise little slave."

"That's not what I was—"

"Here's your assignment: drag that tarp over by the wall and cut off some strips, just as wide as your hand."

Igor snickered and said, "Or as wide as the king's cock?"

"Hmm, it sure is a thick one. Yeah, about that size."

"As you wish, Widow."

She kept flopping it gently, toying with it, and watched Igor drag away the heavy tarp imbued with a paste that was drying out and hardening. He found a dark corner, where the single light, up in the attic from the hatch being open, struggled to reach.

"Hmm," she said, again looking at it. "You sure had a bizarre script for me and the monkey to follow, didn't you?"

He didn't answer.

"Such a twisted imagination. Such perversions from one who would be a king."

She put her other hand on his chest and paused for half a minute.

"Hmm. So quiet now. Not even a tiny breath. Such a big, quiet, fleshy boy for me now."

She looked back at what she held, sighed slowly, then gave it one long pump.

"Hmm. I should just kill you."

She gave it another stroke, then let her hand again rest at its base, aiming it like a gun barrel toward the ceiling. A quick glance over at Igor confirmed that he was quietly at work.

Looking again at the king's royal staff, she said, "Mm," and began slow, steady pulls and didn't pause again.

"You feel that, King Junior. Oh, I know you do. Every touch is adding to the relentless ecstasy that I'm giving you."

She paused her efforts to lie beside the muscular, prone man, and laid her head on his chest.

"Yes, so very quiet now."

She resumed her stroking, pointing the gun barrel right at her face.

"You seemed obsessed with watching me suck that monkey's cock. Hmm, I'd bet that really was quite a sight, perverted king."

He still didn't breathe.

"Were you imagining me in lingerie too?"

Her cheek rested on his completely still, warm and sweaty chest.

"Hmm, that eighty would have gone even crazier for that. Oh, yeah. A soft, sexy human woman forced to suck his monkey cock."

She stared at the bulbous end of it, and she began sliding her hand far enough along to squeeze it, hiding it from view, until she stroked back down to its base.

"Perhaps you'd like to hear what you could have done? Yes, you're not going anywhere."

She grinned at the sight of her hand, unable to get all the way around, as it worked at a steady pace.

"Yes, you could have forced me to dress sexy for the monkey. Lingerie, if I had any. Ooh, you could have tied me up for him too. Did you even think of that? No, you're not as creative as you think. You could have tied me securely, then left me in the room with the eighty. Oh, the things he would have done."

If anything, the king grew in her hand.

"Hmm, he could have let all his friends in for some fun too. Did you even think of that? No. Would you have liked trying to count how many times the tied-up wench got fucked and had to suck a hard monkey cock? Yeah, but it's too late. Too late for all of that."

She picked up the speed, pumping him more steadily.

"Even without all that, you like watching me. You made me suck that cock for you. Oh, yes, you did."

She gasped at the sight of what she was pumping, then squirmed herself down to where her cheek rested on the hot skin stretched over his thick abdominal muscles, and she kept a steady pulling and relaxing with her gaze fixed on the long shaft aimed at her.

"Even my words are adding to your orgasm. An orgasm that you could never have imagined, not as a man. An orgasm that just won't stop."

She shifted around more, getting her lips much closer. Just tipping her head some would have made contact.

"I had a monkey cock in my mouth. Mm-hmm. You made me put that monkey cock in my mouth."

She sighed, then tipped her head forward, kissed his head, then leaned away again, giggling softly.

"I had to kneel quietly for you with that obscene monkey cock in my mouth. Mm-hmm, that's what you wanted, so I did it. I sure did."

She adjusted the aim slightly, so near that she was almost looking at it cross-eyed.

"I didn't care that he was a monkey, and I'll tell you why: because he was only a juicy, sexy treat for me."

She giggled again and said, "Guess what you are. Yes, that's right. Nothing more."

She was about to kiss it again, when she turned her eyes up to see Igor standing close, rubbing his crotch.

Looking at Igor, she said, "Stay very quiet now, juicy king, while I suck your cock too."

She sighed and leaned toward it, taking inside the head and closing her lips around it.

"Mm. Mm-hmm."

She kept her cheek on his belly, his hard king shaft in her mouth, and her hand stroking steadily.

"Torture!" Igor whispered, causing Widow to snort a short laugh but never slow down.

She only pulled her knees in closer, arranged one boot neatly above the other, pointing both heels away, legs curled in, and stroked a few more times before backing away.

"What will happen?" said Igor. "Can he still, you know?"

"Mm. We'll find out."

She sighed and leaned toward the king's staff again and pressed her lips against his skin, lips parted just enough to squeeze the large head comfortably inside, and she held it tight.

"Mm-hmm," she moaned and picked up the pace.

So did Igor.

Holding Igor's gaze, she nodded with her hand at the base.

"Go, Widow!" he whispered. "Do it!"

"Mm."

She gave the shaft a hard, fast stroke, and her eyes opened wide as she angled it up and turned her open mouth up too.

"Oh my, so much!"

She covered it again and gave it another stroke.

"Mm-hmm."

And again. And she kept stroking.

"Mm . . ."

It took a while, but she tipped his rod up and rolled her head enough to look up at the ceiling. And even Igor heard her difficult swallow.

And a second. And a third.

"Oh my, I know now why he was made king."

"A lot? He had a lot?"

She laughed and said, "It was so much that—"

She frowned and turned her head, then spat out a tiny, smoking fireball.

"Uh-oh," said Igor.

"Hmm. I hope I didn't swallow any of that electrified garbage."

"But you swallowed the rest? You swallowed all that cum?"

She sat up and used one finger to wipe around her lips, sucking it then wiping more.

"Mm-hmm. Now, let's see if he's finished."

She stood beside the king and straightened down her skirt, then fluffed her hair back.

Igor stared, and Widow stared, and the seconds crawled past.

And the king gave no hint that he'd had enough.

"Um," said Igor, "I think it throbbed."

"Huh. I saw that too."

They both leaned to have a closer study of the stout post.

The mutant slave panted, almost out of breath, and said, "Could he? Could he do it again?"

"Hmm. Or die trying. Either way, I need to kill the king already."

* * *

Widow stooped down beside Junior, then eased herself down onto her knees. With one hand, she leaned herself on the cushion between his legs, and she held his stiff rod straight up with the other.

"Wow, that's big," said Igor. "Still."

"And he's so very quiet for me. Such a good boy."

"You think he'll cum again?"

She licked her lips and said, "Wouldn't you?"

"Yes! Yes, I—"

"Stop yelling."

"Sorry!"

She leaned forward, aiming her open mouth, but her long hair fell everywhere on both sides of her face. Still holding him, she sat back on her heels.

"Slave, hold my hair."

"Yes! And I won't yell!" he whispered.

He hurried over and reverently gathered her hair, then held all of it straight up with one hand.

"Like this?"

"Yes. Good slave. Do not restrict me or I'll bite you."

"Yes, Widow. Yes. And Widow?"

"Yes?" she said, her mouth close to the king.

"You, um, you're gorgeous."

He kept a hold of her hair as she turned her head and met his gaze. A second passed, then he looked down at the floor.

"Slave."

He winced while he looked into her black eyes.

"Thank you. You . . . you're not disgusting."

"I'm not?"

"Not really. You didn't ask for that, did you?"

"No, Widow. No! I never—"

"No yelling."

"Sorry!" he whispered.

Looking down, with her lips almost touching it, Widow said, "You, King, forced me to beg for monkey cum in my mouth. Hmm, what kind of king is that? I don't know, but perhaps I'll beg for more of yours."

She dropped her mouth onto it, sliding her lips as far down the shaft as she could before coming up for air.

"Hmm, please give me some more cum. Hot king cum."

She dropped down, then twisted around, slurping and sucking before rising up again.

"I want another mouthful. Shoot another hot river for me to swallow. Mm, I'll swallow it all."

She leaned onto it, sucked and licked, and didn't say anymore until Igor tugged on her hair.

"What, slave?"

"Widow, the door! I forgot that—"

"No yelling."

"Sorry! But I never fixed the lock. Anyone could get in here! Maybe Archie!"

"True. We're not completely safe. Fine, I'll suck and bite until he either cums or dies."

"He's a lucky king!"

"Too loud."

"Sorry! Why not stab him? I'll get his sword if—"

"No. That's not how I kill."

"You like to bite!"

"Shh."

She hissed, showing her fangs, and bit into Junior's belly. For half a minute, she fed and didn't let a single drop escape.

Then, she groaned softly while retracting her fangs. She quickly got her lips around his staff and pumped it furiously with her hand.

Still pumping him, she bit again in a fresh place, then sucked and poisoned before putting her lips around his stiff pole again.

Back and forth she went, and the hard shaft in her hand never softened.

"He's not dying, Widow. Maybe he's just too big?"

"And packed with Mortimer's electrical crap."

"Yes. I think he'll cum again, though."

"Yes, I agree. But I need to do both at once."

"You mean—"

"Mm-hmm. Oh, yes. My poisons are getting stronger, and it feels so good."

She stood quickly and stripped off her skirt, gyrating her ass more than necessary and laughing at Igor saying, "Torture!"

She tossed the skirt toward him, then straddled the nearly lifeless but still muscular and erect man on the cushions.

"Oh yeah," she said, holding him up with one hand, "just like this. Mm-hmm."

Wiggling her hips at first to get it started, she gasped when she began to lower herself onto it.

"Oh my God. I'm being impaled."

"He's lucky! You're lucky! I'm—"

"You're going to stop yelling."

"Yes."

After a deep breath, Widow shifted her hips as she slipped down farther and farther, only a small amount at a time.

"Oh, I can't take any more. Hmm, quite the king."

She rose up on the kingly pole and leaned forward, giving Igor, behind her, an unobstructed view of almost all of the king's talents.

"See what I mean?"

While he was whispering "Torture!" she kissed the King's sweaty, bloody, oily chest.

Hissing but before sinking in her fangs, she started raising and lowering her hips, sliding herself along the stout pole. After settling into a steady rhythm, she bit the skin stretched over a chest muscle and moaned while sucking and swallowing every couple of seconds.

"Torture!" Igor whispered, as Widow kept riding the stiff shaft and sucking juices out of him.

A minute passed, and she abruptly stopped her bite and sat up.

"Wait," she said, her voice calm.

Igor kept rubbing himself but slowed down, staying quiet about it.

"When I killed that monkey, my poison was instantly lethal. And I know why."

"Why? Why?"

"Because Pauline, that sweet little girl that I—"

She sighed and reached for both of her breasts and fondled them while licking her lips.

"—that I tied up so nicely. Mm, just a sweet little tied-up girl for me."

Widow moaned and held her breasts up, supporting them underneath.

"Not a massive, sweaty monster. Oh, no. Mm, just a soft, sweet little baby girl."

She gasped up at the ceiling, then looked down again at the prone monster beneath her.

"She was soft and helpless, and she was licking my pussy. Her tongue felt so sweet, and when I bit that foul monkey . . ."

She groaned and reached one hand down between her thighs.

"Mm, my sweet orgasm got even sweeter. That's what did it."

"I'll lick you! I will!"

"You won't."

She placed both palms on the king's muscular chest and began riding his shaft, raising and lowering her hips.

"Make me cum even more, King."

Her tongue kept her lips wet, and her breasts bounced lightly with every movement of her hips.

"Cum if you want, king. Or don't."

She closed her eyes and laughed softly.

"But I'm cumming. I'm cumming with your thick cock impaling me."

She rode it up and down, her eyes closed and her breasts swaying.

"Mm-hmm. So big and hard. In my soft, wet pussy. So soft."

Igor's hand had stopped, and he only stared at the woman riding the nearly-dead man.

"Oh. Mm, that's nice. Yes, like that. Mm, you're a big boy. Such a big—"

She gasped up at the ceiling, then smiled and looked down, never slowing her hips.

"Such a big cock. Mm, a brutal cock. So big in me, so . . . so . . . mm . . ."

She leaned forward, her smile replaced with an unapologetic hissing and snarling, her fangs bared.

And she sank them deep into a region of unbitten skin on his chest.

She kept her hips high, not high enough to lose him, and Igor began rubbing frantically as he watched her taking short, urgent rides down over the thick shaft then reloading for the next stroke.

Moaning, she left her fangs locked on him, sometimes shaking her head like a shark tearing loose meat.

Not many seconds later, her hissing became muffled chuckling, and Junior's kingly pole shriveled, slipped out of her, and lay limp between his legs.

Widow pushed herself back up, then dragged the back of her hand across her lips.

Her soft laughter ended, and she said, "Oh, God."

"What?"

"I killed him."

"Yes!"

"That felt . . . gruesome. My orgasm and his death . . . all the same."

She fell forward onto the dead man's torso, and a few silent sobs shook her.

"No," she whispered, "I can't be such a killer!"

Igor left himself alone and moved to stand where Widow could see him as she kept her cheek against the body's cooling skin.

He stooped down and said, "You had to."

"I know," she said, then sobbed once. "But that's not why I killed him. Not at that moment."

"Why, then? Why?"

"Only because . . . it felt good. Oh God, it felt so good."

Igor stood, then put a hand on Widow's back.

Her hiss was immediate, and he yanked it back before she could say, "Don't touch me."

"Sorry!" he whispered. "Widow, maybe you just have to be, uh, what you . . . are."

She picked her head up, facing the slave mutant, and wiped under one eye.

"A killer?"

"All the sex, too, right?"

She pushed herself up to sit and looked down at Junior's cooling corpse.

"Both. I have no choice."

"I had to accept this," he said, and she looked up.

He was pointing at the dead extra head still hidden away in a small burlap sack.

She only stared, so he added, "I don't think it ever accepted me, though."

Widow laughed once.

"It probably thought I was the freaky thing."

She laughed again and shook her head once, then sat up without any possibility of being impaled.

"If I don't fight this, I don't know how cruel I'll become."

"Not your fault, Widow. Just . . . be."

She fingered around the mix of sweat, blood, and oil on Junior's chest, drawing random lines and squiggles.

"Just be?"

She paused, but Igor didn't answer and neither did Junior.

"Just be," she said. "Oh, mm, just saying that felt good."

"Say it again, Widow!" Igor whispered. "Say it!"

"I'll just be. I have no choice but to just be."

"Yes!"

"Shh."

She looked over toward the eighty, who was still sulking in the corner, and she let the warmed honey bubble into every word.

"Come here."

He pointed a thick, hairy finger at himself.

"Yes. You. I know what you monkeys like more than anything."

Even in the dim corner, his teeth, more brown than white, appeared in a big smile, and he jumped to his feet.

"Widow," said Igor, "you're not really going to—"

"Pauline," she said, her voice normal, "that sweet, obedient little thing, told me to just jump off the cliff. She's right."

"What cliff? Where?"

"The cliff of denying what I'm becoming. What I am."

"A cliff? I don't get it."

"No. But I'm going to. Oh, I'm sure going to get it. And I feel it inside—so much stronger now."

The man-monkey walked over and stood looking down on Widow as she still straddled the weaponless dead man.

"Stand here," she said with extra sweetness, and the eighty stood close by her side.

She looked around him and smiled at the straight, horizontal tail.

"Stay very still. Good monkey."

She reached to her side and worked his pants down, letting his big monkey boner bounce out, then lock itself horizontal like his tail. She kept going, stretching the cloth over and around everything else, then let his pants fall to the floor.

"Step closer, monkey."

He did, and Widow leaned enough to part her lips and quickly take in the head.

"Mm," she moaned softly as she bobbed her own head, wetting as much of his shaft as she could reach.

"Torture!" Igor whispered.

After playfully shaking her head, she let it slip back out and said, "I know what monkeys like."

The monkey man chattered his teeth and said, "Ass."

"Mm-hmm. Want a nice, tight, human woman's ass?"

He squinted, eyes nearly closed, and looked down toward Widow's hips and ass before holding her gaze again.

"No ask."

"You don't have to. I'm offering."

He shook his head and with a jerky sob, he said, "No ask!"

Widow stared for a second, then said, "You didn't ask what?"

He wiped a leathery finger under each eye at the same time.

Wincing his eyes shut, he said, "Be. This."

"Oh my God," Widow said, her voice suddenly normal. "You really—"

"No ask!"

Widow sniffled once and wiped under each of her eyes too.

"No. No, you didn't ask to be that. You were a man once."

He nodded.

"And you never imagined a human woman would offer you her ass," she said, then took his monkey rod back into her mouth and bobbed her head for a minute.

"Ass. Ass?"

"Mm-hmm," she said, then slipped it out just enough to bubble out warm molasses. "A very nice ass. Mm, you're so big that I'm scared."

He grinned and nodded and said, "Scared."

"Mm-hmm, dangerous monkey. And you're so big and slippery now for me."

She sucked it a few more times, held it straight up and licked, then pumped it with her hand while saying, "In the human woman's ass, monkey man. Big monkey cock. In my ass."

"Ass!"

He quickly got on his knees behind her, and she rose up on her hands and knees and shook her hair to one side.

"In the ass, monkey man. We both want it."

His long, hard rod was laying up on Widow, resting between her cheeks and farther still, up onto her back.

"Scared."

Widow whimpered and said, "So scared. So scared of the hard monkey!"

"Ass!"

He lowered the head, and Widow rose up enough to reach for her ass cheeks with both hands and pulled them as far apart as she could. The monkey found the spot and began to push but didn't plunge in.

"Hold on to me, monkey."

He laid his leathery hands on her hips and kept her in place, and Widow, arching her back and jutting her breasts out, put her hands over his.

He grunted and lunged and forced himself partway inside.

Widow gasped at the ceiling, then said, "Yes, like that. Deeper, monkey. So scared!"

"Deep. Scared!"

She still held his hands as he kept her from retreating from his attack, and he gave her a series of short stabs, driving in deeper each time.

"Mm-hmm. Oh my God. Yes, just like that."

The monkey had free reign to slide out, leaving inside just enough for her to squeeze, then rush back in, getting a gasp out of her each time.

While the monkey held her hips, and she held his hands, she said, breathless, "Monkey. Don't fight it. Just be . . . what you are."

"Be?"

"Mm-hmm. Be. Monkeys are rough. Oh, so rough."

He shrieked like a chimp in battle, then grabbed all of her hair in one hand. When he jerked it back, Widow got dragged almost upright, her breasts bouncing and her mouth open wide as she cried out, "Ah!"

She let go of the monkey hand on her hip and used both hands to try to keep her hair from being ripped out, but the monkey howled and shook her head around.

With both hands up, trying to save her mane, her breasts were way out in front and shaking all around.

"Monkey! Oh God, monkey!"

He shrieked again and got his free hand around to roughly squeeze one breast, then the other, almost crushing them with his thick, hairy fingers.

And all the while, he was ramming his merciless monkey rod deep into her ass, each thrust jolting her away and jerking her breasts around.

He pulled her head farther back, causing her to squeal at the ceiling.

"Widow! He's killing you!"

"Quiet, Igor! He's just being . . . a monkey!"

He shrieked and cackled, snapping her head forward and back, still ramming his monkey member deep.

"Mm-hmm. Yes, just like that! Oh!"

Yowling at the ceiling, he let go of Widow's hair and brutalized both of her breasts, squeezing, rubbing them all over, sometimes pinching.

Free of his grasp of her hair, she leaned down to place both palms on Junior's chest, angled her ass up high for the beast, and almost growled as she bit deep into the dead king.

"Mm," she said after a few moments and slipped back out her fangs.

Only seconds later, she smiled and said, "Oh, there we go. Mm, biting and orgasming at the same time! Oh, God!"

"Sure he's dead?" said Igor.

"Mm-hmm. He's still as dead as a dead king can be."

She pushed herself up until she was nearly straight up again.

"So, the monkey made you cum?"

"Mm-hmm. And he still is. What a wild orgasm. Mm."

"So, chase him away now, Widow? He's going to hurt you!"

"Mm . . ."

She found the big hairy hands and put hers over his as he continued to attack her breasts. The man-monkey grunted and nearly crushed them in his strong grip.

"Oh, I don't think so, slave," she said. "Such a good monkey."

"Good," said the monkey. "Ass!"

"Mm-hmm. Cum, monkey. Cum on the human woman, you brutal monkey. You know what to do. You were a man once."

"Cum," he said and gave her a decisive thrust and held it for a second, then slipped his significant tool out and jabbed it up between her ass cheeks, aiming it at her lower back.

"Just like that," she said and reached back with both hands to press her ass cheeks together. "Pump, monkey. Ooh, so smooth. Pump."

Gripping her hips again, the monkey gave his confined post a hard push, then jerked it back, blasting out his first shot, and Widow said, "Uh-huh, there you go."

He pumped again up between her tight ass cheeks.

"Mm. Mm-hmm . . ."

Then, he shrieked and pulled it free, pointed it higher, and kept stroking it with a weathered monkey hand.

"Oh! Oh, mm, just like that. So hot and so much! Such a wild monkey!"

"Wild!"

"Oh, so wild. Good. Good monkey. That was just what I needed."

"Torture!" whispered Igor.

Widow turned her head, didn't smile but winked at Igor, then said, "Kiss me, monkey. Come around and kiss."

"Kiss?"

"Mm-hmm. Be a good monkey man for me."

"Widow, really?" Igor whispered.

"Shh," she whispered back as the man-monkey shuffled around, then stooped down in front of her.

"Kiss?"

"Mm. Yes."

He cackled once at the ceiling, then started leaning toward her, his lips ready. But before he could kiss her lips, he snarled and rose back up onto his knees.

"Widow, um . . ."

The eighty shrieked at the ceiling, then clamped her head between two big, hairy hands. His stiff monkey rod was aimed right at her mouth.

"First. Suck balls!"

Widow groaned and fought to get her head free, but his hold couldn't be challenged. When he shook her head from side to side with one hand and held his hard shaft straight up with the other, howling at the ceiling, Widow gasped.

And he pulled her face into him, covering her so tightly that she couldn't breathe.

"Suck balls!"

"Widow!" yelled Igor.

If she'd hissed first, no one could hear it. She spread her jaws wide, and she clamped down, sending her fangs as deep as they could go into the soft bag of flesh.

He whimpered, and it faded to nothing after less than a second. And when he collapsed, Widow followed him down, her fangs still in him.

Still biting, still sucking and still poisoning, she looked up at Igor.

Who only stared and took another step backwards.

Chapter 59 – The Unmistakable Stink of Him

Widow's knees were still far apart as she straddled Junior's thick legs, but she was lying flat on him, her fangs still in the monkey that she'd just instantly killed with her poisons.

She peeled back her lips, and Igor watched as she slowly backed out her long fangs, moaning the entire time. She turned to face him more directly and licked at her lips, then sat up on the dead king.

She tipped her head back, and he observed what the monkey had sprayed all over her back, most of it too thick to even run down off of her.

"You may lick that up."

"Widow, that's not funny."

"I'm not joking, slave. It's a slave's job."

"Um, sorry, but I'm not that pathetic. Just kill me."

"Hmm. Perhaps I'll allow your defiance this one time. Find me a towel, then."

He rushed into the shadows and hurried back with a torn piece of cloth. He handed it out to her, but she only stared into his eyes.

"Your eyes, Widow. They, um . . ."

"What?"

"I think they're blacker than before. Yes, I'm sure of it."

"They see you quite well," she said. "Mostly, your throat."

He swallowed hard and pulled back the towel.

"Yes, uh, yeah. I'll just, um . . ."

He stooped down behind her and began blotting up the monkey mess, smearing and dabbing until he'd cleaned her skin of it. Then, he tossed it as far from them as he could. It hit the smooth wood floor and didn't slide any farther.

"You must dispose of Junior's body. But stash the juicy monkey man somewhere for later."

"Why not both?"

She pushed herself up and stayed seated, looking down at the dead man.

"Electrical things."

"Oh. Yeah, that's right. Not the best for, um . . ."

"Feeding."

"Yeah. Um, Widow, I don't think I can carry the king up to the roof for the bats."

"He is no longer a king."

"No, but he's still heavy. You didn't, um, lighten him all that much."

Igor grinned and waited, but he only got a blank stare from Widow.

"Sorry!" he whispered. "Uh, how about out the window?"

"Very well. For the boars."

She stood, keeping her boots against the dead man's hips.

"My shirt. Bring it."

Igor squinted at her before saying, "Uh, yes. Yes, Widow."

He handed it to her, and she put it on, then brushed her hair back before beginning the buttons. After finishing as many as she'd wanted buttoned, she remained standing over the body, and Igor stared at her hands as she rubbed them around on her ass cheeks partially covered by the thin blouse fabric.

He mouthed the word, "Torture!" then watched her take a few steps to the side, then turn to watch him.

The small mutant man stooped down and reached under Junior's arms, then grunted while trying to drag him toward the window.

He gave up and tried to catch his breath, looking up at Widow.

"The monkey would have helped."

"Don't ever hint that I should not kill."

"You're really embracing the whole—"

"Shh. You said the attic held moving equipment."

"Oh, yeah! Yes, I did. I mean, it does. Permission to go and—"

"You have *orders* to go and get what you need."

"Yes. Yes, Widow. Thank you."

He bowed, gripped the rope with both hands, and climbed up and out of sight in the attic. Widow scoffed and picked up her skirt, then stepped into it and straightened it out.

Two steps, with heels barely sounding on the wood floor, got her beside the monkey man slumped into a pile. She nudged him with the toe of her boot.

"Hmm. When I want to kill, now, I kill. My poisons know."

She circled around to the other side of him, then stooped down.

"Perhaps I should have only brought you close. That way,"— she leaned forward to whisper, streaked with honey, in his ear— "your cock would still be hard for me."

She waited, offering a modest grin, then scoffed at getting no response.

"Well, my voice won't resurrect the dead. Not yet anyway."

She stood and straightened her skirt again, then looked up at the sound of a button clicking, a motor humming high above, and the sight of a low cart with sturdy wheels being lowered through the hatchway.

Just loud enough for Igor to hear, she said, "Stop."

The moving cart's descent paused immediately.

To herself, she said, "My voice controls the living quite well, though."

Calling out again, she said, "Proceed," and the body of the cart rested on Junior, with none of its four wheels touching the cushions or the floor.

"Close enough."

"Yes, Widow."

He hurried down the rope, and Widow stepped away from both bodies. With crossed arms, she watched the mutant slave man fight with the mass of flesh, and he managed to tip him up onto the cart.

"To the window!"

"For?"

"For the boars, Widow!"

Walking away, she said, "The towel too. They'll eat that as well."

"Yes! Yes, they will!"

He began rolling the cart, and the wheels squeaked, he groaned, and the progress was slow.

Widow had reached the rag used to blot up monkey slop, and she began kicking it toward the window. Without her seeing it, Igor picked up Junior's sword and laid it beside him on the cart, then pushed it up against the wall.

From a distance, Widow scoffed at seeing Igor turn a crank that lifted the cart's platform. He paused the effort only to slide the bolt and swing open the wide plank, then he cranked the body up higher.

She waited, several steps away, and watched as he grunted and rolled the body onto the sill, then gave it a hard shove with both hands, sending it tumbling to the street.

But she gasped when he raised the sword toward the window too.

"Igor, don't you—"

He threw it out, too, then whipped around and stared at her, his eyes big.

"Sorry! Just cleaning out the—"

"And if Archie comes this way? Will he not recognize his sword?"

He swallowed hard, whispered, "Sorry!" then leaned out to look. Widow kicked the cloth closer, then looked with him at the street far below.

"I can go get it," he said. "I'll just—"

"Leave it for now. There are other things that—"

The clattering of many hooves echoed up and down the dark street. Only seconds later, a dozen boars, big and bloated and oily, came into view.

"Shh," she whispered. "Run, slave. Put out that light."

"Yes, Widow."

He hurried up the rope enough to pull the light's chain, then slid quietly onto the cushions and rushed back to Widow's side.

He whispered, "They can't get up here, Widow. They—"

"They would attract attention while they wait for their next handout."

"Oh. Yes. That's very true."

They watched as giant snouts poked and prodded at the body, jockeying for position as they almost bit each other. One chomped at a leg and pulled, but another held an arm, which came loose.

That boar squealed and ran off with another of them growling and chasing it.

They grunted and ripped and chewed, most trotting off with a hot meal. And Widow and Igor looked down on just a smudge where the body had hit and a weak glint off of the sword.

"Solved that problem," Igor said.

"And perhaps created another."

"Huh?"

"Electronics."

"Oh. Not good. And, uh, maybe I shouldn't go right now anyway," he said, pointing.

Widow looked, too, and they watched as a small band of men, some carrying torches, approached The Webber Building.

"Archie," she said, mixing a low hiss with the word.

"How do you know?"

"His scent. The unmistakable stink of him."

* * *

"Boss, I'm exhausted."

676

Blade, who had had his blade taken by Archie before they'd even left the reactor complex, leaned the heavy crate on his shoulder into the nearest brick wall.

"You said you were strong, you son of a bitch."

"But Boss, I've been carrying this thing all over—"

"That thing is my very sexy, mutated, fuckable treat. But hell, you should be tired. Alright, set her down."

"Thanks, Boss."

The tall, thin man heaved the crate containing the mutant girl up and off of his shoulder, then set it down near the building's wall.

"Permission to sit?"

"Fuck, yeah. We all need a break."

Blade sat on the crate, then smirked as the captive mutant girl's tail waved around and slapped him in the face.

"We could still lop that off," he said. "Doesn't have to stick up out of that hole like that."

Sammy said, "He told you, dumbass. That's to hang onto when he, or you, or any of us fucks her through that hole."

Blade groped for the flapping tail, then held it down and rested his back against the wall.

"A hole in a hole. Kind of fucking genius, actually."

Sammy snickered and said, "As long as you don't care which hole you fuck once you get your sleazy cock through the crate hole."

"Who said it's sleazy?"

"I did," said Sammy, "because I know you've been fucking those—"

"Guys," said Archie, grinning at their banter. "You're plenty fucking entertaining, but you might as well be ringing a goddamn dinner bell. Boars, remember?"

"Oh," said Sammy. "Yeah. And fucking bats."

He looked up at the endless blackness beyond the dim glow of the streetlights. Archie looked up, too, then at the two men carrying torches.

"Snuff those out, you fuckers. We go by streetlight light. Keep them ready, though."

"Aye, Boss," said one, and they killed the flames.

"Better. Let's keep the fucking conversation down, alright? You miserable fuckers."

"Boss," whispered one of the Spencer twins, "I think I—"

"Did I fucking say to whisper? No, I sure as fuck didn't. What the hell are you babbling about, Spencer?"

"There's something shiny," he said, pointing across the street, "over there by that post."

"And that's supposed to interest me how?"

"Might be a clue."

"Oh," Archie said, scoffing. "A clue. Something shiny is saying, 'Hey, everyone! The flesh-eating freak that always fucked his momma is here! I'm the proof!'"

Spencer shook his head, grinning, and looked down.

"Hey, don't feel bad. I'm just trying to toughen you up. Why don't you scoot your flea-bitten, sore-crusted ass over there and see what it is?"

He looked up quickly and said, "You mean, because it might be a clue?"

"Fuck. Sure, Spencer. Yeah, it just might fucking be."

"Right away, Boss."

The Spencer twin took his bow with him and when he was halfway across the street, Archie snickered and said, "Maybe it's Junior's spine. Hey, Sammy, would a spine shine enough for a dipshit like that Spencer boy to see it?"

"Uh, doubtful. Something would have eaten it by now too."

"You're fucking right. Fresh spines are probably in high demand in this goddamn dump of a city."

They both looked up when Spencer called out, "Hey, Boss! You won't believe this!" and started walking back, swinging something around.

"Well, I'll fucking be," Archie said, shaking his head. "Is that what I think it is?"

"How would I know what you're thinking?"

"Dammit, Sammy, don't take everything so fucking literal. I mean, is that my sword?"

"Oh, shit. Maybe?"

"Boss!" said Spencer, "I think this is—whoa!"

His boot slid out from under him, and he landed hard on his ass, but he kept the sword raised high.

"Smart," said Archie. "I'd fucking gut him and feed him to—"

"Hey," Spencer said as he touched the street all around him. "Fresh kill, Boss."

"Human?"

"Could be."

"Animal?"

"Could—"

"Fuck, I've heard enough."

He and Sammy and a few others started walking toward the man still seated in a slick area of the street.

"You," Archie said, "get that torch fired up."

"Right, Boss."

He struck a match, touched it, and got the thing blazing.

They gathered around the red smear in the road, and Archie pointed, saying, "That's my fucking sword. Fucking Junior was here."

"Are we sure?" said Sammy.

"You fucker. You think a bat is going to carry a sword around just for fun, then toss it here? Come on. What the fuck."

"Oh, uh, yeah. Probably not."

"Unless . . ."

"Unless what?"

Archie laughed once, then said, "Unless that wet spot is all that's left of Junior."

He aimed a pointing finger all around the limits of the red smear.

"That cannibal fuck got eaten right here. Got himself chopped up, sliced and diced, and everything except fucking barbecued."

"Then, digested?"

"Yeah, Sammy. Way to insert your fucking self into my storytelling."

"Sorry, Boss."

Archie took the sword from Spencer but didn't offer him a hand up. The torch bearer had to do it, and he got pulled down onto the slimy brick pavement.

"Will you guys quit fucking around?"

He pointed the sword at The Webber Building, then jabbed it higher, then higher until he'd aimed the weapon at the roof.

"Guess where we're going, fuckers."

"Not to rescue Junior."

"That's funny, Sammy. No. I sent that mommafucker out here after a nasty wench named Scarlet. No, fuckers, we're on a Scarlet hunt now."

"Yeah, Boss. Because Junior is probably—"

"Piles of steaming boar shit all over this goddamn city. Yeah."

Chapter 60 – More Than Her Own Life

"Those men," said Igor. "You're sure that's Archie and his gang?"

"His employees. Whatever you call them, they're looking for me, if Mortimer is to be believed."

"Why would he lie? Why?"

"Keep whispering, slave. Or one quick bite will drop you to the floor."

"I will!"

"No, Mortimer probably isn't lying. The boars took Junior away, and maybe they—"

She saw the glint of the sword as Archie was stabbing it at the building.

"Um, Widow. He found the sword, so he—"

"Knows that splat on the bricks is probably Junior. Which means, he—"

"Is going to search for you in this building."

Widow scoffed and said, "He will surely try, but it will take time. It's a large building."

"But he knows which rooms to check! There's a puddle!"

"Are you considering yelling again?"

"No, Widow," he whispered. "Not now especially! We should hide."

"We will. Soon."

"What about the monkey? What do we do with that?"

"Leave it. They'll think all the,"—her stomach growled—"cum puddles are from him."

"You're hungry?"

"Always."

"There's food stored in the attic."

"Yes, I know," said Widow. "My favorite kind too."

"How do you know that? How?"

Pushing him aside and closing the shutter plank, she said, "Her name is Marie."

"Oh. Wait, you're going to eat her?"

"Hmm. Sort of. I told you, it's all the same anymore."

"But we don't have time! We have to—"

"Climb the rope. Turn on the light."

"Yes, Widow. Then, we can—"

"Then, use the loops from one hoist for each of her ankles, if they aren't already on her."

"But Widow, we—"

"Lower her to me. Then, lower the other two loops."

"Yes, Widow. Then, I—"

"Then, you'll scurry off into the dark until I summon you."

"Yes, Widow."

She waited in the dark as he mumbled unintelligible cuss words until he found the rope. A few seconds of quiet were followed by the pull chain clinking and adding some light to the attic and the cushions below.

When Igor clicked the button to start one of the hoists, Widow leaned back into the rough planks covering the window and touched her belly with both hands, then she wiggled the fingers of one hand down into her skirt, stretching its elastic waistband.

"Mm, a little girl on a rope."

She chuckled softly and shook her head.

"Not long ago, I would have asked myself what's wrong with me."

Up above, in the attic, Igor dragged things around, sometimes mumbling to himself.

Widow rubbed steadily and said, "Not anymore. Everything is right with me."

She gasped softly at the sound of the hoist and a second later, it got quiet. Right away, another button tap roused the motor again. And a second after that, she saw the very ends of the crafter's hair as she was lowered toward the cushions for her.

"Oh, my little girl. Hmm . . ."

She walked over, stepping lightly in her short boots, then stood on the cushions as the upside-down crafter girl's face passed hers, then her breasts, then her hips and thighs, and Widow said, "Stop."

The click followed her command instantly, and the crafter stopped with her ankles about even with Widow's face. She hugged the girl's legs close with one arm, then looked up and held out her hand.

"Drop the scissors."

"Yes, Widow. You're getting her out of there?"

"No."

"You're leaving her upside-down? Why?"

Widow shivered, staring at the suspended girl, and it led to a smile.

"Because it's right. It's the best. Mm, I feel it just looking at her like this."

"Oh. Um, okay."

He reached around out of sight, then leaned as low as he could and dropped them into her hand.

"Shall I hide myself, Widow?"

"Not yet. Sit quietly and watch, if you wish."

He whispered loudly, "I wish, but with Archie—"

"Shh."

Widow started cutting down along one of Marie's legs, taking her time, then cutting through the waistband of her reactor-issued work pants.

"Hmm," she said when the fabric fell away, leaving one leg and part of her ass exposed.

She cut the other leg the same way, then reached around and wiggled it all out and tossed it up to Igor. The girl's t-shirt, no longer tucked in anywhere, slid down and bunched up but still covered her breasts.

"Oh . . ."

With both hands, she held the girl by the backs of her thighs, pulled her in close, and inhaled. She let her hands slide down until she was holding both ass cheeks, then she kissed each leg, stooping down to give the girl's thighs her attention too.

Still holding her close, Widow looked up and said, "Raise her."

"Yes, Widow."

A click and a whine got Marie started, and Widow waved for a stop after a short distance of travel.

"Hmm," she said while snipping at the girl's t-shirt.

She threw the scraps up to the attic, then the scissors too.

"Mm, such a perfect little girl," she said and gave each of her breasts a brief kiss. "So sweet to offer me all you have."

"Widow, sorry to interrupt, but Archie—"

"Isn't she adorable, slave?"

"Yes, Widow. Yes. But—"

She looked up at the mutant in the attic, keeping her chin snug between the crafter's breasts.

"There's only one way she could be perfect: if she were dressed like a little girl."

"A little girl, Widow?"

"Mm-hmm. Not by force. Oh, no. If she had dressed herself like a pretty little girl just for me. To offer herself to me. Mm, that would be perfect."

While Igor was speaking, she gave each of the crafter girl's nipples a kiss and a soft nibble.

"But Widow, probably no little girl could ever get here. Not with what it takes. You must know that—"

"Slave, I speak not about a true little girl. No. A grown woman who dresses in teasing little girl clothes. Mm, that's what I want."

"Why?"

Widow spun the girl to face away from her, then reached around and fondled her breasts, sometimes rubbing up and down her belly and thighs.

"Why? Some . . . something about a baby girl is just so . . . oh, I don't remember, slave. You shall seek to bring me what I desire."

"Where? How?"

"You figure that out. Keep your eyes open, always searching. Find me what I crave."

"Yes, Widow."

"Mm, so sweet. Slave, hand down a strip."

"Yes."

He reached behind himself, then played out the end of one of the tarp lengths that he'd cut earlier.

Widow took hold of it, and he let the other end fall.

"Oh, just hold still for me, pretty little girl."

She pressed the sticky material against Marie's ankles, then began winding it around, saying, "So nice and still for me."

She got to the end, then smoothed it into the underlying layers.

"Hmm. That's . . . nice. Another one, slave."

Widow started a new binding around the girl's thighs, near her knees. Halfway through winding it, she began to moan.

"Are you okay, Widow?"

"Mm-hmm. Binding my little girl is . . . ooh, it's like . . . an orgasm."

"Just doing that?"

"Mm-hmm."

She finished, smoothed it down, then held her ass cheeks and kissed her thighs, most of those kisses almost touching the tight wrappings that she'd just applied.

Her face still rested between the girl's bare thighs when she looked up and said, "Another strip."

Holding the end of the sticky cloth in one hand, she spun the girl to again face away. Starting near her already bound wrists, she looped the material around the girl's arms, overlapping to give complete coverage, and wound it as far as she could before sealing it like the others.

"Ah, there we go. My little girl is so . . . mm, helpless."

She spun her captive around to face her, pulled her close, and looked up.

"How many straps are left?"

He looked away briefly, then said, "Four, Widow."

"Hand one down."

She took it, fed it around the girl at her waist, and looped it as many times as she could to bind her already bound arms tight into her body.

"Another?"

"No. Not yet. Lower the other hoist."

"Yes, Widow."

He clicked, the motor hummed, and two thick ropes, each with a leather loop, came through the hatchway.

"All the way down to the cushion."

"Yes," he said, then clicked off the hoist when the loops had touched and had begun to lean over.

"Good."

"Should I , um, come down there and—"

"No. Wait there."

She gave the hanging girl a spin, then let her rotate one way until the ropes sent her spinning back the other way.

"Hmm, like a little dance for me. Yes, I know. You're seducing me, little one."

She paused to look down at her boots, then sat near the loops. They slipped over the boots easily, and she gave each a tug and found that they were secure before looking up.

"Slowly, slave. Get me even with my little one."

"Yes, Widow."

To the sound of faint humming far above, as a motor toiled in the perpetual night three stories above the attic floor, Widow lay back and watched as the sturdy ropes lifted first her legs straight up, then her hips left the cushion. Seconds later, she was completely in the air, with her long black mane still touching the cushion. Another second, and her hair was free, too, and Igor stopped the lifting when she was at the same height as the crafter.

Widow reached around first for the girl's breasts.

"Oh, so soft. And such an excited little girl too. Mm."

She gave each nipple a gentle pull, then held the girl's hips to turn her back around.

"Mm, such pretty lips you offer me too."

With one hand holding the back of the girl's head and the other across her bound arms, Widow kissed the girl's lips, then quickly backed away.

"Oh," she said, looking at the girl, "you parted your sweet lips for me? You're just adorable."

She touched one fingertip to her lips, then rubbed along the top, then back along the bottom.

"Mm, such a soft, juicy little thing."

Smiling at Marie again opening her mouth, she said, "Yes, you may. Of course, my little one."

She plunged a finger into the girl's mouth and watched the wet lips close and hold it.

"Oh, such a sweet little girl. Suck, my little one."

She leaned back farther and studied the girl's chest.

"Oh, but you're breathing again? Hmm, let's see about that."

While Widow was holding the crafter's hips with both hands and rotating her to face away, she said, "Watch for a moment, slave. I've become fond of torturing you."

He held a hoist rope in one hand, standing at the edge of the opening, and looked down with his other hand ready, close to his crotch.

"Mm," she said and grabbed the waistband of her skirt with both hands.

Igor started rubbing himself as she wiggled her ass and forced the skirt up, just a small distance at a time and left it around her thighs.

"Mm-hmm," she said. "My precious little girl wants my . . ."

Widow looked up, grinning.

"Uh, pussy?"

"Mm, yes. She adores my pussy."

"I—"

"Shh. I don't want to know."

Widow looked again at her captive.

Igor watched in silence for a few seconds, then whispered, "But Widow! Archie will be here soon! Hurry!"

"Oh, I know, little slave. We're almost ready. Come down with the remaining webs."

"Webs?"

"Straps. Those delightful, sticky strips of tarp."

"Yes, Widow."

Still holding her hips and pulling her bound hands tight between her legs, Widow said, "Oh, such soft fingertips you have, little girl. Yes, touch me so softly. Slowly now, little one. Mm, just like that."

"She's, uh, she's—"

"Mm-hmm. She's touching my pussy. She doesn't want to ever stop."

She tipped her head away, closed her eyes and sighed, and smiled as the crafter used her hands, bound at the wrists, to pleasure Widow high between her thighs.

"She senses, too, that the more of my wetness she touches, the stronger and sweeter is her orgasm."

"She's having, a, um—"

"We both are."

Widow scoffed quietly at the sound of Igor swallowing hard, then she addressed the captured crafter again.

"And your hair is already out of the way for me? Yes, you know that you need a little bite. Let's just see if we can get that troublesome breathing stopped. You need to stay so nice and quiet for me."

Igor had managed to get down to the cushions, still holding the sticky straps, and he watched as Widow bared her fangs, moaned softly, and slipped them into the girl's neck with no sign of resistance.

She moaned and felt Marie's chest with both hands and when her breaths had ceased, she giggled softly before pulling back her sharp teeth.

Rubbing all around the girl's breasts and the surrounding skin, Widow said, "Mm, just like that. My sweet little girl doesn't need air anymore. Only what I offer her."

"You killed her?"

"Mm, no. I know that all she can do now is feel the orgasm my playful little bites gave her."

"Uh, playful?"

"Mm-hmm. She loves those too. And she's ready."

"Ready for what, Widow? You're not going to—"

"Shh. Wrap us together."

"Yes. Um, how?"

"Use the longest one. Bind us at our waists."

"Yes, Widow."

He'd just started with a wider, longer band, and Widow said, "Make our bindings tight, slave. We both want to be bound tight against each other."

"Yes. Yes, Widow."

He spun them together several times, keeping the strap taut, then pressed the end onto the wrappings below. Widow's blouse had sagged enough that he was able to place all of the bindings against only their skin.

"Mm, the little girl's hands are trapped just where I want them. She adores me. Her soft touches tell me so."

"Yes, Widow, of course, but if Archie—"

"Very well, slave. Be sure that the room gives no hint that anyone but the dead monkey has been here. Then, go to the attic and lift me and my precious little lover girl up."

"Um, lover girl?"

"Yes. It must be from my bites. Of one thing I am sure: my sweet, captured little girl loves me more than her own life."

Chapter 61 – You Giant Freak Spider

"Blade, Blade, Blade," Archie said while shaking his head.

In his right hand, he held the recovered sword that he'd lent to Junior. In his left, he still held the one that he'd taken from Blade when ordering him to carry the crate.

He was looking down at the self-proclaimed strong man who remained on the landing just below Widow's floor. He'd set down the crude wooden box with its built-in mutant female and had just sat himself down on it.

"We're almost to the top of this wrecked, fucked up building. Get your sorry goddamn ass and my sweet treat up here."

"Boss, I'm dying. How many more floors?"

Archie called up the stairwell.

"Spencer? How far up have you scouted?"

"All the way, Boss," Spencer yelled, "I'm at the door to the goddamn roof."

Looking back at the man lounging on the crate, Archie said, "See, fucker? Only—"

Spencer, up above, continued, saying, "You want me to check out the roof?"

Archie scoffed and said to Blade, "Interruptions. So fucking rude."

He yelled up to Spencer, "No. No wench would be up there offering her sexy, mutating flesh to the goddamn bats. Come on down."

Blade pleaded, "Can I just wait here with your thing that you want to fuck some more?"

"Are you mocking my sexual appetites?"

"Oh, uh, no, Boss. Never. Right away."

He hefted the heavy crate onto a shoulder and began a slow climb up the remaining steps. Archie nodded, watching his progress, then looked to his right when Sammy called him.

"It's the only door on this floor, Boss."

"Alright. Hold up. I'm babysitting lazy fucker Blade, who's bitching and whining about fucking nothing."

Blade's head was hanging, but he laughed, and Archie joined him.

"You're alright, Blade. I know it isn't easy. We'll rest on this floor, alright?"

"Thanks, Boss."

Breathing heavily, Blade got to the floor, where Archie slapped his back, then laughed at him staggering under the weight, rocking from side to side with it, then letting the crate hit the floor with a dull boom.

* * *

"Widow!" Igor whispered. "They're here! Did you hear that?"

"I heard. My lover and I wish to enter our secret place. Make it fast."

"Yes, Widow!"

He scurried up the rope, hit two buttons but made only one clicking sound, and two hoist motors fired up, their tones just different enough to make clear that each was doing its part.

Widow, strapped together with her heavily bound crafter girl, swayed slowly as the strong ropes lifted them from the room, through the open hatchway, then high enough that Igor could move the pair to one side as the twin hoists scraped along their support beam high above.

"Light the candles, then close the hatch."

"Yes, Widow! Yes!"

He struck a match, and his shaking fingers had only connected with a couple of the tapers before he grunted and threw it to the floor. A quick pull shut off the light mounted to the hatch's underside, and he tipped the thick concrete section closed with only the softest of muffled thuds.

Pausing a moment to look at the two women wrapped together, one naked except for the tight, hardening bindings that Widow had applied to her, the other wearing only short black boots and a black leather skirt around her thighs, Igor groaned softly and used one hand to start rubbing his crotch.

Widow turned at the sound, scoffed, and said, "Open the listening port, slave. Be sure our candlelight isn't seen from below."

"Yes, Widow."

He took one step toward the closed channel to the room below but stopped when Widow said, "You may continue to pleasure yourself."

"Thanks, Widow!"

"Your yelling will get us killed."

"Sorry!" he whispered, then put his ear to the port.

* * *

"Come on. You can rest your miserable ass in the shithole room on this floor."

"Thanks, Boss."

Blade heaved the heavy load back up onto his shoulder, then wobbled and tipped into the hallway's wall.

"Shit," said Archie. "You really are tired as fuck."

"Yeah, Boss."

Archie smirked, then looked toward Widow's door, where Sammy stood, waiting and watching them.

"Well? Let's get the fuck in there already."

693

"Sure, Boss."

Sammy took a step back, then drove a powerful kick into the door, sending it swinging, then bouncing back and needing another kick.

"Did you even try the fucking knob, you fucking idiot?"

Sammy looked down, grinning, and said, "Uh, no. I just kind of wanted to do that."

"Yeah. Fun stuff."

He pointed at the man with a torch.

"Spark that fucking thing, and let's check it out."

"Alright, Boss."

The torch bearer led the way, Sammy and Spencer followed, then Blade with the crated mutant treat girl, whose tail snapped from side to side.

"Boss," said Sammy, pointing around. "Lights."

"Try them."

With torch fire to help navigate the room, they tried most of the nearby fixtures' pull chains, each light mounted in the center of identical square features that, as a matched set, made up the entire ceiling.

"Only this one, Boss."

Archie stepped closer, then turned at the sound of Blade roughly dropping the crate near the door.

"Hey. Show some manners to the lady."

He could barely finish before laughing, and the rest joined him. Still chuckling, he stood under the hatch and studied the dim light. A few seconds later, he tapped the ceiling with the point of the sword that he'd given to Junior. It reached just far enough.

"Concrete ceiling. Like a fucking bomb shelter."

* * *

Igor's self-rubbing came to quick end when he heard Archie stabbing his sword into the hatch. He snapped his head to face Widow.

"Widow!" he whispered. "Hey!"

She backed her lips away from the crafter's neck, gave her soft skin another quick kiss, then turned to view the slave.

"Yes?"

He pointed at the port repeatedly, and she only shook her head.

She mouthed the word, "No," gave the helpless girl another kiss, moaned with her lips pressed into her, then ended it to again look at Igor.

"Fine," she said softly. "Close it. You have an urgent task."

He held his breath and pivoted the lid to cover the opening, then sighed deeply.

"We can speak?" he whispered.

"Softly. No loud noises."

"Good. I'll just stay right where I am."

"You will not. Find that roll of lesser webbing material."

He stood and brushed dust off of his pants while saying, "That gauze stuff?"

"Yes. There is more?"

"Yes, Widow, piles of it."

"Good. I might wish to use piles of it."

"You, um, don't know yet?"

"We shall see where our orgasms take my lover girl and me."

His hand flew to his crotch, and he said, "Right now? You're both still—"

"Yes."

She grinned and added, "Like you can't imagine."

He groaned, staring at Widow's bare legs, covered only by her black leather skirt tight around her thighs and pressed into the crafter's bare legs, and said, "Torture. Such torture."

Widow kissed the girl's neck, then grinned and said, "My little girl's fingers are so busy. So soft and touching me just as I wish."

"She, she is?"

"Mm-hmm. And soon, I will touch her."

"Touch her . . . her . . ."

"Mm, her pussy. Such a soft little lover girl for me."

"It's tor—"

"Retrieve the binding material."

"Yes, Widow."

He scuttled off and was quickly absorbed by the shadows that owned the attic's walls. Moments later, he reappeared with a large roll of plain gauze about as wide as the straps that he'd cut from the tarp.

Looking up at the two bound women, he reached up and showed that his hand was only as high as their shoulders.

"I, uh, can't reach Widow. Unless you want only—"

"We wish to be covered thoroughly. Find something on which to stand."

"Yes, Widow."

He walked directly to a small table and hurried back with it.

Before he could attempt to climb up, Widow said, "Be quiet as if your life depends on it."

"Uh, yours, too, right?"

"Mm. My orgasm tells me not to care very much. Proceed, slave."

"Yes, Widow."

* * *

"If that thing's dead," said Sammy, pointing toward the dead monkey propped against a far wall, "it wasn't no bomb that got his ass."

Archie said, "A monkey? What the fuck?"

"In a locked room, too," said Sammy. "What the fuck indeed."

Scoffing, Archie said, "You don't fucking know it was locked, you and your goddamn greasy boot."

"Maybe the monkey locked himself in?"

"No fucking way, asshole. No monkey's brain could think like that when his balls are about to explode."

"That happens?"

"I've seen it," said Archie.

"Uh, really?"

"No, not fucking really. You fuckers. They do cum a lot, though. I mean, gobs of that shit. I'm a little jealous."

"Eat more bananas."

"You're a funny son of a bitch, Spencer. Maybe I will. Look, I'm just saying that you didn't have to kick the shit out of the goddamn door."

"True. I probably should have—"

"Go check on the goddamn monkey! Shit, you fuckers would forget to breathe if I wasn't here to boss your sorry asses around."

"Uh, right away, Boss," said Sammy.

He looked at the torch carrier and said, "Bring that fire."

"We're going to burn him?"

"What? No, you dumb fuck. Oh, unless the boss says so."

"I don't say so. Since when do we go around burning dead monkeys?"

Sammy, walking toward the monkey, said over his shoulder, "Never too late to start."

Archie grinned at Blade, who slouched on the crate.

"He does have a point. Maybe we should—"

Blade was looking to one side, along the wall, and he jumped up and stepped in that direction.

"What now?"

"Boss, some kind of slimy stuff. Fuck, I know what that is. Somebody's been up here whacking it."

Archie turned toward the monkey and said to the two men's backs, "Ask the dead monkey if he's been whacking his fucking meat up here."

Sammy stopped and looked back, grinning.

"Damn dead monkey would just lie about it, Boss."

"True. Can't trust a damn dead monkey."

Looking toward Blade, he said, "Human or monkey slimy stuff?"

"How the fuck would I know, Boss?"

"Taste it. See if it tastes like bananas."

Blade doubled over, laughing, and said, "As much as I miss bananas . . ."

"Yeah. Not *that* fucking much. Alright, let's assume it was the goddamn monkey that left his slop against the wall."

"Banana slop."

"Yep. Let's assume that too. You fuckers want to know my conclusion?"

"Yeah, Boss."

All waited and listened.

"If the notorious wench Scarlet was ever hiding in this room, that monkey would have . . ."

He looked at Sammy, who only shrugged.

Blade was scratching at his chin, staring, then he shook his head.

The torch bearer shot his unused arm straight up.

Archie scoffed and said, "This isn't fucking grade school."

He dropped it to his side.

"Well?"

"He, he fucking would have fucked the wench in her ass!"

Archie pointed at him and grinned at each of the others before looking his way again.

"Right! You're smart, torch-toting fucker!"

"Can I burn the monkey, then? Can I?"

Archie lost his smile and strode over, then grabbed the torch out of his hand. With it, he continued the walk toward the reclining monkey corpse.

"If anyone is burning the goddamn monkey, it's going to be me."

He stopped and looked back at the rest just long enough to say, "You fuckers."

When he'd resumed his walk, Sammy whispered, "Shit. Just like a goddamn boss."

* * *

"Begin at the very top."

"Cover your boots, Widow?"

"No."

She sighed and added, "My wish would be that my little girl's soft, juicy legs wore very high and pointy heels. Mm."

"Her, uh, her legs are juicy?"

Widow licked Marie's neck, then held the short mutant's gaze.

"She is mostly juice. Mm, such sweet juices. All wrapped in a tasty, sexy package for me."

"Uh, okay, Widow. Yes."

He climbed up onto the table, then tested it by leaning from side to side. The table proved to be prone to tipping along with him.

"Careful, slave."

"Yes, Widow. Uh, look."

He held out the end of the long gauze strip, and it showed a slightly different color than the rest of it.

"What is it?"

"The same paste stuff. I put some of the thickest kind on there."

"Oh, to get it started. Very good. Stick that on her ankle. Do not ever defile my boots."

"That she made for you."

Widow sighed and said, "Now, she provides everything she can to sustain me. I gain strength every time."

"Every time you, uh, bite someone?"

"Every time I feed. Enough with the modest nibbles. I need a long feeding."

"Yes, Widow. You, um, need it?"

"Mm-hmm. To become . . . what I . . . am."

"Yes. Yes, Widow."

He laid the sticky end against one of the crafter's ankles, then began passing the roll around, laying it on in overlapping layers. As he pulled it tight, playing it out, the tied-together women got shifted around and sometimes rotated.

"Slave," Widow said, "do not expect such privileges ever again. You may hold either of us as needed to complete your task."

"I can? I can?"

"Proceed before I change my mind and kill you instead."

"Yes, Widow. Yes!"

"No yelling. Archie."

"Oh, yes," he whispered. "Yes!"

Grinning, he sometimes held one or the other as he moved the roll around them and sometimes, he used both hands for the gauze and leaned his face into soft skin, he didn't seem to care which of them.

Their ankles got covered quickly, and he paused to look at the bare skin of their lower legs, which were even with his face.

He mouthed the word, "Torture!", then wrapped halfway down to their knees.

"Um, leave the skirt there, Widow?"

"Leave the skirt. It feels good as it squeezes into my soft skin."

"Yes, Widow."

"And it's so sweet that my lover girl has found me in a state of undressing."

He looked away and mouthed, "Torture!"

*   *   *

"We're wasting time," Archie said as he took the last few steps and looked down on the monkey. "Fucking around with dead monkeys."

"And puddles of monkey cum," Blade said.

"Yeah. Banana-eating bastards."

"Hear that, Boss?"

He looked up from the monkey and tipped his head.

"Outside?"

"Yeah," said Sammy. "Want me to look?"

Archie looked toward the shuttered window and said, "Yeah. Looks like maybe that fucking shit opens up."

"I'll check it, Boss."

Archie watched Sammy walk over, inspect the bolt, throw it open, then swing out the wide board.

"Huh. Nice setup."

"Yeah, Sammy," said Archie. "No fucking monkey built that."

"Too busy whacking it," said Blade.

"Not anymore," said the one who had held the torch before Archie had taken it. "Maybe the whacking killed him."

"You're a dumb fuck. You all died during sex to get here. Once you're here, though? You can pull all you want on your goddamn—"

"Boss," Sammy said while leaning out and looking down. "Zombies. Lots of them."

Blade said, "Maybe Mortimer's down there. Maybe he knows something?"

"Good thinking, Blade. Keep using that fucking brain before those freaks get their teeth into it."

"Uh, nice. Yeah. Appreciate that advice."

"Well, fuck," said Archie. "If that wench was anywhere in the building, the goddamn horny monkeys would have zeroed in on her goddamn wench scent and fucked her brains out."

Sammy snickered and said, "Out of her ass. Yeah."

"So, fuck the rest of the building. I just want to see what killed this fucker before we go beat the shit out of Mortimer."

"We're going to beat his ass? Why?"

"It's always an option, Sammy."

He leaned over and nudged the monkey around, then got a good clear view of the weakened but still substantial pole hanging out of his pants. Just below that, in a mass of deflated flesh, there were two holes with dried blood.

"Fuck. Fucker got bit. On his horny monkey balls."

"By what?"

"Weird, Sammy," said Archie. "Looks like a spider bite."

Sammy hurried over, stooped down, then whistled.

"Uh, Boss, that would have to be—"

"A big fucking spider. Yeah."

*   *   *

Igor panted rapidly as he held Widow's skirt with one hand and wrapped gauze around two pairs of thighs with his other hand.

"Keep going?"

"Mm-hmm. Wrap us together as two lovers wish to be."

"Yes, Widow."

He continued with shaking hands, winding the stretchy material over their thighs, then beginning to cover their bare asses.

"Mm. More torture for my slave. Spin us slowly and observe our bare asses. You may pause your work to kiss each cheek once."

"I can? Can I?"

"Not if you yell."

"Sorry!"

The crafter's ass was facing him when he got permission to kiss them, so he held the pair of women still with both hands, leaned to kiss one of Marie's cheeks, then the other.

"She's tasty?" said Widow.

"God, yes, Widow! I think I love her too!"

"Yes. Just a slight spin now," she said, "and you will touch your lips to the soft, sweet skin of my bare ass."

"Yes, Widow! Yes!" he whispered.

He spun them around and paused, looking from one cheek to the other and shaking his head.

Forcing his eyes to stay open, he touched his lips to one and held them there.

A few seconds passed, then Widow giggled softly and said, "The other, slave."

"Yes, Widow. Now."

He leaned toward it, and the table rocked enough that it was up on two legs.

"Oh, God!" he said, then held his breath while lowering it quietly onto all four legs.

"Careful, slave."

"Yes!"

Listening to Widow moan and moaning himself, he held the two women and laid his open kiss on her cheek, intentionally missing and getting boldly close to the tight crack that separated one from the other.

"Slave. You test my patience."

He pressed his face hard into her, his nose and mouth completely surrounded by her soft flesh, moaned desperately, then backed away.

"I deserve to die for that. Yes, I do. I'm worthless. I should never have—"

"It's okay. Every touch gives you more of my sweet poisons. When you finish, you have permission to masturbate with your memories."

"Yes, Widow, I will. More than once. Thank you."

"Make ready another of the straps. There are two remaining?"

"Yes, Widow. It's ready."

She let go of Marie to unbutton her blouse.

"Slave, remove this."

"Yes. Yes!"

He pinched the thin material and pulled it back, and she moved her arms as needed to help. He inhaled the garment several times, then let it drop gently to the attic floor.

"Widow, Widow, later, may I—"

"Yes, you may embrace it, inhale my scent, such acts as those. Just don't get any of your vile fluids on it."

"I will, and I won't! Thank you!"

"Mm," Widow said while reaching both arms around Marie. "We both feel my nipples pressing into her. Such a soft, tender little girl."

Igor groaned, watching the two bound, nearly naked women as Widow squeezed her breasts into Marie's bare back.

She sighed, then extended her arms toward the floor.

"Bind us here, slave."

"Yes. Yes, Widow."

He reached the strap's end around, took it in his other hand, stretched it across Marie, then hesitated.

"Yes, there. Bind her breasts. Bind them tightly."

"Yes."

He pulled back hard, compressing Marie's breasts, and looped the band around her and Widow several times, each layer adhering to the one below it, then cinched it up tight before sticking the end to all the rest of the material.

Widow reached back around the girl, and Igor leaned to watch her hands inspecting his work, rubbing all around the breasts that were hidden under tight layers and binding the two women together.

"Good," she said. "Hers will strain against the bindings, and mine will strain against her soft skin."

"Yes, Widow. Yes! Keep wrapping you?"

"Before you continue, hand me the last strap which you cut."

"I knew you'd want it! It's in my—"

"Shh."

"—pocket!"

He handed it to her and waited.

"Spin us. Let my precious little girl face you."

"Yes, Widow."

He gave them a short spin, and he was able to hold Widow's gaze, her eyes very black, as she looked past the unconscious girl's head.

And when Widow grabbed Marie's hair and yanked her head back, causing her mouth to open wide, both of his hands, on their own and needing no guidance from him, went directly to his crotch.

* * *

"Pack up whatever shit you got, and let's get the fuck out of here."

"I got nothing," said Sammy. "You, Spencer? Just the torch?"

"Just the torch."

"Alright, Blade," said Archie as they stood near the door. "It's only a shitpile of flights of stairs down, then—"

Blade sobbed.

"—then out to the street, then to the edge of—"

The tall, thin man hung his head and shook noticeably.

"—edge of the city, then all the fucking way back to—aw, shit. You really are beat, aren't you?"

"Boss, I'm exhausted. I'm as dead as that monkey."

"Close," said Spencer, chuckling. "Go whack it against a wall, and you'll be as dead as him."

Blade scoffed, then smiled.

"You know what?" said Archie. "You're too thin. We need to beef you up some."

"But Boss, carrying that thing only—"

"I mean, when we get back to the reactor, I need a reliable fucker to tend the oven that that swollen muscle-freak bastard used to work. Interested?"

"Uh, that would, um, beef me up?"

"If you do the job right, fuck yeah."

"And I can leave your sex treat mutant girl for someone else to carry?"

"Exactly fucking right. Don't you worry about carrying that feisty little bitch around anymore, alright?"

"Thanks, Boss."

"Fuck yeah," he said and gave him back his blade.

Blade grinned while taking it by its handle, then said, "Thanks for the blade, Boss."

"You'll need a big goddamn fork too."

"Huh?"

"Nothing."

He turned to look at Sammy and Spencer.

"I, uh, have to carry the torch," said Spencer.

"Yeah, he does, and I, um, I have to—"

"Relax, fuckers," said Archie. "We're leaving her."

The other three looked around the room.

"Here? Leave the sex treat here?"

"Yeah!" Archie said with a big grin. "Keep the monkeys alive just a fucking bit longer."

"Huh?"

"Think it through, Sammy."

Sammy looked back at the dead monkey, then the crate with a tail waving around lazily above it, then back at Archie.

"I got it!"

"Tell us, fucker."

"That monkey," he said, pointing at the dead monkey, "died from masturbating too much, right?"

"That and a goddamn giant spider. Go on. We're listening."

"So, if the rest of them that come up here can—"

Blade said, "Fuck the freak girl instead? Is that it?"

"Bingo, fuckers."

Spencer nodded, then said, "As long as I get to burn them."

The other three looked at him, and Archie said, "Sure, Spencer. If you can tell me that that slimy puddle over there is banana-flavored monkey cum."

Spencer stared.

"Right. You're not about to taste that slop, so you're not burning shit. Get your asses out of here."

The other three left, laughing, and Archie paused at the door and turned back to look around the room.

"And you," he yelled, "you giant freak spider. Don't just bite the goddamn monkeys to death. Let them fuck your goddamn spider ass too. You know they'd do it. You'd never stop them. Better yet, suck their fucking monkey cocks before their balls explode!"

"Boss, are you okay?"

"Yeah, Sammy. Just fucking fine."

"Uh, sure. What was that all about?"

He shrugged and said, "Fuck, when will I ever again have the opportunity to say such ludicrous fucking bullshit as that?"

"Fucking never," Sammy said with a big grin.

"Exactly. Come on. Let's go slaughter some fucking monkeys."

"What you got against monkeys? Just because they got bigger balls than you?"

"No, you dumbass. Well, okay. Yeah. I kind of hate that."

"Their balls really are gigantic. The cum never stops. I mean, I've heard that."

"Yep. It's a non-stop cum-splattered nightmare with those freaks."

Chapter 62 – The Truest Love

Igor rubbed with both hands, one inside his pants and the other free roaming. He kept staring even after Widow had turned her attention to the silently gasping crafter girl, naked and bound tightly, her head pulled back by a strong grip on her hair.

"Oh, my sweet little one. You're touching my pussy so softly. Slowly now, my precious little girl."

She held the girl's hair with one hand and snapped the strap with her other hand, straightening it out. She laid it across the girl's open mouth, pulling it to get the same amount on each side.

"Shh, my little girl. Soon, I'll touch your pussy too. We'll touch each other's pussy until I'm done and you're . . . done."

She let go of her hair and held the strap with both hands.

"I know that little girls love any kind of touch from me after they've had my very sweet little bites. Yes, your orgasm only increases with every touch. Even a very cruel touch."

She snapped it back with both hands, digging the cloth in tight and stretching back her cheeks.

"Mm, you love the cruelty. Ooh, so tight between your pretty lips. Let's make sure it doesn't come loose."

She tied a loose knot behind the girl's head, then pulled both ends out to the sides, digging the strand in deeper.

"Hmm, that's better. Such a quiet, cooperative little girl for me. More would be good. Yes, my little one."

Igor rubbed and pulled and stretched himself inside his trousers, watching as Widow gagged the already helpless crafter. She brought one end of the strap around and laid it over her mouth, partly on her chin. The other end did the same from the opposite side, covering her nose too.

"She, uh, she doesn't need to—"

"Hmm, no, slave. She needs only my touch now, gentle or cruel. Never again will she need a breath."

"But she, um, she'll be able to eventually—"

"I'm ruining my little girl on the inside. Mm, I feel it when I bite her. I know just what to give my soft, juicy little girl."

Widow pulled the ends tight and tied another knot behind the girl's head.

"She's going to, uh, die, then?"

Widow paused, holding the straps out to the side, and stared up at the mutant slave. Seconds passed in silence.

"I . . . I am going to live."

A few more seconds passed, then Widow wrapped the material over the girls face again, from both sides, covering her eyes and leaving her entire face coated and hidden.

Widow kissed the back of her wrapped head and said, "So pretty and never to be seen again. Nobody now. Just . . . juicy. Soft and so juicy."

She tied it securely, then reached up to put the fingertips of both hands between the girl's legs.

"Continue the binding, slave. Leave only our heads without webs."

"Without . . ."

Igor fell silent.

"Yes. Do not speak again," she said with her mouth against the girl's neck. "When you have finished, take the candles to a corner, let them sleep, and do not stir until I call to you."

He nodded, not speaking again, then did as he was told, wrapping around their bare asses and hiding away Widow's hands, palms flat against a soft belly and low enough for busy fingertips.

He didn't speak, but he listened while he worked, steadily wrapping them together so completely that the two of them were becoming only a large mass of tightly wound gauze.

"Oh," said Widow, almost whispering, "you are truly my baby girl now. You're my sweet, precious little baby girl. Mm, so soft. So helpless."

He started covering their arms and across Marie's belly and Widow's back.

"Just the sweetest little baby lover girl. So soft and juicy. Mm, so juicy."

Igor stepped down from the table and soon after finished the wrapping. He took a second to look and saw that the two women, locked in an embrace where their fingers had nowhere to go other than where they both wanted them, were encased in what looked like a large cocoon.

"Mm-hmm. Such a soft, juicy little baby girl."

Igor backed away quietly and took the table, candelabra, and Widow's blouse with him.

"Helpless little baby girls are the juiciest. Mm, so juicy for me."

Many steps away, he set down the table and placed the candles on it, then looked back at them. And already, from the candles being so distant, they were no more than a slightly different color of the darkness in the attic.

"Feeling the bindings, feeling the complete helplessness, makes your juices so much sweeter."

He swallowed hard, then unzipped, slowly and quietly, and sat with his back against the wall. Looking back at the odd aberration of the attic's night, and quietly choking a swollen part of himself, he blew out the candles.

He breathed in deeply and without a sound, keeping Widow's blouse covering everything but his eyes gazing into the dark.

The darkness that had flowed like thick syrup and devoured everything in Widow's secret attic.

And he heard, softly in the dark distance, a voice rich with the sweetest of sugary honeys, bubbling with simmering molasses, and blended with nectar so thick that a tear escaped and rolled down his cheek, even as his hand pumped steadily.

"It's time for a very long bite, my soft, juicy little baby girl."

He paused his stroking and held his breath.

"Ours, my precious baby girl, is the truest love you could ever know."

Enjoy the Story?

Thank you for reading! Please consider leaving a review and/or a rating at your favorite bookseller or with your favorite book club. Help your fellow readers meet Widow and the rest of the characters in the Risk and the Killers series!

For more about Edward Allen Karr and his books, visit:

www.LakesideLetters.com

Dying To Be Widow

Is Book Two in the series
Risk and the Killers

Which is the sequel series to
Thrills N Kills in the Hills

Dayzee Dazzle and her best friends, the Kildare Killers, are famous and gorgeous. They're too captivating to be from this planet, and they like it that way. Earthmen can't resist them and rarely survive encounters with them.

They find humor in horror, confront the ghastly with laughter and loss of clothing, and leave dead bodies and satisfied smiles in their wake.

Dayzee Dazzle and the Kildare Killers – Book One
Dayzee Dazzle and her Manic Mansion – Book Two
Dayzee Dazzle and the On-Set Onslaught – Book Three
Dayzee Dazzle and the Cadaver Collectors – Book Four

Have You Met Lin Finity?

She's the powerful star of her own series titled Fringes of
Infinity. In the beginning, she's forced to learn how to control the
unstoppable, magical power she earned at age fifteen. After killing
her abusive uncle with her deadly new ability, she locked it away
inside herself. Now, she's in her forties, and it's back. She calls it
Mayhem. And it's done waiting.

Book One and the Novella are free in e-book format. Just visit
https://www.LakesideLetters.com

Lin Finity and her Mayhem Rising
Lin Finity in Holding On

About the Author

Edward Allen Karr was born, raised, and continues to reside in Ohio, USA. His adult life has followed a meandering path, ranging from working an automotive assembly line to designing space flight hardware. And through all of it, he's seen that life is a captivating and ultimately unexplainable endeavor. His writing seeks to add a splash of wonder to a world already awash in it.

* * *

For more information, please visit:

www.LakesideLetters.com